MY TRANSPORTATION FOR LIFE

VEER SAVARKAR was:

- First political leader who lighted a bonfire of foreign clothes (on 7th July, 1905).
- First India citizen to face a trial in International Court of Justice, Hague.
- First scholar whose title of barrister was withheld for refusing to take oath of allegiance.
- First political prisoner to get two life sentences.
- First writer who despite being deprived of pen and paper, created many literary pieces on walls of Andaman prison with spikes, thorns and even his nails and preserved them for posterity by getting them memorised by his fellow inmates.
- First Indian author to face seizure of his books by two governments, even before they were printed and published.

Tributes Paid to Veer Savarkar by Eminent Persons

"Veer Savarkar led a stormy life of a relentless freedom fighter. He lived an extraordinary life of incessant tireless activity in various fields of national uplift."

—M.S. Golwalkar 'Shriguruji'

"Savarkar means glow, Savarkar means sacrifice, Savarkar means perseverance, Savarkar means element, Savarkar means reason, Savarkar means adolescency, Savarkar means arrow, Savarkar means sword, Savarkar means daze, Savarkar means endurance, Savarkar means bitterness—how many shades his personality had! Poetry and revolution together! The creator in Savarkar flew higher and higher. Savarkar had both highs and lows. His contribution is unforgettable. He will continue to inspire us Indians."

—Atal Bihari Vajpayee

"Veer Savarkar was an exemplary freedom fighter and a great son of India who bore brutalities and atrocities at the hand of Britishers but never gave up. His inspiring life will continue to guide generations to come."

—Lal Krishna Advani

"Veer Savarkar's undying love for India made him fight injustice against our Motherland. He inspired many others to join freedom struggle. His emphasis on social reform and his writing and poetry will continue to ignite the spark of patriotism among people."

—Narendra Modi

"Savarkar ji was a strong votary of an undivided India. His mantra was one nation, one cultural value and nationalism... He was a great patriot, unparalleled freedom fighter and social reformer, great writer, pioneering visionary and strong proponent of Hindu culture."

—Amit Shah

"Mr. Savarkar was one of the earliest revolutionaries who had resorted to remarkable ways of escape. A steady and sturdy worker for the independence of our country, his career was for many a youngster, a legendary one."

—Dr. S. Radhakrishnan

"...if the untouchable class is to be an indispensable part of the Hindu society, then the eradication of mere untouchability will not suffice; but the entire four varnasystem should be uprooted. Very few people have agreed upon the necessity of this. And I'm happy to say, that you are one of them."

—Dr. Babasaheb Ambedkar

"Mr. Savarkar was one of the greatest freedom fighters."

—Dr. Ram Manohar Lohia

MY TRANSPORTATION FOR LIFE

VEER SAVARKAR

Published by
PRABHAT PRAKASHAN PVT. LTD.
4/19 Asaf Ali Road,
New Delhi-110 002 (INDIA)
e-mail: prabhatbooks@gmail.com

ISBN 978-93-5322-764-7
MY TRANSPORTATION FOR LIFE
by VEER SAVARKAR

Edition
2024

Price
₹ 900.00 (Rupees Nine Hundred only)

Printed at
Narula Printers, Delhi

Preface

The Story of the publication of the Book 'My Transportation for Life', originally written in Marathi, is as tortuous and yet as significant as the story of the toils and tortures suffered by its illustrious author.

Many minor freedom fighters have come out with the colourful versions of their internment in jail making the most of what a little they endured there, but Swatantrya Veer V.D. Savarkar in spite of his exceptionally heroic struggle against his most inhuman incarceration and the beastly treatment meted out to him and his co-convicts in the Cellular Jail of the Andamans was reticent to breathe out a word about it all. For, he often wondered if it would be proper and decent to do so, whether it would not bounce back upon him with the charge of boastfulness or whether by doing so, his extraordinary sacrifice and infernal sufferings in the Andarnans might not appear more theatrical and sham than real and horrid. Moreover, he felt whether he would not do a great wrong to his co-sufferers who bravely laid down their lives on the altar of freedom without having the slightest chance of uttering a single word about anything whatsoever.

Granting that a loud and heartrending cry or wail is a natural concomitant or consequence of every agony, whether it be the dying screech of helpless and hapless bird in the jaws of a hawk or, maybe, the national lament of the French people at the sight of the dead body of their beloved Emperor Napoleon brought to Paris from St. Helena - it was still felt unworthy of expression in as much as whatever was worth telling about in the story of the Transportation for Life could not be clearly told because of the stringent government conditions laid down on his release, while whatever little could be written down was bound to be colourless and shallow because of the incoherence that must necessarily creep in the narration. Would it not, therefore, be proper, he felt, to wait till such an auspicious day dawned when he would be able to open out his heart without any hindrance? But, suppose, such a day never dawned! How would his total silence, he wondered, ever affect the course of the world? On the contrary, he felt this slip-shod and inconsistent narration of his turbulent and tumultous life in the Andaman Jail might smack of self-eulogy.

But, constant requests and exhortations by his admirers far and near and the thought that even this incoherent account of his epic struggle might prove edifying and useful to at least some of the readers and might justify, even if partially, the cause for which, and the way in which, he and his compatriots fought and suffered and died, made the author Veer V.D. Savarkar relent a bit and the said 'My Transportation for Life' was published in the weekly 'Kesari' of the celebrated Late Lokmanya Tilak in a series during 1925-26.

But, even that brave national periodical found it difficult to publish the whole account of the 'Transportation for Life'. So, the second part of the story had to be published in another weekly, viz., 'Shraddhanand', from 20th January, 1927 onwards, and eventually the whole work was brought out in May 1927, for the first time.

The author, Swatantrya Veer V.D. Savarkar, as is well known, was implicated by the then Government of India in the Jackson Murder Case of 1909 under Sections 302 and 109 of the Indian Penal Code and was sentenced to the First Transportation for Life on 24th December, 1910 and for the Second Transportation for Life on 30th January, 1911, condemning him in all to rigorous imprisonment for 50 years only to be released in 1960. The terrible Jaws of the Cellular Jail of the Andamans swallowed V.D. Savarkar on 4th July, 1911. But, instead of the jaws of the Cellular Jail, Andaman, crushing its prey to death, the Cellular Jail itself had to be closed for the life termers from India because of the incessant organised agitational movements launched by V.D. Savarkar on various issues breaking down in its wake the tyrannical jailor. Veer V.D. Savarkar was consequently transferred to the inland jails of Calcutta, Ratnagiri and Yervada and, finally, set free on two conditions.

Although it seems that the book was first Published in May 1927, there was no notice given in the weekly Shraddhanand about this publication till the 23rd of June, 1927, when for the first time were announced the Centres at Bombay, Akola, Nagpur and Amravati, where the copies of the book were made available. Maybe, the copies were ready and secretly sold before that date. Within less than three years, i.e., by the beginning of 1930, the first edition of the book seems to have been exhausted. For, a notice inviting publishers to bring out the second edition of the book as also of the same author's poems and life appeared in the issue of Shraddhanand of 29th March, 1930.

Soon a Gujarati translation of the book was published and pop came the government ban on the book on 17th April, 1934 under Rule 19 of the Press Act (Emergency Powers) of 1931. The ban, however, was condemned by various newspapers. The Kesari of 20th April, 1934, for instance, said that the book was widely read by the Marathi-speaking readers for so many years before the ban and yet the peace and order situation in the country was not endangered, and that about three years had elapsed since the passing of the Act under which the book was banned. If the book, the Kesari argued, was not deemed to be transgressing the Provisions of this Act for such a long time, how could it become so very dangerous all of a sudden during the previous week? Only nine days after the ban, i.e., on the 26th of April, 1934, a British Officer was shot at Dhobi Talao, Bombay, by a young fiery worker in Veer Savarkar's group at Ratnagiri, the Late Shri Wamanrao Chavan and within twenty-four hours, Swa. Savarkar's house at Ratnagiri was searched! This attempt at the Life of the British Officer appears to be a violent reaction against the ban.

Immediately following the ban on the book, the office of the Prasthan Publishing House, which had published the Gujarati version of the book, was raided and the Gujarati copies were confiscated. Similarly, the Printer and the Publisher of the Weekly, Prajabandhu, Indranandan Balvantrai Thakor, was served with a notice to pay a security deposit of two thousand rupees.

Thus, the ban which was put on the book, not immediately after the publication of the Marathi edition, but after that of the Gujarati one, gave cause for doubt in the minds of many as to who should have complained to the Government about the dangerous nature of the book. Was it someone, who had been denouncing, all along, the revolutionaries, condemning Shivaji and Rana Pratap as misguided patriots because of their recourse to arms, handing over Pruthvising and other revolutionaries to the government and who, in the name of Hindu-Muslim unity, was trying to appease the Muslims ad nausea?

In 1937, the Late Shree Narayan Rao Savarkar applied, as the

Publisher of the book, for the lifting of the ban; so also did various other individuals and institutions, but in vain. In August 1937, the Late Shree V.V. Sathe, a social worker in Pune, took out a procession in support of the hunger strike started by the prisoners in the Andaman Jail. When, at the end, the procession was converted into a mass meeting in front of the famous Shanwar Wada, Pune, he declared that he would read out a passage on page 191 of the proscribed 'My Transportation for Life' (Marathi) by Veer V.D. Savarkar, in protest against the unjustified ban. The book was immediately snatched away from his hands by the then Sub-Inspector of Police, Shree Devulgaonkar. But soon he and many others in the meeting started singing "Dhanya Shivaji To Ranagaji Dhanyachi Tanaji", also a proscribed ballad by Veer Savarkar on the famous battle of 'Sinhgad'. Various other people vehemently demanded the release of the proscribed books of V.D. Savarkar, while on the Government side, it was given out that the demand was under consideration, which actually meant nothing, and nothing was done.

Once again, in 1945, when the Congress Government took over, the demand was renewed with greater vehemence. Some even declared to publish these proscribed books and sell them openly defying the ban. The ban was finally lifted on the 22nd of May, 1946.

However, ban or no ban, Veer Savarkar's books were surreptitiously published and widely read, although secretly. The second regular and lawful edition of the book was published in 1947, as the Fifth Publication of the Hindu Rashtra Granthamala by M/s Parchure Puranik Ani Mandali.

On the 30th of January, 1948, Gandhiji was assassinated and Veer Savarkar was maliciously implicated in the conspiracy by the first Free Indian Government only to be acquitted honourably. But, people were naturally afraid of buying his books for fear of the Governmental reprisals. So, the book came to the footpaths of Bombay to be sold at a meagre price of a rupee or so. But, this adverse circumstance helped the sale and the book soon came to be sold at its originally printed price.

Besides the Gujarati version of the book, the Kannad and English versions also came out soon. The present English translation of the book was made by Prof. V.N. Naik, M.A., Principal, Narayan Topiwala College, Mulund, Bombay, and was published in 1949 by Sadbhakti Prakashan, Bombay and is now going into its second edition; but, these too had to face the same Gandhi murder turmoil and, hence, the Hindi version of the book could not then be brought out, which, however, was subsequently published in 1966 by the Prithviraj Prakashan, Nagpur. An abridged edition of the book was also published serially in Hinduwani. Even the Sahitya Academya, a Central Government-sponsored organisation, announced its intention to publish the book in all the fourteen Indian languages, but the project seems to have aborted somehow. The reason? Who should know except the Government!

In 1963, the book was published in the first volume of the Samagra Savarkar Vangmaya and again in a separate book form in 1968 by M/s G.P. Parchure Prakashan Mandir. This edition was supplied with ample footnotes by Shree Balarao Savarkar, because the author could not give expression to many of his thoughts, writing as he was under severe restrictions before his release.

Besides being a heart-rending tale of inhuman tortures and indignities heaped on Veer Savarkar in different jails of the Andaman, Ratnagiri and Yervada, it affords a practical demonstration of a heroic struggle given relentlessly, defiantly and with indomitable courage over thirteen long years when utter despair and abysmal gloom haunted him day in and day out. The most astonishing fact is that in spite of the utter ruination of his most promising young age in the hellish darkness of the dungeons of the Andamans and the total frustration of the cause for which he fought and bled and suffered and in the absence of the slightest ray of hope, the author could maintain, when other co-convicts couldn't, and when the temptation to end his life was working heavily on him, the rare equanimity of mind to compose thousands of lines of finest poetry, to think and philosophise, so deeply and thoroughly on so many complex problems that were then, and are still, pestering our motherland and find practical solutions for them which, however loth our rulers might be to acknowledge, will have to be worked on as the situation gets more and more complicated and adverse. One wonders how very vast was the scope of his ideal and how entirely he had thought of the manysided uplift of his motherland! Truly has the poet said:

'Stone-walls do not a prison make
Nor iron bars a cage'

For the indomitable spirit of such a prince of patriots, who was at once a visionary and a stern man of action. Even in the extremity of bondage, he did not waste a single minute of his life without working for the salvation of his motherland. The more the pity that this thorough-bred exceptionally gifted, son of our motherland has so far been neglected so foolishly by us. But, this neglect is, I am afraid, bound to cost us dear. Let us hope wisdom will at last dawn on us in the near future.

Borivli, Bombay

—S.T. Godbole

Contents

PART - I

1
The Gaol at Dongri, Bombay

"You are sentenced to fifty years' transportation. The International Tribunal at Hague has given the judgement that England cannot be constrained to hand you over to France," said Mr. X to me.

"Well, then, I had never depended on any hopes from that quarter. But can I have a copy of the judgement to look at?"

"That does not rest with me, though I will try my very best for you. Yet the fortitude you have shown in hearing the news that has wrung the heart of a stranger like me does not make me think that you will wait for any help from an outsider like me," said my interlocutor almost overwhelmed with feeling.

"Do you really believe that this news or any other news like this does not terrify me? But as I am determined to face this danger and have courted it deliberately, I have now grown impervious to it. Had you been in the same plight, you would have proved as resolute as myself, for everyone can crush such experiences on the threshold of his strong mind. All the same, I am grateful to you, indeed, for your help and sympathy."

Just then I heard someone coming. The gentleman instantly left my room and went his way in the opposite direction. I withdrew a few steps in my cell and kept standing. The word 'fifty' kept on ringing in my ears.

In a moment, those whose footsteps I had heard coming near my cell appeared on the scene. The officer opened the door and his attendant served me my meal. Till the decision of the Hague Tribunal, I was not treated as a prisoner either in food or clothing. Today, I had my usual meal. Perhaps the gaoler had not yet received the order of the Court. I finished my food but did not that day touch the nice things in it. The Officer questioned me about it, "Why, why, Sir, have you not touched these things? Why don't you dine as usual?"

"Of course, I had my fill. But I have taken such things as are common to all the prisoners here. For, who knows, I may be put tomorrow to do the work that they do now. Then I may not get the good food that I have now. The dirty food of a regular prisoner is to be my lot henceforward. Why not, then, make friends with it from now? It will last me for life," I replied with a smile. To it, the Officer impatiently retorted, "No, no, that shall not be. The order has already been received, I hear, to send you back to France. You, to serve your sentence as a prisoner! Never, never. God will not grant it."

At that instant, a watchman came up running, and said that the *jamadar* was following.

The door was slammed. The warden and is attendant proceeded further. Soon after came the Superintendent and informed me, albeit courteously, that thenceforward I was to wear the prisoner's uniform and would be given the food they ate. He conveyed the news that my life sentence of fifty years had commenced from that day.

I got up, took off the clothes I had worn so far, and began putting on those that I was to wear as a prisoner. A thrill of horror vibrated through my whole being. These clothes, I felt, I was to use all my life. No longer I was to part from them. Perhaps, in these very clothes, my dead body may be taken out from the prison door. Faint, shadowy thoughts these—but the mind was overcast by them. The Superintendent kept on talking on sundry things and I tried to divert my mind by engaging myself in that conversation.

As if not to give me the solace I was seeking for, a Sepoy brought to the Superintendent what looked like an iron plate. It was the badge, with the number marked on it, which a prisoner has to wear on his breast. The badge shows the date of his release. What was my date? Am I ever to be free, or death alone was to be the date of my release? I cast my look on the badge and its number with mingled feelings of longing and despair, humour and curiosity. The year of my discharge was 1960. For a moment, I did not take in the full significance of that writing. But, in a minute or two, it flashed upon my mind. I was sentenced in 1910 and I shall have my discharge in 1960!

The British Officer grimly observed, "No fear about it, the benign Government was sure to release you in the year 1960!"

To him, I replied in the same vein, "But Death is kinder. What if it lets me off much earlier?"

Veer Savarkar in contemplation

▲ Picture of Veer Savarkar taken after arrest at Victoria station on 13 March, 1910

Blue Plaque established by Greater London Council on 8 June 1985 in memory of Veer Savarkar ▶

GREATER LONDON COUNCIL
VINAYAK
DAMODAR
SAVARKAR
1883-1966
Indian Patriot
and Philosopher
lived here

Veer Savarkar's birthplace in Bhagur

Andaman's prison where Veer Savarkar spent several years in exile

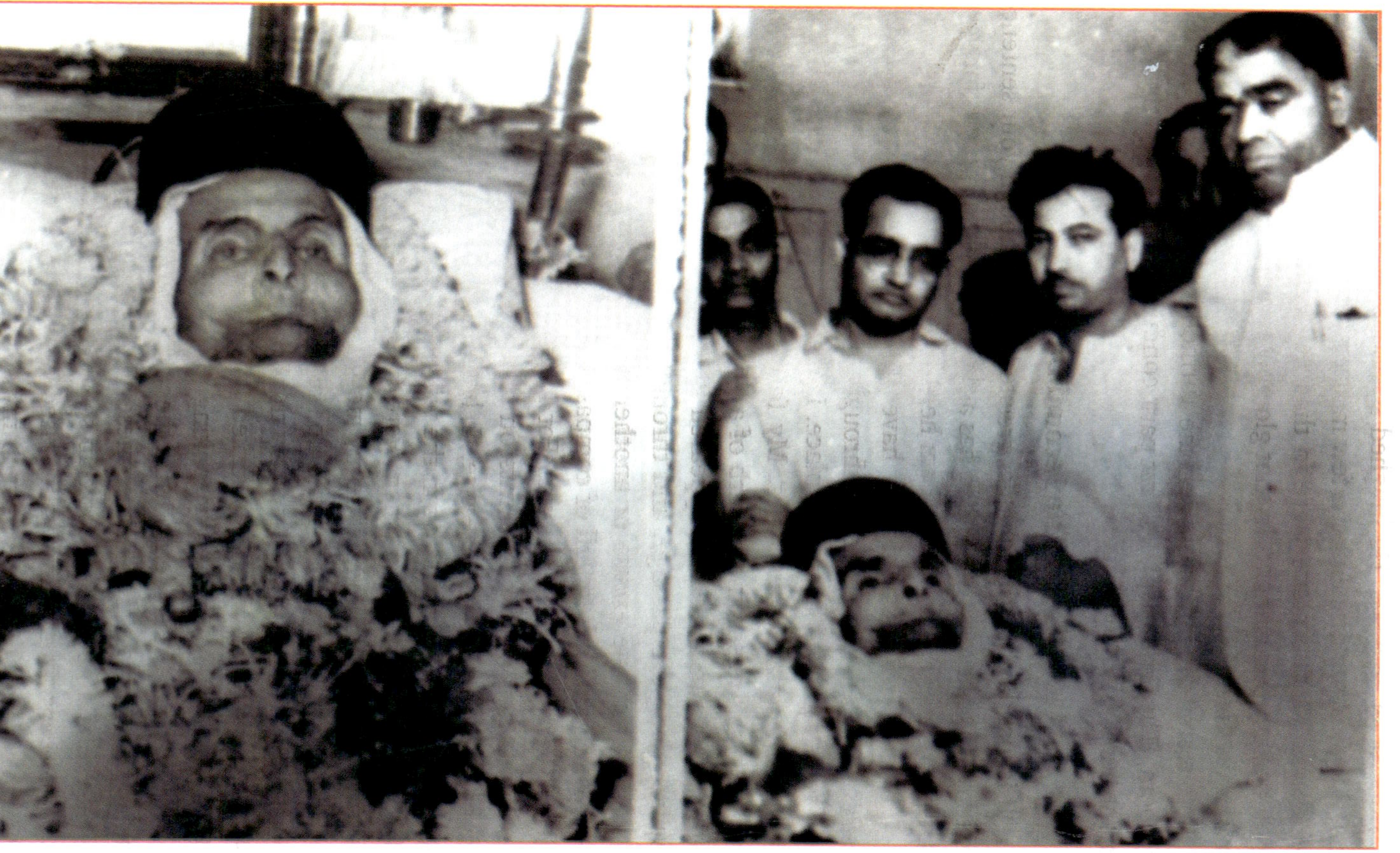

The doyen departs

Both of us laughed. He laughed spontaneously while mine was a forced laugh. After discussing a few matters with me, he left the place. I sat down. We two alone were in that cell confronting each other—myself and my punishment. In that gloomy room, we were staring each other in the face.

The rest of the day's story and the turmoil within, I have depicted in my poem, 'The Saptarishi'. Its first part contains it and I need not dwell upon it here.

The Second Day

"It is just day," so the *jamadar* greeted me, "although your sentence started from yesterday, the Saheb has asked me to take you out for your morning walk as usual, and so I am here."

I went down with him to have my constitutional. During my absence, my cell was searched through and through. My kit and my books were removed from that place. I was having my perambulations in the open square downstairs. My former clothes were not on my person. I was dressed in the garb of a prisoner. And curious eyes were looking on me to see how I appeared in my new vestments. From the hospital, along the passage, and through the windows, they observed me finding out one excuse or another to do so. Some to satisfy their idle curiosity and others full of compassion for me! The gaol of Dongri is in the very heart of the town. For I could see high up and around me, chawls and other tenements on all sides of it. Everyday when I was brought down for exercise, I had noticed people from these neighbouring houses standing in the windows and the galleries to have a look at me. Men and women were there peeping and whispering. They stayed there till I had done my morning walk. Sometimes, evading the watchman, I used to look up, and exchange salutations with them. I was pleased in my heart by the regard they had shown to me. I felt then that we, who had worked for their liberty, were rotting in jails, while they were silently looking on without the least notion of taking revenge. Once I learnt that the guard had administered a stern rebuke to the landlord of one of these chawls. So, I decided to walk in the square and never once look up so that none of them should suffer on my account. During my walk, I used to recite the whole of the **Yoga Sutras**, and recalling each text to my mind, I used to meditate on it. Today, while I was thus absorbed, the guard pulled me up saying that the time was up and I must return to my cell. I climbed up the stairs and went to my room. Being lost in thought, I sat in one part of the room for a long time to come. Suddenly, I heard the knocking on the door and, looking up, saw a Havildar coming in. He had a prisoner with him who carried a bundle on his head. The reverie had made me oblivious of my surroundings. So, I kept on looking at him with vacant eyes, whereupon the Havildar said to me, "Sir, do not please be anxious. God will make the days easy for you. He is a witness to the dire distress, and he will be your stay in it. I and mine, I assure you, were full of tears when we heard of the news. But I assured them all with a pride in my heart that you will never go down under it. Why, then, do I find you taking it so much to heart? Do not think of it." This well-meant exhortation produced quite a different effect upon my mind. It brought to my mind very clearly the fact that some heavy blow had fallen upon me. And a pang went through my heart. Fully recovering myself, I asked the Officer what that bundle was. With a smile, that was forced, he replied, "It is nothing. As a mere matter of prison regulations, I am giving you this piece of work to do. Do it or do not do it, or do as much as you can. It does not matter at all." He, then, took down the coiled rope, he cut it into pieces, and asked the prisoner to show me how I was to break it, spin it and again make threads out of it. It was, as they say, 'picking oakum'.

"This is rigorous imprisonment, then," I concluded, "not simple imprisonment for life!"

The Weary Round

"O, face it, you are condemned to pick oakum, that is all! How foolish you are, O, my mind? What is degrading in it? You think that your life is going to be a waste. But, is not life itself the same process—a weary round, spinning and unspinning, doing and undoing, evolving and dissolving, a tremendous **pis-aller**? The strand of life is woven out of the fusion of five elements. Piecing together the same threads, it is lengthened out, and when the threads and the strand suffer decay, death, with its wooden hammer, pound it into pulp, to restore it back to the elements from which it was drawn. 'Dust thou art and to dust thou shalt return.'

"The morn is followed by the evening and the day follows the night—again a weary round. We live by feeding on the herbs, and then we die. Death consigns our flesh and bones to the earth, to be consumed again by the herbs—the same process over again. The solar system—an array of effulgent stars, and burning nebulae; the earth, an offspring of that system; a stray comet dashes into the body of the earth, and the earth consumes itself into fire and returns to be a nebula!—again a weary round. We are a part of this earth and subject to the same fate, the same law, the same process. I have only to break up this coiled rope, spin out the threads and roll them up again! If the larger process going on in the Universe is worth it, if the life of the Universe is no waste, though it is involved in that procession of time, then why within it should I regard this task as in vain? For is not this the inescapable part of the grander process? It has happened and I must take it as such."

I began to pick oakum. The Havildar and others had left the place. Once again I found myself alone confronting my punishment, each, as it were, making better acquaintance of another.

Soon we became familiar friends. There was no doubt about it. Though without hope, I had still hoped that the Hague Tribunal would come to my rescue. But, there was an end to that hope. It was now certain and beyond the shadow of a doubt that I was doomed to pass the rest of my life, rotting in one cell or another, in this prison or in another far away. What then? I must face it, come what may.

Adversity is the Rule

In my life, crushed as it was under a mountain of calamities that I had brought down upon myself, one rule, bitter though it was to start with, that had sustained me throughout, more than any other, was to take it for granted that the worst always happened and that the mind must be kept ready to bear and endure it.

Those who are unfortunate to be born in time, country or circumstance as adverse as ours, and who yet aspire to rise above them, beating, fighting and conquering them on their way to realise their ideal and to usher in the dawn of a new age, must need to digest the poison administered to their lips by cruel fate. If we once resolve to face up and light the adverse that we know to be our lot here below, the favourable that comes in our way gives us a joy twice blessed, and its faint smile delights us. But hoping for the best makes the worst that befalls doubly cursed for us. The unfortunate ones like us, born in times of utter helplessness, have always to look forward to a fate equally adverse. And, then, the vain hope is apt to crush us completely when the bludgeoning blow of circumstance falls on our heads! Let the fortunate swans of Manas Sarovara, in the exultation of their triumph, feed full on the lotus-fibres, and drink deep of the pearly drops, that float on the crystal waters of that calm lake. But, men like us, who are condemned to wade up to their ears through the miasma of dead waters, defeated efforts, and hopes that turn into dupes, must beware that life for them is ever a grim battle, and they must be prepared in mind and body to pass through the severest ordeal.

The Blow had Fallen

Hardened though I had been to bear the worst that could happen, the blow felled me completely, so terrible was its first reaction upon my mind. Its suddenness almost staggered me. My arrest in London had prepared me for twenty-five years' transportation to the Andamans. My recapture at Marseilles—when the whole world was positive in its conviction that I would be restored back to France—made me conclude that I would be sent to the gallows. But, at last, both these forecasts had proved entirely false. And here I was face to face with a sentence much worse than these and, in its cumulative impact, the direst calamity I had to bear. Fifty years of prison-life, alone and in a solitary cell like this! To pass my life, to count the hours of the day as they sounded and rolled on into months and years till they completed the long, inevitable, unredeemed, dark period of fifty years! What a hell on earth? Yet I had to live it. Well, then, let me plan to live it.

I had already made a plan for myself how I could spend my time in prison during the twenty-five years I had to pass there. The Hague decision had come and gone. The twenty-five years were now to lengthen out into fifty years and I must change my scale accordingly. What work could I undertake during these twenty-five years, so I had thought, that would fulfill my life, that would enable me to pay back the debt owed to my motherland, and to serve my fellowmen ever so little, in the hapless condition of prison-life, where I had no means, and no encouragement to do the task I would like to accomplish? I recalled to my mind the lives of great prisoners from Sir Walter Raleigh down to Prince Kuropatkin. Bunyan, who wrote his **Pilgrim's Progress**, had, at least, the materials to write it with. I have not with me even the end of a broken pencil. I am not allowed the use of it. W.T. Stead wrote articles on non-political topics from the prison where he was confined. I could not do that either. Not a sparrow could come near me. Therefore, I could convey no messages and do no propaganda. It was an offence to have a scrap of paper with me. Hence, any writing was out of question. If I thought of reading and, thus, would add to my knowledge, I could get only one book to read, off and on, and with great difficulty. And mere reading and adding to one's knowledge was as barren as a tree without fruit and flower or as a pond of stagnant water that could not slake the thirst or feed the hunger of one human being, not to speak of thousands whose hunger and thirst it should satisfy. Was I not then the most unfortunate of those who had done some useful and noble work while behind the prison bars? I had to bear greater hardship than they, and I had not their means to relieve it by any congenial work that I liked to do. What can I do then? What plan can I make?

An Epic

When I was but a lad, I remember having decided to write an epic. Write it I will, I said then to myself, though I knew not what an epic was, how I was to write it, and what the subject was that I could weave into it. That desire persisted all along till it had grown into the passion of my life. Caught in the storm and stress of active life, it had seemed to fall in the background. But, now that I lay in the dust of my silent cell, it at once came up before my eyes. Methought that in this cell and in the darkness of the night, condemned as I was to hard labour during the day, I could compose such a poem, though I had not a scrap of paper to write on or a piece of pencil to write it with. None can prevent me from composing verse after verse and writing it on the tablet of my mind. This work I can accomplish even in the direst condition of my prison life. And if I could finish even a single poem in this manner, and, if ever I come back alive from my prison, I could give my garland of verse as an offering at the feet of my motherland, the fruit, as it were, of my twenty-five years' experience of that life. It was no small service that I could render her.

Why should I not then start at once and earnestly? I could no longer undertake any active work in her behalf, I knew it so well. My mind was made up. I was to write at least one long epic during the period of my incarceration. Even if the Hague decision went against me, I thought then, I could do at least this much while under sentence for hard labour.

The idea satisfied the yearning of my heart, and, to that extent, brought peace to my active mind, though for a time only. I learnt that the decision of the Court had gone against me. The period of imprisonment was doubled. A bolt from the blue had fallen upon my head. And yet, I remained unshaken in my resolve. It relieved the gloom of my mind, for I felt, under its spell, that I was not so helpless as I seemed, that I could yet do something towards the fulfilment of my life and the realisation of my dream. The fear that my life was futile was gone forever. The burden was rolled off once and for all. Impatiently, my eager mind counted the days and the lines I could compose everyday. I calculated that from ten to twenty verses a day meant an epic of 50,000 to 100,000 lines at the end of the period. I had to compose the lines, repeat them, carry them in my mind, adding on to them from day to day, till the work was complete. So, I argued with myself. I resolved then to begin at once. I chose the life of Guru Gobind Singh as the subject of my song.

The Life of Guru Gobind Singh

I chose that life because I felt that he was a prince among martyrs. The great men, who have achieved success and have won the cause, no doubt shine like golden domes that crown the summits of palaces. They are, indeed, pinnacles of glory. But I can derive no peace in the present condition of my life by celebrating them in song. On the other hand, I was likely to feel, all the more poignantly, the failure that fate had doled out to me. I must sing, therefore, of those high-souled persons whose failures had contributed to lay the foundations on which these splendid palaces had reared up their heads to constitute the admiration of the world around them. To meditate on such martyrs was an incentive to me "to follow the gleam". Guru Gobind Singh struck me as a man who had triumphed over defeat. Behold him facing utter rout as he sought to slip out of the fortress of **Chamkore**; call to mind the utter annihilation of his family life, the separation of his mother, wife and son, scattered far and wide from him; remember how his sworn disciples had betrayed him in the hour of his great need, and had blamed him for the failure of the cause which he and they had pledged themselves to stand by; and, last, realise how he had proven himself a brave man, brave as a lion, who like Rudra swallowed the poison of defeat, humiliation and woe that destiny had put to his lips, and yet survived as a hero and an incarnation for generations to emulate. The failure of such a man was,

I felt, the fittest subject for my song. It would support me in my hour of sorrow and defeat like a pillar of strength.

It would help and inspire generations to come to erect a splendid edifice of success on the failures, miseries and defeats of the generation to which I belonged.

As I was lost in the contemplation of the bright future, which imagination had depicted for me, my hands were busy uncoiling the hard entangled threads of the oakum before me. That very day I composed some fifteen verses of my song by the time I had finished the hard work allotted to me. My hands were cracked and covered with blisters, and blood oozed out from them.

I cannot say today how long I had to stay in the gaol at Dongri from the time that the Hague decision had gone against me. What was daily routine during that period—you may very well ask me. It was as follows:

Every morning, I had my usual walk in the square below. During that hour, I recited the Yoga Sutras, and thought upon them in their order and context. Then I returned to my cell and set myself to do the work assigned to me as a prisoner on hard labour. While engaged in that work, I composed the lines of my meditated epic. I used to recall the lines composed on previous days, and add to them the fresh ones that I had recently written out in my mind. After the evening meal, when the door was shut upon me, and everything around me was wrapt in perfect silence, I practised concentration and meditation as laid down in the Yogas. I retired to bed punctually at the hour of nine. During all these days, I enjoyed sound sleep. This solitary life, with its fixed routine from minute to minute, wherein I tried my hardest to control the mind by the power of thought and dispassion, sometimes became so intolerable that I felt, on occasions, that my grief and anxiety were sitting on my chest like a nightmare with their grip on my throat that had almost strangled me. In such moments, I could hardly breathe for relief; I tell then that I could even bear this, if I were sure that my cause would prosper through my sufferings. But then? Instantly I recovered from this dark despair, and I was myself over again. The poise came back to my mind as if nothing had happened during the interval.

Sir Henry Cotton

One day the news went abroad that a certain high official in England had forfeited his pension on my account. I could make no head or tail of this report till, a few days after, I fell upon a cutting from the **Kesari** of Poona which I found dropped in a corner of my room. That cutting helped me to piece out the news and gather up all its threads. It was thus: In London, the Indians had a public meeting in connection with the celebration of the New Year. The chief guest of the evening happened to be Sir Henry Cotton, the author of New India, and the president of the Congress Session in Bombay in 1904. In the hall, where the meeting was being held, they had put up my portrait and Sir Henry Cotton happened to notice it. Looking at the portrait, he said a few words in my praise, and regretted that a young man of such adventurous spirit and fervent patriotism should be reduced to a pass that had blighted his life for good. He expressed the hope that the International Court of Justice at Hague would restore me back to France and, thus, save itself from being the instrument of trampling under foot every man's bare right to hold his own opinions without any molestation from the State. This reference to me by Sir Henry Cotton had raised a storm of criticism against him in the political dovecotes of England. To sympathise with Savarkar was such an abomination, even though the praise had not been free from censure! Some suggested that the speaker should be deprived of his knighthood. Others hinted that he should be made to forfeit his pension. Ultimately, the whole incident had proved to be nothing better than the proverbial storm in the tea-cup, though it was not without its repercussions in India. The Indian National Congress was alarmed by the news, and seemed to have lost its balance. Sir William Wedderburn, the president of the Congress session that year, and Surendra Nath Bannerji, one of its most prominent spokesmen, while returning from the annual Congress Session, attended a public meeting at Calcutta, where, speaking on the incident, they put a gloss on Sir Henry Cotton's remarks upon me, and declared that the Congress had nothing to do with Savarkar and his tribe and felt no sympathy whatever for him and his doings. I read this news in the cutting of the **Kesari** noticed above. Strange to say, the **Kesari** itself in its two leaderettes had sought to exonerate Sir Henry Cotton, and, in reference to me in that matter, had used a form of address that was highly insulting to me. It had said, "Sir Henry Cotton did not even know who this Savarkar was, whether he was a black man or a white man." Even nationalist paper like the Kesari at Poona had to write in that tone then. It was a subterfuge, common in those days, to establish one's innocence and prestige by running down Savarkar as a traitor, and by referring to him, in name and style, as the veriest criminal. Every political organisation, at the time, used that handy weapon to save its own skin. It was a cruel irony of fate, indeed, that an English gentleman should speak of Savarkar in glowing terms, while his countrymen at home should refer to him in newspapers and elsewhere in the language of insult and infamy. But, it was not the newspapers that were really to blame in this matter. It only showed the wretched plight to which a foreign rule inevitably reduces a subject nation. It showed that we lost under it even the sense of humanity which, as individuals, we ought to hold, as the minimum that is due from one man to another. What a heavy price this, to pay for bare existence!

Martyr or Rascal

Someone was peeping in through the bars of my door. "How do you do, barrister?" "I am all right, by your grace," I answered. "What is it that you say? Sir, where are you in worth? What am I before you?" he said. He continued that he had a talk with a friend from England from which he had learnt that the whole of Europe was applauding me as a martyr. The newspapers in France and Germany were comparing me with patriots like Woolfetone and Robert Emmett and Mazzini. Even in far off Portugal, newspapers had published a sketch of my life as it came to their hands. The gentleman from Europe had mentioned that he desired to see me, but the man who was talking to me had informed him that it was impossible to grant his request. He was, however, placing himself in the chawl opposite at the time of my usual walk in the square below, and, to satisfy his curiosity, I was asked to look up in that direction. The man indulging in this panegyric suddenly veered round, as it were, and added pointedly, "And, Sir, do you know what an Anglo-Indian Newspaper in Bombay has written about you in its latest issue? Referring to the Hague decision, it has poured its poison upon you." "Let me know, what it has said about me; a public worker is ever eager to know what his opponents, rather than his friends, say of him," I interposed. "The paper is glad over the sentence passed upon you, and in its jubilation, it has written—The rascal has at last met with his fate.' "Well then, the newspapers in Europe have called me a martyr, this paper denounces me as a rascal. The extremes cancel each other, and the real man that I am abides as ever."

The door that was shut upon me in the morning was unlocked only at ten o'clock thereafter. There was not the least chance of its being opened earlier. This rule had habituated me to expect none during the interval, and it had reconciled me completely to the solitude of the cell in which I lay confined. Besides, what little restlessness I had felt at the beginning had by now entirely disappeared. Again, I had lately come upon the means to overcome the tedium of my utter loneliness. Underneath and in the hollow of the tiles overhead and through the cleft in beam over my head, two pigeons used to come and make their home. I used to while away my time watching them. My work went on as usual; only I had something here as diversion for my mind. Today, while I was so pre-occupied, I heard the jarring sound of the door. This was so unusual, indeed, that I at once surmised that something uncommon was going to happen. With eager eyes, I looked up, when the Havildar told me that the Sahib wanted me in the Office below. The word 'follow' had an electric effect upon my mind, as it has upon the mind of every prisoner here. So, anxious he is to escape from the dull monotony of his daily life in the cell. It was not unlike that of a tethered animal which, the moment it learns that the tether had snapped, feels an exhilaration and joy that freedom instills into its frame. I got up. I suppressed my curiosity to know—why the Sahib had ordered me down. It was a rule with me never to make such an enquiry. But the kind-hearted watchman volunteered me the news that "mine had come to see me".

I Meet My Wife

I came into the Office and what did I see? I saw my wife and her brother standing in front of me, and near the barred window. In the garb of a prisoner, in the abject condition writ large upon my countenance, with heavy and chained shackles upon my feet, they saw me coming up to them! A pang went to my heart. Four years ago when I had left them in Bombay to proceed to England for further studies, what glowing picture they had drawn of my returning home as a full-fledged bar-at-law! They must have imagined then that I would come back to them covered with glory, and with prospect of affluence before them. But today and here, they meet me as a prisoner laden with heavy shackles and nothing but blank despair before him. My wife was but nineteen years old, and such a rude shock it must be to her tender heart to see me in this plight. The two were standing on the other side of the window-bars. They dare not even touch my hand. There was nearby a strict and relentless guard of strangers to us. The mind was full of thoughts which would not allow the contact of words to express them. This was going to be the last meeting between us, and the fifty years that were to follow meant perhaps the separation of a life-time. The words of parting were to be uttered in the presence of the gaoler, who was no countryman of ours! He looked at us with eyes that were devoid of any sympathy for us. The meeting told us, as it were, that we were never to meet again on this side of life.

These thoughts passed through my mind like clouds in a summer sky, and they went to my heart to choke it completely. But my will, the sentinel on guard, barred the door against their entrance, and had instantly dispelled them to the winds. Our eyes had met and I sat down before her. I asked if she had recognised me. "Only the dress has changed," I added with a smile, "I am the same as ever. These clothes protect me well from the cold weather." The two outside the window, recovering their good humour, talked to me as if we were together in the privacy of our home. The conversation flowed freely, and, picking up the thread, I assured them that we might meet again if benign providence so willed it. Till then, they must think of life, not as mere multiplication of children, or building of houses, as birds build their nests of straw, but as something higher and nobler than these things. For the usual kind of life, even the crows and kites live. If life meant dedication and service, then they had already lived it. They had broken up their home and their fire-hearth along with it. And they had done it so that thousands may live happily and freely after them. If they thought too much of their personal safety and comfort, let them remember how plague and pestilence had devastated a hundred happy homes. Had they not seen newly wedded couples rent asunder by the cruel hand of death? They must face the inevitable with fortitude. They say here that prisoners are allowed to take their families to the Andamans after a few years' term of imprisonment. I told them that, in that case, I would take them there to establish a home and live happily in each other's company. Otherwise, they must prepare themselves to bear it all with patience, and to live courageously. To which they replied that they would ever try to do so, and that the brother and sister together could take care of each other. They asked me to be no more anxious about them; and what they desired was that I should take care of myself. If that was assured to them, they would get all they wanted. While this talk was passing between us and some words yet remained unuttered on our lips, the Superintendent intervened and warned us that our time was up. I stopped it all at once. My brother-in-law turned to me while he was about to depart, and whispered hurriedly that I should never fail to repeat the mantra he had given me. Every morning I was to repeat the Mantram:

कृष्णाय वासुदेवाय हरये परमात्मने। प्रणतः क्लेशनाशाय गोविंदाय नमोस्तु ते॥

Looking at him wistfully, I promised to carry out his behest. They had departed. Without looking back, I walked inside, clanging my chains as if I could wear them easily. But my mind was not so easy. It repeated vehemently the words I had spoken to them and tried to frighten me. But my will tied it down as a wild animal is tamed under the yoke. Exhaustion and fatigue overcame me completely. As soon as I had entered my cell and the Havildar had locked the door on me, I collapsed on the floor. I had almost fainted when I heard some noise over my head. I looked up and I saw the young little ones of the two pigeons in the tiles above, cooing and crying with a shrill wail. The mother-bird, I learnt, later, had been that very morning shot by the bullet of our gaoler, while she was carrying in her beak food for her youngsters. The little ones waited and waited, and, in sheer desperateness and hunger, flapped their wings and were raising that wail. Alas! It was a picture painted for my eyes of the suffering I was experiencing. The Creator had chosen such a dark and tragic background for it in order to spite me. The tension was too great to bear, and I passed into sleep where I lay on the ground.

"Wake up, how dare you sleep? If the boss sees you sleeping during the hours of work, he will rate us severely for your lapse." So said the warden passing by my door, while he beat the bars with his stick to rouse me from my stupor.

I got up, I picked up the coil; I began to pound it; I spinned and I pulled out the threads—the same dull process over and over again.

It must be a month now that I was serving my sentence in this gaol. All the same, I was being given the same food that I used to get before I was declared a member of this fraternity. Milk was, therefore, a part of my food even now. I had hardly finished my food when the Havildar called me out, and I saw the Superintendent right in front of me. "Take up your bedding," he said. I felt within me that the time had come for my transportation to the Andamans. I came down to the gate of the prison and I saw the prison van drawn up before it. I was put inside, the shutters were down, the door was closed, and I could see nothing around me. Only the rumbling and rolling sound of the carriage wheels told me that I was moving to some place outside the prison I had left behind. Suddenly, the van came to a standstill. I was let down, and, behold! I was in front of another prison-gate. I passed through all the ceremonial of a prisoner to be freshly ushered into its sanctum! I was put into the cell assigned to me for my stay in the new place. This gaol was drearier and more lonely than the one I had left behind. I saw in the distance a warder coming in my direction. Dinner was served. The warder, who put me in this gaol, was not an Indian. He was a foreigner. Casting his look round about him, the European sergeant who had brought me here, bid me good day. I asked him in a low voice where I was, what prison it was. The sergeant spelt the word for me so that the warder in charge may not know what he was saying to me. The word he spelt was **"Byculla"**.

□

2

In the Gaol at Byculla

While climbing up to my cell in the Byculla prison, I felt that I had to go one step higher in solitariness and dejection. For the cell here was more gloomy and far lonelier than the one I had occupied at Dongri. At Dongri, I had no other person near about me, but the noise of the outer world fell upon my ears. I had, besides, a book or two to read, and some sundry articles about me. Here everything of that kind was gone. No noise was heard here of the humming world. Not a soul moved here, and articles of daily use were not here, so that I had no companionship here of any kind whatsoever. For want of these, I felt here completely isolated in mind and body, and, hence more lonely and deserted than ever. I surveyed my room. There was nothing in it to see and inspect. I paced up and down. What must be the condition of my fellow-conspirators and of the revolutionary society we had formed? What plan must we work out for its future?—These thoughts occupied my mind at the moment.

The evening meal was served. A mind tossed on the stormy ocean of politics and full of conflicting thoughts on the subject found some relief in other kind of occupation. After the meals, I cleaned my pots and washed them. I then came up to the door and stood behind its bars. The evening came to pass into night with its philosophic calm. The same day and evening and its thoughts 'too deep for tears' have formed the theme of the second part of my poem—**Saptarshi**.

I submitted two petitions today to the authorities concerned. In one of them I had asked the Government to allow me the quantity of milk to give me in the jail at Dongri. The stopping of it gave me pain in the stomach as I had to eat my bread dry in the prison at Byculla. In the second, I had requested the authorities to permit me the use of my books, one at least out of them, which they had taken away from me at Dongri. If none of them was to be made available to me for reading here, I should at least be permitted here to read the English Bible, I added. The answer to these was—"No milk, shall see about the Bible."

Some days passed and I got a copy of the Bible. For a good long time now, I had read nothing. Hence, I opened the Bible so soon as I had it in my hands. The warder, thereupon, warned me that I was not to read during the day and in working hours. It was not to be kept in the cell; he would give it to me for two hours after the day's work was over. I handed back the book to the warder and resumed my work. As usual, I composed my verses to keep company with the work my hands were plying. At last, the day went down and the Bible came back to me.

The life of Jesus Christ and his Sermon on the Mount had always appealed to me, and I had cherished them both with deep reverence. In France, I had read the New Testament with close attention. I used to read it daily and to meditate upon the text. My verses on Guru Govind Singh had now been finished. Saptarshi was almost drawing to its close. I had not sufficient historical material with me to continue the former and I had no fresh subject in my mind to compose into verse. The life of Jesus Christ suggested itself to me, at this juncture, as a proper theme to weave into a song. The setting for it was furnished by me in the history of the Jews which I had studied with interest and appreciation when I was reading the Old Testament, especially in relation with the bitter struggle of the nation and its heroes for emancipation from the thraldom into which it had passed in its unfortunate history. Their helplessness and anguish and their efforts to set the race free had struck a sympathetic chord in my heart at the time. ...

But why do they not despatch me at once to the Andamans? If a prisoner bound for the Andamans were not sent there within six months from the time that he had begun to run his sentence. The period outside, I had heard, was not to be counted in the sentence itself. Further, I had read in the Andaman Regulations that within six months from the time he had spent in the Andaman Jail, the prisoner was set free on the island itself to do the work he liked, and if he knew the three 'R's, he was given work to supervise over a batch of hundred prisoners, or some similar light and lucrative job to follow it. If there was any truth in what I had heard and read on the subject, then life there was anyway better than the life I was leading here. At least in the

Andamans, under those conditions, I could sit on the sea-beach and watch the waves rolling at my feet. I could inhale draughts of fresh air, I could mingle in the crowd, and make contacts with the people. I could then do some work for enlightening the people and be of use to them in several other ways. Ten years more, and I could take my family there and set up a house for myself. Life for me would not then be so hard to endure. In this vein of thought, I suddenly remembered those who had suffered for me and had been sentenced for ten or fifteen years of hard labour. What of them? I thought. Are they not doomed to spend their lives in dark cells! Some of them were my friends from childhood; others my trusted colleagues; others, again, were my staunch followers. Most of them looked up to me, loved me and adored me. And I could do nothing for them or for their bereaved families! These calamities had befallen them on my account; they had suffered for me. Right or wrong, they had a clear grievance against me. Out of many such, I recalled those who had old parents to look after. Fate had taken from these parents the staff of their lives. For two out of them and their parents again, I felt deeply grieved. And last, what of that friend of mine, a hero indeed, who had suffered hardships that one could not bear narrating? He had not breathed a word of reproach against me for all that he had endured so bravely. And those young men, again, O, it made my heart too full to remember them all. What were my sorrows, what were my trials compared to these? I must forget mine in theirs. Again, the mind would recoil from these musings. Have I lingered behind? It would ask me. Have I not borne the brunt and faced the music? Why then should I brood over the inevitable and be lost in grief? My work was their work. And we must be all burden-bearers and burden-sharers. And the worst to bear was yet to come. It was but the beginning. The end? Who knows of it, and who dared forecast it?

Long before this, I had submitted an appeal in which I prayed that the sentences passed upon me should run concurrently. Among the reasons I had given to support my plea, I had quoted relevant sections of the Penal Code which had laid it down that a life-sentence meant a period in a man's life which was the period of his active work. In England, it was reckoned, at the longest, to be no more than fourteen years. In India, commensurate with the offence, it could not extend beyond twenty-five years. Here I was sentenced to run a full period of fifty years' hard labour. According to the Penal Code then and its interpretation of what constituted a life-sentence, I must take two lives to finish up my sentence, if it were to run consecutively. That was, on the face of it, ridiculous. If I were to survive these fifty years across the seas in the Andaman islands, it would really mean, my rebirth—being dead once, and being born again legally speaking to put through my second sentence of twenty-five years. And what a horrible death-in-life it was to endure the first twenty-five years in the prison-house of the Andamans! So, I appealed to them that the two sentences passed upon me should be made to run concurrently. The year of my discharge should not be 1960, but twenty-five years earlier. That would save them the ridicule of the step they had taken.

I got today a communication from the Government saying that the decision of the Court that my two sentences shall run consecutively was final and the Government saw no reason to alter it. A gentleman had come to me personally to report the contents of the communique. Adopting its technical language, he remarked jocularly, "My dear Savarkar, the Government had, at last, decided that you were to run your first life-sentence first, and your second life-sentence after it, that is, you have to take a second life to run it full." To which I replied in the same vein, "Yes, indeed, but I have, at least, the consolation that for this purpose, it has subscribed to the Hindu doctrine of re-birth, and had disowned the Christian doctrine of resurrection."

The dinner so early today? How was it? The prison meant the strictest regimentation. Everything was to happen there punctually upon the hour. Not a minute too early, not a minute too late, even if a prisoner were at the door of death itself. If the prisoner were to starve and die, none could give him a morsel to eat before the prescribed hour. Death, if it so chose, may wait for its victim, the dinner shall not wait upon death. How can I account, then, for its arrival earlier? Yes, it may be the shadow of some coming event. The European Officer in duty upon me—I looked at him with expectant eyes. He pretended to push his hat backwards, and taking his hand behind it, waved it twice. It was a sign to me that I was to be removed from here to some far-off place.

I finished my dinner. The verses that I had scrawled on the prison-wall with the help of a pointed stone, I read rapidly, and treasured them up in my memory. I rubbed off the scored lines as hurriedly as I had read them. I did not desire to leave any trace of them behind me. Hardly had I finished the job, when the Havildar at the door called out "Come away". He opened the door and let me out. The gaoler handed me over to the European sergeant as if I was some goods or chattel to carry over. Motor, station, railway, and station once again! That was all I knew of it. The station where they got me down was Thana. And my destination from there was to be the gaol at Thana.

□

3
At Thana

It seemed to be all bustle and noise in the prison at Thana. Everyone was, as it were, on the tiptoe of expectation. A prisoner sentenced to fifty years' transportation to the Andamans, a bar-at-law was arriving! The Officers in charge had issued the strictest orders that none was to look at me even with an eye askance. A part of the prison was purged clean of its prisoners and warders. It was kept apart for my occupation. But nothing could repress the curiosity of its inmates to have a look at me. My cell was guarded by the worst known warders of the place. They were, one and all, Musalmans and the wickedest of them, into the bargain. There was preternatural calm and solitude about me. My meal was served in due time, but I could hardly touch a morsel thereof. It consisted of hard-baked jwari bread and some vegetables ill-cooked and too sour to taste. I broke the bread, put the piece of it in my mouth, could hardly bite it and had to wash it down with water. Only a little of it I could eat. Then came evening, the door was closed, and I lay on my bed for sleep. It was now completely dark, for night had followed, when I heard gentle tapping on the door. I heard the voice of someone calling. It came from somewhere, I felt, as if in fear and trembling. I turned round and saw and discovered that the wickedest of my warders was beckoning on to me. I went to the door when, all eyes and ears, he whispered to me, "Sire, we have heard about your daring and valour; I am a slave to one so brave as you; I will do all that I can for you, no fear about it. Today I have brought you some news which I may pray you will keep strictly to yourself, for woe to me if it were to leak out. You are a hero, and I feel sure that you will never let me down. But I must warn you all the same." So, he carried on in a suppressed tone, and then coming up very close to me, whispered, "Your brother is here." "What brother?" I asked him. He replied that it was my younger brother. And he left precipitately as if he was anxious not to be caught in the act by any casual observer. For my part, I withdrew inside.

The Younger Brother

My younger brother! A youth hardly twenty years old, and so many of the same age with him. A bomb was thrown in Ahmedabad at Lord Minto, the Viceroy of India, and my brother was put under arrest as a suspect in that case. He had to undergo much persecution on that account but he did not flinch, though he was then but eighteen years old. He was soon after released as innocent of the crime, and returned home to rest. But hardly had he laid his head on the pillow when he was arrested for a conspiracy and crime of a political character, and was sent to jail as an under-trial prisoner. For one long year, he had to pass through all the agonies of mind and body—intimidation, threats, torture and persecution. But he bore them all well with stern determination and, even in that tender age, did not fall from his vow. This was my younger brother. Orphaned from his childhood, I, his elder brother, was like a father to him. He never knew to live apart from me and cried like a child when I had to stay away from him even for a day. And this was so until very recently. To find him in the same place, in shackles like myself, and undergoing the hard labour of grinding corn, was an experience harrowing in itself. To add to it he was to learn from me today, as I had learnt about him, that I was here on a life-sentence and on my way to the Andamans. He had heard of that sentence, no doubt, but they had all hoped that the Hague Tribunal would turn it down and order me back to France. In that expectation, my brother, and others like him, would drown their own suffering. But now that the slender thread of hope had given way, and I was to be transported for life, how can I be the bearer of that news to him? Oh that I should be the person of all others to break it to him! One of his elder brothers had already gone to the Andamans. And now I was to follow him there! I was to meet him no more. Already orphaned in the loss of his parents, this brother of mine was to be doubly orphaned now. When he realises that the Andamans for me meant no sight of me for him any longer, what a blow it will be for him, and how it will break his tender heart! In case he is set free, to whom will he go for help and shelter? Who will shelter him? Who will look after his education? The lad shall have to go from door to door, and every door will be shut against him. With contracted brows, they will look at him and turn him out as a prisoner, a convict, an outlaw, and a man to be shunned.

On the rising tide of grief, these thoughts lifted their heads to be drowned with the ebb tide that followed it. But they suffocated me all the same.

My Master, Have It

The warden returned. He came up very near to me. It was completely dark by this time and he whispered, "Master, take it." He put a slate into my hands, and expostulated, "The Superintendent has warned the wardens against giving you any news of your brother on pain of ten years' rigorous imprisonment across the seas. If you were to breathe a word of it, then I am finished." So saying, he instantly left me and went his way with measured steps and with creaking noise of his shoes in the corridor.

The slate was a letter to me from my dear brother, my younger brother, Bal as we called him. A lantern was burning at a distance, and the writing was dimly visible in its light. I read the letter with feeling of affection welling up in my heart. It contained not a word of sorrow, repentance or defeat. On the other hand, it breathed an assurance that, come what may, he would never budge an inch from the vow that he had taken. He was prepared to face the worst in fulfilment of that vow. I decided to indite an answer. In the Andamans, we can send only one letter home during the year. But sometimes that opportunity even is denied to us. I felt, therefore, that this was the last chance I had to write to my dear Bal. I beckoned to the warden who was patrolling in the corridor. He came up with stealthy steps. Let the night fall, and then he would do what he could, he said to me, and went away.

I must have completed half the period of my sleep when I was awakened from it by some noise near my door. Startled from my sleep, I got up, and, behold, 'the warden was tapping with his staff against the bars. He signed me to write on, and brought his lantern close unto me. I was amazed to find him so sympathetic to me, knowing as I did, what risk he was running for his life if he was found communicating with me. And who was he? He was a notorious and hardened dacoit with not a spark of kindness in his cruel heart. I simply wondered then as I have wondered since when I had a similar experience in my later life. And I had no small measure of such happy surprises. I tried to thank him, but he stopped me, adding that the first thing I was to do was to finish the letter forthwith.

Do or Die

And yet I doubted that the man might deceive me. Who knows, he may hand over the written slate straight to the gaoler and would then put me in a fix. I had passed years of my young life dodging the detectives set on me. Therefore, I put no name in the letter that I wrote. I mentioned no names and referred to no places. Nor did I write about any specific plan for the future. I pointed out that I was going to the Andamans by putting the necessary asterisks to indicate the name. And I added, "If, according to regulations in that quarter I could take the members of my family to that place after five or ten years, then I would spend the rest of my life in the acquisition of knowledge. If it were not given to me to step my foot once again on the soil of India, my projected epic, like that of the sage Valmiki, will announce me to the world through the mouths of my disciples, my Lavas and Kushas, who would sing it throughout the length and breadth of my dear motherland. This service was enough to fulfil my life's work. But if they were not to release me even after the completion of my first life-sentence, then? I shall try to escape by any means available to me or perish in the act. This was my firm resolve and there was no relenting from it. Do not think of me, and do not shed tears of sorrow that you have failed in your life. Some fuel had to burn in a steam-engine that the steam may rise up from it and the engine begin to move. Are we not that fuel that the fire may burn and the flames rise up and spread far and wide? To burn thus is in itself a great act." The warden coughed and warned me to finish up in time. I put the slate near the door and withdrew inside. I said to the warden while he was about to leave, "I do not wish that you should suffer the least for me. Do this bold act if only you feel like doing it. Don't risk it." "What boldness is there in this?" he replied with a smile, "Sir, I am no ordinary thief, no coward soul is mine. I have attacked a whole village with open eyes. I have plundered it in the teeth of them all. I have escaped fighting while they had pursued us. I am fearless, and, hence, I am out to serve one like you. Where is daring here? I know not. It is only two months from now and I am free. The daring is on your side; for you laugh in the face of adversity."

He delivered the Letter

He went and gave the letter faithfully to my brother. I had not forgotten the definition of valour he had given to me. The dacoit considered the thief as his inferior and despised him even as, among the untouchables, the **mang** does not touch the **domba.** Next day, I sought to bring the truth home to him that pillaging and loot may involve daring of a kind, but, as it was selfish, it was by no means either laudable or meritorious. I did not put it so to him directly, but by means of a parable, I set him right on the matter. He seemed to understand me all right. Never since then did he boast to me of his exploits as a dacoit.

It was not even two days after my arrival at Thana when my brother—now Dr. Savarkar—was removed elsewhere. The Officers knew that we were never to meet each other thereafter, but they did not arrange for our meeting together here and behind the prison-bars, when only the partition on a wall separated us, one from the other. For years together, after this event, I did not know where he went, when he was set free, and what he did in life. No information was given to me about him by the authorities or by anyone else who knew him.

Behold My Tiger!

The head of wardens in this jail was particularly appointed in charge of the lonely part of it, where, for the time being, I was kept in custody. He was stout in body, light-hearted and funny in disposition, ever smiling, but the most secretive of all the wardens in that gaol. Naturally, the European Officers of that place confided in him. He always tried to draw me into conversation. Real or apparent, perhaps it was a mingled feeling, he was full of compassion for me. He tried to give me as much good food as possible. He never gave me the slightest trouble. He ever connived my talking with anyone else. He discussed politics with me and sought to impress me that I had ruined my life by following the wild goose chase. Coming and going, he called other wardens near my door and, pointing at me, would exclaim, "Behold my tiger. A man should be like him." Then he would sing a skit: "Marvellous is thy deed, O Fate, marvellous thy play. Thou hast trapped a tiger in a spider's net I say." And then he would eye me significantly and go into a dance while he chanted those lines again and again. Sometimes he raised a discussion in which he put a question and answered its pros and cons, all by himself. "How mighty is this Government," he would say, "how funny that these few brats who would beat it! And, look here, these aspire to take the raj back from the British Government!" Then with this argument on his lips, he would flourish his stick around him, take a few steps forward, and whirl himself round in a dance. Suddenly, he would put a question to the company of wardens he had gathered round him. He would ask one of them, "Why, O, Ramya, do you think that the wind is cut to pieces by my passes at it?" And the company would burst into a peal of laughter. They could not but laugh, for was it not their Havildar, their chief, who had cracked the joke? Perhaps, they would suffer if they showed reticence. But the chief would turn round on them and ejaculate, "Fools, why do you laugh? Do not these few brats do the same to the British Government? I beat the wind with my stick. My lord, here, would blow up the Government with his daring conspiracy. Am I so ridiculous after all? Is not his venture as foolish as mine?"

The Coquette

Sometimes, as I was bathing, he used to stare at me, and calling out the wardens under him, would address them, "Oh Gondya, behold his body! It is like the bar of pure gold. How well-knit the arms, how full-developed the chest! Evidently, he must be a fine wrestler in his day." Suddenly, he would change the tone. In a piteous tone, he would say to me, "Sire, what a splendid young man you are, and what the devil have you done with your youth? This was your time to serenade with some fine girl abroad and be lost in her embraces. Instead of spending your time in England in such pleasure, here you are, hardly turned twenty-five and with but a fringe of moustache on your lips, embracing these heavy iron chains and shackles. How do you love to fall into their arms, I wonder." At other times, he would burst, "No, indeed, these are not your deeds. Some big men have made a cat's paw of you, that is all. They have feathered their nest and lined their coats very well, indeed, and at your expense. How they must have duped you with fine promises and then, in the nick of time, let you down! O, Sir, I am so happy, I am far happier than you are. I draw my wages all right. I have my pension as a retired servant. I get fifty to sixty rupees every month. I jingle the coin in my pocket and am carefree. While you, with your fine appearance, your youth, your noble profession, high status and with the daughter of a minister for your wife, you have shattered your life completely, and have forfeited the bliss of paradise on earth. All for the country, you say, Pooh!" I bore it all patiently. But sometimes it became too much for me to put up with this nonsense. With folded hands and in a sneer, he would say to me: "Tell me verily, my master, how you were going to win the raj. When do you think you will be set free? There is going to be a big Darbar at Delhi in coming December (he evidently referred to the coronation of King George V); do you think that it will bring you amnesty and pardon?" To which I would reply calmly, "What is that jubilee to us? Yet I hope to get out ten or twelve years hence, if times prove propitious." Then he would make a wry face and say, "No, they will never release you. They will torture you and make you rot in the gaol and they will take you out with your corpse, not a minute earlier." It became impossible for me, at times, to save myself from this harsh man's cruel badinage. Whenever he would call some five or ten wardens to gather round him, and would address me in their presence as "behold, my hero", and would jig and dance and jeer at me with the flourish of his stick, I felt I would die of it, so piercingly it went to my heart to watch him. He was, as it were, taking out a caged tiger for show round the circus ring. This show, for children to laugh at and to enjoy, was so much painful to me. I chafed at it and felt that being sent to the gallows was better than life in that condition. This was like piercing red-hot iron into a heart already lacerated with grief.

The Crown of Thorns

Often and often did I repeat to myself the text from the Yoga Sutra which enjoined that a man must be as much prepared, while in prison, to pass through agonies of the mind as he had to suffer tortures of the body. If that suffering were to damp his courage and his ardent spirit, then he must conclude that the courage and the spirit were but a momentary phase. If they enjoy the show, why should you not as well enjoy it? You do not do so because you do not possess that detachment of mind which makes a man rise above personal considerations. When you know who you are, what you did, and why you did it, what do you care if they parody you? How do you lose anything thereby? Do you not know that long before you, others, who were messengers of God, had to wear their crown of thorns. The notorious criminals rotting in jails had not spared them from jibes and jokes. The world worships them today as saints and seers, as "prophets, priests and kings", in spite of those jibes. It touches their feet and bows its head before them. Thoughts like these reconciled me to the conduct of that man. It is now sixteen years since that day, and I cannot yet say if the man, as some persons used to say of him, was deliberately put upon me to torture my soul and damp my courage, or he was merely a fool who had sincerely felt for me and had expressed that sympathy in such an outrageous manner. Whatever that be, the song that he was singing then still rings in my ears: "Marvellous, is thy deed, O, Fate, marvellous is thy play. Thou hast trapped a tiger in a spider's net, I say."

"What news?" I asked him one day. To which he replied, "What news can I give you, Sir? You have well-nigh perished for them and you cannot still forget them. What kind of people are they? And what is their service to the country? You are arrested, and they have gone into hiding, they have covered their faces; not one of them bothers the least about you. What news, then, can I give you? 'After me the deluge'—that is all I can say about it."

A Confirmed Rogue

The coronation ceremony in England had come and gone. Dame rumour was busy saying that many a prisoner was to get his release presently. The Havildar had just talked to me about it when the officer, who occasionally conveyed the news to me of the outside world, came up to me and hurriedly said, "A brahmin in Madras of Shakta persuation had killed Collector Mr. Ashe by a rifle shot. The Officer, it is said, had something to do with the trial of Chidambaram Pillay. What is your opinion about it?" When the Havildar saw me that afternoon, he pointedly put to me the same question. "Well, have you any friends in Madras?" he asked. "I do not know, I cannot say, I am confined within the four walls of this prison. How can I then know anything about them?" I answered. "Besides, you had just said, don't you remember, that they had all gone underground, they had covered their faces and spoke not a word about me." The Havildar nodded to his friends significantly, and, pointing at me, uttered: "What a confirmed rogue, a double-distilled essence, is he?" I have not yet caught the import of his observation. Perhaps he thought that I had already known what he was saying to me, and my reply to him made him realise that I was not to be drawn out so easily.

My Spectacles on Sale

All my belongings here were a pair of spectacles and a miniature copy of Bhagwadgita. This morning the Havildar demanded them of me. "The Saheb wants them," he observed. I knew not what it meant. Presently, the Superintendent followed, and I asked him why I was deprived of my pair of spectacles. To this he gave the following explanation. I was a conspirator; the rule was that a convict of that type lost all his property to the State. Government had, therefore, confiscated all my belongings. My trunks, clothing and books had already been taken in possession on my arrest in London. And, presently, these articles were to be sold by public auction. The money so recovered will be appropriated by the State. That my anna-worth of Gita and my spectacles, the last things I had with me, should also be taken away from me, grieved even my fellow-prisoners. And some of the wardens resolved that they would not purchase a single thing of mine to be sold by public auction. I had to expostulate with them so that they might change their mind. I told them, "Look here, in that baggage, there were costly clothes. Lest anyone else should get them for a trifle, I would be very pleased that you should go in for their purchase. If you desisted, a foreigner might have them practically as a loot. I would prefer that they fall to the lot of my own countrymen. I feel if you and your children used my clothes and other articles, they would be put to good use." I persuaded some of my wardens, the sensible ones among them, to go in for them. On the following day, my copy of the Bhagwatgita and my pair of spectacles were restored to me with the understanding that I was to use them as property belonging to Government.

The Party Bound for the Andamans

The prison today is all agog. A party bound for the Andamans is to arrive here. The party is known in prison parlance as 'chalan'. Of all the convicts in the presidency, those who are branded as hardened criminals are always sentenced for transportation. Out of those, the worst are picked out and detailed to confinement in prisons scattered all over the province. After a few days, they are roll-called and inspected. Such of them, as are unfit to be stayed in their own country and in local surroundings, are then dispatched to the gaol in Thana. Here they rally and reside for some time whence they are put on a steamer bound for the Andamans. These are designated as 'chalan' for they proceed from here for their destination across the seas. The thief, the murderer, the incendiary, the prisoner, the heartless dacoit and the cold-blooded killer—all downright cruel and fiercest of the fierce—a troop of these, a veritable procession of them was to march today into the prison at Thana. Hence, this stir and excitement inside.

The arrival of this gang was a signal for holiday-making and mirth within the prison-walls. For it relieved them for a day from the hard routine of their normal life. They pine for such relaxation. The slightest change from it is enough for them to forget the monotony of their dull existence. A crow flying up in the air meets with an accident and drops down one of its wings. Sparrows peck at sparrows with their beaks. And the prisoners look up, feel interested and, lost in that contemplation, forget the worries of their hard lot in this house. Today it was the chalan coming. Everyone, from the *jamadar* down to the lowest in the rank, was full of the news. Everyone seemed to be in a hurry. A set of rooms was kept apart for the confinement of these prisoners from abroad. It was located in one of the eastern wings of the old fortification. Today the rooms were swept clean, the provisions were arranged for and clothes were counted and put together. Every other arrangement for the accommodation of the chalan was well-nigh complete. Half of the prisoners were pre-occupied in this work, others loitered about as busy-bodies and none of them had eyes or ears for anything else about them, so completely were they absorbed in expectation of the show that was coming.

The Party Arrives

It was three o'clock in the afternoon. Everyone in prison asked of his neighbour why the chalan had not yet arrived. Just at the moment there was stir and bustle near the main gate of our prison. Every inmate was seen moving to and fro. "Has the chalan come?" "What's it that is coming?" "Yes, right near the gate." "How many are they?" "How do they look?" There was a shower of these questions and there was trepidation and movement, confusion and excitement all over the place. It affected not only the prisoners but the wardens as well. For the latter felt as tired of their job as the prisoners themselves. On a sudden we heard the sound of measured footfall and of clanging chains and shackles every moment approaching nearer and ringing clearer. The prisoner and the warden, one and all of them, were seen gathered in small crowds and by the passage, forgetful of or ignoring their normal life, and with eyes alert to witness the procession coming in. They seemed to be crouching low lest anyone may detect them off duty. At last, it came in—the chalan came in. How hideous to behold! There was in it a type of every kind. One looked very fierce, another hard and cruel, a third an incarnation of terror, a fourth thick-set and firm, a fifth coal-black in complexion—the rest a miscellaneous crew of varied features, some, indeed of presentable appearance among them. How they walked—some of them in the party! One walked upright and with chest in prominence, another strided with a heavy tramp as if he was returning as a hero of hundred battles. A third treaded as if he was bent to make mother earth fall at his feet, a fourth proceeded with a hang-dog look, nervous and ashamed to look up. The party was moving to its quarters in a row of two each. It was guarded by armed sepoys on either side of it. Between the measured paces of the regular soldiers and the clanging footfalls of the prisoners, it was a sight full of fun, nay, of grim humour.

The Master-Criminal

Look at that Musalman from Sindh. He is the super-dacoit. Behold him, stern of face with a jungle of thick hair crowning his head and hanging down his neck. He wears thick and pointed moustaches and a beard to match them. He rolls his protuberant eyes all around him. He flaunts his prisoner's garb, and wears the chains of his shackles like a girdle round his waist, as if he was decked out for a Kingship. He does it all nonchalantly. He has put his bedding under the armpit. He is calling out someone uproariously. He laughs and sports and walks along as if he was a victor returning home in triumph. The wardens say of him that it is his third turn to go to the Andamans. He was twice there before, each time sentenced to hard labour and transportation. And now he is transported for life. He boasts and brags that he had worked there as a *jamadar*, and that he was a terror to other prisoners in that colony. As an instance he tells, so the wardens report to me, that in a fit of rage he knocked down a young fellow with the bludgeoning blow of his stick, The blow had broken the skull and the victim had expired the day following. The dacoit-*jamadar* had felled the lad for being too intimate with his enemy. And he had taken no permission from the *jamadar* to talk to him. The *jamadar* had reported that the boy had fallen from the edge of an embankment where he was dêtailed for duty; hence the accident and the death.

And he had escaped scot-free! The new recruits to crime he

flabbergasted by telling that all the officers in the gaol at the Andamans were his friends. His return there meant his sure reinstatement in the old post. In support, he referred to them as this and that and the other Mr. So and So. So much did he impress the youngsters in the party by this tall talk, that, ever after, they attended upon him as his minions and propitiated him by flattery and service. Of course, the youngsters did this to save themselves from shame, and from the rigours of their punishment in the horrible prison to which they were being transported. The party on its way to Thana was regaled with plantains, coconuts, sweets and money-gifts by the passers-by on the route. These young recruits passed on the money to their future *jamadar,* and champooed his feet on the way. He, on his side, promised them cushy jobs, with the influence he had with Mr. Diggin or Mr. Montford. So, he spun yarns and thoroughly enjoyed himself. The gullibles in the party had to pay the price.

This one stabbed his Sister

Observe in the same gang this boy who is yet in his teens—not more than nineteen at the most. What did he do to deserve the company of that master-criminal—the dacoit we have described above? Well, one day he kicked his sister for abusing him as she found him in the company of moral rakes—those who indulged in *bhang* and took to evil ways. He killed her under the intoxication of that narcotic. He stabbed her in that frenzy and she died. Now he walks in that line bent under the heavy load he carried on his head. He limps for the heavy weight that binds his feet. He cannot bear the shackles on his feet and the load on his head. And he fears that once in that prison beyond the seas, he can never more see his kith and kin, his land of birth and his intimates at home. Between these two extremes—the dacoit at the one end and this boy at the other—one saw in this procession a variety of fierceness, shamelessness and cruelty. Behold this rank and file marching on—one by one, one after another—with their chains ringing to rhythm. It was a hideous sight to see. Indeed, it was a spectacle that none looked on without humiliation and disgust.

At last, the procession passed through the main gate. The gaoler came forth to inspect it. The news of his arrival on the scene made the onlookers run helter-skelter. Each of them escaped as he could, and pretended to resume his work. The wardens on the scene cried out, "No more noise, get on with your work." As if they were unaware of what was happening only a minute before! As if they themselves had not shared the sight and the fun with those whom they now presumed to reprimand! As if everything then was being carried out according to law and discipline!

A kindly Officer

On the following day, I was ushered into the presence of a Committee which was to examine me. It was to say if I was fit in body and mind, by age and several other things, to be transported to the Andamans. A kindly officer said to me at the time, "If you would really not go there, I shall try my very best, use all my influence, to keep you here. I shall not fail you." I said to him, "I am very grateful to you for your kind wishes. But it is not in the power of the Government of Bombay to keep me back in India. And I would not trouble you and you need not trouble yourself where we know we are helpless." I was then examined by the Committee. The officer was present at the examination. I had high fever; nevertheless, I was weighed and the board reported that I was fit to be carried over. And I was ordered to proceed to the Andamans. I took my bedding under the armpit. I carried my utensils in my hand, and I walked on to the place reserved for the chalan. I crossed the threshold and entered the eastern wing of the old fortification. This was the threshold of my entry into the Andamans. India lost me and I lost India. I was definitely bound for the Andamans.

□

4

On the Way

The portion of the prison-house reserved for the chalan's confinement in the gaol at Thana was to me like crossing the threshold and entering the precincts of the Andamans. The room in which I was locked up in that outlying part of the gaol, though a solitary cell, was within hearing of the rooms occupied by the prisoners in the chalan. I could hear from my room the noise they created, the sighs they heaved, their wails, their talks and their good cheer, clearly enough to divert me from the long loneliness of my own cell. My mind, oppressed as it was with dejection and grief, felt relieved by this company of prisoners near me. They were really hilarious, for, as I know, man laughs even in the dungeon-hole of utter calamity, overbearing grief, and unbearable tortures of body and mind. Such is his resilience. Perhaps, that horrid laughter is the acme of all laughters as it unburdens the soul of all the horrors of underground imprisonment. Man laughs when he is reduced to extremes, and his grief laughs with him when he grows callous to it, as if he has thrown it off himself to pass it on to the shoulders of callousness itself. Excessive joy or the ecstasy of joy, if you will, makes a man burst into tears. Similarly, an excess of grief bursts out into broad laughter. It is said that in the days of the French Revolution, when inhuman bloodshed, slaughter, guillotining and murder had been the order of the day; when no man's head was safe on his shoulders; when the premier and leader of today found himself to be the arch-traitor of tomorrow, with the guillotine waiting to chop off his head; when things had passed into the reign of terror, theatres in Paris were full to over-crowding, as they were never before, and wine flowed freely in the taverns of the city. Hilarity, mirth, merriment and brutal murder kept each other company, and danced and laughed and roared in sheer recklessness. "Let us eat, drink and be merry for tomorrow we die." That seemed to be the obsession of them all.

Reckless Laughter

The same was the experience during the great world war of 1914-1918. The officers and the crew on the German submarines had to do the hardest and the most dangerous duty during that period. With their head on their hands, they had to dive deep underneath the sea and expect death in that bottomless pit every moment of their breathing life; they had to torpedo boats and steamers plying above, at the risk of their lives. In that precarious state, they had to come up on the surface for rest and refreshment. And they ate and drank to their heart's content in the restaurants that were specially provided for them. Their slogan was—"Enjoy till thou goest mad! Enjoy, for tomorrow we die! Laugh till you go mad, and tomorrow be a morsel to fill the jaws of death!" In these pleasure-houses, the frenzy of laughter sometimes overstepped the bounds of decency, and let itself go in reckless dancing and mirth. For the reveller knew to certainty that his name, that was today on the dancing card, was to be enrolled tomorrow in the casualities of death. Verily the laughter of sorrow is the most hideous of all laughters.

These prisoners, deprived of all the good things of life and reduced to a condition of existence which beasts even may tremble to live in, their hands and feet bound in chains, their hearts seared and deadened by a career of crime, some of them, being new to sin, feeling the stings of conscience within them, fretting and fuming with anger, sighing and sobbing for grief, were still roaring with laughter—a hundred of them and more were weeping and laughing at the same time. The poignancy of their grief found no relief in light fun and humour. They reeled with the intoxication of the obscene of which they drank deep in this hell on earth. Some came from the province of Sindh, others from Dharwar, some belonged to Kathiawad and Gujarat, and others again were drawn from the Konkan. They talked in different tongues; their thoughts and feelings were so diverse, one from the other; they scarcely understood each other. But the obscene formed the common bond between them all. That had become their national language in which they could thoroughly participate and fully enjoy. This social union had come to them as an opportunity of a life-time, and they used it to the full and abandoned themselves completely to its pleasures and pastimes. The evening was the hour when this rebellious mood of frank and free indulgence in the obscene and the broadly humorous found its fullest outburst. The whole wing on that side of the prison was one pandemonium of shouts and cries, of abuses and peals of laughter, and of irrepressible utterance of coarse and foul language. But in this orgy of self-indulgence even, there ran an undercurrent of honour and duty. Human nature is, indeed, a strange amalgam of conflicting elements. These convicts indulged in this uproarious pastime as if it was a duty which they owed to themselves. If the lowest of the low had not laid this flattering unction to their souls, they could not have shamelessly gone in for the kind of life they were leading. The meanest and the most case-hardened among them egged on others, less perverse and less inured to these ways, by the slogans "O, my brethren, sing, O, you fools, go on, for the name and notoriety of our outward-bound phalanx." And they stressed their homily by adding that when they had been last in this place, they had all caught hold of the prison-bars and shaken them with all their might. They had hurled their pots and pans against the walls and the wardens were hard put to it to control them and restore silence. They cajoled, they wept, they went down on their knees and they doled out to each one of us a little tobacco as a solatium. "Shout, shout, O, you nincompoops, do not disgrace the name of this gang."

Its Fair Name

For it had made a name—this chalan to the Andamans—in the prison-world of those days. It was no mean institution or a body of men. To aspire to the membership of that notorious gang was no mean achievement. We had to pass through several examinations for admission to that status. It began with the ordinary lock up; the magistrate's court; the criminal session of the High Court; the jury; and the final verdict. Through these many sieves, we had to pass before we became eligible for the corps that was ordered for the Andamans, sent to transportation for life. The troop here was made up of the picked ones of this corps. They constituted the representative leaders of their several provinces. And it was the crown and culmination of the Underworld of crime. It had, indeed, a reputation to maintain, for whenever it came to Thana all the wardens of the place—the warden, the *jamadar*, the *havildar*, the gaoler and the Superintendent—had a fright. The bars must be broken, the walls must collapse, heads must be shattered, a warden or two must have their thrashing, and twenty or more of the gang must receive their whipping and lashing, and their skins must cut open and bleed till this hell on earth would have its quietus. This was our chalan, with this tradition to maintain. The wardens must wheedle them, if they at all cared for their lives. The chalan would incur disgrace if it did not bear up to this age-long reputation. The old ones of the gang admonished its recent members in the following words, "Why did you at all go in for crime, if you did not feel like coming up to the standard? Today we are the inheritors of its fame, and we must keep it. We should not tarnish it. Therefore, shout, cry, raise an uproar, dance and abuse. Oh, brothers, we are jealous guardians and cannot afford to lower its name."

Indeed, they felt that was their code of honour. When they indulged in the obscene and the slang common to their tribe, when they danced and jibed, an applause greeted them from all sides of the house. When someone appealed to maintain the honour of the chalan, whistling, clapping, the clanging of chains followed their pranks. And the whole atmosphere resounded to that noise. Thus, the wheel ran on and completed its full circle—victims as they were of their brute instincts and sensual appetites. This continued far into the night till the midnight hour had sounded its arrival. The pride of the chalan as an institution made the warden bend before it. The Superintendent lost his self-importance, and all had to eat the humble pie before this outrageous multitude. The only way to soften it was to offer them tobacco and beg of them to maintain silence, to talk if they liked, without being a nuisance to the rest of the colony. The officers were anxious, above everything else, to hand over the party intact when it left the place and was taken in charge by those who were to give it safe conduct, under proper escort, to its last destination. It was, indeed, a heavy strain on their minds and the tension was relieved when the chalan had quitted the place in the same condition and numbers that it had entered it.

We always follow the tradition of the community where we belong to. There was no finer example of this **esprit de corps** than this chalan and its behaviour in our midst. If indulgence in the vulgar and the obscene is the rule, abstention becomes a sin and a crime. In the days of our Holi, that man is a disgrace who abhors the time-honoured practice of mud-slinging. The rest laugh and jeer at him for not falling into line with them. Such is communalism and its practice all over the world. That is, verily, the way of all flesh.

The Prestige of a Barrister

I may have suffered the same fate but I escaped because I happened to be a bar-at-law, a member of the legal profession, and, hence, a man of prestige. The criminal class, and the worst of that class, fears a barrister as they do not fear or revere a poet, a man of learning, a saint or an astute statesman, even if the last be the Premier of England. Utter the name of a barrister and you will see the most hardened criminal raise his brows and ejaculate, "Is it?" The reason for it was plain enough. Men whose life is spent in thieving and dacoity, in courts and prisons, fear and respect him who can unearth their sins, unravel their threads, and expose them to the world by his legal acumen or can shield them by equal chicanery from the arm of the law. He can prove them guilty or not guilty according to the position he takes up towards them. How can they not quail before him? Or how can they fail to regard him as their saviour? They look upon him as an extraordinary being, and, as such, fear him. The criminal class fears the lawyer and seeks to curry his favour. Stories go round about him in the prison-world, not unlike those one hears about the great Birbal and his monarch. The prisoner in the dock trembles before the lawyer as people in Birbal's time quaked before him. In brief, I must say that my professional degree, if it had served me for nothing else, did serve me in this, that it spared me the insolence and insult of neighbours around me. The most confirmed criminal at once felt humbled before me.

I was standing that night near the door of my room. And I quietly watched them in their revelry, dance and riotous behaviour. For many days now, I had never heard such noise, never witnessed such a scene. The mind fretting in solitude should have recoiled from the obscenity and riotry of the scene. But it happened to me otherwise. It was like an ignited match thrown into a tin of kerosene. All my repressed feeling flared up and in that blaze, I stood there and lost myself in the show. And as I watched its progress, the mind analysed the emotion and traced its genesis to the wretched condition of my own heart. The heart in its woe-be-gone condition could not help turning outside for any relief it might have there. I watched the show because I could do nothing else and in order to forget myself in the ecstasy and revolt of grief I witnessed without me. I did not participate in it, and I found rest and sleep when the whole show had stopped on the admonition of its leader not to disturb me. He seemed to forgive me for not joining in the revelry. As the clock struck eleven, the noise had reached its peak, when the wardens reminded the party that my sleep was spoiled by their uproar. They had the goodness to listen and to end their shouting. It was about twelve midnight that my eyes drooped and I fell asleep.

As I woke up in the morning, the idea came into my head that my elder brother, who was now a prisoner in the Andamans, may have proceeded with a chalan like this and must have stayed in this prison before being carried over. I asked the warder about him but, as he was new to his post, he could give me no information on the subject. An older man, after further enquiry, told me that my brother did occupy the very cell in which I was locked up now. The old man had left when my brother's image came up before my eyes. He had to undergo considerable persecution here, as I had learnt from a co-accused in my trial. And I saw him vividly as he must have stood up under these tortures. He must have faced them unbending like the elephant at bay, as it stands rooted to the spot, while the rider rains upon its head blow after blow of his trident that it may move forward. Behind the bars of the prison-door, he, like an eagle, may have beaten his wings against them. He must have sat here thinking of me. He must have said of himself that it did not very much matter to him, if he was transported to the Andamans, so long as I was free to carry on the work behind him. If these were his musings, what will he say when he knows that I was going the same way as he. What a shock will it be to him? Would that mean I do not meet him in the Andamans, and that we live in different parts of the island?

I think that if only I had suffered by myself, the agonies of my mind would not be one-fiftieth of what they are now. But now that I see my brother before me as he must have suffered, when I hear what he had endured, the thought of it is simply beyond my patience to put up with. My heart was cleft in twain and I felt that I was collapsing under the blow like the banyan tree suddenly breaking down.

I asked an officer who I could trust, if my brother had to pass through any tortures in this place. He replied, "Not here. He suffered terribly at Yeravada, as some of the co-accused with you informed me at the time." This assurance from him gave me a sort of relief. At least, in this cell, he must have slept in peace. I asked the same officer about Wamanrao Joshi, Soman and other fellow-workers who had passed a period of their sentence at Thana.

Brethren, start we for the Sea

Only two or three days after, our army of prisoners was taken out to proceed to the Andamans. I had shackles on my feet. I wore a chaddar, a *banian* and a short scarf over it. That was our uniform on the way to the steamer and across. For my bed, I had a rough blanket and a hempen carpet which too could not be rolled into a bedding and was, therefore, hard to carry. Somehow, I took it under my armpit, and carrying my tin-pot and tin-plate in the other hand, I stood ready near my door to fall into the line. The gang came on in a file, clanging their chains in measured steps. They saluted everyone on the way. "Come on brethren, we are proceeding to the Andamans," they repeated as they marched on. The party came near the main gate and, one by one, they passed across. The soldiers were ready, fully armed to give it an escort along the road. The party walked on to the station under the full guard of the soldiers.

I was left behind, I wondered why. A motor car came up to the door, two big sergeants got down from it. I was put into it and they stepped in after me. The door was shut and the car started. I was not taken along the road like the rest because they feared that the crowd, who knew of my departure, had stationed itself on the road in scattered groups to have a sight of me. Besides I was a culprit who had run away at Marseilles. Perhaps, I may be spirited away in the same fashion by some member of the secret societies, of which there were many in those days. A mine may spring up beneath my feet, and, who knows, I may disappear on a sudden. These and other reasons of safety had decided the authorities to take me to the station all by myself, in a car, and along a different route. They did not want to repeat the mistake that they had committed at Marseilles.

Whenever I was thus taken from one place to another in a special car and under a special guard, my fellow-prisoners thought highly of me. They used to say, "Why, he is a king; they take him out in a car; why should he tramp with us along the road?" Others said, "Evidently Government is afraid of him. Otherwise, they would not have given him a car to go in." My effort to run away from the steamer-boat at Marseilles did do me some good after all! It procured me a car to enjoy a long drive. It created in the mind of these prisoners a sort of reverence for me. And, further, right or wrong, the more the authorities tried to belittle me, the greater the respect they showed to me.

We came to the station and I was shoved in a separate compartment. The other end of my hand-cuffs was tied to the hand of the officer who was charged to carry me. Poor man, he had to be a prisoner like myself for the time-being. There were shackles on my feet as well. Not only did I wear hand-cuffs, but my two hands were tied together by a chain between them. I could not tuck up my *dhoti*, the officer had to do it for me. If I had to go to the lavatory, he had, perforce, to accompany me, as he and I were holding together by a common chain. So also about sleep. Such wretched experience and dirty life I had to pass through during my journeys, to and fro, from one place to another.

Although they had quietly put me in a separate compartment, people had noted my transit all night. They approached my compartment with eager expectation and, as ruthlessly, they were turned out from that place. They were not only Indians but counted some Europeans among the number. These could come close to me, open the shutters of my compartment and address me in polite or rude words as they liked, and leave. There was no restriction or forbidding in their case. The train started, but at every station, where it stopped in the journey, I found the shutters of my window put down. Since the time I had left England, I was never allowed to travel in any compartment with windows up. But the officer with me in this compartment had, as if by pre-arrangement, kept the window shutters up so that the European visitors should have a full look of me. A large crowd of them had come near my compartment. Some of these men had lifted up their women-folk on their shoulders so that they might see me clearly. One beckoned on to me to stand up. "There is he; that is Savarkar," went up the cry from all sides as I stood up. The European ladies and gentlemen on the station platform, of course, did not come so near me as I could talk to them. Four or five of them did come close enough. But I did not exchange a word with them. I did not enquire who they were. They were all polite to me; only rarely, I met with insolence from them. And if anyone of them was rude to me, I paid him back in the same coin. I simply cold-shouldered him, and so he melted away.

Those hot Plains

The windows of my compartment were always kept shut. Across the bars in another compartment was huddled up the party bound for the Andaman islands. They were all in an uproar on that side. Those were hot summer days. The heat of the Sun overhead was like that of a burning furnace. A marriage party going in that train would have found the journey unbearable. I was only a prisoner sent to transportation for life. How then must have I felt it? The plains all about us were exuding hot vapour, and correspondingly it was steaming hot in the train. And both vied, as it were, with the dreariness and burning heat of the heart within. My soul and body were oppressed by both. In this state of mind and body, I found the train running at full speed through the Mogul territory on its way to Madras. In desperateness, I recalled to mind the treck of prisoners in Russia marched in exile to the bleak regions of Siberia. Their miseries made me cry, You have not yet experienced a fraction of them. This is not a mere matter of words. As thou sowest, so shalt thou reap. And he alone will reap who had dared to sow.

The train was leaping acoss village after village, town after town, through gardens and forests, across the rivers and over the valleys, along the mountains, up hill and down dale like a maddened tigress carrying in its mouth the prey which was no other than myself. The train was delivering me to the Andamans with the rapidity of a lightning. Will it bring me back to my own country with the same speed? Will it bring me back at all? How can it bring me back and when? Vain imaginings these and obstinate questionings! But the mind that hopes against hope cannot escape them. In far-off Siberia, many a prisoner dies with the name of dear Russia on his burning lips. So, may I die far away from dear India, and in the Andamans, breathing the last word—my motherland!

The train arrived at Madras. I was taken down from my compartment and was kept under guard apart from my fellow prisoners in the train. An officer had accompanied the train right through the journey. Between every two stations, he would come to my compartment, talk to the officer in it, have a look at me and go back. I thought he was to leave us now as we had reached Madras. He approached me now and wished me goodbye. He seemed to be overcome with feeling as he said, "I do hope, my friend, you will be let off in the coming coronation ceremony at Delhi." That was to be in December. I answered, "Thanks for your good wishes. My wounds are so raw that nothing can heal them. It would be folly for me to bank upon this hope." The officer assured me to the contrary as if he was in the know of things. "Believe me, you will be free before long; goodbye. Nothing will efface from my mind the impression of this your dignified courage." Other officers also took leave of me in the same manner. Having heard all sorts of report about my behaviour at Marseilles, they had conjectured that, in the journey, I would prove a horrible nuisance to them, I would hate the Englishman as a devil, I would burn with rage against him. They took me naturally enough for a ruffian, a braggart and an indecent fellow—a veritable miscreant in short. But I gave them no trouble whatsoever. And they could pass me on safely to the officers in Madras. At long last! they said to themselves, and heaved a sigh of relief. They found me a fine fellow, and taking off their hats and wishing me, they departed.

I was now in Madras where its Collector, Mr. Ashe, was done to death by a man of the Abhinav Bharat Society. And the officers suspected that it had some connection with the Central Association of that name in Europe of which I happened to be the leading figure. I had, therefore, expected that they would directly or indirectly sound me upon the incident. When I was arrested in England and was being brought back to India, I had not the slightest notion that the Vice President of the Abhinav Bharat, Mr. Aiyer, whose premature death since, we were all mourning as a great loss to the country, had proceeded to India. He had reached Pondicherry from Europe bearing all the rigours of the journey, when warrants were hanging over his head and the police were on his track all along the coast. He had eluded them all by assuming various disguises and offering excuses and making pretences as time and occasion had suggested themselves to him. At Pondicherry, he took charge of a branch of the Abhinav Bharat, and had compassed the end of Collector Ashe through the instrument of the Shakta Brahmin. Such was the suspicion of the secret police against Mr. Aiyer. And I learnt this seven or eight years after my incarceration, in the Andamans, having then read the secret report about him. But while I was proceeding to the Andamans. I had no knowledge whatever of the return of Mr. Aiyer to India. I had, no doubt, information about this murder and I had also suspicion in my mind that someone from the Abhinav Bharat Mandal had done the deed. Presuming that I may know nothing about it and yet seeking to worm out some information from me, if he could about the Mandal, especially of its branch in Madras, an Indian Officer dressed in an up-to-date European style saw me while I was in that city. A steamer called Maharaja was anchored in the port to take us to the Andamans. All the prisoners were conveyed on board the ship, in a boat full-packed with them. I alone was left behind on the port. The officers, including this Indian, presently arrived in a special boat to convey me on the steamer. I got into the boat. It was a rule with me to talk to none in these circumstances. For I was a prisoner and if I began talking, anyone could put a stop to it. The Indian Officer opened conversation with me on several ordinary topics and, on a sudden, showed anxiety to know from me the history of my Society in England and its present state. I told him that it was for him to enlighten me upon it. How can I know anything about it from any person in India? "That is true enough," he interposed in order to encourage me. "And what poor plots they are after all? They could not count even four members to support them." Smilingly, I retorted, "It was then for you to swell the number." "Nonsense, we in Madras are level-headed fellows. We are not wild and senseless like young men on your side. If anyone were to preach sedition or revolution here, he will not get a single person to follow him." He kept on talking in this strain just to make me blurt out, by way of protest, the names of well-known revolutionaries in Madras. He was looking at me from time to time if I was about to fall into his trap. After a white he himself said, "What is your experience in this matter?" I retorted, "You ought to know it better than myself." "I feel," he continued, "that everything in Madras is quiet." I smiled and replied, "Yes, are you quite sure about it?" He caught the meaning of my remark. The other officers smiled significantly, and interposed. "He knows all about the Ashe business. Only he is trying to pump you out, as you are trying to pump him."

The boat touched the steamer Maharaja which had come from the Andamans. I was lifted up, with handcuffs on, the ladder of the steamer and taken on the deck. While I was climbing up, a whole crowd had gathered around to watch the scene. All the passengers on board the ship, all officers, all men in the boats around her, and other spectators, had come out to see me. They saw me entering the steamer. They rivetted their eyes on me, as we witness a corpse being lied on the bier. With eager eyes and bare-faced shame, they kept on gazing.

Yes, climbing into that steamer to be transported for life was like putting a live man in his own coffin. Hundreds and thousands must have gone to the Andaman Islands during these years, and not ten in a thousand had returned alive to India! Young men of 18, as soon as they put their step on that steamer, became old and the shadow of death was visible on their faces. When a man is put upon the bier, his relatives conclude that he had left the world forever, and, overcome with bereavement, watch the corpse with vacant eyes. Even so, the spectators watched us as we climbed into that steamer, and felt that we were dead to the motherland we were leaving behind. The people, watching the scene, fixed their eyes upon me with the same feeling in their hearts. I was dead to the outside world—that feeling was writ large on their faces. Really, I was being put on my funeral pier. The only difference was that I felt what was happening to me while my corpse would have felt nothing. Thousands looking at me in this plight were simply indifferent and altogether cold. They were looking at me as they would have seen any corpse passing along the road. "Poor man, he is dead and gone!" says the passer-by and forgets him the next moment. It was a pain to me to see them gaping at me—my fellow-countrymen that they were—more than that the consciousness that my transportation was to mean a death-in-life for me, could give me. If but a single one out of these my compatriots was to tell me, "Go, my brother, go, I and others like me swear that we shall make India free and fulfil your vow," I would have felt my funeral pier as soft as a bed strewn with flowers.

□

5
The Black Sea

They took me on the ladder and put me in the ground floor of that steamer. A portion with strong iron bars was set apart in that place, no better than a long and narrow cage to accommodate twenty or thirty of us, in which were to be huddled prisoners on transportation at least fifty in number. We were no better there than cattle huddled up on board the steamer. I saw in that iron cage all the prisoners—the chalan—the whole of it, from Thana—arrayed and standing cheek by jowl in the file. They were cribbed and cabined into a space too small to hold them. As I saw them, I wondered whether I was to be put in the same place with them, when the door of that partitioned room opened to welcome me. Yes, I found my place in that crowd and in rank and file. In England, I had suffered from bronchitis, and it had left its traces which always made my breathing hard in a narrow and congested room. I also had some pain in the chest due to such hard breathing. So, I pointed out to a European Officer, who accompanied us, that it would be dangerous to lock me up in such a place. He conveyed the information to the doctor in charge of the steamer. The doctor asked me to stay there for a while, and then, he would let me know about it. If anything went wrong, he assured me, he would certainly arrange for me elsewhere. In the meanwhile, he selected for me a spot in a far-off corner of the same apartment, and ordered me to spread my bedding on that spot. How this special favour to me worked out in the end, I shall narrate as I go on.

A gentleman came up to me while this was going on and broached the topic of my escape at Marseilles and my arrest thereafter. In my turn, I spoke to him frankly on the subject. Thereafter, he said, "We have deliberately come here to see you. May God grant that you return safe and back to your motherland. That is all our prayer to Him, and a very sincere wish, we assure you." And the European gentleman and other officers left the steamer bidding me good-bye and showing me reverence by taking off their hats. There was only one person among them who seemed to be displeased by their behaviour to a miscreant and convict like me. He despised me altogether as unworthy of this courtesy. He looked at me full of scorn, and went away without wishing me.

The Steamer Starts

The siren sounded, the funnel roared. It was a rude shock to us. The boat rolled and began to move. The partition in which we were pigeon-holed had, high up, two or three window-like holes fixed with glass. Hanging on to them, some unfortunate prisoners were casting their wistful glances at the receding harbour and fortification. The wall of the fortification became invisible when one of them burst out, "O, brethren, our home we have left, left have we our home." He was so overpowered by that thought that he instantly sank to the ground. His wail sent two prisoners from Satara—peasants they were—into an outburst of tears. "No hope, now of seeing our country again, not the least hope!" they added. To them the retort came, "Do not weep my brothers, we are doomed for transportation, and no amount of weeping can save us." It came from the most hardened criminals among the party, who had already served their term in the Andamans once and were going back to it again. They consoled others like dispassionate philosophers standing in their midst. One of them suddenly turned round, and pointing his finger at me, exclaimed, "Behold him, he is a barrister, Officers take off their hats to him. What is our grief before him? Brothers, let us not think of ourselves, let us think of him." At this, they gradually gathered around me. Everyone put me the same question, though they all knew it: "What, Sir, is your term of penal servitude?" I gave to them the iron plate with the figure writ large upon it. I had been tired of repeating the figure 'fifty' over and over again. When the full realisation of this fact had come home to them, those, who were sentenced, among them, to fifteen years' transportation, gathered courage and felt considerably relieved in mind. Looking at me, they learnt to forget their own grief.

The Dirt on the Steamer

The evening came. It was blazing hot and the crowd was unbearable. The party of fifty, who were my immediate neighbours on the ship, came from the dirtiest class of Indian population. Hindus, Muslims, thieves, dacoits, they were all inured to filth, cruelty and crime. Some of them were striken with foul diseases, some knew not what it was to brush their teeth, and all had piled their beddings one upon the other, and lay by each other without an inch of space between them. In this crowd, I made my bed and lay upon it. My feet touched their heads, and their feet came up near my mouth. If I turned on the other side, I found that mouth had nearly touched mouth. I lay on my back. Right in front of me, I saw a big cask almost half cut and open. It was placed a little apart from the thick of the crowd, with a little open space near it. The space on my side of the partition and in the corner that accommodated me was not so full of prisoners as that on the other. It was a little roomier and, hence, I was put there. But a horrible stink greeted my nostrils from that direction. And I had to stop my nose to avoid it. A neighbour pointed at the cask in the front. And I discovered that they used it all during the night as a chamber-pot and commode. One of them was actually seated upon it at the time to ease himself. And he was almost about to leave it in shame. I signed him not to do so. "The claims of the body cannot be put off. There was no shame in answering the call of nature. In a moment, I may follow you. Do it freely. We cannot help it. We cannot afford to feel ashamed in this wretched condition. I can smell, you think; do you think you have no nose? Why, then, should I feel the stink more than you?" At this, the hardened one among them came up to me and said, "Sir, we are used to this I am the one who has been once to the island across and I know this practice too well. But you do not. Come over on the other side where there is not much dirt. And I take your place here." My heart melted when I heard him say this. His generous offer was a wonder to me. I said, "O, my God, even in the hearts of the most sinful ones, thou makest thy abode, turning into a shrine of worship and prayer. Thou turnest what is dirty mind untouchable into the holiest of the holy—the sacred basil—pot it becomes, when it was no more than a sink of filth and crime."

I thanked him for the offer and said, "I could get a little breeze, a draft of fresh air from this side and so the doctor had put me here. I could recline near the bars and stretch myself a little more comfortably than the rest of you. The officer had no idea, perhaps, of this cask right under my nose. But I consider this even as a concession to me. So, you need not worry. Why should I put you in the midst of dirt by exchanging my place with yours? I also must inure myself to this kind of life." The night came and I beheld a file of them going one after another to that cask. Filth and stink had reached their peak of nausea and disgust. I shut my eyes and pretended to be fast asleep so that they may have no compunction on my account. Within me, I said, "Alas! this was veritable hell on earth and I had to pass through it." But reason admonished, "True enough, but it all depends upon our thinking. Don't you know that this place was assigned to you as a favour; then, why should you grumble? Why would you not reconcile yourself to it? Maybe, God desires by putting you here, that you should overcome your pride, your self-conceit, your separateness from the rest, your sense of superiority. The best of sages, saints, seers and yogis refrain from the '*sadhana*' which has come in your way to conquer and burn into dust the pride of caste, gotra, race, class and character and merge themselves into the universe and be one with its Creator. Why not use it to the full then? Do you not know the story of Trilinga Swami? He was arraigned before a Magistrate on the charge of obscene conduct. In the course of the trial, the Magistrate observed, "These call themselves Advaitis? Why do they eat food and not cowdung?" The Swami laughed, answered the call of nature right in front of the Magistrate, and before anyone could stop him, ate his own excreta!"

Ramkrishna Paramahansa

The story goes of Ramkrishna Paramahansa which enforces the same moral. He had exhausted all the *sadhanas* of experience of unity with the Divine. One *sadhana* alone remained, and that was the hardest to practise. In order to practise it, he went to Calcutta and in the vicinity of the town where all the sewers of the town deposit its excreta. He turned it up and down with his own hands. He put five blades of straw into the dirt and sucked the besmeared blades with his own mouth! You only smell it by the nose while the prisoners are seated on the cask to use it as their commode and you try to run away from the cask because the stink is too much for your nostrils. But while you seek to run away from it, how can you escape from the one which you carry on your person wherever you go? You may hide it underneath your garment, but as the saint has put it, "The more you hide it, the more it is exposed, and the more it fills the atmosphere with its foul smell." Ramdas is still clearer on the point when he says, "You may eat the choicest meal. It is bound to be reduced to part feces and part vomit. Drink the water of the pure and holy Ganges. It cannot help itself from turning into urine." And the process is common to man—be he prince or pauper. None can wash out the dirt in his own stomach. If this be the fact true for all time, then you must put up with the stink and filth outside of you as you bear it within and of your own body. If one is no nuisance to you, the other must be borne as no nuisance. If eating is the need of the body, purging is as much its indispensable need. And both the processes are equally beneficial to the human system. Why the world is like this, why the body and its senses feel happy in certain function and despise others as degrading to them, is more than man can either understand and explain. Only nature, which created us, can explain and justify. This antagonism is beyond human intelligence to grasp. Perhaps it is nature's play and nature enjoys it. Or nature is helpless to do other than it has done.

Such conflicts between reason and sentiment, such battle between their opposing forces on the theatre of my mind was a comedy to enjoy. Henceforward, I felt nothing of the close contiguity of dirt I have mentioned. I went to sleep at past midnight. The hour, I believe, was one o'clock at night and I had sound sleep during the rest of the time. While on board that steamer, I never more showed my inconvenience and discomfort. The placidity of my temper was a surprise to fellow-prisoners. One or two of them even passed strictures upon my behaviour. They said that their suspicion of me as a dirty man of an extremely low caste was more than justified by my recent conduct. This they said behind me and only among themselves.

The attitude of the Europeans

The travellers and some of the Indian officers on board the ship desired to express their feeling of reverence for me by doing me service of one kind or another. They often used to pay me a casual visit. Some of the European soldiers treated me very politely. I was given some English newspapers to read as also some magazines. We got on with nothing else to eat but fried grams and peas. But the officers insisted that I should have something better. I did not know what special things I should ask for and it was difficult for them to make an exception in my case. As a result, some philanthropic merchants on board that steamer arranged a dinner for all of us with the permission of the Captain. It consisted of rice, fish and pickles and several other preparations. The whole of the prison-world in that steamer welcomed it with joy after two days of practical fasting and I was the cause of it. They were duly grateful to me for it. They were all taken for half-an-hour during the day along with me on the deck of the ship to have a whiff of fresh air, and we were all treated during that time much better and with greater ease than in the prison-hold below. Naturally, the prisoners expressed their gratitude to me in the following words. They said, "It is our good fortune, Sir, that we have your company in this voyage. What a piece of good luck it has proved to be!" To which I would reply, "Well then, it was right, after all, that I was sentenced to transportation for life. You, at least, welcome it, it seems."

Day and night I used to enter into conversation with them. And the one thing I tried to impress upon them was that they should even think of their country. And it was their duty to work for its freedom, and so on and so forth. When anyone spoke to me, full of passion and sincerity, that it grieved his heart to find me in this pitiable condition, my answer to him always was, "Then you must be ready to fight. India must be fully armed to fight and win her freedom, whatever be the cost of that struggle, whatever the ordeal she has to pass through to reach the goal. Then not only I but ship after-ship laden with her cargo of prisoners shall be crossing the seas to go to the Andamans. You should realise this beforehand, for whoever reaps has to sow, and whoever sows has to reap." From the ordinary sailor to the highest officer of the ship, from the prisoner right up to the soldier, I had become an instrument of political discussion all round. Some of them heard things that they had never heard before. What had never suggested itself to them up to that time did suggest itself to them now. And conviction came to them on matters of which they were never convinced previously.

Barrie Baba

Another important matter, which harassed my mind during the voyage and did not give it rest, was to know the kind of treatment meted out to the prisoners during their term of imprisonment in the Andamans. That was the one question I put to everyone whom I met on the boat, the one question I pursued all along the route. The party of soldiers accompanying the prisoners was one prime source of that information. They were, as it were, the arch-priests of that temple, and its authorised version. Whenever one uttered the name—transportation for life—the first response that came from that quarter was the word—

Barrie Baba. The one happened to be the synonym for the other. When even the worst of the prisoners showed the slightest spirit of rowdyism or indulged in noisy mutual recrimination, the soldiers rebuked them with the exclamation, "Wait, you seem to be too proud of your devilry. But remember that once you face Barrie Baba, all this will at once disappear. You will shake and shiver before him like aspen leaves." As I felt that this mysterious personage and myself were soon to be lifelong intimates, I was curious to know who and what Barrie Baba was. But I decided that it was no use questioning the sepoys about him. About the Andamans, they assured me that, within six months of my stay in that place, I would get my release from hard labour in the prison-house, and be detailed for some work in the office itself. An intelligent and educated man like me, they further added, might even be put in charge of a whole district in that place, had a good chance there, during ten years, to make his pile, have a home for himself and to pass the rest of his life in happiness and peace. That was their constant refrain as they talked to me on that subject. Am I being taken to the Andamans, I asked myself, to be rewarded for my revolutionary activities in India? It was well then that I was caught at Marseilles! If life in the Andamans is as they depict it, it will not be harder than the days of bitter exile I had to pass in Europe wandering from place to place, and begging from door to door for refuge and shelter. Maybe, what they tell me is true. But will it fall to my lot to share it? No, that cannot be for me. It was no better than a mirage in my case. I knew what had happened to my brother, and to others who were the first batch of political prisoners to be transported to that place. Shall I ever meet them? And what of my elder brother? Shall there be any chance of my seeing him? Who knows?

None could say anything definitely about it. I was told, however, that he was there in that prison. And I was probably taken to be confined in the same place. Of that, at least, there was no doubt in their minds.

Today, they are all saying it, our steamer will touch the port of the Andaman Islands. The hour was six in the morning, when the prisoners were brought up on the deck in serried ranks. The laskars and other servants on the ship were busy cleaning the steamer. The sun came up and the temperature went up along with it. It was burning hot on the deck. With the nearer approach to the island, the transportation sentence wore a gloomier aspect. It had come so near to us, and the prisoners seemed scared by the thought. The thoughts of helplessness, separation, and grief, that were held in abeyance during the voyage, rose up rebelliously in my mind, like big fishes in the ocean that are tossed up on its surface in stormy weather. They created a storm in my heart. The shadow of transportation had completely darkened my soul.

The sea is calm like a lake, and the boat glides smoothly on its bosom, like children, in colder climates, skating on the winter snow. The sun is looking down on the earth with his fixed and glaring eye. It seems he is dazed by the triumph of man over the elements, as withessed by this steaming boat sailing defiantly over the element beneath. An ocean—a vast, endless expanse of water—"The deep calling unto the deep." The boat—what a funny thing it is before his terrible might and his broad bosom—almost "a cockle-shell", as were. But a small room in her, known as the captain's cabin, dominates the whole scene. The man in that cabin with his helm and rudder handles the sea like a tamed elephant. His compass and needle help him ride the sea as the trident helps the rider master and drive the elephant. What a conquest is this of mind over matter! One day the very sun will be equally amazed to witness man's victory over himself, and gaze at this very earth for that triumph. Man shall have then conquered his devilish instincts and the brute and the tiger in him shall be no more. Those who suffer and those who make them suffer shall have been an ugly dream of the past, and man shall live with man as a brother, tied to one another by the common bond of love. All other bonds shall snap, and freedom and goodwill prevail in the world of man. A glorious day will dawn on the kingdom of man. And the sun will look down upon the earth from his place high in the heavens as now, but with a heart full of rejoicing for the millennium that had arrived. Freedom will reign supreme then but for its allegiance to love. On that day alone shall have fructified the endeavours, the sacrifices, the supreme struggles, and the high and unquenched hopes, of all the martyrs of the Earth. And 'nune dimitis' will be the song sung on earth in honour of their souls. Happy the man who saw this promised land in the distance; happier he, who strove to bring it nearer; and happiest he, who has the fortune to enter it. Would that I be one of that shining company! At least, some share of it will surely fall to me. What a glorious future that will be!

The Present

But the present? What is your state today? Dream, an empty dream, a foolish dream—"the golden morrow" that you so delusively paint on "the midnight sky of sorrow". Ages have rolled on since the Vedic Rishis had painted the golden scene. Man has ever been its dupe. It offers us a gleam of light in the dark; the horrible night of the present. Behold the sea, mighty, unfathomable, incomprehensible! A veritable giant in strength and power. And this little boat glides softly dancing on its bosom. But the sea lets her go it, that is all. He watches her play—the play of this gnat on his body. In a moment, he may chafe and grow angry, and shake his giant body! A slap from him and she is finished. So is the bold inventiveness of man. If this mighty power rises and overspreads the land in a deluge, its single wave and spray are enough to shatter the boat to pieces, its Atlantean waves can swallow continents, and none shall know thereafter what was Asia and where was Europe! How puny is man! And of the race of this creature, I am today the weakest and the most contemptible specimen. I am here squatting, in a corner, in the midst of the outlaws and the outcast of the world—the meanest and the self-condemned specimens of humanity on earth. I have to sit in a row with them, unseen, unwept and unsung. Manacled, gyved, bound on wrist and feet, here I am among them. So mean that the scavengers of the place are filled with pity; so abject that the hewers of wood and drawers of water could shout at me, "O, prisoner, get away from this place, sit there." And I am compelled to obey them!

The sea was calm, snoring like a giant. The boat was slowing down like the pulse of a dying man. The sun overhead was burning like a furnace. The weather was unbearably warm. We were very close to the Andamans. The travellers and officers behaved with me now as perfect strangers. They were reticent and curt. They kept themselves at a distance. The shadow of transportation had extended itself to cover and darken my countenance.

□

6
The Andamans

The group of islands, including the Andamans and the Nicobars, constitute a link not only with the past history of India, but also with her development in the world of tomorrow. As such, no Indian can afford to be ignorant about this group of islands. India of today is bound to have cultural contacts with other parts of the world; and the Andamans are a part of it that she is bound to influence.

This group of islands is six hundred miles distant from the city of Calcutta, and spreads like a long range in the Bay of Bengal. It is not an unbroken range of land. The islands are dotted and scattered along the entire area of the Bay interspersed with the waters of the sea flowing between them. Of this group, the Andamans constitute the largest range. In the map, you will notice the group divided into three parts—the northern, the southern, and the middle or the centre. It has the shape of an elongated circle—of an ovum or an egg. Hence its name—the Andamans. Some have traced the origin of that name to Hanuman, the monkey-god of the Ramayana. But there is no reason to believe in its authenticity. The North Andamans is 51 miles in length; the middle portion is 59 miles; and the southern part of it is 49 miles. The island of Rutland has the length of 11 miles. The whole is known as the Greater Andaman. At the top of its southern territory, there is a portion of land known as the lesser Andaman with an area of 30 by 17 miles. This last is a long stretch of dense forest which remains uncolonised to this day. The forest is so dense that the rays of the Sun cannot penetrate it during the best part of the day. It rises sheer from the sea-beach into a height of mountain wall that protects it on the rear, and has in the mid-area dark, thick jungles yet untrodden by the feet of civilised man. The forest officers of the place have, however, succeeded, at tremendous cost and labour, in making a survey of this portion and marked the spots and the trees in it which they are now to indicate on the chart of these islands. The highest mountain peak in this range is three thousand feet above the sea-level; and the point is known as Sandal Mount. There are no big rivers crossing the forest; only streams and rivulets trickle down from the mountain into the valley below.

The hot-bed of Malaria

As the place is full of jungles, rainfall there is continuous throughout the year. Even in autumn it rains a drizzle. But, in between, the sun glares fiercely overhead. In the part of the forest, where spaces of the jungle happen to be cleared for cultivation and residence and gardens of coconut trees are found planted, the climate and the seasons have changed to conform to the tropical parts of our own country. The main seasons, however, are the summer season and the rainy season, with winter only peeping in to disappear. The sea not only engirdles the island group on all sides of it, but rushes between the range so as to cover and divide it into several portions of two islands each. The islands have greater length than breadth, and are, thus, full of creeks and marshy places. The dry leaves of the jungle trees accumulate in these watery marshes. They lie upon them in thick layers and become breeding places for malaria, all over the area. In addition to malarial mosquitoes, the jungle is full of a variety of flies which make the spot a nuisance to its stray inhabitants. The flies hum and spread over the place in thick swarms, and cover it with their regular network. The big ones stand up on their wiry and long legs and swing in the air to the humming tune. They appear to the onlooker, as they swing, like a black long line, and one wonders whether it is one big fly or a continuous row of them.

Leeches and Serpents

Besides the flies that are carriers of malaria all over the region, there is a pest of leeches that are found in this part, here, there and everywhere. In mud, on leaves and underneath the layers of dry leaves, they lie in thick masses, as they are also found hanging on trees, clinging to their branches, and stuck to their foliage. In the hot sun, they go into their hiding; with rain drizzling, they emerge on the top. The smell of human flesh is a joy to them, and they fall from trees and leaves like a shower of continual rain-drops. They stick to the soles of your feet; they stick fast to your calves and thighs; and they suck blood from wherever they glue themselves. The hardened *badmashes*, the most unashamed criminals, who defy the worst punishment in jail, quake and shiver when they are sent out into this forest to cut and clear the jungle. It is the fear of the leeches that makes them quail. When they return from their work at sunset, one finds their bodies bathed in blood. For leeches have pierced them, and through the holes that they have bored into their bodies, jets of blood are found flowing. And there are not one or two of these that invade them thus. They come in swarms. While one catches them in handfuls and throws them off his body, leeches drop down upon him in a heap from trees above his head, or crawl up his feet from the earth below him. From all sides, they stick to his body like limpets and suck his blood all night.

This jungle contains a species of serpents only less hurtful than the leeches. But their bite is fatal to the life of man. This species is one foot in length and an inch or more in thickness. They are so venomous that a man bitten by them is struck down with paralysis, and the pangs that they give are simply unbearable. The ordinary variety of serpents is not to be found here. There is, here and there, a kind known as the viper which is extremely poisonous, and there is an occasional specimen of the python. Uninhabited by man, the species have grown into an enormous number. That they devour one another is the only control upon their abnormal growth. Tigers, lions, bears and other carnivorous animals are not here. Now and then you come across a wild boar. There are no Indian birds in this jungle. The British Government has tried recently to import and naturalise in these parts the cuckoo, the parrot, the peacock, the squirrel, the *baj* and the *maina*. It has even introduced here the ubiquitous crow. They have brought here the deer, the dog, the jackal, and other tamed animals. Hence, today, the jungle resounds with the sound of Indian birds and beasts.

The wonders of the sea, in this part of the world, are as boundless as those of the jungle. Conches, shells and hailstones, of variegated shapes and colours, convoluted and lined, strew its sandy beach in overwhelming proportion. The creator here proves himself a wonderful artist and painter. His handiwork is simply marvellous. Who can describe its beauty and grandeur? The shells and conches are arrayed within and without with lines of shaded colour that excel the beauty of the rainbow. If a human artist were to transfer to his canvass a fraction of this glorious display in line and colour, he would make himself immortal. He will furnish forth a specimen of art worthy to find its place in any museum of the world. Nature, as it were, is behaving like a prodigal in lavishing her plenty, in minerals, stones, reptiles and other creatures, on the foreshore of this bell of sea round the islands. The procession of an emperor goes along the road of a busy thorough-fare, and leaves the whole path behind him strewn with flowers of gold and pearl, which his admirers shower upon him in the passage. So do the conches, shells and hailstones lie here like sprays of colour thrown off the brush of a master artist. Fishes, crocodiles, alligators and sea-snakes rise and fall on the sea-shore with the ebb and tide of its rolling billows. Of how many shapes are they indeed! Some with a sword-like pointed tail, ready to cut our feet and flesh with its lash; others with the mouth of a horse; others, again, with tails that flash with the charge of electricity; others having human faces; an endless variety of them which only a few travellers in these regions have enumerated and described in their works. Many and varied are these creatures to be seen rolling on the sea-beach or sorting on its waves in the vicinity of these islands.

Andaman and Hindusthan

A reference to this range of islands is found in the works of Marco Polo and Nicolo, as also in the earlier writings of Arabian and European travellers. But India must have had contact with them far earlier than this. There are allusions in India's ancient history to sea-voyages from Magadha kingdom in the north to Ceylon in the south. Similarly, the Andhras, the Tamils and other people in the south had carried invasion into the heart of Burma, Siam, Pegu and Java, as we know from their ancient history. The conclusion cannot, therefore, be escaped that the Indian travellers of those days had some personal knowledge of these islands. The specific mention of their names is found in the annals of the Pandya kings, and in the description of a naval war in the 11th century A.D. The sea-faring monarch of this dynasty invaded and conquered Pegu, and while returning home with his naval forces, he landed on the Andaman and the Nicobar islands to plant his flag and establish his rule over these regions. This account finds its mention in the contemporary records of that monarch's rule. However, we do not find in these islands today any traces or landmarks of these visitors either as travellers or conquerors. An officer had told me, while I was in the prison of that place, that excavations in these parts had discovered relics of ancient palaces. I cannot vouch for the authenticity of that report, and I have had no time since then to investigate personally into that question. So much, however, is beyond dispute that Indians knew something of these islands and that they ruled and stayed on them for some time in their past history.

The condition of these Islands

However that may be, it made no change whatever in the life of the aborigines of that place. As the natural condition of these islands shows no traces of the agricultural and other cultivation of the soil by its early colonists, so the life of its natives reveals no effect of the cultural influence of India upon it, either in the field of religion or in intellectual and moral life.

The Andamans is a small island engirdled by the sea. It demanded a long and continued influence of India to reclaim it for civilisation and progress, from its wild and savage environment. The wilderness of nature and the wildness of man could only be conquered by permanent impression in that soil of civilised life, with all the accompaniments necessary for the stabilisation of such a life. As soon as the contact and influence are withdrawn, the island relapses into its state of barbarism. And this law holds not only for the natives of the soil, but also for others who have to dwell there, for some reason or another, for a good long time. In the Great War of 1914-18, steamers could not ply between India and the Andamans for four months at a stretch, and provisions of all kinds were entirely cut off during the period. The result was that the inhabitants of this island had to go without clothing; had to feed on flesh for want of cereals and rice, and agriculture perished for want of necessary implements and seeds. The suspension of civilised life took the island back to fifty years. Imagine then how the Hindu colonists of that island, in its remote past must have suffered a setback for want of any communication with the outside world. In those days, crossing the seas was regarded as a sacrilege. No wonder if the civilised Hindus themselves had turned into savages during the period that they had dwelt among them in order to civilise them. Having lost all touch with their own countrymen, they must have either withered away, or been absorbed in the people with whom they had comc to stay.

The aborigines in the Andamans today resemble in life and habits similar to aboriginal tribes in other parts of the world. The groups of islands that of the around Java contain savages who look like monkeys.

One or two savages from the Nicobars, brought here as prisoners, had a three-inch-long bone, at the lower end of the spinal cord. They found it impossible to sit comfortably in a chair. The doctor of the place drew my attention to them. That bone had no hair on it and no tuft of hair at the end of it. Their faces and chins exactly resembled those of the monkey. Such savages, with the tail and appearance of a monkey, are occasionally to be seen even in the Andamans. The only difference between them and their originals is the latter's want of speech and the former's use of some kind of language. The tribe of savages in the Andamans known as Javra have men and women from four to four-and-a-half feet tall. They have a coal-black complexion, hard, short hair standing on their skulls, which they tie in tufts on the top of their heads, like the Negroes of Africa. They have no hair on their chin and upper lips; they move about stark naked and wear not a rag upon their person. They besmear their bodies with red earth, like some sadhus in India, and thus satisfy their lack of clothing. The women-folk, the most ostentatious of them, wear as a piece of additional ornament, a leaf round their waist. The Javras live a kind of austere and simple life of which the ascetic, scorning every kind of pleasure in this world as sin, yet only may dream to realise. They are primitives, remote from any temptation natural to civilised and human existence. They know no match-boxes, no clothes, no bullock carts, much less, therefore, do they know vicious habits of railways, ocean-liners, aeroplanes and mills. They know no chairs to sit on, and no shoes to wear, no house to live in and no art of agriculture either. They do not cook their food and use no machine, neither the *Charakha*, nor the spinning wheel. Civilisation and its accompaniments, which are considered by a certain school of devotees to be the enemy of plain living and high thinking and a danger to mankind, the Javras know not and desire not. They are not only strangers to it, but they dislike it. The simplest and the most ascetic among us have, at least, the need of a loin-cloth round their body. But the Javra not only does not wear it, but is not even tempted to wear it. Are they, therefore, contented and happy? By no means. They cultivate no soil, hold no plough and use no bank-notes. But for a fish in a creek, or a little space in it that he may call his own, he will fight like any other human being; he will jealously guard it; and be full of anxiety lest he might lose it. Not even the Kaiser of Germany, or the Czar of Russia will, as jealously, guard his possessions, as the Javra will guard his own. The Javra has to struggle for his edibles everyday of his life—which are roots underground, fruits on the top of trees, fish in the waters, and flesh of the hunted animal on earth. He works and fights for it as hard as a civilised man fights hard for his daily subsistence. He has to hunt and angle, pluck and dig, as much as we have to plough the soil, sow the seed, and reap the corn. He has to depend upon chance more than we have to depend on it for his daily subsistence.

A Hail-shower of Arrows

There is another tribe in these parts as savage as the Javras. The men of this tribe are taller than the Javras, and, in some respects, more progressive than they. Perhaps, this tribe is a cross-breed between the early colonists and the aborigines of the place. The Javras are monogamous and know the use of the bow and arrow to perfection. The bow they use is six feet in length. They are fine shots with the bow. With the help of this weapon, they have still maintained their freedom. Of course, they cannot hold their own against the rifle and the aeroplane. Even then, they are still free, and the Englishman has failed to conquer them. The Javras come out from the forest, lie in ambush, and attack Government camps or the policeman's cabins, or stray prisoners. They are, of course, driven back to their haunts in the dark recesses of the forest, but the Government forces do not pursue them further, for it is so very dangerous to do so. It is not so easy to beat and conquer brave people like the Javras, to stand the hail-shower of their arrows, as it is to conquer and subdue a province of India. That question is not urgent at the present moment; and the Javras roam about unmolested in these jungles. They settle in batches, in the empty spaces of their jungles, and they lead a life as their ancestors had lived it centuries ago. They go about naked; they hunt after wild boars; they eat raw flesh; they worship ghosts and dead bodies; and they enjoy the life that they live. If one were to denounce them to their face that they are barbarious, the eldest of the tribe will not scruple to flay the person alive on the spot, and consume his flesh as his choicest morsel of food.

Cannibals

For thc Javras are still cannibals. Daring European travellers have penetrated into these parts, have made friends with the Javras, and left behind them interesting records of their dialect and their manners and customs. Some of the prisoners in the Andamans have succeeded in making themselves intimate with these cannibals, and have enjoyed hospitality at their hands. They have returned alive to tell us about them. The story is conclusive on one point and in favour of the Javras. They never kill those who surrender themselves to them. However, they regard British Officers and civilised men as their natural enemies, and, coming out of their jungles to pry, they kill them if they catch them. They eat man raw, or roast him by hanging his body on the fire, and thus devour him. They start out for hunting with the dawn of day. Everyone carries his bow and arrow across his shoulders. The women go out for fishing and catching small game. The tribe usually settles under one roof. The big game belongs to all. They share it all in common. The fruit and the honey each one keeps for himself. At sunset, they light fire and keep the big game hanging on it. The roasted part is cut into pieces and all make a common meal on it. Occasionally, after the meal, they indulge in a common dance: males and females mingle and dance together. They appoint a king to rule them and they hold him in high reverence. After the dance, pell-mell and stark-naked, they sleep in a circle around the fire that they kindle at sunset.

Some runaways from our prison tell us that when they treated the Javras to some preparation of vegetables which was the product of their own cultivation, the latter were wonderstruck by it. When anyone dies among them, his dead body is kept hanging on a tree for some days. Then they pelt it with stones and drop it down. Nobody knows how they dispose it off subsequently. Nothing is yet known about their religious beliefs and practices. Yet, they fear dead bodies, are afraid of ghosts, and fear is the prime element in their faith and worship. Beyond that stage, they seem to know nothing of God and Religion. One of their tribes, many years back, had gone over to the British and had sought their shelter and protection. The members of that tribe have incurred the hatred of the aborigines as much as any civilised man. Though the Javras pass their lives in seclusion, and in isolation from the rest of the world, country liquor and foreign brandy have begun, slowly but surely, to penetrate their hearths and homes.

Their Occupation

The Javras that made friends with the British officers in the Andamans have learnt some kind of trade and business as a result of their contact with the outside world. They gather beautiful conches and shells and other stones on the sea-shore, and bring them to English officers in their cabins. They also sell these articles in exchange for glass toys and trinkets, sugar and tobacco. They stay for a while in the adjoining chawls built for that purpose, and again return and disappear in the dark regions of the dense forest that is their home. Occasionally, they also sell honey. The Government collects all these things from them for export to foreign countries. The conches polished and set in silver or gold fetch a fancy price in the markets of Europe. These Javras, as a result of their contact with the Europeans, are domesticated enough to put a piece of cloth round their loins. And their women cover their parts with a single big leaf or with a garland of leaves round their waists. Their contact with the settlers has produced a generation, which is the hybrid of two races. The Javra women are found to cohabit with soldiers and other Europeans in the settlement and their children show a distinct mark of this fusion in their white complexion and European features. The Hindus in that settlement have also taken to wife the Javra women, and the children born of that union are fairer in complexion than their parents. These children, when they grow into young men and women, are given a sort of education which finds employment for them in Government service. A woman or two have turned nurses, and become governesses in private families. The wife of the Chief Commissioner of the Andamans had, for her companion in the family, one of the trained Javra women.

The modern history of the Andamans begins somewhere from 1766 A.D. Prior to that date, convicts from India were sent to Singapore, Penang, Malacca and Tenasserim islands to serve their term of transportation. Engineer Colebrooke and Captain Blair were the two Englishmen who, in 1766, tried to turn the Andamans into a regular settlement. Before that time, many a British boat foundered and was stranded on the shore of these islands. We can still read the horrible accounts of these mishaps. When Captain Blair selected this spot for settlement, its climate and temperature were altogether detrimental to the health of settlers in that place. The first convicts brought to settle there perished almost to a man. Port Blair, the present harbour of the Andaman islands, derives its name from its early founder, no other than Captain Blair himself. The captives in the Indian Mutiny of 1857-58, soldiers to be counted in their thousands, were also sentenced and despatched to this place to serve their term of imprisonment. And this was the beginning of settlement in the Andamans. When I was in the prison of the Andamans, an old man, who was one of the surviving convicts of the place and captives in the Indian Mutiny, sent me a message of congratulations for my incarceration in this prison for an attempt to overthrow the Raj similar to the one they had planned in their day.

I heard, later on, that the old convict had been released after serving sixty years of transportation, on the occasion of a durbar or some similar celebration. The settlement began with imprisonment, in this place, of soldiers involved in the Indian Mutiny of 1857. And here I am today to end it as a convict in the conspiracy case of 1907-08. What a strange coincidence this is! Some persons involved in the conspiracy and revolt of Wasudev Balwant Phadke were also sent to serve their imprisonment in the Andamans. One or two of them happened to be discharged from this place about the time or some time after I had reached the settlement. Some Hindu culprits involved in the Hindu-Muslim riots of 1893 had also been here, as I was told. The Manipur Conspiracy Case had contributed its quota to this prison. And members of the Manipur Royal Family had been put on parole, and lived their lives in a place on the settlement, set apart for that purpose. Such is the story of these islands since they were selected for the imprisonment of political prisoners or prisoners involved in similar trials. Hundreds of them, before me, had passed their lives under hard labour in the jail of the Andaman island. But none had so far recorded the story of their imprisonment as I am led to do it now. None had tried so far to stamp it on the heart of India. It is, indeed, a peculiar conjunction of events that impels me to narrate that tale. Thousands of Indians in that place have their claim for consideration, sympathy and duty on the whole of India. They belong to not one province and owe allegiance to Mother India alone, in spite of their difference in caste and creed, in party and other persuasion. The fact is being realised today, however dimly, more than at any time in India's previous history. It is principally the political prisoners of India who have brought this home to the heart of her people.

Port Blair

Port Blair is the name of the harbour and the main island of this settlement. The Andamans contain, by and large, a collection of Burmese and Indian prisoners. As such, during the last sixty or seventy years, its population happens to be mainly composed of Indians. In the Nicobar Islands, on the other hand, the Burmese and the Malayans form their naturalised and settled population.

These islands, therefore, are lost today to Indian culture and to contact with Hindu Society. The Andamans are having less and less of Indian prisoners now. So, there is every fear of their being cut off from contact with India, and the settlement itself being denuded of its Indian population. I, therefore, think it to be my duty to write a few words here on this question in order to draw the attention of the Indian public to a matter of such vital importance. I take upon myself all the blame of having neglected it before.

So soon as the number of Indian prisoners being sent to the Andamans had begun to decline, the officers of the place planned to divide the whole island into plots, and to put out for sale, the right of Government plantation in coconut and betel-nut trees, to the intending purchasers. They intended by this ruse to purchase the whole settlement for themselves and turn it out into a personal estate. As a result, the best part of this land with its gardens and plantations is gradually passing into the hands of European and Anglo-Indian settlers on the island. There are almost no Indian merchants in the Andamans, rich enough to bid for the purchase of these estates. The merchants in India know nothing about the deal. So, the land is going cheap to the settlers mentioned above, with the result that the islands, before long, will be completely lost to India. Such of the local merchants as have purchased a few of these plots and plantations are without resource in proper men from India to develop them, and to enrich themselves with the wealth they contain. A golden opportunity for possessing these lands and developing them as fruitful economic projects is being thus denied to India. The jungles also, out here, are being let out on cheap rent for clearing and colonisation. And Christian missionaries and their societies are taking full advantage of this facility. They have prepared a scheme to transplant Santal and other tribes in India to the Andamans, convert them to Christianity, and settle them in vast colonies on the jungles made available to them for clearing, cutting and exploitation. No Indian or Hindu merchant ever thinks of utilising this opportunity. None of them has even so much as paid attention to the immense possibilities of such a project.

Go and Colonise

When the Andamans were an entirely prison settlement, others found it difficult to open it for trade and business. But now this difficulty will not arise. Hence, it is up to the merchants in India to purchase land

and plantations in that part of the world, and they should not fail to turn this opportunity to advantage. Full information about it cannot be given here for obvious reasons. They should write to the Chief Commissioner of Andamans for the information they need. It is profitable by far to purchase acres of land in the Andamans that are being sold for a song than to enter into endless litigation for over a span-worth of land in Indian courts. That is a policy of mass ignorance and perversity, not unlike that of the frogs in the pond. They may exclaim, "Oh, we are fighting for our ancestral property!" But these foolish and stay-at-home persons should remember that it is a foolish and idle boast to swear by our ancestral inheritance; it is credible to be proud of what we have earned by our own efforts. The latter win the blessings of their God and their country as well. God and the country smile on those who earn by the sweat of their brow. The Indian legislatures discussed the problem of the Andamans only so long as Indian prisoners were being deported to that place. But our councillors seem to have forgotten the Andamans with the discontinuance of that practice. It is regrettable that they should do so. For, there are yet in the Andamans ten thousand people who are Indians in blood and religion. Besides this, four generations of Indian political prisoners have sacrificed their lives, and the ashes of some of these have mixed with the soil of that country. The islands, which have thus witnessed the hardships of so many Indians, cannot be considered to be negligible. Apart from these patriotic and political considerations, the soil is rich in natural products like tea, rubber, sugarcane, coconut and betel-nut, and is undergoing rapid development in the shape of tea plantations, rubber cultivation, the growth of sugarcane and gardens of coconut trees and betel-nut trees. And it admits of still more intensive and wider cultivation and development. Shall India have no share in this process? Should the foreign European settler be allowed to have the monopoly of it? During the last fifty years, only a small portion of these islands has been brought under cultivation. Its vast jungles still remain to be cut, cleared and explored for human habitation. The jungles are capable of giving us twice the yield that they are giving now. It is up to the members of our central legislature to demand full information on the existing condition and growth, and the future possibilities of these islands, as also about the future plans of the Government as regards their parcelling out the cultivable soil for sale. They must insist on knowing if there is behind these plans a policy of exploiting the islands for the exclusive use and permanent domination of foreign settlers on the soil, and whether they will put the soil out for open sale and advertise it in India. It is also necessary that some members should visit and tour the islands to see their condition first-hand and to ascertain the economic condition of ten thousand of their own countrymen who happen to be its permanent residents.

They must become the mouthpiece of those who cannot speak for themselves, and exponents all of India's interest in these islands. Let a member of the Arya Samaj visit the place to give them proper knowledge of their mother tongue and religion. The Indians have tried hard that the mother tongue that their children should learn shall be Hindi, but Urdu is being forced upon them. And the medium of instruction in these schools is Urdu and not Hindi or Hindusthani. If preachers, leaders and organisers go there to agitate, organise and educate the Indian population in their own rights, and if officials come to be properly informed and guided in these matters, many things will be set right that are now subject to the policy of drift and let-alonism, or of exploitation and monopoly in favour of those who happen to be its present masters—the men on the spot. In the present chapter, I have drawn the pointed attention of the reader to certain outstanding factors of the present situation, other matters, equally vital, being left for consideration in the narrative of the story and in their proper place in the course of that narration.

Indianise the European Names

The many divisions of the Andaman Islands are known today by their English names. But the Indians domiciled in those parts use their Indian equivalents in common parlance. And if an expert were to go into them, he can know for himself how effectively they have converted them into thorough-bred Indian names. For instance, "Shore-point" has become "Suvar Peth", "Dundas point" is "Danda peth", so on and so forth. Gokulban, Baratang and Kalatang are some Indian equivalents that are worth noting. New and unknown things are always best known and expressed through the familiar and the well-known. As in knowledge, so also in the evolution of language and its expression, the law is well illustrated by the equivalents that we have quoted. Indianisation of foreign words proceeds along natural lines and its spontaneous development takes place as the foreign words pass from lip to lip of the common man.

In every division of this island, barracks are built and a factory is attached to each barrack, where the prisoners are confined and made to work. Thus, Phoenix Bay barracks accommodate four hundred prisoners who are skilled artisans in metal work. Iron, brass and tortoise shell are turned into beautiful articles by skilled prisoners in the factory attached to these barracks. Chatham division has a saw mill for sawing planks of trees felled in the surrounding jungles. Kalatang is famous for its tea plantations. The prisoners are so much overworked and sweated on these plantations that they shudder to be detailed there for labour. Cutting down a jungle is a task still more exhausting and arduous than work in these plantations. In the earliest stages of prison-life in the Andamans, it was a practice to set the prisoners free so soon as they had landed on its soil. Later on, they came to be confined in prison-cells and had to undergo hard work under Government control and supervision. The free ones had applied themselves to the cultivation of land, and they grew rice upon it. When they had multiplied from generation to generation, their progeny was designated as 'free', to distinguish it from their immediate and remote prisoner-ancestors. Today these later generations contain some well-educated and decent persons. The last stage was to build a big and self-contained prison-house where prisoners from India could be straightaway confined for a stipulated period and freed or not freed and live their own lives on the island, according to the sweet will of the officers in charge. The local criminals were also confined in this jail. This prison has come to be known all over the place as Silver Jail or Cellular Jail, wherein it was meant that political prisoners should spend their long term in solitary confinement, and not a sound of their groans and agonies was to reach from it to the world without. But providence had willed it otherwise. And today, it is the political prisoner's cry that is heard resounding on the shores of India.

□

7

We reach Andamans

Our steamer had entered the port of the Andamans and her anchor was cast with ringing chain into its waters. She had stopped, and boats and officers' launches were seen gathering around her to remove the prisoners. We had to wait for a long time before we were let down into the boats. I cast a glance around me to survey the place where I was to pass the rest of my life. My fellow-prisoners, who had been there before me, and, occasionally, some sepoys explained to me the topography of the island. There was the Ras Island, the headquarters of the Chief Commissioner of the Andamans. The island ornamented the sea like a palace built in the land of the fairies. It was, indeed, small in size compared with other islands. But it was so picturesque and compact that it could not fail to ravish the mind of even a prisoner in chains like me. On the other side of the island, the foreshore of the sea was fringed by a long line of coconut trees waving their crests in the gentle breeze overhead. Beyond, one observed clusters of mango trees, betel-nut trees, and pipal trees. On the wharf were crowds of people filling the whole atmosphere with their humming voices. Higher up and just on one end of the climb, we saw a stately building in perfect seclusion and enclosed within circular walls and shaded by a thick grove of coconut trees. All around it were gardens of coconut, betel-nut and plantain trees. They stood there like royal menials waving their fans and holding their umbrella over the head of this "grand monarque". The building, with its perfect calm, struck us as the mansion of a happy, solitude-loving rich man or the manse of a retired clergyman. We inquired of our neighbours, and a sepoy told us that it was the very "Silver Jail" of Barrie Baba. The guards on board the steamer had referred to that name more than once to rebuke the unruly prisoners in their charge. And the sepoys were not mistaken in their belief that its mere mention was enough to strike terror into their hearts. The man, who told us the name, kindly added that, as we were presently going to that place, he need say no more about Barrie Baba and his residence. We were let down the boat one after another in a line, and each one carried his bedding on his head and the pot and pan in his hand. Landing on the pier, other prisoners were at once marched in a line up the steep climb, under the strict escort of regulars and warders from the prison beyond. I, alone, was kept waiting on the wharf, and in charge of European Officers. Thus segregated from the rest, I sat there, and it suddenly struck me that the islands were so located in the Bay of Bengal that they constituted the bastion in the naval fortification of India from the East. As such they had an abiding importance in the future defence of our country.

The eastern islands of Andaman and Nicobar are gateways into the Bay of Bengal. If they were not to come under the control of India and if they were not properly guarded and fortified, any foe from the East can easily launch a naval attack and knock straightaway at the door of Calcutta. But under her control, they can be turned into a formidable naval base for the defence of India from the East. It can then be equipped with a fleet of aeroplanes and a strong detachment of fighting ships that will guard its waters day and night and hold in bay any attack on the shores of India. The population of the Andamans and the present state of its culture being Indian, the islands themselves must form a political province of India. The Lakhadives and the Maldives, lost to India in her early history, exposed us to European incursions from the next-door islands of Bombay and Goa. The native rulers of those days could devise no efficient means, at the time, to stave off these inroads. We should all learn from these mistakes of the past, and profiting by that experience, raise an effective line of fortifications covering in their range Lakhadive and Maldive islands in the West, Ceylon in the South, and the Andamans and the Nicobars in the East of India. We must turn this base of defence into a naval fortress, not unlike the formidable Sindhu Durga in the glorious days of Shivaji. Today Singapore constitutes our first line of fortified defence. The Andamans are its natural front line. For, like Ceylon, they form a natural link with India and also her cultural heritage.

Get up, on with your Bedding

While the future navy of India with its base in the courtyard of the Andmans was floating on the sea of my imagination and guarding its fortifications of the historical Sindhu Durga, the sepoy rudely awakened me from my dreamland with the words, "Get up, on with your bedding." He used high words because he knew that his officer was hearing him. It was his faith that the more insolent his language is, the quicker will be his promotion. These insulting words were a prelude to my humiliating position in the prison-house of the Andamans. I got up, I took the bedding on my head, my pots and pans in one hand, and, girding up the chains round my waist, I stood ready for further orders. The mind suffers pain like the body hurled suddenly from a great steep height into the deep valley below. Disillusioned and consigning to the future the glorious picture I had drawn, I stood up to face the grim reality of the present. I was led from the wharf to go up a steep ascent. With heavy weights on my legs and with bare feet, I could not walk up as rapidly as I wished. The warder, beside me, was goading me on to quicken my pace. The European Officer once rebuked him not to trouble me. In my climb upwards, one thought was persisting in my mind. It harassed me with the question, "You are going up this climb to your prison, will you ever go down by the same road to freedom?" In a short time, we reached the top, and saw the main gate of the "Silver Jail" in front of me. The gate began to grate on its hinges. It opened, I went in, and it was shut behind me. I felt that I had entered the jaws of death.

Mr. Barrie

As I stepped in, two sergeants held me on either side and made me stand up. At the same time, I heard a whisper going around among the warders that Mr. Barrie was coming. They seemed to have seen none more cruel and hard-hearted than he, and they watched my face to see what impression that name had made upon me. But I was absorbed in looking at the decorations in the space between the two iron doors that had folded upon me with their tremendous size. The high wall of that mighty prison was adorned at the top with a festoon of manacles of every size and shape, and worked into the form of hideous-looking flowers. Heavy shackles for the feet, iron bands for the arms, and several similar instruments of torture were hanging down from the wall, right in front of me. They had a grimness and beauty all their own, for they were befitting ornaments of the horrible dungeon I had entered. The bayonets, the rifles, the shackles, the handcuffs—these were the proper layout of that hall of torture, of that big ghastly prison, as appropriate to it as the neat and fine garments that become an executioner, when he escorts his victim to the block. I had read many a work dealing with the history of revolutionary movements all over the world, and also autobiographies of martyrs in those struggles for independence. The descriptions in those works of the prisons, in which they were confined, were harrowing enough. And they had exactly reproduced, I felt, what I was seeing before me now. The two surly sergeants had made me stand up, that I might behold the scene and be thoroughly downcast in soul by it. The hideous scene was staring me in the face and I was staring at it with an eye as stern as the scene itself. I did not turn my gaze from him, as he did not lower his eyes before mine. We seemed to understand each other, and rightly had we measured each other's strength. I had a mysterious satisfaction that I was here experiencing what I had read in the books, and that I was standing up in the jaws of this horrible monster, as it were, without being ground down by its teeth. I stood calm and composed, fearless in mind and body, and without a tremour in my limbs. I had written a poem "The Two Images" in the Briston prison in London. Lines in that poem came up in my mind now. I began to revolve those lines; and my heart thrilled with their utterance: "Victory to the Goddess of Freedom".

Mr. Barrie's Counsel of Perfection

I had almost recovered from this maelstrom of emotion when I beheld a stout, corpulent European Officer, carrying in his hand a big stick as formidable as himself, standing right in front of me and watching me from head to foot. This was Mr. Barrie and he had announced his name that it might fall upon my ears before he was himself on the scene. He had expected me to look out for him with fear in my eyes, to cower down before him, but I had not noticed him as my mind was absorbed in the feeling of defiance which it had conjured up as a reaction against the fearful present that was facing me. In those few minutes he kept on watching me. My eyes caught him in that process when he gruffly turned to the sergeant and said, "Leave him; he is not a tiger." Then, pointing his big stick at me, he went on, "Well, are you the man who tried to escape at Marseilles?" I answered his bold query in a similar independent but self-controlled tone. "Yes, why do you ask me that question?" The tone lowered slightly the temper of the man before me. And he added, as if in a mood of curiosity, "Why did you do that?" "You ask me the reason why? Well, one of the reasons was to spare myself all future trouble." "But did you not invite the trouble upon yourself?" "Yes, but that was because I felt that it was my duty to do so. And I may add, Mr. Barrie, that I also felt that it was my duty to be rid of it." "Look here," said he, "I am not an Englishman. I am an Irishman." He pretended to be as frank with me as I was frank with him. I intervened, "But I would not have hated you for being an Englishman. I have spent the best years of my life in England, and I am an admirer of the virtues that characterise an Englishman." "I tell you that I am an Irishman," he replied, "to let you know that I also have taken my part in activities like yours for the liberation of Ireland. I was young then as you are now. But since that time, I am a changed man. Look here, I tell it to you as a friend," he continued, "you are young and I am pretty old in years. I have seen many more winters than you have." I smiled and interrupted him, "And don't you think that, perhaps, that may be the reason of the change that has come over you? Not increasing wisdom but dwindling energy?" The man was non-plussed and he retorted, "You are a lawyer and I am a layman, and I have but little education. But you are a prisoner, and I am the gaoler of this prison. So, don't reject my advice as useless, murders are murders, and they will never bring independence." "Of course, I know it, but may I ask you, why don't you convey this to the Sinfeiners in Ireland? Besides, who told you that I had favoured murders?" He, then, changed the subject and said, "The Superintendent will be here presently. It is against the rules that a man in my position should discuss politics with you. But my heart feels it poignantly that a man like you, educated, scholarly, and famous, should find himself in the company of the most hardened criminals in the world. It was thus that I was impelled to talk to you. Let bygones be bygones. I have nothing to do with them. I ask you to observe strictly the regulations of this place. You are a prisoner here and it is my duty to warn you about them. Don't break them and I will not interfere. Otherwise I shall have to punish." What unconscious humour it was that he should be talking to a political prisoner like me, and yet be warning that I was not to break my rules of prison discipline in this place!

"I would give you one more tip," and it is this: "You will be involving yourself in a terrible mess if ever you try to run away from this place. The prison is surrounded on all sides by vast, dense, impenetrable jungles; the cruellest of aborigines make their abode in them; they are cannibals. If they catch you, they kill you, and make a meal of tender, young bodies like yours, as easily as we may eat cucumbers! Do not, please, treat it as a joke; don't chaff; the *jamadar* here will tell you if it is not true." The *jamadar* saluted him, of course, and said, "Every word of it is true, Sahib."

"I know it, but too well," I added. "The first book I ordered and read, when I knew that I was to be sent to the Andamans, was the Government Report of these islands. I fully realise that Port Blair is not Marseilles."

"So far so good, act as I like, and I shall prove myself useful to you. *Jamadar*, take him in, and show him up to his room on the top floor of barrack number seven. Lock him up."

□

8

The First Week in My Cell

The *jamadar* led me to Chawl No. 7. On the way lay a big reservoir of water. The *jamadar* asked me to take my bath there. I had not taken my bath for four or five days. My body was full of sweat and dirt. The sea-voyage had done it. I was delighted with the permission to bathe. But I had no garment to change. The *jamadar* gave me a piece of cloth no better than a suspender. I had never entered my bath in that naked condition. What then? Was not to wear it for bath and for my labour all my life here? The mind revolted, but then said, "Fool! did not a saint like Ramdas use the same apparel? The world knows what you carry within it. From whom are you hiding it now? Has not Milton described it as 'honour dishonourable'?" There was a sect in Europe which considered it a sin to wear clothes. For Adam and Eve never wore any. Their followers adopted the same mode of life. And they called themselves Adamites. Even today, if not for religion, then for hygiene, colonies of men and women in certain regions of the world go about as nudists except in the cold season. They expose their bodies to sunlight as a matter of health. For, certain doctors in the West condemn the practice of excessive clothing as harmful to a man's health. In Europe, they wear too many clothes for fashion's sake. They seldom expose their bodies to sunlight. From birth to death, they wrap themselves up in clothes, and the health of these people had suffered. So, doctors had opined, and the people had followed them. I was thinking all this over while I was donning the strip of cloth that was given to me by the *jamadar*. The *jamadar* had watched, with delight, the trepidation and shame of many a person here when he was called upon to take a bath in this dress or absence of dress. But he was disappointed in me and, perhaps, he set me down as the most shameless of them all! I went to the tank and was about to dip my pot into it, when the *jamadar* cried out, "Not so here, you are a prisoner, you first stand up; I will say, 'take the water'; you will then bend down and dip the pot in the reservoir. I will then say, 'rub your body clean'; then you will clean it with your hands. I will say, 'have one more'; then you will dip your pot for a second round, and so on. The whole bath has to be finished in three pot-fuls of water." This order of the Pathan *jamadar* simply surprised me. I was a resident of Nasik, a place of pilgrimage where hundreds bathed freely on the banks of the Godavari. I was accustomed, however, to the ritual of the bath finished with scanty water, I laughed to myself and finished my bath here in the same mood. That was a pious act done within my sea; this I had to do when I was transported beyond it. One was white and the other was black water! That was all the difference between the two. The priest here was my bearded *jamadar* and a Mohomedan! As I poured the water on my person, I felt a strange sensation. I shut my eyes and could see nothing. I felt like burning all over the body. "Was the *jamadar* wrong in his recital?" I asked myself. Just then, I happened to gargle my mouth, and, instantly, spewed out the water. Was it salt water I was bathing in? The tongue tasted it as salt. I asked the *jamadar* about it. He retorted, "Was ever seawater sweet?" It was then that I realised that I had a sea-bath here. Sweet water is scarce throughout the Andamans. They all use sea-water for bathing, for washing clothes, and for several miscellaneous purposes. And the water is conveyed in pipes and stored in the reservoir for such use.

The whole body had become sticky. The hair had become hard and stiffened. It was better I had not bathed in it. But I thought over again, and realised that it was to be my daily habit in this prison. In London and Paris, I had enjoyed the luxury of a Turkish Bath. Should I not enjoy in India the pleasure of the "Andamanish Bath" by way of change? The expiation of all my sins as a patriot and nationalist could not be done by washing in warm water and with soaps and fragrant oils and under shower baths. It has to be done in pots of sea-water drawn from the reservoir, with the mantra of the *jamadar* priest; "Now dip the pot for water," repeated by him thrice, and no more.

I put on my clothes and walked on till I came in front of a three-storiyed building of stone and mortar. It was solidly barred from top to bottom. Every floor of it had separate rooms equally barred. The building had no wood-work in it. It was entirely fireproof. It had broad steps reaching up from one floor to another. It was all white-washed and clean without. The stair case and the symmetry of the rooms gave it the appearance of a big, roomy mansion. And the heart delighted at the sight. "This was then chawl number seven. It was here I was to stay on the top-floor, and in a room all to myself, and barred and bolted from without," I said to myself. A fine place this, me thought, I shall have free and fresh breeze to breathe in. I shall have plenty of light in it. If this tenement had been my own, I would have gone down as a rich man in my society. And for four months in summer, I would have used it as a pleasure-resort, with this fine green court-yard around it. If I drive away from my mind the notion that it is a prison after all, I can still be happy in it. Speaking for its use alone, it is true enough that the pleasure or the pain of it, as the Vedantist puts it, arises from the fact that it does or does not belong to me. Let me then be entirely indifferent to the notion of mine and thine, which is the seed of all our miseries in this world, as far as in me lies, I shall try to be indifferent about it, and derive all the joy that I can from it. The building is mine so long as I occupy it. It is a fine building and I pay no rent for it. What if they call it a prison? Let me pass my days in it as happily and as long as I must.

But, then, how long and for how many days? Ah! there is the rub! According to prison regulations, I may be free within six months. If the gaoler is particularly harsh to me, then, at the most, within a year. The wardens had told me that three years were the limit here. The Silver Jail knew not a single instance of a prisoner being detained within its portals for more than three years, Hence, I concluded that I would be let off after three years. But, facing the worst, as it had been a rule of life with me, I took it for granted that, at the longest, they will confine me in this room for a period of five years. I, therefore, decided to accept the situation, stay in this fine building for five years, and spend the time in composing the epic that I had already planned in the jail at Dongri. This I took as the Government order as well as a matter of personal choice.

I was revelling in this play of fancy when I climbed up to the third floor of the building, and stood near the door of my room. The whole of that chawl was emptied of its inmates because I was to come there. There were a hundred and fifty prisoners in that chawl. Only three wardens, the worst of their kind as being taletellers, sinners, men of evil propensities, dare-devils, and, for that reason, in the good books of their officers, were retained in the whole building as guards on me. The rest of the prisoners who had denounced them were ordered to vacate the place. All three of them were Musalmans—two Baluchis and one Pathan. All political prisoners had Musalmans for their wardens. And myself was especially given in their charge. Those who were detailed to keep watch and ward on my room took great pride in that mission. For, thereby, they could boast all over the settlement that they were in the special confidence of their superiors. They were appointed to their place because the officers wanted through them all the information that they could get about the political prisoners in their charge—their possible machinations and their secret communications. And the officers could use the wardens as convenient tools to perpetrate any kind of cruelty, to trump up any kind of charge against the prisoners in their charge. They were apt for these nefarious deeds and, being of so much service to them, the officers usually connived at their gross misdemeanour and their immoral action, if only they held in check their Hindu prisoners and succeeded in terrorising them. A large portion of political prisoners in that jail being Hindus, and I being among them, these wards were regarded by us as the greatest terror of our lives. It was not unlike the visitation and influence of a malignant deity. We were Hindus and a Hindu warden may be kind towards us. Hence, the authorities put upon us Musalman wardens who reported our movements to them either in an exaggerated form, or invented stories about us and systematically and heartlessly maltreated us to curry favour with their masters. Since the time that the Silver Jail began to be filled with political prisoners, the Hindu wardens had fallen from the favour of their masters, and had, consequently, suffered in their rise and promotion.

Moreover, the Pathans, as a rule, were bigoted Mohomedans, and were especially notorious for their fanatical hatred of the Hindus. The officers had pampered them to serve their own ends. To persecute the Hindus was natural to them. The result was that they began to harass them all the more and justified their action by reporting fibs against their fellow-prisoners—the Hindu wardens. "Barrie Baba", as the gaoler was called, would never countenance or entertain any complaint against his own favourites. Consequently, the Pathan wardens had nothing to fear in that quarter. Not only did the Hindu wardens suffer in promotion and disfavour, but the Muslim wardens succeeded more and more in ousting them from their jobs and replacing them by their Pathan brethren. The Pathan always sides with a Pathan. This fact, if it had been a fraternity of good men, would have been a blessing. But here it helped them to connive at the persecution practised by prisoners of their own community against the Hindu prisoners in the jail. For the Baluchi, the Sindhi, and the Pathan prisoners had wardens belonging to their own religion while the Hindu prisoners were systematically denied that favour. So, that the Hindus suffered doubly. First, from their fellow-prisoners, the Muslims, and secondly, from their Muslim wardern. Since our admission in that prison, the situation in this respect had considerably worsened. The Hindu prisoners and the Hindu wardens had a hell of their lives in that place. How these happenings had their inevitable repercussions, the reader will know in the course of this narrative and in its proper place. We have barely referred to this matter here precisely because the reader may grasp their significance later on. The Pathans, the Sindhis and the Baluchi Muslims, with a few exceptions, were, one and all, cruel and unscrupulous persons, and were full of fanatical hatred for the Hindus. Not so the Musalmans from the Punjab, and less even than they, those of Bengal, Tamil province and Maharashtra. But the fanatical section always belittled and held up to laughter their co-religionists from other parts of India. It twitted them as "half kafirs". And this constant jibe compelled them, very often and perhaps inevitably, to follow in the foot-steps of their wicked brethren. That emulation did not help them, however, to ingratiate themselves into the favour of their masters, the European Officers. They were always inclined to favour those who were, according to them, their best servants, that is, tyrants and persecutors of prisoners in their charge.

That was one of the reasons for placing me under the close supervision of the most seasoned of these Pathan wardens. He wore the designation of *jamadar* or Petty Officer, that is a warden, who was himself a prisoner, promoted to a higher rank in the settlement. There were three such *jamadars* appointed to the task of keeping a close supervision on my movements. The *jamadar*, who had brought me to my quarters in this chawl, handed me over to these wardens, closed the room, locked it, and went away.

Next morning, these wardens presented themselves before my room and announced that the Sahib was coming and I was to stand up. I came to the door, which was nothing but a barred entrance into my room. Mr. Barrie had come up with his European friends. He had acquired a special importance with them since my arrival in this gaol. The Europeans in the locality, men and women, were naturally curious to see me and talk to me. And for that purpose, they had to burn incense before the demi-god, Mr. Barrie. Mr. Barrie pretended that he was taking them to my room under great risk, and they had to request him, again and again, before he would accede to their importunities. He brought them here under great secrecy, and showed me to them from a distance and, sometimes, allowed them to approach me closer, all the while making a show that he had done them a great favour and that he was indeed anxious how to explain it to his superiors or how to get over the hurdle. With a solemn air, he marched them away always ending with the expostulation: "That will do! That will do." The intending visitors had to go to Mr. Barrie's bungalow fifteen times over, before he would yield to their cajoling. I know many a European sergeant and his wife and daughter who had to flatter him thus.

The word "Sarkar" made me wake up and stand before the door according to prison regulations. The first thing I could see through the barred entrance was not Mr. Barrie but the protruding part of his nether region—the stomach. For it bulged out defiant of the world, and ran before him, as it were, to display its circumambient rotundity, not dissimilar to the spherical apparatus in the classroom to explain to the school-children the size and shape of mother Earth. Over this circumference, Mr. Barrie had tied his leather-belt. And it marked faithfully the equatorial line on the Earth's surface.

The Indian Mutiny Discussed

Mr. Barrie began his talk with me in the following words-"They may be telling you that I am your jailor. Is it not?" I only smiled. He added, "And I assure you I am your friend." The European friends who had accompanied him remained silent. For Mr. Barrie never allowed anyone to talk to me directly, except some like him, and to whom he could not deny that privilege. "I like to converse with an educated man like you. Therefore, I come here, sometimes, without any particular reason to do so. They say that you have written an account of the Indian Mutiny of 1857. Am I right in it?" While he was uttering these sentences, I simply listened, with a smile on my lips and an eye upon his countenance. I found out that he had opened the conversation to sound my mind upon the subject, to press the key and start the music. I was inclined on my side to let him go on and listen, as I felt that the talk may afford me relaxation from the very dull time I had in the solitude of this room.

However, I intervened, "I have read a number of books on the Indian Mutiny. That is a fact." "Don't you feel fed up with those monsters of cruelty? Can you put up with their monstrosities? What horrors have they not committed? My father was himself a victim of that Mutiny. He used to tell us that the wicked Nanasaheb had personally tortured English women and put into their mouths XXX. Will you not call them monsters? What else are they?" I asked him if his father was an eye-witness of the scene. He replied, instantly, that a colonel was an eye-witness when such things happened in Lucknow, and he had reported them to his father. "Then, it must be a downright lie, for Nanasaheb was not then at Lucknow. He was in Cawnpore when English men and women were imprisoned at Lucknow." Pretending not to hear me, Mr. Barrie continued, "A thousand instances like this have happened." I replied, "Very true, but there are also a thousand canards to keep them company. And as the instance you have quoted has proved to be a hear-say, so it may be with others as well."

One of the visitors who appeared to be a polite gentleman intervened to remark, "But, on the whole, don't you think that Nanasaheb, Tatya Tope and other mutineers like them were selfish men? Will you not recoil from them with contempt?" To him my answer was, "If you desire to discuss the Indian Mutiny with me in this place and when I am a prisoner here, I am ready to do so. You must forget, however, for the time being, that I am standing before my jailor, and concede that I am your equal. Otherwise, it will be like shutting up my mouth while you indulge in criticism against my country and its past history in a manner insulting to her. That will be entirely a one-sided affair to which, as gentlemen, you will not subscribe. It will be not only despicable conduct but an act of utter cowardice." Mr. Barrie said, "By no means, Mr. Savarkar. I have already told you that I have come here as a friend. Discuss the matter freely."

"Then, I express my opinion without any reservation. I know that you regard me as an extremist. As such, you will find my views altogether one-sided and unpalatable. I open this discussion to make you think if they are really so. I have never concealed them and I find no reason to conceal them now. This is purely a question of history and if I am to suffer for my opinion on it, I shall not hide it, for I shall never tolerate anyone distorting the history of my country and misrepresenting the principal characters in it. For, to put up with such distortion, I regard as timidity and a sin. The British Government had itself appointed a Commission to review a report on the actions of Nanasaheb in this Mutiny. And the report has completely exonerated him. The charges made against him, in the particular episode you have mentioned, have been found by the Commission to be baseless and exaggerated statements. They were declared to be emanations from the wicked brain of some soldiers in the English camp at the time."

Who, Pray, is not Selfish?

"You have described Nanasaheb and Tatya Tope as selfish men." "Yes, for Nanasaheb wanted back his Raj, and Tatya wanted to pass for a hero," said the visitor. I replied, "Yes indeed, but is it not true also that Victor Emmanuel wanted to be the King of Italy, that George Washington desired to be the first President of the American Republic, and Garibaldi wished to be a hero? But, strictly speaking, they all fought for the independence of their own country!" "Then, you also raised the revolt to seek independence," Mr. Barrie interposed. "That is a different issue altogether. The Indian Mutiny of 1857 does not necessarily justify any revolutionary activity today. Nor are we precluded from any such action on the ground that nothing of that kind had happened in 1857. The inference on either side is not only absurd but foolish as well." The visitor, it seemed, had read a book or two on Indian Mutiny. He retorted, "Then you mean to say that the slaughter of English women at Cawnpore by the mutineers is a concocted story?" "I have never said that," I answered. "It is a fact and it is a deplorable fact. But the issue is who was responsible for the carnage, and how did it at all happen? The women in that prison-camp were first treated as prisoners of war. And this is proved from the evidence of the survivors, and of those who had independently testified to the fact. I have reproduced that evidence in my work on the subject. When the British army marched on Cawnpore, it set fire to the villages round about Allahabad and kept them burning. And in that fire were destroyed the females of those who had participated in the Indian Revolt. The news inflamed the Indian regiments that had joined the Mutiny. Meanwhile, the English women, who had been confined as prisoners of war, had sent secret missives to the army marching on Cawnpore. Their messages happened to be intercepted by soldiers in the Indian camp. All this had contributed additional fuel to the fire that was already burning, with the result that you describe as the wholesale slaughter of English women by Indian soldiers.

Both are Equally Guilty or Not Guilty

"If we are to regard these acts as blameworthy, we must blame in an equal measure the excesses of the British army, which were partly responsible for these actions. Do you regard Cromwell's action in Ireland, the massacre he carried on at Drogheda, as an act of monstrous cruelty? Are you ashamed of it? In times of fierce national crisis and revolution, such things are bound to happen. And however regrettable in themselves the incidents may be, they do not justify the perversion of the motive behind such struggles and revolts. Nanasaheb's forces may have put to the sword many an English woman without his sanction or knowledge. But what of ten times as many women burnt to death in the campaign of fire and loot that the British army had carried in the villages round about Allahabad? Statues have been erected to the Generals of this army in England. Neile writes in his diary about it, 'It was my duty to follow this policy of cruelty for the good of my country.' Cannot the same words be used in defence of excesses perpetrated by the army of mutineers? If at all there is guilt in these actions, both the sides are equally responsible for it, more or less; or we must exonerate them both from such a charge." The visitor said on this, "I grant that the revolt was a War of Independence. I also admit that allegations made by one side against the other in that struggle are mere fabrications. The Indian soldiers may not have committed all the indecent acts that are being attributed to them. But what is the moral that we may derive from it now? What is the lesson we are learning today?"

"That is none of my business. I have discussed the whole position in the spirit of history. I am not going to descant here on its present-day applications. I think I have said enough on the point consistent with my position today. I cannot go into that question further at the present moment."

"Well, we shall leave it here today. Some other time we may open it again," Mr. Barrie concluded, as if spontaneously, and left the place, after enquiring sympathetically about my health.

An Experiment in Verse

For two days after, I had no work to do in my cell. I asked for books to read, and I was told that I would get them only after a month or two of observation of my conduct as a prisoner. Not a soul moved here with whom I could exchange a word. I resumed my originally planned work of composing poems. I continued with what I had already done elsewhere. But I had no means with me in this place to do the kind of literary work I had intended to complete. It taxed my mind to the utmost to keep it going. For a single date and a single right word, I had to scratch my brain for weeks together. However brilliant the fancy, I had to abandon it for want of material to translate it into beautiful and apt imagery in words. I had to draw exclusively on the stores of my memory for anything I could think or write. For years, this was the only capital I could use.

The first secret Missive

It was the fourth or the fifth day of my residence here. No other prisoner was let into the whole building from whom I might gather any news. I had just finished my morning meal and I was resting in my room. It was afternoon. Suddenly I heard a stone knocking against the bars of my room. The stone fell on the ground. It was again hurled at me. It came through the bars and fell right in front of the door. I was standing and went forward to see what it was when the warden, who had thrown it at me, directed me to pick it up. He at once disappeared from the scene. I picked it up and found a piece of paper bound up to the stone. It was a missive to me. I opened the note when I heard a hue and cry in the compound below. I got up considerably startled. I came forward and saw my warden calling out the petty officer above him. I at once concluded that it had something to do with the stone. Evidently the Pathan warden must have seen another warden throwing the stone up to me. And he was calling the petty officer either to catch him or to search my room to find out what it was that he had thrown. In a moment, the officer was near my door. I could not make up my mind to destroy the missive. For he who had brought it to me at such a great risk must be knowing that it had some important news to convey. But I could not conceal it either, for there was no place to do it. In a minute, they will open the lock and if they discover the letter, all those implicated in the act were bound to suffer. The warden who had brought it, the man who gave it to him, and myself, its recipient, will all be involved in the crime. I resolved, while I stood in the corner of the room with my face turned to the *jamadar*, and yet hiding my body from him, to secrete it on my person where the *jamadar* could not find it. I had no other alternative in the matter. I turned it in a manner that the writing on it might remain clean and intact. The petty officer came in. He questioned me in a high and insolent tone about the letter. He asked me who had picked up the stone. I answered that I knew nothing about it. The Pathan warden at the door was lost in brown study as he feared no danger whatever, when the stone was being hurled at me. The noise of the stone had roused him from his day-dream, and he saw the warden below beckoning on to me. Suspecting something amiss, he raised the cry that had brought the *jamadar* to my room. The warden was a Hindu, and anything that could damn him was a gain to the Pathans, for one of them could easily take the place of the dismissed man. That was another reason for all this hullabaloo. The petty officer was also a Musalman. He searched me through and through. He searched my shorts and my waist-coat. He pressed them all over with his hands. And, at last, he found nothing. Nor did they discover anything on the Hindu warden. And the matter ended there.

A Warning

After they had left the place and after I had assured myself that everything was normal, I took out that paper and read it. The note described to me the situation in that prison, and warned me to be very cautious. Convicts in the Manik Tola Bomb Case in Bengal and three or four editors of Swarajya at Allahabad were all the political prisoners in the jail at that time. The man who had sent that note to me was one of that numbers and an old Bengali friend of mine. He specially warned me to trust none for the mere reason that he was a political prisoner. He had hinted that some of them had turned into Government spies whose only business was to propitiate the gaoler in order to save themselves from the hard labour of turning the oil-mill. They had not only communicated to him the names of the conspirators who were out, but had started backbiting those who were in. Such men should by no means be trusted, and no confidence should be given to them. That was what the paper conveyed to me.

This division in the Bengali revolutionary camp did not surprise me. For, I knew that their leaders' arrest had dispirited them and the convicts were busy exposing one another and betraying the cause even in the jail at Calcutta. This was, indeed, an unpardonable action and disgraceful apostasy. All the same, it was folly to tar them all with the same brush. There were many among them who still showed high courage and were staunch in their loyalty to the cause. And even those, whose unbearable hardships had made them fail, must be given their due for past service, for sterling patriotism, and for their sincere sacrifice for the side they had taken. None can forget their solid qualities, and, yet, be just to them.

The Spies at Work

The ring leaders in the Bengal Conspiracy Case who, as convicts, had been transported to the Andamans, found it hard to bear the trials of prison-life and thought, naturally enough, to somehow escape its harrowing experience. Some of them, therefore, conspired to spy on the movements of their colleagues and disciples, and even on me, who had come there but lately and who knew them not. They reported us secretly to the prison authorities. They had no scruples about their doings. They did not hesitate to carry on this nefarious business. But we must remember that they were led on to it by the horrible sufferings, the insults and humiliations, and the physical tortures that they had to endure in this prison. Those, who do not bend or bow under these bludgeonings, have, alone, the right to cast any stone at them; not a Tom, Dick or Harry, who comfortably sits in his arm-chair, and keeps on barking at the world.

I had known similar backslidings among political prisoners and conspirators in Ireland, Russia and Italy, and in similar circumstances of physical pain, mental agony, and moral disgrace. And, in some instances, the backslidings and apostasy were more disgusting than I had known in my own country. Not only politics but religion also had such examples to show and to hold up to shame. It was, therefore, unwise to brand a community or a province as particularly guilty of that crime. And it was worse still to let oneself be depressed by it.

"Say it Out"

Hence, I was not shocked by what I had read. On the other hand, I pitied those who had been frightened by it. I may give here a specific instance in point. A prominent Bengali conspirator, who was not more than thirty at the time, used to discourse to his loyal disciples on the Bhagvatgita in order to impress upon them the mortality of the body and the immortality of the soul. He would quote in support the famous text: "No weapon can slay it, no fire can burn it." The young men who heard him had become fearless of death and were ready to face the worst ordeal for the cause they were championing. But when the leader and fiery writer was himself sentenced to imprisonment in this jail and saw its stonewalls, and had to faint one day under the grinding labour of running the oil-mill, which even two powerful bullocks could not go round easily, then the body avenged itself upon the soul by trampling it underfoot. His courage failed him and he could no longer bear the hardships of that labour. Again, it was not a question of a day or two. It was a prolonged agony of a life-time. To refuse to work meant added labour and increased agonies. In this dark despair, life cried hoarse to be spared that labour at any cost. What was the way out of it? Where was the outlet from the enclosing walls of these unbearable calamities? There was only one way and one gate. The way was filth and the gate narrow. That was to report against one's fellow-conspirators. That board—"Say it out"—was ever hanging on the road and pointing to the gate. And who, do you think, carried tales about this man's despair to the authorities? A friend and no one else. And that friend again, who had himself desired a similar escape! The matter was reported by the gaoler to the authorities in Calcutta. At last, fine promises were made to him in order to trap him completely in the net. A drowning man is known to catch at a straw. So, our Bengali writer and preacher went in jail and fell. To enact the drama, the gaoler one day brought in that jail the highest officer of the island. The political prisoners were busy going round the mill. The officer came to the entrance of this man's cell. The man shouted, "A petition, Sir." The officer echoed, "What do you want?"

He proceeded a few paces, returned and awaited the prisoner. The latter knelt, folded his hands, and prayed: "Do what you will, Sir, but free me from these tortures; that is all I beg of you." The officer replied: "You may report to the gaoler." The curtain was rung down on the scene, and the drama ended.

The Betrayal

After the officer had gone, the gaoler sent him ink and paper as pre-arranged. The man started reporting on the Calcutta Conspiracy Case. He gave all the information about it, right or wrong, true or false, as suited his purpose. Naturally, all the other persons involved in the Conspiracy regarded the action as a cruel betrayal. And the man himself had the conscience to feel that he was doing a bad act, though he was too enfeebled in mind to desist from it. He wrote a letter to his friend as follows: "I can no longer bear the suffering. The only alternative to it is suicide. I attempted it, but dare not attempt it again. You may kill me as you have killed other betrayers of the cause before this. I will not blame you. I must propitiate the officer by betraying you. I must give him all possible information in order to save myself from the tortures of the body. I have lost control over my mind." He sent this strange epistle to his friend and passed the other letter, with the names and information in it, to the jailor.

On the third day, he was taken off from the hard labour of turning the mill and given the lighter work of picking oakum. He was neither removed from his cell, nor let off from the prison.

The man had, at least, the honesty of feeling that he was doing a reprehensible act, and of acknowledging the fact. Two of his other partners in the act had parted company with their conscience. These found, in my coming to that prison, an opportunity of their life-time. To report everything about me to the jailor, to invent stories for that purpose when truth had proved of no avail; anyhow to compass the end of ridding themselves of the hardships of the prison-life, though they trembled in the act; to prove false to themselves—all this they achieved without the least compunction of the soul. So much were they lost to all sense of shame and decency.

It was thus that I was caught between these two inescapable alternatives. I continued my life here on the horns of a dilemma. Whosoever reported against me at once became the favourite of the jailor, and got some facility or another in this prison. So, to carry tales about me had become, with some of them, a regular and fashionable business. It was no surprise to me that mean and wretched fellows should ply this trade. But that these decent men, coming from respectable families, should have stooped so low in order to make their lives easy, and to get some concessions, here and there, was, indeed, a surprise and degradation beyond my imagining. But they did it, making hay while the sun shone! Every facility that they had won by this means was an added burden to my suffering in the jail. But that story I shall unfold, as I go on, in this narrative.

The note sent on to me had a reference to all intrigues of prison-life. One section was reporting against the other, and the warning was conveyed that I should be on my guard against the traitors. The letter was couched in a spirit of sincerity and earnestness. I, therefore, decided that until I had convinced myself of the facts, I was to cherish no suspicion in my mind about those who, in the past, had proved themselves bold, fearless, sincere and devoted servants of their country. And even if I knew that they had fallen now, I was to cast no aspersion upon their character and on their former service. The only thing I was to do was to walk warily in my contacts with them and throughout my stay in this prison.

Pardon Me, Please; Enough of It

A day or two after this incident, I saw a crowd of prisoners, excluding political prisoners, gathered in the foreyard of my chawl. Two hundred in number, they were employed in the work of peeling, breaking and cutting to pieces the coconut fruit gathered, in a heap, before them. From his sequestered place on the third floor of my chawl, the Pathan warden was looking on with eager eyes. He felt a hungering for a coconut or two from that heap. His mouth watered to drink the water and to eat the luscious sweet inside it. His appetite was whetted by what he saw right under his nose. He was a favourite with his master, and who will not fear him? Who dares deny him what he asks? The Pathan went down into the courtyard, and slapping a prisoner in the face, charged him of eating a coconut. "Look at his mouth, it is too full of it," he fired. By this threat at the outset, he had created an atmosphere, as he felt, favourable to his game. For, he was confident that none could say no to him, if he were now to ask for the choicest fruit from that heap. The king of fruit is known in the producer's parlance as "Dahi-Naral"—that is a coconut fruit full of curd-milk-sweet inside it. Presently, he saw the fruit secreted in the hand of a Madrasi man who was a recent arrival in that prison. Straightaway my Pathan warden went up to him and said, "O, you scoundrel, hand over that fruit to me." But the Madrasi man seemed to be recalcitrant. He was the most notorious dacoit in his part of the country. He was a Tamil and, before being sent here for transportation, he had seen life in many a prison and many times in his own province. He was sentenced here for only ten years' imprisonment, which he treated as a trifle. He did not know Hindusthani language and could very well put off the importunate warden by pretending not to understand him. He faced up to him and ejaculated "Ille, Ille"—meaning that he had no fruit with him. That was his peculiar way of putting off anyone who happened to press him. He had secured the particular fruit by palming off an anna worth of good tobacco to the prisoner whose business it was to break the coconuts. How can then a hardened criminal like him part with his booty to this Pathan Warden? But the haughty warden was sure in his self-importance that a mere Hindu dare not deny him what he had asked. The warden abused the Madrasi prisoner and ordered him to part with the coconut forthwith. The Tamil man at first proceeded on the principle of discretion being the better part of valour. Piteously he wailed, "I have not it, surely, I have not it," pretending ignorance and feigning madness. The Pathan was furious. He flew into a rage. As the quarrel was with a Hindu, it soon turned into a question of religion, and fanaticism put the fat into the fire. He showered abuse after abuse upon his victim. He called him names. "Kafir, scoundrel, let me uproot his tuft of hair," were some of his choicest epithets. "A Hindu, a villain, yes, I must pull it out," so he went on. And he put his hand to the Tamil man's sacred tuft of hair. Being ignorant of Hindusthani, he seemed to be confounded by the Pathan's ejaculations and outburst. He thought that the Pathan was asking him to do some good piece of work, and that he was angry because the latter was not doing it. But when the Pathan tried to wrest the fruit from him, the Madrasi prisoner came to close grips with him. It was a veritable wrestle and tug of war between the two. None of them cried out halt after it had begun. For, both of them had fastened their attention on the bone of contention, which was the "curd-milk-coconut".

The whole crowd was enjoying the scene and the Pathan was having the worst of it. The crowd began to titter and jeer, and the game was getting too hot for my warden. Instantly, he lifted his bludgeon and gave a heavy blow on the Tamil man's head. He also wrenched his tuft of hair and had almost uprooted it. The Pathan kept on raining blow after blow, and showering abuse after abuse. 'Kafir, scoundrel" was the constant refrain. All of a sudden, the scene changed: The prisoner had lost his temper. Without uttering a word and putting his hand straight to his antagonist's beard, he lifted him bodily off the ground and dashed him down in the dust. The Pathan measured his full length upon the earth and the Hindu prisoner sat firmly on his chest. He planted his knee upon it, and gave slap after slap into his face. The crowd watched the fight with gaping eyes. It did not raise any alarm, for the Pathan man was extremely unpopular with one and all of them. I was watching the whole show from my room, and I was nearly bursting into laughter. The Fez which the warden wore, his turban thereon, all lay in the dust on the ground. Muttering within his lips, the Tamil prisoner was still belabouring him. He had held fast his beard, and was slapping him in the face. The Pathan broke down completely. No more abusive words danced on his lips. The coconut? There was no more of it. Instead was the rider belabouring his mule under the stride. Two or three minutes had thus gone and the Pathan, while the slaps were still hot in his face, begged of his opponent to halt. "Enough, enough, my man, enough, I beg of you, enough." These were the words that trembled on his lips, so done up was he by the hard drubbing that the Madrasi had given him. But this exasperated him still more. Showering abuse for abuse, the prisoner rained fisticuffs on the head of the Pathan. It was the dialect that had made confusion worse confounded. The Pathan had said in Hindusthani—*Maph karo*—pardon me. The Madrasi caught only the first letter of it, Ma, which in Tamil meant mother. He took it as the most insulting abuse that one man can utter to another. And so he attaced the Pathan all the more vehemently, never understanding that the fellow was all along begging for mercy. "Ma", "Ma", replied the prisoner, and at every repetition, felled him with bludgeoning blows. At last, the inevitable had happened. The petty officer had arrived, the crowd rushed on the scene, and the combatants were separated. The Madrasi kept on gibbering—*Sahcb-hum tum mar* with gesticulations, which indicated that if the Pathan were to take the complaint to the gaoler, he will not stop short of throttling him. The Pathan is constitutionally a bully and a coward; the threat of the Madrasi, one better than him, completely unnerved him. Again he had broken the law himself, for he had left his post on the top floor, and gone down into the crowd to purloin a coconut. That must go against him. So, he ended the quarrel there, and, adjusting his dishevelled hair and turban, returned to his place on the top floor of my building. So was his greed satisfied. For three or more of the sweet coconuts, he had received blow after blow on his mouth and had to swallow them quietly.

"What's the matter? Why this hullabaloo?" I asked him. The warden replied haughtily, as if I had not witnessed the scene, "O, Sir, there was a man there, the rascal that he is, who wanted to steal the curd-milk-coconut." I gave him abound thrashing." "Well done," I answered, "a thief, and, at that, one who would thieve again, and also in prison! He deserved what he got." The Pathan and myself knew well who the thief was, and who gave the thrashing.

□

9

Early History of the Political Prisoners

The Cult of the Bomb

The first batch of political prisoners sent to the Andamans consisted of Bengalis involved in the Manik Tola Bomb Case, and two gentlemen from Maharashtra, namely Mr. Ganesh Savarkar and Mr. Wamanrao Joshi. Soon after them came another batch of six persons from Bengal, implicated in the trial for political dacoity. Of all these, three from Bengal and two from Maharashtra happened to be sentenced to transportation for life. Others, who were all Bengalis, had been sentenced for three to ten years' imprisonment. When I reached the Andamans, there were the Bengali persons, I have mentioned, and four editors of Swarajya from Allahabad with seven to ten years' imprisonment against them. The latter were sentenced for sedition and treason against the Government and, not like us, for revolutionary crime against the State. Some of these editors were deadly against all revolution and had not even understood its theory or known its practice. Their association with us had this advantage that they had begun to know both the theory and practice of revolutionary movement and had begun to sympathise with it. I must be satisfied with this general statement today for I do not recollect now the trials in which these men were involved, their names, and their opinions on the issues in question. I remember another being there in addition to those I have already named. As the majority of the first batch were Bengalis, we were all, in prison parlance, known as Bengalis, later on, the number was swelled by an influx from the Punjab in their hundreds, and several from other provinces as well. So, we came to be designated now by the hybrid name—the Bomb-makers.

Politicals or Men of the Tongue

Those who had never heard the name—political prisoner—could not understand what it really signified. Thousands of such prisoners could, on the other hand, form a distinct notion of bomb-throwing and, hence, the generic name of bomb-throwers by which all of us were recognised in the jail at Andaman. Whenever Mr. Barrie had to send for anyone of us or all of us, he would order the *jamadar* in the following words: "Go and fetch Bomb-golawalla No. 7" or "Go, and gather quickly all the bomb-throwers and shut them up." All understood that order and did accordingly. When I had entered the place, I enlightened my fellow-countrymen on the distinction between the bomb-thrower and the political prisoner. I told them we were not charged with the crime of bomb-throwing. We were charged and sentenced for agitation to fight the Government, and win and establish Swaraj. Some of us, no doubt, used pistols and bombs and rifles, but others fought only with their pens. Many had not even seen a bomb; what then of using it! What we all of us, exercised most, was our tongue. You should, therefore, call us men of the tongue, if not men of the pen. Surely the appellation 'bomb-thrower' does not fit us. To this, my disciples answered humorously, "Tell us then the right name for you, we shall adopt it." "We are rightly called political prisoners. If you cannot easily utter it, then abridge it if you please in your vernacular as Raj-Kaidi." This word was picked up quickly, and they could pronounce it easily. Henceforward, "political prisoner" became our common designation. Mr. Barrie did not welcome the change. He never put up with it. If anyone addressed us as 'Babu', Mr. Barrie would shout at him, "What Babu, who is Babu here? They are all prisoners, you fool." Mr. Barrie, of course, distinguished between prisoners who knew to read and write and those who did not. He had no objection to call the former 'Babus' But he resented that name being bestowed upon us. How then will he allow others to call us political prisoners?

'D' Ticket

"You are not political prisoners"—that was Mr. Barrie's slogan to the end of the chapter. If any prisoner pronounced that name in his presence, the Sahib would go at him, "Ah! What political prisoner? There is none here of that kind. They are all of a common class like you. Ticket No. D marks the so-called politicals, as it brands you all and the worst among you." The letter D signified 'dangerous' And the badge that we wore had this letter inscribed on it. The clothes we were given to wear also had badges with that letter. With all Mr. Barrie's objection to these appellations, from the first day to the last, I came to be known as "Bada Babu" Even Mr. Barrie, at times, would say, "Go, Havildar and fetch here the Bada Babu No. 7." As my fellow-countrymen in that prison learnt to distinguish between ordinary prisoners and political prisoners, they all called us by that name. The word had the smell of Swaraj and that was why Mr. Barrie hated the word. On the other hand, I desired to stamp the word 'Swaraj' upon their hearts. So, I particularly stressed the point that, when referring to us, they should all mention us as political prisoners and, in course of time, that word became a current coin in the terminology of the Silver Jail.

An Offering to a Cruel Deity (A Sop to Cerberus)

The political prisoners in the Andamans, before my arrival there, were all put together in one chawl. They had one Pathan warder to watch over them. The hard upper covering of the coconut fruit was broken into pieces, dried in the sun and was given to the prisoners to pick out threads from them. 'Picking oakum' is the technical term for this kind of hard labour in the prison. This labour was hard enough but was not so exhausting and soul-racking as the grinding mill to which they were yoked later on. Ordinary prisoners who could hardly spell the three 'R's were employed in this prison for light desk-work and they at once became 'Babus'. But political prisoners were shut out from that work and given hard labour, the kind of which their hands had never done. Surely, they knew better the art of reading and writing than the prisonrs who had hardly spelt its rudiments. Perhaps, this was their very disqualification for clerkship within the prison-door.

Though picking oakum was a task hard enough, its tedium was relieved by the company of prisoners working in the same chawl. An educated man desires company and association with his equals and, therefore, this mode of working was a solace to him. One or two of these prisoners were ailing and milk was provided for them. It was given to the Pathan warder as an offering to God.

And the God—the Pathan—on that account was less cruel to them. All these factors made prison-life for political prisoners less endurable than it is today. My elder brother was in the same chawl.

Months passed on in this manner when a high official from Calcutta came to the Andamans to inspect the prison. When he saw the political prisoners picking oakum in the same tenement and in one another's company, he was, of course, put out by it. He passed severe strictures upon local officers for ordering things in this manner. These men, he said, were not ordinary criminals—the thieves, the robbers, the murderers, the dacoits and others of that fry. They were entirely submissive and, therefore, praiseworthy men. But political prisoners! They are the worst prisoners in the world and they must be treated in this prison in a way that will break their spirit and completely demoralise them. This high policy the official from Calcutta had impressed thoroughly on the mind of the rude, matter-of-fact, soldierly officers.

The Oil-Mill

And everything changed since that time in this prison. A new era had begun. The political prisoners were split up, and put in different chawls, and one in each cell of that chawl. If their talk with another excited the slightest suspicion, handcuffs were put on them, and they were subjected to all kinds of punishment. On the tank for a bath or in a row for their meal, if they merely signed to one another to inquire after health, the sentence for that infringement was to keep a man standing with handcuffs on, for seven days. And to crown it all, the sentence of picking oakum was substituted by work round the grinding oil mill. Yes, they had determined to break our spirit and to demoralise us. So, they gave us that hard work to do for two months continuously, then one month on picking oakum, again the grinding work on the mill. We were to be yoked like animals to the handle that turned the wheel. Hardly out of bed, we were ordered to wear a strip of cloth, were shut up in our cells and made to turn the wheel of the oil-mill. Coconut pieces were put in, the empty and hollow space to be crushed by the wheel passing over them, and its turning became heavier as the space was fuller. Twenty turns of the wheel were enough to drain away the strength of the strongest cooly and the worst, brawny *badmash*. No dacoit who was not past twenty was put on that work. But the poor political prisoner was fit to do it at any age. And the doctor in charge ever certified that he could do it! It was the medical science of the Andamans that had upheld the doctor! So, the poor creature had to go half the round of the wheel by pushing the handle with his hands, and the other half was completed by hanging on to it with all his might. So much physical strength had to be expended on crushing the coconut pieces for oil. Youths of twenty or more, who in their lives had not done any physical labour, were put upon that labour. They were all educated young men of delicate constitution. From six to ten in the morning, they were yoked to the wheel which they turned round and round till their breath had become heavy. Some of them had fainted many times during the process. They had to sit down for sheer exhaustion and helplessness. Ordinarily, all work had to be stopped between ten and twelve. But this 'Kolu', as the oil-mill labour was called, had to continue throughout. The door was opened only when meal was announced. The man came in and served the meal in the pan and went away and the door was shut. If after washing his hands one were to wipe away the perspiration on his body, the *jamadar*—the worst of gangsters in the whole lot—would go at him with loud abuse. There was no water for washing hands. Drinking water was to be had only by propitiating the *jamadar*. While you were at Kolu, you felt very thirsty. The waterman gave no water except for a consideration which was to palm off to him some tobacco in exchange. If one spoke to the *jamadar* his retort was, "A prisoner is given only two cups of water and you have already consumed three. Whence can I bring you more water? From your father?" We have put down the retort of the *jamadar* in the decent language possible. If water could not be had for wash and drink, what can be said of water for bathing?

Must Finish Your Quota

What of bath? Even of our usual meal it was the same story. The dinner being served, the door of the prison-cell was locked, and the *jamadar* was upon us to see, not if we had dined well, but if we had not already begun our round of the grinding oil-mill! He paraded through the chawl, halting before each room and announcing to its inmates in bad and threatening words that, come what may, the usual quota had to be completed by evening. He added that otherwise the prisoner would get a sound thrashing from him and some additional punishment from his superior. When we heard this shouting, while we were just at our meal, the morsel in our hand would not go down, and we had to stop eating all at once. For everyone of us had seen how a man who had failed to do his quota had a belabouring of kicks and fisticuffs from the august *jamadar*, in addition to his bludgeoning him with the stick. The anticipation of this terror took away all appetite, though we were, all of us, indeed, very hungry. We got up, and began our work of pushing the handle and going round the mill like a yoked buffalo, with perspiration dripping down from our face, and its beads falling into the dish we were carrying in the other hand. I have seen prisoners working in this pitiable condition, swallowing, anyhow, the food in their plate, and running round the mill at the same time. The claims of hunger could not be put off while the demand of labour was equally excruciating. The work of the 'Kolu' had to be carried on in this condition till five o'clock in the evening with the hurried meal preceding it, the mode, whereof I have already described. Out of a hundred, only one with a callous body could hardly complete his daily quota of thirty pounds of coconut oil. The rest took two days, at the least, to crush so much oil out of dried coconut pulp. The novitiates, the simpletons, the inexperienced, and the honest were the greatest sufferers in the process. They always got the severest beating from the *jamadar*, when they poured out before him the quantity of oil they had crushed from the substance; and they went back to their cells with tears in their eyes and groaning with pain. I see their weeping faces vividly even to this day!

The 'Kolu' Work at Night

In spite of this, if any day, none of them could finish the quota allotted to them for the day, Mr. Barrie would come upon the scene when they were all sitting down for their expected evening meal and announce to the assembly that there would be no grab for them, as they had not done the work; and none would get anything to eat till he had finished his quota. Imagine a prisoner rising with the day; beginning his work at six; toiling at it till eleven; and continuing it without rest till 5 o'clock in the evening; with the morning meal half-finished and hurriedly gulped down or hardly eaten at all; and you will realise the cruelty and injustice of this punishment, if you can at all picture it to yourself. For it beggared description. Some forty or fifty persons could not go through their work with all their will to finish it. But Mr. Barrie would not realise the hardship and the harshness of the imposition. He would bring his chair in the chawl, sit upon it, and would see the slackers, as he imagined these fifty helpless creatures to be, going on with their work far into the night. The rest of the prison was, of course, closed for work at night, and no one dared report against Mr. Barrie that this part of the chawl was being treated at night to this grinding piece of work. If anyone dared he was sure to be falsely charged for some offence and put to trouble. Everywhere was the stillness of night; but here the mill creaked on till 8 or 9 P.M. In the meanwhile, Mr. Barrie dozed in his chair; woke up at intervals, his mouth full of abuse, and cursing the labourers that they had not yet finished their day's work. "Woe be to them," he would exclaim, "punish them now; do not reserve it for the morrow; cane them, *jamadar,* within an inch of their lives; the scoundrels are idlers, they are slackers, no mercy on them." And presently, he would doze again and snore.

Pretext of Ailment

None was spared, among political prisoners, from the rack of that inhuman toil. Most of them were unaccustomed to any kind of physical labour; the best part of them were college youths; some had not turned sixteen or seventeen; they were tender in age and body. But they were forced, for months on end, to do this grinding work—Kolu. Their tortures knew no bounds. Among them many had fallen ill, and preferred death to this work. As they became worse, they were declared to be feigning illness. If their bodies burned with high fever, they were shut in their own cells and were never taken for treatment to the prisoner hospital, for they were all "honourable men"—political prisoners! The thief, the dacoit, the cut-throat had his bed in the prison hospital, but not the poor political prisoner! That was the ethics of prison-life at Port Blair! Fever, motion, vomitting were obvious diseases. But not so, head-ache, heart-ache, stomach-ache and heavy breathing! If political prisoners showed such symptoms, then the diagnosis was invariably that they were feigning! And the reason given was—they were shirkers. The most hardened of convicts in this prison knew drugs that would make them vomit, pass motions, and even to burn with high fever. And they would use them cleverly when they desired a transfer from the prison-bed to the hospital-cot; no doubt about their feigning in order to avoid work. But if the prisoners preferred 103 to 104 degrees of high temperature to their work on the oil mill, then the fault was not of the prisoner but of the inhuman torture that was such work. And to such racking toil was a political prisoner yoked as soon as he had crossed into the prison! And worse still, if he really fell ill due to the effect of his work, he was sent mercilessly back to it with the reason that he was only feigning it. To such kind of soul-racking labour was my elder brother yoked. And he was the first to be yoked to it, because he belonged to the first batch of political prisoners transported to the Andamans.

An Experiment to Tame Him

My brother was suffering from hemicrany as a chronic complaint even while he was free. The hardships of prison-life, physical and mental, with the added work of the grinding mill, had not subdued him, but had made him fierce and fearless. Not a word had escaped his lips about his fellow-prisoners, no piece of information could thus be wrung out of him, and he never prayed for any leniency from the authorities. That was why Mr. Barrie was persistent in his efforts to 'convert' him, though he had no scruples to treat all political prisoners as if they were animals in his menagerie. In this plight and as a result of Mr. Barrie's coaxings, one day the hemicrany came down upon him with a vengeance. As the day went up with my brother's work round the grinding mill, his headache also pursued him with an increasing pain. He could not bear the heat of the sun, and yet the sweating workhad to be carried on, for the *jamadar* was ever behind him shouting: "Crush, crush, grind on at the oil mill, don't relax, for I know nothing but to get the work done. Go on." Overborne by this, my brother petitioned to the Superintendent on his rounds that he was suffering from a severe attack of hemicrany. The Superintendent said that it was not his business to attend to him, and the doctor should be sent for. The doctor was an Indian and would say, when he did not find the patient suffering from fever, that there was nothing wrong with him. He directed that the patient should be referred to the jailor. The thermometer, of course, did not register fever. And there was no other test there to detect hemicrany. Hence, it must be feigning, especially so with a political prisoner like Ganesh Savarkar.

I Alone can Say who is Ill

The doctor realised the untruth of his statement. But he was more afraid of Mr. Barrie than of lying. For he knew that the former would constantly goad him in these words: "Doctor, you know but too well that you are a Hindu and these political prisoners are Hindus. There is no knowing when they will let you down. If anyone sees you talking to them without my permission, he may report you to the authorities. So, please, be careful. If you care for your job you must not say anything about them, do anything for them; you hold a degree but I have more experience than you. I know who feign illness and who do not; so that, be guided by me in these matters. When I say a man is well, he is well; when I say a man is ill, he is ill. Understand me, will you?" He said this as if lightly, and, smiling to himself, he went forward. Once, an hospital assistant realised the pitiable case of my brother and could not contain himself. My brother had severe pain in the head, and the doctor saw him dashing it against the prison wall, and yet carry on his grinding work unintermittedly. The doctor came up to him and told him that he was removing him to the hospital as an observation case. He asked him to take up his bed and proceed. My brother was making ready to depart, when, on a sudden, Mr. Barrie confronted him, dashing his stick upon the floor. He accosted the *jamadar* gruffy, "Where is this bomb-thrower going?" The *jamadar* shivered all over, and said, "It is under the doctor's orders, Sir, that I am taking him to the hospital for observation." "Why the hell, did you not ask me? Who is the wretched doctor to give the law here?" Mr. Barrie's voice went like an echo and a thunder throughout the whole building. "Take him back to work," he ordered, "I shall take care of the doctor. I must rate you as well; you, to take him out without my orders?" And he saw the patient back into his cell and at work again. He had the door locked before he went away. The doctor, strictly speaking, was not under the gaoler but under the Superintendent of that jail. But the Hindu jailor and his Hindu myrmidons took great care that no news about the political prisoners reached the ears of the Superintendent. As a sequel, the doctor had to eat his words; he apologized to the jailor, and solemnly resolved never more to interfere with the political prisoners, and did not take a single patient from them to the hospital without the permission of the Superintendent. For all others, the hospital remained an open door. Prisoners with ten years' sentence against them, those who had broken open the prison itself, had free access to it under any pretext of illness. Permission was never denied to them. It was for the doctor to decide if he would keep the patient or discharge him. Of course, the jailor had no voice in that decision. But, for political prisoners, the hospital ever remained a closed door. With hemicrany and the hard labour of the grinding mill, my brother felt dead-tired by the time he had finished it, and delivered his quantum of oil to the blessed *jamadar*. Sweated and exhausted, he tottered to his cell and threw himself at full length on the wooden plank of his bed in that prison, where he groaned the whole night for the pain all over his body. The day dawned again; hemicrany, the *jamadar*, the insult to the Indian doctor and the tortures of the oil-mill, stood like grim spectres before him. Weeks, months he had spent in this dire condition, and they were to be his inevitable lot, all his life.

Enough of this Life

Who can describe the suffering—these agonies of mind and body? I may give you an instance, however, to point the moral. Of all the hardships of prison-life in the Silver Jail of the Andamans—gruelling work, scanty food and clothing, occasional thrashing and others-none was so annoying and disgusting as its provision for urinals and lavatories. The prisoners had to control the demands of nature, of hours together, for want of these arrangements in the cell itself. Morning, noon and evening—these were the only hours when prisoners were let off for this purpose and at stated time only. It was an outrage to ask the *jamadar* for this convenience at any other moment than the stipulated hour. The prisoners were locked in their cells at six or seven o'clock in the evening and the lock was opened only after six the next morning. A sort of clay-pot was given them to use it for that purpose during the night. As I have already told you, the prison is called Cellular Jail, because the prisoners in that jail were confined each in a separate, solitary cell. During twelve hours of the night, the warders insisted that the prisoner shall have no occasion to ease himself. The pot was so diminutive in size that one could not discharge into it even once during the night. As for nature's call, one had to go down on his knees to the *jamadar* to let him out. The warder may or may not take the call seriously. He may be reluctant himself or he may fear the Officer. The prisoner had, therefore, to check it till the morning. If the warder relaxed and carried the matter to the *jamadar*, the *jamadar* would severely rate the convict for the call at such an odd hour. He would severely reprimand the warden also for having heard the prisoner. He would or would not report to the doctor as his fancy or memory may guide him! The doctor's report on the ailment was never made, or made only in one case out of a hundred. That report had to go to Mr. Barrie and Mr. Barrie would take action upon it at his own sweet will. Imagine the prisoner's condition during the night and during this process of red-tape, particularly when the call was not normal but an abnormal and sudden ailment! In the morning, Mr. Barrie would sit in judgement upon it, rebuke sternly the warder and the *jamadar* for their lapse of duty. When he brayed in this fashion there was no answering him. The prisoner was also cross-examined by Mr. Barrie. And if the former said that he could not help the call of nature, Mr. Barrie turned round upon him fiercely with the ejaculation, "Why the devil did you have it?" And if the wretched creature had the courage to say, "I got it because I got it," the *jamadar* would give a slap in the face and scold him for giving such an insolent answer. Usually, the prisoner was let off only with this cannonade of words. But Mr. Barrie's particular kindness to the prisoner always ended in an order to put him immediately on the grinding mill!

A Pinch of Tobacco

In this unbearable state of mind, some prisoners found it impossible to control the call of nature and answered it on the floor of their cells. The cell was eight by ten feet, and the prisoner had to sleep with his head near the nuisance he had committed. As soon as the lock was opened for the day, he had to persuade the sweeper to clean the room of the filth. He promised him the much desired tobacco in return. It was well if the scavenger agreed to do so. Otherwise, he would cry out for the *jamadar* and break the fact to him. The *jamadar* kicked the prisoner and rained fisticuffs on him if he was meek enough to bear them. If he resisted, the *jamadar* instantly took him to Mr. Barrie and lodged a complaint against him. The complaint was that the prisoner had dirtied the room. Mr. Barrie passed orders that the prisoner was to clean the room himself or was to be put in the stocks for three to four days. Standing in the stocks meant continuous stoppage of urine and secretion, compulsorily so for four or five hours on end. The sentence was executed between six and ten in the morning, and from twelve to five in the afternoon, during which the prisoner had to stand with chains on hand which were fastened to the top above him. During this period, he was not to be let off for either of the two functions.

This hardship all had to bear equally but the stringency of it was felt more by the political prisoners than by others. For, whether they worked or not during the day, they were in solitary confinement all along. So during the day, as also at night, to answer the call of nature was prevented in their case as it could not be prevented in the case of other prisoners. Betimes, they had to relieve themselves either on the floor or on the side-wall of their cells. The other prisoners felt neither compunction nor shame about it. They would let themselves off in the face of the passer-by and roar into laughter for doing it. But the political prisoners could not be so brazen-faced. It was a trial to them, when, in spite of themselves, they could not help answering it either in the room or on the wall or right in the public eye. The jail regulations condemned as a crime what was simply a function of the human body without making decent provision to discharge it decently. The jail punished the act, as it had banned from its precincts its other needs like wholesome food and decent clothing. It considered all the three useless luxuries.

Ethics of the Andamans

My elder brother had to suffer terribly for the perpetration of the crime. And he was given the alternative to pick oakum by way of relief. And he contracted dysentery. He had griping pain in the stomach as one of its symptoms. The pain and the sensation were acute after each meal. But once the door was locked in the morning, it was opened only for the evening meal. Other patients were removed to the hospital for the treatment of the disease. And they could ease themselves comfortably—if comfort that be called—in that place. But a political prisoner was an exception to the rule, till he was entirely bed-ridden by the ailment. When in his cell, the pot that was furnished him was also equally ailing! The doctor, unless the ailment was acute, could not certify removal. So, he had the hell of his life in that sickness. My brother informed the warder and the *jamadar* of his acute ailment. But it took two days to reach the ears of the doctor in charge. The sickness had aggravated into diarrhoea. The badly boiled rice made the complaint still more acute and persistent. Added to it the work of picking oakum and close confinement. So, he had to discharge it all over the room. And when the evening revealed it, he had to bear all the abuse about it. The matter was exposed all over the prison, additional punishment followed with disgrace to crown it all. To avoid it all, my bother covered the nuisance under a heap of rubbish in that room and when he was released in the evening for removing the rubbish, he removed the nuisance along with it and swept the room clean. Whenever he was put in the stocks and hands were manacled, he had to go for days together without the function. But, diarrhoea and dysentery could not be put off. So, he had to do the double function standing in the stocks and was punished for it. This was not an occasional trial with him as with many other political prisoners. It had become his ordeal for years. He had to stay and sleep in that dirtied room and in that wretched condition of his body all along, and throughout the many years of his stay in the Cellular Jail.

The cattle yoked to the cart or the plough are treated better in this respect than the human material in this prison-house of ours. It is considered a cruelty to obstruct them as they obstruct us here at night and during the period of close confinement. A political prisoner in this jail was worse off than the cattle under the yoke. He did not enjoy the freedom of movement that the dumb-driven animals enjoyed under the whip of their drivers. The ethics of prison-life in the Andamans condemned asking for such freedom between twelve and six during the day and in the night that followed it. We petitioned to the Commissioner of Prisons against it. But Mr. Barrie interfered, and deposed that the complaint was fake. He brought in as his witness the *jamadar* of the place and piteously moaned, "Look here, Sir, ask him if I treat them so badly. It is all a fabrication against me; it is their trump-up to damn me; they lodge this complaint to disgrace me." The Commissioner and the other Officers with him exonerated Mr. Barrie and warned the complainants not to make such allegations against an honest servant of the Crown. Why should political prisoners, of all others, file such a petition? Why should the rest not make any grievance of it? The fact of it was that these did not suffer that way; they did not suffer as much; and, last, they bore it meekly for fear that Mr. Barrie might belabour them with kicks and caning, and detail them for the horrible grind of the oil-mill—the eternal rack of the 'Kolu'! So, they dared not utter a word against Mr. Barrie.

The right of Nature

We had to take up the matter, at long last, with the Government of India that this political right be secured to us against all injunctions. We got the primitive right of answering the calls of nature established in our favour by carrying an agitation till the grievance had reached the Home Member of that Government. How we achieved it will be narrated during the course of the story. When the Home Secretary happened to visit the place and went about inspecting the prison-cells, some of us took the complaint before him. As usual, Mr. Barrie protested, when one Mr. Nanda Gopal—a Punjabi and fellow-prisoner—challenged him on the spot and offered to take the Home Member round the cells that he may see them for himself and be convinced. He added, "You have only to step in, Sir, and smell the corners of our rooms and be assured if the arrangement in our prison for urinals and lavatories does suffice or help us in our lock up in these cells. Your nose will be our best witness." Although this outrageous language got for him the rebuke of silence from the authorities, and although the political renegades among us sought to flatter Mr. Barrie by denouncing his language and challenging it as unbecoming and insolent in the extreme, the Home Member caught the force of it and severely remonstrated with Mr. Barrie for his prison-management. Thenceforward, this disgusting practice had almost ended. At least, it ceased to be harassing as before, and no more so rigorously enforced. It reminded me constantly of the text of the Yoga-Sutra—the disgust for the body going along with attraction for the same in another. Nanda, Gopal himself had an experience similar to my brother's. Hence, Mr. Barrie had condemned his outburst as an act of malice against himself.

The First Strike

The series of endless hardships described above ended in a manner that came as a surprise to the jail authorities. The political prisoners reacted to it each in his own ways. The general trend among them was to obey and do the allotted work as far as it lay in them to put up with it. But when the discipline and its rigid enforcement had become too harsh, well-nigh impossible to endure, then the question that faced one and all was "to live or not to live".

It was no longer an academic discussion, no mere philosophising, but a stern reality. And it effected two extremes in a different way. The one extreme was but to practise abject flattery and be relieved of it. Among these were those who had lost heart and the control of their minds. Safety first, safety at all costs had become an obsession with them. At the other end were those who, suppressed and downcast as they were by all the rigours of their prison-life, were now out to fight it out to the finish, and never submit at the cost of self-respect and honour. Fight, fight to the last ditch. That had become a slogan with them. There were those in the centre whom their inner voice had told not to seek death but live, so long as you can live without being false to your principles, and work up politically to remove the grievance. At the same time, if life with self-respect became an impossibility, they would, of course, prefer death to it and without a moment's hesitation.

I have already described to you the type that chose for safety at any cost. The other which went on for fight, and those who counselled discrimination, resolved to join hands and go on passive resistance against the unendurable rigours and humiliations of our prison existence. As a first step, they were to refuse work that involved hard labour. And it materialised in the political prisoners' non-co-operation with the "Kolu"—the grinding mill that had ground down their lives. This was the first strike in the history of the Silver Jail. It was a strike on a small scale, but the very act was regarded as an impossibility under the stern regime of Mr. Barrie, and its beginning created a stir and excitement in the prison-world, the like of which it had not witnessed before. Mr. Barrie regarded it as a great personal insult, and was infuriated by it. Poor Mr. Barrie! This was but the beginning of the end. And the insult was nothing compared with what he had to face in the sequel.

The Demi-God of Port Blair

To all other prisoners and occasionally to us also Mr. Barrie would sometime harangue as follows: "Listen, ye prisoners. In the Universe there is one God, and He lives in the Heavens above. But in Port Blair there are two: one, the God of Heaven, and another, the God of Earth. Indeed, the God of Earth in Port Blair—that is myself. The God of Heaven will reward you when you go above. But this God of Port Blair will reward you here and now. So, ye prisoners, behave well. You may complain to any superior against me, my word shall prevail; I hold my own. Mind ye well." One day to make a display of his power before us and to show us how they all trembled in his presence, as also to dazzle us by the display, Mr. Barrie arranged all prisoners before him in a row of two each, and while the petty officers and *jamadar*s were standing in front of it, he suddenly rushed into the seated line and asked a petty officer if it was day or night. The petty officer, new to his task, replied that it was day. Seeming to fly into a rage, Mr. Barrie affirmed that it was night. The petty officer said it was day, and Mr. Barrie persisted it was night. Not content with the duck, Mr. Barrie suddenly turned to his trusted servant and questioned, "Well, *jamadar*, is it day or night now? I am sure it is complete dark and night." The *jamadar* replied, "Yes, Sir, it is night." Mr. Barrie remarked significantly, "You speak aright, but you will realise that you don't tutor your petty officer aright. Well, take care, let not this happen again." And, indeed, the trusted servant of "Barrie Baba" never failed to improve upon the lesson.

A Slight to God

The man, who ruled the prison with an iron hand, who made the prisoners tremble in their shoes, could not bear the slight to his authority by political prisoners like us. It is no surprise that he was terribly annoyed by it. Up to that time, even the *jamadar* dared pour fowl abuse upon us, and Mr. Barrie had instigated him to do so. And the *jamadar* and his lieutenant slapped anyone of us in the face if he was found talking or had not finished his day's work. And if he happened to report the incident to the jailor, the latter would laugh outright in his face. The same political prisoners had now turned against the Pathan warder to the extent of returning word for word, abuse for abuse, and slap for slap. Two of our political prisoners, who had stopped all work, did not spare Mr. Barrie himself from such humiliation. They began to show him up as he had never been shown up before.

Mr. Barrie Exposed

I give here one example of how they made fun of him. Mr. .... had been sentenced to ten years' imprisonment in this jail. He came from a respectable family in Punjab, and was himself a man of education and culture. For the first time that he was put on the grinding mill, the gentleman entered his cell, did the work in a leisurely fashion till ten o'clock, and came down for dinner pot upon the hour. The prisoners put on the grinding mill were not allowed to bathe or dine before they had finished their allotted task. But this man did not mind it. He straightaway went for his bath, had his full time of it, and quietly sat down for his meal. By this time, the other prisoners had already been driven back to their work by their warders, with abuses and fisticuffs amply bestowed upon them. The man in question had his shower of abuse like others, but, as if it was not meant for him, he went on unperturbed until he had his full. The warder and the petty officer goaded him on to hasten and go back to work. But they could not move him from his seat. They sent for the Havildar. He tried his best to bring the man round. But the latter quietly said to him, "Look here, Havildar, I must have a full bite for each morsel that I take in, or else I may not digest it. To gulp down one's food was a sure way to spoil the stomach and I won't do it." Discomfitted, the Havildar took the complaint to Mr. Barrie. All others used to be frightened out of their wits to hear that Mr. Barrie was coming. Mr. Barrie came and this gentleman kept on eating as if nothing had happened. Mr. Barrie shouted at him and expostulated, "All the prisoners have gone back to their work, and you are still at your meals. Do you take yourself to be a gentleman-at-large? Who will finish your work? I will break your bones, remember it too well." Biting slowly and, deliberately the food in his mouth, he said to Mr. Barrie, with a calm and smiling face, "Sir, I am not idling away my time. Medical science insists that a man must give, at least, ten bites to every morsel that he chews. Our digestion, you know well, begins with this process in the mouth, and one dare not hurry over it." Full of fury, Mr. Barrie abused him for that information, and declared with a loud voice that he would proceed against him the following morning for such breach of discipline. Softly our prisoner answered, "Look here, Sir, from ten to twelve is our time for rest, during which you have often forced us back to work. If anyone is unlawful in this affair is it not you? I have broken no law." Mr. Barrie was taken aback, for he did break the law, as the prisoner had brought it home to him. Mr. Barrie told him to go on with his food as long as he liked, but when he had finished it, he must return to work forthwith, and that if he did not finish in time his allotted work, he would not spare him, for anything in the world, but flay him alive with the strikes of his cane. He said this and walked away, sad at heart and stamping his feet for the insult he had received before all the prisoners in that part of the building. How much he would have liked to thrash and make an example of him before the whole world! But he knew full well that, in spite of kicks and fisticuffs, the political prisoners had gone beyond his power to control them and was, therefore, uneasy at heart that they were on the verge of a general strike.

Another Principle

The gentleman had, at length, finished his dinner. And the petty officer, the *jamadar* and the Havildar felt relieved in mind. They brought him to his cell and locked him in for his usual round of work. They beseeched him to proceed with the work as he had finished his food as he had desired. For, if the prisoner failed in his task, it was the *jamadar* that incurred severe censure from Mr. Barrie. Having tried thus to win him by flattery, they left the place for their usual rounds. When they returned after a time, with the full expectation that the prisoner was hard at work, to their utter dismay, they found him at full length in his bed, fast asleep and snoring and with a Konkat covering his body and face. The *jamadar* was full of exasperation and shouted, "O, the devil that you are, what is wrong with you that you pester me so? It is already twelve now, you had your meal, why don't you begin work, I wonder." Our prisoner opened his eyes, signed them not to make such an uproar. He then said, "*jamadar*, if I were to turn the oil-mill immediately after my meal, I shall not digest my food. To take a little nap after meals was a good rule of health; my grand-father always used to tell me so." The prisoners all round burst into a roar of laughter. The *jamadar* lost his temper, but had no courage to go and beat the prisoner. Instead, he gave hard slaps in the face of some of the jeerers. In the evening, the gentleman delivered to the *jamadar* fifteen pounds of coconut oil he had pressed from the oil-mill. That was, according to the prison-calculation, half-a-day's work. Others could not have given even that much quantity of oil, but he was a strong and sturdy fellow, so he could do it. We have already spoken of his courage. He was punished for his slackness, he was kept on reduced ration, and, at last, the Superintendent had to promise that they would take him off the oil-mill if only he gave them his complete quota for three days in continuation. The prisoner, it must be admitted to his credit, completed his three days' work, taking leave, for the time, of his strict medical observance. Mr. Barrie, puffed up by this success, broke the promise and sent him back to the oil-mill. The prisoner flatly refused to go back. He said that he was not an ox to be tied so to the grinding wheel. "We are all men," he added, "and must be treated as such." Thus began the prisoners' first strike in the Andamans.

The political prisoners on strike were subjected to all kinds of punishments in succession. Hand-cuffs, shackles, solitary confinement and other regular forms of punishment were inflicted upon them to last for a week. But the prison authorities gave them punishments severer than these in order to put down the strike. They were, in some cases, against the sanction of the prison-regulations. Thus, the prisoner, whose story we have already related, was made to subsist on 'Conji' for ten days continuously, when other punishments had proved in his case of no avail to subdue him. No prisoner could be put on 'Conji' for ten days in succession. It was a clear violation of the prison-rules. Sometimes three days on Conji was a limit. And it was inflicted to tame down the prisoner by weakening his power of resistance. But the prison-calendar did not include this form of punishment. Later on, when a high official from the Government of India visited the place, we drew his attention to this fact and Mr. Barrie flatly denied that he ever had recourse to it. The prisoners subjected to this ordeal have declared to me on oath that they were not only kept on Conji but, at the same time, they were treated to large doses of quinine, so that they felt dizzy; their stomachs turned, and they had suffered in body and mind beyond any power of human endurance. But it availed not in the least to overcome their passive resistance. Their unity and their courage and its unfavourable effect on the mind of fellow-prisoners at last compelled the authorities to surrender to their demand, which was never to put political prisoners for work on the oil-mill. The authorities had to assure them on the point, in order that the strike may be called off. They pledged their word that "Kolu" shall be administered only in rare instances and the political prisoners shall be detailed for lighter work outside the prison-walls. From what they had heard of this kind of work they had inferred that it would mean more freedom for them. And once the right was conceded, it was sure to pave the way for further concession, namely, after five years' term of imprisonment in the jail they would be entirely free to work on their own within the bounds of those islands, and in ten years' time, they shall have the privilege of setting up an independent home there with the necessary 'ticket' of the prison authorities themselves. These considerations led the political prisoners to conclude that the relaxation as regards work on the oil-mill was the thin end of the wedge and, therefore, it would not be unwise or cowardly on their part to call off the strike although it was not to be done all at once. Some of these prisoners had already filled their one year's term of imprisonment, and they would be set free immediately to go on work outside the prison. These began to go back to work one by one and, thus, the strike had gradually come to an end. Within a few days, the first batch of political prisoners was sent out to do all kinds of sundry work. Some of them had to dig in the mud, others to load their buckets with the mud so dug out, others were detailed to sweep the streets, and others, again, to carry loadfuls of coconut fruit-so on and so forth.

Yoked to the Carriage

In the Andamans, it is the fashion for the Government officers to drive in carriages to which, instead of harnessing bullocks or horses, they harness convicts from the Silver Jail. It was a common sight in the streets of this island to meet such carriages. The prisoners ran them over steep climbs nearly breathless with that exertion and received epithets from their inmates, like "Go on, you scoundrels, run on quickly." A few of them, I knew, had refused to drive in carriages driven by these human animals. But there was none among the prisoners themselves to offer resistance. This fact was, later on, brought home to them by Mr. Barrie's indiscretion. He had no penetration of intellect to perceive the folly of his action. But the outrage became too patent when, in order to impress upon the Superintendent the recalcitrance of political prisoners, he had arranged with the *jamadars* to make the daring experiment of yoking the stoutest and the most daring among them to such carriages. The experiment was made on a batch recently set free to work outside. But the experiment failed and failed miserably. When the *jamadar* concerned proceeded to carry out the orders of his master, those selected for that humiliating operation refused to move. They refused to be harnessed to the carriage like dumb-driven animals. "We are not oxen or horses that we should be made to pull the carriage," that was the firm reply they gave. Mr. Barrie felt that he had got what he wanted. He, at once, called the attention of the Superintendent to this act of disobedience and remarked, "Now, you can judge for yourself how vile and hopeless they are; they wanted to be free and we have given them freedom; and yet they would not do what we bid them to do! They will not pull the carriage; what other work can I give to them that they deem unobjectionable? And if I detail them for lighter work or work that they consider decent, others may blame me for being partial to them. So, I am in a fix here."

The God-fearing Mr. Barrie

But had not the same god-fearing Mr. Barrie swallowed all his scruples, when he had given the lightest of work to those who least deserved it? He had appointed in his office or at his residence men to do work who did not know how to spell their rudiments. He had selected for desk-work some of the worst characters in that jail. And he had bestowed such favour upon those of the political prisoners who had served him as spies, or who had won light jobs by sheer flattery and similar demeaning behaviour. Where had his conscience gone when he had shown these preferences and exclusions? The definition of favouritism in Mr. Barrie's vocabulary of words was evidently an action that had inevitably led to the fall of his favourites! When I reached that prison, the condition of political prisoners was as I have described above.

This I came to learn within a month's time of my being in that prison. Some of these prisoners were definitely against the policy of strike as a matter of conviction. Others had decided to give implicit obedience. These Mr. Barrie had used to sow dissensions between the strikers, and to bring home to them that strike was a great blunder. Between stern resisters, who would use abuse for abuse, insolence against insolence, he sought, through these renegades, to create aversion for such tactics, as being quite unbecoming to them as well-bred young men. Naturally, they desired to seek my opinion on all these matters. Not they alone but Mr. Barrie himself was anxious to know what I thought of it. He had striven his hardest to pump me out upon the whole question. After a fortnight of close and secluded life in my cell, he brought me down on the chawl nearby, and on its ground-floor to work there during the day.

Picking Oakum

There I was to pick one pound of oakum on the first day. Usually, the piece of work to do for an ordinary prisoner is no less than one-and-a-half or two pounds of oakum. Mr. Barrie declared that it was a favour done to me as a special case and in consideration of my superior status. So, he harangued briefly to his listeners. The work may be less and inspired by added kindness, as Mr. Barrie sought to put it; but this kindness did not make the oakum less hard for my hands to ply with, and there was no kindness in it to soften the labour for me. My muscles were swollen by it and the pain it gave me was unbearable. My palms blistered and blood flowed from its cracks. I showed them to the Superintendent and asked him if he could not change it. I exhorted him to give me a respite from it for a few days at least. To it the inevitable answer was, "That is the experience of all of them here. Take it as a favour that we gave you one pound to do, and not like others, one-and-half or two pounds a day." And the Superintendent went away. I had to do the picking all the same. And the material I had picked was stained with the drops of my blood. Mr. Barrie was careful to note if it was one pound. He did not care to note the drops that had stained it. He had no time for such attention.

Rascals! I will Cane You

And yet not a day passed when he had not exchanged a few words with me. Gradually, he introduced, in his ten minutes' daily talk with me, reference to the attitude of political prisoners under him. Others were strictly banned from carrying information from one of them to the other or even to convey greetings from one to other. And if anyone was caught in the act, the punishment visited upon him was reduction from his post as a warden or a week's hard labour on the oil-mill. But the same information Mr. Barrie was free to carry from one member to another; only it was to be an information to sow dissension and to create division among them. Mr. Barrie knew well that I had all the past information about these prisoners and it had come to me in spite of his strict watch to the contrary. Why not then put forth one's own point of view? So, had Mr. Barrie thought to himself and would open his talk with me upon that subject. He would bestow full praise upon those who had turned informants; he severely censured those who had gone on strike, who had resisted his authority, who would not tolerate his abuse, and who burnt no incense at his shrine. And he indulged in panegyric or censure to convince the person he talked to, that he should never follow in the wake of the recalcitrants and the resisters but behave in a manner that became him as a man of high education and culture. In this lay his good finally and truly. This appeal to me I heard with perfect silence. I neither endorsed nor contradicted him so far as I could help it. But sometimes his conversation became intolerable, full as it was of jibes, abuse, scandal and misrepresentation of those who, I knew, did not deserve them. To say ditto to him was impossible for me. To be silent was equally unpardonable. Mr. Barrie ever sought to draw me out. "What do you say to that? How does it strike you?" That was his constant refrain. To quote only one instance out of many; he would describe the gentleman who had given him the utmost trouble and with whom, I have already told, began our strike in this prison, as an insane fellow and as a man of low birth. And he capped the observation by praising me to the skies. He would draw me out to know what I thought of the man and his action, if it was not an action of a mad man and an idiot.

Mr. Barrie's Plot

I could no more listen to him with patience, and I told him plainly that I knew some of the persons whom he had mentioned; yet, the account he had given to me about them did not make me think that they had done anything unbecoming to them, or which went to show that they were off their minds. If their sufferings had become intolerable and if the prison authorities had begun to punish them in defiance of their own regulations, what remedy had they against them, and what other method could they hit upon, except that of striking work, and of passive resistance? And it was true as much of ordinary prisoners as of political prisoners. Desperate diseases demanded desperate remedies. I added, "Whatever you may tell me about Mr. ......, he looks a gentleman. He is no rogue or a mere quill-driver." My plain answer exasperated Mr. Barrie. He grew red in the face and he brought his conversation abruptly to an end, but next day, he arranged another drama to influence me. The political prisoners that were sent out for work every morning returned to their cells at about eleven in the afternoon to have their morning meal. They had been asked that day to take their seats for dinner near me. They had not yet finished their bath, their clothes were all dirty with the mud they had worked in. It had covered their body and their clothing. In that wretched condition, they were standing right in front of me. Suddenly, Mr. Barrie came there and began scolding them. He looked at me, and then turning his back upon me said to the batch in a stern voice, "How is it that you have not thrown in as many buckets of mud as your *jamadar* had directed you to throw? Look here, I shall not tolerate this any longer. I will give you a sound thrashing." Then turning to the *jamadar* he continued, "Look here, *jamadar*, if these fellows do not complete their task by the afternoon, bring them up to me. I will cane them all right. I will cane them on the buttocks till they burst." As if to excuse himself for uttering such foul language within my hearing, he addressed me, "Mr. Savarkar, a man like you ought not to mix with such people. They are a despicable lot. You are well-bred and a gentleman. These wretches will go back to their homes after running their term of eight or ten years in this prison, and the world will forget them. That is not so with you. You have to pass here full fifty years of your precious life; and you are no mere political prisoner. You will lose much if you associate with them, go on strike with them, or sympathise with them. Even talking with them is fraught with danger to your future. Whatever you intend to do, do it on your own. You take care of yourself never forgetting your ticket. Do you understand me?"

You are no Political Prisoner

I did not answer his last question and went on dining which, not a little, abashed him. He left the place repeating, "This is to your interest. You are not a political prisoner; you are an ordinary convict with a sentence of fifty years to run." It was for the first time I learnt that I was not a political prisoner. I do not know how many times this was dinned into my ears by the gaoler, the Superintendent and other officers of the place.

Mr. Barrie had gone. He had arranged this show of scolding the political prisoners to give me an object-lesson of what was in store for me and thus to cower me down into submission to him. It filled me with compassion for the political prisoners to see them used by Mr. Barrie as an object-lesson for me. Its effect on me was, however, quite the contrary of what Mr. Barrie had counted upon. It did not damp my courage. It emboldened me to make a common cause with them, to bear all the insults that they had borne, so that they may feel less the language used by Mr. Barrie against them, the taunts he had given them as vagrants, wretches and the scum of society. He had made me realise deeply, as I had not done before, all the mental agony through which they had passed and I resolved to soften it by fully throwing in my lot with them. I began to talk to them openly, I asked them their names, and looking at their pale faces. I said to them, "Do not feel small, do not be dispirited by what Mr. Barrie said of you in my presence. What he says of you today, he will say of me the day after. Thereby, he does not insult you and me; he only insults and degrades himself. We are helpless today, the world holds us in disgrace today, but a day is sure to come when it will honour you, perhaps, raise statues to you in this very place where they revile you, and thousands will visit this place to offer their tributes to you as martyrs to the cause." My speech did not go home to their hearts as it should have done; for many of them did not fully understand the significance of what I had said to them. At least, they did not feel so deeply as I felt it myself, in addressing to them. I did not note on their faces any sign of animation, courage and heroism. On the other hand, I found them in dark despair. Only one of them seemed to be roused and put me the question: "Do you really feel all this?" I answered, "It may happen as I have described it to you. I think it ought to happen."

No sooner had I finished what I had to say to them, than the petty officer and the warden raised a howl near me saying, "Babu, what is coming over you? If Mr. Barrie were to know that you were talking to them, he is sure to make a public example of us. Come away, we respect you. But if you are to continue like this, then..." They pulled me from that place, and locked me back in my own cell.

□

10

I See My Elder Brother

Myself and my elder brother were in the same jail, and we had not seen each other yet. His heart received a shock to know that I was here. And the news of his sufferings had wrung my heart. But a day came to prove unto me that these happenings in the past were almost nothing in our experience of life. Joy is scarcely fraught with such pain as that day brought to us both.

I was naturally very anxious to meet my brother. I tackled the warden and the petty officer to use some means, by which I may have even a passing glimpse of him, and that we may so meet that none else could be present near about us. I had insisted on secrecy because Mr. Barrie, and others of whom I had enquired about him, had told me that they had peremptory orders from their superiors not to tell me if he was or was not in that prison. What of our meeting each other then? Once I heard that my brother had a bad headache and I enquired if that was true, and if true, why they had not removed him to the hospital, and if it was not unnatural, in that condition, to keep him confined in his lonely cell. The Superintendent asked me to mind my own business, and that I should not dabble in other people's affairs. He scolded the *jamadar* and questioned him as to how I could get any information at all of my brother being in that prison. He admonished him further for his negligence, for otherwise, I could not get that news and told him to find out the source there of. I was trying my utmost, therefore, to see him at any cost, for I knew that he and I were never to meet again in this life. When I proceeded to England in 1906, my brother was among the persons who had come to see me off. Since then, I had not seen him at all till I saw him here. At times, I felt that it was better that we should not meet each other for the meeting would be exceedingly painful to him. But not to meet would be an act of cowardice. It would show lack of strength on my part to see adversity in the face. The elephant of calamity had already trampled us down under foot; what then, of a slight rap with his proboscis? And, after all, to avoid it was to spare oneself the shedding of some hot tears! That would be wanting in fortitude. To weep, to shed tears in a meeting between brothers, was an act of piety, the reward of merit through many births. At last, a warden did it for me. He had manoeuvred for our meeting in the evening, when all of us used to come together for our daily roll-call. Even then all were not let off at the same time. A batch came up, as another was sent away, in serial order. Availing himself of that opportunity, the warden set off our batch while the batch to which my brother belonged was delivering its quota to the *jamadar* detailed for that work. I got hurriedly into my batch and came on the scene of action. And I saw my brother returning and our eyes had met. He had seen me bound for England, full of pride and great expectation. He saw me now in the abject condition of defeated hopes, with ashes of my failures rubbed all over my body. It was a meeting and a sight that astounded him. The only expression of grief that passed his lips was "Tatya! How are you here?"

It went like a poniard into my heart. My warden instantly pulled me back lest anyone should notice us, and the meeting may grow into words. He was afraid that it may lead to consternation in the crowd, and that would expose all of us to severe punishment by the jailor. We came, we saw, and we separated. That was all of my meeting with my brother. But his words to me I could never forget. Later on he sent me a note drenched in tears: "I had hoped that you were there to carry on our work to success, to win India's battle for freedom. I felt nothing, therefore, of the sentence of transportation passed on me. I treated it as a trifle. For, it was a sacrifice for my country in a cause which you were out to lead on to success. The thought braced me; it made my sufferings a happy portent for the future. But now?........You were in Paris then, how then did you come to be inveigled? Who is there after you to keep "Abhinava Bharat" alive and its activity going? How will it function? Your ability, your capacity, and your power have all gone for nothing; they are buried in the dungeon of this prison. And what of our young brother, Bal? I saw you face to face. And still my eyes would not believe what they had seen. I am confounded by the sight. Alas!

Alas! How came you to be here? It taxed all my patience to reply to that note. Every question that he had put to me had raised many questions, which were already preying upon my mind. To brush aside all the yearnings of my heart; to drown the sorrow of my personal failures and of hopes associated with my success, now no more; to console my brother and to pull up myself was a task too great for me at the moment. Yet my will came to my rescue. I swallowed the bitter cup of misfortune. I penned a letter to convince him that "the prize was in the process", and that failure and shame in such a cause were nothing in comparison with the God-given opportunity to fight in such a struggle.

It was a Singular Good Fortune!

Was it not to do what we have done? Why then mourn for the past? My power and intelligence would have been as nought, if I had feared and trembled in the hour of my trial, like Arjuna on the battlefield of Kurukshetra. I did not fail in my duty—in my Dharma as we may put it. I had betrayed none. I faced up; I burnt myself into ashes; I exhorted my allies to face danger as their duty had called upon them to do; and I passed through the fiery ordeal which I had insisted that others should pass through. That is fearlessness, that is patience and fortitude; and you have done it as much as I have. Ours is the victory and not defeat. For failure is no crime as low aim is. Failure is a matter of chance, of adverse fate which none can avert. A Napolean dies as exile at St. Helena on a foreign soil and on a bed of thorns. Does it take away aught from his past triumphs and victories, from his intrinsic greatness? His battle of Austerlitz will ever remain a shining monument to his genius as a warrior; a hero of hundred battles that he was. A Laxmibai of Jhansi falls at the second or third stroke of battle! An unknown soldier dies at the first shot. Is her or his valour the less praiseworthy for such a defeat and death? If I had lived free exposing others to the cannon shot, exposing them to win the battle, but not to see the victory, I would not be worth the name of a leader. I chose to be in their ranks and suffer the fate that they had suffered. That is the test of worth and will to power. And we have passed the test, and I feel proud of it more than of success and the golden opinions we would have won in consequence of that success. We are both in this prison, but we are going on all the same. We are doomed to rot and die here, we know. And those, for whom we had paid our hostages to fortune, may be cursing us, no doubt. But that is our life's ideal, as great as to thrive and rise on the tide of fortune, and to hear the applauses of the crowd, and the drums of victory beating in our ears. For, failures are but stepping stones to success. We have served our country by our failures; let others serve her by their successes. Yet we consider our failures as glorious as they may regard their successes. The tears of blood that we shed in this dungeon, and our forgotten lives on this earth, are as valuable assets of final victory as the trumpets and drums sounded in the hour of victory in the fields.

What of Our Cause?

"You ask me that question. And my answer to it is no other than the song I composed on the day the High Court was to deliver its judgment against me. Those thoughts and feelings shall inspire me when my transportation has thrust me into the jaws of death itself. The lines I wrote in that song run thus: The Indian battleline of three hundred million soldiers of liberty led by the charioteer Shri Krishna, and by the warrior Rama, heroes of Hind, and her invincible ideal, shall not fall back because we are not in it. It will hem in the enemy; it will beat and conquer; it will hold fast the flag of victory and freedom; and it will plant it firm-Hind's Oriflamme', on the snowy summits of the eternal Himalayas—the abode of our holy trinity—Brahma, Vishnu and Mahesh. Glory to them; glory to Hind; and victory to the battleline of a three hundred million soldiers of freedom, the soldiers of Hind. That is my faith and that is my solace."

Such was the letter I wrote to my brother and saw that it reached him safely. It heartened him, and it gave me new zest, new hope, and new courage to do the work I did.

□

11
I am Put on the Oil-Mill

For nearly a month after my entry into the Silver Jail, I did the work of picking oakum. Everyone was wondering how I was not put on the oil-mill. The optimist said, "Now, how can they put 'a barrister-babu' like me on the oil-mill?" I said to him, "They will put me on it with the same mouth that they pronounced the sentence of transportation for life on me!" At last, one day, the Superintendent came to me and said, "From tomorrow you shall have to work on the oil-mill. Oakum must have hardened your hands by now, and you can very well take up that work forthwith." At this, Mr. Barrie laughed and said in a banter, "Now you are promoted to a higher form." That evening, Mr. Barrie sent for me in his office. In his conversations with me, he had already learnt that I was in full sympathy with the strike that political prisoners in this gaol had organised; and that I had denounced those who reviled the strikers and their fearless stand as work of a fraternity of insolent, indecent and foolish folk. Their mouths had by now been shut by my attitude towards the strike and the strikers. The secret reports that were being conveyed to Mr. Barrie, from day to day, had almost convinced him that, before long, I was going to join their ranks and to be one of these indecent fools—nay, the very 'prince of fools'. Mr. Barrie had called me to know if I was going to passively resist the new task that had been assigned to me by him and his like. He was anxious to dissuade me from that course. After talking on other sundry matters, he, at last, came to the point, and said, "You will please realise that I am helpless here, and I must follow the orders of my superiors. They have written to say that you shall be put on the oil-mill, and I had no hand in that business. However, I have persuaded the Superintendent, realising your worth, to relax the order in your favour. You shall have to do the work only for a fortnight. I will not put you on it repeatedly as I have to do in other cases. I know you well, I know your worth, I would have you go on with it and not resist it. Go, do it, I will help you as far as I can. Only do not compel me to punish you." To which I answered, "I will do the best I can. I will work as far as I can help it. My life is already a heap of ashes, and I have no desire to bring more trouble on my head." Mr. Barrie pretended to be overcome, and said, "Look here, I am telling you all this in your best interest. You have fifty years to pass in this jail. It gives a shock to me to realise it. So, I pray that you will keep aloof from all further entanglements. Let others do what they like. You should have nothing to do with them." His constant allusion to my sentence had ceased to shock me or to unnerve me. The more he repeated it, the more callous I became towards it. It was like the artillery man, whom the constant sound of the whizzing cannon-ball had ceased to frighten and unnerve. The next morning I was yoked to the oil-mill.

I had my solitary cell in Barrack No. 7. The oil-mill work had to be done in a cell of Barrack No. 6, close by. So, they removed me there early in the morning. In a sense, I was delighted with the change of quarters. For, there I saw some of the political prisoners and they could occasionally exchange a few words with me. I entered the cell and found a Burmese prisoner put to work with me on the same oil-mill. He was there, I was told, to lighten my work. Were not two to a yoke better, anyway, than one? But I must not, they insisted, in anyway, slacken; I must push the handle and go round the mill continuously, unfailing and unresting. I had been better treated than any other political prisoner but it was 'Kolu' after all. The labour on it, however lightened, was more than enough to exhaust one who was not habituated to the task. I put on the barest piece of loin-cloth round my waist. My work began precisely on the hour of six and it continued unbroken till ten. The continuous round gave me a sensation of dizziness. My body ached all through, and, as I lay upon the plank of a bed for rest and sleep, I felt feverish so that I could not sleep soundly, as I did before. Wake up I must the next morning and resume the work. So, it went on for a week, and I had not finished my quota. One day Mr. Barrie came to my room and said loftily, "A prisoner in the next room gives me his daily quota of thirty pounds of coconut oil, at 2 o'clock sharp, every afternoon. You have worked till evening and still you fall short of two pounds. You must be ashamed of it." I replied, "Yes, you are right; I must be ashamed of it. But when? If I had been inured to hard physical labour like him from my early childhood. Each one to his work, that I know too well. Let him compose a sonnet in an hour. I will do it for you in half an hour. You will not, on that account, be justified in crying shame upon that prisoner; you cannot say that he had shirked the work. He can well retort, 'Nobody taught me the art of poetry in my childhood. Hence, you cannot expect me to do it now.' You employ in your office unlettered peasants, robbers and dacoits for writing work. If they do not speak fine English like you, surely enough, you do not blame them. And they are not ashamed of that drawback. Equally, I need not be ashamed if I cannot turn out as much work from the oil-mill as my next-door prisoner does. Those really are to be ashamed of it who yoke intellectuals like us to the oil-mill, and employ hodmen to do the work of a desk. They fail both ways, for they do not get the best out of either."

Generous Friends come to My Help

While I was turning the oil-mill, one or two of the political prisoners, my neighbours, who could slip in unnoticed, always came to help me from time to time. Some of them washed my clothes, even with my protests to the contrary, though they had more than enough of their own hardships to bear. And they cleaned and washed my drinking pot and my dining plate as well. The petty officer and the *jamadar* often reproved them for it, and even beat them occasionally, but like true friends, they helped me on in my daily work. I tried many times to stop them. I washed their clothes without their knowledge, which, when they learnt, gave them exceeding pain. They literally went down on their knees and besought me to refrain from it. When I realised that my not allowing them to do my work, and my doing their work on the sly, both harassed their mind, I thought it the better part to let them do what they liked. On the whole, I found all of them affectionately disposed towards me. Their selfless devotion for me touched my heart. Sometimes, there was a regular rivalry among them to serve me, and it went the length of making them jealous of one another. Then I had to let them wash my clothes by turn. My heart still goes out in gratitude to these political prisoners when I recall their unstinted generosity and their deep friendship for me. I also feel it my duty to put on record in these pages all that I owe, in help and kindness, to my ordinary brethren in that jail, and for the respect they ever paid to me. I can tell many a story of their "unremembered acts of kindness and love". But I must not do so, and I record here my deep gratitude to them all.

The Mind Revolts

To speak to none, to discuss with none, and to keep on looking at my naked body so shabby, so dust-covered, so sweated by the work on the oil-mill, a work that I had to do for the best part of the day. The body used to be full of perspiration, the dust thrown up by the turning wheel of the mill as it crushed and ground down the pieces of dry coconut fruit for oil, with other dust mixed up in it had clung to it all over—this was the experience from which the mind revolted with disgust. It went on like this from hour to hour, from day to day, and, who knows, it might continue from month to month, and lengthen out into years. I began to hate myself. "Why should I bear it?" my mind asked me, "this your body and this your power, of what use are they to you now?" What will you, and what can you, do with them to liberate your country to revive its spirit, and to cover it with glory? Nothing, nothing at all, now and forever. Your body, your mind, your will and your power—they are all dust now in this darkness of your prison-house. And no more will you see light, no more the way out. The world knows not of your sufferings, and will not care to know. What effect, then, can it have upon the world? Thus, you are of no use to yourself, no use to the world, nothing for the cause, nothing for mankind. A burden you are on earth, why then live? Why not end it all? A cord, a noose, a pull, and finish!" So did my mind torture me and argue with me.

End it All

Your power to will and to persist was given to you to agitate the minds of your people, not unlike Mount Meru of Indian legend given to the Gods and the Demons to churn the ocean. Now they will be used by you to churn what? No better than to use the rod of Mount Meru to churn the curds for butter-milk! Why disgrace your gifts thus? Again and again the mind would revert to the same topic. "To live is futile; to die is honour", it would persist in admonition. Novalis and other foreign writers have said much in defence of suicide. It sometimes becomes an act of duty, as they preached it. And I recalled all their sayings in this perturbed state of my mind.

One day, in the hottest part of the noon—and it was particularly warm that day—I was turning the 'Kolu', almost panting for my breath. All of a sudden, I felt I was fainting and sat on the ground. My stomach had become hard like stone; the bowels within had stiffened; I supported myself against the wall; I shut my eyes and fell into a stupor. I do not know how long I was in that senseless condition. Suddenly, I woke up from that deep state of unconsciousness. For a few minutes, I knew not where I was, and what I was doing. I had lost all sense of time and space. Deep peace of nescience, state of perfect bliss, complete self-forgetfulness, body, mind and soul merged into one, and the sense of personality gone from them—this was what I seemed to experience in that happy mood which lasted but for a few minutes. Life in death and death in life, as it seemed to me then! And then I came to myself, objects around me became clearer, one after another. And I resumed my work. My mind was ever goading me: "Why don't you finish that work? Death is no torture. You have experienced it now, complete self-forgetfulness and the peace of nescience. Thousands of prisoners have used the means to attain that nirvana. Why do you hold back? Don't, take a piece of string and strangle yourself. End all this trouble thus. Why not?"

The Lure at Suicide

The whole day passed in this obsession of mind. Suicide—that one word was luring me on. Death was nothing but that indifferent state I had lately experienced. And it was, indeed, better than my present state. Twice did this mood come over me. Once I was re-arrested at Marseilles and was proceeding through Aden to India. The sea was a blazing furnace of fire, so hot we felt round about Aden; I was then in the lock up on a cabin, distressed in mind and heated in body. And now in the Andamans, working on 'Kolu', when the brain became dull and the body failed me. A wrestle within me between reason and desire, when reason had almost gone under! The same was to happen to me twice in the future. That night as I lay on my bed, my eyes were rivetted on the barred window, where I had known that prisoners before me in the room had hanged themselves and taken leave of their lives. I listened to that controversy between reason and desire as a third person, and I wove it into a poem later on. Again and again the voice of reason would admonish the voice of desire in some such words: "Fool, how proud, how vain you are! Let us believe that you were meant to do great deeds of heroism and national uplift. But what of it now? The human machine is now useless for you; now you say. Maybe, granted that it is true. Have not thousand such machines been completely shattered prior to this? Why not use the machine that God gave you for humbler ends? Why break it with your own hands? Silent, unknown tortures—to bear and endure them—is also a part of its work. In national work, on a stupendous scale, one has to fight and conquer from point to point, from stage to stage. This may be a stage in your onward march to success. This is, perhaps, the hardest stage, the tightest corner that you have to turn. Will you turn away from this part of duty? Rather stay on and fight, fight at bay if you must. That is also a compliment to the human machine, which you will so recklessly destroy. And if you must die then.

Die Fighting

Kill one enemy of the country and then expire. Why die like a coward? Your tribulations must influence the country, however small that influence may be. And if you don't believe it, and if you conclude that they shall have no repercussions outside, even then why need you hang yourself? It is dying like a dog. They did not send you to the gallows. Consider why? Were they smitten with compassion? No; they did not hang you because they thought it impolitic to do so. Now, if you hang yourself, you will be only playing into their hands. You will add to the failures and ruin of your party. Why, then, quit the world thus? It will be a distinct disservice to the cause, which, you yearn, should prosper. You are a soldier in this war of freedom. Then die like a hero. Do not commit suicide, but kill and die in the fight." Reason, when it argued with desire in this fashion, convinced and won me over to her side. I had become desperate. That mood of desperation was conquered, and I recovered my poise once again.

If I Resolve to Die, I Die only Thus

Not only did I make up my mind to die bravely, but I persuaded all my friends and disciples in that jail that it was their duty, in virtue of the pledge they had taken, to die like heroes. I, thus, saved many a lonely and wretched human being in that place from the verge of suicide.

While working at the oil-mill and with all the fatigue that the work involved for body and mind, I had one compensation in it and that was the chance I got there to talk to my political friends. These came to me either by connivance of their *jamadars* and wardens, or by eluding their watch. They kept on talking to me as long as they could safely do so. Most of that conversation took place after five in the evening while others were busy arranging for our dinner, and during the hurry and bustle of that business. We gathered together then on the resting place of the reservoir in front of us. One of us kept the watch and the rest engaged themselves in talk. We had free and candid exchange of opinion on the question which had all along occupied our minds and for which we had sacrificed our lives. The talk went on like a fresh breeze through our souls and thoroughly revived us. The fire that had smouldered blazed once more. Insults and humiliations were welcomed as acts of grace. What we had suffered paled into insignificance, and what was to come we resolved to face as "the stern daughter of the voice of God", would dictate it to us. These moments of freedom from the harrowing teeth of the Kolu were, indeed, blessings from that Goddess. Most of the political prisoners of my time were not more than twenty-five years old. I found their education defective and incomplete. They had read nothing of history, politics and economics. It was not a strange experience, and that did not diminish aught from their patriotism and self-sacrifice. On the other hand, I felt a sort of respect for them because they had suffered so much for the cause inspired by noble motive and thorough disinterestedness. If only they had added adequate knowledge to their sterling enthusiasm, they would have better fitted themselves to advance the cause so near to their heart. I, therefore, resolved to make up the defect in them by proper study and wise guidance. First, it was necessary to awaken in them this desire for study and guidance. And my conversation with them had this principal object behind it. I began my work as soon as I was set to my new labour on the oil-mill. Some of them had begun to despair that their life had gone in vain. I had to draw them out of this "slough of despond". I quoted to them examples from history. Those who had doubts, I gave reasons to overcome that doubt. Those who were merely caught in the whirlwind of agitation, I convinced why it was right to do what they had done. I, thus, succeeded in reinforcing their will and confirming their zeal. After the tiresome and soul-killing toil of the day, the evening meeting was a happy, though brief, respite to them all. They talked freely, they imagined boldly; they revelled in happy dreams of the future; and they recovered the balance of their minds and the poise of their souls. Their courage to face and to endure was deepened; its blurited edge had recovered its sharpness; and, when they dispersed, they went away, each to his cell, taking leave of one-another, like happy and loving brothers. It was there that I enrolled them and other prisoners of the settlement as members of my "Abhinava Bharat". It was here that they took their solemn oath to be true to the cause and serve it ever with their lives.

□

12

Consolidation and Propaganda in the Andamans

While I worked on the 'Kolu', I had an opportunity of knowing much, not only of the condition of the political prisoners inside the jail, but also of the situation in the Andamans as a whole. In spite of a thousand obstacles in their way, those who had learnt to love and admire me put themselves into contact with me and gave me news about the islands. I, therefore, felt that even from this prison, I could do some work of consolidating our forces in the Andamans. Of course, it demanded strenuous efforts and I was prepared for it.

The Work Begins

To rot here and suffer all kinds of hardship had become the part of our daily duty, and we had to bear that burden all our life. May we not, then, take this additional burden upon our shoulders which was an essential part of our service to the country? Why not, then, acquire the double merit, for which providence had marked us out? We would suffer gladly for her in this prison, and we would work strenuously for her outside. Inspired by this feeling, I set out on that larger work by first educating those whom I considered to be in my charge.

Education of Political Prisoners

Within a fortnight, I put myself in contact with such of the political prisoners as had come into our struggle by the force of driving whirlwind, as it were, and whose convictions were yet shaky about the means we had employed. They did not entirely favour our adoption of violent methods to reach the goal of independence. I explained to them the whole position; and, while the jailor had put me under the yoke to tame me down, I made these men take an oath to join us in the proposed work of consolidation. This was the beginning of my work for the Andamans. How that work developed and spread out, I cannot narrate in full in these pages. I will tell as much of it as I can during the course of this story.

About a fortnight had passed when I was relieved of my work on the oil-mill. I was put upon the work of weaving the strand. This was the easiest of all hard labour in this jail and it was considered a piece of good luck to have it. After a few days' practice at it, I found it easy to weave the strand, and I felt that the strain on my body and my mind had considerably lessened. I had been taken back to my room on the topfloor of Barrack No. 7. But on this occasion, I had, for my neighbours, two to four political prisoners. They were there in spite of the jailor, it seemed, for the jailor and the other authorities of the prison had made it a point never to bring them into touch with me. But when all the possible cells outside this chawl were full of them, they could not but accommodate four of them in the building that I had occupied. The Superintendent and the jailor told me plainly, on more than one occasion, that if I would turn them into moderates, I could have the company of educated men to live with. Whenever a new recruit came in this prison, he was always locked up in a cell near to those of such 'educated' political prisoners. But none was kept for a long time in one cell, or in the same group. To avoid risk, their place and their grouping were changed periodically.

That was a Holiday in this Prison

Such a day was always marked in the prison calendar as a holiday for all of us. For this change of batches and places occupied the best part of the day, during which we had no work to do. Besides, prisoners, moving from one place to another, always jostled one another. Thence they could at least see one another and, at times, exchange a few words as well. But the best of it all was that we could know then who were the newcomers to this jail. We could make their acquaintance as well as secure their membership. Though I was invariably confined in chawl No. 7, and although, as a rule, no other prisoners were sent to this chawl, I found this day the best holiday of the month. For, I could see on that day my elder brother going from one place to another. And if I could pre-arrange it, I could also exchange a few words with him on that day.

As this mode of exchanging prisoners and places, everyone or two months, afforded us an opportunity of contacting one another and of exchanging a few words between us, so we had other means at our disposal to establish communication with one another. Each room in our chawl had a barred window at the top and an iron grating on the floor and in the side wall for purposes of ventilation. The seven divisions of the Silver Jail were built in the form of petals spreading out from a common centre. As such, the courtyard of one opened on the backyard of another. And a man standing in the barrack of one division could see and communicate with a man standing in the barrack of another. One from the chawl of one division could communicate with the rear of another division, and one from the rear of another could carry on with another in the courtyard of another division. Each had only to hang up to the barred window at the top or peep through the trellised grating at the bottom.

Talking from the top Windows

But to hang on to the top window was a dangerous experiment. Therefore, we put the plank, on which we slept at night, straight up beneath the window and, supporting ourselves on the edge, peeped through the window-bars to talk to a man who, from his window, was talking to us. But the hands and feet had a heavy strain on them in this process. We often talked to a person on the floor beneath ours. Sometimes, in this brief talk, we exchanged thoughts and solved doubts on politics and political economy. Suddenly, if we heard the footsteps of a *jamadar* coming in our direction, we had to throw ourselves down from a height of twelve feet, which meant falling sheer on our buttocks. The teacher and the disciple had to disengage themselves from common study without a minute's notice, and both were hard put to it to escape unnoticed. Many a political prisoner received a severe shock to his nether part and even an occasional injury to his body in this unusual art of learning. The second way in which we carried on our communications was to talk through the trellised iron grating in the side-wall close to the floor. The grating was so fixed at the base of the wall, that none could see through it in the room beyond. It was a cleft in the wall, so to say, for pure ventilation and nothing more. Sometimes, on the other side of the grating, prisoners were made to sit for dinner. It was an opportunity for conveying messages to one another. The dinner was prolonged on their side, and, putting our mouth close to the trellis-work, we spoke on this side. It was a telephone call between the two.

The grating was the machine, which, in prison-parlance, came to be recognised by the name of telephone. Only the trusted ones exchanged messages on this telephone. It began with ringing the bars with one's dining plate; and that was the call which started the message. When the telephone would not work, we started the telegraph.

Thus, through several devices improvised on the spot, we kept our touch with one another; and the business went on more briskly, the more they tried to prevent it. They would detach and separate us; they would prevent us from talking by signs; and they would put all sorts of obstacles in our way. But, undaunted, we went on with our propaganda work in the prison. As I have said above, it began with the two or three political prisoners who had been lodged in the same chawl as I. Soon after, I was taken away from the work on the oil-mill. And I began to teach them. They were not all uneducated men; they had all passed their matriculation examination, and had spent some time in the F.Y. classes of their college. But they had no education in political science and constitutional history. When I started giving it, the first difficulty I felt was of suitable books.

Lack of Books

I was deprived, at Thana, of the few books that I had. The books, in possession of certain prisoners in the Andamans, were of an insignificant character. The books of Ramakrishna Paramahansa, of Swami Vivekanand, of Tolstoy like 'My Religion' and others, of Mrs. Annie Besant on theosophy and her theosophical magazines, were all our stock-in-trade. Of these books, they could get to read only on Sundays. The warder carried them from door-to-door like vegetables in a net-like bag, and distributed them to the prisoners. In the evening, he took the books back again. Everyday a prisoner got one book to read from his own collection between the hours of four and six in the evening. It had also to be returned to the warder at a fixed time. The prisoner was prevented from reading anything during the working hours. And he could not read at night because it was complete dark then. Again, the strict regulation of the prison forbade one political prisoner from transferring the book that he was reading to his next door neighbour. Mr. Barrie had laid down the law that each was to read his own book, and no exchange of books was to be tolerated. An ordinary illiterate prisoner could not finish a small book during a week. But to ask a political prisoner to confine himself to one small book during the week was the height of tyranny. If anyone broke the law so laid down, the warder and the *jamadar* had the opportunity of their life to show him up. He was dragged to Mr. Barrie, tried by him, and the book, snatched from his hands, was evidence enough to punish him. The *jamadar* exulted in the detection of this offence and Mr. Barrie was proud of his servant's masterly vigilance.

"This Fellow gave and that Fellow received it!"

That was the howl they raised and the Superintendent was in extreme anger. The trial was enacted and those, guilty of the offence, were sentenced to be manacled for four continuous days. To read a book not his own for a few hours of the day got him the punishment of standing up for four days with the chains on his hands fastened to the ceiling above his head! The sentence was passed upon them, no doubt, to help them meditate on the sayings of Ramakrishna Paramahansa which he or they had read in the book so purloined! Mr. Barrie was their greatest enemy in that respect. The great 'pandit' opined that the reading of books had turned the heads of these youths. About a certain gentleman, he had said to me distinctly that it was the reading of books on theosophy that had made him mad. He, of course, referred to the political prisoner, who had defied all the prison orders about dining, resting and working on the 'Kolu'. He objected to the books of Ramakrishna Paramahansa and to books on theosophy as hair-brained trash. Maybe, but what of books on politics, the hardheaded stuff that they were? No, he would allow them neither. He was a learned man, indeed, for he had not progressed beyond his fifth form. And he was to decide what books the prisoners were to read or not to read. Mr. Barrie opened a book, turned over its few pages; if it was not intelligible to him, he at once condemned it as "nonsense and trash"; a rigmarole he called it and threw away. On the other hand, a book may approve itself to him by its jejuneness and poor stuff; but if it contained a word like 'nation', or 'country', it was at once put under lock and key by Mr. Barrie, segregated like plague germ, declared untouchable like high treason. Mr. Barrie used to say, "We cannot allow our prisoners to read this dangerous stuff, for these, with their frequent allusions to countries and nations, had turned these men into violent agitators." What of books on theosophy and Yoga? His answer was, he would not let them in; but the Superintendent had allowed them and he had to submit.

A Hater of Books

There were many reasons why Mr. Barrie hated books. One of them was that he had himself very poor education and was smitten with jealousy for the political prisoners who were better educated than himself. Secondly, these did not bend their knees to this demi-God of Port Blair; they burnt no incense before him. Some of the Superintendents also objected strongly to any kind of reading. A prisoner may chew tobacco before him and many times Mr. Barrie did not mind it, and he called it kindness and leniency. But if a prisoner was found with a slate or pencil or with a book, Mr. Barrie would fly into rage and burst out, "You scoundrel, you want to read and write. This is no school. Why did you not learn it at your father's? Send him on to the oil-mill, put him on 'Kolu', confiscate his book, his slate and pencil."

Their Effect

In a sense and from his point of view, Mr. Barrie was right. We know how in their exile, the Pandavas used to be down-pressed; how they would pity and condemn themselves. They were tortured by their minds for what they had brought upon themselves; despair and melancholy overcast their souls, and they forgot their own valour and greatness. Then Dhaumya and other sages narrated to them stories of Nala and Rama to put courage in their hearts and leach them to defy misfortune and cruelties of fate. And these stories from the past put a new hope in their hearts. Similarly, stirring acts of former heroes in history, poetry and romance, or discourses on the immortality of the soul from the Upanishads and the Bhagwadgita would prove a tonic to the shattered hearts of our political prisoners. That would imbue them with the spirit of defiance. That would fortify them against all onslaughts of the severest persecutions of prison-life. Was it for this that they were incarcerated in the Andamans? How could, then, the doorkeeper of the Silver Jail let in such incendiary stuff within its portals? Will he not be false to his charge? Will he be true to himself and his calling if he allowed such matter to spread among his prisoners and influence their minds?

But their argument against reading books was just our argument for reading them.

I began my work of teaching them without any books to start with. They learnt and taught by word of mouth. We used to gather every evening on the reservoir of our prison. I utilised this time to give them talks on history. Sometimes we were interrupted, sometimes punished for disobedience, and sometimes we could go on with these evening meetings with the connivance of our wardens. And on occasions, even if the political prisoners were caught in the act, they told the warders boldly that they were having some talk; of course, they had to face the consequence of being hand-manacled. This way, week after week, we continued to meet and I discoursed to the political prisoners on the History of India from its early beginnings in the Vedas down to our own day. I drew their attention, particularly to the heroic deeds of the past, acquaint them with the lives of its outstanding personalities, and of epoch-makers in that history. I then took them similarly through a course of European history told them of heroes like Napoleon, Mazzini and Garibaldi and gave them an insight into the contemporary history of tottering Russia and the great revolution that was going on there against its monarchy. From that course in very broad outline, I took them in a course on the elements of economics, politics and theory of government. The lectures were followed by discussions and the political prisoners, who would gather together for them, began to take deep interest in the subject. As their number increased in the prison, and as the wave of strike and resistance, fight and opposition, spread like wild fire among them, the Officers, just to pacify them, allowed us to sit together for a longer time, read what we liked, talk as we chose, so that we may work and not trouble them any further. At this stage, mere conversation of an evening took a turn into a regular meeting for settled study.

The Sunday Meeting

Throughout the week, we continued to meet every evening at our appointed place on the reservoir. But, in addition, on every Sunday morning till the hour of nine, I used to sit together with nine or ten of them who happened to be in my immediate neighbourhood and gave them regular lessons in subjects that I have already mentioned. At nine, we were taken out for weighing our bodies or cutting grass. I used to allot to each of them a particular subject for study. The student had just to tell me what he already knew about it. Then I carried on discussion with him. And we ended with the singing of our national song. This meeting was all a hurried business and not like an elaborate study in a class-room. For, in the very midst of it, someone would announce the arrival of Mr. Barrie, or we were afraid that a *jamadar* would appear suddenly on the scene. Then we were all told off to cut grass, and asked to disperse. As soon as we smelt a cat, we ran helter-skelter to our holes, like the proverbial mice. The lecturer and the audience had both to cut short the meeting, and distribute themselves, some on the field, some behind the iron-sheets and some to clean their pots and pans. And we met again as soon as the alarm was no more, as described in the famous lines of the poet, "Let the legions thunder past and plunged in deep thought again." After their rout, some faint-hearted individuals would point out in self-condemnation, the futility of it all, when I had to remind them of the prayers of the early flying Christians. When these had to follow Christ, in defiance of the tyranny of the Romans and the persecution of the Jews, they lived up to his Commandments by praying in catacombs, round the graveyard and in prison vaults, whenever five of them could assemble and hearten one another. Sometimes they had just knelt down in these secret places lifting up their faces to God, when they would hear the foot-falls of the Roman legion pursuing them, and instantly they had to disperse and hide themselves. But, when it had passed by, they would return and pray as before.

Such were our Prayers Also

The Sunday meetings had as their adjunct prayer and bhajan to end them. This addition I had made so that our spirit may be sustained in the depressing atmosphere of our normal prison-life, so that our meeting and our prayer were of a like nature to that of the early Christians. I kept on this Sunday bhajan for years together in my prison-life. We had discussions—political, religious, literary, linguistic and scientific at these weekly meetings. I felt happy that what I had at our Sunday meetings at Nasik in my very early life, what I continued in Poona, and later on in Bombay, and when I had gone abroad, in England and elsewhere, I could resume in the Andamans and in the Silver Jail presided over by a man like Mr. Barrie. I could, thus, keep up my resolution. I could offer my daily sacrifice, I could perform my daily 'yadnya' in the little space of the family pre-hearth (my prison) as I had performed it in the spacious spaces of the world's altar. And that was how, by the grace of God, I could keep the fire burning. In addition to 'flying meetings', we had discovered other means for the propagation of knowledge. These were the high, spacious, white-washed walls of our apartments. With the pointed thorns of the cordage plant, we used these walls as our writing tablets. For, in the prison-cell no political prisoner was allowed the use of a scrap of paper or the end of a pencil to write on it. The thorn was our writing instrument and the wall was the paper to write on. The prisoner, in spite of close scrutiny and strict vigilance, managed to have on his person pencil and paper to write on. He concealed them in his tuft of hair, in his mouth, from one hand to another, and, last of all, where they could least suspect to find them. Search them how you will, the things were never found out. But these were not enough for the propagation of knowledge. And I am not going to let you, besides, into all the secrets of our prison-life. Some tricks and stratagems and subterfuges one must always keep to oneself, perhaps, for future use! With all our handicaps, the prison-wall proved to us of immense use in writing out our notes and discourses on the subject of study on its spacious surface. The very first year a difficulty arose to damp our spirits. We were studying the elements of Geology from a book published by the R.P.A. Series. It was my habit from boyhood onwards to summarise a book and note its important passages in a separate exercise-book. And this habit proved of immense use to me. For, I could draw upon my memory to reproduce the contents of the important books I had read and even to quote notable passages from them. Accordingly, I made an outline of geological time from that book on a sheet of paper that I somehow procured for that purpose. I returned the book on the following day and, when my room was locked for the evening, I took out the paper and began to read it, when, to my surprise, the overseer came up, stamping his shoes, approached my room and opened the door. He searched my room right through. It was not an unusual experience for me, for my room was searched like this three times previously and during the same day. Let any-one whisper into the ears of Mr. Barrie that "Bada Babu" had something with him, and 'search' was the order that followed. When he had found that not even in two percent of such reports was there any substance, he gave it up. But this change came after seven or eight years. That day, however, when the overseer surprised me in the act of reading that paper, it became impossible for me to hide it.

A sudden onslaught

The overseer picked it up and asked me what it was. I told him that it contained my notes. Whereupon he strictly enjoined me that I was not to make notes in this fashion from any book given me in this prison. But, anxious as he was to make a political capital out of this episode, he subjected that paper to the closest scrutiny. He held it up in light and against the just lighted lamp, and began to read it minutely. What did he find in it? Words like Pliocene, Miocene, Neolithic, which were abracadabra to him. "What cipher is this?" he questioned me and showed from his face that at last he had caught me. I told him in a light-hearted mood, "it was the language of geology". He then muttered something to himself and smiling at the *jamadar*, asked him to bring me to his office the following morning, and that he was going to prosecute me. Accordingly, I was taken to the office the following day, I was tried for the offence, but, it being my first offence in that prison, I was warned and discharged. And for two following weeks, I had been to get no book to read. The question then arose how I was to summarise and make notes of the books I was reading. The political prisoners must have luminaries of the weekly lectures I had given them. How were they otherwise to remember and make progress in their knowledge? Where was I to get so much paper and writing material? And, if at all I could procure it, where was the place to hide it? Suppose I were to write sheet after sheet who will be able to read them under the very nose of the supervising warder and *jamadar*? All of a sudden, and while I was cudgelling my brains, I suddenly happened to look at the wall and there I found the paper to write on. A whitewashed wall—a paper—a broad sheet to write on! What a relief the discovery gave me.

The Wall—A Paper; The Cordage Plant—Thorn—A Pencil

I had already tried an experiment of that kind in the jail at Byculla when I wrote on the wall with the sharpened point of a stone. I sought to perfect it in the Silver Jail of the Andamans. And I made a full use of it till my release from here after a full period of fourteen years' imprisonment. I used to hide a pointed nail in the bolt of my door. And as soon as I was locked up inside the room and the door was shut, I would begin to write on the wall with that pencil in columns which I drew upon it. All the walls of the 7th chawl were, thus, scrawled over and each constituted for me a book by itself. For example, the cell, in which I was confined to weave the stranded cord was written with a full outline of Spencer's 'First Principles'. My poem 'Kamala' was composed and copied in full on the walls of this seventh division. In another cell I wrote all the definitions of political economy as I had learnt from Mill's Work on the subject.

My object was that when I was changed from that room to another, a political prisoner, brought in there, may learn those definitions as he was learning that subject from me. With a little management such a student could succeed being put up in this lock-up. He could then learn them off in a month before his turn came for transference elsewhere. As I was being changed from division to division, I saw to it that every division and every cell in that division had its writings on the walls from my improvised pen. And the political prisoners who had turned students took the fullest advantage of these written tablets—their books of study in this lonely place of a prison house.

I utilised in this manner all my opportunity to train them. Three means I employed in that laborious task of self-education. These were lectures delivered at Sunday meetings, oral instruction on every other occasion of personal contact, and, lastly, the use of the prison-walls for purposes of writing.

One Great Drawback

But the life of these writings on the wall could not be longer than one year. They could not last for centuries like inscriptions on the bricks of Babylon. Every year the walls were being whitewashed, and, as the process went on, the writings on the wall began to perish. They were completely effaced. Hence, the month before this operation was my month of serious and intensive repetition, not unlike the time-honoured recital of the Rig Vedas. I had to recall all the verses that I had composed in my mind and scribbled on these walls, and learn them by heart during this transition period. But there was one advantage in using this wall as a sheet of paper to write on. For, though the writing lasted only for a year, the fresh wash on it gave us a new blank sheet of paper to write on for a whole year once again. The paper as such was subject to the processes of time. It was bound to get old and worm-eaten. But these walls for fourteen long years furnished a broad sheet that was ever new and ever white to write on. Sometimes, while the white-wash was proceeding, our secret would come to light. But such a thing rarely happened. For the writing was carefully rubbed out before the process and the faint lines that survived made any deciphering an impossibility. Besides, I wrote in Marathi and on abstruse subjects like political economy. This made the task of deciphering a hopeless job altogether. Mr. Barrie could not read the writing, much less could he decipher it. He was so learned and wise after all, that he finally opined that it was a wicked attempt to spoil and disfigure government property. My brother was caught in this prison using the thorn of the cordage plant and was punished for it. His offence was to write comments on Vivekanada's lectures on Vedanta, in which he had raised some doubts and answered some objections. The book was his own and he had marked certain passages in it and written some marginal notes. These markings and annotations were made in the margin of the book with thorn. And this was his cognisable crime according to the prison's penal code. Mr. Barrie's words were, "This is a jail, this is not a school; if you wanted to learn, why did you not learn when at home? Why did you come here? Don't fight, don't read, only work—yes work. I know nothing else here."

What Avails it to Learn?

These obstacles to learning were external; but there was one great internal obstacle, and that was that some of the prisoners themselves were averse to learning. Being political prisoners they cared nothing for knowledge. Their motto was action. What do we want with pure knowledge?—they would say. Action and sacrifice, that is what we need. I had to make them realise that many of them, when they were released after seven or eight years, shall have to play their part in the Indian world. Let them not read anything then, if they felt that it was no use reading. But here they must add to their knowledge even for the sake of their ideals, rather than rot without knowledge as they were bound to do, if they did not make a special effort to keep their minds active. I further brought home to them the fact that if winning freedom was difficult enough, retaining it after it had been won was more difficult still. And until their minds were trained perfectly, they would never realise this fact of politics and political advancement. In a free nation, no constructive work can be undertaken by those who were ignorant of subjects like history, economics and science of politics and government. I cited to them the instance of Persia. Revolution in Persia set the people free. But because the political revolutionaries were ill-equipped in the art of government, in the essentials of good government and of reform and progress, when power came to them, they had to depend upon foreign experts in finance and economics, in the knowledge of trade and business organisation, and to carry on with the help of these experts, it led to chaos and confusion, all over the field, in the economic, industrial and public life of Persia; it led to maladministration, indiscipline and nepotism in public servants. Want of knowledge was the root of all these evils. Mere destructive action, leading to anarchy and the reign of terror, and resulting in dictatorship, benefits no nation. On the other hand, it sets back the clock of progress. This has been ever the lesson of history. And its best illustration is the French Revolution of 1789. Blind fury is ever national suicide; and if it is not controlled in time, it exposes a country to danger from without as well as to danger within its own domains. That is the lesson of that revolution for all time to come. The story of the Chinese Republic from its early beginning down to this day conveys the same lesson. That was because the leaders of the Chinese Revolution were inept in the art of government. And they had to import administrators from abroad to establish peace, order and good government. These were naturally interested in their own countries and exploited the anarchy in China to serve their own ends; and China remained as backward as it was in the pre-revolutionary era. Hence, no political revolutionary, if he really loved his own country, can afford to be ignorant and to trade on the ignorance of his own countrymen. The more they know the practical art of good government, sound administration, and of the management of their country in every walk of public life, the better it is for them and their country when they came into their own. In this respect, the so-called 'moderates' were better equipped than their friends, the extremists. And political prisoners must learn to follow in their footsteps. The moderates can claim among them economists, administrators, and statesmen of the highest rank like Gokhale, R.C. Dutt, Ranade and Sir T. Madavrao. I asked them frankly, "Have you anyone to rival them?" Hence to waste their time in idleness in this prison was sheer folly and shortsightedness. It was equally useless to be rotting and despondent. They had better keep their minds well employed and active by study and hard thinking on problems they shall have to tackle hereafter. And the subjects indispensable for future equipment were Constitutional history, politics and economics.

I said, "Everyone who presumes to think of his own country, to dabble in politics, and to aspire to political leadership, must need possess full and deep knowledge of subjects like politics, economics and constitutional history. To be wanting in such knowledge is to spell yourself inefficient and unfit for responsible self-government, or for high administrative offices in it. As in religion, so in politics, action with knowledge is the key to salvation. At present, you are working out the nation's destiny by self-immolation and service which are apparent failures. But if this service and self-immolation are to fructify in success and commonwealth, then here it is: when you have plenty of time before you, a number of years to be passed in enforced idleness, you must add knowledge to service and vision to self-sacrifice. Heroism, to do or die, is not enough. It must be illumined by deep learning ripening into wisdom." I exhorted them finally to cast off gloom and despondency, and apply themselves to knowledge which was their proper work there.

□

13

Correspondence with India and Means of Information

A prisoner in the Andamans was permitted to write only one letter home during the year. The letter had, perforce, to be as brief as possible. Again, it was to be an open letter, to be censored first by the jailor, next by the colonial officer, and to be despatched if approved by them. Every prisoner was warned that the letter shall not be forwarded if it breathed a single word against the jail authorities. Thus, only a slip of a letter could be sent by him home once every year. Even this small facility was taken away from him for the year if he was found guilty of the slightest offence like talking to a fellow-prisoner, committing nuisance outside the stated hours, not sitting in a line, so on and so forth. One can imagine how difficult it was to be free from any trivial offence of the kind we have mentioned, during the course of three hundred and sixty-five days. It was impossible, therefore, for any prisoner in the Andamans to convey any news about him to the outside world. It need not be said that it was also impossible for the outside world to send any news to him. The prisoner, in these circumstances, could not write even two lines, every year without fail, to inform his people at home that he was alive.

The worst kind of gagging

Moreover, the letters that were officially sent from here through the Government of India could contain no reference to our ill-treatment and persecution in this jail. Nor was there any scope for publication of such description of jail-life anywhere else. For, the Jail Inspection Committee never, visited our jail. Occasionally, a magistrate condescended to pay a visit to us. But, as a rule, he did not report against Mr. Barrie and his doings here. All petitions to the Indian Government from our side had to pass through the colonial officer—the Commissioner—who threw them away or rejected outright the petitions that contained complaints against the administration. Who would then care for us? Not the Jail Committee, for there was no fear of its regular visit, nor Mr. Barrie and the Superintendents, for they were personally concerned in these matters or the Commissioner, who always sided with them. The highest official would step in if only there was such a thing here as riots or an open rebellion. But the local men took very good care that the news should not, at least, officially reach the ears of the highest authority. So, the five functionaries of the Silver Jail were the sole masters of the situation and not a word went out from this prison about the real position here. These functionaries disposed of all complaints, petitions and counter-statements without any hindrance from the outside world. In case an obvious injustice was found out in that disposal, to make it reach the higher authorities or to ventilate it publicly had become a process more difficult here than in the prisons of India. And the ready means, available to prisoners in India to send news with their brethren on going home after their release, were denied altogether to the outgoing and the incoming prisoners of this jail. For, whoever came here had to stay on for twenty to twenty-five years. And the least period was never less than ten years. And, then, there was the question of his ever going out alive, for the Andamans was such a wretched place for the prisoner to dwell in, whether inside or outside its prison-walls. How, then, were we to take our complaints to the public place and hang them on the gates of India?

Ways and Means to Do It

The political prisoners were thus faced in my time, with the question of making the public known what they were suffering in this place. The only way to keep body and life together and release themselves from the persecution and tyranny of officers of this jail was to bring the facts to the ears of the highest authorities in India. For, the local officers told us that the kind of treatment meted out to us by them was according to orders from the Government of India, and that they were not to blame for it. Even to ascertain the truth or otherwise of this allegation, it was imperative that India should know about it, that. the matter be brought to her notice. When a prisoner was taken to the Andamans, India knew as much of it as she knew about Honolulu. After all, it was transportation out of India! What little was known of these islands by Indians came to us when political prisoners began to be sent there for suffering their term of imprisonment. But the public and the newspaper-world of India had no clear notion of them. And the same was the condition for years together of the Government of India. The annual report to them came in substance to being 'all well' in that settlement. And the officials never cared to enquire closely into that business. Perhaps, they thought that once the political prisoners were deported to that place, they need not further bother about them.

With all these circumstances against them, the political prisoners were busy devising means to communicate with the Government of India. For, it was with them the question oft 'to be or not to be', if not of release from this dungeon of a prison-house. It was all well to confer and conclude, but who will bell the cat and how, that problem still remained. There was among us a prisoner from U.P. named Hotilal, who had been sentenced to ten years' imprisonment. He, in collusion with a friend, offered to bell the cat. The strike of political prisoners and the strife between them and the local authorities, which I have described in a former chapter, and the sequel of these happenings had contributed not a little to have a sobering effect upon a few level-headed men among the ordinary prisoners. And out of them, some had begun to cherish the wild hope that these editors, professors and barristers would agitate and finally make the officers bend before them. They also hoped that if they rendered a timely help to the political prisoners now, they would reap its reward by securing for themselves an earlier release from this jail. Mr. Hotilal managed to procure some paper from these hopefuls and wrote out a long letter full of our grievances.

Hotilal's Letter

This Hotilal had made things very hot for all officers of the prison from Mr. Barrie downwards during the days of our strike against being put on the 'Kolu'. He was a man from Northern India and spoke Hindi as his mother-tongue. But he had an equal command over Urdu and English. He had travelled all over the world including Russia, China and Japan, and had seen and enjoyed life to the fulest. He was imprisoned in a solitary cell, apart from all others, as one of the "irreclaimables". A strict watch and ward was kept on his movements. In that cell, notwithstanding the surveillance upon him, he had written that three-columned article upon us. None knew anything of it except his two or three most trusted friends. One fine morning, Mr. Hotilal managed to smuggle out the letter with one of them, who was being sent for work outside the prison. Hotilal had put his signature on it and had also put upon it the number of the cell and the chawl, in which he was locked up. He contrived to send out that letter despite the strictest watch upon all his actions. He did it in the rush of prisoners going out for their day's work. It went out of the Silver Jail no doubt, but it had yet to cross the barrier of the Andaman Islands, which itself was a big prison-settlement. But the letter travelled all the same. It travelled in the envelope of a trusted friend on voyage and reached its post at Calcutta safe and sound. It went into the hands of the famous publicist and leader, no other than Surendranath Bannerji of Calcutta and the editor of *The Bengali*. In those days of terrorism and Press Act, Mr. Bannerji published it entire in his widely circulated daily, and wrote a leaderette on it. As soon as *The Bengali* had published the letter, other newspapers had no hesitation in taking shelter behind that paper and writing their own comments upon it. At last, the letter became a subject of questions and replies on the floor of the Imperial Legislative Council.

If it was difficult to send out news from the Andamans, it was equally difficult to get the news from India in that place, and still more difficult for it to reach us in our jail. Hence, those who had done the coup were naturally anxious to know if the surreptitious letter had reached its destination or if the friend who took it across had dropped it in the sea, or had delivered it straight into the hands of the Government. While they were so nervous about it, all of a sudden we got the news straight from the horse's mouth, from Mr. Barrie himself. He played the postman for us in the following manner.

Mr. Barrie Inflamed

One morning, without any apparent reason, Mr. Barrie came to our quarters in uproar and all red with anger. He had gone through all the seven divisions of the prison-house dashing his big stick upon the floor and showering abuse upon everyone he met on his way. The warder, the petty officer, the *jamadar* and the poor prisoner had each his full share of recrimination and abuse. The prisoners were confounded with this sudden outburst of temper. The petty officer could not account for it and all of us were dumb-founded. Mr. Barrie kept on shouting, "You rascals and rogues, I will teach you a lesson for it that you will never forget. What kind of watch is this? I will pound you all into dust." With all these ejaculations, he would not let us know what had happened. In the Andamans there is a kind of reptile known as centipede. Mr. Barrie's 'dance of death' and fury, his wild gestures and grimaces made the frightened prisoners indulge in the humour that he was so whimming and contorting because he was bitten by that reptile. In the course of his peregrination he came to the cell of Hotilal and shouted out to him to stand up. He rebuked him, "Why don't you stand up? You are the greatest liar in the world." And he went on like this, which others could not explain, but which the wily Hotilal understood well. And he also inferred that the shot that had wounded Mr. Barrie and gave him such a pain was none other than the long letter that he had indited and managed to send abroad. Perhaps, the letter had reached its destination and had been published. And the news of it carried to the Andamans was the cause of his sudden outburst. After wasting hot words on Hotilal, Mr. Barrie issued a fiat that no political prisoner was to come within ten feet of one another and the violation of that order meant a sack for the warder, the petty officer and the *jamadar* without fear or favour. The prisoners were no longer to come together for dinner. They were to sit apart, one from the other, and none else was to be within the shadow of his body. Issuing these strict orders Mr. Barrie left the place. Those who were in the secret knew the cause of it all, and concluded that the letter had done its work. In a day or two after, we learnt that Mr. Barrie had referred to the letter in his talk to his confidants—the 'gentlemen' political prisoners who had become his allies. He enquired of them how the letter had gone out and who had taken it. The 'gentlemen' assured us that nothing could be more foolish than that action. And they informed us further that *The Bengali,* which had published it, was prosecuted for the offence and its press was confiscated on that account. "Mr. Hotilal's folly had cost *The Bengali* the loss of a press worth from two to three lakhs of rupees! And we shall all be liable to severe treatment as the consequence of that blunder. Hotilal will suffer the most for having made false allegations. All of us would also suffer in consequence. What a reckless act it was and how contumacious!" That was what the allies would say to us; it was no better than the echo of what Mr. Barrie was saying to them, sure that it would reach our ears and frighten us.

The Echoes of Mr. Barrie

These renegades and time-servers, however, forgot that the letter in question had exposed the sufferings that they themselves had undergone. And when an opportunity came to them later on, they had not refrained from the 'folly' which they had condemned in other political prisoners. They were playing the double game of propitiating Mr. Barrie with the condemnation of Hotilal and of being ready at the same time to welcome any relief that would come to them by the publication of that letter in the press of India. However, all other political prisoners did not hesitate to congratulate Hotilal on his astute move and his brave action. They did it openly, unafraid of any consequences that might follow. They answered the objections of the detractors that they had nothing to lose and everything to gain by that step. For, already the officers of the jail were treating them harshly enough. Worse they could not do. And to put an end to that harsh and inhuman treatment, the first step was to expose it to the daylight of public criticism. It would mean, for the time being, relentless suffering but the price had to be paid for the object all had in view. And this was no question of any single individual. It concerned and affected the future of political prisoners as a class.

Political Prisoners as a Class

After the first batch of political prisoners had been transported to the Andamans, and in the conditions obtaining then in India, the political prisoners had almost become an institution in the country, and they were sure to arrive in the Andamans no longer in batches of ten and twenty, but in a growing volume of a hundred and a thousand prisoners. The fact was obvious and resistance by the early batches was necessary to relieve the yoke on those who would follow them there. Either they bear the yoke themselves or shall have to resist more fiercely and on a tremendous scale to put an end to the evil. Why not then begin now and face the consequences? Why not make the path of our successors easier? Why not strive and fight to raise the status of political prisoners as a class? I would go further and say to them, while I was there, that the task which had fallen to our lot was much nobler and wider; and that was to improve the condition of prison-life in India as common to all its inmates and to see that we did not merely work to ameliorate it for a class known as political prisoners.

Raise the Status of All

It was to improve prison-conditions as a whole that we were striving, and, therefore, we must agitate and rouse public opinion by every means at our disposal—letters, strikes, petitions and stiff resistance—in scorn of consequence to ourselves. Even if we were to fail and reap greater trouble than relief, doing the work as a duty, we must be ever prepared for it. This reasoning produced a desirable effect on the mind of the political prisoners and they openly supported Hotilal's action, that he had done the right thing in sending that letter to Calcutta. All felt within their hearts that he was right, but now by far, a large number came out in the open to defend him. The stir and excitement over the letter had lasted for two weeks. After the first reaction had passed, Mr. Barrie began to worm out the secret by flattering those who had despatched it. "What can we do? Everything happens here as directed by the Indian Government", so he began excusing himself to me. Once he said, "Look here that Hotilal of yours has killed the newspaper Bengali; it was for that letter that Government has confiscated its press. I answered: "I do not really understand why it should be so. I am afraid the news is entirely false." "Taking for granted that it is true," I added, "the action of the Government should not deter any publicist from printing in his newspaper what he is convinced to be right and fair. Not only one but ten presses, the Government confiscates, but the price is worth paying if it helps the cause of the political prisoners and relieves them from the kind of harsh and humiliating treatment that is meted out to them in this prison. That was the only way to improve conditions here. The Government should have taken note of that letter and started proper investigations. If the allegations proved true, then steps should be taken to remove the grievances. If they were proved to be false, being made by Hotilal over his own signature, the authorities should take him severely to task for having made them. How can the confiscating of the press help in such matters?" I concluded.

But was the press really confiscated? How was I to know about it? It was very difficult to get any news from India. The political prisoners were always very anxious to get news about their families, of what had happened to their property and their people after they had left India. But they were still more anxious about the news of their country, what was its political condition, and what was the state of the agitation in which they had taken such an active part.

How is My Country!

That was what many a political prisoner was anxious to know. The party of revolution was most ascendant in the country when I had left it. In what condition it was now, when political prisoners were all sentenced and sent to jail? Crushed as that party was under the heel of power, it may have gone down. But were other political parties doing something for the emancipation of the country, shielded as they were under the aegis of the ruling power? How were we to know this and other news of the world? What should we do to have it? Whenever one political prisoner met another, the first question that was asked was how the country was faring. If first even a single item of news came to them, they felt, for the time being, that there was nothing wrong with them and they kept on discussing the item for the whole day in small groups of two or three. Such was the curiosity of youth that remained unsatisfied here. The political condition of their country made them more restless than their personal grievances. A lover is always keen to get the news of his beloved. Our political prisoners were equally keen about the news of their mother country, for they had sacrificed their all in her service. No newspaper could reach him in this prison and no letter; all political news was expunged from such newspapers as were given to him. Hence, the only anxiety that ever preyed upon his heart was how to get at the news.

The First Source was the 'Chalan'

And yet they devised means after means and succeeded in getting news, however scanty, of the outside world. The first source of such news was, of course, the Chalan. Every month the convicts transported to the Andamans landed on its shores to be taken to the Silver Jail. It was a gang of 50 prisoners. The importance of the party during the first month of its prison-life was so great that even the petty officers from the warders to the *jamadars* sought to be in their good books. For, everyone tried to get some news of his village or town from the prisoner belonging to his own part of the country. Common language, common native place constituted an affinity between them. He got something to know from the fellow-countryman about his relatives and friends from this common source. To meet a man belonging to our part of the world and speaking the same language begets an attraction for us and affects us like a woman who meets someone coming from her paternal home in a far-off place where she happens to stay with her husband, a man, living in a foreign country and on the continent of Europe, experiences the same emotion, the welling up of the heart, when he sees there a person who is a native of his own village and country and talks in the same mother-tongue. Here we were banished from India to the Andamans and passing our lives in isolation and prison. No wonder, therefore, that an in-coming party of prisoners should evoke such feeling in the hearts of those who had spent many years there. The slogan indicative of this common bond between us was:

My Countryman, A Man of My Native Place

This was the title of the new-comer in relation to one older than himself in the experience and the habitation of the Silver Jail. And the title sounded sweet in the ears of the incoming man and was more precious in his eyes than any other title in the Andamans. The title 'Mulkhi' was stretched to signify my countryman when its meaning was a man from one's native place in India. How the linguistic divisions of India were more natural than its territorial divisions, as they obtain today, was brought home to us in this jail more than anywhere outside it. When a Mahar from Maharashtra began to speak Marathi, the heart of a Marathi Brahmin went out to him spontaneously and he felt that the Mahar was his brother and fellowman. The feeling that the latter came from his own province and, perhaps, his native place too, made him give that untouchable of Hindu Society all the help he could in this place. Fellow-feeling and brotherhood got the better in such a condition of differences of caste and the taboos that the caste had brought into being. Whenever a new Chalan arrived in this place from India, the old birds here inquired of their kith and kin, but even before that, the political prisoner invariably sought information from the coming party of the political condition of their dear Motherland.

A large number of the party were illiterate and ignorant men and they had the least notion of the political upheaval in India so that they could give but poor information about it to our political friends. Only when a great political trial was going on, and they happened to be in the court as arrested men for certain other crimes, or when they happened, for the time being, to be locked up in the same prison as the political prisoners, and when something in that connection had casually come to their ears, then alone some persons, in that part, used to give our friends piecemeal information on it in their broken and muddled words. In case an educated prisoner happened to be in that company, it was an effort and a trouble to us to glean information from him. For, in whatever division he was locked up, there the political prisoners managed to make their way and contact him or sent him oral messages for such news. They gave him no rest till he had told them something. And how much they had to entreat him earnestly for that news! They would even help him on the sly in his labour of picking oakum, in order to propitiate him for the news. But even an educated prisoner was not up to the task of picking political news. If he were asked about any political party, its agitation and its power at the time that he had left them, he would fumble for he had no answer to give. He would often end that he had no knowledge of it, and everything was quiet there. And that answer was a damper on the enthusiasm of our sentimental political prisoners. If there was one piece of information that he could definitely give them, it was about the arrest of some great political leader or of the immediate arrival of the King Emperor to India. "The Emperor is coming"; "There was a great show at Delhi"; "A big Lord had been killed"—that was all their definite talk. This news came ready to them because it had spread like a conflagration throughout India, in all its market-places and thoroughfares. Minus this, he could tell nothing about the Indian National Congress, or of the Imperial Legislative Council, of Swadeshi, of the struggle for Swaraj. Of course, I am narrating here experience of my first five years of prison-life in the Andamans. What change came over will come later on in this book.

It is interesting to note here a few—stratagems we employed to get information from the Chalan. A few of the political prisoners in India used to meet some of the prisoners bound for the Andamans, and they would pass on letters to them to be conveyed to their friends in the Silver Jail. They knew that the letters would be taken charge of by officers in that jail. So, the trick that they used was to put the letters well-concealed within the pages of an ordinary, innocent book bound specially for that purpose. In the body of the binding. the letter was enclosed so that none could detect it. The book happened to be duly delivered to the political prisoner concerned and along with the book went the letter to the proper person.

A Letter behind the Badge

After a time, the stratagem became too patent to be used safely by the emissary abroad. Another was quickly resorted to, and that was to secret the letter in the badge itself. Every prisoner had to wear a badge with its marked number hanging on his chest as soon as he became the regular convict in a prison. The letter was written on the inner side of the iron-plate, which was seldom exposed to view. And, thus, the news was conveyed safely to its proper quarters. The son of a great Punjabi leader sent me a missive from a prison in the Punjab, where he was serving his seven years' term of imprisonment by resorting to this trick. The prisoner through whom he had sent me the letter was in the Punjab jail before he was deported to the Andamans. He carried the badge on his person, and though he was searched fifty times and stripped naked to discover anything he might hide on his person, the thing remained undetected until it had reached me. No one suspected the iron-plate as the carrier of that message. The prisoner had taken good care all along the transit that the letter written on the back of the plate was not rubbed off. And he handed the strange missive to me as soon as he was inside the jail. I read the letter and handed him back the iron-plate with all the letters erased from it. Thus, the news percolated to us through the prison-walls of the Silver Jail. The Chalan was an invaluable agency for such news. And yet the news was so inadequate, fragmentary and intermittent that none of us was satisfied by it, for it did not inform us fully of what we were most anxious to know. To satisfy the craving, the only way was to have a newspaper sent to us from the outside world. And this was the hardest nut to crack. The time of which I am writing was one when no prisoner could have even the sight of a newspaper in this jail. It was much easier to let an elephant pass through its portals than to let even a scrap of a newspaper in. A prisoner may be pardoned for the former offence but never for the latter. We were content, in these circumstances, if we got at even small pieces of a newspaper properly smuggled in. Some political prisoners had agreed even to draw carriages, in which the officers drove from place to place, as part of their prison work, with this objective in view. They even carried out carts full of garbage, took them to the officers' bungalows, that they might load their garbage on these carts and discover in the process old newspaper or its cuttings. They discovered them and concealed them in the planks of the lumber on the carts on their way back to the jail. They used to hide them well in the drain pipes of our building for safe custody. And in their movements during the day, they would read them all right. Funny was their experience of such reading. One scrap told them of Edinburgh; another of the cricket-world in England; a third delighted them with a column and half of a vulgar and serial fiction. Some came from wrappings round old shoes, and others from wrappings of clothes sent to a washerman. But these contained no news from India. Whenever we came upon a scrap of the 'Times of India' or of a wire from London, we were on the qui vive, but to be disappointed soon after.

'Foreign Mail'

The newspaper scrappings, thus imported into our jail, sometimes brought us striking news and without our least expectation of it. One such was Sir Valentine Chirol's article on India and Indian revolutionaries in an issue of the *London Times*. Another gave us a full report of the Congress presidential address. A third, of which I have the clearest remembrance, was a full one-columned report of the Tuticorin trial. When they got the scrap, they handed it over to me with eagerness and attention. That we could procure this piece of news and pass it on safely to all political prisoners made the prisoners realise to the full the utility of drawing these carts full of garbage to and from the prison and they never felt the hardship of months for the gain they had reaped from it. The dumping ground of this foreign mail was the lavatory of officers' bungalows. It contained scraps from the daily *Times* stored away for daily use. Or they were thrown there on the floor carelessly after the officers had read and done with them. The political prisoners bribed the scavenger in charge to collect them and put them in the garbage for carts to carry. And after they had been picked out and stowed away, we read them as we have pointed out above.

Sometimes, 'The Local Mail' kept company with 'The Foreign Mail' for proper delivery to us. The factory attached to our jail wanted nails and other articles for use. They came in the factory, parcels of them wrapped up in newspapers. The prisoners picked up these wrappings. Whenever they read the word 'India' in them, their curiosity was sure to be roused by it and the scrap passed forthwith to the political prisoner. Often, the piece of paper was so lull of dirt that it had to be held with blades of straw and picked up from the garbage. Small chips of coconut shells and cord had to be employed to spread it out for reading. But, even then we never failed to read it. We read in such a bit, a portion of Gokhale's last speech on Free and Compulsory Education Bill—the finest portion of it full of despair over the opposition of Government to its enactment. We read also from the same source a report of his having introduced the Bill in the Imperial Legislative Council. How it gladdened our hearts to know of it. The spread of free and compulsory education all over India would dot the whole land with schools that will so richly contribute to the literacy of India. A new mill opened; an old tax removed; a trial going on; a bomb thrown revealing the underground activity of revolutionary societies; a riot breaking out; a new book published; a new poet coming up;—whatever the news conveyed to us in a far-off place like the Andamans, even though it be through such a dirty source, it sent a thrill of joy through our hearts, for we felt that we were linked by it to our dear country and it marked some progress for it. The political prisoner hungered for such news, great and small, pleasant or unpleasant, for it gave us a topic for discussion in that dark, lonely dungeon of the Andamans. Dear India, we, your forsaken children, ever thought of you in the dreariness and rigour of that lonely residence. We were rudely torn from your breast, Mother India, but we never forgot you; and we forgot our personal cares and sorrows in thinking of you and reading about you. In that news, we felt your pulse and marked its beats. And we passed our years in this prison forecasting her pains and joys, and experiencing them by the news that filtered down to us through this channel.

Another Source of Information

In addition to Chalan and 'The Mail', we established another agency of communication with the outside world. It was to send some of our prisoners detailed for outside work to certain Indians settled in the colony of the Andamans. These gentlemen were full of sympathy for us, but they were not habitual readers of newspapers. Even if they agreed to read them for us, they could not communicate news from it to men whom we sent to them, and these, again, were not so trained in mind as to carry the report faithfully to us. There were very few among them to keep correspondence with us. And even if they had dared it, harder still it was for anyone in the prison to convey such letters to us. For, those caught in the act were liable to severest punishment. They lost their jobs, and suffered in so many other ways. I had advised them not to do that. Even then a few undertook that risk, imbued with the spirit of patriotism, which they had derived from their contact with political prisoners, and through the lectures they had heard. They did it as .a part of their duty This did not happen during the first three years of my life in that prison, and in the beginning, we had to beg of them so much to do it for us! The political prisoners had nothing to give them in return. But they parted even with a portion of their daily bread so that their appetite for news should be partially attended to. They had semi-starved themselves that they might get some news every evening about their dear motherland from the outside world.

Over and above the improvised agencies for getting news of which we have written in the foregoing pages, suddenly, we got the news from the authorities themselves. Mr. Barrie himself would blurt it out to us. Others also brought it to us occasionally out of absent-mindedness or because they were overcome with fits of sympathy for us. Mr. Barrie's news was ever bad news—a curse more than a blessing. Whatever to the detriment of India, whatever was damaging to our cause and was bound to fill our hearts with despair or told us about the weakness and disintegration of our past flowed freely from his lips, and he took pains to come over and communicate it gleefully to us. He told it to us and listened to our comments upon it, which he carefully noted in his diary and journal. Even then we were not slow to thank him for whatever he gave us. For a man, worth the name, always likes to hear news unfavourable to one whom he loves, as he loves heartily to hear great, good tidings about him or her. News that is good news brings satisfaction to his soul, while bad news makes him ready, body and soul, to run to the rescue of his beloved person. It nerves his arms and fortifies his soul to fight for and save the person from the impending calamity. We shall have occasion as we go on to hear more about this matter. But, as a sample of Mr. Barrie's behaviour with us, I give the following incident. When Mr. Gokhale, the great patriot of India, had died, Mr. Barrie rushed up to me and said, "Well, Sir, you always want news, Mr. Savarkar, here is something for you, Gokhale is dead!"

Gokhale dead!

He brought this sad and tragic news to me in the evening when I had satdown for my meal. The news was so sudden and so unexpected that I could not believe it for a moment. I burst into tears, whereupon Mr. Barrie said, "But was he not against you?" I uttered, "By no means; I have learnt in a college of which he was the head. We had differences, but we were not enemies. He was one of the best products of our age, and an undaunted patriot and a sincere servant of India." On this, Mr.

Barrie went on, "What then of the evidence in your trial of a conspiracy against him? And what of his observation that until you were caught and punished, there will be no peace in India?" I answered promptly, "Do not, please, believe in such hear-say reports. It is no use. We had intimate talks with each other and we cherished deep affection and reverence for each other. And this can be borne out by those who were present on the occasion. My way of doing things may not approve itself to him from his own standpoint of service of the country. But that does not detract from his sterling patriotism, and as for revolutionary and secret societies, I may say that when he attacked them in a speech or two in England and when some of the members of the Abhinava Bharat Mandal, at a secret meeting, spoke of finishing him off, I stood up and censured them severely for even a thought of doing harm to his body. I condemned it as a reprehensible act to attack anyone for honest difference of opinion, and much less a man who was our own in blood and race and whose service to the country was unimpeachable. This would be downright heinous act and an unpardonable sin, and saw that the resolution, that they had put down was thrown out by the meeting. My friends themselves will bear me out in what I am telling you today. If every Indian were as patriotic and as dedicated to the service of India as Mr. Gokhale, our country would take immense strides forward towards emancipation and all-round progress."

Mr. Barrie noted down every word of what I said to him. I saw his notes long after the incident. In those notes, he had made one surprising observation which was: "however different these Maharashtrians appeared on the surface, they were at heart one with the other."

While I am narrating this episode, I am reminded of a similar utterance of great patriot of India. While I was in England, Hardayal told me much about Tilak. He narrated to me about him the following story. While in India, Hardayal once went, to Poona to pay a visit to Tilak. And then he paid a similar visit, to his rival Gokhale. He had travelled all over India paying visits, to the leaders of India in opposite camps. And he had heard from them nothing but abuse and misrepresentation of one another. But Tilak and Gokhale were free from this foible. Each of them tried in his own way to persuade Hardayal to join his own party, but not a word they breathed about each other, to traduce character or misrepresent work. Not a word of malice or vilification escaped their mouth. On the other hand, what they spoke of one another was full of appreciation and reverence. Tilak said, "Do see Gokhale once." And Gokhale said, "You have done well in seeing Tilak." And he added, "That you have put up with him is as it should be, for the next generation is going to be his." After telling me this story, Hardayal remarked, "The conviction that we are

Hundred plus five Before our common enemy, I find deep-rooted in the heart of the Maharashtrian alone; and it is not so evident anywhere else in India. The Marathas forget their petty jealousies and quarrels in a national cause. Their leaders have learnt the art more than others. And I have experienced the truth of it many times in my life."

The political prisoners during the first three years of my stay in this jail had, facing all difficulties and using all possible means, devised a news-service from India to the Andamans, and from the Andamans to India. As time went on and conditions improved, they grew in power and then correspondence with India proved more effective. New means were added on to the old, the details of which we shall narrate as we go on.

It was through this new source that we learnt before long that it was Mr. Barrie's invention, pure and simple, that *The Bengali* was prosecuted for publishing Hotilal's letter and its press was confiscated in consequence. And he had spread the news through his minions to demoralise political prisoners in his charge. A few days after, we procured a cutting from the paper itself and we learnt that it was the first paper in India to publish the news that I, as a convict in this prison, was put upon the hard work of turning the oil-mill. The news was, thereafter, published in American papers. And our workers of the Abhinava Bharat in that part of the world improvised a cartoon and circularised it in the press there, and distributed its copies all over the States. I shall narrate its effect on India when I deal with the story of convicts in the Lahore Conspiracy Case since their arrival in this settlement.

□

14

The Coronation Ceremony of 1911—and its shadow on the prison in the Andamans

As narrated in the previous chapter, the publication of Mr. Hotilal's letter by *The Bengali* created a flutter in the official dovecotes. In the wake of that stir and excitement was created an atmosphere of sudden hope in the prison at Andamans. A thick rumour was abroad that all political prisoners, including myself, would be released in a month or two after the Coronation Durbar at Delhi to follow the King-Emperor's Coronation in London. The date given was December 1911.

The Hope of Release

In the days of famine, thousands of starving population turn into beggars for food, and their minds alternate between hope and fear when corn comes for distribution among them. Everyone hopes that he shall have his share of the corn, but at the same time that he fears and trembles that the corn will be spent up by the time his turn comes to have his own share and, perhaps, he shall have to go without it, and a struggle ensues for securing one's share before everyone else. So was it with us in that prison since we had heard the news of that Durbar. The phase mostcommon in those days with us was 'Jubilee was coming', the inference being that either release or remittance of sentence was sure to come along with it. The news soon spread all over the settlement and every prisoner's face was bright with hope. Each prisoner was now in a flattering mood as he knew that if his number was to come in the list of prisoners recommended for release, he must no more be sulky with those with whom rested his recommendation or otherwise. For, after all, good conduct was the test, and to certify good conduct remained entirely in the hands of the jailor and other officers associated with him in the management and supervision of the jail. So, the prisoners were bent, in these days, on doing their work smoothly while the officers were determined on exacting as much work from them as they could. If any prisoner demurred, the plea was put forward in the following words, "Brother, remember there are few days now for you to stay here. Your name and number are already being sent forward." In this sanguine state of mind, the cry of Jubilee coming made the life of the prisoner full of joy for a month or two afterwards. Hope springs eternal in the human breast. Those who were transported for life and who had, therefore, no hope whatever of returning to their homes as free men, could expect release only if something impossible were to happen.

The Jubilee is Coming

When any news of an impossible happening drifted on to us, the mind was attracted more by the chance of its turning true than could be induced to discover its impossibility, and hope led to wishful thinking all over the place. Hence, almost every year, and, certainly every two or three years, "the Jubilee was coming", and "release or remittance of sentence was a surety"—these would become the talk of the whole prison; and the poor, disappointed inmates, taken in by that rumour, experienced a sort of relief in their minds, till the rumour had proved altogether a hoax. This had gone on now for ever, and whenever it started again, prisoners still persisted in believing it, and if anyone sought to disillusion them, if anyone assured them that it was like the proverbial straw at which the drowning man caught, they became furious with him for thus damping their hopes.

One always gets angry with another, who says that there is absolutely no hope of release from a danger or who contradicts a rumour leading to such a hope, even though in cooler moments of reflection, he himself may have come to the same conclusion. That is a peculiar trait of human nature, to which very few are exceptions. And I myself have passed through the same experience. When I was sentenced to twenty-five years' transportation on the first charge in the High Court of Bombay, I was ninety-nine percent certain, that if the second charge was proved against me, I would be sent to the gallows. And in all conscience, I was preparing myself in mind to face such a fate. And yet, when a visitor to me in the jail at Dongri drew the same inference, I became very angry and had to control myself lest my anger might burst out in harsh words to him. I remember the occasion too well to forget it even now.

But the memory of that experience hardened my mind against entertaining any foolish hope of release on the occasion of the Durbar at Delhi. Other prisoners were too sanguine to disbelieve it. Most of them began marking time and planning for their journey homeward. They went the length of fixing the route by which they would go, and they thought out beforehand what they would do when they had reached their destination! But the wonder of it was that some of these were here on a term of seven, ten or fourteen year's hard labour, of which they had not yet completed even one-half or two years at the most. I could never believe that these would get their discharge for anything in the world, when the Government had put them there at such a huge expense and at considerable trouble to itself. These were dangerous men in its eyes and, I was convinced, that the prison-doors would never open for their release. All the same miracles do happen even in such cases as history tells us about them. Ireland, Italy and Russia had furnished instances of them. But it was ever wise never to count upon such miracles in individual and personal cases, though one had every right of hoping against all hope. Life becomes endurable and work a matter of course when one disabuses his mind of such exceptions. It was my constant advice to fellow-prisoners never to build on such foolish rumours and to prepare themselves always for what was inevitably in store for them. But nothing could conquer their irrepressible hope and their wishful thinking. Some were put out with me for my eternal doubt and pessimism. Others swore by the prophesy of Aravinda Ghosh. When Aravinda got his discharge, while others with him were sentenced to long terms of hard labour in India or across the seas, he had addressed them from the prisoner's dock in the following words: "Go, you young men go, you are sentenced today, but I assure you that you will come back free within three years from now."

Aravinda's vision of Krishna

The rumour then was that Aravinda Ghosh, as a prisoner on trial, had a vision of Krishna in the jail, in which he was confined during the hearing of the case, and it was this vision that had emboldened him to make that prophesy. Naturally, these prisoners had put their implicit faith in it. If the prisoners from Calcutta, caught in the Bomb

Conspiracy Case, were bound to be free, why not the prisoners from Agra and Punjab, who had spread sedition by their writing? And if all these were sure to be let off, why should the three Maharashtrians alone lag behind? Thus, the logical chain was complete, based as it was on that great prophecy of Aravinda Ghosh. All will be free then—that was the firm conviction of them all. The question now remained was how to count these three years, from what date to what date. In whatever order of time we counted them, the reckoning did not fit in with the date of the Jubilee or the Coronation Durbar at Delhi. However, with an amount of hairsplitting, common to all logical disputants, somehow they made it according as they were anxious to interprete it. According to them, the period of three years had definitely marked out the month of December—the Coronation Durbar Day—as the day of general amnesty and pardon, and therefore, the day of our liberation. There was, as such, no end to our hope. We were to be free; we were to see the faces of our dear ones as fresh as they were when we were taken away from them. Two or three years would not make such a difference. We shall tell them the story of our prison-life in the freedom and happiness and love of our hearths and homes. What a pleasant dream it was! The men from Bengal were flush with it and they wanted their Maharashtrian friends to come to their homes and make a sojourn there! So also with the Punjabis, who extended similar kind invitations to me. Everything was fixed for the journey, none thought of any hindrances in their way.

Of course, I was among the invitees. Men in my division of the jail flocked round me and talked to me with candour and affection. Everyone came to me and accosted me, "Tatya, do please come with me; do please pay a visit to our side of the country." Bengal and Punjab were equally enthusiastic in welcoming me. And, if I seemed indifferent or hopeless of my release, they tried their hardest to shake off my despair and indifference. Everyone of them was deeply pained to realise the hardship of my imprisonment of fifty years to run in that jail. And then deep sympathy for me made them more happy over my own release than their own.

At last, the blessed day came nearer. It was to dawn tomorrow. The news went abroad that orders had already been passed and received for our release on that day. Even the officers believed that it was to happen accordingly. We learnt later that something was on the anvil. This was the eve before that day. We were all of us in a line for our evening meal.

My political friends were sitting beside me. The *jamadar* himself was in a jubilant mood for he was also hoping to be released along with us. The only item that had remained to be settled was by what train we were to leave from Calcutta for our respective homes. As we were, thus, in the very height of our hopes, one Mirza Khan came running up to me and, almost out of breath for the news, pressed my hand and told me, "Barrister Babu, you are let off." This man was the worst of his kind among the prison-warders. The dirty canal through which Mr. Barrie's palaver flowed on to us claimed him as its very own. There were three of them who were similar channels of his messages to us. They constituted the trident in the hands of the demi-god of Port Blair. It was this trident with which he always pierced our hearts in this prison. But today, its sharp end had blunted. The Khan beamed with kindness upon me. These wretched minions are opportunists all. They are kind or cruel as occasion suits them. Tomorrow, all of us were to be free, were to leave the prison. What, then, was he to gain by being cruel to me? Perhaps as a free man, I may be of help to him. Knowing me as a man of law, he would require my services to defend him as the accused in a future case of dacoity or similar crime. It may happen like that, who knows. So, it was discreet now to be on good terms with me. At least, it would cost him nothing to behave thus with me now. So, Khan pressed my hand and, in anticipation, felicitated me. And he made the news public to all the rest of them.

Bada Babu Released

"But who told you this," I asked him with a smile. He said, "But why need anyone tell me this? Mr. Barrie himself has issued orders to assemble all the *jamadars* in his office tomorrow. For, the prisoners have to be arrayed and sent off to their respective places on the island and to be put on the boat that will take them home." "But how do you say from that I am included in that number?" Khan replied, "I put a definite question about it to Mr. Barrie and he laughed." Then it was on this slender thread of hope that he had built up this news. All the same, I must confess that it gladdened my heart to hear it. I also had my castles in the air. I shall go home; will meet my brother, and I will embrace him deeply. All released souls will wake up as from a bad dream and gather together like humming bees, these were the musings I indulged in. And with a wave of joy, it filled my whole being. I knew that it was only a dream and yet it brought to me peace and happiness. In the direst condition of overwhelming misfortune, what man is there that will not clutch at such a hope for relief and consolation? It does blunt the sharp edge of calamity that is ever at our breast.

The happy news made all of them fall into my arms and embrace me. Everyone of them was eager to say, "Now, at least, you will take it as true. Now you are sure of it," I shook my head and said, "No." When the most enthusiastic and forward among them, Ram Hari by name, caught hold of my iron chain, and my breastplate with its marked number, and said, "Tomorrow, this plate will be broken, and the chain shall fall to pieces." I again answered, "It may be true about you, but not so about me. Yet your release will gladden my heart as much as mine. For, it will mean much more good tiding for my country." Damped by my answer, the prisoner pulled the chain and the plate with such loving passion and vehemence that the plate fell off from my neck, and it slightly scratched my neck as well. But he took it as a good omen, and the news went like fire all over the prison. This made assurance doubly sure for those who were locked in other divisions of that place. I alone expostulated with him that this good omen was to cost me heavily in the future for it was sure to bring on me added punishment and suffering. And, at last, my forecast proved truer than the much announced prophesy of Aravinda Ghosh.

The Day Dawns

When tomorrow came, all of us were called near the main gate of our prison. But myself and a young man from Bengal were not so called to begin with. The assembly stood there anxious to know their fate. They expected every moment that the gate would open and they will hear either about their release, or, at least, some mitigation in their term of imprisonment. As they were looking about them, they saw the Superintendent coming up towards them. Then followed Mr. Barrie in full uniform as the custodian of the place. They called the prisoners one by one; my name was not among them. Fortunately for me, my brother's name was in the list. He was the last to be called out. The officers announced that each of the prisoners, whose names were called, had a remission of one month in a year in his total period of sentence. Accordingly, I was entitled, at the minimum, to fifty months' mitigation. But I was told that I had neither release nor remission.

Even ordinary prisoners on simple imprisonment were given that remission but not I. That day was celebrated for us by rice and potatoes boiled together for our feast. And I, of course, had my share in that feast. So, the Coronation Day of King George V set over me without release or remission. It brought us potatoes and rice and it brought for me, in addition, punishment for the badge that had fallen from my neck. I must thank Mr. Barrie specially for his address to me that evening in which he said, "I am very sorry, indeed, that the man with the longest punishment in this jail should not get even a day's remission on this happy day. But I must also remind you that a prisoner like you, who had not felt the slightest compunction of soul for the horrible deeds he had done, did not deserve that mercy at the hands of government. While others are mere political prisoners, you come under the category of a 'common murderer'. You cannot claim, therefore, the concession given to other prisoners on this great occasion." I replied, "I knew this before you had told me. I often told them that I was regarded as a dangerous man and an anarchist, and I expected no release at any time from the Government responsible for my incarceration. I am not a political prisoner, I am not an ordinary prisoner either; so you will kindly take away from me this dish of potato and rice, which is not my due because I am an anarchist and as you put it, 'a common murderer' at that."

The Coronation Ceremony of 1911 had ended without release for a single political prisoner and without even a day's remission for me. In the morning, when they had been brought out of their cells, they expected that they would not be returning to them in the evening. That before sunset they were bound to be free and to start on their way to India, or to wait somewhere for the boat to take them to India. But they had to bury themselves once more into their solitary cells as before. Of all the occasions that I recall in my prison-life, when the darkest shadow of despair, fear and melancholy had overcast the faces of the inmates, this was perhaps the worst of its kind. Although I expected nothing from this day, I could not escape the contagion of despair that had infected the rest of my fellow-prisoners. What I had foretold lay confined within the four walls of my cell. Outside utter darkness prevailed all about the prison-barracks. The atmosphere of despondence and gloom prevailed all around me.

The hope of individual freedom had proved a dupe. But what of my country as a whole? I also tried my best to get information about the death-trap of revolutionary struggle, which had gone on for the last four or five years. Had India got some additional rights in commemoration of that Coronation Durbar? That was what I was most anxious to know. The few prisoners who were being sent out for work, and who were given work in different parts of the island settlement, were always ordered in if they fell ill instead of being treated in a hospital outside its walls. When they returned with their bedding for treatment in the prison-hospital, they always brought to us some news of the outside world. They often got newspapers to read in that world and whenever a political prisoner had special news for his fellow-prisoners inside the jail, he contrived to fall ill and return to the prison-hospital. While all of us were so anxious for news from our country, one such prisoner suddenly returned to the hospital in the jail. It was not difficult for us to conjecture what sort of illness it was. The prisoner, we concluded, had some important news to give us and hence the illness. Next day, I came as usual for my bath on the reservoir at about ten o'clock when a prisoner in the chawl across shouted out to me from the top window of his cell and called out my name. I turned round and saw him looking at me from the backyard of his own chawl. He was in the second floor room of that tenement. As soon as our eyes had met, he told me that the Partition of Bengal had gone.

I could not believe it. And I questioned him, "Partition of Bengal? The settled fact is unsettled?" He smiled and answered "yes." I told him it might be news as faked as that of our release, and perhaps he was indulging in a guess as foolish as that. My friend assured me that it was not so, and that the news was authentic news. I left my bath there, and contrived to circulate the good news through all the seven divisions of the Silver Jail. Soon after, we learnt that the Capital of India was transferred from Calcutta to Delhi. But this news was not so important after all. The restoration of united Bengal had behind it an orientation of policy fraught with wider political consequences than the removal of capital to Delhi. It was the triumph of an agitation that filled our hearts with deep satisfaction. And in that joy, we forgot our personal disappointment. If the political question affecting our country was to be solved in such a successful manner, it did not matter in the least to any of us if we were within the prison or without it.

No Matter if we are Here

These words fell from the lips of every young prisoner when he had heard that good tiding. The partition or non-partition of Bengal was in itself a minor matter compared with the triumph of the principle involved. The deeper satisfaction came from the fact that we had made the Government bend down to our wishes. Further, it discovered to us the new method of achieving the goal. It created in us a fresh hope and instilled in us a new faith that what we would we could. Someone asked me if I was content with the single achievement. Will not this lay to rest our revolutionary campaign? I answered, "No, this achievement will inspire confidence; it will give a fillip to our movement as the surest method of winning freedom for India. The people are bound to feel that the revolutionary programme that annulled the partition of Bengal would also fructify in bringing them Swaraj." He who had experienced that quinine was the surest remedy against malaria, would not fail to use it against malarial fever whenever he was attacked by it.

Ujjain or Delhi

I was not in the least sorry that the capital of India was removed to Delhi. For, whenever we discussed among ourselves which should be the future capital of India, I had always expressed my preference for Ujjain. But I never failed to add that though from the standpoint of history, culture, industry and art as also from its geographical position and military importance, I regarded that city as the best-fitted in the whole of India to be its capital, I had no objection to Delhi taking that place, and I felt that the probability was more in favour of Delhi than Ujjain. According to my conjecture and forecast, Delhi had become the capital of India, and I felt no regret for the fact. Of course, personally it would have pleased me to see Ujjain as the capital of India.

□

15
The Prisoner's Food in the Andamans

While these changes were going on in India between the end of 1911 and the beginning of 1912, I had nearly finished my one-year of imprisonment in the island of the Andamans. In spite of bad food and inhuman treatment in that prison, I had managed to keep normal health, on the whole, during the period. I may, therefore, give here a general idea of the kind of food we were served in this prison.

A Prisoner's Ration

The quantity of daily food allowed to a prisoner in this jail, measured by prison-regulations, was both sufficient and nutritious. But there was no end of trouble for the food to reach the mouth of the prisoner himself in quality as well as in quantity. The prisoners from Punjab and the Pathans consume, mainly, wheat as their staple food. The large number of wardens and *jamadars* in the jail came to be drawn from the Mussulman prisoners hailing from Punjab and the North-West Frontier of India. And they were appointed, for the most part, as supervisors over convicts detailed for the hardest labour in this prison. Hence, they could easily deprive the prisoners in charge of the large quantity of wheat bread allotted to them as their daily food. They did it by coercion, tempetation or both. As a result, these hard-worked prisoners generally went without bread and had to feed themselves exclusively on boiled rice. When the meal was being served to them, they had to put their quantity of bread in the bowl of the Pathan and the Panjabi warder and be content with rice alone. And if anyone refused to pay this daily toll, prompt came the threat from the warder that he would make a hell for the prisoner who would not part with his bread to him. And the warden never failed to shape the deed to the word. He harassed the poor prisoner in his work, he made false allegations against him, he got him tried for faked charges, and he got him punished for those charges. A large number of these wicked warders consisted of Mussulmans from Sindh, Punjab and the N.W.F. Province. And the prisoners under them were mostly Hindus. The Hindu prisoners were persecuted by the Mussulman warders as a matter of religion and fanaticism, and their complaints never reached the ears of the custodians of the jail. For the warders and the *jamadar*s were all-in-all in that work, and saw to it that their own actions were not reported to the authorities above them. The warders took their meals in prison and, therefore, they could part with their rice to the prisoners in exchange for bread. But the petty officer and the *jamadar* did not dine in prison because they were regarded as officers. They were not allowed to do so. But the law did not prevent them from making a meal of the food allotted to the prisoners. So, they took away the bread of the prisoners without giving them anything in return. Besides, this way of satisfying their hunger saved them all the bother of having a kitchen in their own quarters. It saved them a lot of expenditure also. The prisoners had to part with all their bread to these officers in the first place and got no rice from them in return. If they did not do so, they were sure to suffer in consequence and get beating from them into the bargain. Mirza Khan was the worst offender among them. He regarded himself as the right-hand man of Mr. Barrie, May, he was "Chhota Barrie".

Throughout the Silver Jail, Mirza Khan strutted out as miniature Mr. Barrie. He made a sign, he had only to wink at a warder to get for him ten or twelve chapatis a day from the prisoners' dole for the day. He would walk along the line of the prisoners, when the meal was being served to them, with his eye on him who collected his ration of bread from the prisoners. If a Hindu prisoner were to show the impudence to refuse, he would, at once, turn round upon him and find fault with him, there and then, for some mistake or another. He was not sitting in a line, he was looking insolently at the *jamadar*; so on and so forth was the expression of his grudge against him. And, shouting at him, he gave him two sharp raps on the back with his big stick.

Every week a prisoner used to get half-a-coconut full of curds. This was a gala day for the petty officers and the *jamadar*s. For, they filled their pots with the curds and drank it off on the spot. Hardly, a particle of it was allowed to be served to the prisoners before them. They seldom touched a drop of it. Once a Hindu prisoner, instead of parting it to the warder, poured it straight upon the rice. When the news was conveyed to the *jamadar*, he straightaway rushed into the line where Hindu prisoners were dining, picked up the empty coconut-shell and pointing it out to him said, "O you scoundrel, why did you have this leaking shell?" It was an offence to use such a shell in the prison-ethics of the Andamans. The Baluchi *jamadar* instantly caught hold of his tuft of hair, and kept on kicking him all the time. The hair had almost been wrenched when he exclaimed, "Kafir, kafir with the tuft of hair," and abused him into the bargain. The prisoner raised a hue and cry and Mirza Khan came on the scene. He noticed that the quarrel was between one of his own and the Hindu prisoner opposite to him. He carried him to the jailor to frame a charge against him. I was watching it all from my own place. I beckoned to the prisoner to call me in as a witness. And I was sent for. I put before the trying officers the facts of the case as I had seen them. Mirza Khan, thereupon, began to shout at me. He said, "Sir, this Bada Babu is ever found to complain against Mussulman warders and he tells lies against them." I told the jailor, "Granted that I always give false evidence, I shall add one more to it now. Go and search instantly the shed in which the Baluchi officer has hidden his pot of stolen curds. Come along and I will show it to you myself." The jailor was obliged to accompany me. He got up and followed me to the shed and he found the pot, well-concealed behind a heap of coconut shells. I further deposed that the Baluchi *jamadar* had pulled the prisoner's tuft hair, had called him kafir, and had kicked him recklessly and for no misdemeanour whatever. On hearing this, the Superintendent became red with anger, called the *jamadar* in front of him, and, in order to teach a severe lesson to the rest of them, pulled off his belt and dismissed him from the job. He was reduced to the status of an ordinary prisoner and sent back to hard labour along with them. Thus ended the scuffle between the *jamadar* and his victim—the poor convict who refused to be deprived of his share of curds by the lordly Baluchi who posed as *jamadar* over him. The kafir's tuft of hair had pulled all right the beard of the Gaji Mussulman!

Thus, we tried to save the Hindu prisoners from the tyranny and persecution of Mirza Khan—the 'Chhota Barrie' of the Silver Jail. Occasionally, the latter would put us in a tight corner in order to take revenge for the lesson we had taught him, and we had to suffer a great deal on that score. We shall refer to these incidents in the course of our story. Suffice it to say here that only the political prisoners here dared to challenge him and to defy his authority. Others were meek as dumb-driven cattle before him. Out of these again only five to ten persons would carry complaints against him to the highest authorities. What we seek to emphasise in this place is the fact that though the prison-regulations were fair about the food to be given to the prisoners, they did not properly safeguard against its loot before it reached the hands of the prisoners themselves. In consequence, the prisoners were normally semi-starved while the petty officer, the *jamadar* and the warder systematically fed fat upon them.

Apart from this, there was another drawback in it, and that was about its nutrition. Give a man insufficient food to eat, let there be no bread in it, but whatever you give him let it be properly cooked. Here the rice that was served was not well-boiled, and the bread was half-baked or burnt. Do not serve bread in the form of half-baked dough and do not give rice that is as good as raw. Many a time we had to pray to the authorities to remedy this evil. Of course, the prison had a big kitchen for nearly eight hundred persons. But the cooks and caterers in it were all dirty men and some of them stricken with foul and dangerous diseases. Their dirty clothes, their perspiring bodies, the perspiration dripping down into the big pots of curry and rice, which they brought out to serve—all this we saw with our own eyes. And we had to eat such food to satisfy our hunger. Neither the cooks nor the servants were to blame in the matter. In the hot blazing sun, they had to do the work. And there were only five of them to cook for eight hundred persons. They had undertaken the task because they could themselves eat freely of it in the privacy of the kitchen. And even if they refused to work, none could set them free from it as they were taken from the prisoners themselves. In these circumstances, there was nothing like *taste in the food* served to the prisoners. A man enters the prison and puts the word taste outside it. Again, the prisoners were not royal guests to be treated to the choicest dishes. They were to be made to feel, as we understood it so well, that they were cut off from their kith or kin; that they were secluded in this dungeon for some crime either against society or government. Therefore, taste was no question here. Moreover, there was yet no distinction made between prisoners with simple imprisonment and convicts on hard labour. Again, political prisoners had not there been yet put in a class apart. Hence, these could not claim better food or different food from ordinary convicts condemned to rigorous imprisonment. We did not, therefore, complain against tasteless food. Our grievance was that the food should be clean, well-cooked and healthy.

The food in the Andaman Jail broke all rules of hygiene, nutrition and careful cookery. We were several times accused of false complaints and punished for them. But as political prisoners had to serve the longest terms in that prison, sheer tenacity and constant protests did not go altogether unheeded. And those, who had survived the ordeal, found, at long last, a considerable improvement in it. And the change in the dietary proved beneficial to all of us. I may close here with a few instances of how bad the food could be.

Kerosene Oil in Conjee!

Occasionally, we found kerosene oil mixed in conjee. The conjee had to be boiled very early in the morning. A big pot of enormous size was set on the fire-hearth, and rice and water were poured to the brim in it for boiling. Every now and then, the cook had to look in to see that it was properly boiling. He could not watch it well without a light. There was not sufficient light in the kitchen that he could dispense with the lamp. He often carried his kerosene lamp right above the boiling pot. With half-sleepy eyes, he did that work. The dirty lamp sometimes leaked or the man spilled kerosene from it as he lifted it right into the boiling pot. The pot contained conjee for eight hundred persons; as such, it could not be thrown out. The cooks were afraid of bringing the matter to the notice of the *jamadar*, and he himself could not report it to the jailor. For, the cooks as well as the *jamadar*s were liable to punishment for gross negligence, so that the conjee was served to us as it was. This happened, at least, once in every two months and it went on till the time of our release. But the political prisoners would not take it quietly, and they raised loud complaint about it. Once they refused to have that conjee altogether and the man had to report about it to the jailor. The jailor, as was usual with him, came to the spot and began to scold us. He shouted at a prisoner near us, and asked, "Do you really tell me that the conjee has kerosene into it?" He knew what answer to give when the jailor roared at him. He straightaway said "No Sir, Bada Babu tells a lie."

Mr. Barrie forthwith came up to me and spoke to me, fretting and fuming, "All of them don't smell kerosene in their conjee; how is it that you alone smell it? Well, I am going to take you to task for it." And he went away and all the prisoners that day had to swallow that kerosene-mixed conjee. For, if we did not drink it, we had to go without food that day and do our daily work on an empty stomach. But more than that we would be violating the prison-regulation that Whatever is put in the plate shall be eaten. It shall not be thrown out. Some of them may be given insufficient food, and some more than enough; but all must consume whatever was placed before them. Weak or strong, everyone must have his ration to keep him going. But the rule is not generally observed in all its strictness. But when it is sought to be enforced literally, the prisoner has to suffer from it. I have seen instances of warders forcing the prisoners to pick up the food they had thrown into the dustbin because they had enough of it, and make them eat it. I have already told you how we were compelled to gulp down the kerosene-mixed conjee. If some prisoners had thrown it off, we could have easily proved that it did contain kerosene. Speaking for myself, I did throw it, and Mr. Barrie threatened me with punishment for that act of disobedience. It was my good fortune that the matter did not go beyond that threat. He pretended to forget it all, and I was relieved in mind about it.

The political prisoners carried these complaints straight to the Superintendent. As a rule, the Superintendent laughed them out and did not entertain them. But, sometimes, when he was in good mood, he did not fail to castigate those who were the cause of these complaints. Of course, he did not do it openly, though Mr. Barrie was often hard put to it to get over these complaints. He often resorted to the practice of advising us through the mouths of traitors in our camp. At his instigation, they would say to us, "It is only the selfish men who quarrel over food."

To them our answer was that we would eat the worst kind of food, and even starve for days together, if, thereby, we could secure better food for hundreds of our companions in this jail. If we were bent upon mere livelihood, we were not beggars at home, earning one shilling a day in the streets of Ireland, to come in this jail for mere subsistence. This remark had a reference to Mr. Barrie's condition before he came to the Andamans as jailor of the Silver Jail. He was reduced to beggary in Ireland, his native country; scraping together some money, he had made his way to India and had come into his own as a white-skinned man. He had proved both bold and unscrupulous, and, hence, had got the job he was holding then. After this episode, all the political prisoners kept these confidants of Mr. Barrie severely at arm's length and even openly denounced them. The rest of the prisoners asked them point-blank, if they themselves had not confessed that the conjee had kerosene oil in it. These gentlemen shamelessly replied that it was a mean act to protest in matters of food as it proved utter selfishness of those who complained against it. These fellows had no scruples of conscience to watch for an hour together to steal a piece of dry coconut and their action was, of course, most honest and most unselfish!

The Selfish among Political Prisoners

Those of us, who had gone over to the enemy, and repeated parrot-like their master's voice, had no shame whatever to eat a piece of bread and a slice of fruit—the off scourings—from their master's table, when, at the same time, they called us "men who looked after their bellies", because we fought for better food on behalf of our fellow prisoners. If a man offered them *chutney* and onion on the sly, they had no conscience to reject them.

But the political prisoners were not foolish or faint-hearted to be taken in by this sanctimonious advice, or to care for these cowardly preachers. They persisted in catching hold of half-baked chapatis, kerosene-mixed conjee ill-boiled vegetables or insufficient quantity of rice, and similar bad stuff in the prisoner's daily ration and bringing it promptly to the notice of the authorities. This made them popular with their brethern in that prison. These looked upon us as a Godsend. Though they had not the stuff in them to stand up to Mr. Barrie's fulminations or give their evidence against him, they helped us in many other ways out of sheer gratitude. If the political prisoners had derived no sympathy from them, if they had not won their affection and reverence, their lot in that prison would have been beyond endurance. They were not alone in their fear of Mr. Barrie, but many a political prisoner himself could not summon up courage to give evidence against Mr. Barrie. Once a political prisoner found kerosene in his conjee, he refused to eat it and four others did the same. Other prisoners followed suit. The wave began to spread all over the prison. In a moment, Mr. Barrie got the news and came up to us. He approached the first man with a threatening look and said, "You, man from the North, you are spoiling the discipline of this place. You are instigating revolt. Look at others among you who utter not a word against that food." And he turned round to one of his minions and asked him, "Well, Mister, does it contain kerosene or does it not? Tell me." The gentleman replied, "Speaking for myself, I don't smell it." Well, that was final with Mr. Barrie. If a whole tin of kerosene oil was emptied into the conjee, Mr. Barrie would not have, therafter, smelt it. He praised his man and went away.

A Centipede and a Serpent in the Vegetables

We have already described the kind of centipede to be found in the Andamans. It is one-and-a-half-foot long and has deadly poison in its fang. Every morning, a batch of prisoners was sent out to bring vegetables for the prison. On the wayside and in the jungle-area grows a kind of esculent vegetable much liked by Indians. And, in between, grow different kinds of green vegetables. The prisoners cut them with their sweeping scythes and bring heaps of them in carts back to the prison. Then they are sorted and bound, into sheaves and with four curved instruments cut them into pieces. The vegetables, so cut, are then piled into separate heaps to be taken into the kitchen for dressing and boiling. That was the process of serving greens to the prisoners. Nothing was cooked carefully; everything was done in a hurry and, therefore, reptiles went into the boiling vessel along with the greens. When it was served out to us, sometimes we discovered in the vegetable boiled pieces of these reptiles. But the sauce to these strange dishes was furnished by the spicy words of Mr. Barrie. He praised the greens, mixed with these pieces of boiled flesh, to the skies and interspersed that praise with showers of abuse on us who objected to it.

Whenever we lifted up these pieces of centipedes and serpents from the boiled vegetables and showed them to Mr. Barrie, he would exclaim, "O, it tastes very well." If we complained to the Superintendent, he would say ditto to Mr. Barrie. We had, then, no other alternative than to throw out the pieces and eat the vegetables. For, there was nothing else on our plates to eat bread or rice with. If we went without food, that was going to give us no respite from our routine work. Mr. Barrie knew this too well and would, therefore, not care. Occasionally, the discussion between me and my friends on this matter brought some condemnation to Mr. Barrie. On one such occasion he came to me and sought to pacify me with these words: "Oh Savarkar, don't you think much of these scoundrels." "If you so choose," he added, "I will ask the man to prepare it separately for you. But do not expose its defects before them. They are no better than beasts. They will override me in no time. Thousands before them have eaten these boiled centipedes, but not a single death has occurred as its result."

It seemed that Mr. Barrie would improve matters only after a fatality had occurred in the jail in consequence of such eating. He had another card up his sleeves to silence us in this matter. When he saw that neither cajoling nor threat were to stop us from protests and complaints against this kind of food and other mismanagement in this prison, he would throw the blame of it all on the Hindu warder or petty officer.

Hindu *Jamadar*, The Cause of It

Whenever we lodged the complaint that there was kerosene in the conjee or the vegetables had no oil in them, and, perhaps, the oil was stolen instead of being put in the boiled vegetable, Mirza Khan used to defend himself before Mr. Barrie that the mischief was all the doing of the Hindu petty officer, and not he but the Hindu officer was responsible for it. Mr Barrie, of course, supported Mirza Khan and added that he shall have to proceed against the Hindu petty officer. In this situation, not wishing to make a scapegoat of an innocent person and knowing that the decision would be his dismissal and supercession by a Mussulman *jamadar*, we preferred to remain silent and not press the matter any further. At least, that was my attitude, all along, in such cases in my prison-life.

Later on, these complaints began to produce their desired effect and the prisoners got better food than they had ever done before. This was the result of continuous and relentless vigilance and agitation. In five or six years, a distinct improvement had taken place precisely because of these efforts on our part to set things right at any cost. The change of Superintendent had also much to do with the reform. The new Superintendent was a gentleman and a fair-minded officer. His appointment over this prison was also the fruit of ventilating our grievances in the Indian newspapers and their discussion in the Central Legislature of India. The Andamans had, thereby, become the topic of the day and the Government of India could no longer ignore it as in the past. The Superintendent, kind-hearted as he was, could not avoid moving with the times and the prisoners had benefitted by the change.

In addition to bad, insufficient, and sometimes unhealthy food, we had to suffer as much from the way in which we were handled while we were at our morning and evening meal. The prisoners were seated in a line in the hot noon-day sun or in drenching rain. None could sit out of the line. To avoid this nuisance, the prisoners, as soon as the food was served in their respective plates, would hasten to go under a shelter from the sun and the rain, but the petty officer in charge abused them and Mr. Barrie proceeded against them for having broken the line. And the Superintendent would punish the offenders for encouraging disobedience among others of their number. All the same, the toughest among us never gave up the practice of sitting for dinner in the shade as protection from sun and rain.

And this was not the rule only for the prisoners inside but also for those who were sent to work outside. Other officers treated these batches no better than Mr. Barrie himself. Sometimes these were made to take their meal standing. Their clothes were wet with rain, their bodies shivered with cold, and they held their plates in one hand and dined with another all the while standing, and the drops of rain falling on the bread and rice in their plates. And this mode of serving and eating was not an exception but the rule with the prisoners working outside the jail and in different parts of the island settlement. Those alone escaped from this imposition who had the privilege given too them to cook for themselves and eat independent of the rest. But no political prisoner, detailed for work outside, was ever given that freedom. He had to suffer all along and yet he did not shrink from the struggle to relieve the misery of his fellow-prisoners in and out of the prison-walls of the Silver Jail. The political prisoners suffered continuously and exceptionally; they incurred the severe displeasure of their custodians, but they did not give up till they had seen that things were changing for the better in the prison where they had to serve the longest term of incarceration. Besides this hardship of the sun and the rain over their heads, they had another grievance and that was the petty officer who never gave them sufficient time to finish their meals. The time given was very brief, and, as soon as it was up, the petty officer went round shouting, "The time is up, get up." And the prisoners had to stand up and leave, whether or not they had finished the food in their plates. The remainder had to be thrown into the dustbin. If they refrained or hesitated, the petty officer would rush into the line, brandishing his stick, and knock the plates out of their hands, and he would also give a blow or two to some of them. Stragglers were then hauled up before the jailor and the Superintendent invariably punished them. It took us five years of persistence and agitation to change all this. The prisoners were gradually allowed to sit in the shade, to take their meals without unnecessary hurry and bustle; they were seldom semi-starved and the 'Zulum' of the petty officer, the *jamadar* and the jailor on the top of them had almost come to an end. At the end of the fifth or the sixth year of my prison-life, Mr. Barrie had almost ceased to address us as scoundrels, or to say to us that we were sent there for work and not for eating. All his rigour and hauteur had gone for nothing and he had become soft as putty. This is the record of years reckoning up to 1914-16 from the day I went into the prison in 1910. We shall see presently to what further development this change in food had led. It was almost the beginning of the end.

□

16

Suicide, Mental Derangement, Arrests, The second and the third Strike

In the first six months of my sentence in the Andamans, I was treated as a prisoner in solitary confinement. As a matter of fact, almost all other prisoners were sent outside the prison for their work after they had finished their term of six months of simple or hard labour in the prison itself. But at the time that they were taken out, I was released from my lonely cell. Even then I was not allowed to mix with other men, but only made to sit in the gallery and opposite the door of my own room all by myself. Other political prisoners were free to talk and move with neighbours in their own block and those in common work with them. I alone was kept apart and all alone by myself. A special watch was kept on me to prevent me from any intercourse with other people of my class. For the whole day, I sat in the gallery and in front of my room busy, in making coils of rope—my daily labour at the time. With the evening I was sent back to my own room and locked for the night. Years went on in this round of dull routine. The only exception of it being my hours of dinner, morning and evening. For two hours in the day, I could see human faces and exchange words with them.

During all this period, I had kept myself rigidly to the time-table I had chalked out in the Thana Jail. My object ever had been, while working for public good, to adhere strictly to the rules of prison-life and thus, by good conduct, shorten the period that would entitle me to be sent for work outside the prison-walls. I felt that if I was so taken out, I would be better able to do some propaganda work in these islands as also plan for my release from the Silver Jail. Hence, though I did my best to improve the conditions of our life inside the prison and to change its regulations, I ever took care not to come in the clutches of law and to give no occasion for the officers to frame any charges against me. The one excuse that these officers always found for stopping the prisoners from going out was that these had refused to do their normal work in the prison itself. Hence, I was extremely cautious that none of them had any chance to make that accusation against me. What little I could do for my fellow-prisoners in the prison itself, I would have multiplied a hundred-fold if I were free to help them from the outside. Again, that would have considerably facilitated my freedom from the settlement itself. Hence, I patiently followed the course I had chalked out for myself and was biding my time to get out of this prison.

The prisoners, who got the first opportunity to work outside, were all convicts sentenced from three to five years' hard labour. None with transportation for life went out with them. And they had to do as much hard work in the settlement as they had to do inside. I would still induce them to remain outside, for their remaining outside would pave the way for others to follow them and, in course of time, as their number would increase, their propaganda outside would grow with them in strength and volume. So, I would beseech them to give no opportunity to the authorities to send them back to their own cells. Agreeing with me, they had all remained outside till the day of the Coronation in December 1911. After the first strike and after the Coronation, some four more were let out from this prison, and my brother and myself were not in that number. The letting-off of these four prisoners had, at least, this good side to it that political prisoners could be so let off. And I hoped I could take full advantage of the precedent. Hence, I worked on with hope and courage waiting for the day when I could be as free as the three or four who had gone ahead. But news began to filter in that these political prisoners had a very hard time of it even outside the prison-walls. They were given such heart-breaking work to do that they preferred to it the swallowing of some drug that would bring on illness and get them back to the kind of life they had left behind. We always think of medicines that cure a malady. They thought of potions which would bring them one. Strange, indeed, is the psychology of prison-life!

Give me medicine for Fever and Diarrhea!

When any prisoner asked this favour of another in a suppressed voice and with a dejected mind, it did not imply that he demanded mixture to drive out these maladies but to induce them into him. A man, it was reported, gets high fever if he swallows the paste of 'Kanheri' roots; another told me that the easiest way to get loose continuous motions, with blood in them, was to drink the paste of red berries called "Gunja". If a thread soaked in some liquid—I forgot which—were sewn into a wound, another said, the wound remained raw and open for six months on end. This was the talk of the prison. And if I questioned the authenticity of these reports, they told me that the medicines were tried and found effective for these purposes. Prisoners, put on the oil-mill or sent out to cut down the jungles or detailed to pick oakum and weave the threads into a coil of rope, were so much done up with the work and felt such a terror for it, that they preferred anything else to going on with it. Hence, they would resort to these dangerous shrubs, roots and berries or would make a wound to their feet, with the scythe they carried, to fall ill and come back into the hospital. They would sow a thread into that wound to keep it from healing. They would prick their throats with a needle and to convince the physician in charge that the blood had come out with their spit and from their chest. Any of these tricks they employed for purposes of escape from the toil under which they were being ground down in their prison-life.

Others feigned madness, and, to prove that they were really mad, would besmear their faces with urine and excreta, and, occasionally ate them also.

To convince the doctor and obtain his certificate to be transferred to the hospital was the one aim of these self-imposed tortures. I have seen such specimens in the prison with my own eyes, and travellers spending a week in the Andaman Settlement have testified what I have stated here. These prisoners would dupe the doctor endlessly with these methods, and it became hard for him, at times, to mark the genuine from the counterfeit. These criminals were hauled up before the Magistrate and were caned for their dishonest practices, after they had been cured and released from the hospital. The offence was obvious, the practice objectionable, but it cannot be gainsaid that the prisoners were forced into these tricks of having 104 to 105 degrees of high fever or getting continuous blood-stained stools, and suffering pain in the stomach, by the horrors of the prison-life, to which they were doomed for all their crimes. Some of them were seasoned convicts and not new comers, and still they did it, which only shows how hard the work must have been. If dacoits, robbers and other confirmed and dangerous criminals found it beyond their endurance to go through the hard labour, it is easy to imagine how the political prisoners must have felt about it. I need not describe their wretched condition and the horror of their lot in the Silver Jail of the Andamans.

Disease was Better than this Labour

I quote here specific instances of such prisoners and describe the tortures of their lives in their own words. One such political prisoner was Babu Upendra Nath Banerji. He says about himself: "Most of the prisoners that had come before me in this jail from the Indian Mutiny of 1857 onwards, on transportation for life, did not return alive to India. I learnt this fact and realised the horror of it while I was myself passing through the sentence of hard labour. I often felt that I should take a rope and put an end to my life forthwith to end all my troubles. But I could not summon up courage to do it. I kept on crushing the coconut pieces for oil by going round the grinding mill patiently and without any complaint. One day, working from morning till evening, I felt my body stark and stiff like a plank of wood; I found my palms blustered over; I saw blood trickling from the cracks in my hand; and yet, at the end of it, the yield had not come to the regular quantity of 30 lbs. a day. I felt I was swooning; I heard abuses hurled at me by the petty officer in charge; I felt them like whips against my heart, and, at last, I was dragged before the jailor. He abused me downright with the choicest slang and threatened me with caning. I was brought back from the office and seated in my place for the evening meal. Grief, pain and insult choked my throat and I could not swallow a morsel of the food put before me. A Hindu petty officer took pity upon me, and whispered to the cook to serve me more rice. He said, 'The Babu is stricken with grief. He cannot eat his bread, give him some more rice.' This made me cry aloud and burst into a loud wail. I tried to control myself and stop this exhibition. A blow with a stick would have been borne at that time better than these words of pity and compassion from the mouth of my fellow-prisoner—the Hindu petty officer."

Better Die than Suffer Insult

A young man named Indu Bhushan Roy was convicted of guilt in the Maniktola Bomb Case and sentenced to ten years' rigorous imprisonment in the Andamans. He had also to suffer from hard labour on the 'Kolu' and had his full taste of similar soul-killing experience. He was one of those who were sent out to work. But he found the work outside more fatiguing and humiliating than the labour inside. He had thought he would get some concessions, but, instead, he found that he had more rigorous work to do in the settlement. If a prisoner outside happened to fall ill, he was sent to a hospital relatively better than the hospital in the jail. But if a political prisoner became sick, he was punished all the more for that sickness. For if he had fever or suffered from loose stools, he was made to walk the distance of four miles, carrying his own bed to the jail, and was instantly locked up in his own cell. Indu Bhushan was fed up with it and returned to the jail of his own accord. Chains were put on his arms and hands, and he was marched on to his old residence; but he refused to go back to his work in the settlement. He was punished for this recalcitrance. No sooner was Indu put in his cell than Mr. Barrie came on the scene. He said, "Well, you have returned! You think, perhaps, that by coming here you will be spared all work. Nothing of the kind." And turning to the *jamadar* he ordered, "Put him on the oil-mill, and at once." Indu Bhushan was immediately marched off to work on the 'Kolu.' He was simply disgusted with his own life. I tried my hardest to help him bear up. I told him to think of me who had fifty years' burden on him to live in this jail, whereas he had to live there only for ten years. While he was taking his quota of oil to the *jamadar*, I again met him and could address only a few words of solace. He said, "No, I cannot bear it; better death than life in such disgrace." That was his constant refrain. I argued with him, I entreated him, I tried to soften him. I ended, "For the sake of our country, Oh my brother, we have to sacrifice our self, our life, and even our honour at times. We owe this duty to her at any cost. You are very young, you are not even twenty-five, of the same age as myself. You have better hopes to be free and alive than I have. So, cheer up, suffer and live, so that, when free, you will serve the country as before." These words were exchanged in a hurry and on the sly. Two or four days passed off. Every evening I saw Indu Bhushan returning from the 'Kolu', dead tired, with drops of perspiration on his face, the chaff of the coconut clinging like saw-dust to his body from top to toe, chains clanging on his feet, a weight of about 30 lbs. on his head, and a sack of chaff on his shoulders. I saw him coming up bent down under this weight, and staggering to the place. All of us were in the same plight. One fine morning, as our doors were unlocked for the day and we were all coming out, a warden approached us and, requesting not to disclose his name, broke the news that Indu had hanged himself last night.

I was astounded by the news. Only yesterday evening, I had seen him—a man in the prime of youth—before he went into his cell for the night. I had exchanged a few words with him. And in the morning, he was found dangling from the top window, hanged by a noose made of his torn clothes! His neck broken, his tongue lolling out, his feet dangling, his throat strangulated by a cord whose one end lay tied to the bar of the window, and corpse suspending from it in the mid-air. The young man must have found life too burdensome, for the loss of his self-respect, to bear and to endure. Dark deep shadow had spread over the whole building. Once in two months we had found such incident happening. But Indu Bhushan was the first political prisoner of his kind to put an end to his life thus. I was saying to myself, "Who knows, one day your fate will be the same as his. He died tired of his ten years' sentence and you, you will tire of your fifty years and quit the stage like him."

But Mr. Barrie gave me no time for these musings, for such melancholy brooding. For, he announced within three hours, not that Indu Bhushan had got tired of life and committed suicide, but that he had done himself to death in a fit of insanity and personal quarrel. Indu had tied a slip of paper round his neck which Mr. Barrie had cleverly removed and concealed. That was what the prisoners present were saying of him. He tutored the *jamadar*, the warder and the petty officer at the postmortem upon Indu's body to depose that they saw nothing to conclude that the deceased was tired of his life, or that the work in that prison was too much for him. Before the officers, brought together for the post-mortem, the political prisoners on the side of Mr. Barrie supported his statement and the immediate custodians of the dead man swore that he had hanged himself in a fit of insanity. But we, on the other side, sent message after message to assure the officers that the deceased was not an insane person, that he did not commit suicide on a sudden, that he had done it deliberately and as the result of the hardships and insults he had to bear in that prison. The officers were requested to call independent evidence to prove the truth of our deposition, and we suggested for that purpose the name of a person whom Mr. Barrie could not browbeat. The officers accepted our offer and the witness gave his evidence undeterred by the circumstances around him. He was one of the editors of an Allahabad newspaper 'Swaraj', who were all sentenced for sedition and came here as political prisoners. He proved to the hilt that the deceased was a victim of the tortures he had to suffer in the prison presided over by Mr. Barrie. These had created in him a disgust for life and he had ended it by suicide. I had told all of them about the conversation I had with Indu Bhushan. And I wanted myself to give evidence. But Mr. Barrie would not call me. In the evening Mr. Barrie came to me and told me whining, "Indu Bhushan has left a note behind in which he says plainly that he had ended his life as the result of some personal quarrel." I turned round upon Mr. Barrie and asked him, "Why did you not produce that note?"

"Why did you not put in this note as evidence in your favour? It would have supported you much better than mere argument and logic," I said to Mr. Barrie. I continued, "Please show me the note even now. I know the conversation Indu had with me only two or three days previous to this happening. I know what he had said to other prisoners in the same trying circumstances. He had told me and them that he had no desire to live for ten years in such hard conditions. He had said so several times and yet you dare say that he committed suicide in a fit of insanity. Granting that it was so, the question remains how at all a man strong and young like him could suddenly go mad. He was an arch-conspirator; he had faced treachery, imprisonment, transportation for life, hardships of prison-life and at last death by hanging with calmness and indifference and with a smile on his face. He had never shown temper in hot discussion with his friends, and had not given even the slightest indication of an unbalanced mind. Political prisoners are accustomed to such discussions and to sharp difference of opinion among themselves, and yet none of them has shown such a sign of weakness. Why then should these affect the mind of Indu Bhushan? Indu Bhushan was a man of strong mind. What had made his mind so weak now? What was the cause of it? It could be no other than the harsh treatment that he received in this prison. He was treated here harshly. Therefore, he chose to work outside; there also he had to pass through the same kind of torture and humiliation. He returned here sick and woe-begone. You put him in his cell and straightaway ordered him to work on the oil-mill. All this had contributed to his weakness. He openly said that he was tired of his life and would put an end to it. That is why, he hanged himself. It was no case of suicide through insanity as you put it. If he has really written what you say, then there must be some reason for his insanity." I talked so to Mr. Barrie. Mr. Barrie bore deep grudge against me chiefly for this plain-speaking. But even those, who flattered Mr. Barrie then and deposed that Indu Bhushan killed himself in a fit of insanity, say openly in the history of their prison-life, now that the circumstances had changed entirely, that the cause of his death was no other than the very hard conditions of jail-life in the Andamans. Thanks to them, for they tell the truth at long last. For, many continue to tell lies because they had told them once. Rare are the men who confess the truth they had deliberately hidden before.

Among the books found in Indu Bhushan's room was one on theosophy. And it gave Mr. Barrie an easy brush to white-wash the case. He succeeded in impressing upon his superiors from the Chief Commissioner downwards that it was theosophy that had softened his brain. Theosophy led its devotee to practise Yoga and Yoga, with its breathing exercises and other conditions of the body, had a bad effect upon the brain! We do not know if he was able to convince the Government of India by this kind of logic. But it is a fact that the Government showed no solicitude for investigating into the case, though Indu's elder brother fought hard for such an enquiry. Indu had hanged himself and the shock of it made the survivors count their days in this prison. They were afraid that theirs would be the next turn to follow him in the same way. Mr. Barrie became more and more impudent. He began to boast publicly that the incident had not at all affected his career and influence. On the other hand, he had begun to send reports that prisoners in the Andamans were never before so well-cared for, and that they had nothing to complain about it; but just at that moment, an incident happened to upset his whole story.

Poor Indu could not narrate his own story. But the man about whom we are writing now has given a record of his own impressions.

Ullaskar Dutt

Ullaskar Dutt was sentenced to long imprisonment in the jail at the Andamans. He was released from it after thirteen years of hard labour and he wrote out from memory an account of his experiences during that period. Let us, therefore, hear from his own mouth the story of his prison-life. He was convicted as a conspirator in the Manik Tola Bomb Case and the Magistrate who sentenced him praised the convict in the following words, "Ullaskar is one of the noblest boys I have ever seen, but he is too idealistic." What havoc his incarceration had made upon his body and mind is clear from his own version about it. He says, "I was yoked to the oil-mill similar to those we see in India for crushing oil from coconut and sesame. It is the bullock that is made to run the grinding mill in India. And even the bullock cannot turn out more than 16 lbs. of mustard seed oil during the day. In the Andaman jail, men were yoked to the handle of the turning wheel instead of bullocks, and it was imposed upon them to yield by their hard day's work 80 lbs. of coconut oil! Three prisoners were yoked to the handle of one mill. And they had to work continuously from morning to evening with a brief interval for their bath and morning meal. The interval actually given us came to no more than a few minutes. We were made to run round the oil-mill unlike the beast which could plod on slowly. We had the fear in our hearts that, otherwise, we shall not be completing our daily quota of oil. If any one of us was found to slacken his pace, the *jamadar* was in attendance to be labour him with his big stick. If that bludgeoning did not hasten the pace, there was another way of compelling him to do so. He was tied hand and foot to the handle of the turning wheel and others were ordered to run at full speed. Then the poor man was dragged along the ground like a man tied to the chariot wheel. His body was scratched all over and blood came out from it. His head was knocked on the floor and was bruised. I have seen with my own eyes the effect of this mode of getting work done. What man can make of man? These words of the poet escaped my lips after watching the process and its torture. When I came back in my cell in the evening, I found myself completely washed out by the process. I was not sure that I would be alive the following morning to continue that harrowing work. Yet I remained alive and did the work all right during the day. We all used to say about it, that we are fated to do that work and we must pay the price! All the prisoners working with us were, however, released from it in six months and sent to work outside. Other batches came in, worked on it for the fixed period and were sent out like their predecessors. But myself and other political prisoners were tied down to the same sweating toil. For years together, it went on like this without respite and without change of work. At last, a day came when I was ordered abroad. But the change was no better than from the frying pan into the fire. For, I was sent to work in a district in a factory of bricks. I had to run for the whole day, to and fro, carrying bricks that were wet and not baked yet in fire. This work was exhausting enough for an ordinary labourer. And he was given a daily quantity of milk as an inducement to it. But the poor prisoner hardly got that milk to drink when the petty officer or the tindal would pounce upon his plate and empty it down his own throat. I got my share of milk also and I at once drank it without looking anywhere about me. A few days after the tindal was in fury against me for not offering him the 'naivedya', he changed me on a labour which was not entitled to milk. Later on, he gave me the hardest work to do on the settlement. I had to climb up a steep ascent, draw two buckets of water out of a well, tie them at both ends of a pole, and carry the buckets with the pole on my shoulders to the bungalow of an officer. The weight of the buckets and water came to a maund, the ascent to the hill was steep and every moment there was the danger of my foot slipping on it, and myself falling down into the valley below. The work had to be done for the whole day, going up and down the steep climb. I used to be dead tired at the end of the day though I carried on for many days. At last, I was fed up with it and refused to do it any longer. A charge of disobedience and of shirking work was framed against me. The Magistrate tried his best to persuade me; he asked me to rest for a few days in the hospital and begin again, but I had made up my mind against it. We, political prisoners, who do what we will to conform to the rules of the prison and the settlement, were shown no consideration by the jail authorities. Why should we then bend down to their wishes? The more we toiled, the more they made us toil. Let them do their worst to our bodies, let us, at least, keep the soul free. They may rule over my body, but I am master of my soul. I shall not, of myself, enslave my body to them. I was given three months' additional sentence of hard labour, and I was sent back to be locked up again in my cell. The same Silver Jail, the same Mr. Barrie standing near the gate! As soon as he saw me, he roared, "This is not an open field, beware, this is a prison-house. If you go against its discipline, I will thrash you with my cane. I will give you thirty stripes of it, each of which will go deep into your flesh." I answered, "You may cut my body to pieces. I am no longer going to work here, for I think that to work according to your orders is a crime against my conscience." Instantly, Mr. Barrie ordered that chains should be put upon my hands, and I should be suspended by them in my own cell for a week continuously. All of a sudden I saw a strange scene before me. I imagined, now I say that I imagined, though it was at the time as real as the body I touch, that Mr. Barrie, my jailor, said to me that I had insulted him. And in order to wipe out the insult, he had challenged me to a duel with him.

I will fight You

He asked me to choose one who would fight for me. Mr. Savarkar, he added, will take your side. And he telephoned to Savarkar accordingly. A form thinner than Savarkar came up before me. The jailor asked him if he would fight in a duel on my behalf. Mr. Savarkar seemed to agree. Instantly, Mr. Barrie gave him a gauntlet to throw down and a sword to handle. I watched the duel between the two.

A Duel between Savarkar and Barrie

The duel was keenly fought on either side. At last, our side had won. Mr. Savarkar had beaten Mr. Barrie, and Mr. Barrie's countenance had fallen. I was in an ecstasy of joy and I wanted to clap. Suddenly, I came to myself, and the vision had gone. I was in my room in manacles and hanging down with my hands tied up to the top of my cell. I felt I would have fever on. I reclined as I could against the wall. The rays of the sun were falling hot upon my body. The temperature had gone up, the fever had flared. I passed into unconsciousness and saw in that state a person putting a phial of poison to my lips and forcing it down my throat. In came the doctor; I was shivering with cold and the temperature had risen. I was tossing restlessly with the manacles on. Twice before this I had fever on and I had requested the authorities to take off the handcuffs, but to no purpose. Today, the doctor had them removed at once. I fainted and passed into fits of convulsion."

It was Noon Then

We had all known that Ullaskar Dutt had been put in chains, but we had no knowledge whatever, at that time, as was later on described in his own account of it, that his mind had gone so weak as to see the hallucination that he has recorded in that narrative or that he was burning with such high fever as to pass into delirium. We came and stood in front of his room when we heard a piercing cry and the confusion that followed.

It shocked our heart. It was a usual occurrence in this prison, and the consequences were ever the same. That was the reason of the fright. Five or six petty officers were found ever, in such scene, to sit firmly on the chest of the poor rowdy prisoner locked up in his room, thrash him thoroughly and then run away. And then the cry of helplessness resounded through the whole block of that building. That was our usual experience. Hence, we feared that Ullas was, perhaps, meted out the same treatment. The slogan among us about it was 'to make one straight'.

Mr. Barrie and his myrmidons used to say openly that if they were "to make straight" a prisoner or two of these political prisoners, everything would be calm and quiet and normal in the jail they ruled. I asked the warder whose cry it was that I had heard, and what all this noise about was. He said he did not know. Heartrending cries, one after another, had filled the whole atmosphere. I saw some of them dragging a man from block No. 5. There were ten of them trying to lift him up and carrying him to the hospital. The cry was coming from him. He cried, he fell on the ground, they were all in an uproar! I saw this from a distance when the warder came running to me and whispered that Ullaskar had gone insane!

Yes! Burning in the hot sun with fever of 107 degrees, manacled and tied up, what else could happen to him than the loss of his brain? The brain and the body, which had been both outraged by excessive pressure upon them, had suddenly gone to pieces. Already he was so weakened in mind that he would easily pass into delirium tremens. He saw hallucinations and visions. The brain was out of gear and the body was out of joint. The latter had repeated fits and convulsions, and ten persons could not control it. The doctor somehow managed to take him to the hospital. Ullaskar was a young man full of laughter and mirth. He would crack jokes and make fun while hearing in court the sentence of death passed upon him. The spirit of humour did not forsake him even in his present state of delirium. The whole night he sent piercing cries of pain that rent the whole building around him. At the same time, like a ventriloquist, he filled the atmosphere with the sounds and notes of all sorts of birds, whose chirping music he had heard before and would burst into laughter.

We had no Sleep that Night

If a young man of this jovial mood, ever smiling, ever witty, one whom not the sentence of death even could repress, the fearless Ullaskar could go mad, then what of us who were passing through a similar ordeal of prison-life? How long could our nerves stand the strain? Such thoughts passed through our minds that night, especially of those who were under life-sentence, and every cry from the hospital that fell upon our ears made us fear and tremble. We were hoping against hope, however, that other officers in the jail would yet look after him, and nurse him back into sanity and health. The morning came, and what did we find? We found that the cries had grown more frequent and harsher in sound. Ama, Ama—mother, mother—that was the sound we heard repeatedly. It wrung our hearts and deafened our ears. What was really the matter? None would tell us. Some said, they were giving him shocks from an electric battery to discover if he was really mad or was only feigning madness. I thought it might be so, but I could not believe it till I had seen with my own eyes. And now, I will relate it to you as Ullaskar himself has written about it in his own narrative.

An Electric Battery

"Even in this semi-conscious state of mind and under severe pain of the body, I could clearly feel that the Medical Superintendent had played his electric battery upon me, the shocks of which were impossible for me to stand. The electric current went through my whole body like the force of lightening. Every nerve, fibre and muscle in it seemed to be torn by it. The demon seemed to possess it. And I uttered such words as had never passed my lips before. I roared as I had never done before, and suddenly I relapsed into unconsciousness. I was in this state of unconsciousness for three continuous days and nights. And my friends told me about it when I awoke from it."

We, his friends, had felt that Ullas had passed away. The cries I had heard were cries that he uttered when the battery was applied to him. Why was he given those shocks! Was that a remedy for his fever or for his delirium!

When after eight or ten days he had somewhat recovered his senses, he began to hear his relatives calling out to him full of pity and sorrow. Their cries, he felt, were appealing to him. He concluded from them that he was the cause of all their troubles, of all their grief. What a wretched being he was, a disgrace to his family, a thorn in their sides, a blot on their fair name! Overwhelmed with sorrow and repentence, he tore a garment upon his body. Out of its shreds, he made a rope, and in the rear window of his lock-up, he attached the rope and put its noose round his neck, as so many before him had done and expired.

Trying to Hang Himself

The watch and ward man detected him in time. Ullas relieved the knot and came down. That saved his life. The Superintendent, who had used the battery, was on leave and another had taken his place. He was known to be a fair-minded man. Next day, when he saw the shreds of the torn garment, he spoke to Ullas words that deprecated the act but were full of sympathy for him. He said to Ullas, "Though I am an Englishman and a Government servant here, and though our interests differ, and I cannot approve the deeds of you, revolutionaries, allow me to say this to you, believing as I do, that you did all for the freedom of your country and as your duty to her, that you need not blame yourself for them or censure your own conduct. You are yet very young; you will go back to your own country after serving your full term here; then why go in for such a cowardly act, why hang yourself? I know full well the source of all your troubles and your persecution in this jail. Excessive hard labour has undermined your constitution. But I alone cannot help you out of it. For, as a government servant I cannot countermand the orders of a superior authority which enforces such hard labour upon you. I must abide by these orders. But if you feel it a relief and if you will not object to it, I will arrange to remove you from here to the mental hospital."

To the Lunatic Asylum

And Ullas at once agreed to the proposal. He was then removed to that hospital. He had his fits, his convulsions, his lock-jaws in that hospital, though he was much better there, both physically and mentally, than in the place he had left behind. When he, occasionally, recovered his senses, he felt happy that he was free from the tortures of jail-life. He stayed in the lunatic asylum for a total period of 12 to 14 years. After a short stay in the Andamans, he was removed to Madras and he got his discharge from there after a period of fourteen years.

Four days after I had heard those heart-rending cries reaching our ears from Ullas's cell that afternoon, Mr. Barrie came to have a talk with me. It was a rule with me never to talk with an officer myself. They came to talk to me and I never hesitated to be frank in my opinions when I talked to them. Barrie knew this full well and, when anything extraordinary had happened in the jail, he came to me to know what I thought of it. That day he came to me full of smiles. Mr. Barrie was so wicked of heart that his geniality even could not be free from taint.

He was Cruel Even in his Geniality

As soon as he saw me, he began, "Well, when are you going to be mad?" I retorted with anger, "After you, surely." Then he turned to the story of Ullas. I at once reminded him, "You had said about Indu Bhushan, you remember, that he had hanged himself because he was mad and not because he had suffered from excessive hard labour in this jail? And, then, I had asked you what was the cause of his madness. Why, then, Ullas had gone mad? Can you give me the reason for it? Dare you say, now, that it was anything else than the sufferings in this prison-life? Here they have no hope, no future to look to and no relief in their present state. Day and night they are ground down with labour; day and night they suffer insult and humiliation from you and your creatures. How can they bear it? What wonder that they are off their brains? It is unbearable suffering that brings on insanity and it is insanity that ends in suicide. Ullas and his life are standing testimonials to this fact and you cannot deny it. You manacled him, you kept him hanging for eight days in his cell, he went into fits and loud wailing. That took him to the hospital and that brought him to the stage of madness and he attempted suicide." At once, Mr. Barrie changed his front, and said, "But who told you that Ullas is mad? He only pretends madness."

A Pretence!

I answered, "Then let us see him and we shall decide for ourselves." He retorted, "Do you want to suggest that I am lying? I say that Ullas is not mad and he pretends madness in order to escape work." I replied, "Then I must say that if Ullas is not mad, then he who says so is mad. Do treat us fairly henceforth, treat us as political prisoners, or at least, as ordinary prisoners. Do end this suffering. Else we shall have no other way out of it but strike. Not that we shall always win against you; entrenched as you are behind power and authority, the fight is bound to go against us. But we shall have done our best to expose injustice and defend our honour. And that is a great satisfaction."

For eight months after this, Mr. Barrie had kept on reiterating that Ullas was not mad but had feigned madness. If there were a large number of prisoners in this jail capable of feigning equal madness, Mr. Barrie's power to distinguish the true from the false would have been blunted long, long ago. The fount of sympathy had already been dried up. But Mr. Barrie was not such a cruel man in his behaviour outside. As soon as he stepped out of the prison, he became a human being; inside it he was a beast. We shall have occasion to describe him fully as we go along.

It had come to this then. We had tremendous hard work in the prison and we had equally hard labour without. And yet I ever advised my political friends to prefer the latter to the former. Because outside you could do some propaganda work for which there was no scope behind the prison-walls.

Resolved to go out at any Cost

As soon as I had completed my one year in the Silver Jail, I began sending petition after petition to be sent out for work. During one year and a half, I had the misfortune to be caught by Mr. Barrie and appear twice before the Magistrate on charges framed by him against me. First, on having written an anonymous letter to a person outside the prison for some news and press-cuttings from him. Unfortunately, the man to whom I had entrusted the letter happened to be Mr. Barrie's spy upon my movements and the letter went straight to him. I had not mentioned the name of the man to whom the letter was to be delivered. A certain man would meet him at a certain place to whom the letter was to be given. That was the direction I had given to Mr. Barrie's man. Hence, that man's name could not come out in the trial. But I was punished for it by one month's solitary confinement. The next occasion for coming into Mr. Barrie's clutches was the first strike. I had discussed in a letter how the strike was to be organised and carried on, and I was about to circulate it among the political prisoners. On a sudden, my room was searched. The officers had just stepped in when I threw the letter away. Somebody got hold of it and handed it over to the authorities. It was written in Modi script and the officers could not ascertain who was its writer. Mr. Barrie got it read by one of his confidents. But the political prisoner dared not depose before me, when the case was on, that it was written by me. For, he feared his other friends in the prison. Whereupon, Mr. Barrie got his Bengali clerk to declare that the letter was written in Bengali, and to read it out before the Superintendent. But a friend on our side gave evidence to prove that the letter was not written in Bengali. "Damn me," said he, "if a single Bengali alphabet appears in that letter." The Superintendent was non-plussed, but Mr. Barrie held his own, and shouted, "Oh, Sir, these political prisoners have conspired not to give true evidence." At last, the clerk's word was accepted as truth and I was sentenced to be manacled for a week.

While so manacled, I appealed to the Chief Commissioner that he should make a thorough investigation and decide if the letter, put in evidence, was written in Bengali or Modi. The complaint was against false evidence about the letter in question. It did not matter to me if the sentence passed upon me was not annulled. The Commissioner replied that the letter contained not a single word in Bengali. The clerk had deposed otherwise and had read the letter clearly and boldly in the Bengali script and had interpreted it to mean that I had advised the prisoners to go on hunger strike. The Superintendent, when he knew of the report of the Commissioner upon the letter, was simply in a rage. He sent for the clerk and asked Mr. Barrie to go out. He threatened the clerk with punishment if he were not to tell the whole truth. The clerk was terribly frightened and blurted out, "Sir, I am only a prisoner. I have to do what Mr. Barrie orders me to do. I swore that the letter was in Bengali and I drew upon my wit to read its contents as if it was a Bengali script. It is not so, but I read what I was made to repeat in original Bengali. It was all under Mr. Barrie's instruction that I did it." The Superintendent was beside himself with anger, but to save Mr. Barrie, he dismissed the clerk as the guilty person, he removed him from the job and informed me that, as I said it, the letter was not in Bengali and that he had taken proper steps against the clerk who had misled the court.

Mr. Barrie was Scolded

The Superintendent gave it hot to Mr. Barrie and warned him against practising such a deceit upon him. Whenever, in rare cases, the political prisoners taught Mr. Barrie a lesson, he used to be as meek as a lamb with them during the succeeding weeks. He then recollected that he was an Irishman. He said to us, "Oh my friends, I am an Irishman; when I was young I hated the English as you hate them now. I have been a conspirator myself; I behave like this now simply because I am a government servant, and I have to carry out orders. Why do you consider me your enemy? If you suffer, it is the government to blame and not I. I am innocent." He used to be loquacious and ended his rigmarole with an apt story. He used to give us, during these weeks of expiation, a paper to read as an occasional act of favour. And we did make a full use of such facility and thanked him for it, taking him to be honest for the time being, and wasting no more flattering words on him. For, we had to give even the devil his due.

Excepting these two cases against me, the rest of my period was completed without any flaw. As such, I kept on sending petitions for outdoor work as it was my due after the lapse of one year and a half in that prison. For other prisoners, who had been sent out before me had not only cases against them, but had also gone on strike. My brother had already put in two-and-a-half years. Some time I got an answer as follows: "You are not a political prisoner; you are classed as an ordinary prisoner." And I used to reply, "Ordinary prisoners include thieves, robbers and dacoits. They also have among them some who have broken open prisons, escaped from them, are hardened criminals and sentenced several times. But they are also detailed for out-door work and have become petty officers and *jamadars* in this prison. If I am an ordinary prisoner, then I must get the same concessions as they. I should have been let out long ago. You should have appointed me as a petty officer or a *jamadar*. For, I have not against me any charges of breach of discipline in this prison." At long last, the Chief Commissioner wrote categorically that I was not to be sent out For any work outside the prison-walls. The reason he had given for this final decision was that though my conduct in that prison was exemplary, I had a very dangerous past behind me. If the past conduct was the criterion of decision, where was the point in the remark that my present conduct was unexceptionable? The sum and substance of it all was that I may behave well or ill, I was always to be treated as a prisoner. There was no getting out of that position even for a slight concession.

While I was being dealt with in this manner inside the prison, the political prisoners, who were sent for work outside the prison, were being treated more harshly than before. All of us had begun to think that it was part of our duty to make an organised move to retaliate on behalf of Indu Bhushan, the account of whose tragic end I have given in the previous pages. They had misrepresented him and they had sought to prove that he had done himself to death in a fit of insanity. We felt that we must do something to set things right in this affair. And we decided after considerable discussion and deliberation that strike was the only weapon that could bring the authorities to their senses. We further felt that we must be recognised as political prisoners not only for purposes of maltreatment, but also for purposes of due concessions, that whether we were kept inside the prison or sent out on the settlement, we must be given comparatively light work to do, some writing work inside according to our ability, or some light work outside according to our status. Nothing should be forced upon us simply to undermine our health as was being purposely done then. Political prisoners, other than those who had been transported here on life-sentence, should be treated like ordinary prisoners, so on and so forth. We put down these demands in a serial order, and we selected two of us as our representatives to submit the petition personally to the authorities. In the petition, I had pointed out that prisoners on transportation for life did not get even the ordinary facilities of other prisoners, like sending and receiving letters, or occasional meeting with relatives and friends, or facility to read and write, or to be taken up as petty officers. We were not recognised as ordinary prisoners entitled to these concessions and we got no facilities as prisoners belonging to a special class. If we claimed any rights as political prisoners, we were put off with the excuse that ordinary prisoners would resent the partiality shown to us, and the prison-officers would not be a party to such a decision. To sum up, we were subjected, as political prisoners, to all the disabilities of prison-life in India and the Andamans, without the compensating facilities afforded to ordinary prisoners in all the jails of India, as well as in the Cellular Jail of the Andamans. I ended the petition with a solemn warning that no longer shall we tolerate such treatment of political prisoners in the jail presided over by Mr. Barrie. 'No relief, no concession, then no work'—that was our final resolution on the matter. And, in carrying out of this solemn covenant, we were prepared for the worst. Our petition, like all other petitions before it, went for nothing, and strike was the weapon we decided to employ. One by one, the political prisoners outside began to retire to their cells in the Silver Jail. The prisoners inside stopped all work on the fixed day and, thus, the strike began. This was the second strike during my period in the prison of the Andamans.

My brother had joined the strike on its first day. Prisoners were handled severely for this species of non-cooperation. Batch after batch of civil resisters was hauled up before the Superintendent, and sentences were passed upon them of putting on handcuffs, or chains on the arms, or shackles on the feet, or solitary confinement in the cells. Every block of the Silver Jail, and every room in that block witnessed the scene of prisoners hanging with their manacled hands tied to the top above. Some tried to squat on the ground with the chains on their hands and feet. Others offered stern resistance when shackles were being put on their feet. Others deliberately broke the rule of perfect silence and kept on talking loudly with one another. Others, again, refused to stand up, when Barrie would come to see them. Most of them had stopped work. When Mr. Barrie came, the petty officers announced him as 'Sircar'. Ordinary prisoners, off their guard, would stand up. But the political prisoners, to a man, firmly sat upon the ground, and it took three men to dislodge them, each one from his seat and put him on his feet. Mr. Barrie would not like the exhibition of enforced respect, and he could not continue this exhibition endlessly. The political prisoners were given no food as retaliation against their stopping of work.

Food stopped or cut Down

Some of these were given very scanty food to eat and others were put on conjee without salt from weekend to weekend. Some skirmishing also began between the guardians of law and these passive resisters. So, there were obvious signs of impending disaster all about the prison. When the news came to my ears, I sent for Mr. Barrie and warned him to take care. I added, "They are at present only civil resisters. They disobey the law and you punish them for disobedience. And I don't blame you for that. But if you are going to punish them in a manner to infringe your own regulations, then these infuriated young men will not fail to retaliate. They will return blow for blow.

They realise that you will crush them. But they are like vipers. Even a worm turns, and they will not fail to sting you to the quick before you are able to scotch them. The responsibility of all this will rest on your petty officers who hammer them, and who set on each one of them, three of your creatures to pinion them and beat them down. Your petty officers are cruel, they are bullies and cowards. They abuse and they beat. The Pathan, the Punjabi, and the Musalman—they are your agents in this nefarious business. But, be sure about it, abuse will meet with abuse and blow will meet with blow, before long. Our political prisoners are up to that game if you would have it. The Pathan and the Mussulman petty officers will stand aghast when they get such abuses from them—the choicest abuses, the like of which they may never have heard before. And abuse invariably leads to blows. And I have already warned you of the consequences; so you had better muzzle your men." This warning was not without its effect on Mr. Barrie. He misrepresented me, all the same, to his superiors as the arch-instigator of the strike, and of violence that would come in its wake. I had not yet gone on strike myself. For, I was expecting everyday my annual letter from home. I had asked the political prisoners to wait till they had received their letters. Besides, my letter always contained fuller news of events in India, and that had afforded to all of us ample matter for discussion later on. It used to be circulated throughout the prison for perusal by political prisoners. As the time was near for receiving the letter, I had decided to postpone going on strike till the receipt of that letter. As I have mentioned above, my brother had already stopped work and joined the strike.

As the strike went on, Mr. Barrie began to meet with insult from every quarter, as he had never done before that time. All the prisoners seemed to view things differently. They behaved with perfect indifference. He tried his utmost to re-establish his influence over them by striking terror into their hearts. How hard put to it he was! Sometime this led to funny incidents. Among the political prisoners, some knew English nominally, but they talked to Mr. Barrie in his own tongue like others. Mr. Barrie took it into his head that these prisoners wielded influence over the rest, because they were able to speak to him in English. He told them one day that they had no right to use English in their talks with him. He said, "You do not know good English and, therefore, you must express yourself like common prisoners in Hindusthani alone."

Well, they began to act up to his precept. No sooner said than done. The very first sentence they spoke in Hindi was to the effect, "We don't regard English as the language of the Gods. You addressed us in English and we replied in English that was all. It is not a shame to us that we cannot speak English well; the more shameful thing, indeed, is that, being born an Irishman, you do not know your mother-tongue, which is Irish. It is a credit to us that we don't talk such fine English as to make us forget our mother-tongue. You ought to be ashamed that you speak English so well and altogether forget your native Irish." Mr. Barrie, exposed to this barrage of Hindi sentences that all understood so well in this prison, became an object of ridicule to all of them. They began to stare at him with gaping eyes. Whenever he talked to us in English, they did not understand him so well, and our answers to him in English lost all their significance and innuendo for them. And though really crestfallen, he used to stand to his ground as if he was a hero and a victor. But now he stood thoroughly exposed, and every prisoner henceforth answered him straight in Hindi, and more so the political prisoners than anyone else. Question and answer followed like an exchange of bullet-shots. The Northerners among us were fine Hindi speakers. To Barrie, they gave answers as he deserved. If he talked to them politely, they returned the compliment in choicest Hindi. But if he was rough, coarse and abusive to them, they retaliated in Hindi, which he could never cope with in abuse, satire, innuendo and brutal frankness. So, he was confounded and scared by their talk to them in Hindi. He would have fain returned to English, if it was possible for him to eat his own words. I may give here a few samples of these quick repartees. One day he said to a political prisoner in his usual way, "You, Hindusthanis, are all slaves." He was full of exultation over this jibe, for he showed through it, he imagined, how he was looking down upon them. Out came the prompt answer from a political prisoner, "Indians, if they are slaves at all, are slaves of Englishmen. We are not your slaves. You are the slave of slaves, for England holds Ireland in subjection. We Indians are prepared to fight for freedom with our lives. But you serve those who throw a few crumbs of office at you. You bark like dogs for the master who feeds them. You regard as your own the British Empire that has enslaved your people as much as they have enslaved us, and are proud to be the watch-dogs of that Empire. You bark and bite at us because we do not recognise this Empire as our own." This retort in Hindi to the supercilious Mr. Barrie made all the prisoners giggle with laughter, and Mr. Barrie became red in the face with shame and anger. It was he that had begun the discussion and introduced politics, and he was floored in that discussion. The only recourse left to him was to shout out. And he did shout, "No more of your Hindi, speak in English."

But now the political prisoners would not listen to him. "You ordered us to speak in Hindi. You forbade us to speak in English. Now we will stick to that order. No more of English for us." Thenceforward, not once did he say to anyone that he must talk to him in Hindi. He learnt the lesson of his life, and expressed a desire that we should all address him in English alone.

Many things had happened in this prison to spoil its discipline and lower the prestige of its authorities. And the resistance of political prisoners made that discipline and prestige totter to their fall. All the weapons in the armoury of its officers had spent themselves. Only caning remained to be used with such frequency as the other weapons were used. The officers were at their wit's end—what to do with us. They threatened us to beat with cane, but none of us minded that threat. At last, the Chief Commissioner asked the Superintendent as also Mr. Barrie to make overtures to us. He told us through them to return to work. He promised that he would give light work to us, and assured us that he would see that the political prisoners would be sent out for work like ordinary prisoners. And lastly, he also promised that he would definitely take up our case with the higher authorities to determine our status as a class of political prisoners. So, some among us resumed work, and, as soon as it was resumed, they were given lighter work to do, and they were also sent abroad. When we got the news, a change of opinion began that we should not now strain too much. I had always considered it desirable that my friends, the political prisoners, should have the freedom of going out for work in the settlement, for I was sure that it would help me in my propaganda, and would pave the way for my escape from the prison. So, I advised them to call off the strike and go to work. If all of them were not treated equally in the matter of outdoor work, we were free to declare strike once again. Within a few days, the prisoners resumed their normal life and my brother was one of them. The officers kept their word and sent many political prisoners on light work outside the prison, such as watching the coconuts, sweeping the streets and so on. If they had continued this policy, the strike would have ended at once. But they refused permission to the ringleaders to work outside. My brother, Mr. Wamanrao Joshi, Hotilal, Nani Gopal and two or three others were denied that right. Of course, I was out of question. I had never given up my work even during the progress of the strike, though I did not escape the charge that I was their ring-leader. It was well that the political prisoners, who had been punished many more times than myself for breach of discipline in and outside the prison, were chosen, after the strike, to be detailed for that work as before. They had gone on strike as their last recourse against the tyranny of their prison-life. I asked the officers why a thing that was just in their case should not be so in mine. The only answer they could give me was the remark of the Chief Commissioner that "my previous history in India had prevented them from doing so". I answered to it that there were others like me involved in that history and sentenced to life-imprisonment for the same offence, but they had got the relief that was being denied to me. The previous record of that jail was that a prisoner was set free to go out and work on the settlement without regard to his previous history, if in the prison itself he had done nothing to violate its regulations. Besides, there were instances in that record of those who had been granted the concession in spite of the fact that they were prisoners on two to three years' sentence and were clapped in this jail for the offence of breaking open and escaping from prisons in India. Invariably, the reply was that the Government of India had ordered not to give me that relief. How long and for how many years was this ban to continue in my case? That they could not say definitly, I, therefore, decided to appeal directly to the Government of India.

They would not let me Appeal

I was, therefore, in a fix. My brother was in the prison much earlier than I came in. But even he was not being let out though he had been long assured of the concession. While discussing and arguing in this fashion, the Superintendent of the jail said to me, "Your protests are, no doubt, unanswerable, but, there is no doubt, it is you who encourage the strike." To it my answer was, "But those who were actually in the strike have already been sent out. Why do you then come in the way of one who, like me, has only approved of the strike? Is my offence really graver than theirs? Is it not against all laws of the British Code? Just consider why I had not encouraged strike so far, or if I had done it, why did not my friends approve of it before? Why should there have been a strike at the moment when it happened? Did I encourage Indu Bhushan to hang himself? Did I teach Ullaskar to go mad? It is not I but the regulations of this jail; its hard physical labour; its mental agonies; its insults; and its whole system that are to be held responsible for the strike." This way of reasoning convinced the Superintendent as also Mr. Barrie. Their stock answer was, "We are helpless; everything rested with the Government of India. It is their order that has compelled us to keep you in this prison." While I was fighting out my case, a new episode occurred and matters were carried to extremes. Among those political prisoners, who had held out to the last in the last strike, there was a Bengali youth sixteen or seventeen years old. He was a Brahmin lad from a respectable family. His name was Nani Gopal.

Nani Gopal was sentenced to fourteen years' rigorous imprisonment for throwing a bomb on the running motor of a high-police officer in Bengal. He was a lad of sixteen and in spite of prison-regulations to the contrary, he was put on the hard labour of the oil-mill. A struggle went on and he offered resistance. He had to suffer terribly in the last strike. He was segregated from his elders on the ground that they were spoiling him. But he did not give in. He resisted all the same. He was kept standing with manacles on. The more they punished him, the wilder he became. They punished him for the stoppage of work, but he gave up even washing his own clothes. He was given clothes made of gunny bags. He gave up wearing clothes, altogether. They held him fast on the ground and put those clothes upon him, and sewed them on his body, but he tore them off at night. Thereafter, he was put in chains. Hands and feet were both tied up. But during the night he managed to break the lock, snap the chains and set himself free. They abused him for the act, but he did not reply. He was punished for refusing to answer any question, and he refused to stand up before the officers. Then he was sent to solitary confinement and he refused to come out of his cell. He would not turn out even for bath. Then he was bodily lifted, stark-naked to be washed on the reservoir. He was stretched flat upon it, and the *Bhangis* washed his body. They rubbed his body with a piece of dry coconut shreds. And they rubbed it so hard that the skin was almost blood-red with the rubbing. The skin burnt, but he was not to be beaten. The Pathan warder, when he was alone with me, abused him in vulgar and indecent language. Nani Gopal went about naked during the day and they deprived him of one of his blankets at night. He threw off the other along with the first. So, he remained day and night stripped in body and at night shivering with cold on the bare floor of his prison cell. His contention was that the prison authorities should rank him among political prisoners.

Recognise me as a Political Prisoner

That was his contention all along. He never cared. He said what kind of food they gave him, for that was with him a minor matter. But the question of rank was not so insignificant for it was a question of honour with him. "We are," he said, "political prisoners and not thieves, robbers and dacoits." And the matter had to be decided once and for all. The Chief Commissioner informed him that status would never be given to him, do what he will. Nani Gopal would not surrender when the Chief Commissioner visited him personally and told him to his face, "You think that if you continue in this state you will melt our hearts, frighten us, and compel us to yield. That shall not be. We do not care even if you die. Believe it." The officers may not yield, but his behaviour gave them no rest, gave them furiously to think, was obvious to all of us. It was a creed with Mr. Barrie that two or three sharp raps with a cane were bound to bring a political prisoner to his knees. That was his experience with other prisoners in the jail. On the other hand, some of us quoted the order of Lord Morley that such a punishment was strictly forbidden in the case of political prisoners. We, therefore, thought that Mr. Barrie's words were but an empty threat. However, I did not fail to warn them that Mr. Barrie might carry out his threat in spite of Lord Morley, for in this prison he was his own master, and, if it came to that, he would get an order changed, that they must go on strike bearing this fact full well in their minds. The Burmese lads of sixteen and twenty took twenty or thirty strokes of the cane on their palms without wincing, because they were accustomed to that form of punishment from their early boyhood. They may also get accustomed to it, and take as many canes as Mr. Barrie gave them. This made Nani Gopal face the threat of the Chief Commissioner unconcerned. He would obey none, he would bend before none, and he would do no work, leave alone the 'Kolu'. In sheer desperation, the officers felt inclined to support Mr. Barrie and decided, at last, to resort to caning.

Nani Gopal was to be Caned

Mr. Barrie was the first to inform me of it and confidentially.

I told him frankly that though he was speaking to me confidentially, he was speaking as an officer that he had given me the news intentionally, that I may pass it on to my friends. I had, however, to warn him that if he ever used the cane on Nani Gopal its effect on all of us would be tremendous, and the consequences to him and to the prison would be terrible. All the political prisoners would be roused as they were never before roused in that jail. He had to recall, I told him how dangerous these men were and what horror and violence they were capable of once they were inflamed in mind. Their past deeds were witnesses to this fact and he had to think a hundred times before he caned Nani Gopal. I knew, I further told him, that his might was supreme to theirs and they would be crushed. But they will not fail to do, and will not shrink from doing, all they can. For the present, they only protest and offer civil resistance. But if he resorted to inhuman punishment like caning, they will unfailingly resort to violence and then anything might happen.

They will Shed blood and Not Refrain

"I do not say," I asked Mr. Barrie to note, "what should happen, but what cannot but happen." Mr. Barrie pretended to smile, but really he was startled. The punishment was announced, the frame was set up, we were all locked up in our rooms, every precaution was taken to prevent a riot and revolt. We were all ears to hear the piercing cry go forth from the mouth of Nani Gopal with the spurt of blood from his lacerated body. A warder came and informed us that Nani had been removed from that prison. He went away and presently an overseer came up to volunteer the information that the victim was thrashed within an inch of his life, and in indecent language he added, "Nani's had been rent into twain. I answered him calmly, "Nani has not suffered in the least, and I may tell you that if anyone has come worse off in this business, it is not he. For, I know that he has been transferred from this place elsewhere." The overseer was simply astonished and went back without making any reply. The petty officer soon learnt the mischief that the overseer was spreading. He issued orders to apprehend the man and went away in anger.

The news was correct, the sentence was pronounced, but no one was prepared to execute it. They telephoned to the Chief Commissioner, but he hesitated to give the final order. At last, Nani was taken down from the frame, the order was cancelled, and he was removed from the jail to be confined in a district prison for a few days. The Chief Commissioner carried but all this on the telephone, and the danger was avoided. That Nani Gopal was spared the ordeal made us all happy, but he himself felt bitterly disappointed. For, he was determined to bear the caning and hold out to the end. He was flush with it and now it had all gone. His courage extorted the admiration of his enemies. He was taken out of our midst and far away, perhaps with the belief that they would be able to tame him down in the new prison. Soon, they discovered how mistaken they were in this belief. For, in that new place, he, at once, went on hunger strike.

When Nani Gopal was among us, we had all along tried our best to dissuade him from that step. For three days, he went in that prison without a particle of food. But none paid the slightest attention to him. He did not eat and he did not speak. He lay on the ground without food and water. He was brought back to the Silver Jail, but he would not give up. Some five or six days it had continued like this, when they forced the food into him through a tube, as was allowed by the regulations of the prison. He was made to inhale milk through the nose. While this was going on in the prison itself, something happened outside that fell upon us like a bombshell.

The political prisoners, detailed for outside work, went, about from district to district and established contact with those who had become free and set up a house for themselves over the entire settlement. This was strictly forbidden by law, though all prisoners without exception fully availed themselves of the opportunity of work outside to move freely among the people in the locality where they worked. The political prisoners were specially interested in the spread of Swadeshi among those with whom they came in contact and to get from them bits of news that they would communicate to us inside the prison. There were in the settlement families of former prisoners of the Silver Jail. The new generation among them was free citizens and as such got reports of happenings in India without let or hindrance. We spread through them, by poems and articles, the spirit of Swadeshi all over the settlement. The articles sent out by us through this agency assumed the form of a circulating newspaper, and it helped build up the influence of political prisoners in the world around them. The news of this spreading influence was carried to the ears of the authorities in an exaggerated manner, so that before long, it was interpreted by them as a regular conspiracy. By this time, the letters, surreptitiously passed from here to India about the suicide of Indu Bhushan and the insanity of Ullas, had gone to their proper quarters. And they found their place and publicity in the newspaper world of India. This fact and the knowledge of it in the jail itself created a flutter in the official dovecotes. Even the most commonplace news was to us, prisoners of the Andamans, good tidings of great joy. A question about us in the Legislative Council gave us the strength and the hope to bear it all with patience here for a month following. For, we had begun to think of ourselves as the neglected ones of the earth, whom anyone could trample under foot with impunity; it had filled us with dark despair about our life. This news came as a ray of hope to illumine that darkness. And hope revived and with it courage, when we realised that our sufferings were not all in vain, but had in them the power to stir other men even as a drop of oil serves to flare up the burning fire into flame.

And it happened like that on the day I am writing about. Who must have sent the news to India and carried the letters was a matter of discussion among the jail authorities. And as they could not get at the source, they became more irritated than ever. Days went on in this way. When I was informed in reply to my former petitions that I was allowed to move out, and the officers would send me out on the following Monday, I was surprised at the reply! I felt that my brother also would be allowed to go out. I learnt by heart all the lines of poetry that I had scribbled on the walls of my room, and waited for the promised Monday to arrive. I was not sure all the same that they would keep their word. Monday dawned. Some prisoners were sent out, and I was not among them. I lay confined in my own cell. On the third day, the Superintendent came to me, and I asked him about it. As he was honest of word, he felt ashamed of himself as he was the man who had given me the news of the promised relief. The Chief Commissioner, he said, had gone to Rangoon and that I would know about it after his return. I felt doubtful about it. The Commissioner had gone to Rangoon to see the Lieutenant Governor, and, as soon as he had returned, there began, one fine morning, a regular campaign of arrest in the Andamans instead of my being sent out of the Silver Jail, as promised by the Superintendent when he saw me last.

Mass Arrests

Some were manacled, others were detained, and others again had their rooms searched. From the political prisoners, the campaign spread out to the houses of free citizens, of *jamadars* and tindels. The search and arrest party was manned entirely by European officers. And it did its work with terrible efficiency. It threatened, it shouted, it scolded and it terrorised, till the whole of the colony was stricken with nervousness and fear. The cause of all this noise and fury was that the officers had information of a bomb-factory started in the island by political prisoners working in the settlement. And it was not altogether without foundation. But the search and the arrests afforded no clue to it. Even a cracker did not come out in the search, not to speak of a bomb. The informant was a Bengali gentleman, Lalmohan by name. On two other occasions, he had similarly put the officers on a false trail. The officers were, of course, furious with him. It was the same warder who was suspected by them of delivering Hotilal's letter from the prison to its proper quarters. The warder had perhaps raised the canard to propitiate the gods he had displeased. However that be, the political prisoners suffered terribly by this tale-telling of Lalmohan. Rumours were afloat that a bomb was found in an adjoining brook; that letters were intercepted by the police containing the plan of chartering boats to take the prisoners across the seas. No one was sure of what he was saying and what he had heard. The only thing one was sure of was the wholesale arrest of political prisoners and their being clapped back into their cells. Now, we knew why the Chief Commissioner had gone to Rangoon. Mr. Barrie's stock went high up in the market. He dared say to the Commissioner himself that he was always telling him that these were dangerous men and never to be trusted. But, he continued, the Commissioner had always blamed him. They did not behave well even to him. They deserved nothing but kicks.

It gave me great anxiety about the future in store for me. I had already suffered enough in one conspiracy case, and I feared what this case would bring to me. We had already been on transportation for life, my life-sentence was fifty years. The Gods that did me that ill-turn may involve me in this and deal even worse with me. I never more thought of being sent out in the settlement. The manufacturing of bombs and the chartering of boats had made that out of question. The officers behaved insolently towards me and told me openly that I should no more think of it. They had final orders from the Government of India that I was not to be released from this jail till I had run my full sentence of fifty years or till I was dead before that time.

Who can describe the state of their mind, when these political prisoners heard these words from their officers? Some like me on life-sentence, all utterly helpless and locked up in their respective cells, with this new charge possibly hanging over their heads, and the nature of that charge still a mystery to them! A few days passed in this disordered and apprehensive state of mind, and they could not see their way out of it.

But this bewilderment continued no further and we were soon able to plan our future course. First of all, we made up our minds to entertain no unnecessary fears. Next, three of us were to write to the authorities to let them know definitely what the charge against them was. Thirdly, if our offence was bomb-making, plotting to escape from this place, conspiracy, or general revolt, we were to ask them to start criminal prosecution against us. The suspicion was, of course, against those of us who had been working outside the prison and the petition was forwarded in their names. They got a reply that the officers had not sufficient evidence in their hands to launch a prosecution. Then, they insisted on work outside the prison, when they were warned not to think of it. The ordinary suits in the Andamans were filed before a court without a pleader to conduct either the prosecution or the defence, without either assessors or a jury. And if a man like Mr. Barrie, who was an expert in concocting evidence, could not prosecute us before such a court, the conclusion was inescapable that the whole story must be both imaginary and exaggerated. But whatever the nature of the evidence, it was enough to damn us with the Government of India. For, it would afford them material enough to send highly coloured reports about miscreants in this prison, so that they could be doomed for life to rot in this jail. It was particularly so in an individual case like mine.

We have said above how our letters had reached India and how their publication in the newspaper had created a stir there. To this was added the report of a bomb-factory in the Andamans. The Government of India, therefore, decided to depute its own officer to ascertain the truth behind these two reports. And no less a person than the Home Member himself—Sir Reginald Craddock, afterwards Governor of Burma—undertook the voyage on that mission.

Usually, the arrival of such an officer to the Andamans, in itself a very rare occurrence, was kept a close secret from the inmates of the Silver Jail. None knew his name; often he came as a stranger and went as a stranger. His inspection of the prison was almost a farce, for the prisoners were seldom asked questions or gave answers. They looked upon him as a casual visitor and never took him seriously. He, therefore, did not know their real grievances and was often guided by those who chaperoned him. As a result, he went back to report that all was well in the Andamans, and there everything ended.

But, this time the political prisoners had got previous news of the arrival of the Home Member to the Andamans. And they were prepared to make the full use of this opportunity. They informed the jail authorities that some of us wanted to have a personal talk with that distinguished visitor. The authorities asked them how they had come to know of his impending visit, and who had told them about it. But we were not to be cowed down by such threats. When the officer was going the round of our prison, he was sure to pass by our cells. And if we were not allowed to talk to him, we had decided to invite his attention to us by raising a hullabaloo as he went along our blocks. It was no matter to us if we were punished for it after the event. They had tried this method on former occasions and suffered punishment for it. But 1913 was different in this respect from all the years before it. Sir Reginald Craddock came. A few prisoners were called out to meet him. Questions were put and answered. Some were told that they were the enemies of the Government and deserved nothing short of death. Others were told that they should never talk of being sent out for they were sentenced for high treason and they had conspired against the King. When some of us asked for proofs, the answer was that though they could not prove, they knew enough of it. My interview with Sir Reginald began on a different note altogether. Sir Reginald began, "Savarkar, to what a wretched state have you reduced yourself? I have studied all your books. If you had applied all your talents to nobler ends, there was no high place in Government service which was beyond you to fill and adorn. But you chose to fall into this wretched condition." To which I answered, "I am grateful to you for your kind wishes. I may tell you, however, that it is entirely in your hands to take me out of this. Mr. Gokhale has just brought in his resolution on compulsory education in the Imperial Legislative Council. If it is accepted by the Government, and if such measures of progress are assured to my people that they may rise as a nation, then not only myself, but all my friends who are dubbed as revolutionaries will be ready to turn to the path of peace. They must be thinking similarly, I feel sure, as I am speaking to you now."

Sir Reginald: How do you know this? Do you know where they are?

Myself: How is that possible? Am I not here confined in a solitary cell, and under your close watch and ward? But I know their minds as they know mine, and, hence, I draw this inference. If we advance definitely through methods of peace, it is immoral for us to enter on methods of violence. That is a principle with me, and I feel sure it is equally sound to them.

Sir Reginald: I am sorry you are entirely wrong there, for they are still advocating terrorism and they still swear by you. In India and in America, your followers are still busy with their plans of secret societies and revolutionary activities.

Myself: I know it for the first time from you. How can I prevent anyone from swearing by me? Why do you take it that I can influence them from here for the simple reason that they call me their leader? (The reference here was to the Gadar movement and its newspaper in America started by Har Dayal and other members of the Abhinav Bharat Mandal)

Sir Reginald: (After a little conversation on the subject) If you are really prepared to stand by what you have said just now, I may think of permitting you to write a letter embodying your views.

Myself: I shall be very glad, indeed, to write such a letter. But it must be sent by me independently.

Sir Reginald: It must go through us or through me at least.

Myself: Will it not mean that it was written under your pressure? I should write, I think, independently.

Sir Reginald: I cannot allow it.

Myself: Then, I am sorry, I cannot write it, for I feel that to write through your government will make it suspect.

Sir Reginald: (Looking at me closely as if we thoroughly understood each other): Well, what are your grievances? May I know them?

I then told him the full story of sufferings in the Silver Jail. I also described to him the disabilities and hardships of political prisoners as well, when the Chief Commissioner who was present on the occasion interposed, "But you, political prisoner, have you not murdered? Are you not violent? Have you not conspired to destroy the Government in power? If Russia were ruling here, they would all have been sent to Siberia or straightaway shot in the back. It is the British Government that is treating you so leniently. And it is your good fortune that you are under that Government."

Myself: I am sure, however, that Russia would not have disarmed India. Today, Russia enrols inhabitants in Siberia as well as foreigners in its army, and appoints them to responsible military posts. And it would have appointed Indians to the same posts, and if it had treated us as you do, we would have beaten them, as we beat and conquered the Mogal Emperors of India.

Sir Reginald: Your Hindu Rajas would have treated you much worse than we are alleged to be treating you now. Do you not know how they tied rebels to the foot of an elephant and crushed them?

Myself: Yes, I know it. And I know also that in England they dragged a prisoner along the street for felony and hanged him. But these are things of the past by which none should swear today. You don't hang a thief today in England. The fact is that the benefits of civilisation, wherever they may originate, are shared by all alike. Formerly, a traitor was trampled under the foot of an elephant, but the victor punished a king by sending him to the block. Charles I and the English rebellion are instances in point. On both the sides, the rule now is to follow civilised methods and, as you seemed to agree with us, we appeal to you to treat and judge us accordingly. If you say that you will treat us barbarously, we shall face the situation as best as we can.

After this long digression into history, we returned to the main subject. Some questions and answers passed between us about the management of the prisoners in our jail. Finally, I was told that the Government of India would reply, as it thought fit, on the subject under discussion. Sir Reginald Craddock came and went. But no reply was sent to us from India. The authorities in the Andamans told us to be satisfied with the interview, and reconcile ourselves to the status quo. But we decided that something had to be done; we could not take it lying low. With this decision made, we went on strike for the third time.

The third Strike

Except one or two, all of us struck work. Sentence after sentence were passed upon us of six months' imprisonment in chains. It was now one-month-and-a-half that Nani Gopal had gone on hunger strike. Only a little quantity of milk was dully administered to him through the nose. He was reduced to skin and bones. Even then this lad was sentenced to stand for a whole week with chains on his hands and feet. But he remained firm, nothing could deter him. But others, deeply touched by his sufferings—some six or seven in number—went on sympathetic hunger strike. They were put in chains and subjected to similar punishment. I had, by this time, my expected letter from India. But it was not given to me on the ground that it contained some objectionable matter. And I immediately joined in the strike. I was sentenced to stand for two weeks in a framework of fetters for my feet. This punishment was followed by chains for hands and feet interlinked with a chain between them. My informants told me the contents of that objectionable letter. There was in it a reference to the criticism of Keir Hardie in Parliament on my imprisonment in this jail.

Keir Hardie's Criticism

The gist of that criticism was that while in Ireland, the Government had taken no steps against those who had threatened open rebellion, who had raised armies to fight the partisans of Home Rule on the soil of England, a man like Savarkar, whose only crime had been to distribute pistols among his fellow-conspirators, was sentenced by the Indian Government to fifty years' transportation to the Andamans. If I had received the letter, the jailor felt that criticism in particular against my incarceration might go to our heads and it might lead to the intensification of strike in that jail. Hence, the letter was withheld from me. In the manifesto about the strike, we had made three principal demands: (1) As political prisoners, we should have all the privileges of the first class; or (2) We should, otherwise, be put in the category of ordinary prisoners, given all the facilities accorded to them and the periodical visit to this jail be permitted to members of our families; or (3) We should be sent back to serve our term in the jails of India, so that we may get all the facilities of that jail life, including reduction in the period of the sentence on certificate of good behaviour. During the strike, we defied all ordinary regulations of the prison. We were locked up separately and under strict guard. So, it had become difficult for us to communicate with one another. Even "the telephone method", described in previous pages, was no longer available to us. It broke down completely because we could not reach the iron-grating near the floor of our cell and in the wall to talk. Well, if the telephone had stopped, we hit upon the method of telegraph, and that again of the wireless telegraph. It went on splendidly for a long time. We had shackles on our feet and they had manacles on their hands. We rang them on the bars of our doors, according to a particular code. And the news went round not only through the three or four adjoining rooms, but through all the storeys of the near-by blocks. And in this mode of communication there was no scope for the warders to betray us. We carried on the communication in English to start with. My brother remodelled it into Nagari. Thus, we had a pure Swadeshi telegraphic code and message to run through the whole building. Marconi may have invented the wireless for the world, my brother hit upon the plan for our prison before Marconi's invention had reached the world of the Andamans.

Oh, now I Remember

By the way, as I am writing, I remember what the Capital of Calcutta had written about my brother. It had published the news that my brother had been appointed in this jail to run the wireless. You will please understand, my reader, that the news was not altogether without foundation! In vain, did we threaten the Capital with a suit and exact its apology! Yes, my brother was, indeed, working the code; the mistake lay in the fact that he communicated by it with two or three rooms close by, and not, as it had alleged, with Germany during the outbreak of the first World War. But what is 'space' and 'time' to the philosopher of the Capital?

We conveyed our messages through this device to all the political prisoners in our jail, and whatever we proposed to do, we did, all as one man. Mr. Barrie was ever at the throat of the warders to extort how the communication was effected and how combined action was undertaken. The Pathan warders were ignorant blockheads. They made no head or tail out of the sounds they heard. They did not grasp why the handcuffs were sounded or knocked in a particular manner. If any one of them shouted out to enquire, we said we were keeping tune to the singing of religious songs, which we recited inwardly. At last, one of them suspected foul play. He made out sound responding to sound in regular sequence all over the building and in the rooms of the prisoners. And he reported his suspicion to Mr. Barrie. One night Mr. Barrie went silently over all the blocks in the building. He heard these sounds and their rhythmic beats. It was not difficult for him to make out what it was. He went back with an order to the warders not to let the devils make these noises. But who would listen to the warders? Who would obey the order? Were we not out for passive resistance?

During this period of noise and disobedience, we were taken out everyday for our dinner for one hour in the morning and one hour in the evening. Mr. Barrie kept standing before us during the hour, lest we might talk to one another. For two or three days at the beginning, everything went on quietly. On the fifth day, however, while all of us had sat down to our meal and we were eating it, each from his own plate, we heard someone lecturing to us. The opening words that fell on our ears were, "Brothers! We are free!"

Everyone was startled and looked up. And behold, here was Nani Gopal who had uttered the words to defy the 'silence' order of Mr. Barrie.

And he went on: "Brethren, we are all born free. It is our birthright to speak to one another with love and kind greetings. If an enemy were to deprive us of that right, we must challenge him. Here I am speaking to you and will continue speaking." Hardly had these words escaped his lips, when, bursting with rage, Mr. Barrie, Mirza Khan and the Pathan warder rushed at him. Nothing daunted, Nani Gopal went on with his eloquent discourse. He was lifted up bodily out of us and locked in the room. Still he had kept on talking and had not finished his peroration. The political prisoners could not contain themselves for laughter, and Mr. Barrie's anger knew no bounds Pathan or Hindu.

Mirza Khan presently came to my room. He could not hold his peace; he seemed eager to unburden his heart to me, and said, "Bada Babu, that young fellow is your true disciple, I mean Nani Gopal. He is loyal to the core. His daring becomes a Pathan like me more than anyone else. He is verily a Pathan lad." I answered, "Bada *jamadar*, you are wrong. Your father was a Pathan and you are a Pathan. If he were a Pathan, he would not have rotten in this jail for the sake of his country; he would have, like you, licked the shoes of Mr. Barrie and would not have defied him. If Mr. Barrie said it was night you would say 'yea' to him even though it was day. It is because Nani Gopal is a born Hindu that he is so brave. I am full of admiration for his daring and intelligence. But if all the Pathans were brave and all the Hindus were cowards, how could the Hindus have overthrown the Pathan or the Mussulman Raj in India?"

The Hunger Strike Ends

I was always against the suicidal policy of hunger-strike, as I regarded it as ruinous to the individual and ruinous to the cause. That was not the way to fight the enemy, I maintained strongly. My view had its desired effect on the mind of our friends and they gave up the hunger-strike. The hardest nut to crack was Nani Gopal. He would not yield. He was on the verge of death. I, therefore, employed all extreme measure to overcome his resistance. I threatened him with hunger-strike if he would not give up his own. And the following day I acted up to my word.

I went on Hunger-Strike

The news that I had stopped taking my food went like wild fire round the prison. The officers were full of fear. It was all stir and excitement among them. The Chief Commissioner expostulated with the Superintendent to put an end to it. I was tried for this new offence. But in the trial, instead of punishing me, they exhorted me to break the fast. I told them why I had gone on hunger-strike, and asked them to permit me to speak to Nani Gopal. When Nani heard the news that I had declared three days' hunger-strike, he was stricken with grief. I was taken to his cell by Mr. Barrie. I saw him and he agreed to break his fast. I took him aside and whispered, "Do not die like a woman; if you must need die, die fighting like a hero. Kill your enemy and then take leave of this world."

He Dines and I Break My Fast

From this time onwards, we had our two meals, and had plenty of coconuts to eat in addition to them. The quantity of daily ration had been reduced for strikers. Yet they consumed it all and would not work. Why do you starve yourselves? Take as much food from them as, you can, grow fat and don't work, This was the mantra I gave them and they followed it to the letter. All forms of punishment by the jailor were exhausted in our case. And we were hauled up before the Magistrate. Some got two months, some four, and Nani Gopal was given one year's rigorous punishment. But the strike continued all the same. At last, the Government of India had to come out with a special notification on the subject. It was about the new order of things affecting us as political prisoners in the Silver Jail of the Andamans.

The New Order

What did the notification say? What was there in it so that our officers read it out to us so grandiloquently? Well, the following were some important items in that notification:

(1) All the prisoners who were sentenced to a definite period of time, short of life-sentence shall be sent back to their respective prison in India, where the remission of their sentences will be duly considered and followed.

(2) Prisoners on life-sentence shall be detained in this prison for a continuous period of fourteen years, whereafter they will be set free for some labour of a light character. This shall operate only in the case of those prisoners who give proof of good behaviour during their period of incarceration.

(3) During the period of fourteen years, the prisoner shall be given

decent food to eat, and decent clothes to wear. After five years, he shall be allowed to cook his own food and given from twelve annas to a rupee per month as his pocket allowance.

The end of the third Strike

From the concessions granted in the notification, it is easy to realise that many of them had confirmed to the demands made by the strikers. Although the notification had stated that the order was final, we knew what to think of them, for, in the opinion of the political prisoners, nothing was a settled fact that could not be unsettled. However, we decided to accept what had come to us, and to end the dispute for the present. We, therefore, called off the strike and resumed work.

Soon after, the term-convicts began to be sent back to the prisons in India. We, who were left behind, did not fail to remind them that in India, they must give as much publicity as they could to the prevailing harsh condition in the Andamans, and with every chalan despatched to the Andamans, they had to send us news from India. As these political prisoners were distributed all over India, it was easier for them to do this double work. And be it said to their credit that they did their part remarkably well. After the exit of the term-convicts, those who had remained behind on life-sentence like me were very few in number. There were one or two term-convicts still with us. We were all allowed in batches to cook our own food. As such, we got clean and well-cooked food to eat. Some of us were detailed for work in the printing press, in the library, and on map-drawing, of which we shall write in its due place. And each of them earned about ₹ 10 a month from such work. Those who had not seen a single rupee since their incarceration, had now with them five to ten rupees every month, a change in their status equivalent to that of a millionaire among beggars. So, many of those were at their beck and call for anything they needed. Don't think it was a miracle. That was bound to happen in a prison like the Silver Jail, and in a place like the Andamans.

About those on Life-Sentence

All this was no less than a revolution in the life of a political prisoner. But to what extent was I benefited by it? Not very much indeed! I was given no writing work to do. I was not appointed to supervise any factory. The only satisfaction I had was to see my friends in better condition than myself. Myself and my brother had to weave the same strand, and do the same work. Later on, my brother and Wamanrao Joshi were transferred to the cooking department, and they cooked for all of us. I was the same solitary prisoner, in the same solitary cell, and in the same block No. 7. The administration of the Silver Jail in my time had one policy to follow, and Mr. Barrie had defined it to me many times before. The keynote of that policy was: “Savarkar was the father of unrest in the Andamans; he was to be given no quarter and shown no mercy.”

We have reached the year 1914 in our narrative. Here ends the first part of the history of our agitation in the Andamans. The political prisoners in the Silver Jail were mainly responsible for that agitation. We now enter on an epoch fraught with immense changes in the world as the result of the First World War. It had also its repercussions, mainly political, on India. And these affected, in no small degree, life in the Andamans as well, and changed the course of its future history. In the years till 1914, the political prisoners had directed all the energy of their mind and will to improve their own condition in the prison-life of the Andamans. And the first part of our narrative describes that struggle. After 1914, they concentrated their work on the awakening of the people in the Andamans and on putting new life into them. This remarkable difference between the two periods naturally divides our narrative also. We end its first part here, and will give the rest of the story in the part that follows.

□

PART - II

1
Consolidation and Propaganda in the Andamans

In the first part of this narrative, I have given an account, not of prisoner's life and condition only but mainly that of the political convicts in the prison-house of the Andamans. The story is brought down to the year 1914. The struggle, the courage, the tenacity of will, and the fight for principle of the political prisoners, during the period, had their effect on other Hindu prisoners in that jail and had instilled into them the spirit of social and cooperative endeavour. They had gradually begun to realise the meaning and significance of words like 'country', 'religion', and 'service' in relation to themselves and to the larger community of which they were also social units. The Mussulman warder, as also the Mussulman prisoner, had each his copy of the Koran to read in the jail. And, sometimes they apparently read the Koran to put off their normal work. This facility was dented to their Hindu brethren in that jail. These had no religious books given them to read and understand. They could keep none of them themselves; and it was an offence to read them openly. Either the superior officer strictly banned them, or the lesser man—the Mussulman *jamadar*—would not get them any copy of their religious scriptures. If a few of them even on a holiday gathered together sometime to read and hear the Ramayana of Tulsidas, the Muslim warder or *jamadar* would suddenly disperse the assembly by force and loud abuse. I had seen these happenings myself, and several times, looking at the pictures in such a book, they denounced as indecent; and they regarded it as a religious duty not to allow prisoners to see and read such stuff. Not tolerating such interference and coercion, the political prisoners often carried the matter to the superior officers. And this knocking at the door resulted, in the long run, in the prisoners' freedom to keep a religious book. After his day's work, from that time onwards, the prisoner could openly keep also a slate and pencil to con his alphabets and write them.

There was extreme partiality on the part of the authorities as regards their holidays. On a Mohammedan holiday, the Mussulman prisoner was allowed to spend the whole day in idleness and free talk with his fellow-men. The Hindu prisoner, on the other hand, got very few holidays in the first instance. Some holidays were not even recognised as holidays for Hindu prisoners of that jail. And when they got the holiday at all, their warders and *jamadars* gave them the Hobson's choice at work or solitary confinement in their own cells. The prisoners, at this threat, went quietly to work for they knew by experience what the other alternative had meant for them. To put an end to this glaring partiality, I induced all of them to stop work and also joined them in the strike. When the Superintendent came on the spot and found the atmosphere too hot for him, he turned to me and spouted, "The Hindus shall have their due holidays but they must not make such a grievance of it. If they do so again, they shall be handled severely. I forgive them now, for, I do not ordinarily like to punish them."

As I have written above, the prisoners were given the facility of keeping a slate and pencil. The question remained of procuring books for them. The ordinary prisoners came as a rule from families ignorant of books. If they ordered books, they would get instead parcels of rich pairs of shoes, never a book worth two annas apiece! To ask the Government to provide books for them to learn their three ₹ was bound to prove mere waste of ink and paper. That a book or two was spared them was in itself an act of favour. I, therefore, got these books through our own parcels from home, and distributed them widely among these prisoners. Elementary books of geography and history, readers and books on arithmetic—these I gave them. And days passed on in this arrangement.

Soon, we set up a central organisation to do the work with method and precision.

I have already told of the beginning we had made to take within our fold, by solemn oath and declaration, prisoners who had no training whatever in the political work they had done. I have also narrated the efforts made to educate them in the ideals of social service which included the service of their country. I had begun later on to include in that organisation ordinary prisoners as well, and to instil into them similar principles. These prisoners, when they went for outside work after six months' or one year's stay in that prison, started similar organisations in the centres of their work. It was these organisations that imposed a rising scale of fees from one anna in a rupee to eight annas in five rupees, as an educational cess, on persons in their respective localities. Some of the skilled political prisoners earned as much as forty rupees a month. And when the political prisoners had won freedom for work outside, they spread the net wider and got ordinary traders and other independent men to subscribe to this education fund, and also to interest themselves in the general politics of their country. Those, who were pledged by solemn oath to carry on the task, had also done their work splendidly in the districts where they went. The political prisoners and others had got themselves acquainted with the independent settlers in these islands. These had come there on business or on mechanical jobs in factories, as doctors and lawyers or as officers in other lines of service. They were all, more or less, educated men, and they also, as the result of our acquaintance with them, had pledged themselves to Swadeshi. They paid five percent of their monthly income to our organisation. Some of them took advantage of our institution to learn Hindi, both to read and write. We had organised a library of select books on Constitutional History, on the History of Politics, on Economics and on the Science of Government, according to a list I had already drawn up for the purpose. They either purchased these books for themselves, or read them from our library. The funds of the association and its general management were looked after by us without any correspondence or written constitution. We had to work secretly because we had to count upon the opposition of the jail officers to our programme.

We provided the prisoners with books, slates, pencils and readers to begin with. There was yet another difficulty in our way. The jailor was sure to question them how these books had come to them. Many a prisoner had suffered punishment for keeping books and writing material with him. If a warder told that he had received the book from me, he was sure to lose his job or be sent back to work on the 'Kolu'. He was forbidden to talk with a political prisoner. What then of accepting a book from him? Therefore, when a warder went out on a holiday the book had to be sent in with him as a gift from a relative. So, we spread the readers among prisoners in this jail.

More than this difficulty, there was another that we had to overcome and that was the reluctance of the prisoner himself. Whenever one asked him to begin reading and writing, the stock question that he put was, "What was the use of it?" If we dwelt on their intellectual benefit, or their national importance, it was out of his power to understand us. Again, Mr. Barrie was particularly cross with those who liked to read and write. And the prisoner had no desire to incur Mr. Barrie's displeasure. By no means. Still we tried to educate those who came in close contact with us; we offered him to teach English as soon as he had finished his Marathi; we showed him its advantage by pointing out that it would lead to some post associated with the office; that he would be a 'Munshi' or a clerk. That would mean an honour for him. Many prisoners learnt to read and write because that would lead them to that post. There were also a few who learnt the language for its own sake, because it was their mother-tongue, or it would enable them to read religious works in that language. There were also some among them who learnt to spell their rudiments after they had passed their youth, and only as a national call. All honour to them.

How strenuous the work was, you can imagine from the fact that we had to begin everything in that education from the very beginning. We had to teach them the A.B.C. of their vernacular alphabets; we had to take them through the formation of words through these alphabets; we had to plod on with them that they might remember them, write them and make them into simple sentences. And all this work had to be done secretly and regularly. We had to wheedle them into pursuing their lessons from day to day. Sometimes, the prisoners would not accept the slates and pencils that we gave them free for writing their lessons; others refused to talk to us for fear we might open to them the subject of learning. We gave them tips to induce them to read and write. We paid them in the currency of the Andamans. Rupees, annas and pais were not so important a currency with them as what they called "Sukka", that is, payment in quantities in tobacco. If we gave a prisoner two pinchfuls of tobacco, he would bestow upon his teacher the favour of reading his lessons with him for fifteen to twenty minutes at the most. This heartbreaking work was hard to pursue from day to day, and my collaborators simply refused to go on with it after a few days' experience. This was a waste of time, energy and talent, as they put it to me. They were themselves graduates and double graduates and it was hard on them to be giving lessons in rudiments to ignorant, dull-headed, disinclined pupils like the thieves, dacoits, murderers, swindlers, and hardened criminals in this jail. While teaching them the three ₹ they had so many times to flatter them, and break their heads over them. Whenever this mood came over myself or other teachers, I would talk in the following words, "You think it a waste of your energy; what better work can you do for your country, what more important work can you accomplish while you are here? He who would assure me of such work, I shall relieve him at once of this drudgery. But to waste one's time in idle brooding or in useless discussion is worse than this drudgery. For, this, at least, means to raise the fallen by teaching them to read and write; it is to infuse into them the right sense of looking at things; it is to imbue them with the spirit of service and mutual help. Is it not service to the country, the hardest it may be, but sterling service, all the same? Remember again that we pass resolutions to establish schools of primary education, free and compulsory all over the country. Some men must come forward to teach in these schools. Some must dedicate their lives for this work. Why then, not do that thankless task ourselves? Are we only meant for drawing fat salaries and filling top-jobs and passing on drudgery and hard work to others? Is this not unfair? Is it just for us who call ourselves servants of the people? Real and faithful national work must begin with the uplift of the down-fallen and the down-trodden. Great missionaries in the West dedicate their lives to spread education among prisoners and in jails of their own countries. In Russia, thousands of revolutionaries have spent their lives in going from village to village and educating the masses, their unfortunate and ignorant brethren. Why then should we grudge to do it here? By our teaching, we are not only making them learn to spell their rudiments; but we are opening the windows of their soul upon the world, and making them understand their best interests in life. In contact with us, they come to know of their country, of their nation, and of their people. They imbibe right notions into them from us. When we tell them stories of great men from our history of the past, light shines in their eyes. Are they the really fallen ones? Then what are we? We were not born emancipated. If we have improved and are 'twice-born' now, they also can improve and take their rank with us. Hence, so long as we cannot do better work than this, that long we must do this, for that is real national service, however laborious, disappointing and nerve-racking it may be. To educate the fallen into seeing right and feeling right, to give them as much of literary, intellectual, moral and national education as it is in our power to give them is a duty we must do as long as we are in this prison."

As we kept on working with this faith, gradually there arose from among these outcasts of society men so generous, so selfless, so pure in life and conduct, so strong of purpose, so tenacious of will, that their zeal in the national cause put to shame some of the best workers among us. And before the former self-praise became a fatuity and a shame.

We Started a Library

Having provided reading books and writing material for ordinary prisoners in the jail, I set myself to the task of founding a decent library for the use of the political prisoners themselves. We called upon all of them to put their own collection of books together. Seeing the circular, Mr. Barrie, as usual, strongly opposed the move. He realised that we were bent upon carrying it out, and communicated to the Superintendent that the political prisoners were unwilling to part with their valuable collection of books and hand it over into the common stock. He brought forward his own pawns to support the move. These good men informed the Superintendent that they were opposed to this common collection, whereupon the Superintendent asked us how we could bring all the books together and form a common library, when a large number of political prisoners disapproved of that proposal. I proposed to the Superintendent to have a referendum on that subject, and he would know the truth of the matter. On this, Mr. Barrie went round and threatened everyone of them that if they voted for a common library, he would burn such books from it as bore pencil marks on them or notes in their margin, by one who was not the owner of those books.

In spite of this and other threats by Mr. Barrie, when the Superintendent came the next day to sound our opinion, all of us voted in favour except the two or three among us who were the henchmen of Mr. Barrie. As regards Mr. Barrie's threat of burning the books, I said, "In the proposed collection, I have my own precious and valuable books worth three hundred rupees; and I must have a library in this prison for free and common use by all the political prisoners, and I do not mind if you bum my books out of the collection. Every prison has a library of its own provided by the Government. But none of us can use it. Now we start a library on our own, and we lend our books for that purpose. We have sought your permission to help us. Why then should you find it hard to grant our request?" The Superintendent was a man of progressive views. He agreed to our proposal and started a library, only omitting from the collection the books of those who had objected to it. Every Sunday, a political prisoner could go to the library and get such books issued to him as he wanted for his reading during the week. The library gave them an opportunity of reading books on a variety of subjects, and such of our political prisoners as had no chance of ordering books from home could read them freely in the library. Those of us who could order out books from home, timed our orders in a manner that the parcels came to each one of us one after the other; and not all at the same time. Again, we arranged matters between us that each parcel should contain a different set of books. The avoidance of overlapping in time and books, enabled us to read many books and on many subjects, without multiplying copies of the same books. We procured in this manner books in Bengali, Hindi, Panjabi and Sanskrit without unnecessary burden upon a single individual. We had a parcel of books addressed to one or the other of us. So, we had a full and growing stock of new books and of literary and religious magazines. And these kept us abreast of news in India many times, to fight hard for magazines. We have already referred to Mr. Barrie's way of assessing their worth. But a level-headed Superintendent was in charge for some time, and he showed considerable good sense in the choice of books. As regards magazines, however, he dared not go against the opinion of Mr. Barrie. For, Mr. Barrie, he knew, would not hesitate to report against him to the Chief Commissioner that the Superintendent was giving to us magazines full of seditious writing. Hence, magazines like the **Modem Rcvicw** and thc **Indian Review** found access to our library only after taking up the matter with the Commissioner himself. I always used to argue that the magazines that had not been proscribed by the Government of India ought not to be banned in the Andamans. And there should be no objection to their reading by a class of educated men like the political prisoners in this place. For a book or a magazine that had passed the thousand-eyed scrutiny of censorship in India must be considered free from sedition and from any other objectionable reading matter in them. That a man of the intellectual calibre of Mr. Barrie should sit in judgement upon us was to declare that censorship purblind. This argument weighed with the Commissioner and we got these magazines all right for our perusal in the library. However, with the change of that Superintendent, Mr. Barrie found his chance once more to interfere with our work. Sometimes he would tear off pages from a magazine; at another time, he would blacken the objectionable portion in it with an ink-roller from his printing press, so on and so forth. And, yet, we got what we wanted and fought for more. Once or twice, Mr. Barrie intercepted parcels of books that had been sent to us after the lapse of a year, and informed us that they were not received. We had information that they had been delivered in the jail. We, therefore, wrote to the Superintendent who discovered that they had been received a month before. Mr. Barrie had to look very small in that episode. He found it very hard to make up with the Superintendent. To obtain books and magazines, we had sometimes to strike our work. We had opened the library against his wish, and he gave us considerable trouble over it.

Passing through all these difficulties, the library became a model institution in our jail. It contained from one to two thousand books in different languages and on different subjects. It contained choicest books on these subjects. Those who had kept aloof from it at the start, now began to take full advantage of it by sending their own books to that collection. Even the Superintendent became proud of that institution. He sanctioned new cupboards for it, gave it an independent hall to house in, and got all old and tattered books bound for it. He appointed three political prisoners to supervise that work and to take proper care of the books. They knew the art of book-binding, did their job thoroughly well, so much so that the Government began sending its orders for book-binding to the jail from that time onwards. Some of them were excellent photographers, and they got orders for photo-enlargements from European officers in our jail, with the permission of the authorities themselves. Thus, these were released from hard manual labour, and got an opportunity for doing work that was entirely to their taste. Of course, these relatively easy jobs fell to the lot of those who were the favourites of Mr. Barrie. They did not go to those who had done their best work in that line. Mr. Barrie and they put spokes in our wheel and he did his best to pay his debt back to those who had obliged him.

The Origin of Vainayak Vritta

The library contained biographies of Raja Ram Mohan Roy, Ishwar Chandra Vidyasagar, and other great men of Bengal in the original Bengali language. It included works of Navin Sen Roy and Rabindranath Tagore, and books by Jogeshchandra and others in original Bengali. It had complete Sanskrit editions of the Mahabharat, the Ramayan and the Yoga Vashistha. Lives and works of Vivekananda and Ramakrishna Paramahansa, and magazines bearing on the subject of religion and philosophy constituted a special feature of the library. We had these in duplicate and triplicate copies, so that the political prisoners read them repeatedly and with avidity. It was through the study of these books that I mastered the Bengali language then. While in London and when I was engaged on the study of all available material for my book on the Indian Mutiny of 1857, I came across a work on the subject written in Bengali by Babu Rajanikanta. The book was styled "The History of the Sepoy War". I had it read to me by a Bengali friend in London. I knew at that time to read and speak in Bengali. But I could not master the script and was unable to write in Bengali. I mastered it later on, and I can write it now; yet I must say that while I can make them out when I read Bengali books, they somehow slip from my memory when I undertake to write Bengali. Life and sayings of Ramakrishna Paramahansa, reminiscences of Rabindranath Tagore, his dramas like Chitra, I read all of them from the library of the Silver Jail. I then turned to the study of old Bengali as in the Ramayana and in the Mahabharata written in Bengali metre known as the 'payara' metre. This special metre was used by Michael Madhusudan Dutt in his own Bengali poems. He slightly modified it to suit his own blank verse. His poems like 'Meghanad Vadha', 'Kurukshetra' and others made me familiar with this form of unrhymed verse. It taught to me to appreciate English blank verse. And, at last, I succeeded in adapting it to Marathi metre after the model of English blank verse. I have employed it to the full in my longer narrative verse known as 'Gomantak.' Since then, it has come to be known as 'Vainayak Vritta'.

As for Marathi books, we had a good collection of the works of ancient Marathi poets from Dnyaneshwar to Moropant inclusive. We had works on scientific subjects like those of Dikshit. We had Marathi serial readers for the use of ordinary prisoners; we had works on Indian History in Marathi from its early days to the close of the Maratha Period, and a special, comprehensive selection of books on Maratha History. We had, besides, a full and complete translation in Marathi of the Mahabharata, all the Baroda series of the Dwaita and the Advaita Bhashyas or commentaries and the translation into Marathi of the entire text of the 'Brahma Sutras'. In all, this section came to about two hundred volumes. My friend and collaborator, Mr. Wamanrao Joshi of Nagpur, made a full use of this collection.

All the Hindi books in the library had to be paid for through our own pockets. We ordered them in a large number because I was of the opinion that every Indian should study Hindi as his national language. I purchased for that purpose selected Hindi books, magazines and readers, and stocked them in our library. Later on, there was, by far, a large addition of political prisoners from Punjab and U.P., and Hindi books began to come in a growing number.

The principal and the largest section in our library, of course, consisted of English books. Herbert Spencer's volumes on Synthetic Philosophy, including his 'First Principles', and Sociology and Ethics; all the works of John Stuart Mill; of Darwin, Huxley and Tyndals, and Haeckel; the writings of Carlyle and Emerson; of historians like Macaulay and Gibbon; of poets like Shakespeare, Milton and Pope, constituted its main feature. We had in it Abbot's Life of Napoleon, the Life of Prince Bismark, of Garibaldi and Mazzini, with Mazzini's complete works. The library contained historical works bearing on England, Italy, America and India. We had novels ranging from Charles Dickens to Count Leo Tolstoy; and we had works of Kropatkin. The library had English writings of Vivekananda and Ramtirtha; works of the German Historian Trietske and of the German Philosopher Nietzche. Plato's Republic, Aristotle's Politics and Bluntchili's Theory of the State as well as Rousseau's Social Contract, found their place on its shelves. Our political friends had, thus, succeeded in bringing into one place the most representative collection of books on subjects of general interest and of deep educational value, in almost all the vernaculars of India, and in the English language. It was a fine library of about two thousand volumes available to all the inmates of the Silver Jail; and all could profit by it, if they had the desire in them to read and improve. Books on theosophy abounded in this collection. We had to carry on a long struggle for securing works on politics for this library. Excepting one liberal-minded Superintendent, all other officers of this jail regarded this library with deep suspicion. It was an eye-sore to them. When a high official from India happened to visit this jail, the first concern of Mr. Barrie was to hide these works on politics from the official's gaze. Mr. Barrie was afraid that if the officer saw them, he was sure to take him to task for it. But as time went on, everything passed muster with him. In the course of time, the officers themselves offered their collection of books for keeping in our library, and issued books from the library for their own personal use. One of these officers presented to our library all his books on theosophy from the works of Mrs. Annie Besant down to the latest work of Krishna Murti on "My Gurudeo".

I read all these books carefully. Not a single book in that library I had left unread. Some of them I read over again, and I made my companions study works on politics, political history and economics with particular attention. I made them write summaries and discourses on them so that the knowledge they had derived from these books should remain a permanent treasure with them. Our Sunday meetings developed, in course of time, into lectures by them on the different subjects they had studied. Books like Bluntchili's 'The Theory of the State' I taught them in the spirit of a regular college class.

All the Sanskrit books in the library belonged to us. None was bought from outside. Most of them were translations with the Sanskrit text embodied in them. All Upanishads, the Rig Veda, the Ramayana and the Mahabharata, the Brahma Sutras, the Sankhya texts, the Karikas of Ishwar Chandra, the Yoga Sutras, all these works we studied here in translations and along with their originals.

Whenever a new book in Bengali, Marathi, Sanskrit or English was published, we ordered a copy of it for our library, if we found it worth having. Thus, though we were far away from our homes, and from the world, we could know everything that was happening there, and had our finger on the pulse of every moment in that world. Away from it, far far away from it, as we were, these movements and this new information communicated a new hope to our hearts, and a new energy to our brain. I used several other ways to inspire the hearts of my political friends with the highest sentiment, long before the library had taken its present form. For instance, I set them a question to state the names of national leaders in Indian history from the fall of the Peshwas down to our times. I told them I would select from them the twelve who top the list, by the total number of votes against their names. The discussion went on for a week and the names were at last submitted. In the list there was no name from among the leaders of the Mutiny of 1857. One alone had mentioned the name of Laxmibai of Jhansi. I called them together and discussed the mutiny with them in several meetings through lectures, conversation, and by questions and answers. I brought the book on the Indian Mutiny by Rajanikant. I pointed out to them how his designation that it was the Sepoy War was a mistake. I showed that it was really a revolutionary movement, a war of independence on a larger scale. Thereafter, everyone of them knew who were Tatya Tope, Nanasaheb Peshwa, Kunwar Singh and Laxmibai. They became familiar names to them.

My Study of the Koran

Thomas A Kempis' "Imitation of Christ" was a favourite book of mine. When I began the study of the Koran in England, I read it first in its English translation. Then I turned to its Bengali version. Back to India, I read it in Marathi. I read it in the original with a Mohommadan friend, who always told me that its beauty and spirit could only be felt by its study in the tongue it was delivered. I read the scripture page by page with him, washing my hands and feet and sitting apart and with my mind concentrated on the text. I made my friend recite the suras and translate them into Hindi for me, as we studied the text together from day-to-day, at a stated hour, and in a devoted frame of mind. I then read Mohommad Ali's modern version of the Koran in English. I had already read the English Bible twice. I had studied the ten principal Upanishads, finishing each of them in one month, and taking one whole year to complete them. I used to read them and ponder every night with deep thought and meditation. All of a sudden, I fell upon the Yoga Vashistha, and I found it of such absorbing interest that I have come to regard it ever since as the best work on the Vedanta Philosophy. The propositions were so logical, the verse is so beautiful, and the exposition is so thorough and penetrating that the soul loses itself in raptures over it. Such a fine combination of philosophy and poetry is a gift reserved only for Sanskrit poets. Look at the eleventh chapter of the Bhagwadgita, and remark the manifestation in it of the Divine Spirit as cosmic force, embracing in its sweep both the one and the manifold. Note, again, the verses in Kalidas on the manifestation of Vishnu, or note in his Kumar Sambhava those grand lines in which the Poet compresses the vastness and majesty of thought into the setting of a beautiful lake-like flowing stanza of charming verse.

And, indeed, there cannot be any antagonism between poetry and philosophy. Poetry is the expression of beauty, and that alone is beauty, which communicates ineffable and perfect bliss; and nothing can bring perfect bliss but truth. "Beauty is truth and truth is beauty." And that alone is truth that communicates to the soul the feeling of doubtless and deepest satisfaction above the conflicting suggestions of the senses, the emotions and the reasoning faculty of man. That is peace, that is pure contemplation of truth, that is ecstatic beauty and joy. Hence, the highest poetry fulfils itself by locking herself in deep excellences of truth.

As I went on studying Vedanta Philosophy, I began to experience one feeling above everything else. And it was that the study of these books relaxed every fibre and nerve of my mind, and merged me completely in the contemplation of the Universal, to the extent that I completely turned away from fruitless action in the world of man. It destroyed my will to power and my power to act. "The highest attainment was inaction." This text resounded continuously in my brain. And words like 'the service of my country', 'altruism and humanity' faded into the background as useless phantoms. Before this supreme goal, they appeared as transient and childish pastimes. A similar feeling of higher pessimism was breathed upon me when I read master-works on geology and astronomy. But for different reasons. These works describing as they did the earth and the starry heavens, brought home to me infinity of time and space, and, correspondingly puniness of man and the briefness of his life on this tiny globe. Why then struggle, why work and strive, why not live like lotus-eaters? That is what I felt. For all this was to end and to be lost in the depth of space and time. The study of Vedanta did not fill the heart of man with this kind of cynicism and despair. It did commend inaction; but in order to reveal to us the deeper joy and the higher realisation of our being, it exhorted man to cast off spurious dolls, but to endow him with something higher, deeper and more abiding than the fleeting pleasures of this world. In Vedanta the abandonment of action was in itself supreme self-realisation and supreme bliss. Not so the mood of despair and utter futility brought on by the study of geology and astronomy. In Vedanta, man is the master and the maker of his being, the spark of the divine, the emanation from the fount of life. To Science, man is the creature of nature, and subject to her mutations, and heading for the final dissolution of the universe into the vast emptiness of space and time. When I used to be lost in the reading of the Yoga Vashistha, the coil of rope I was weaving dropped automatically from my hands, and, for hours on end, I lost the sense of possessing the body and the senses associated with that body. My foot would not move and my hand was at a standstill. I felt the deeper yearning to surrender it all. All propaganda, all work seemed such a worthless task, a sheer waste of life. At last, the mind and the matter asserted their sway over the body and swung it back to work again.

On the other hand, when I read history and the other sciences, the will to power asserted itself with tremendous impact. When I read about revolutionary upheavals in the East and the West, tottering thrones and empires to their fall, the news went to my brain like heady wine, and I felt that I should forthwith break the bars of my prison-door and escape, in order to hold up the flag of independent India, and plant it on the Himalayas. I felt I must rush into the fray, be in the thick of the battle, fight and win, or lose and be in the dust. These conflicts were all on the battlefield of my mind, and when I recovered from them, I used often to laugh at myself. What a plaything I was to be so tossed between these emotions. But this is not the occasion for a synthesis of these questionings, imaginings and feelings. Hence, I mark the end of these musings with a 'Yet', and hasten on with the main narrative.

A Travelling Library

There were educated men even among ordinary prisoners. And of those whom we had taught to read and write, we found some men of talent and intelligence who proved to be keen on reading books of history and other serious subjects. We had to open for them another library well-stocked with Hindi and Marathi books. Where were we to open it? And who will provide books for it? The officers were dead against providing such reading facility for ordinary prisoners. They would connive at their chewing tobacco, carrying tales, and indulging openly in any unseemly vice. But if ten of them were to open and manage a reading room for themselves, it would be a serious offence in their eyes. Hence, we had to provide them this convenience on our own, and through an organisation we had already started for outdoor propaganda and work, mention of which we have already made in a former chapter. From the secret funds of this secret association we procured books on economics, history, fiction and novel, and made them accessible to ordinary prisoners. We ordered them on the address of Hindu officers outside the jail. We did not stock them in one place, and we circulated them among intending readers. By turns, the books passed from hand-to-hand and were duly returned to the place from where they were being circulated among the readers. The movement spread all over the settlement, and we added Hindi and Marathi newspapers to the circulation of books. I had also prepared a list of books on general politics which were read accordingly by the Hindu officers themselves. Every man, who earned a monthly salary of seventy-five or hundred rupees, had his small library at home full of such select books. We were always pressing for such a home library and we largely succeeded in our efforts.

Another advantage of training ordinary Hindu prisoners was that as soon as they could read and write in Hindi and English, and had learnt English up to the third standard, they could get jobs as Munshis. Thus, many of our trained prisoners had gradually spread over the whole island, in districts and at the centre, as clerks, writers, munshis and petty officers. They were freed from their hardships of manual labour and could save from four to five rupees per month.

And they became available to us for our propaganda of "Swadeshi" all over the place, among prisoners as well as free citizens, without any interference with their settled and usual work. And there was a distinct improvement in their private and personal life. They were intellectually better and morally purer. There were less quarrels among them because they were now free from the common vices of their class like drinking and theft, riotry and beating, wickedness and deceit. The main object of putting them in prison and segregating them from society in this settlement was, thus, bearing its fruit. It was for the Government to introduce these measures, but it never cared for their improvement, for that was not its ideal and goal. What it cared for most was to exact as much work from them as it could, and to punish them severely if they failed to give that much work. The officers appointed on prisons had no better outlook than this, and we were forced to undertake the work of improving them without their knowledge. Otherwise, there was no need for secrecy in such a laudable enterprise.

□

2
The *'Shuddhi'* Movement in the Andamans

I was sent to the Andamans in 1911, and I soon found out that some Hindu prisoners had been converted to Islam and assumed Muslim names after their transportation to the Andamans. And when I traced the genesis of this change, I found that the Hindus in that place never found it worth while to think of, and took it as a matter of course. What was there in it, they felt, that one should look into its origin or trace it to its cause? The Andamans were, in fact, under the supreme authority of the British people, and if at all Hindus were to be converted under that rule to any faith, that faith was Christianity and not Islam. Till 1857, both in prisons and in the armies, the ruling authorities had encouraged the spread of Christianity. But after the terrible catastrophe of that war of Independence, the British authorities seldom interfered with religion and did not encourage conversion. However, even today, the Christian missionaries try to convert the so-called criminal tribes in India to their own faith. At least, they exert considerable influence over their lives and social habits. But I dare say, with all my knowledge and experience about it, that prisons are never utilised by the authorities to convert Hindu prisoners into Christians by propaganda or by any other similar influence. Sometime, a Christian missionary comes there to offer a prayer. But none of the prisoners are compelled to attend that prayer. With very rare exceptions, no concealed or open effort, either official or non-official, is made throughout the Andamans to convert Hindus to Christianity. And no officer was found to use his influence in that direction. The exception was brought home to me in a strange manner. And I shall mention it in its due place. But I can bear out, by my fourteen years' experience, the fact that not even four examples can be quoted of forcible conversion of Hindus by Christian missionaries of that place. Nor was any temptation or bribe used by them for that purpose.

How strange is it, then, that under such a power and in the prison and the islands under its suzerainty, the Pathan and other Mussulman warders, petty officers and *jamadars* of that prison could convert the Hindu prisoners to Islam by methods of conversion and coercion. Leave alone the prisoners who knew by their age what they were doing. But what of lads of tender age who were so forcibly converted to Islam by their Muslim warders? Is it not the duty of the British officers to care for their spiritual welfare, as it is their care to look after their physical and moral well-being? Is it not, at least, their charge to guard them from such conversion till they come of age? It is as sacred as to protect the property of a minor from spoliation and misuse. But in the prison of the Andamans, this is a duty totally neglected by its officers. And I go further and say that in all the prisons of India such conversion to Islam is going on systematically under the very nose of the jailors themselves. And it is the Mussulman warder, *jamadar* and petty officer who are doing it without let or hindrance. Fourteen years of prison experience made me assert, without fear and favour, that prison-mosque converts in one year more Hindus to Islam than the Jamma Masjid of Delhi or Bombay is found to do it. The organised efforts of Hassan Nizami to catch Hindus in the net of Islam are not so dangerous as the insidious and wicked way of conversion practised in this jail-masjid of India and the Andamans.

The Preliminaries of Conversion

There are no appointed persons to bring about conversion in jails, nor is there any organisation behind it. Every Muslim is trained from his very childhood to regard the conversion of a kafir to his own faith as his sacred duty. He is told that, thereby, he will be forgiven all his sins and abide in the heaven of Allah with all its pleasure and ease to be his, from eternity to eternity. This is, in truth, the mainspring of conversion of Hindus to Islam throughout the prison-world of India. The process begins in big cities like Bombay, Calcutta, Delhi, Lahore and Madras in the gangs of thieves, robbers and dacoits with their own dens to lurk in. The Mussulman gang of criminals do not consider it a sin in the eye of God to raid a Hindu village and to loot and burn the property of a Hindu sowcar. Nay, it is a matter of pride to the gang to have successfully brought off the coup. I have met maulvis who have condoned these crimes and declared their perpetrators innocent beings. Those who know anything about this side of human life will bear me out when I say that in places like Bombay, every den of thieves and robbers has its 'mahant' or high priest to propitiate its tutelary deity. Ostensibly, each of these mahants is a decent shopkeeper doing his own particular trade. "Honest, decent and above-board" is his reputation in the ordinary world. Young boys as novitiates are given to work under him. And, in course of time, they turn out clever pick-pockets and cut-purses. Then they are promoted to the job of cat-burglars—those who enter people's houses through windows by climbing over the pipes and by breaking open the doors. Then they are put upon the work of breaking safes, and finally in the highest standard of a highway man, stopping men to stand and deliver, with a knife pointed to their chest. At last they are initiated into the gang itself which plans and executes organised raids and dacoities. It is these street-arabs that often go to jail. The mahant, the leader, the high-priest is ever safe, he never leaves his place and is never taken in. The profession lives and thrives on the continuous recruitment of these lads into the gangs.

The Dens of Hindu Thieves

In the dens of Hindu thieves, you will find a large number of helpless orphans and vagabonds belonging to many faiths. But these don't dine together, eat together and mix together, for the Hindu religion does not sanction such practice and allows no conversion from one religion to another. Hence, in the dens of Hindu thieves, presided over by Hindu mahants, you will find but a sprinkling of Muslim lads. And those who are in it practise the usual trade of thieving, pickpocketing and street-hooliganism. But they are never decoyed from Islam. They retain their faith intact, whatever they do or become otherwise. In case the Hindu lads and the Hindu mahants mess with their Muslim fellows, it is the former that go down and are corrupted. The lads and recruits in Muslim gangs from the fold of Hinduism inevitably catch the faith of their Muslim fellows and mahants and gradually drift into Islam. They learn thieving and other crimes that take them to jail. They commit all sorts of sins from cheating, lying and pilfering to rape, incest and murder. As occasion demands, they assume disguises in which they have to cut their sacred tuft of hair and grow a beard. And if once or twice they are made to eat flesh and break bread with their Mohomedan companions, they are stamped as Muslims and swear by Muslim names. In order to cheat the police in their track, they circumcise themselves and throw off their sacred thread. Once this change is achieved, they remain Muslims forever. Besides, in their own homes as Hindus, they are brought up to regard the slightest departure from these conventions as utter ruin of faith. In this way, hundreds of Hindu lads and young men are becoming Muslims in the haunts of thieves and criminals in the city of Bombay. Their castes, if they learn of their breaking bread and eating meat with Muslims, excommunicate them. And the moulvi-mahant is ever ready to receive them with open arms into the fold of Islam. He tells them, "My friend, you are already a Mussulman; now do *namaz*, get circumcised, you will have a fine girl for a wife, and I shall make you happy." As the mahant has on his record these vagabond lads, he has also at his disposal a large number of girls who are as reckless as the boys. Thus, step by step, the vagabond thief climbs into Mohomedanism, and is lost for good to the Hindu religion. The way and the path is not only familiar to the moulvi-mahant at the top, but also to his henchmen in the craft. And these often lure the Hindu lads into that way. The source of it all from top to bottom is the fanatical belief that to turn a kafir into a Mussulman is absolution from all sins and the surest gateway to heaven. Those who are saved from the dens in this city, are converted to Islam in the prison that follows them. The Muslim warders and *jamadars* are adept in this art and other Mohomedan prisoners help in the process. The former do it openly with all the weapons of offence and defence available to them. Others proceed indirectly and tempt them into ways from which there is no going back.

If this is the situation in India, what can you say of the Andamans? There the warders, the petty officers, and the *jamadars* are double-distilled rascals and bigoted Mussulmans—the tribe of Pathans, Baluchis and Sindhees. The political prisoners, of all others, suffer most at their hands, because the bulk of them are Hindus. These officers subject them to the hardest labour, threaten them with the severest punishment and lodge false complaints against them. They, thus, make their lives a hell for them, and out-and-out tell them to become Mussulmans to escape from these throes. The young, the ignorant and the helpless easily succumb to them. How this is being practised I have already indicated in the first part of this book. As I began noticing this, I felt an urge within me to put an end to it. Every week or fortnight I had seen one Hindu prisoner at dinner sitting in the rank of his Mohomedan fellows. It was impossible for me to witness the scene. But I was only a prisoner here; what could I do to save them?

I tried hard to infuriate the Hindu prisoners against this act of sacrilege. But one and all of them I found so callous. Each one of them used to say, "What is it to me?" and "What do I care?"

The Opposition Begins

Leave alone the ordinary Hindu prisoners, it was the same with the political prisoners as well. They dared not put a fight against conversion, and for obvious reasons. For, they were already suffering enough, and they were not willing to put an additional strain on their patience. Having done the most ceaseless daring work in the country, they were paying for it heartily in this jail. And in the prison again, they had to struggle and fight for their very existence. How then can their mind and body bear the additional burden I was putting on them? This work had to be done by others and not by them. Hence, they often used to say, "Leave alone this trouble, for the time being, it is already hard for us to be constantly fighting with the *jamadar* for our right to live. We are not willing to expose ourselves to his malice all the more by opposing him on the ground of conversion." I did not blame them, but I certainly blamed three or four of them who dismissed the effort as a sheer waste of time, as a foolish action. For, they were, thus, shielding their own cowardice, and their conduct deserved censure from me. Others went even further in order to insinuate themselves into the favour of the *jamadar* and save their skin. They used to show to them that they were themselves going to adopt the Muslim faith. How could they, then, openly join a movement to resist conversion? The next step with them was, that when some of us tried to save the Hindu prisoners from the jaws of Islam and the battle was joined on that account, to denounce our action as foolish and to propitiate the *jamadar* by addressing their coreligionists in the following words: "What is pollution or purity in this? These are after all the dregs of society,convicts, sinners, and the meanest of mankind, unredeemed and irreclaimable miscreants. What is it to Hinduism if they are in it or out of it? What difference does it make? Those who embrace Islam by threat or bribe, how are they better as Hindus? To keep them in Hinduism is utter folly and childish nonsense." That was also the vein in which the Superintendent, the jailor and the Commissioner tried to argue with me on the point. And the self-conceited, hypo-critical Mussulman said the same thing to me. Those who are against the *Shuddhi* movement are often found to object to reconversion and purification on similar grounds. Not only those who are hypocrites, but those also who are honest and sincere in their opinions. It is, therefore, imperative that I should clear all misconceptions on this burning question.

Is the *Shuddhi* Movement So Childish?

If it is a foolish waste of time and a childish pursuit to retain in Hinduism those born in it, maybe, sinners, criminals and the miscreants of society, how can one explain the Muslim campaign, now going on for a thousand years, to win this riff-raff, condemned class of Hindu society for Islam? The Mussulmans have waged wars for it, they have put men and women to the sword, they have burnt and looted houses—in short they have declared *Jehad*—for effecting this mass conversion. Is this a childish game? May be the Mussulmans are a bigoted and fanatical race. But even the level-headed, thoughtful Christians in Europe and America have raised vast sums, sent their missionaries, not only to Indian cities and towns, but to the backwoods of India and the jungles of Africa to win the unregenerate and the heathens for Christianity. They have worked among savages, among criminal tribes and the depressed classes and sought, by fair means or foul, to bring them within the Christian fold. The missionaries have suffered for them, paid with their lives for them, spent their monies on them, flattered them, bribed them, coerced them and persuaded them. They have done all this for the sake of Christ. Is this also a childish act? Of what use are these sinners and criminals to them? Why shouldn't then the Hindus seek to save them where they are? They are of as much use to Hindus as they are as converts to Islam and Christianity. I may as well ask the Christian missionary and the Mohomedan moulvi why they should be so keen on their conversion. Why do they taint and tarnish their purer faith by assimilation of such wretched souls into it? Why not let us retain them? They are after all born Hindus and our kith and kin. Do not waste millions of your precious money on their conversion, and we shall not pursue the useless task of *Shuddhi* and reconversion.

Evidently, the Christian missionary and the Mohomedan moulvi undertake the task as a religious duty. They convert heathens, the fallen, the criminals, and the derelicts—for the salvation of their souls. Why then do you blame us if we seek to keep them in their own religion and work for their uplift and redemption as Hindus? We believe fervently in the Gita doctrine that the salvation of man lies in dying in his own religion. And we seek to save their souls and redeem them for Hindu society on that principle. Hindu religion and Hindu culture have in them the power to work such redemption. That is our faith and we act up to it.

It is the Sinful that Need Salvation

The individual whom you try to convert may be a wicked man, a sinner or a drunkard. But after deep thought, you have learnt the social law that if you make him a Christian or a Mohomedan by means fair or foul, and if you change his name, you are really adding to your strength. In course of time, children come into his family and it grows. The children become Muslims and Christians by name, birth and association. And they turn out better than their parents and add in number to the well-to-do, educated, well-behaved number of Muslim citizens. And, in that proportion, the Hindu society loses its good members. The history of Canada and Australia is an instance in point. England started deporting to those colonies her criminals and her unemployed families. Today, the grandchildren and the great-grandchildren of these first inhabitants have built up prosperous dominions and commonwealths and powerful self-governing nations out of these colonies. Where are those criminals and outcastes of society sent to Botany Bay in those days and where is the Commonwealth of Australia today? You are dragging today by your shovels dregs of Hindu society into your soil, and you know how to use these dregs to manure and enrich it. And, in course of a few generations, the soil so enriched will yield you an abundant harvest. The fields will smile and wave with their dancing ears of golden corn.

We have come to realise this law of social growth and, hence, we are following in your footsteps. We will no longer let any Hindu boy or girl, man or woman, however fallen they may be, pass into another religion, and we shall not fail to reconvert those whom you may have duped into embracing your faith. This is the rationale of the *Shuddhi* movement, which we have resolved to launch, and no specious argument can divert us from our true path.

A Hindu thief is less harmful to Hindu culture than a Mohomedan thief. The former will only rob, the latter will break the temple he has robbed, he will break the idol in it and give a shattering blow on the head of a kafir, while running away from the place of robbery. He will spill his blood to save his soul in heaven. This difference between the two has ever to be borne in mind by everyone as a probability. Hence, persuading as we must a thief to give his thieving, a drunkard to give up his drink, and a greedy wicked man to give up his greed and wickedness, we must not give him up, as a Hindu, to any other faith or religion than his own. It is the duty of every Hindu to persuade a Hindu to remain a Hindu. It is a principle to be followed as vital to his community and culture for the preservation and progress of both.

But there is another valid reason: Why must the cult of *Shuddhi* be propagated throughout the Hindu society? And why, above all, must our boys and girls, our young men and women, be persuaded to adopt it?

It is well if a Hindu thief gives up thieving, but even if he does not give it up, he must be made to remain a Hindu. The theft is a sin, no doubt, but to cease to be a Hindu is a greater sin, and a social and national sin. Persuade a Hindu thief not to commit that sin. Everyone who calls himself a Hindu must impress it upon the most abandoned Hindu that it is not well for, him to change his religion. He must strive his hardest to do it. For our ancestors committed the greatest blunder when they allowed such persons to go out of their fold, in pride of self-sufficiency and moral superiority. "Let them go where they choose," said they, "We are sufficient unto ourselves." "He is, after all, a wretched being, let him be a Mohomedan, a Christian or whatever he will. It is nothing to us." And what was the result? For one person whom they so neglected, there arose, hundred years ago, hundred Muslims and Christians to be born enemies of Hinduism, Hindu society and Hindu culture. Aurangzeb was born to such an abandoned Rajput woman. The Moplas of Malabar are by blood and bone half-Hindus. They have forgotten the mothers who gave them birth, and today, they swear by their fathers and behave as bitter enemies of the Hindus. Whence this difference in one generation or two? The difference has arisen by their conversion to Islam, by "the childish play" of the moulvi who cut their tuft of hair and made them grow a beard.

The Childish Play of Great Men

Thus, even for its name, the meanest man or the most useless man must be kept a Hindu if he happens to be born a Hindu. We as Hindus have lost terribly for not playing the game that others have played. It has affected us detrimentally, as we should come to realise after the Malabar riots. We must not now, for our very existence and preservation, refrain from playing the "childish game" of pulling out a convert's beard, and making him wear a tuft of hair instead. We must change his Christian or Muslim name into a Hindu name; we must give him a *Tulsi* leaf to eat and we must declare that he is purified and accepted back into his own faith. Our leaders must play the game as the Christian and the Muslim leaders have played it in the past and are playing it today. We must admit these sinful men in our society not for themselves but for their progeny which, otherwise, will be lost to it. It is first, our social duty, and it is a religious duty as well. Who knows that a Valmiki may not be born to anyone of these Hindu robbers, dacoits and highwaymen? You denounce and disown them today as being more holy, more pious Hindus than they are. This is a pride and self-righteousness highly injurious to the future of Hinduism and Hindu culture. A pirate robber and highwayman wrote the Ramayan, which is the admiration of the world. Let, therefore, a Hindu, however depressed, criminal and abandoned in character he may be, repeat the name of Ram, however wrongly he may utter it to start with. Make it worth his while to do it. Do not shun him, do not revile him, do not turn him out. Treat him as your own brother, make him love his religion. Then he will recite that holy name properly, and it is sure to be good for him.

Inspired by this conviction, I taught the Hindu prisoners of our jail, and chiefly its political prisoners, to rescue the worst of Hindu prisoners from the grip of Islam, to save them from the coercion and blandishments of their Pathan *jamadars*. For six or seven years, these thoughts had been passing in my mind and these words had been dancing on my lips. In 1913, that is a year-and-a-half or two years after my coming to the Andamans, the first complaint was lodged by me against a forcible conversion in our jail. This was the first resistance I offered. I carried on the campaign of resistance and *Shuddhi*, which began in that year to the end of 1921-22, that is till the day I was transferred to a prison in Hindusthan. My friends, the political prisoners, and my friends, the ordinary prisoners, gave me considerable co-operation in that work, and gave the moment, the impetus, and the drive it had received. I did not give up even when I was a prisoner in India. For that, attempts were made on my life by Pathan *goondas* from time to time. There were riots on that account in that jail itself. My brother was actually injured in such a strife. But we never gave up the movement. The movement went on and one appreciable result of it was that forcible conversion in the Andamans had become a thing of the past, and the reconversion of the forcibly converted by *Shuddhi* became an established fact.

Shuddhi in the Andamans

The usual way of conversion in the Silver Jail of the Andamans was as follows:

As soon as the Chalan came in that prison or whenever, later on, a suitable opportunity was found for the purpose, the young and the simple-minded lads out of Hindu prisoners were taken in charge by the head of the Mussulman warders and *jamadars*, the notorious Mirza Khan, and at once put on hard labour. The Musalman warder or petty officer, in their immediate charge, lost no time in browbeating and thrashing them on the one hand, and in offering them baits on the other in order to force them into Islam. He would give them, with that end in view, tobacco to chew and sweetmeats to eat. On such an occasion, he treated these gullible lads with extreme kindness. When these boys were beaten and worked to the point of crying, he would openly advise them to become Muslims and all their troubles would be over. Gradually, these new victims were caught in his net, and at last the ceremony of conversion came to be completed, by making them, openly abandon their seats for meal among the Hindu prisoners and go into the rank of Muslim prisoners. They were then served Mohomedan food so that there was no more chance left open for them to rejoin their Hindu friends. The Hindu and the Mohomedan kitchens were kept separate in this jail and the cooks were Hindus or Mohomedans, according to the kitchen they looked after. Once the Hindu lads were discovered dining with the Mohomedans, they were sure to be banned by the Hindus. This was, therefore, an effective mode and final stroke of absorbing them in the Islamic faith. They were at once baptised with Muslim names. If anyone called them by their former names, Mirza Khan would growl at them, and his myrmidons would threaten them with severe punishment. "He is now a Musulman" they would say, "and you must call him by his new name, beware." This was all the ceremony through which these poor lads were made to pass to be the followers of the new faith. No circumcision, no recital of the *Koran*, no *namaz*, was necessary in their case. Tobacco was their circumcision, hard labour their *Koran*, and dining with Muslims was their *namaz*.

The Hindu Prisoners, Themselves, Against *Shuddhi*

Generally, these were the means employed to convert them. Some of them were, later on, circumcised. When they passed from the prison, they registered their names as Mussulmans. None of the officers cared to enquire how they had happened to change their names. None asked them if they were converted by force and bribes or were converts through the intelligent study of the *Koran*. When they went out to settle in the colony, the officers to watch them were also Mussulmans. The officers outside converted the Hindus by pursuing similar methods. And if, fortunately enough, they happened to be thrown into the company of Hindus and showed their desire to cast off their borrowed feathers, it was the Hindus themselves who threw the greatest obstacles in their way. If they tried to mix among them they shouted at them as polluted beings, and reminded them, that they had lost their caste by dining with Mohomedans. And they at once turned them out as untouchables. I have seen that a convert Muslim takes on his own Hindu name and sits for his meal among his former coreligionists, whereas he is driven out by the Hindus with a hue and cry much worse than the Mussulmans would have raised against him. They make him sit down with the Mussulmans, at any cost. And this made the task of Mirza Khan much easier to accomplish. He had only to put a Hindu prisoner into a tight corner; he had to make him dine with a Mussulman, and all was done. He need not then keep the new convert under his eye; he need no more give him a pinch of tobacco; he need not make him do the *Nimaz*. For the rest was done by the Hindus themselves to keep the convert safe under his paw. Only one day he had to do his business thoroughly to make a Hindu convert, and for the rest of his life and generations after, it was Hindus themselves who detained him in that fold. If this was what happened in India, the same was the case in the Andamans also. For, Hinduism was not better there than in the mother-country, and the shadow of the latter was bound to fall upon the former. In this manner, everyone or two months, at least three to four Hindus were found going over to Islam in this settlement. And when they had married and settled, whether in the Andamans or in India, their children were bound to belong to Islam. And after a generation or two they developed fanaticism that made them forget and disown that they had come of Hindu ancestry. Not only that, they hated Hinduism as only converts could do it. If a Hindu woman married a Mohomedan, she became a Muslim forthwith. But if a Muslim woman married a Hindu, she could never become a Hindu. For, who would admit her to the fold of Hinduism? The Hindus would, by no means, welcome her, and her Hindu husband was compelled to be a Mussulman! He was treated as Mussulman and was presently ex-communicated from Hindu society. I resolved to put an end to this suicidal policy. And in 1910, when a Brahmin boy was hemmed in by Mussulmans, I openly tried to save him. As the instance is typical of many that followed, I may as well narrate it here in full. This boy hailed from the North of India and was about twenty years old. He was a thief and had undergone conviction for that offence. He was, in consequence, a thoroughly spoilt youth, though he was still proud of his Brahminism. The moment he saw the Andamans and the jail, and realised that he was transported to that place, he was in a fright. And, then, he was about to be put on 'Kolu'. In this frame of mind, the Mussulman warders surrounded him. It was the slogan of this wicked gang that a Hindu boy was first to be crushed by hard labour—straightened out as they put it—then he was to be spoilt, and last, get him converted to Islam. The boy had already succumbed to pollution at the first temptation, and now, he was to be taken for dinner with his Muslim prisoners. I sent him a word that on no account was he to submit himself to dine with them. He was not to give up his Hinduism thus. To this, the boy answered that he had no other help than this, for, otherwise, Mirza Khan was sure to put him on the oil-mill. It was useless to preach that he should put up with that hard labour for the sake of his religion. For, that was not going to influence a rake like him. I must help him against Mirza Khan and I could not do it from my cell, where I was in solitary confinement. At last, I carried the whole news to Mr. Barrie, at a private meeting with him. Not that Mr. Barrie was altogether ignorant of such happenings under his very nose, he did nothing in the matter. On the contrary, he turned round upon me and questioned me how I had come to know about it. He added, "Let alone these evil fellows, why should you bother with these derelicts?" He put me off with questions and cross-questions, and went away. I next took up the matter with the Superintendent. But as Mr. Barrie had primed him full on the topic, he gave me the stock answer that it did not matter if such evil persons were Hindus or Muslims. I argued with him in defence, in the same way that I had argued on the subject with my Hindu friends. Then, the Superintendent clinched the point by asking me how I was going to prevent it. I answered that I had no objection to conversion if it happened as a free wish on the part of the convert. But the warders and the *jamadars* made converts by harassing the Hindus, by putting them on hard labour, by bribery and coercion. That was highly objectionable and must be resisted. The Superintendent informed me to catch them in the act, and then he would certainly resist it, and bring them severely to book for it.

The Superintendent left, and Mr. Barrie and Mirza Khan were very much angered. For, in my conversation with him, I had to expose many of their machinations. To ask me to catch them in the act was, in Mr. Barrie's opinion, an encroachment upon his rights and the violation of his orders. Among the Mohomedan prisoners, everyone was gnashing his teeth at me. For, to them, Hindus were a negligible quantity. And the complaint was against their so-called individual privilege of a Mussulman to convert a Hindu. They had never heard such a thing in their lives. Barrie decided to teach me a lesson and ordered Mirza Khan and the angry Mussulman warders to tutor the boy to declare that he was embracing Islam of his own accord. Next day, he was brought to our block, though his cell was in another block, and Mirza Khan gave him food along with the Muslim prisoners in our block. He went away after showering indecent abuse upon me without uttering my name. The Hindu lad was, for the whole day, called by his Muslim name. This was done to humiliate me by showing how helpless I was before them. I had, of course, to quietly pocket that insult. Next morning, a Mussulman warder was giving two or three annas worth of tobacco to the Brahmin boy when I saw him, and I drew the attention of the Hindu warder to that act. He went down on his knees before me and requested that he should be spared the step of catching the Mussulman warder in the act of bribery, as that would mean Mirza Khan's grudge against him. I then raised a cry and gathered together a number of persons, and, sending for the petty officer, asked him to search the boy himself. If the petty officer desisted, I warned him, I would take the matter to the Superintendent. He had to search the boy, when he found on his person the quantity of tobacco palmed off to him by the petty Mussulman warder. All this noise brought Mirza Khan on the spot. He questioned the lad as to who had offered tobacco to him, and he gave him the name of that warder. Mirza

Khan kept me in the lock-up and took the boy to Mr. Barrie for further disposal. On fuller enquiry into the matter, I found that nothing had happened. I asked Mr. Barrie about it in the evening, he replied that he was the man to do anything that was to be done in that business, and I had no right to interfere in it. He added that I was only a prisoner like the rest of them, and could only say anything about myself, and, that, if I were to dabble in matters that did not personally affect me, I was liable to punishment for such interference. Two days after, the Superintendent came on his usual rounds, when I called out to him with the usual cry: "A petition please." The Superintendent was a man who used to be put out by any complaint lodged to him on any other day than he had fixed for it during the week. He, at once, went at me furiously, saying that I had no business to speak about others, and that I should speak only for myself. I answered straight to him: "I am bent upon submitting the petition for the boy, do what you will with it. The political prisoners are reported to you by the ordinary warders on the charge of merely speaking to one another. Their notes are intercepted by them without any let or hindrance; as such I had the right to complain to you on a matter that I regard as the most serious, namely, bribing a boy in order to convert him from one faith to another." These hot words of mine had their effect on the Superintendent, whose duty was to listen to every complaint we made to him. He came up to the door of my room, and asked me what the matter was. I said to him, "I caught the Mussulman warder giving tobacco to the Brahmin lad. I had a search made upon his person. I drew the attention of Mr. Barrie to it. And yet no step was taken by him against the warder in question." The Superintendent was confused and angry. He asked Mr. Barrie petulantly what the matter was. He called for the Mussulman warder. In the meanwhile, Mr. Barrie winked at Mirza Khan, and the latter came forward and deposed, "Sire, the complainant had himself put the tobacco on the person of the lad in order to bring the Mussulman warder into scrape." The Superintendent questioned the boy, who was honest enough to depose that I had not done it. The Superintendent understood how it was. When Mirza Khan tried to interpose, he silenced him with a stern rebuke and said to me, "What have you got to say upon the conversion generally?" I told him in brief, "If any man in this prison desired to read the Bible or study the Koran, I had no objection to it. He should get the permission of the superior officer for that purpose, and if he then felt honestly the urge within him to change from one religion to another, I would not interfere. But for such a conversion, either in the prison or in the settlement, he must have the sanction of the authorities concerned. And the authorities before giving such a sanction must convince themselves by proper investigation that there was nothing in the act like bribery or coercion by one party of another. And in the case of a minor, no conversion should at all be permitted. This is about the settlement generally. In the prison, conversion had to be banned entirely." The Superintendent assured me that about conversion in the Andamans, it was the Chief Commissioner who would decide, and he would speak to him. As for the prison itself, the matter stood as follows. If anyone were to change his religion of his own accord, he cannot prevent it. He will not, however, permit anyone to effect forcible conversion. Mr. Barrie hotly interposed at this point with the remark that even to prevent that kind of conversion would be a hard task for the authorities, for they had pledged themselves to the policy of non-interference. I said to Mr. Barrie, "I am also fighting for religious liberty, that is, for no forcible conversion of any man by any other man in this prison. A free and willing conversion stands on a different footing altogether from conversion by coercion and bribery. The bulk of the warders, petty officers and *jamadars* in this prison being Muslims by faith, they can buttress up their action by any means they like. While the Hindus, on the other hand, have to go unheard. For instance, if I were found talking with a fellow-prisoner, he and I are at once punished for it. Hence, Mr. Barrie's non-interference reduces itself in plain terms to this: That his Muslim henchmen will be free to "do what they like, while their Hindu victims will not be free to complain against them". On this Mr. Barrie argued, "There are Hindu warders and tindals enough here, why do they not instruct the prisoners under them in their own tenets?" "Well," I said promptly, "that was because you, Mr. Barrie, were not lost in love with them, as you are with the Muslim warders. You are partial to the latter, and severe on the former. And if this instruction in tenets was to be the ruling order of the prison, then the whole prison will turn into a mosque and a temple with endless controversies between the two about the truth of these opposing tenets. Further, according to the rules of this jail, not even a tindal or a warder was to exchange a single word with the prisoner except on business, prison discipline demands, for this reason as well, no encouragement to talks on rival religions inside this building." The Superintendent clinched the argument by a remark, the truth of which came home to me. He confronted me straight and asked, "Why don't you, Hindus, convert Muslims to the Hindu faith? Why do you ever shout at others?"

This was, no doubt, a valid charge and it went home. I had to make a reply and I said, "Hinduism does not believe in conversion because it swears by the liberal doctrine, 'to each man his own faith'. Religion is not a matter of changing colour so that we may wear one religion one day, and a different one on the day following. But when it has to face today cults and powers wedded to spread their religion by sword or out of worldly considerations, Hinduism will not be wise to adhere to its liberal doctrine, for then, the doctrine will either fail or be misrepresented."

"We have in past history instances of reconversion by purification even in Hinduism. The Arya Samaj of India has been practising '*Shuddhi*' in modern days. Swami Vivekananda and his noble disciple Sister Nivedita are recent instances in point. He converted her from Christianity to Hinduism and changed her original name of Miss Margaret Noble into the Hindu name of Nivedita and accepted her as a disciple and a worker in his mission of Ramakrishna Paramahansa. We have her books in the library here and you may judge for yourself. Hinduism has forbidden conversion so far, not because it has doubts of its own worth, but because it feels sincerely that man can attain salvation through the gateway of every religion in the world, only if he remains true to it in life. It further maintains that religion is one though religions are many in this world. Hinduism does not regard religion as a means of social cohesion, consolidation and power. I regard this attitude as a blunder in the world of today. But I cannot shut my eyes to the great principle which has inspired that attitude. And I must say that it is a noble principle and the most liberal attitude imaginable."

The Superintendent was a man of culture, and, as far as lay in him, he ever tried to be fair to all. I have referred to this trait in him before, and I shall have occasion to mention it again. He listened to my explanation with perfect composure, and seemed to be impressed by it. He became, at once, serious and replied in a calm tone, "I will think over the matter; for the present I order that the Brahmin boy has to sit with the Hindus for his morning and evening meals, and that he shall not partake it of the Muslims. And if any Mussulman were to tempt him or offer him his own food, let that man remember that he shall not go scot-free." He addressed later on straight to Mirza Khan by fixing his eyes straight upon him. Mirza Khan trembled in his shoes, and made a low bow to him. The Superintendent left the prison.

The threat was all right, and it, no doubt, went home. But the real difficulty came in after. The Superintendent may order that the boy shall take his meals with us alone. But how were the Hindu prisoners to be made to admit him to sit in a line with them? Had he not dined, if only for a day or two, with the Mohomedans? We had defeated the Mohomedans, but how were we to win over the Hindus? That was the crux of the matter. Mr. Barrie had seen through it and kept quiet on the first day. For, the Superintendent himself had lectured to him on that business. I sent message after—message to my Hindu brethren that they should now agree, and admit the boy in their line. But there was suppressed opposition to it throughout the rank and file. In the Andamans, all Hindus dined together, irrespective of their caste distinctions. They sat in the same line, and the Mussulmans alone were seated in a row separate from them. I, therefore, expostulated with them that here was an opportunity, the first of its kind in this prison, to rescue a foolish Hindu lad from the grip of the wicked Mirza Khan who had never before winced for anything he did in the world. Mirza Khan was out to use him and convert him. And the Hindus must now show their mettle to save him. If they were to forego their right on that occasion, Mr. Barrie was sure to make a capital out of it. He will send a counter-report to the Superintendent and make him look small for deciding in their favour. Mirza Khan will then dance upon their chests and be more impudent and overbearing than ever before. He was crestfallen today, but will strut like a cock tomorrow. So, I argued with them endlessly but they would not make a definite answer. I and two others literally folded our hands to them, and personally appealed to them. At last, one or two of them were stricken with shame. And almost all agreed that the boy should sit at the extreme end of the line, and myself and two others be seated close to him. And, further, this was to be accomplished by eluding the lynx-eyed Mirza Khan. What a trouble it was to all of us! But it had to be done at any cost.

At last, the boy began gradually to sit with us for dinner and the Hindus, who agreed with us, also reconciled themselves to it. Mr. Barrie had lost the game. Yet insidiously the Muslims went on with their work, for there was no fiat to the contrary from the Superintendent upon the policy as a whole. But there was a difference in position, and that was an important difference. The Mohomedans had ceased to bully and to browbeat the Hindus on this particular matter. They behaved with caution. But that had deepened their hatred for us. Mr. Barrie kept going on with his incitement work in favour of conversion.

The news went round the whole of the Andamans that I had put an effective check upon the machinations of Mussulman warders in this prison to bring about forcible conversion of Hindu boys to Islam. Some of our prisoners were from Northern India. They had heard Arya Samajists and they started helping us. Before my going to the Andamans, some enthusiasts had already opened a branch of the Arya Samaj in that settlement. But they were unable so far to do any organised work there for the propagation of the Arya Samaj doctrines or to do any kind of *Shuddhi* movement. They had not even a notion of what could be done in this direction and in that place. They were gratified to learn of our efforts and began to help us. Later on some of them took the most enthusiastic part in the propagation of *Shuddhi* tenets. Some independent officers also joined us in that work.

A prisoner, who had imbibed the principles of the Arya Samaj in his own country and who was for some time working on the settlement, was sent back to the Silver Jail just at that time. He was himself a *goonda* and defied the Muslim *goondas* in our jail. He had served his sentence of transportation in the jail, was sent out to settle in the Andamans when again he entered on a terrible career of crime, and was, on that account, sent back to this prison. He was a terror, all over the place, to the Mussulman *goondas*. He was a seasoned jail-bird, expert in every form of crime from ordinary theft to breaking open prisons, smuggling narcotics like opium, street brawls and similar anti-social crimes. The Mussulman dared not look at Hindu boys, whom he had once taken under his wings. For whosoever harassed those, whom he had regarded as his protegees and friends, came in for a severe thrashing from him in defiance of all prison regulations. And he effaced the man completely by exposing some of his secrets. And, curious as it was of note, he had a fanatical faith in Hinduism, as his Muslim rivals had a fanatical faith in Islam. That had lent a sharp edge to his attack on them. He was gratified to behold the frustration and disgrace of his Muslim opponents as the result of our *Shuddhi* movement, and he promised to give us his utmost help in that agitation. I was now resolved not to take things meekly. For, we had to deal, everyday of our lives, with persons who were typically wicked and low-minded. It was impossible for us to cope with them in their abuses, thievish tendencies, beating and in their mean and devilish actions. Their ways were not our ways and I decided, henceforward, to carry out the principle of setting a thief to catch a thief, of confronting a scoundrel with a scoundrel and an insolent man with insolence incarnate. I set this Hindu *goonda* his first task to save a Hindu youth of twenty-five back to Hinduism. The young man always expressed his desire to be reconverted to Hinduism. I put this man on him to accomplish the task.

I remembered the words of the Superintendent who had admonished me for mere talk and had exhorted me to convert Muslims to Hinduism. As soon as I caught hold of this man, I had made up my mind to begin the work, and to take that youth back to Hinduism. The prisoner I had chosen for that work took it so seriously that he succeeded before long in preparing the man's mind for reconversion, as also of a younger person who was an intimate of that youth. He never bothered who knew it; he began his work openly. He was, as I have said, a seasoned jail-bird, but, not being a political prisoner, he was appointed a 'Mukadam', in charge of ten persons. I was myself in solitary confinement. I, therefore, advised him to carry out the purification and reconversation within the precincts of his factory. This was the first experiment in *Shuddhi* in the jail of the Andamans.

On Sunday, while Mirza Khan and the Muslim warders under him were busy attending to the prisoners washing their clothes on the reservoir, my man, the Hindu Mukadam, quietly took the two persons aside—the young convert of 25 and the boy who was his friend—he made them bathe, put on fresh clothes, and he brought them round to declare that they had made up their minds to return to Hinduism. These two made the declaration before three Hindus. The Mukadam made them eat leaves of the sacred Tulsi plant, recited to them some *slokas* from the Bhagvatgita, and he read to them a chapter from the Ramayana of Tulsidas. And the purification ceremony was done. He then distributed as "prasad" the "*shira*" he had specially prepared for the occasion. Before Mirza Khan could realise what had happened, everyone had retired to his room as if nothing was the matter. The two persons, thenceforward, gave up doing *namaz*, and all of us began calling them by Hindu names. When the Mussulmans still hailed them as converts, they never answered them. They began to read the Ramayana of Tulsidas and sat with us for dinner.

This reconversion and *Shuddhi* created a great sensation in the Andamans. For a few days after the incident, Mr. Barrie and his creatures said nothing about it. He knew that if he were to complain about it to the Superintendent, we may rake up the whole past against them. Moreover, the Mussulmans had hopes that the whole show would end soon, and the Hindus themselves would oppose me.

And it did turn out as they had predicted. For, one of the Hindu tindals gave vent to the suppressed feeling of resentment for my action among the Hindu prisoners, and punished me by not allowing me to touch their water. As they always feared political prisoners, they did not take their protest further and did not ventilate it too much, though they did not give up harassing me. They constantly twitted me, by openly hailing me as '*Bhangi*-Babu'.

I must say, however, that much as they insulted me and continued their pin-pricking me, the party of '*Bhangi*-Babus' began to grow in number and to gather in strength so that, at last, the leader of these tindals was himself compelled to join it. And in two or three years' time this 'Thakur' himself became the most enthusiastic champion of *Shuddhi*, and reconversion to Hinduism, and he gave us his strong support in pursuing the campaign. The appellation '*Bhangi*-Babu' was bestowed upon me as a title to signify one who had no scruples to dine with a Mussulman who was reconverted to Hinduism.

I did not convey the story of this *Shuddhi* to the ears of the Superintendent. For, if Mr. Barrie would permit us to carry on our propaganda of Hinduism in the prison, and did not obstruct us as he had not obstructed the Mussulmans, there was no point in informing the Superintendent about the event in question. For, I did not like to pick an unnecessary quarrel with Mr. Barrie. Mr. Barrie was, indeed, indifferent to the future of Islam or Hinduism. He favoured the Muslim warders and *jamadars* because they had proved ready instruments in his hands to harass and torture the prisoners, and, especially the Hindu prisoners, and to keep a strict watch over us as political prisoners. If he were now to oppose openly the *Shuddhi* movement, he knew but too well that we shall not fail to report him to the Superintendent, and, as the latter had been on our side, he was not sure that he would not get a scolding from him for such interference. For all these reasons, Mr. Barrie did not say a word about our latest activities to the Superintendent.

And I had kept the movement going on. Just at this time, some three or four prisoners from Ceylon had come to our prison on the charge of rioting and similar violent action. They were sent on transportation for life. They became friends with us, and they were duly registered as members of our organisation. One of them had been already a convert to Christianity. We talked to him about the matter once or twice, and requested him to be converted back to Hinduism. Two out of three, who were more competent, soon got work as writers outside the prison. We assured the Ceylonese Christian that we would try our best to secure a similar job for him too. This practical offer induced him to become a Hindu. And by our ready method of purification, we soon made him a Hindu. In the Silver Jail, occasionally, a clergyman paid a visit to offer prayer for those who were Christians. He came to us just after we had converted a sheep from his flock. The Ceylonese Christian told him frankly that he was no more a Christian and the news astounded him. He carried the matter to the Superintendent and the latter started an enquiry. And our activities became a subject of discussion among the authorities. It must be said to the credit of the officers that they showed no temper over the matter. The investigation was conducted in a judicial frame of mind.

Just before this incident, report reached my ears that the Mussulmans had plotted to catch a Bengali prisoner into their net. He was a young boy and an addict to '*ganja*' and, in the intoxication, had stabbed a person. He was 18 years old and was sentenced for that purpose. As soon as he was admitted into the jail, Mirza Khan took a fancy for him and managed to keep him under his Mussulman warders. Having felt that they had assimilated him completely with them, they made up their mind to convert him to Islam. So soon as I got the news, I set upon him a young Hindu prisoner to dissuade him from that course. This young man was a *goonda* of *goondas* in the Andamans. Having served his sentence for ten years in this prison, he always had about him plenty of money. He always carried from ten to twelve guineas in the pouch of his throat. Four times, he had run from the settlement to be in hiding in the dark jungles of the Andamans. Though he was a dare-devil and had committed horrible deeds to survive in the adverse conditions of prison-life, he was not a man of wicked heart. He was a man inclined to virtue and with deep faith in God. He was loyal to his friends. He was prepared to run any risk to save a friend. We decided that this Hindu should stay just where they had kept that boy and, at the proper time, expose the whole plot. Although the political prisoners were forbidden to move from one place to another without the permission of Mr. Barrie, the task of transferring ordinary prisoners was assigned to a munshi. The Hindu prisoner in question tipped the *munshi* to the tune of two rupees and got himself changed to a room adjoining the room of this young boy. Within eight days of his stay in that room, the boy became his intimate friend. The elder man talked to him seriously on religion, country and caste, and completely got him under his influence. As a result, the boy unfolded to him the whole story of their dealings with him and their future plans to capture him for Islam. The boy further added that he hated Mirza Khan bitterly, but could not resist him and his like openly for fear they would persecute him all the more for such resistance. It was for his older friend to protect and save him from them. The Hindu friend had made up his mind about the matter and consulted me about it. With my consent and approval, he finally decided that he was to lie low till the last day, and to catch them in the very act of conversion. One Sunday, the Muslim tindal in charge of the block, and, who had taken the lead in the boy's conversion to Islam, approached the boy and asked him to wait outside his room, when others were properly locked up in their respective cells. Thereafter, some five or ten of them involved in the plot seated themselves beside the reservoir and opened a packet of sweets (*Jilebi*), from which they were to ask the boy to partake with them. Everything was ready for the ceremony—water, *jilebi* and men who were to partake them from one pot and one packet. The boy was brought down, he was made to recite '*Kalma*', and he was told the occasion and the importance of their coming together that day. He was plainly warned that if that day, he declined or hesitated to be a convert to Islam, he would lose all the facilities they had given him so far, he would be regarded as ungrateful wretch, and no further mercy would be shown to him. He would be subdued by the hardest labour that would fall to his lot thereafter. While the threat and the initiation were going on together in a sequestered spot near the reservoir, a European officer suddenly appeared on the scene, and saw with his own eyes the plight of the boy before them. Our Hindu friend was with the officer to witness the deed.

Early in the morning, while the Muslim tindals were engaged in their business, he had quietly slipped out of his cell. Nobody hindered him on the way, as the other warders were beholden to him for the tips and other favours he had occasionally passed on to them. As soon as he had left his own block behind, he directed his steps to the office and informed the officer on the spot that he was catching a thief red-handed, and the officer should accompany him. The officer at once got up and went with him to ascertain for himself the truth of the report. As I had known the exact time of the ceremony, they were all caught in the very act, with all the material they had brought together for the proposed conversion. The Mussulmans, the young lad who was to be their prey, the pot of water, the packet of sweets, and last of all, the kalma, the *namaz* and everything else, the officer saw in the process of the initiation ceremony. The Hindu prisoner had timed his arrival so well that none could escape, and all should be caught in the very net they had spread for their intended victim.

The Mussulman tindal collapsed on the spot. His former acts were enough to condemn him. For, he was the man who had made himself familiar with the boy, had smuggled the sweets into the prison, and had gathered together the Mussulmans for the initiation ceremony. And now, he was caught in the act of conversion itself. So that the cup of his iniquities had filled to the brim. The elder Hindu prisoner told the officer the whole story as he had known it. The Muslim tindal was charged with the offence and a suit was launched against him. Even Mr. Barrie dared not to defend him. The lad, in his evidence before the court, put the whole case, as it had happened to him, to the Superintendent in charge. The Superintendent was fully convinced that what we had told him all along about conversion in this prison was not at all a fib. The Mussulmans sought to implicate me in the trial by deposing that the Hindus were doing the same with the Mussulmans in that jail, like the preaching and propaganda of their faith and conversion of Muslims to Hinduism. I was called, therefore, to put in my defence. I, of course, closed with it as an opportunity to explain to the Superintendent, once again, the whole position on the issue in question, I reminded the Superintendent of his retort to me that I was always complaining against the Mussulmans but was doing nothing myself in favour of Hinduism, that I was not converting Mussulmans to Hinduism as they were converting Hindus to Islam.

The challenge implied that the Muslims were not weak minded enough to embrace another faith, whereas the Hindus had not even the power in them to retain the adherents in their own faith. How can they convert the Muslims when they cannot keep their own?

But it was a mistaken view of the whole position. If the Hindus mean it, they can absorb others in their own faith and I had proved it by my *Shuddhi* movement in this prison. Both the Muslim prisoners and the Superintendent, I averred, must have realised the fact by what they had seen. Formerly in this prison, the Hindu prisoners had complained that the Muslims forced them into conversion. Now the Muslim prisoners have begun to shout that they are worse sufferers in that respect. If the Superintendent desired to put an end to this mess, I concluded, the only means for it was to stop conversion altogether by ordering that the authorities will not sanction it, and that the mere dining together or the change of names shall not be accepted as the test of conversion.

Consulting the Commissioner, the Superintendent soon issued an order to the jailor that he shall not countenance conversion. The prison was not the place, it declared, for conversion in any form or shape, either by common dinner or by mere change of names. They were not even to think or discuss about the matter. This put an end to the Mussulman petty officers or their underlings in this prison trying by every means to gather Hindus into their fold. The Hindus had never been keen on it, and had not started the propaganda with that aim in view. So that within the jurisdiction of the prison, at least, the fanaticism of the Muslims to convert Hindus had come to an end. It had been definitely checkmated and "Othello's occupation was gone."

I had another wonderful experience in this affair. It was that I could touch the heart of the so called *goonda* and rouse his social sense and patriotism more quickly than of the so-called decent-minded people in Hindu society. The other educated people showed little courage to plunge in this struggle and work with the sacrifice and the spirit of service evinced by these fallen and sinful creatures. And the reason for it was plain enough. The *goonda* is by habit a daredevil and is tenacious in the line he chalks out for himself. I think that his tenacity and devilry are but perversions of courage and will, which are signs of manliness and virtue. These qualities of the heart are running to waste in the *goonda*, but they could be used, as I found out in the *Shuddhi* movement, to noble ends if the incentive to them came from love of one's own religion, and pride for one's own culture—in short, of love of one's own country and community. It was I who had given them the objective to work for, but gradually, as they had proceeded in that work, they began to love that work for its own sake; their instinctive daring gave them the spur to devote themselves to the cause with pride and selflessness all their own. No further incentive was needed to goad them on in that work. What a change it had made in their lives! Some of them began reading Tulsidas' Ramayana, and they did it regularly. Others took to learning and self-education. Others, again, gave their money for the *Shuddhi* movement. Those who had been typical hoarders gave liberally to the cause. A Hindu boy—a new arrival in the prison—could be safely put in their charge. These boys got all that they needed from these workers. Hence, no longer could the Muslim warders tempt them, hoodwink them, or take them under their wings.

The more the Hindu prisoners came to be impregnated with love and pride for their own faith, the more did the Mussulmans began to chafe against them. And as Mr. Barrie was ever ready to instigate them, we had to suffer much from them. It was not a mere physical suffering but mental torture as well as torture to the soul. How much I suffered from them, I cannot adequately describe. Sometimes showers of indecent abuse was poured over my head from their quarters. Mr. Barrie had detailed some of them to harass me thus throughout the day. These were the worst of their kind and had a free run of all the wards in that prison. They stood for hours together before my room or my chawl, and flung at me their choicest epithets of abuse. And the officers stood nearby to enjoy them, and giggle in laughter. I was no match for them in this contest. And even if I could improvise similar abusive language, it would not heal the bruises on my soul, and it could inflict no pain on them. For, such vulgarity was their usual pastime. I had, however, to bear it with patience. My cause was, however, taken up by the Hindu *goondas*, and they succeeded in silencing them. For, in that jargon of abuse and vulgarism, these had proved their masters. They did not complain against the Mussulman *goondas*, for they knew that Mr. Barrie would not entertain any complaint against them. But one Hindu warder devised a more effective plan to damn them. He secreted in the bedding of a Mussulman warder, knives, tobacco, money and other articles he was not allowed to keep with him. And one day when the Superintendent came on an inspection tour, he quietly placed the bedding with its contents before him. In consequence the Muslim warder was dismissed from office, discharged from his duty, punished and sent out on hard work outside the prison. There he was caned for some dispute with the Hindu prisoners. They dealt in a similar fashion with other members of the gang with the help of the political prisoners in the jail, catching them somehow upon the hip and beating them at their own game. In course of time, the whole gang was completely routed and there was an end to all our troubles. The Muslim *goonda*, infuriated by our *Shuddhi* movement, had, at last, come to his senses.

The *Shuddhi* Movement outside the Prison

As the political prisoners, trained in the organisation that I have already described in previous pages, went out in increasing numbers in the settlement of the Andamans, they carried with them the torch of *Shuddhi* to the locality, in which they were called upon to do their normal daily work. And the movement gathered in strength and volume as these mixed and moved among the people. This agitation, all round, deepened the people's love for Hinduism, and their resentment for those who had persecuted the Hindus or tried to convert them to their own faith. The suffering and the awakening contributed greatly to the fusion of the people, and to minimise, if not altogether abolish, the distinctions among them, as Hindus, of province, caste and custom, and to their consolidation in these parts as one society. Let there come news of someone converted, and the whole community of the Hindu prisoners in that settlement was alive to the need of retaining him. In this manner, even the Hindus, who had embraced Islam eight or ten years before I had reached the place, were, by this *Shuddhi* movement, reconverted to Hinduism. They dined freely with their Hindu brethren and without any objection by the Hindus themselves. I may give here only one instance to point the moral and to adorn the tale. There was an old man of fifty by name Tulshi. This fellow was a veteran in all kinds of vices. He was a first class thief and a first-class gambler. Realising that in the Andamans the Mussulman was in power everywhere, and hating the taboos in Hinduism on food and drink, he had embraced Islam. But when he knew by our *Shuddhi* movement that one did not cease to be a Hindu by food and drink with his fellows of any caste or creed, or religion, and when public opinion of the community concerned had veered round to the view, Tulshi found it impossible to continue as a Mussulman, and felt keenly that he must be a Hindu as before. He was so steeped in his borrowed habits that he had even forgotten his old Hindu name, and one had to remind him of it. Everyone took him for a Muslim and he wrote and signed as a Muslim. But the stir and excitement of the Hindu revival around him awakened his deep-seated love for his own faith, and made him throw off his borrowed garments. Continuing to be a Mussulman for a period of fifteen years, he reverted at the age of fifty to his own religion. We christened him Tulshi, and as Tulshi, he is now known throughout the island. Everyday he reads his Ramayana, and wears as a mark of Hinduism, the usual '*tilak*' on his forehead, and they do not forbid this reconverted Hindu from dining in a row with them. As this difficulty disappeared, it became easier for us to retain those whom we had reconverted and correspondingly more difficult for the Muslims to convert Hindus to their faith.

If a Muslim or a Christian does not lose his caste by taking his food with a Hindu, why should a Hindu alone lose his caste and religion by dining in the company of Christians and Muslims or eating the food that they set? Was it because the Hindu had lost his power of digestion? How did it happen, I wonder. A Hindu must now eat and drink with the Mussulman and the Christian, and digesting his food, survive as a Hindu. The whole world has been feasting on you and you are the only people starving! We must now learn, O, my brothers, to feed on the food of the whole world and yet remain staunch Hindus. That is the only way of our salvation! That constitutes the salvaging of Hindu culture, Hindu religion and Hindu civilisation. I have been preaching this all along and in different contexts. I have sought to impress this truth on the mind of my co-religionists. I may quote only one instance to illustrate my argument.

There come to the Andamans, as it is a coaling station, steamers laden with coal. Coal is stored up in the harbour to provide passing ships and steamers the coal that they need occasionally for their voyage to and fro. Once, when a ship with the cargo of coal in her happened to be at anchor in that port, thousands of prisoners were put on the labour from day-break to empty the coal and to stock it in the appointed warehouses. The prisoners could get no food during the day, as they were so busy with the work. So, usually they were given four handfuls of gram each, as a substitute for their morning meal. They worked like this from early morn till three in the afternoon when alone they were sent back to the settlement to have meal. Sacks full of gram were ordered for the purpose on the day of such work. Hindus and Muslims did not take from the same sack but separately. On that particular day, the Hindu prisoners, dead tired with their work, their bodies full of perspiration, and their faces and hands besmeared with coal dust, returned to the spot where these things were being served to them. It was 12 noon and they were very hungry. And what did they find? They found that the Muslim prisoners who had preceded them had already opened the sacks reserved for Hindus and had been making a full meal but of them! These Hindu prisoners belonged to the Thakur caste in Hindusthan, who would not eat the food touched by the Mussulmans. Here were sacks full of grams and parched rice. But they would not touch a particle because the Mohomedans had touched them. The officer in charge of them all was a Mohomedan. And when he saw the Hindu prisoners so starving themselves, he burst into a fit of laughter. He did not attend to them, he made no arrangement for their food, and the Mohomedan *goondas* had their full feast and fun out of it. For, they ate their own ration all right, and finished that which the Hindus would not touch. So, these had to toil and starve for the whole day without a particle out of the sacks meant for them. The same thing happened to them on the following day. The Muslims had touched two sacks of gram reserved for the Hindus, and the Hindus had to go without food in consequence. The European officers did not bother to know what was happening near them. They would not care and pitied the starving Hindus for such ludicrous nonsense and folly.

I came to know of the incident in the evening of the first day. I rebuked them severely, such of them as were the inmates of my prison, for this foolish and suicidal custom. "Look here," I told them, "how this way of yours is going to harm you. Suppose, you Thakurs prepare '*jilebi*' one day; and the whole of it is touched by the Muslims; they eat it all and you go without it. Another day, you bring *pedhas* and a Christian touches them. You throw them and the Christians feast upon them. Where is this going to take you in the end? This foolish notion of purity and impurity, of pollution by touch, has landed the Hindus into misery and starvation. They remain poor because they would not cross the seas; they would eat from nobody and eat with nobody, and they starve in the midst of plenty. They don't do business and others steal a march over them and exploit them. It is no sin to let others carry your riches away from your own country; to let others devour your food. It is no sin or pollution to let others fatten on you. But if you eat your own food touched by others, it is a great sin. Do not eat another man's food, I grant it. But do not allow anyone else to eat your food; that is merit and not sin. Simple touch does not desecrate it. And the eating of food so desecrated is no sin before man and God. Do not be so foolish, so asinine. If the gram and the parched rice handled by the Muslims became Muslim-tainted food, then why should not your touch make their food Hindu food and purified food for you? Go, you fools, tomorrow when your work is done, rush, some of you, to the sacks reserved for Muslims, and devour the gram in them. If they cry and complain, say to them that your touch had polluted them because it had turned the grains into kafirs! Our grains do not get polluted by the touch of the Muslims, remember it well, and their ration is certainly polluted by our touch, don't forget it. So, eat both and don't starve. Your sin, if it is any sin, be upon my head, I assure you. Why, on earth, do you let yourselves starve?"

As I thus brought them round by harsh and plain-speaking words, some hundred and fifty of them agreed to do as I had bidden them to do. On the third day, these men, without waiting for their fellows, ran straight to the bags of grain reserved for the Muslim prisoners, and began to feed full upon them. The Muslims, of course, were angered by this act. The Hindus reminded them of what they had themselves done on two previous days. "You felt then that you had polluted the thing and we would not touch it. Now we touch the bags and they are ours, and we eat the contents as food of the Hindus." This talk the European officer overheard and could not help laughing over it. He did not punish the Hindu prisoners. On the other hand, he congratulated them for doing away with the foolish notion, which had kept them from that food for two days before. When others saw how well they had fed themselves, they also began to have their share in that feast. From the following days, the Muslims never dared open the bags reserved for the Hindus, for they knew that it would no longer serve them to play that dirty trick.

I, thus, succeeded largely to drive away from their minds the silly notions about food, and drink, sleeping and sitting, which, in the name of pollution and non-pollution, had done so much harm to the Hindu society. As a result, the Hindu way of life became as convenient for us in prison as were the Christian and the Muslim ways to their followers. Life became easier and we, as Hindus, were enabled to face our hardships with better courage and greater fearlessness. This had one other effect as well. Many a Hindu in this prison, who had gone over to Islam disgusted with these taboos, was converted back to Hinduism by this change of outlook on life and religion. And many a Hindu, who was inclined to that faith, naturally remained in his own religion. Occasionally, I succeeded in converting a Christian to Hindu faith. Let me mention in this connection the story of a Telangi Brahmin warder. This prisoner was forty years old. He had come from Telangana. He was a Christian by descent. His parents, or grandparents, a generation ago, had accepted Christianity. I saw him reading the Ramayana in his native tongue and since then, I began to take interest in him. I kept an eye on him and began to know more of him. He had also learnt English and knew it tolerably well. I promised him the post of a Munshi, if he would improve his English and teach it to other prisoners in the jail.

That offer made him come to me to learn English. Of course, he had to meet me for that purpose warily. Soon he became my staunch follower. I told him about our country, its history and its national leaders, and how it was the duty of everyone of us to work for her. This drew him more closely to me and he expressed his earnest wish that he should be taken back into Hinduism. He was a man of strong will, and, though I tried to dissuade him from it, he would not listen to me. At last, I agreed to perform the *Shuddhi* and convert him back to Hinduism. So, he became a Hindu and also adopted a Hindu name. He wrote to the Government that, in the register of prisoners, his name should be entered as a Hindu. When the priest came, he did not attend his prayers as a Christian. Mr. Barrie was very angry with him and threatened that he would take him off from the duty of a warder. But the Superintendent paid no heed to Mr. Barrie. After his conversion, the Brahmin went to the Hindu temple on holidays like Dussera and Divali taking special permission for that purpose. He wore a tilak on his forehead and began the study of Vivekanand's writings. He read stories of great valour from Indian history, and contributed regularly to our organisation the monthly sum of four *annas* out of his slender purse of twelve *annas* a month.

From the prison, the *Shuddhi* movement began to spread outwards among the free inhabitants of the Andamans. There was in it an independent Hindu world of merchants, tradesmen, soldiers and children of prisoners, who had settled in that land. There were in the

Andamans Hindu temples built by these permanent settlers, and these were not so far open to the outcastes. It was difficult to get converts to Hinduism admitted into them. But, in the process of time, that custom fell into abeyance and on big holidays they were open to all who called themselves Hindus or were Hindus by conversion. These entered the temples without restriction, participated in the recital of the Ramayana, took darshan of the idol, and were admitted to public dinners.

With all this progress in the *Shuddhi* movement we had clashes with the Muslims, from time to time, which sometimes resulted in open riots. Just about 1920, a shameless and insolent *goonda* among Muslim prisoners had kept a Gujarati boy as his paramour, and, in due course, this relationship between the two would have led to the boy's conversion to Islam and the corresponding funeral of Hinduism in his soul. My brother came to know about it and managed to detach the boy from his *goonda* friend. At my instance, the Hindu Munshi transferred him from that ward to a room in another, near the room of a trusted Hindu prisoner. Enraged by this transfer, the Mohomedan *goonda* came up to my brother when he had just finished his bath and was wiping his face with a towel, and attacked him. He gave a severe blow on his nose, which made him faint on the spot. Blood began to stream down from his nose and he fell senseless on the ground. The prisoners around him came running up to him from all sides and, at last, caught the *goonda*. What did Mr. Barrie do to him? He openly complimented the *goonda* on his brave action. And he said to others, "How fine it would be if someone was to handle Savarkar in a similar fashion." But one who was not cowed down under the shadow of death, was not to be put down by the curses of a man like Mr. Barrie. Savarkar's movement suffered no setback by this threat, but the *goonda* was soon brought to book for his nasty act. He was caned twice for similar other offences, and was finally put into solitary confinement in a room near my own. He then became meek as a lamb. He then confessed that it was Mr. Barrie who had set him on to attack my brother. Otherwise, he would not have done it; he dared not do it. How much of truth there was in that story either he or Mr. Barrie alone could say.

I had to undergo personally so many hardships in these matters that I felt, at times, I should stop all these movements and mind my own lot in this prison, a lot that was already so hapless, helpless and hard to bear. Yet the urge within would not let me rest on my oars; it would not let me do nothing for those around me. To be doing something for the uplift and education of my countrymen had been the breath of my nostrils; to give up the struggle was simply not to exist. Yet I felt, betimes, that to suffer thus personally in jail, was in itself a sort of expiation and service for my motherland, and I should desist from anything outside the sphere of such service and such expiation. Let others take up the burden from me, and let each one of them share it and carry on. But I saw before me a Hindu prisoner caught in the meshes of this mood of pessimism did not last long, for whenever Mussulman intrigue or any prisoner mercilessly handled by the jail authorities. I could not repress the overpowering impulse in me to plunge into the fray and help these helpless creatures out. I thought the injury and insult to them as personal injury and insult. And further that I could not take it lying down. I used to control my surging emotion by meditation. I am inclined to believe that, when a man feels keenly the insult of his community, nation and religion, and his helplessness to retaliate; when his position is no better than that of a tiger in the cage; some such expression as the Sant Ramdas uttered in similar circumstances, cannot help escaping his lips Ramdas admonished himself as follows:

"The self is already torn to pieces; let the burden of the world be the self for you; wake up my soul and be ready for repeated sacrifice."

I meditated upon these verses of Ramdas to restore to my tortured mind the poise it needed so badly. For, my mind was inflamed by what I had to bear of the daily insult to my religion and nation in this prison.

My temperament was averse from the kind of detachment that would allow me to abstain from pursuing any activities for the resuscitation of Hinduism, for doing away with the foolish customs which had dragged her into the mire. I had to inspire the Hindus with a new faith and with a spirit of nationalism calculated to restore Hinduism to its high status. No doubt, it was an uphill task, for, in its pursuit, I had to face the opposition not only of the officers and their Mussulman henchmen but ridicule and contumely of men belonging to my own religion. And this exposed me to terrible mental worry, physical exertion and irrational opposition from the people themselves.

Within a short time, I had won for the cause the active cooperation of some of the political and ordinary prisoners in this jail. I am not permitted to give their names here as I do not know if they will like it, and if it is safe for them as well. At the proper time, I will mention them, for I must not fail to pay the debt of gratitude I owe to them. Among the political prisoners from Punjab, there were many who proved themselves bold and resolute in the defence of their own religion and culture, in the promotion of education and in the cause of *Shuddhi* and conversion. It did not matter to them, in the least, who the person was to whom they imparted instruction, whom they saved from conversion, or whom they converted to Hinduism. He may be the lowest of the low, the very dregs of society; it was enough for them that he was a Hindu or he was willing to be converted to Hinduism. But till I had thoroughly instructed these willing workers in the principles of '*Shuddhi*' and '*Sangathan*', I could not but bear the whole burden myself. The only persons who came forward to help me were some from the ordinary prisoners in this jail.

In this self-imposed task of mine, I had to face the same kind of disputes, quarrels and fights between Hindus and Muslims in the several districts of these islands, as I had to face them in the jail itself in our earlier struggle for *Shuddhi* and conversion. I have described some of the latter in my narrative earlier. Let me give an instance or two of such fights outside the jail. In the district of 'Hardu', the quarrel between the two parties was taken up to the officers when they told us that they would not officially recognise conversion or reconversion within their own jurisdiction, which meant that a man's religion shall continue the same that he had at the time of entering the Andaman Islands. This ruling gave a blow to the Muslims, who had converted Hindus to their faith after the latter had stepped into the Andamans. Their change of religion and change of names had gone for nothing, and they were not liable to be sued in a court of law by their Muslim friends for return to their own religion and to their own names as Hindus. Much less did they fear for it the displeasure or anger of the officials concerned.

The change in these circumstances compelled the Muslim converts to look up their original names and caste in the prisoners' register. I had also to search up in the register the real names of those boy-prisoners who had been reported in their personal tickets, without any let or hindrance, as belonging to Muslim faith. I had noted the Mussulman clerk of the jail writing out tickets under such false names and religion. I, therefore, decided to scan the entire register of prisoners in the Andamans and prepare the census of Hindus among them. I had to search up for that purpose all the papers giving a full and faithful record of these prisoners, such papers as they had particularly brought with them from their respective prisons in India for purposes of entry into the Island and the prison of the Andamans. For, then alone I could make out who were Hindus and who were Mussulmans, and who had been turned into Mussulmans by conversion and who were again reconverted from Islam to Hindu faith. I could trace those who were passed off as Muslims on false tickets issued to them by the clever Munshi of that jail. But how and where and from whom was I to procure these papers dating back, in many cases, to several years?

A Golden Opportunity

Fortunately enough, chance favoured me miraculously in my projected work. In the last census of the Andamans, following the census in India, the bulk of the work was done through the prisoners themselves. And many of these men happened to be my trusted friends. In that census the authorities had entrusted to me the task of preparing the whole record and allowed me to sit in the office for that work. That story I shall narrate in its own place later on. I make a mention of it here in connection with the *Shuddhi* movement.

The last census in India was taken during the days of the acute differences among the Hindus in all parts of the country. And the Andamans were not without its repercussions of those differences. When we began the census work in the Andamans, it was my ambition to make it an accurate and full record of its population according to caste, creed, race and colour. I had made up my mind to remove from it all the discrepancies and errors of the past, and all the misrepresentations in it about conversion and reconversion. I wanted to give a true and complete picture in that census of the existing Hindu population in the settlement of the Andamans. I and my co-workers on that task sent messages to that effect throughout the districts of the settlement. The most important part of the work had to be done in our own office. The census-forms, properly filled in, had to come to this central place. We had to compare them with the corresponding original records of all the prisoners in that island. We had to check them as regards name, village, religion, and caste from their original warrants kept in the jail-record. So, many political prisoners came forward to help me in that strenuous task, and the jail authorities permitted them to assist me in it.

One difficulty arose at the start to interfere with that work. The Arya Samajists resolved that they would mark themselves in the census-forms as 'Arya' instead of as 'Hindu'. This was in consequence of their past misunderstanding about Hindus and Hinduism. And the Sikhs followed the Arya Samajists for the same reason. The obstinacy of both was bound to affect the census record of the Hindu community as a whole.

I need not discuss here the comprehensive term 'Hindu', as it covers our whole history and culture from the remote past to the recent present. I have written about it in a separate book called 'Hinduism' in Marathi and the issue is settled for the Arya Samajists by the writings of leaders like Lala Lajpat Rai, Swami Shraddhanand and Bhai Parmanand. The comprehensive movement of Hindu *Sangathan* has given a quietus today to this wrangle between Hindus, Sanatanists, Aryasamajists and Sikhs. Suffice it to say here that the definition of Hinduism and Hindus, which I had arrived at in England to prevent further divisions in our society, and to consolidate the Hindus as one community of the people of India, was my beacon light in the disputes over the question in the prison. I taught in the Andamans political as well as non-political prisoners to prevent disintegration, and to integrate the mass on a higher level of synthesis and understanding. My definition of a Hindu is simply this: A man who recognises our country as the land of his birth and religion is a Hindu. And I impressed it upon all whom I welcomed as true Hindus, namely the Arya Samajists, the Sikhs and the Jains. The book containing the exposition of this definition is in the market today. And there the reader who wants to know its fuller treatment, may find it. The definition as stated by me in Sanskrit in my work on 'Hinduism' is:

"From the ocean to the Indus the whole land of Bharata
Is my fatherland, is my sacred country
And that makes me a Hindu."

That is the definition of a Hindu, which I have given in my book on Hinduism. All thoughtful men and all members of the Hindu Mahasabha, in all its branches, have accepted it. In the Andamans, it was put forth but recently, and it took so much of my energy and power of persuasion then to convince people of the truth and the utility of that definition. I had to argue with every man, whom I met there, to bring it home to him. One instance, however exaggerated it may be, I must give here to show how sectarianism is apt to destroy our essential unity as Hindus. The Sikhs have among them various sects like Akali, Sahajadhari and Keshadhari. In the census movement that

I have already mentioned the Keshadharis insisted that in the forms supplied to them they would mark themselves as Keshadharis and not as Sikhs. I pointed out to them how it was detrimental to the interest of the community as a whole that, though belonging to it, they should fill the form as Keshadharis. The tendency was bound to divide and destroy the community inch by inch, when what we needed most in India, both politically and socially, was not minute sub-divisions and disintegration but fusion and integration. This weighed with them home what, and all my Sikh workers succeeded in effecting a compromise. The Sikhs were to make a representation to the authorities and fill in the census-form as Hindus though within brackets they were to show themselves as Sikhs. This was a fair compromise. For, their prison-warrants had followed the same procedure. First the prisoner's name, then his sect, then his particular caste, like the Jat and the Mahajabi—that was the order in which they were noted in their warrants. The mention of caste made them Hindus without distinction, whatever may be their sect and name. Every Sikh possessed his prisoner's sheet. And not one of them had claimed in it that he was not a Jat and was only a Sikh. And the nomenclatures "Jats'" and "Sodhis" were clearly Hindu nomenclatures because they belonged to Hindu castes. And these had no objection, besides, to dine along with other Hindus. This procedure helped a great deal to spread and popularise my definition of Hindu mill Hinduism throughout the community of Hindu prisoners in mil settlement. Even the officers interested themselves in the discussion and gave it a serious consideration.

At last, when all forms were received in our office and were duly classified and tabulated, we found to our satisfaction that men of all castes and sects in Hindu society in which the Sikhs were also included had noted themselves by no other nomenclature but that of the simple Hindu. We had to spend days and days in the careful inspection of the prisoners' original warrants. These revealed to us many funny things. An originally depressed class man had changed his caste so many times in these warrants as he passed from prison to prison that ultimately he came out in them as a Brahmin. The *Bhangi* had effected the gradual change with a distinct motive. As a Brahmin, he had a good chance of being selected for the cooking department of the prison. That a *Bhangi* should rise by this process to be a Brahmin was curious enough. But what was more surprising and insulting in the revelation of the records was the fact that so many Hindus came out ultimately as Muslims in them, and it was due to the fact that thereby they had set themselves free from all the horrors and tortures of the prison-life. There was evident in them fraudulence and coercion all along the pages. I drew the attention of my friends to that fact, and showed what a change the *Shuddhi* movement had effected in their condition within but two years. In the final copy of the report, we had counted all as Hindus, who were originally Hindus, including in them reconverts from Islam to Hinduism. It showed us clearly the triumph of the *Shuddhi* movement and the stopping of all efforts to convert Hindus to Islam. We could note from it the number of Hindus so converted as also of those taken back to Hinduism. And we could also count those who yet remained to be reconverted.

If the agitation in the Andamans had not done all this, but had only awakened the conscience of the Hindus to the possibility that a Mussulman can also be converted to Hinduism, I would have achieved a great deal. For, up to that time the question always put to us was, "A Hindu can become a Mussulman, no doubt, but how can a Mussulman be admitted into Hinduism?" Hundreds of Hindus had asked me that question and sincerely believed that there was no answer for it. But none put such a conundrum before us any longer. For, the *Shuddhi* movement had shown that it could be done, and we had done it. The food touched or prepared by the Muslims could be eaten by the Hindu without tarring his stomach and making him lose his caste and religion. Hinduism was not so anaemic as that; and the Hindus in the Andamans had realised the fact as they had not done it before. This was a great achievement of the *Shuddhi* movement in that part of the world. For, there are in the so-called wise and liberty-loving Hindus of India bigoted champions of Hinduism who, seriously enough, still seek to confound us by the same conundrum. This awakening in the Andamans was not confined to the few but had spread all over the place and the roots of the new feeling had gone deep down into the soil of the Andamans, in illustration, whereof I quote one or two incidents that happened there after I had left the Andamans.

Before we started the *Shuddhi* movement and the *Sangathan* movement in the Andamans, a Hindu woman, who happened to marry a Mussulman, had to become a Mussulman. She dared not ask the Mussulman husband to be a Hindu and she could not remain a Hindu after marrying the Mussulman. The Hindus, having very squeamish notions of marriage as handed down by custom and tradition, no Hindu prisoner ever offered himself to marry a Mussulman woman. On the other hand, the Mussulman was ever ready to have a Hindu woman not only as his wife but even as his keep. He never let go such an opportunity, for it was his faith that to spoil a kafir woman in that way was his sacred duty, for it added, in her children, to the number of Mussulmans in the world. To him a woman was nothing but a breeding ground and an object of enjoyment. As the Hindus in the Andamans began more and more to realise this state of things, they became more and more vigilant not to let a Hindu woman pass into the fold of Islam. A woman of the Thakur tribe had spoilt herself in matters of food and drink in the company of a Mussulman. Later on, she made up her mind to marry him. And she threatened to embrace Islam and marry her Mussulman companion if the Hindus did not take her back purified, and find for her a Hindu husband. The Mussulmans were only too willing to accept her. In this critical situation, a Hindu decided to marry her, just with the object of saving her and her children for Hindu society. But against his fair offer of marriage to her, the Muslims raised a cry that the woman was, for all practical purposes; a Mussulman, and cannot marry a Hindu man. The Hindus had to report the matter to the officers against this claim of the Mussulmans. A Hindu woman and a convert to Islam could marry a Muslim; but though unmarried, she cannot be reconverted to Hinduism and cannot marry a Hindu! That was the position and the issue raised. This outrageous and absurd claim of Muslims had its justification in the foolish and ante-dated custom and tradition of Hinduism itself. This fact no Hindu can afford to forget. But in the Andamans the Hindus in a body protested against the claim, and, as a result, the officers decided that as the woman was a Hindu when she came in the Andamans, and change of religion was not allowed during her continuance in the islands as a prisoner, she was a Hindu and free to choose a Hindu husband. This silenced all opposition to her *Shuddhi* and to her marriage in Hindu society. The Thakur woman was married to the man who had offered to take her, and they remained Hindus thereafter.

I may mention here another instance in point. As a matter of fact, there are thousands of Mussulmans who do not do their *namaz* even once during the day. But just to spite the Hindu prisoners, they insist on that practice in this prison—and these Mussulmans are the worst dacoits and criminals of that place. If a party of prisoners was sent out for work on the islands, the Muslim section in it did the *namaz* five to seven times during the day, for that obtained respite from the officers in their day's work on grounds of religion, and the Hindus were hard put to it to finish the day's allotted labour, while the Muslims safely escaped all the rigour of it. It is very interesting to note on such an occasion what apparent absorption in prayer these Muslim miscreants put on. They spend a good deal of time in washing their hands and feet, they slowly clean and stroke their beard; they sit long with eyes shut after the *namaz* is done; and they assume an air of quiescence and deep contemplation. One may feel, as he looks at them, as if they had passed in all yogi practices like "Pranayam", "Karma", "Japa" and "meditation", leading up to final ecstasy or beatitude. There were only two items wanting in it to complete the show—either a pot of milk or line of fishes in front of them, and hard labour in the prison itself! For, in the first item, their attitude will be no better than that of a cat or crane watching for its prey, and, in the second, that of the miscreants silent and lost in prayer to evade the work before them.

They resorted to another trick in order to harass their Hindu brethren in prison and to defy the prison regulation in the spirit of a *goonda*. That was to cry 'baang' early at day-break. The term 'baang' meant a call to prayer from the top of a minaret to the faithful ones in Islam. And it is to be uttered with the topmost note of one's voice. In the prison, this was definitely an intolerable nuisance, for, at that hour, all were fast asleep after the day's exhausting work, and it was liable to censure and interdiction by the authorities. The man who, for years, opened the prison gate with the utmost reluctance and straightaway lapsed into sleep at day time, had, sometimes, the frenzy in him to get up and utter this piercing cry, and disturb the peace of the entire prison. Who can then say that it was all well-meant, and not an action just to tease and harass the Hindu Section of the Jail? *Namaz* may be a solemn duty of every Muslim under the sun; but to cry 'baang' at an odd hour and in prison is not enjoined, surely enough, by his religion. But to shield themselves behind a religious sanction and be able, at the same time, to make themselves a nuisance to others was a chance too tempting for them to forego. It was an intoxication with 'baang', which they were not prepared to miss.

The Conch-Blowing by the Hindus

The Mussulman prisoners were stricken with this frenzy in the prison-house of the Andamans. Each one of them, from his respective cell, began one early morning to cry 'baang'. The whole prison was roused by this clamour. The Burmese and the Hindu prisoners suffered the most by this uproar. The officers rebuked the Mussulmans for creating the noise but they did not stop it. On the other hand, they maintained that it was a religious act and they must perform it. The Burmese prisoners were hand-in-glove with the Hindus in their *Shuddhi* and *Sangathan* movements. And the Mussulman could not convert a single Burmese in the Andamans. For, the Burmese do not regard inter-dining as loss of caste and religion. They are the followers of Buddha and they feel that they are much nearer the Hindus than the Mussulmans. They do not object to meat in any form and style, and they will take it from Muslims, Christians and Jews and yet remain Buddhists. Hence, the Mussulmans could not prevail upon the Burmese in this respect. Only two means were open to the Muslims to convert the non-Muslims. One was the sword which had, long ago, broken in their hands. And the other was persuasion and argument of which they knew nothing; the Muslim community, as a whole, is at cross-purposes always with the method of persuasion. Hence, they could not convert the Hindus in the Andamans by these two weapons. Their only resource was *goonda*ism and commensality. But in these two matters, the Burmese were powerful enough to beat them at their own game, or even one better than they. For, the Burmese ate hog's flesh, which was an anathema to the Muslims, and they ate mice and other flesh which would make the Muslims shudder. We would deliberately talk to them on Buddhism and praise it, and would listen to their reciting verses from the Mahabharata and the Ramayana. We observed their holidays and our holidays together. Hence, they were drawn closer to our *Sangathan* movement. Moreover, the youngsters among them were always exposed to the coarsest jests and the hardest treatment of the Muslims. Hence, they were convinced that if anything could save them it was the *Sangathan* of the Hindus alone and nothing else. And it was a fact that the strength of the movement had saved them from that cruel treatment and drawn them still closer to us by ties of love and mutual devotion.

The incident of the 'baang' had been as much an annoyance to them as to the Hindus. The Hindus were in rage because by that act, the Mussulmans desired to flaunt the Muslim religion in their faces. The officers would not give them any protection. In these circumstances and as a counter-blast, the Hindus started their prayers early in the morning. Once I had checkmated the *namaz* by confronting it with a Hindu devotee and his bhajan. And the Hindus adopted the same method to silence the Muslims. It was not a question of one or two Mussulmans. It was a dispute between one community and another. As the Hindus began their prayers in a loud tone, the officers who had maintained silence towards their rivals, launched prosecutions against the Hindus. One-by-one, they were charged and punished for the act. Their plea was that to offer such morning prayers was not an essential part of Hindu religion. To which the Hindus answered that if not prayer, at least blowing on the conch early in the morning was an essential part of the Hindu worship. Therefore, one of our enthusiasts, who had taken a leading part in this affair and who was a prominent member of our organisation, procured a conch and secreted it in his cell. The following morning at dawn, just when the Muslims had begun their 'baang', this member began to blow vociferously upon his conch. The kafir conch in its sound and volume proved more powerful than the Muslims cry of the 'baang'. The tomtom of the drum was lost in the sound of the kettle-drum. The 'baang', the Muslims felt, was desecrated by the conch. They were angered and shouted abuse. The enthusiast was punished for the offence. Thereafter, the Burmese and the Hindu prisoners began to blow on their several conches. At last, the united and bold action made the 'baang' withdraw into its shell. Their protest with the officers had gone in vain. The Hindu's right to blow on the conch as an act of worship was recognised and they were asked to stop the 'baang' before the Hindus could be asked to cease blowing on the conch. Thus, the 'baang' came to an end and the conch ceased to blow. What was impossible for reason to do, that the sound of the conch could do for us. The *goondas* were subdued by the conch, as they would never have been subdued by an appeal to commonsense.

It is our sad fortune to refer endlessly to the misdeeds of our Muslim brethren in this record of prison-life, and of the *Shuddhi* and the *Sangathan* movements as part of that life. It is because they formed the most fanatical and the most mischievous element in the entire colony of prisoners in the Andamans. With the rest of the good and honest

Mussulmans, whom I met with in the islands, I was always on the best of terms. They respected me and I respected them, as I enjoyed the respect of all other prisoners in that colony. Minus the particular question of coercive conversion I always tried to see that justice was done to all of them and I took the side of justice against tyranny and oppression in every case and about every person, irrespective of his caste, creed and religion. If I succeeded in changing the hell of the Silver Jail into a habitable place on earth for all its inmates, and that by incurring the wrath of its authorities, the advantages of the change went as much to the Muslims as to the Hindus, and both of them showed equal gratitude to me for it. That I was throughout just and fair to all is borne out by the fact that if I blamed the Muslims for the conversion of the Hindus I did not conceal the fact that most of it was due to the foolish notions about religion entertained by orthodox Hindus themselves. Conversion followed as a natural consequence from the obscurantism of Hindu society about purity and impurity, touchability and untouchability, conversion and reconversion.

I always used to assert, while engaged on these activities, that both the *Shuddhi* and the *Sangathan* movements in Hindu society were not the means of antagonism between the two communities of India, but of their abiding unity on the basis of right knowledge and right understanding.

This was the motive inspiring my agitation in the Andamans. I began my work of *Shuddhi* in the year 1913 and fought my first battle in its favour in the same year. From that date to 1920-21, I did that work in the Andamans; from 1921-24, I continued it in my prison-days in India; and from my release in 1924, I have been pursuing it to this day. And I have invariably carried it on in the interests of freedom, justice and fair-play for all. I have no hatred in my heart for the Christian, the Mussulman, and the heathen, or for those whom they style as primitive barbarians. I do not look down upon anyone of them with scorn and contempt. I only oppose that section of it vehemently, which is oppressive and violent towards another. For, I believe firmly that the *Shuddhi* movement itself will build a bridge of permanent union between the Hindus and the Muslims, and will bring good to both and lasting advantage to India as a whole.

□

3

The World War (1914) and Its Menace to the Andamans

The reader must have gathered from the first Chapter of this section, how, we, political prisoners, were handicapped for news from India, and how, later on, that is, after my transportation to the Silver Jail, matters became easier for us to procure news from India and circulate it in the Andamans. Officers like Mr. Barrie spread among us canards from India to harass and frighten us at the start of our prison-life here, whereas after two years, we gave him the correct news about the position in India, so that faked news found no soil to take root in these islands since that date onwards. I give here one or two very funny instances of how they tried to fool and frighten us then.

A Bomb on the Governor-General

In the viceregal procession to the Coronation Durbar in Delhi in 1912, a bomb was thrown at Lord Hardinge, the then Viceroy of India, somewhere in the vicinity of the Chandni Chowk, when a stampede ensued, and, before the procession could move onwards, the elephant with its Howdah, in which Lord Hardinge was seated, had to be taken out of it. Except for the shock of the incident, the Viceroy had suffered no material injury. This was reported as confidential news to the Chief Commissioner of the Andamans, but we got it through our sources right at the time that it was flashed to the Chief Commissioner. Depending upon it and in order to verify it, for it was likely to be full of discrepancies as it came to us, I asked an officer who came to the prison next morning on his usual round, "Has the Coronation Durbar Ceremony at Delhi passed off all right?" As he had no news of it till that time, he answered, "Yes, of course; you revolutionaries must certainly have been staggered to witness this formidable display of our imperial prestige." I simply laughed to myself at this expression of arrogance, and he was touched to the quick by my indifference. He returned to the office and Mr. Barrie put into his hands the special wire he had received from Delhi. He, instantly, flared up in abuse and said, "Surely enough these fellows must have some inkling of it." Mr. Barrie was astounded at the remark. He started a secret enquiry and found that the news had been the talk of the entire prison. He created a scene in his office. One of my young friends, by name Mr. Nair, was in the office at the time, for he had to attend it as a clerk. Mr. Barrie cast his suspicion upon poor Mr. Nair. He pestered him for two days after to tell him who had brought the news to me. He threatened him with caning. The young man was a spirited individual. With pen in hand he stood up and invited Mr. Barrie to cane him there and then. Mr. Nair was taken to the Superintendent, who found no proof against him to confirm Mr. Barrie's suspicion. He was punctual and clever in his work and pet, on that account, of the Superintendent. The Superintendent let him off with a warning that he was to keep no connection with me, and that, if he was found doing so, the Superintendent would order caning him as punishment for the offence. This young man continued his association with me in spite of the threat, and we were intimate with each other till my release from that jail. In my final year, the officers themselves appointed him and me to work together. That is all that I have to say of him for the present.

I had a particular motive to let Mr. Barrie understand that we had already known of the bomb incident at Delhi, that, with one or two experiences of a similar character, he might cease his pin-prickings and realise the futility of his effort to hide the news from us. And the result of it was, as I had anticipated, he was amazed to learn that he could hide no news from us. And, on occasions, he plainly told me as well as the Superintendent that it was not only impossible for a man like him to prevent the political prisoners from talking to one another, but to prevent news also from reaching them from the outside world. He added, "Even if the devil be sent here as a jailor instead of me, he will not be able to stop it." This sentence, he used to repeat to us, every now and then, and, in course of time, he became very lenient to us in the matter of news. He connived at us almost, only catching such news-monger as he could let escape. On the other hand, he and the other officers of the place adopted towards us a different line of policy, which was to give the news to us straight as it came to them. The bazar and other news about any happening in the world reached us often in an exaggerated and garbled form, for those who brought it could not report it faithfully to us out of their sheer illiteracy and ignorance. For instance, about the Delhi affair, they reported to us as follows: "Four big officials were done to death by the bomb", which was evidently a false news. Why then prevent us from getting the correct news rather than let such false news filter down to us from the bazar? The officers reasoned about the matter. "The mischief created by the report of correct news was any day less harmful than the mischief of false and exaggerated news from unreliable sources." It was this experience that had at last brought the officers to their senses. How I wished that they had seen the wisdom of it long ago! They now began to give us newspapers to read. And when they came to us from Mr. Barrie himself, we had no need for getting the kind of news that we used to procure from the outside. We were saved all the bother of it; and we got faithful news without being put to any trouble for it.

To avenge himself on us for the news of Delhi that we got before him, Mr. Barrie spread the news in our jail that my younger brother was arrested in connection with the incident at Delhi.

My Younger Brother in the Delhi Incident

This was no impossible news, and I learnt later that he had to suffer a great deal in connection with that incident. But, as I did not know anything about it at that time, I was naturally anxious to know the truth about it. That very afternoon the Superintendent asked me if I had a younger brother and if he was yet free. Before I could give him any answer, Mr. Barrie, as was usual with him, wickedly remarked, "O, if he is free, you will soon find him here." Slightly annoyed by it, I said, "Any man from India can come here. For, the whole of India is a vast prison-house, as much as Ireland. What wonder then that my brother should be here?" Mr. Barrie was an Irishman, and he looked crestfallen. Then the Superintendent put in, "I do not know anything of it, but am I right when I say that he is a bit of a coward?" I asked him, just to pump him out, "How do you say so?" The Superintendent answered, "I say so because he wired to the police as soon as he got the news from Delhi that it should note that he was at Calcutta. He informed the police that they should not involve him in it." To which I retorted, "Then I may consider him the wisest man in Calcutta. Evidently, he had not thrown it, but even if he had thrown the bomb, this was the cleverest way to mislead the police. He was no coward. He is a brave man, for, he knows to attack and yet escape."

Evidently, these remarks were dictated by vehemence and passion. The Superintendent was taken aback and went away without making any answer.

For two or three days after this conversation, I was really restless in mind about my brother. Repeatedly, those verses came to my mind in which I had embodied my deepest conviction:

"I have not taken this vow blindly; or in the course of nature, just to win popularity and fame. This ordeal is extremely painful; burns the soul like fire. I know it and I have taken it as the Sati takes her vow that she will immolate herself on the funeral pyre of her husband." I brought the verses vividly to my mind, repeated them to myself, and was prepared for the worst. So was I consoling myself when I learnt the truth, and was completely relieved in mind.

I may give here another instance of how Mr. Barrie used to tease us. One day he came and asked us, "Who is this Har Dayal?"

I answered, "You know him. He is the man to whom the Home Member, Sir Reginald Craddock, had referred as the leader of the revolutionary movement in America, in his conversation with me in this jail." I further enquired of him if he had any special information to give me about him. Mr. Barrie told me of Har Dayal, as if in confidence, that he was brought to Bombay on the charge of murder. I was simply stunned by that news. That one of our great revolutionary leaders should have been so arrested and was to meet the same fate as I, was too much for me to bear. How unhappy my country was, indeed, that the same destiny that was mine should be his. I recalled my own arrest, my trial, my hardships, and my transportation to this jail. I sent out secretly warders to ascertain what the truth there was in the news that Mr. Barrie had given me. They could not remember the name of Har Dayal. So, I made them repeat it. What a miserable condition, this, of our motherland, that those, who had lived in other lands and had worked there for her freedom at tremendous risk to their own lives, should not be known even by name to her own ungrateful children! The thought almost maddened me with grief. My fellow-prisoners had to pour water over my head to cool my heated brain. The Superintendent came in the wake of Mr. Barrie, and put me the same question, over and over again. I retorted that, indeed, I had the honour of knowing him as my very intimate friend. He informed me that Har Dayal was accused of murder, and he had implicated himself in the bomb-incident in Delhi. I said; "Maybe, but that does not lower him, in the least, in my esteem; and my friendship will ever remain the same for him." The Superintendent made out from these curt replies that I was not in my usual humorous and polite mood, that the news had completely upset my temper. He at once changed the topic and, after a time, left me. The political prisoners grew anxious that I should give such rash answers to him. I told them that I knew lull well what I was doing, that we must not take it quietly when they talked in such terms of Har Dayal, that we must not disown him because he was under arrest, as they had told us, about it. That would be sheer cowardice on our part and I was not the man to behave so. Har Dayal was my friend and I was prepared to suffer any punishment for saying so. The political prisoners ought to learn this, if they did not learn anything else. That was the only way to show our gratitude to Har Dayal.

Gradually, I became appeased in mind and set about getting the news for myself. Within two days, I learnt that Har Dayal was under arrest in America and was released on bail. We kept on asking Mr. Barrie where Har Dayal was, if he was in Bombay or taken to Delhi, free or under arrest. He deceived himself that we were absolutely in the dark about him. One day, he told us that Har Dayal was tried and sentenced, and would soon be despatched in Chalan to Port Blair. We all giggled at him. I told him to put Har Dayal in the room next to my own, so that I might talk to him freely and fully. Poor Mr. Barrie took it all seriously and said he would think of it. It was too much for all of us, and the whole company burst into laughter. Mr. Barrie realised then that we were all fooling him to the top of his bent, and that we had all known that he was telling us lies. Days went by and we learnt that Har Dayal had given the slip to the police in America, and that the American Government itself had helped him in the escape. However, that may have been, the news had lifted a burden from our hearts. Now that I am on the subject, I may as well narrate a similar episode about another leader in India, how the authorities in this jail often spoke in contempt about the Indian worthies in order to spite us. This was during the days that my health was completely shattered and I was removed to the hospital for treatment and rest. I was confined to bed at the time and the Chief Commissioner visited the hospital to see me. He was a man, who had always been polite to me. In the course of his conversation with me, he said that he had the good fortune to meet Surendranath Banerji on board the ship that carried him from Europe to India.

Surendranath Banerji

The Chief Commissioner continued, "I met him on the steamer and, after we were introduced to each other, the topic turning on the Andamans, Surendranath put me a question about your health. He asked me if he would be permitted to visit the Andamans to see the state of political prisoners for himself, and, if, in that case, he could personally see you and enquire about you." I, at once, asked the Chief Commissioner what he had said to Surendranath about that proposal. "I told him," said the Commissioner, "you can come there by all means. I shall write to you definitely about it." "But, look here, Savarkar, where can I put him? I have no better place to accommodate him than the block where you are put up, and in the room next door to yours." I replied to him in lighthearted raillery, "Well, if you really mean it, there is the Chief Commissioner's bungalow; for two days the Chief Commissioner may very well stay here and accommodate Surendranath in his bungalow." I must say here in passing that the veteran leader of Bengal took interest in me and other political prisoners in the Andamans as no other leader did before or after him. He ventilated their grievances in his paper 'The Bengali', and he ventilated them in the Legislative Council; he gave us all the help he could. I must pay my tribute to him here, though I regret that the old fighter is no more in the world to read it.

In the first part, we had brought down the story of my prison-life to the middle of 1914. The strike brought us material concessions, which enabled us to continue our work as before. As soon as the Chief Commissioner learnt of it, he sent me a personal letter of congratulation, perhaps because he felt that was the end of all his troubles in the administration of the prison. And I began to think how I was to pass the remaining fourteen years in that prison in the same chawl and in the same cell. When I entered the prison, I had believed that I should not be passing more than five years in that room but now fourteen long years loomed before me as a dark long tunnel, through which I was to pass before I entered the light on the other side.

As soon as I had learnt of my transportation for life, I had read up all the regulations of the prison in the Andamans and I had written to my wife a letter in verse assuring her of a home in the Andamans after a period of five years, during which she should possess her soul in patience. We would have then a cottage and a garden in that place trellised over with creepers and plants of fragrant flowers like jasmin and its varieties, in which we shall dwell together united in love and peace, though far away from our kith and kin in India.

But even this hope had turned into a dupe. I found in these years a series of misfortunes befalling me, the last of which I discovered to beat all others before it, in its hardship for me. In the agony of mind, the dream of a happy home and of flowers trailing down by little cottage door had withered into shadows and insignificance. They could not bring to my parched soul even a dew-drop of refreshment and solace.

To add to this desolation and grief, only a few of us happened to be detained here when the rest of my political compatriots had been sent back to India, and could look forward to the remission of their sentences in their respective jails in India. We found our separation from them the gloomiest experience of our life. Our extreme solitude on this account would sometime become unendurable. A deep yearning came into the soul to call out someone by name, to ask someone to come and sit beside me. But in that heartless prison, who was there to answer to my affectionate call? My mind thus began to prey upon itself. Nights were found too long and did not pass quickly into day-break. No new friends to make, no new work to organise, no new food for hope, the mind dwelt constantly on past memories, long-gone and forgotten activities, on friends in these years; and it played with these fantasies. But one does not feed on sugar and rice by merely drawing their picture on a piece of paper. These famished longings and thoughts sometime rebelled against me like unruly and riotous bands of robbers. Nothing that I could do would suppress them. The hunger was left unsatisfied; and it made the heart restless. This used to be my experience in prison for months together in succession. How much harassed by loneliness, how much eager for the society of friends, how much yearning and restless for friendship and love, and yet how much keen on duty to be done, my mind was during this period, none could know and describe except the few, who had pined away with me in that prison. Do what we will to satisfy the authorities with our day's work, there was no hope in it for our discharge from that prison. There was only one way out of this dire position. That was a chance of escape from the settlement, when and if, we were sent out for our daily labour. And with that aim, we were punctulious in attending to our daily work in prison. But when I learnt that I was to stay and work for fourteen long years within the precincts of the Silver Jail alone, that chance again faded out of my view. In retrospect today, I cannot say how I must have passed those days in that place. Months went by in these musings when, all of a sudden, as bolt from the blue, news came to us of a war having broken out between England and some foreign power.

First, we could put no faith in this news from the marketplace. For, the prisoners had been long in the habit of catching at some such thread of news in their helpless condition. Every four or five months, someone would start the canard of a jubilee or a similar celebration, in which the prisoners were sure to get their freedom, and the prisoners welcomed the news in the hope of the drowning man catching at a straw. And it was bound to prove a hoax. Another news came floating in on a similar rising tide. The news of war was the most hopeful news of them all. But we did not yet know between whom the war had broken. For, the prison-world knew only of two powers under the sun, the British power in India and England, and the Amir of Afghanistan. The Muslim section of it knew, besides, of Turkey and its Sultan. Therefore, when it was definitely known that war had broken out, it must be a war between the British and the Amir, or between Britain and Turkey. Britain had nothing to lose in her war either with Afghanistan or Turkey. Hence, for two or three days subsequently, I paid no attention to that news. Later on, news had filtered that the English monarch had gone to war with his son-in-law. But who was this precious son-in-law? Outsiders used to hint of Germany. But those who brought the news to me spoke often of an English Princess married to a foreigner on the continent of Europe. It was a war, they said to me, between these two sides. They could make some meaning of this relationship. But to me, it came as a puzzle to think out an English Princess, married to a foreigner, on the continent. After much trouble, I got a note written to me from the outside. And from that note I could make out that the war could be no other than between England and Germany, and that it had already begun between Germany and France.

So, this was a war between England and Germany!—a prophesy I had made years ago. This was, indeed, a golden opportunity. But it came when I had found myself helpless and behind the prison-bars. As I have told many times before, what I write down here expresses my passing moods of the day, as they overpowered me in my prison at the time. They do not necessarily represent what I feel about the happenings today. They are, so to say, history leaves from my diary, and not their justification today.

It was the activity of the Abhinav Bharat that had drawn the attention of Germany to India. When I was in Europe, I had long conversations with German, French, Irish, Turkish (the young Turks as they were called) and other diverse agitators and patriots, from which I found out that they did not know anything of India, that there were people like Indians in the whole world. India as a nation did not exist for them. It was a dead civilisation—this India—which they thought could not be used conveniently even as a second fiddle to England in international affairs and in international politics. It was the propaganda carried on in England, through newspapers and other agencies by the Abhinav Bharat Mandal, which drew the attention of Germany to the existence and political importance of India. It interested all far-sighted politicians and leaders in her future. And more so in France and Germany than anywhere else, for the members of the Mandal had worked intensively in those countries on behalf of India. I may mention particularly the lecturing tour of Madame Cama in Germany, which I have already mentioned earlier. Subsequently, German newspapers published articles on India from the pen of some of our workers. Then came the episode of Madanlal Dhingra and the shooting of Sir Curzon Wylie by that revolutionary. Madanlal Dhingra went to the gallows like a hero, and the British C.I.D. were set after our workers all over the field. This created an awakening in France and Germany about India, and faith in the power of our organisation. Madanlal Dhingra had made a reference to Germany in his final spirited statement to the court that had tried him. My book on the Indian Mutiny of 1857 was in the press at that time, and the police were keen on knowing where it was being printed, and, therefore, it had come in a large number in Germany to keep a close watch on our movements. Some of the German officials had already informed me about it. I was warned to leave England in time so that I might not be arrested in England itself. This message came to me through one of our workers in Germany, who got the news from an agent in the German police itself. When the Abhinav Bharat's newspaper "Sword" began its publication in England, I wrote an article in its first issue predicting war between Germany and England within six years. I had written in it a long article over the Kiel Canal. It was then that I had shown that such a war would be a golden opportunity for India. Later on, my hazardous attempt to escape at Marseilles and many international issues it had raised, made our movement, its hopes and ambitions, and sacrifices we had made on its behalf, the topic of discussion all over Europe. These upheavals not only in India, but at the door of Europe itself, had brought the realisation to Europe that India was a live nation, that it would prove a thorn in the side of England, and, therefore, would be a handy weapon in its hands for future use. England and Germany, being on bitter terms with each other, this notion swayed the mind of Germany more than that of anyone else. The German officials tried consequently to establish a direct contact with our workers. One or two of our outstanding leaders had made their permanent home in Germany for that purpose. And those of us who had settled in America wrote in our newspaper, 'Gadar', published in that country, that Germany would soon go to war with England, and, therefore, they must be ready to use the opportunity to make the final effort to liberate India. We used to know about it in our prison in the Andamans.

I have given a brief account of this past history here so that the reader may realise what bitter disappointment the news of war brought to us because, though we had known that the war was coming for many years now, it came at a time when we were prisoners in the Andamans, and as such, helpless to make any use of it, as we had planned it to do in the long past. It is unnecessary to dwell further on our ambitions and plans at the time.

Even in this helpless state of mind and body, I determined to take full advantage of this rare opportunity in the life-time of a nation to further the cause near my heart in such ways as I could adopt for that purpose.

In the meanwhile, the Superintendent himself told me one day, while he had come to inspect the prison, that war had broken out in Europe on an international scale and Turkey had joined the side of Germany in that war. It was decided, he added, to raise funds in Port Blair to support the war and start a magazine, to which writers in that place were to be invited to contribute. He asked me to give an article or a poem for that magazine.

I wrote a long poem in English and gave it to the Superintendent, as he had asked for it. From time to time, I used to write short poems, which the officers of the place were not unfamiliar with. I doubted, however, if this poem, considering the feelings it had expressed, would pass muster with them. But the projected magazine never saw the light of the day, and the matter rested there.

However, when I learnt that Turkey had gone over to Germany in that war, I had to change the plans I had made to take advantage of that war for the freedom of India. The siding of Turkey with Germany, as against England, roused all my suspicions about Pan-Islamism and I scented in that move a future danger to India. I discovered that Turkey in this war had made it possible for Germany to stretch her long arm to India and create a critical situation in India itself. This was, indeed, a circumstance favourable to my designs. For then England was bound to grant India all the rights that she would demand, or India herself could wrest them as the result of the exhaustion of England and Germany both, battered as they would be in this terrible combat between two mighty foes, not unlike the fight of two powerful elephants joined in life-and-death struggle with each other. Broken, battered, bleeding and exhausted they will lie on the field with victory to neither, and with full advantage to others who knew to profit by the situation. But I also feared that in this grim struggle between two mighty powers the Muslims in India might find their devil's opportunity to invite the Muslim hordes from the North to ravage India and to conquer it, instigated in that effort by the machinations in Russia.

Thinking calmly over all these near and remote consequences of the war, I settled my own line of action, and, as the beginning of it, I resolved to send a long letter on the subject to the Government of India. I cannot here give my reader what line of action I had settled in my mind to follow. But I may summarise in outline the letter I had sent to the Government of India.

The Superintendent agreed to forward the letter and I wrote in it as follows: I wrote that I felt it my duty, as intimately connected with the revolutionary movement in India, to inform the Government, in its distracted state of mind, what I thought about the present situation in India vis-à-vis the war between England and Germany. It was our ideal, I wrote, to win independence for India and it remained our ideal even that day. But we were not sworn to violent means alone to achieve that independence. If any other sure means were available to us before for that purpose, we would not have gone in at all for terrorist and revolutionary methods.

What was true about the means was equally true about the end.

Politics and Government had for their aim to endow man with the rights of citizenship, and to create in each country representative institutions to maintain those rights by the method of law and order. We had for our goal the creation of the parliament of man and the federation of the world. We wanted this federation to be the guardian of freedom and peace, justice and equal rights all over the world. All distinctions of race and language, of creed and colour, of territory and boundaries, ought to be submerged in this parliament and this federation, for the unification of man, and for the promotion of peace and goodwill on earth.

Hence, we were friends to all political institutions and arrangements which promoted this cause. We welcomed them as steps on the path leading up to the temple of peace. We were not enemies of the groups of nations or of empires that materially helped the cause by a union of countries in a common bond of loyalty and government. The countries in the Union and the Empire had to be endowed with freedom and self-government as means to their progress and prosperity.

These being our principles of action, we were ready and willing to be friends of the British Empire, if it equipped India with a form of government, vital for her freedom and her progress, and commensurate with her capacity to run such a government in the peculiar situation, in which she happened to be placed at the time. If this became a practical proposition, from Ireland on the one side to India on the other, an empire would emerge from the process, which can no longer be the British Empire. Until it assumed any other suitable name, it might well be called "The Aryan Empire".

If the statesmen of the Empire had the vision and the daring to effect the change, their first task would be to raise the continent of India to the status of colonial self -government, if they could not see their way, in the midst of the war, to grant her the independence she desired. And as the beginning of that self-government, they must, in the Central Legislative Council at Delhi, accept the principle of the elected majority and of representative government through that majority. If this was achieved, if we felt certain that it was going to be achieved, we, the revolutionaries of the past, would stop all our violent sanctions, and help England whole-heartedly in her present war with Germany.

Let the Government give us a chance to prove our bona fides. Let them release us to convince the people that England was willing to break the chains that had held India in thrall. We pledged our word of honour that we would exert our utmost to bring recruits to the Indian army in large numbers that would equip her to stave off the invasion of India from the North by the forces of Afghanistan and Turkey, and to march to any front that needed her presence to fight the foe and beat him. We would offer ourselves as volunteers to serve in that army in defence of India and for the victory of England. Release us, I said, equip India with colonial self-government, and win the loyalty and love of her people. That would assure to the Government all the co-operation that it needed from the people in the present crisis. Let it not miss that splendid opportunity. In case the Government suspected, I wrote in conclusion, my motive in writing the letter, I offered to do without any release for myself personally. Let them release all the political prisoners in the country leaving me alone in my own cell in the Andamans. I shall rejoice in their freedom as if it was my own. The Government was right in suspecting me; perhaps, when free, I might lead an agitation to break the peace in India. I had not written the letter to seek my own liberation, or to compel them to set me free along with other political prisoners involved in similar or the same political conspiracies. Hence, I had made the proposal to keep me back and set all others free.

This letter, in substance, I had forwarded to the Government of India. All other Governments were setting their political prisoners free at that time. Even political prisoners in Ireland were set free. I had given in my letter all the instances of such liberation as had come to my knowledge then. I was not a fool to conclude that my letter would be the charter of our freedom. But I knew that, apart from its immediate effect, letters of this kind had told in the long run, along with agitation in the country to support them.

I wrote this letter in September 1914 and I received Government's reply to it at the end of December. The answer was brief. It informed me that the Governor General had read the letter and noted all its contents, although no official reply could be sent to it for the present. In the present circumstances of the situation, the Government found it impossible to give effect to my suggestions.

I had reason to infer, even from this brief answer, that I had helped by it the efforts of far-seeing leaders in the country to win more rights for India. The Government had known by it that we revolutionaries and conspirators were behind the demands of the constitutionalists in the country. And it must have exercised some pressure upon it to be willing to listen to them. "Give us rights and take our help and co-operation." "No rights, no co-operation." That was my plea all along. I impressed it upon my colleagues in the prison, and, to the end of the war, I acted up to that precept. If the political prisoners were released with the concessions to back them up, they were to co-operate in filling the army with young recruits and help the Government to win the war. I persuaded many to that view though I had to linger alone in this prison.

With the beginning of the war and for a month-and-a-half after I had sent the letter, myself and the officers of the jail were on most cordial terms. But an occasion arose when a sharp altercation became inevitable. For, as news about the war came on to me, I passed it on to other prisoners. The early reports of the war were, all, of the advance of Germany The officers sought to conceal them. Mr. Barrie behaved very queerly at times. He began telling them of victories of England all over the field. He spun long yarns about them. His motive was that we should not lose faith in British power and in its prestige over the Empire. The moment we felt that these were tottering to their fall, there would be, he imagined, riots and confusion all over the settlement. That was Mr. Barrie's fear about it. Knowing this full well, two or three of the political prisoners, who were his henchmen, outdid him in showing up Germany as a weak and wicked nation, and in belauding England as an embodiment of righteous indignation against Germany's betrayal. For, they received the reward of this praise in this world, at the very moment, and in the prison of the Andamans itself. The Lord God of the Silver Jail, Mr. Barrie, relieved them of hard labour; let them mingle freely with other prisoners; and appointed them as Mukadams. Two or four of us had proved quite useless for that task. For, we could not tell the prisoners that England, like the Knight of chivalry and romance, was out to save the lambs of Belgium and other smaller countries from the jaws of the tiger that was Germany. We did expose the selfish ambition of Germany for a place in the sun, but we did not shield England from its greed for power, and its jealousy of Germany's growing might. We did not observe the day of German victory as a day of mourning. We gave the news as it came to us without gloss or criticism. Only we pointed out how each move on the battlefield would affect the politics of India. We felt that it was a fine opportunity to enlighten the prison-world of the Andamans on the politics of India, and of the burning question of the hour.

For, as soon as war began in Europe, all the people in the Andamans, as in India, felt an excitement and a thrill passing through them. The excitement in the Andamans was not due to any interest in politics, or any anxiety for the future of their country, as it was due to the expectation that it would mean their freedom from the prison. It was selfish desire that was its cause. Hence, the future of the war had become a matter of personal interest to them. Even the most ignorant among them knew stories of old emperors and *rajas* when their kingdoms were overthrown, and the prisoners had won their freedom. And these stories from the legendary or the historical past had become today the gossip of the entire colony. And from these instances in the past, they drew conclusions to suit their own wishes in the present. A certain king was killed and his kingdom was won by another. And from this instance, they inferred that if the Emperor of Germany was made captive, the war would come to an end; and if England was defeated, all the prisoners would be at once set free. On the floating wave of self-delusion, the prisoners sailed their ship of hope from day to day.

When the warders passed their cells at night on their usual rounds, lantern in hand, the prisoners would anxiously ask for news of war. And the self-sufficient ignorant warder would tell them anything that came to his lips as its innermost news. Drawing upon the talks in the town, the warder would paint before their eyes a scene of the British Monarch standing on the top of a hill and watching his own army. He wears the crown on his head, and a sword dangles at his side. What if the German Emperor suddenly shot him with an arrow? But he would not do so. For, was he not the son-in-law of the English King? His wife, the Empress, would come in, and stop her husband from it, will she not? Some such guesses and fantasies they would weave from their minds and discuss them with hilarity among themselves. It was funny to hear them talking thus. The warder in these chats with his prisoners hardly knew how time had flown, how three hours had sped, and his patrolling was at an end. The prisoner did not feel the arduousness of the labour on Kolu, while he was wrapt in such conversation. For, the jolliest of them, feeling the heaviness of the handle they were pushing along the rut, regaled themselves with the exclamation, "Friend Kolu, turn and turn. It is only for a few days now that we shall be working on you. None will turn you, then, round and round. Then rest and rust." One would set the tune and the rest would make the chorus, "Yes, dear Kolu, turn, for we are to be with you for a few days now." In that frenzied mood, they would turn the wheel faster and faster, and often did the work of an hour in half the time. This was true not only of prisoners on hard labour, but also of petty officers and *jamadars* ordered to watch on them. They themselves were prisoners on twenty to twenty-five years' term of imprisonment. Tindals and petty officers used somehow to finish their duty as supervisors—three to four hours at the most—and spent the rest of the day mourning their lot. But since the outbreak of the war, they brought some news from the world without, and kept on discussing it with the veteran convicts and drew a pleasant picture of instant freedom by the overthrow of British rule in India as the result of the conquest of Great Britain by Germany. They tattered the news to pieces, even as the Kolu would crush the coconut pieces into oil by turning round and round on them. While he was wrapt in this talk, another petty officer came up and then the former realised that his time was over and he must leave the scene. "Three hours gone, how quickly time passes, the hour has sounded. I must leave. I knew not how it had gone,"—such was the mutual greeting between the relieving and the retiring petty officer in those days. They had forgotten their task of persecuting the poor prisoners; the hard discipline of the prison had relaxed; the petty officer and the prisoners had developed the spirit of comradeship, and the tie was the common news about the war and its Idle forecasts. Otherwise, they used to quarrel as soon as they saw one another; they would growl like dogs; they began abusing each other; and there used to be resentment and discontent all around. The war had changed this: there was eagerness and curiosity on the one side, and the willing loquacity on the other. Whatever be the news for the day, the only end to it was, "Well, only a few days now, and we are free." That was the form of leave-taking between the petty officer and his ward.

I resolved to take full advantage of this eagerness for war-news among the prisoners, though I knew that it had no deeper root in their heart than the selfish longing to be free. But the awakening should not be allowed to spend Itself on nothing. I desired to plant in their hearts love for their country and interest in the politics, with which her future was so intimately bound up. Everyone approached me for news. Even the Mussulmans, who bore me a grudge on account of the *Shuddhi* movement, were reconciled to me by this common need. And they listened to me with patience and devotion. As for the political prisoners, who had allied themselves with Mr. Barrie, they gave them news about the war after the pattern of their master. But I myself, and others along with me, told them frankly what we knew about it. And this bait of daily and faithful news had caught; it made them learn to read and write as I guided them.

Among the millions and millions of India's teeming population, the whole world was divided into two or three States. If one happened to be a Hindu, the boundaries of the world did not stretch for him beyond England, on the one side, and Kabul, on the other. All his knowledge of Geography and politics did not go beyond this range. He was surprised to learn that there were other kingdoms in the world besides these. He knew them not even by their names. The Britisher and the Afghan-Ungrez and the Amir—these were his familiar figures. If one were a Mussulman, he would add to them the name of Turkey. So that, for days together after the war had started, they believed that it was a war between England and Turkey—between the King of England and the Sultan of Turkey. They never thought that there could be any other kingdom on this habitable globe. They were familiar with Mussulmans, on the one hand, and Britishers, on the other. Taking advantage of the war, I asked them to repeat the names of all countries in the world, to understand the map of the world, and the maps of several countries along with it, before I agreed to give them any news. With a piece of brick, I used to draw these outline maps on the whitewashed walls of the prison-rooms and explain them to the prisoners. My political colleagues helped me considerably in that work. Those who would never learn geography for anything in the world, became its apt pupils for the sake of the news that they wanted from me. Germany, France, Austria, Russia, Egypt, Belgium and Servia became to them as familiar names as England, Afghanistan and Turkey. I had made them repeat the names and had pointed out their location on the maps I drew for them. And I explained to them the news of war in the light of geography that they had thus studied. To the cleverer ones among them, I explained the constitution of these countries. They knew no other word before than the King. Hence, they interpreted the news in the light of that term. The King of France had to fall back; the king of America was angry—that was the terminology they employed. And when anyone of us told them that there was no king of France or America, their question was, "Who fought the war then?" Their idea of warfare they had derived from what little they knew of legendary lore, from the stories they had heard from the Mahabharata, for instance. The war or the battle was to them nothing better than a combat or a duel between two rival princes. The King of Russia was weak, he was not strong of thews and sinews; the King of Germany was a giant in strength and, hence, he would crack the King of Russia like a betel-nut. That was their surmise and hope. So, whenever they wanted to weigh and balance victory and defeat between the parties, they measured their strength by the personal prowess of their kings. How does the King of Belgium or any other king fight? That was the typical question they asked. Is he a fine rider? Does he know horsemanship? The manner in which they described the Kaiser of Germany was very amusing. He was, they told us, a finely built man, almost possessing the physical strength and form of our Bhima. He shattered with the blows of his fisticuff the gates of fortresses. Once he held the King of France by his neck like a cat and hurled him down. Who was taller—the Czar of Russia or the Emperor of Germany?—I remember clearly one prisoner putting the question to me. I told him that the Russians, as a rule, were taller and broader than the Germans. And his face showed bewilderment, for he was doubtful, how, in these circumstances, Germany could ever beat Russia? I wanted to drive this notion about the king from the mind of my listeners. I wanted them to grasp what was the State and the politics of the State. What was the Republican form of the State, and what a constitutional monarchy! I told them broadly how the people were governed; who made laws for them; who declared war or peace; and who made treaties. I further explained to them, in the simplest terms possible, what was a representative government and a legislature, and the relation between them and a monarch or a president of a Republic. I further told them the difference between the monarch and the president and how France and America were Republican States. I enjoined upon them to remember these facts well before I would give them the news that they wanted. Within one year, most of them gave correct answers on these points. They could understand the difference between international and national politics, and the relation between the two, as also the geographical importance of these states dotted all over the world. And the more they knew, the more I gave them to know. And during these years, they showed extreme eagerness to know everything about the war. For, the knowledge of geography, maps, and politics had made the news so vivid and interesting to them. They became so enamoured of it, that before long, they would themselves locate the news on the map and ask me to enlighten them upon it. The temptation for news made them procure from outside newspapers for themselves and read them. This work I did for them during the duration of the war.

While I was busy teaching them the geography of the world and widening their knowledge of it, I was particular to teach them more about the geography and the map of India, of its political conditions, and of its situation in the world around us. The prisoners felt, at first, a strange fascination for Germany. They had lisped the word 'English' too often to like it. For he, the prisoner felt, never treated him well, and Germany, he concluded, if it beat England, was sure to set him free. Hence, he did not like anyone denouncing Germany. So, when I explained to my political friends as well as to other prisoners the possible consequences of Germany's conquest of India, I made it clear to them that it was a mistake to suppose that Germany would not harass and persecute India, and that it would be no advantage to us to change one master for another. It was up to us to be ready to play our cards well during the fluctuations of the war, and it would not do for us to be counting on the victory of Germany to win freedom for ourselves. This fact they found too unpalatable to digest. And then, I would narrate to them the story of the potter and his donkey. One potter fell, and another mounted the seat. What was it to the miserable donkey, he remained a donkey all the same. So, it was no good speculating on the victory of Germany. It was foolish to think that it would make any difference in our status. I then explained to them what must be done by us to reap the fullest advantage for India from this great world war, and what was the advantage that we were likely to reap from it. I convinced the prisoners that if Germany became the ruler of India, she would ride roughshod over us. But when I said that Turkey or Afghanistan would mete out the same treatment to us, the Mussulman section would demur to that statement. For, the Sultan of Turkey was a god to them. How many stories and legends had grown round him as the Kalipha in their sacred writings! They were taught in their cradle to worship the name of that Sultan with feelings of sanctity and reverence. That personage was to invade India and I said that his rule will bring no good to India. What a blasphemy to say so. That the rule of the Sultan over India would be a foreign rule was a proposition beyond their understanding. If a moulvi prisoner in our jail, who knew something of history, were told of the invasion of the Arabs over Persia; of Persians over the Pathans; of Pathans over Pathans; and of all these together over the Mussulmans of India; and if one further enumerated to him the horrors they had perpetrated over their coreligionists in India, he would still maintain that the invasion of India by Turkey and the establishment of the Sultan's power in India could not but be a blessing to her. The fanaticism of the Mussulman disqualified him to think nationally and to be a patriot of India, and if this was helped by the ignorance of the world history, then he was bound to think fanatically. Every Mussulman knew the name of the King-Emperor of India. But the Kaiser was a strange name to him. He used to hear everyday strange stories of him, and to convey them from mouth to mouth. They wondered how the Kaiser had become so mighty, and discussed the matter between themselves. At last, they came to the conclusion that the fact was due to his alliance with Sultan of Turkey, who was the anointed of the lord and sacred to them.

The Sultan is to Rule India, now Hindus, See to It, that You turn Mussulmans

The war began after the *Shuddhi* movement. With the participation of Turkey in that war, the Mussulmans, disabled by the *Shuddhi* movement, got the name of the Sultan as a fresh weapon in their hands to make a renewed effort to convert Hindus to their faith. And they began to talk openly to the Hindu prisoners as follows: "Germany is sure to beat England and conquer India. The Sultan of Turkey will personally crown the German Kaiser as the Emperor of India, and the Muslims will be a power in India. As such Mussulmans will get high positions and big jobs in the Indian Empire. Those, who will not be Muslims then, are going to be severely punished."

When they brought the report of this open talk to me, I used to ask them what was the man who talked thus. They said that it had been printed in a Urdu paper that was available in the bazar. With wry and long faces, the poor prisoners would come to me to know if there was any truth in it. "Is it a fact, Bada Babu, that the Sultan of Turkey is to be the ruler of India and that he is going to grant amnesty to all the Muslim prisoners in India?" So, they would ask me often, and add that on this ground they were being exhorted to convert themselves into Mussulmans. I lost no time in exposing the hollowness of these stories, and in showing up those who had helped to spread them all over the colony. So, slowly but surely, the prisoners had learnt a great deal about Turkey and had measured her at its proper worth. Whenever the Mussulman moulvi prisoners bragged of Turkey, they flung into their faces what they had learnt from me. They quoted sentence after sentence from my talk to them on the subject and silenced them. "Your Sultan is no tiger but is the tiger's skin stuffed with saw-dust. A small State like that of Bulgaria beat him hollow; Servia compelled him to bite the dust; Greece succeeded in throwing off his yoke. During the last ten years, poor man is being twisted round and round and finds his throne tottering. This Sultan of lathe and straw was to invade India; one blow from England was enough to finish him. What if Germany adopts him? What value has that in the hierarchy of nations? If he was, indeed, so powerful, why did he not go against England so long? To say of this man of shreds and patches that he has made Germany mighty and will bring her victory! Where is the Kaiser of Germany and where the Sultan of Turkey? Where is the Royal elephant of the Gods, and where the sorry nag of a beggar!" The Hindu prisoners used to strip them of their self-conceit by flinging these words at them.

I used to instruct the more literate among us by comparing the strength of Germany with that of the Sultan of Turkey. I used to give them facts and figures about the army, the air-force, and the dreadnoughts of the Germans, and make the whole position clear to them from statistics and tables. I told the Mussulmans that they should not mislead themselves. Whatever victory Turkey would achieve, it would be due, I told them, to its reinforcement by Germany. German arms and ammunition, German instruction in the strategy of warfare and German generalship constituted the real might of Turkey. I gave them all the information on the subject, as I got it from true sources. Whatever news came to my hands from time to time, I explained it fully to them. We used to study and discuss these things in our weekly and peripatetic meetings and lectures, about which I have mentioned in a former chapter. I then lectured to them on Turkey and the activities of the new party led by Enver Pasha. It was known as the party of Young Turkey, many of whose members had taken their education in France and Germany. I had bestowed due praise on the efforts of leaders like Enver Baig to revive Turkey and put a new spirit in her. I had also told how it would benefit India if Turkey were to join her forces with Germany in its war with England. I explained it to them, according to my viewpoint then, and I expressed my full sympathy with the Turkish movement. But I would not tolerate exaggeration and empty bragging. Hence, the Mussulmans were always gnashing their teeth at me.

I had to expose them often by humour and laughter. Once, for a whole week, the Mussulmans at Port Blair and in this prison spread the rumour that the German Kaiser had embraced Mohomedanism. The Sultan had plainly told the Kaiser that he should expect no military assistance from him till he had converted himself to Islam. "I stay with you on the battlefield only on that condition, otherwise I withdraw with my whole army. I go back to my country." That was the ultimatum, so went the rumour, that the Sultan had given to the Kaiser. The Kaiser was alarmed and he became a Mussulman! This fib they uttered before the Hindu prisoners in order to spite them. "Was there any truth in this?" they went about asking. At last, one of the enthusiasts in our camp, who was an Arya Samajist, said to me that this bubble had to be pricked. I told him, "My dear friend, how can we prove or disprove it? You know that a lie must be met by a lie; a canard can only be exploded by a canard; and I will tell you how to do it. Tomorrow, as soon as you come back to the prison from your work, go on proclaiming with as much emphasis as you can that the 'Kaiser' had become an 'Arya'. The Mussulman in the Andamans pronounce the word 'Arya' with a long 'a'. Whenever you see Muslim prisoners in conference and chatting together, go and gather together and say out: "The Kaiser has become an 'Arya'. And if they asked for the proof, fire off that you had read it in the bazaar in a Hindi paper."

The Kaiser Becomes an Arya Samajist

And it was done. The news went round the prison the following evening that the Kaiser had become an Arya Samajist. The Mussulmans lay low and sought to discover what it was all about. They found out, at last, that the news was brought into the prison by a Hindu warder. On the third day, they met him in a block where they were to do common duty for the night, and the Hindu warder, without waiting to be questioned by his colleagues, announced to Hindu prisoners that the German Kaiser had turned an Arya Samajist. The Mussulmans became fidgety over it, and questioned him what proof he had about the story. The Hindu warder asked them promptly what proof they had to say that hc had become a Mussulman. They said that they had read the news in an Urdu paper, to which the Hindu retorted that he had read it in a Hindi paper. They asked him to produce the Hindi paper and the Hindu asked them to get the

Urdu paper. The Mussulmans, so discomfited, began to shout that 'Arya' was the religion of the kafirs. Nothing daunted, the Hindu replied that Islam was the religion of the heathens. So, it had nearly come to blows, but there it stopped.

The report of the quarrel was next day taken to the *jamadar*. He was also one of those who had believed and declared that the Kaiser was converted to Islam. But what was the poor man to do when every time that they said that the Kaiser had become a Mussulman, the Hindus were ready with the retort that he had become an Arya Samajist. Ultimately, the Mussulmans ceased talking about it, and the rumour was effectively scotched.

The fact of Turkey entering the war on the side of Germany against England fired the imagination of the Muslims, and man, woman and child began to dream of Muslim Raj in India. And when, occasionally, they came to hear that the Amir of Afghanistan had made a common cause with the Germans and the Turks, their enthusiasm knew no bounds. The Pathans were so enraptured by the prospect that their tongues began to wag like the croaking of frogs in a pool of water before the advent of the monsoon. If one Pathan raised one rumour, another multiplied it tenfold, and so long as Enver Pasha was in the field, he was reported to have decimated thousands of British regiments or taken the city of Basra. About the Amir of Afghanistan, the reports were still more extravagant. It was not enough for him to cross the Indus, but he must knock today at the door of Lahore, and march another day on Sirhind. The petty officers, moving in and out of prison, brought in fantastic news that produced a convulsion among the prisoners. One told us that the Amir had taken the city of Lahore. Another reported that Kaiser had seized London. And, when asked for confirmation, they both excused themselves by pointing to this munshi or that who had given them the news, or by saying that they had read it in an Urdu newspaper.

But behind the ridiculous behaviour of the Pathans there was one quality that I never failed to impress upon those, who simply laughed at them. I always asked my Hindu brethren not to forget how enthused they were, to a man, over the prospect of Muslim Raj in India, or over the invasion of India by a Muslim power. This pride of race and religion was a virtue worthy of emulation, and it was this pride that would instantly translate itself into action at the right moment and with the right opportunity. The Hindus lacked this pride, this fervour, this unity of action, and, therefore, they had suffered.

This was a matter of compliment for the Pathans but was full of menace to the Hindus, and the Hindus must be ever vigilant about it. Eternal vigilance was the price of liberty. Also they had to bear it well in mind that the Mussulman imbibed this religious fervour and this spirit of pan-Islamism with his mother's milk. In every Muslim household, he was taught from his childhood to love his religion and to stand by the Muslim Raj. What had the Hindus to show in comparison with this fervour, with this ardent, burning passion? Not one in ten thousand Hindus knew or cared to know what Hindusthan was, what was Hindu power, Hindu Raj, or the meaning of the term 'Hindu' was. What then of a common bond of sympathy among them? The Pathans had, at the moment, only one place to call their own and that was Kabul. But they swear by it at all times, while they eat, drink and sleep. The Hindus have a place which is their own, but very few know of it, and know that the place goes by the name of Nepal. Crores of them cannot tell if the Nepalese is a Hindu or a Muslim. And the educated classes among them think and are found to declare that Nepal is no part of Hindusthan and that it was a different country altogether, more akin to China, Persia and Afghanistan and as foreign as Serbia. I have seen some of them holding an argument with me on the subject.

Whenever in my talks with the prisoners in the Andamans, I maintained that Nepal, being a Hindu Kingdom, can be made a good nucleus of Hindu *Sangathan*, they showed their doubt about it, and presumed to imagine that Nepal was, like Tibet, inhabited by primitive people, and was an insignificantly small country of foreigners. I was hard put to it to convince them by argument that the truth was far otherwise.

As I conveyed the news of war, from day to day, to my fellow-prisoners, plain and unvarnished, as it came to me, the partisans of Turkey, our friends—the Mussulmans—often showed me their bitterest hatred. And for the same reason, when I presented the English side of the war as faithfully, Mr. Barrie and the Superintendent were equally put out with me. The Superintendent, at the time, was a jingo imperialist, and he looked upon my work as an act of wickedness. He watched me with a severe eye as an enemy of his country. Just at the time, the Andamans felt the first shock of the war; the report had come that a German submarine was plying in its waters, and the officers had been arranging the defence of Port Blair against the attack of the enemy. The prisoners in the jail were all put upon the work of preparing tarpaulins and similar material to shield the British regiments from the sudden onslaught. The officers became still more adverse to me in that crisis. For, in order to prepare gunny-bags, the prisoners had to be put on the task of picking oakum and work five or six times as much as they had done before.

They had each to pick ten pounds of oakum everyday, where before they picked only two pounds of it. The prisoners were put to that hard work under pain of severe thrashing. The political prisoners were few in number—only those on transportation for life. All the rest were sent out to India after our third strike. The political prisoners were themselves appointed by Mr. Barrie to supervise the work, and to exact it from the prisoners. If we proved helpful to the authorities in exacting work from the prisoners, there was every chance of our being relieved of all work and of being appointed warders. Barrie saw this and delegated the task to us. He told us: "Do nothing, but see to it that these youngsters give us their full day's work." And this device of Mr. Barrie proved a success. Unfortunately, the prisoners given in my charge, I discovered, could give no more than three pounds a day each of picked oakum. And they complained that they were not bound to give more work as the present war was not theirs and India had nothing to do with it. "Take from us, of course, our normal quota of two pounds a day. We are bound to give it. But to compel us to turn out ten pounds because of the war, is a task that we are not going to put up with." What answer could I give them on this? I myself thought that they were right. None dare thrash the prisoners under my charge. The prisoners knew it full well. Therefore, they would do their normal quota and something more, and stopped there. In the evening, Mr. Barrie found out that my section had done much less than ten pounds for every prisoner, but had done much more than his share of two pounds a day. Mr. Barrie, therefore, began his barking. He stripped the tindal of his belt and made things hot for me. In the night, the Mussulman petty officers reported to him that I was preaching sedition to my section of prisoners. Next day, the Superintendent deposed me from my new office, and, by way of punishment, put me on picking oakum. I put on my strip of suspender and began the work. At the end of the day, I could hardly do one pound with the utmost of my labour. When it was found that I did just as much work as I could, and would not receive any help to fill my quota from other prisoners in my section, the other prisoners also ceased overworking themselves. I was, therefore, segregated from them and put again in my cell on the top floor of block number 7. I was asked there to resume my task of picking oakum.

The tindal, who had complained to Mr. Barrie about my preaching sedition to the section in my charge, had himself sworn against the Government before me by the name of God. Other tale-tellers had done the same. But I did not report against them. They attributed to me all sorts of offences and continued inventing stories about me, because they were sure that I was not the man to betray them. It became easy for them, by these means, to curry favour with the authorities of the jail to feather their own nests.

It was at this time, as I have already mentioned the fact in the chapter on *Shuddhi* movement, that the Mussulman warders and petty officers were set on to harass me for hours together by indecent abuse within the hearing of those who had come to look up to me with reverence and affection. They were given full freedom to talk about me in foul language all over the prison, and they continued to pester me all along.

But then incidents happened one after another, which encouraged me to carry on my work even in the depressing atmosphere of my prison-life.

The Submarine Emden and the Havoc it worked

The first event that diverted the attention of the officers at Port Blair from us, and consequently brought us some relief from the troubles described above, was the advent of the Emden in the sea around the Andamans. Soon came the report that the Emden had bombarded Madras. The authorities tried to keep it a dead secret, but this made wilder rumours spread all over the settlement. Never in the whole history of these islands had the officers found themselves so militarily unprepared and in such panicky atmosphere. There was hurry and bustle all over the place to rally the armed forces to protect the islands from similar attack. Next to the prison they set up an arsenal and an ammunition depot. Trenches were dug out all round the prison-wall and British soldiers were posted in them to guard the prison. A regiment of British soldiers was ordered out from Calcutta. The officers were detailed to guard the shore day and night. Within a few days, British warships or men-of-war were sailing on the seas around the Andamans. French submarines and Russian Dreadnoughts touched at Port Blair and passed on. The naval officers on board these warships visited the jail from time to time. The Captain of a Russian submarine, on his visit to the jail, had a long talk with me. He told me that Europe still remembered that I was a prisoner in the Andamans. The visits of these officers and their occasional talk were not without their consolation to me in the solitude of my cell.

These movements made it clear to us that in the strategy of the war in Europe the enemy had marked out these islands as a point of attack in the Eastern waters. Recalling to my mind the activities of the Abhinav Bharat Mandal and the other Indian revolutionary societies in the West, I had guessed that if at all war were to break out in Europe between Germany and England, these islands were bound to be the point of attack in the movement of the war from the West to the East. Mr. Barrie and other officers of the jail tried their level best to keep us in the dark about the movements of the troops along our shores, but I had divined, in spite of the secrecy maintained by them, that the Emden was hovering about the place to level its attack on the Andamans. News filtered in, that it was seen approaching our shores and that it had created a consternation all over the settlement. The harbour of Port Blair was not of such value to her. Why then did the submarine ply in these waters? I felt it was to bombard the Silver Jail and to set all of us free. I can say freely now how a doctor friend had managed to send me a message in the Andamans that the Abhinav Bharat and other revolutionary societies in Europe had contacted the Kaiser and arranged that a submarine should come over here to bombard the place and release us. It was then to rush into Burma and help create a violent revolution in India by all arms and ammunition necessary for that task. The ordinary prisoners were full of high hopes. They changed the slogan of "a free days now" to the password of "today or tomorrow". "Brother, today or tomorrow, we shall be free", that was a mode of greeting that had become common among them.

On a sudden, one would come panting and report to us that the German submarine had come and was sighted by the officers. They had turned their binoculars in her direction and were busy spying her movements. The Europeans on the island had left their bungalows and were running truly enough helter-skelter. The German submarine and the German navy had, for sometimes, become a scare to the handful of British soldiers, posted to guard these islands. And they feared that in the event of such a crisis, the prisoners themselves would turn against the European settlers. And this feeling was not altogether groundless, for the number of soldiers and the amount of arms and ammunition in that place was not sufficient to guard the place against an ordinary riot. The Andamans was no more than a drop in the ocean. What then would be their plight if a German Dreadnought or a German submarine were to bombard the place in such a helpless position? But brought up in the traditions of a great Empire, the Britishers held together and had decided to guard the place at all cost. They did not yield themselves to panic but made full preparations to hold the foe at bay. That the flying visit of a submarine should create a panic among the wives and children of the Europeans on that island was no surprise to me. The surprise of it was that a handful of them should maintain their hold over us for four continuous and trying years of the war, and in the midst of thousands of prisoners and other people on the island, who regarded them as their enemies and whose faith in their power was completely shaken by the catastrophe. Not a coconut plant was allowed to be uprooted from its soil, not a prisoner escaped from his daily quota of two pounds of picked oakum, or the portion of woven strand that was his usual labour. The same regulations, the same discipline, the same round of labour, the same order in the prison and the outside, went on with the regularity of the clock-work.

This nature of an Englishman, this tenacity of will, this pugnacity of temper, the Peshwas had failed to discern in the decline of their power. And today, as then, the population of Hindusthan is ignorant of it as ever. It is this trait in us that filled me with dismay. In the thick of the war, rumours floated on to us that, that day London had fallen, and that the German Dreadnoughts were bound to attack and take the Andamans overnight. The prisoners were dead sure about the authenticity of the news. They had, of course, no answer to give when we questioned them on the point. They would tell us that they had got it from this, that or another source. Some said it came to them from the waiter or the cook of a particular officer. Another said that it was the head-cook of the Chief Commissioner, who had given the news to him. He had himself seen the Chief Commissioner break open the post and reading the letter had dropped down in the chair, and dashed his hat on the table. Mr. Barrie was seen in tears, and his little daughter had thrust her head into the knees, and was lost in fear.

Such were the bits of news purveyed to us by the prisoners, and such were the proofs that they produced to support them. I was reminded by them of the alarming and false news in the days of the last Peshwa, Bajirao II. What reporters were those on whom the Peshwa depended! One correspondent reported to him of the big victory won by Yeshwantrao Holkar over the English and in support of the news, the wise-acre stressed the fact that the political resident at Garpir, while reading a communique, had flung his hat on the floor! The same evidence and the same inference still obsessed the mind of the people of India even today. The Britisher has not gone and wears his hat fast on his head. We are the fools for all that.

Indeed, during the last hundred-and-fifty years of British rule in India, there has been no change whatever in these traits of British character. They are born politicians, strong-willed administrators and tough fighters. And we have not changed either. We have remained the same gullible people, incapable of appreciating British character and ignorant of the ways and means to effectively confront them. The Britishers have not forgotten much during the last hundred-and-fifty years. And we have not learnt very much from them. The word-for-word report conveyed to me of the Sahib dashing his hat on the ground, spontaneously made me retort: "Fools! the Sahib was no Indian to do it. He was an Englishman and no coward. You would find one in a thousand Britishers, whom you could call a coward. The rest would not budge an inch. They fight to the last and win. Behold how among a thousand lambs like you, five of them live like lions, brave, fearless and stern. A Sahib to dash his hat on the ground for fear! Nay, the weather was warm and he did it, Barrie's daughter to thrust her head between the knees because she was frightened! No, she must be sleepy because she played too much, and was dozing. How do you know that the news of the submarine had scared her?"

Though it was foolish to be elated by the news, true or false, of British reverses and to exclaim, "O, brother, we are free, today or tomorrow," it was no less short-sighted to affirm that, while kingdoms and empires were tumbling down in the earthquake of war, the god in India would stand firm on its pedestal, and the shock of the war could never make him totter and fall. My information of movements abroad, the hovering of the German submarine about the Andamans, and the intensive British preparations to defend them, made me conclude that it was equally foolish to say that nothing would come out of it, that we must ever remain weak, and rot and weep for ever in this jail. I still believed that the Emden was plying in these waters according to plan, and the plan was no other than to get us free. Once or twice, I felt that the event was imminent. For the Emden, moving around, had almost hemmed us in. The wireless messages sent by the Chief Commissioner to Calcutta for monetary help were duly intercepted and released by the Emden, and when the ship laden with money was on her way to the Andamans, the submarine caught her and looted the treasure. The Andamans felt keenly the shortage of food stuffs once or twice, for the ships could not ply the water, for months together, from Rangoon, Calcutta and Madras to this place. In this situation, none could say definitely how long we could hold out, and when we would be compelled to surrender to the enemy. And then?

Not to be provided against this contingency would have been a reckless attitude of mind. For, then, we would be missing an opportunity of a life-time. So, we began thinking out what we were to do, if we were suddenly caught in this deluge, if the German submarine bombarded the Andamans and captured it, and if, in consequence, the prisoners of the Silver Jail were all forthwith let loose.......

The plans of the submarine were clear to my mind as I knew the movements of the Indian revolutionaries abroad. In that light, I made the position clear to my political colleagues as well as to other prisoners in my confidence. And I prepared a line of action to meet such an emergency. I communicated it to all of them that they might be ready for the day and be not caught napping. "Do not believe like fools that the Britishers can be so easily overthrown," I told them. But restricting ourselves to the Andamans, and in case the Emden succeeds in capturing and turning it into a centre for a possible revolution in India, we must be prepared to defend ourselves and do our duty to our country. We are not to be misled by foolish hope or useless despair. Whatever we decide upon, we must decide by wise and selfless attitude of mind. It was my effort, during these trying days of doubt and hope to awaken in the prisoners the sense of caution, alertness and duty.

The publication of the Rowlatt Committee's Report, in subsequent years had made it evident that the Emden had such designs in approaching the shores of the Andamans, and that my forecast was not altogether without foundation. The account of revolutionary activities in India outside, given in that Report, and their connection with Germany, makes it plain enough that, at least, during the first year of war, their plans were definitely to capture the Andamans and release us. And I know that these were not idle speculations but had nearly succeeded in the Emden's prowling activities about these shores. The European officers on these islands, in their later reports, confirmed our fears of such possible happenings.

I have already narrated in the early pages of this work, how, after the capture of Emden, the Government was definitely in the know of these matters and how they set up the defence of this prison as a military fortress. A turn-coat among us had, at once, carried to the ears of Mr. Barrie a report that negotiations were going on for the German aeroplane to swoop down upon the prison and take Savarkar out and away from this place. As if to checkmate this fictitious move, Mr. Barrie planted a fully armed posse of soldiers on a platform in the centre of our prison. This was in addition to the regiment of British soldiers specially detailed to be on patrolling duty all over the prison. This order continued for many months after the cessation of the war in Europe. After the incident of the Emden, I was subjected to the strictest surveillance.

And that gave the traitors among us a chance to raise all sorts of rumours against me, and to convey them to the jailor and the Superintendent above him. They were busy propitiating these tin-gods in any manner they liked.

When a regiment of British soldiers came to be planted in the island, this mood of our friends had found a special outlet to vent itself against us. The Tommies had no means of amusement and recreation in the barren and sordid atmosphere of this prison. Our friends were kind enough to furnish the entertainment. They invented all sorts of stories about me and about my former revolutionary activities, about my machinations in this prison, and about my secret connections with Germany. Full of fervour and spice they told the stories to the soldiers in order to entertain them. What those stories were, how the soldiers were regaled by them, what the officers said about me in their serious discussions over the possible movements of the Emden—full of the real and imaginary in them—all this finds its proper place in what the famous 'Ditcher' of the 'Capital' of Calcutta wrote of these events later on in his weekly notes for that paper. I may mention more about it as I pass on.

It was not so easy there to control us, and especially the political prisoners! The officers and the authorities must have imagined that our transportation to the jail in the Andamans was our death-in-life, the end of all our activities, our burial in the graveyard of the Andamans, from which no resurrection was possible. And, therefore, they need no more think of us and be anxious over us. But the world had not forgotten though we lay buried here. On the other hand, they thought and spoke and wrote about the Andamans in the world without, because of the political prisoners confined in that island. And the jail had been turned into a living fortress, strongly armed and keenly guarded, and the seas were protected by dreadnoughts and submarines, for fear of our escape from it, in order to keep us safe within.

That our compatriots in India should so remember us, so cherish our memory, when we lay as prisoners in the Andamans and dead to the world without, filled our hearts with gratitude to them. And even in that dark dungeon of a prison-house, in the conditions of utter despair and horrid physical and mental torture, this living memory about us gave us hope and courage, which I feel it my duty to record in these pages. Everyday we were in fear that a fresh charge of sedition and high treason might be trumped up against us as the result of a systematic campaign of misrepresentation going on against us during these days of war. And who did misrepresent us and carry tales against us? Our own men, the renegades among us, who had allied themselves with Mr. Barrie to save their own skins!

But even in this daily suspense and anxiety, we felt gratified that the war had made the Indian question an issue of International importance. This world earthquake was sure to fructify our hopes about India, that the desert of India would smile again like paradise—thoughts like these elated us, but a reaction also came that the war may end in turning the whole world into a desert with India included in it.

We swung like a pendulum between smiles and tears; and yet did not fail to rise above the darkness of despair and peep at the dawn that was sure to follow it. To end with the words of the poet, we ever "painted on the midnight sky of sorrow, the golden morrow".

□

4

(1914-1918) Political Prisoners Again Flood The Andamans!

While these manoeuverings of the German submarine in the waters of the Andamans were in progress to attack the islands, I happened to receive a press-cutting from a friend which contained the heading "Mutiny at Meerut". This cutting was thrown into my cell by a political prisoner employed as a writer in the office below.

About the month of May last, a plot was discovered in India to start a revolution with an army at Meerut rising in mutiny against the Government. Several arrests were made. Some were tried and sent to the gallows. As I read the headline, a thrill went through my heart and all over the body.

In 1857, in the same town of Meerut, and about the month of May, Indian regiments had broken into open revolt against their masters. That also was a spark of fire thrown up from the furnace of revolution that was preparing all over the country. What was to be the end of this recent mutiny at Meerut, I wondered. Was it a spark of a general revolution?

If it were confined to Meerut alone, the Government would not make such a mountain of it; it would not so broadcast it all over the country. What a difference it indicated, all the same, between India ten years ago and India now! Discontents, petitions, appeals, protests, censures, conspiracies, riots, action and reaction, revolvers, bombs, fights, and the revolt of an army—the widespread rumours about it! What a change had the whirling of time introduced in India in these ten years!

Since the War of Independence in 1857, the word mutiny had been expunged from the political vocabulary of India. The idea had faded out of her political sky. In the conflagration of the European War of 1914, it had risen phoenix-like to inflame that sky, and the daring of the people had risen to its highest point in that thermometer.

On that day and during the week, the mutiny at Meerut had become the absorbing topic of discussion for all of us in that prison. Then came in its wake the news of conspiracy and revolt in Lahore and Punjab. Within a few days thereafter, the soldiers, who had refused to go on the front and regiments of them, were being deported as prisoners to the Andamans; and we had first-hand proof of the agitation going on in India.

Our last strike had ended in the beginning of 1914. And, thereafter, we alone, some few on transportation for life, were detained here, while all other political prisoners were sent back to India. Of that I have already written. But in the turmoil and confusion of this war, who was to follow that rule? All political convicted for conspiracies and revolutionary movements on the eve of the Great War were being sent for incarceration, batch after batch, to this jail, and this change had become, convenient for us to secure the latest reliable news of agitation all over the country, and of war in Europe.

The German submarines had, for sometimes, blocked the passage in the seas of the Andamans. They had captured and detained one or two merchant ships during the period; as such there was no communication by sea between India and the Andamans, and no prisoners from India could be sent to the prison in the Andamans. When these submarines were destroyed by the warships of Japan, Russia and Great Britain, the sea became a safe passage for traffic between India and the Andamans and the system of sending Chalans from India to these islands was resumed as before.

And one day, we found a party of political prisoners entering the Silver Jail. This was the first batch of convicts in the Lahore Conspiracy case and consisted, for the most part, of Sikhs involved in the Gadar trial.

On seeing them, I exclaimed, forgetting for a while, their pitiable condition in the jail, "Behold these Sikhs, they have come here at last as I had predicted."

When I was taking a leading part in the Indian revolutionary activities in England, I had a discussion one day with my Sikh colleague, Sirdar Harnam Singh, on the subject of national awakening among the Sikhs in India. There were at that time many Sikh students taking their education in England. Punjab being the centre of recruitment for the Indian army, it was easy for these young students on their return to India to spread the cult of nationalism from hut to hut, and village to village throughout the Sikh community in Punjab. I told my friend how to do it and drew up a scheme for that purpose. I emphasised the need of such work as I regarded the Sikhs as part of the Hindu community as a whole. My friend, Sirdar Harnam Singh, seemed to have no hopes about it. He said that the Sikhs, as a community, were extremely clannish, they had no vision and interest beyond their particular habitations in Punjab. They had no national outlook, and he doubted very much if they could ever be persuaded to think and feel as nationalists. Their religious fervour on behalf of the Panth and the Sangha was a great obstacle to their being converted to the view that they were Indians, and they were one politically with the Hindus of India. I said to my friend, then, "Look here, you are a Sikh, you come from a Sirdar family of moderate views in politics. You take your education in England and you have become one of us, a nationalist, a revolutionary like myself, and ready to sacrifice everything for your country. If a Sikh, like you, can, in such a short time, be this, why not all other Sikhs? I have studied the history of the Sikhs closely and I know what type of men you are. If you agree to work up the scheme, I have outlined for you, and talk about it, discuss it with every Sikh, whom you meet here and in India. I feel sure that within five years you will witness a great change in them, and they will all range themselves on our side. I have no doubt about it." This was said somewhere between 1908 and 1909.

I remembered the meeting and the conversation when I saw the Sikh prisoners pouring into the jail of the Andamans. And I said to my friends, "They have come as I told they would."

Now remained the Nepalese to be one with us. If the Gurkha along with the Sikhs were absorbed in the camp of Hindu *Sangathan*, all Hindus would be one and would present a solid front to the rest of India.

These feelings would well up within me, according to the changing phases of thought, through which I was passing at the moment. After the batch of Sikh convicts, came in batches of political prisoners in Punjab sentenced in conspiracy case in different parts of the province. Several batches of soldiers were transported to this place for refusing to go to Rangoon, Singapore, Basra and other fronts; and there were among them convicts in revolutionary conspiracies. Their advent in this prison surcharged the atmosphere with shades and differences of live political opinion. About a hundred-and-fifty political prisoners had gathered in this prison as convicts for different kinds of offences. There were those who had mutinied at Singapore; others who had proceeded to Rangoon via Siam to spread sedition in the army and raise a rebellion; others again were involved in Benares Conspiracy Case; there were some from Bengal charged and sentenced for political dacoit; and all sentenced to long terms of imprisonment. It is impossible here to give a full story of all their adventures, their daring exploits, their secret movements, and their mysterious plans. We cannot even mention their names in this edition. We have to leave that task for the future.

Among these recent arrivals, there was only one man, whom I had known personally and he was Professor Permanand. However, I had referred to all of them in my previous talks with the prisoners, so that when they came in this prison, there was a complete change in their political outlook. They heard from these recent arrivals about their ideals, about their self-sacrifice; they heard stories of those who had been sent to the gallows or had died fighting, of their plots and conspiracies; they heard discriptions of battlefronts in France, and of the war as it was being fought. This first-hand information had worked such a revolution in their thoughts and behaviour. We had already endeavoured to educate them in these high matters and to make them capable of thinking about them and of playing their part in the political life of their country. But personal contact with these new men had helped considerably widen their interest and deepen that knowledge.

Though I knew only Professor Permanand among them, most of them knew me. They had read my contributions to the press; they had studied my books. Their reverence for me made them eager to see me as soon as they had stepped into the prison. The prison officials took all possible measures to keep them apart from me; but, considering their strength of numbers, it was impossible for the authorities to detach them entirely from me; and soon myself and they could establish perfect communication with one another. They told me that newspaper 'Gadar' in America had published translations in Hindi, Urdu and Punjabi, of my book on the Indian Mutiny of 1857. One of the prominent leaders of the 'Gadar Movement' in America, Pandit Jagatram by name, who, in the Lahore Conspiracy Case, refused to defend himself, though the charge against him would have brought upon him the sentence of death, and who confessed that he had done what he was charged with, further told me: "I was once an easy-going man; one who loved pleasure and knew nothing else of importance in life. I did not dabble at all in politics. But one day, I happened to get your book on Indian Mutiny to read. I sat out for one whole day and one whole night and finished the book. I set it aside, and, with it, I also set aside my former mode of life. I took an oath that I will work for the freedom of my country, and here I am today with you." Just in a vein of humour, I said, "Well then, that book of mine had obtained for you a ticket for the Andamans."

Another, who had served long in the Indian army and had earned much wealth in business in the latter part of his life, an old Sikh gentleman told me that it was the reading of articles in the 'Gadar', that had converted him to a revolutionary movement for the freedom of India. He enlisted himself in that movement and gave all his fortune to it, though anonymously. And, as a result, he had achieved transportation to the jail of the Andamans. Speaking to me on the subject, he said, progressive people in China, who knew about India and her present struggle, always enquired: 'Where is Mr. Savarkar? In which prison is he locked up?' And, then, the old gentleman had told them about my hardships here and they expressed their bitter grief for my misery and suffering. When in England, I used to write on India in the newspapers connected with the Chinese revolutionary movement led by Dr. Sun-Yet-Sen. Some of them remembered me as late as the years 1915 and 1916. And I had the consolation that my work had not all gone in vain.

Referring to the Kolu, I am reminded of a story of its publicity in America. Its publicity had induced some of the brave Sikhs, who had now come here as prisoners, to join our movement in America. They told me, "A cartoon, showing you yoked to the oil-mill, was published in one of our papers in America. I got the newspaper from a newsboy hawking it about in the streets of America. As we saw the cartoon, we were deeply pained by the sight and were full of tears. While men like you, we felt, were sacrificing their all for their country, we were wasting our lives in spending lavishly on drink and enjoying ourselves. And the thought made us ashamed of ourselves." This revulsion of feeling made them take life seriously, join our movement, forego their wealth and suffer as others had suffered for the independence of India. They left America, came back to India and joined in conspiracies for the overthrow of the British Raj. And here, they were now in the prison of the Andamans along with us, and sentenced like us to serve long terms of imprisonment across the seas.

Many were the episodes they told me of their own experience about the matter. I have narrated here only one or two of them. The last of these surprised me most, though it was a pleasant surprise. For, whenever I turned the Kolu in the solitude of my room and was done up by the exertion, I always used to console myself by the thought that I would bear it all, if the knowledge of it to the world outside were only to pour oil into the flames of discontent that I knew were spreading all over the country. But I was in despair about it. For, how was the story of my hardships to reach the ears of those, who were so far away from me? I have already referred to this mood and how I controlled it by the power of thought! But when my Sikh friend told me the story, I said to myself, "Yes, I must bear it all, for it is never lost, it produces its effects in due time. That is the only way that one can put fat in the fire and make it burn. An agitation succeeds finally on the strength of tenacity and patience of its sufferers. Here was the proof of it. Every drop of oil that fell into the vat below, as I turned the wheel that ground down and crushed the dried coconut-kernels in the rut and the well, was a spark that had kept blazing the sacred fire of discontent already aflame all over the country. Here was a clear evidence of that influence.

One of the Sikhs in the prison informed me that his copy of my prescribed book on the Indian Mutiny of 1857 had gone into the hands of a friend in Brazil. The book was so popular with Indians everywhere that the copy in Brazil was sold for a sum of ₹ 150. In addition to this personal news, I got all the information I wanted of what had happened in Siam, Canada, Singapore, America, Europe, Bengal and Punjab as a result of our secret movements and conspiracies in that part of the world, from the mouths of leaders and followers who had taken an active part in them from the incident of the Komagata Maru down to the violent uprising in Punjab during the days of this war. Part of it was known to the world, and part of it had yet remained in the dark. I had planned to write a complete history of all these efforts and struggles in one connected narrative beginning with 1909 and bringing it down to the close of the first Great War. But I found it impossible to complete such a story in the prison at Andamans. And I had slender hopes to write it ever, for I had never expected then to be free and to enjoy sufficient leisure and peace of mind to complete the task that I had proposed to myself. My fellow-prisoners, the Sikhs, ever encouraged and always insisted that I should undertake the work, when I would twit them that the task of the present generation was to make history and the task of the following generation was to write it, which it may or it may not do. After all, writing history was a secondary business, making it was the prime part.

As soon as the first batch of convicts in the Lahore Conspiracy Case in Punjab reached the Andamans, the jail authorities adopted all measures to keep it under strict control. Profiting by past experience, however, the work on Kolu was given only to those in the batch, whom they found strong and able-bodied to do it. But we warned the newcomers that it was but the thin end of the wedge, and that they would be wise to refuse to do it from the very start. We know that the authorities dare not remain stubborn with these forty to fifty prisoners, with by far a larger total of prisoners at that time in the jail, than it was when we had resisted, struck work and finally won in banishing the Kolu from our daily ration of hard labour. The authorities proposed, as a result of this protest, that they were to work on the Kolu for a week and no more. We suggested that the prisoners should agree to the compromise and get on to work. All our earlier struggles, on behalf of political prisoners, had, thus, proved of immense value to those who came after. But now the quarrel turned on the work of picking oakum. Many of the convicts in this batch were spirited young men, fire-eaters, most of them, and it was foolish to expect that they would prostrate themselves on the very first day before the petty officers and the *jamadar*s put on supervising their work. When in the evening each one of them went to the *jamadar* to hand over to him his day's quota of work, the tindal and the *jamadar* ventured to behave very rudely with him, for which they got from him and from all the reward they deserved. Of course, the *jamadar* took the affair to the jailor, and, as a result, the boldest and the most spirited of them, one Parmanand by name, was sent for by Mr. Barrie for personal enquiry.

The Convict Beats Mr. Barrie

This young Parmanand was a different type altogether from Professor Parmanand. Later on, he became one of the most shining men and teachers who had studied deeply and read widely during the long years of self-education in this prison, which, for that reason, may be well compared to the University of Nalanda in ancient India. They had not only qualified themselves for that high position by mere erudition, but by their spirit of sacrifice, by their sense of service and by their sterling character. Well, young Parmanand was made to appear before Mr. Barrie, and Mr. Barrie, as was usual with him, began by insulting young Parmanand. He first ordered him to stand erect. Parmanand had stood before him as any ordinary decent man would stand. But Mr. Barrie would not be satisfied and, in fury, addressed foul words to him, for abuses were his ingrained habit. But the spirited young man was not accustomed to them. As soon as the young man had heard these words, he brushed aside his warders on either side, rushed forward, and gave a sharp slap in the face of Mr. Barrie right in the office where he was sitting to try the young man. Seeing him coming like a tiger, Mr. Barrie shouted and tried to rise from the chair, and the blow crashed on his hat, the chair was upset and Mr. Barrie ran out crying, "Catch him, catch him." Mr. Parmanand was overpowered, beaten all over the body with stick and fisticuffs, till his lips, his face and back began to bleed. Mr. Barrie hurriedly rang up the Superintendent. He reported that there was riot in the prison, and there was consternation all over the colony. The cry went round that a bomb-thrower had thrashed the warders and had beaten Mr. Barrie. The Superintendent arrived and ordered caning for Parmanand. He was tied to the frame work and given twenty stripes with the cane. Every stroke made a deep cut in the body and blood spouted from the wound. His whole body was a mass of lacerated flesh. The cane cut the flesh and pieces fell out with each stroke of it. Yet Parmanand did not wince and uttered not a word. I have heard prisoners bellowing under the inhuman punishment—the most hardened criminals and the *goondas* among them. But young Parmanand stood still. Mr. Barrie went on, "Beat him, beat him with all your strength." The caning was done and Parmanand bore it unperturbed.

It has to be noted that he was not taken to the hospital for dressing the wounds but marched straight to his cell and locked up. This was the first occasion for a political prisoner to be punished this way.

Young Parmanand felt nothing, nor did the other political prisoners feel for him. For, they knew that Parmanand was the aggressor and had beaten Mr. Barrie. They did not think it a heavy price to pay for Mr. Barrie's disgrace throughout the prison and for the fear it had engendered in the hearts of them all for political prisoners as a class. The spirited action of Parmanand was a lesson to them all. Parmanand had defied prison-regulations and he was caned for that defiance. There we were quits. But Mr. Barrie was not entitled to abuse Parmanand. And he had abused him and, therefore, we had a right to show our resentment for that action. So, there was a sympathetic strike in the prison. The Superintendent and Mr. Barrie went round pacifying the strikers. The Superintendent pledged his word that Mr. Barrie shall no longer abuse the prisoners. The strikers were requested to resume work, no matter how much they did it or did not do it. After this, the strike, of course, came to an end.

The resistance offered by the first batch to the high-handedness of Mr. Barrie made life easier for those who came after it. Even then, Mr. Barrie would, now and then, try to exercise his authority and extract additional work from one or another minor political prisoners. Sometime, he would ask them to weave four pounds of coiled rope instead of three, and sometime he would exact more quantity of picked oakum from them. Sometimes, he would slyly seek to put someone on the Kolu, so on and so forth. But these political prisoners would not tolerate anything from him. And if he threatened caning, they would straightaway tell him, in that case, they would all stop work at once. The spirited and the daring among them beat Mr. Barrie on all scores. These daily scuffles always led someone or another of these political prisoners to resist Mr. Barrie. They never gave Mr. Barrie more work than what the prison-regulations had laid down for them. And, sometimes, they gave much less. Everyday they had to put up on the prison-gate the roll of those present and absent in their record of daily work. Since the entry of political prisoners in that jail the absentees on the roll were never marked as zero. The resistance in some form or another, had continued from day to day and, therefore, neither Mr. Barrie nor the Superintendent dared continue his policy of repression any longer, or carry things in his usual high-handed manner.

The Warders Carry Complaints Against Me

I have narrated in the last chapter with what suspicion and severity they treated me in this prison. And when these new batches of prisoners had begun to come in, their rigour towards me was even greater, for they knew that the newcomers would look up to me with reverence and affection, and, therefore, they must keep me isolated from them as lay in their power to do. Mr. Barrie took the lead in the matter. And when he found that he had failed, he set his henchmen—our political renegades—

to do that dirty work for him. He and they left no opportunity to damn me in their eyes; he left no stone unturned to destroy their faith in me, and to divide them from me by poisoning their minds about me. That continued till the end of the chapter, and he chafed that he could not succeed. He used to tell all the prisoners, "Do not run after Savarkar; you will unnecessarily incur the wrath of your superiors by depending upon him. He is a clever fellow and a shirker; do please listen to me. I shall give you all the comforts you need here; I will make your life easy. And if you don't believe me, ask these fellows, they are also political prisoners, they will convince you of my good faith. How very modest and gentlemanly they are! I have given them responsible offices in this jail, while your Savarkar still rots in his cell picking oakum." While Mr. Barrie went on talking in this vein to the prisoners, he reported about me to his superiors in the following terms: "This man is, indeed, the source of all our troubles. He praises Germany; he gives news to the prisoners about the reverses of England; he incites them to plots and conspiracies; he dares not take the lead himself for he is afraid of his own skin; he fears punishment, but he is behind the scene, all the time. He will inflame the Sikhs against us counting upon their respect for him. Nothing that I may do will diminish his hold upon all the political prisoners here. He is, indeed, a dare devil." "He had a motive in thus misrepresenting me to them as an irreclaimable and confirmed revolutionary. For then, it was easy for him to saddle me with every disturbance in the jail, and show himself as an innocent being to his masters. This was due to the instigation of Mr. Savarkar," was always the burden of his song.

Though Mr. Barrie considered himself a wily fellow and an expert in the art of lying, he was, indeed, a shallow minded officer and a fool. When he tried the same arts of deception upon us, political prisoners, that he had tried upon others, it made me simply laugh at his self-delusion. Once it came into his head to show me but a portion of what he had written about me to his superiors. He wanted, thereby, to cower me down, and make me give up the leadership of the party I had built up in the prison. With this object in view, one day he sent for me in his office. He started with praising me lavishly for my intelligence and scholarship, and for my fearlessness in public life. And the same Mr. Barrie had been representing me to my friends as a shirker. Then he began reproving me for the misuse I was making of these high qualities. He, then, pretended that he had all good wishes for me and yet was bound to report against me as he had reported. If I were to see these reports, he added, I would wake up in time and mend my ways. He was showing those reports to me against all prison regulations, because, indeed, he loved me, he concluded. And then Mr. Barrie took out his diary, and read to me a portion of it from day to day. What I have quoted above are the sentences from his daily diary as I could recall them. I must state here that every petition, that I had sent from here to the Government of India bore Mr. Barrie's inevitable comment: "It was all a lie and that Savarkar was not a man to be won over by any facilities or concessions that the Government might grant him. He was not to be intimidated either by the severest punishment it might think of meting out to him." Mr. Barrie was foolish enough to show this to me and to tell me that I was not to reveal it to anyone else.

Mr. Barrie's Gentility in Harshness

In this record of my experiences in the Andamans, I had to expose so frequently the wicked disposition of Mr. Barrie. But there was another side to it, which I must not omit to mention in this narrative, for I regard it as an act of justice to give every man his due, and not to blame him except when he deserves the blame. In the position of a jailor, as he was, and of a prison, in which the worst class of criminals in the whole of India was sent for custody and proper management, it was but natural for a man like Mr. Barrie to be stern and severe, and to come down with a heavy hand, sometimes, on the rebellious mob that he was called upon to rule. And I often told him that if he did so, he was not to blame for it. Years of contact with such a class of people had developed that temper into an ingrained habit of his mind. At least, that was true enough about his prison administration. He was hard, cruel and autocratic in that office. He could not discriminate good and bad. He really believed that he was the demi-god of Port Blair. And that was a blemish, a defect in him. The bother and fuss of prison administration were both the amusement and the concern of his solitary life. Yet, out of prison and in the midst of his friends and family, he was not a cruel man or a martinet. And he allowed himself to be flattered and fooled by anyone, who chose to do so. He was not a learned man and yet desired to show off his learning by repeating some stock quotations from English poetry. He knew only a few of them and when one pressed him, he repeated these five or six poems with the pose of a born actor. Occasionally, he had a fit to dazzle me by his erudition. And then, he would repeat them all to me in one breath. Leaving aside his behaviour with me as a jailor, I must say that he cherished a sincere regard for me. Whenever some merchants, editors or military men visited the Andamans on business, they often visited the prison to see me. In the days of war, the naval officers on submarines came here to enquire after me and exchanged a few words with me. That also may be the reason of his high esteem for me. Among the members of his family, his wife was a saintly woman and his only daughter of seventeen had been to Rangoon, where she had passed her Matriculation and was reading for the Teacher's Diploma. Mr. Barrie's wickedness was considerably softened by the influence of these two women. The prisoners often told me that they often restrained him in his hard conduct towards them. Both the wife and the daughter felt deep personal sympathy for me. Miss Barrie from her very childhood till Mr. Barrie's death, whenever she happened to be in the Andamans during her holidays from Rangoon, used to visit the prison, talk with me for half-an-hour or so on topics of general interest. And she left always with a word of sympathy for me. Individually, and on such occasions. I behaved with Mr. Barrie with perfect familiarity and good will. On occasions, Mr. Barrie sent me fruit from his own garden, and he did so with a wish that I should be on good terms with him. I accepted the gift with sincere gratitude, and I keep it on record in these pages. But whenever he found that I would not give up my political friends in that prison, or abandon activities like *Shuddhi* and the spread of education that I had undertaken for the uplift of prisoners, in his jail, he repented for his kindness towards me. And for some days after, he used to be very harsh on me. Those of our political prisoners who had been won over by such kindness and those who desired for nothing but selfish ease, were always invited by him for a personal talk with him. But strange as it may seem, he always invited me along with them. The only difference he made between them and me was that while, giving them some writing work he seated them in chairs, he made me stand in front of him like an ordinary prisoner. It was done deliberately and with a motive to humiliate me before them, to make me repent for my obstinate conduct with him, and for my refusal to give up public work as a concession to his kindness.

Mr. Barrie and the members of his family, as also the friends read the poems I used to compose for them, would listen with interest to the story of my life, and it must be said to their credit that they showed due appreciation for it. On the whole, they regarded me with a feeling of respect and I often wrote some English poems for them. On one day in the year, Mr. Barrie had made it a rule of his life to be on terms of perfect cordiality with me. And that was Christmas. It was impossible for him, on that day, to shake off completely the traditional influences of the religion of Irish Roman Catholicism on his mind. The demigod of Port Blair, the autocrat and tyrant of the Silver Jail, came out that day an extremely different man—a man full of kindness and warmth for all. On that day, the political prisoners, with all their efforts to annoy him, did not disturb the calmness of his face. No scorn or contempt or anger was visible on it, even to the extent of raising an eyebrow. He invited them for Christmas in his office and treated them to tea, milk and other sweets. I would say to him at that time that he had better give us a newspaper or two to read rather than entertain us to tea and sweetmeats. Mr. Barrie, to be fair to him, gave us the newspapers and sent us sweetmeats to follow them. If I could not go to his office that day, he sent the sweets to my room. That day, he never treated anyone harshly, and, as far as possible, heard no complaints against him.

Who were these Tale-tellers?

Mr. Barrie's shrewdness was as defective as his kindliness. He was ever crooked in his kindness as he was foolish in his shrewdness. For he had in his temperament that trait of foolishness that disqualifies a man from knowing his limitations. The shrewdness he boasted of may have served him very well, perhaps, in dealing with the ordinary class of prisoners in his jail. And he imagined that it could work effectively in all cases and with all persons. That he should have shown and read to me his diary in the office was, in his view, an act of remarkable shrewdness to trap me in. But it was I, who scored against him in that business, because I knew, in spite of myself, what he had been writing against me to his superiors. It was he who was exposed and not I. And I had the further advantage of glancing through his diary, though he did his best to hide those pages from me in which he had been writing in praise of those among us who had gone over to his side. After he had finished with it, Mr. Barrie said to me with an air of self-importance, "Well now, you have seen my diary, what do you think of it?"

I answered him contemptuously, "Well, it is a precious document, indeed. The Great Caesar of Ancient Rome wrote a diary, and you have written one. May I call it a village Caesar's journal? I believe there are only two diaries in the world of such unparalleled importance. And I thank my stars for reading them both."

Mr. Barrie was, of course, put out by this retort. But he took it all in the spirit of a joke and said, "But it will be good for you to lay to heart the lesson it conveys. The Government has so much evidence against you, so many reports like these to condemn you. Beware, even now, I put it to you as a friend. Have nothing to do with those newcomers—your friends, the Sikhs and the Punjabis. They are, all of them, wild fellows, uneducated, illiterate, loafers and vagabonds-hewers of wood and drawers of water. They have joined you and your organisation to line their own pockets. They turned dacoits for selfish gain and nothing more. A man like you ought not to demean himself even by a word with them."

I answered him coolly and with deliberation somewhat as follows: "He is a truly educated man, who, smitten with grief for others seeks to make them happy, whatever it may cost him in personal ease and well-being. The Punjabi and Sikh prisoners may not know English, but to know English is not to be educated. What the educated have not done for their country, these so-called ignorant person have done for it. They have given their life for her, they have sacrificed their all for her, they are brave and bold peasants and workmen, and I regard them in no way inferior to political prisoners. What even ten in a thousand educated Indians have not done for. India, that sacrifice of life and property have these men done for their motherland. I shall, therefore, never keep myself aloof from them. For, they are as much mine as the political prisoners in this jail."

It was Mr. Barrie's nature to brook no opposition. Whenever he condemned anyone, one must say yes to him, and then he was pleased. I knew this trait in him and yet could not take it calmly that he should traduce the Sikh and the Punjabi prisoners in my presence. I had to support them against this vilification. Mr. Barrie was, therefore, irritated by my reply, and he bore a constant grudge to me. But he could do nothing to me, could frame no charge against me and could not implicate me as I gave him no chance to do it. He kept on fretting and fuming for a long time, and at last set on me some *goondas* to involve me in some plot or another that he may catch me.

The *goondas*, so encouraged, began to frame up some thing against me, of which I shall give here an instance or two. One of the ragamuffins, a Christian prisoner, concealed a knife in the urinal of my chawl. And he tutored another of his tribe, a Hindu, to depose that I had concealed it there to stab an officer of the jail. Fortunately enough this Hindu prisoner knew of me because I was the leader of the *Sangathan* movement. And he came to me and told me all about it. I exposed the plot to Mr. Barrie and threatened to take the matter to the Superintendent if he sought to hush it up. Of course, Mr. Barrie had to submit and I came safe out of the matter.

The second instance of the kind was as follows:

A Mussulman convict, who was an out-and-out ruffian and who was caned and placed in an iron cage right near my cell, had managed to induce a Muslim warder to partially saw overnight the two iron bars of the main entrance to the block right in front of my room. It was his plot to escape from the cage and the chawl, if he could, by breaking the bars, or to say to the authorities that I got them partially broken to make my own escape. A Burmese prisoner was also involved in the plot. If the ruffian could not escape, then reporting against me would win his pardon straightaway. A tindal on his evening round noticed that the bars were slightly bent, and that very night the culprit had plotted to make his escape. Thus, the conspiracy proved abortive, whereupon the prisoner in the cage reported that it was I who had contrived to get the bars partially bent and broken. In the investigation on the matter, the Burmese was also implicated in the plot, the two Mussulmans having suspected him to have broken the secret. But his arrest led to an evidence by him, which brought the whole truth in the daylight. The ruffian in the cage and his Muslim accomplice were thoroughly exposed in the trial and I was saved. I told the Superintendent without mincing words how these frame-ups against me by the worst elements in the prison were due to the incitement of Mr. Barrie who had told all of them to keep a strict watch on me.

Mr. Barrie did not rest there. He tried to involve me in a plot of a different nature than the one indicated by the two instances I have given above.

In the batch of Punjabi prisoners, who had been recently deported to the Andamans, there was a political prisoner Chatarsingh by name. He was a teacher in a Sikh High School. When a high European official had come to inspect the school, this man had attempted to stab him. The prisoner belonged to a revolutionary society in Punjab. On that offence, he was tried and sentenced to serve his life-sentence in the Andamans. Chatarsingh was a short-tempered and irascible person. The Sikhs grew long hair and beards. And they wanted soap to wash them clean, but they were not given this or any ordinary facility in this prison, and they were subjected to constant persecution and abuse by the warders in charge. Infuriated by this harsh treatment, Chatarsingh one day attacked the Superintendent, who had come to the prison to supervise the prisoners that were being weighed that day. The Superintendent rolled over the chair and, therefore, no harm was done to him. But a cry went round that the Superintendent was attacked and the tindals, warders and *jamadars* gathered round, overpowered Chatarsingh and gave him a sound thrashing. It was the Superintendent himself who came to the help of Chatarsingh and freed him from the warders. Mr. Barrie, so soon as he got the news, reported that it was I who had set Chatarsingh on the Superintendent. Only one day before this incident, I had a conversation with the Superintendent in which I asked him if he favoured Home Rule for India. Taking advantage of this question, Mr. Barrie had said that it was evidence enough to prove me as an instigator of Chatarsingh. Some four political prisoners had openly denounced Chatarsingh for this cowardly attack and I had spoken nothing about it. Mr. Barrie questioned me for the silence and I replied, "You had yourself given orders that no prisoner shall meddle in the doings of another. When my brother was ailing and I told you in his behalf that he should be removed to the hospital, you had warned me that it was none of my business; you may be brothers outside, but you come here as prisoners, you said then, and. therefore, none was to speak for another. Why then should you expect me to intervene in this affair?" The third thing was that when it was known that Chatarsingh was to be administered caning, I had interposed along with other prisoners that he had been sufficiently punished for the violation of the prison-regulations by the sound drubbing that the tindals and warders, rushing on him, had given him. The Superintendent had escaped without injury, hence, there was no need or justification for caning Chatarsingh. Mr. Barrie pieced these facts together to frame up a charge that I was at the bottom of the whole mischief. Chatarsingh had been locked up in a cage since that day for a number of years. A slip that came into the hands of Professor

Parmanand made him deduce and publish: "Mr. Barrie had worked up the whole matter. He saw in the incident his chance to inflame the mind of the Superintendent against the political prisoners as a class, and he simply rejoiced over it. And, therefore, casting all the blame on Savarkar brothers, he wanted to pluck out the very root of the discontent in that prison. He, therefore, gave it abroad that Savarkars were very glad to foment such spirit among them, and the officers were not without being a party to it." (See Professor Parmanand's Reminiscences.)

I Lose My Health

Between the year 1915 and 1916, my health began to fail in this prison. My constitution had held up against all hardships it had to bear since my arrest in London in 1910. I had to pass my life since that date in British prison, in the many prisons of India and in the Andamans. I had to endure all sorts of inconveniences, of mental and physical suffering added to my family cares during the period. My constitution had already been undermined by my exertions and worries in regard to my political activities and the constant risks and anxieties imposed by these activities. Bad food, insanitary mode of living, and hard labour in this prison had brought it to the breaking point by the year 1915. But from that year, my digestive power had been interfered with by the unnutritious and ill-cooked food it had to swallow and assimilate. I had, many times, drawn the attention of the Superintendent to the state of my failing health, but none seemed to pay any attention to it. Once or twice during the period, I had high fever, but I was not sent to the hospital for any treatment, and as soon as the fever had subsided, I was made to do my usual work and to eat the same food. I developed dysentery out of this, but I was not given a drop of milk, which was given to the ordinary prisoners as a reward for their good work. Hence, I had to live on ill-cooked rice and dal of the prison ration. The bread served to us being almost raw, I gave up eating it and suffered from loss of weight. In course of time, my stomach refused to digest dal. So, I had to do without it and ate rice with water as my curry on it. I continued on this diet for days in order to avoid an attack of dysentery. The dysentery gave a griping pain in the stomach, made me go for stools at odd hours, and it was a great trouble to me in the cell where I lay confined. The fever had become almost chronic, I had temperature everyday, and the attacks of dysentery were more frequent. At last, I could not take rice even, for it was served half-raw every third or fourth day. The doctor was to be sent only if dysentery proved to be acute. And the measure of that acuteness was left for the jailor to decide. There were occasions in my malady when I literally prayed to God that it may be given me to discharge the whole fluid right in front of the doctor that he might be convinced that I was really suffering from dysentery! For, if he made me sit for stools when I had no discharge or not a drop of blood in it, suddenly the decision would go against me that there was nothing the matter with me and that I was only feigning. This experience I had many a time in this my chronic ailment, that often at night I felt griping pain in the stomach followed by high fever, I discharged blood and had stools. But when the doctor came, all these symptoms had disappeared, and the doctor declared me to be a doubtful case with no treatment to follow. So when very rarely, these symptoms synchronised with the arrival of the doctor, I really thanked them. For, then I was put on a different meal and given milk along it and I recouped quickly. But then I was instantly put to work and relapse followed. The same food, the same work and the same malady—this followed unbroken for months together.

At this time, my brother got the concession to cook for himself, according to the settlement of the political prisoners' general strike in 1914. My brother got his own ration and after his morning work he prepared his own food in a corner of the kitchen set apart for him. Soon after, Mr. Wamanrao Joshi of Nagpur was given the same concession and joined him. As they began to cook their food together, they felt much better and improved in health. Similarly, all the convicts in the Manik Tola Bomb Case were clubbed together for their own food. My brother used to send me some vegetable and bread out of his own food. He managed to send it unnoticed to me. I was not given that facility at the time to cook for myself. When I got it, I was given no partner to cook along with me. And I used to get fever, as soon as I had cooked for myself. Even these exertions were too much for my poor health. So, I depended entirely upon what my brother could smuggle on to me, served in coconut shells. I relished the curry and the chapati very well, but when any day, the expert cook, my brother, was unable to send it, I had to eat my rice with water. For, the prison curry was unpalatable and there was no milk given to me to mix with my rice.

All this brought on a rapid decline in my health, while my general work and the hardship of prison life multiplied correspondingly. Every night, I began to have high temperature. But as it declined or disappeared in the morning, the authorities took no notice of it, and I had to pass day after day without medicine to cure it. My brother declined in health because he had attacks of hemicrany and suffered from the effects of the poor foodstuff given to him. After a time, both of us were given a little quantity of milk. But we could no longer digest it for want of health.

Just then a Bengali prisoner, an M.A. of the Calcutta University, honest and intelligent, had to strike work, for his delicate constitution did not enable him to complete his daily quota of two pounds of picked oakum, while the authorities insisted that he must complete it. He suffered punishment for it from time to time and, at last, it came to caning him. The University graduate bore the caning with patience and fortitude as the officers gave it with obstinate and contemptible ill-will. This tussle went on for months and though it was unsupportable for the individual, other political prisoners benefited by it, for, deterred by his example, the officers could not compel them to do excessive work, much less put them on the Kolu.

Just then, matters came to a crisis and we had all to go on the fourth strike.

□

5

The fourth Strike and My Ill-Health

The misfortune, to which I have referred at the end of the last chapter, happened thus: There was a political prisoner among us by the name Bhan Singh. He was a Sikh, and for skirmishing with his tindal and the petty officer, he was locked up in the cell and Mr. Barrie was sent for by the tindal and the petty officer combined. Mr. Barrie entered the cell and abused him, and the Sikh prisoner returned abuse-for-abuse. Mr. Barrie was enraged and signed to the petty officer and the tindal to give him a sound beating. Instantly, five of them entered his room with big sticks and began to belabour him. The prisoner did his best to resist the attack, but, being well-stricken in years, could not stand up to them. They felled him on the ground and bludgeoned him all night. The cries of the prisoner were heard all over the place. "I am undone, brothers, I am undone, save me," yelled the prisoner. Four or five of the political prisoners, who were nearest to him on the ground floor, alarmed and enraged by the cries, rushed out of their rooms for his rescue, and went up the chawl with anything as a weapon that they could lay their hands upon. Mr. Barrie was there to bar the entrance. When he saw these men running up the staircase, he quietly slipped from the place by another passage; of course, he had stopped the beating before he managed to leave the place. This incident I narrate here, as it was faithfully reported to me by these political prisoners, was confirmed by others. And they put it in writing for the information of the officers concerned therein. And this is what they had stated in their representation:

"As soon as we heard the cry of the prisoner from the floor above us and in the next block, we at once concluded that it was the usual method of the petty officers to hammer sense into the head of the prisoner. In the meanwhile we gathered that the victim was poor, old Bhan Singh. The petty officer, who had gone in with others to effect the process on Mr. Barrie's orders, but who himself did not beat him, vouched for the truth of it." That was the time for dinner, and I made up my mind along with two other leading men amongst us to issue letters to all the prisoners in the seven wings of the Silver Jail inviting them to condemn the action. The political prisoners, far from being cowed down by the incident, were all in a rage, and began to talk of general strike. One or two of them went the length of suggesting death for Mr. Barrie. But Mr. Barrie got wind of this commotion, and realising the terrible reaction that was in store for him, he, as was his nature, got frightened and came in the evening to see me. I told him very plainly that his terrorism had reached its limit. Of course, all of us shall have to pay for it, but he will no more get off scot-free. He cast all the blame on Bhan Singh and added that he had bitten him. I said, "Maybe, it was true, but the right course was not to beat him as he did, but to punish him in the proper way by proceeding against him. You have hammered him so much that he has vomitted blood, and this was borne out by all the prisoners here, and it was a fact that he could not deny."

Next day, when the Superintendent came to inspect the prison, a deputation of political prisoners waited on him and demanded full investigation in the matter, and the punishment of Mr. Barrie as the abettor of the deed. But the Superintendent threatened those who had rescued Bhan Singh. And that was the genesis of the fourth general strike in Silver Jail.

Just at the time news came from India that the Secretary of State for India, Mr. Edwin Montagu, was proceeding to India in connection with the new reforms, I felt that the visit of Mr. Montagu to India was an opportune moment to give publicity to the real state of things about the political prisoners in the Andamans, and strike was the only weapon by which we could draw India's attention to us. The immediate cause of the general strike was, no doubt, the cruel persecution of poor Bhan Singh by Mr. Barrie.

Some of the political prisoners were of the opinion that the lead in the strike should be taken by the older members among us, that is by those who had spent more years in that prison. It was also for them to formulate demands on behalf of us all. But I explained to them how the purpose of the strike might be defeated by such steps and how our cause was likely to suffer by it. If I were openly to lead them, Mr.

Barrie and the authorities over him would get the opportunity they needed to take off all the concessions, which had come to me and old political prisoners, according to jail rules, and put me back in solitary confinement. And the essential publicity of the strike by correspondence, personal messages and similar other methods will suffer, and the means of getting news from India through newspapers and other sources would come to an end. If I were isolated from them, it would be impossible to organize a unified plan of action to hold the strikers together against all machinations to divide them, and to attend to similar work of cohesion and moral pressure. Again, up to that time, we seniors had borne the brunt of the struggle that had undermined our health. And now to be again put in chains and solitary confinement, to go back to bad food and expose ourselves to caning, was to expect too much from us, for it was to risk our very life, and that sacrifice on our part was not due to an occasional resistance like strike. To risk one's life for such a petty object was to kill the national movement itself; and if I was to plunge in the strike, I must not withdraw from it, whatever the cost be of such a strike. Hence, it was for the young and the energetic among us to shoulder the burden, and these hundred and odd persons must by turns keep up the agitation and all the activities connected with it. The last and the most important reason for my abstaining from it was that I would have forfeited, thereby, my right of sending a letter to India. It was a rule that a letter was allowed to be sent annually by one whose record during the year was clear of any punishment. If I were punished or went on strike, my right would go along with it, and to be deprived of my right was not only to harm the strike, but, more important than that, to lose the chance of working for the freedom of the political prisoners themselves.

It was known to all of them that my younger brother was carrying on a propaganda in India under my name to secure the release of all political prisoners in India. And my annual letter to him strengthened his hands to carry on the work. Copies were made of my letter and sent to almost all the leaders in the country. Some of them were published in local newspapers. Patriots made their own copies of the letter and preserved them. That my letter was copied and sent to Paris, where Indians made their own copies and preserved them, was stated in the 'Foreward' newspaper by Barrister Asaf Ali himself at the time. In my annual letter, I never mentioned the complaints of prisoners in this jail. I emphasized the kind of agitation that had to be carried on in India for amnesty to political prisoners in the Andamans; I pointed out how our leaders had hesitated to tackle the question; how the Government refused to designate me and other revolutionaries as political prisoners; how it was sheer perversity on the part of the rulers not to call us by that name; and how, therefore, the people ought to take up the question of injustice to us. I also expressed in those annual letters, my views on social, religious and political matters of consequence to the whole country. During the war, we had a liberal-minded Superintendent in our prison, who allowed me to write freely on all these matters in letters sent by me to my brother in India. He only objected to information about happenings in the prison Itself. He used invariably to censor such news. Otherwise, he would let them pass in spite of Mr. Barrie's fretting against it. I took the fullest advantage of the facility afforded to me by the generous Superintendent. Matters regarding prison-administration I managed to send on through other sources, and, from time to time, they found due publicity in Indian newspapers. But there was, of course, a world of difference between anonymous news and authenticated letters like mine. My letters travelled in copies from the council hall to the house of an ordinary citizen, and had greater effect on the public mind. Again, out of ten communications sent on surreptitiously, one would reach India and perhaps half of it could find its place in the newspaper. But my annual letter reached India with the imprimatur of the Government itself, and, therefore, had a wider publicity in the Indian world. I had, therefore, made it a principle not to do anything in the prison which would forfeit my right to indite such communications, for they meant continuous stirring up and awakening in India on behalf of all political prisoners.

For, these and for other reasons, I settled about the strike that those alone of the new political prisoners should go on strike who could stand the strain right through, that we, the old ones, including Mr. Vamanrao Joshi and my elder brother, were to be excluded from it, that others, who were as old in prison as ourselves, were out of question, because they had carried tales to Mr. Barrie and had denied even the knowledge of Bhan Singh being beaten in his cell by tindals and warders. I further arranged that two out of the strikers should present a memorandum to the authorities on the main question that political prisoners shall not be treated as ordinary criminals, and they were to hang their case on the recent incident of Bhan Singh. If the memorandum was refuted by the authorities, the able-bodied among them should threaten to go on hunger-strike, and none should carry their resistance so far as to be locked up in solitary confinement and rot there, and none was to go on hunger-strike to the verge of death. I took upon myself the task of advertising the strike in the whole world, to win moral support in its favour, and to raise an agitation that it might come to a successful termination. I also promised to continue other public work like that of education throughout the settlement of the Andamans. My being out of the strike helped materially the smooth conduct of all other activities so needed to hold the team together and to give the cause strength and cohesion that might lead it on to success.

On a fixed day, batches of political prisoners in the different wards of the jail struck work simultaneously. About a hundred prisoners had joined the strike. Such a large number had never before organised such a strike. The hold of the authorities over the prisoners had considerably slackened during the interval of the first and the fourth strike. As such, this strike proved very effective. Never in the long history of the Andamans had a strike on such a large scale been organised or had lasted for such a long period of time.

From the beginning of the strike right to the end, Mr. Barrie tried hard to poison the minds of political prisoners against me. He stood for half-an-hour everyday before the cells of these prisoners and say to them, "Look here, Mr. Savarkar makes you dance to his tune; he is deceiving you, clear enough, for he himself is keeping back, as he is afraid of punishment. You are fools. Behave like that wise man among you-he, of course, referred to one of his henchmen-who has nothing to do with the strike. That will be to your good, I assure you." But they were more than a match to Mr. Barrie. They knew him but too well. If Savarkar was to behave like one of Mr. Barrie's men, they said to themselves, his lot would have been far easier long ago. But he did not like to live by flattering Mr. Barrie, they were sure of it. They were aware how long and what kinds of punishment I had undergone in that prison. Chains perpendicularly tying up hands at the one end and feet at the other; chains on hands and feet separately; chains on the arm; and solitary confinement on end. He had passed through all these ordeals, added to hunger strike for a day or two. And all this they could verify for themselves from the records of that prison. All of them had gone on strike as their duty, and some of them were so enraged that they would not have stopped at strike alone, but would have gone in for violent action, but for my bidding them not to do so. And most of them saw sufficient cause in Mr. Barrie's revilings and misrepresentations, for me to stand by. Some of them openly laughed at him and told him, "How is it, Mister, that you are day and night so much afraid of him, if you really think him to be coward at heart?"

All Mr. Barrie's efforts failed to create a diversion between us, as also failed the efforts of his allies to sow dissensions among us. The strike went on vigorously. Poor Bhan Singh, however, did not improve from the shattering blow to his health, given by the drubbing he had got from his tindals and warders. Within a week's time, he began to vomit blood and had to be removed to the prison hospital for treatment. I was also there after the shattering of my own health, and we met. He showed me the scars on his back. In that hospital, he soon developed consumption, and it was so rapid that two months after he died of it. Bhan Singh was only a peasant, but such a sterling patriot was rarely to be found among the class of educated men in India. He was transported for life for service to his country and he expired in the Andamans a year and a half after. Every political prisoner thought like me about him.

The authorities would not entertain the statement on the strike and its causes presented by two of the strike leaders, appointed for the purpose. Accordingly, as previously settled, the two went on hunger-strike. One of them was a sixty-year-old Sikh political prisoner, Sardar Sohansingh. The other was a spirited Rajput young man from the Punjab, named Prithvi Singh. For twelve days, they lay confined in their prison cell without a morsel of food. At last, the authorities had to yield and admit their written statement. The statement embodied all the grievances of the strikers from the demand that they should be treated like political prisoners in England down to their demand for soap and water to wash their hair. As their statement was received by the authorities, the venerable sixty-year-old Sikh called off the hunger-strike, which was meant to force that statement upon their attention. But the spirited young Rajput refused to listen to him and continued the hunger-strike individually for two weeks more. It was sheer passion on his part to do so. After the lapse of two weeks, they began administering milk to him through the nose by a tube. The young man grew emaciated in body, but his spirit refused to yield to the craving of the flesh. His temper rose as his body began to sink. He gave up wearing garments, he took no blanket to protect himself against cold; hungry, stark naked, in heat and cold, he lay on the cemented floor of his own cell and behind locked doors. He followed the practice of Nani Gopal and talked with none. Why should he talk to those who would not mind him? Whatever was to be told had been already embodied in the petition before them. That was his attitude to them, as also his reason for silence. He expressed himself in these words and never spoke again. The Commissioner came to ask what he had to say. But not one word would he say to him. For full six months, he continued like this without a break. He lay in his room for full six months, without food, without clothing, without a word, and his well-built body was reduced to skin and bones. I tried my hardest to save the life of such an honest, patriotic, promising young man. At last, I contrived to meet him. I rebuked him. I told him the story of Rana Pratap Singh, who regarded it a valorous act to retreat four or five miles from a battlefield rather than fight the enemy on the spot and be put to the sword along with his army. I told him about the battle of Haldighat and quoted similar episodes from his heroic life. One was not right in giving up his precious life without exacting full price for it. If one resolved to die, he must die fighting. Patriotic service meant heroism and extorting cent-per-cent for the sacrifice made, and not the death of a man by hunger and in a lonely cell like a rat. If one killed himself in the name of his country in this fashion, one was harming and not helping the cause of his country. The young Rujput seemed to be touched by this appeal to his conscience. He relaxed, and promised me not to end his life by suicide. And I felt relieved in mind.

But I could not break this to his friends; and they blamed me for not dissuading him from that course. I had to put up with this censure silently, for I had given my word to Prithvi Singh not to reveal the promise he had given me. I had asked the doctor to inform me from time to time about his condition, and especially when it had reached its breaking point.

Often the warders and other petty officers addressed him roughly that he might utter a word in retort. It came to the breaking point one day. Bound by a vow, he could not return abuse for abuse. His body was burning with fever and his mind could not bear the foul words of the warder. In sheer desperation, the young man got up, ran to the wall, and began beating his head against it. They were alarmed. The Superintendent ordered that two warders should be on the watch in his room during the night, for fear he might commit suicide.

At last, the doctor in confidence broke the news to me that his health had reached a point, where he might either die or go mad for life. I induced all the political prisoners to write a letter to him requesting him to break the fast, and that none would say that he had been beaten or surrendered, if he broke it. The letter said that it was a mandate to him from his fellow-prisoners, and that he must keep his word that he would never fast unto death. The time had come to act up to that promise and he must not fail them. I added my voice to that petition and the obstinate young man at last gave in and took his food.

I had always told them that it was utter folly on their part to throw away their lives by fast unto death for an occasional and useful weapon like the strike, though we may bear all other suffering incidental to that move. No patriot, no political prisoner worth the name, was to give up his life in this manner for the cause he held sacred. The proud men went on hunger-strike occasionally, and they had resolved to go on hunger-strike in a body during the continuance of the general strike, but I had never supported them, on the other hand, I had always denounced them, of course, without unduly deprecating their action. Today, some of those, whom I had drawn from the jaws of death were doing great national work in the country. I know no more of the brave Punjabi, Prithvi Singh, what he is doing and where he is. I may write of him in future when I know more about him.

On the day the strike was declared in this prison, I had asked permission of the authorities to address a personal letter to Mr. Montagu. Commenting on it and referring slyly to the strike, Mr. Barrie ejaculated, "Well, you have accorded a fine reception to Mr. Montagu."

Although, it was true enough that the strike was launched at Port Blair, as our salute to Mr. Montagu, I got the permission from the authorities to address a personal letter to the Secretary of State for India, on the ground that I had kept myself aloof from it. The authorities could not legally deny that permission to me. But there was another reason for it as well.

I had, no doubt, in my mind from the information on the subject I had personally received from the discussions I had with officials as also from newspapers in India, that the one thing, which Mr. Montagu was anxious to ascertain, while in India, was how far the reforms he had intended to introduce in the administration and the Government of India would satisfy her political prisoners in India and outside. On the eve of the Morley-Minto Reforms, I was in England, and I had known then, from what the high officials then talked about them as also from the public utterances of a leader like Gokhale, who happened to be in England at the time, that their main object was either to satisfy the revolutionaries or to save others from going over to the extremists among them. "To rally the moderates," was a phrase used by Lord Morley himself at that time. When men like Tilak were endeavouring to present a united front in their demand of reforms for India on the arrival of Montagu in India, it was up to the political prisoners like us to support them. I deemed it my duty, therefore, to communicate to Mr. Montague the minimum of reforms that would satisfy us, who then would be ready to follow the path of peaceful progress in India. Mr. Montague had interviewed representatives of all political parties in India. It was obvious that he could not openly interview representatives of an organisation like ours. And yet, he was anxious to know our about opinion on the matter under discussion. Hence, the officers discussed the question with me, though in an indirect manner. To them, some of us gave very discouraging answers. They would say, "No, we have nothing to do with politics; we do not desire freedom for India at this moment. What we want is peace, to think of God and lead an undisturbed life. What we pray for is our own release." Others, and the fire-eaters among them, repeated to the officers the pledges they had taken for the independence of India. They had nothing else to say to them. In these circumstances, they welcomed my offer to write to Mr. Montagu a balanced statement of our aims and objects, our methods, and our future attitude to the proposed reforms. It would have pleased the authorities better if the political prisoners, who had gone under their wings, had drafted the memorandum. But, somehow, none of them would come forward to undertake the task. Again, they realised that the authorities in India would prefer my signed letter to any memorandum on our behalf without an authority behind it. The rules of the prison could not come in my way, for I had not joined the strike and was no obstructionist. So, at length, permission was granted to me to forward my letter to Mr. Montagu through the Governor General of India, and I despatched the letter accordingly.

It was necessary that the contents of the letter should be known in India in order that the letter should produce its desired effect. It was not enough for that purpose that Mr. Montagu alone, or the Governor

General along with him, should read it. For, in that case, the hands of the Indian leaders would not be strengthened for demanding the reforms that would bring back the revolutionaries to the paths of peace. I was anxious to give as much help to them as it was possible for me to give them in my present condition of life. And, therefore, in my annual letter to my brother, I outlined what I was going to put in my communication to Mr. Montagu. As the letter also indicates, the state of my mind, at that moment, I give its bare outline here for the information of my readers. It will also convince him how much I was working in this jail for the release of my colleagues and of political prisoners as a class. The original letter is printed in full in an English book entitled, "Echo from the Andamans." The curious reader may get to read the letter in full in the pages of that book. It embodies all the letters I had sent from the Andamans to India. However, to proceed with the narrative, the gist of the letter was as follows:

"I am glad that the Maharashtra Provincial Conference has passed a resolution asking the government to grant amnesty to all the political prisoners. It is important to note that a similar resolution was adopted by that Conference in its session at Nasik. This shows that the Bombay Provincial Conference is more keen, courageous and persistent in its demand for our release than any other Provincial Conference in the whole of India. And we, political prisoners, are grateful to the Conference for its efforts in our cause. So far as I know, a similar resolution was passed on our behalf by Conferences in the United Provinces and the Andhra. The resolution passed at the Andhra Conferences was all-inclusive and full of sincerity. It is clear from this expression of opinion that the heart of the people of Andhra goes out in sympathy towards those who have served and sacrificed for the freedom of the Motherland, according to their honest convictions, even though the convictions may not commend themselves to the Andhra people on grounds of method of work, and the ways and means adopted by them to reach the goal. That these political prisoners should court prison and suffer, as they have suffered, has, no doubt, appealed to their heart. You write to me that the articles appear in newspapers and magazines on the question of our release. I wonder then why the Indian National Congress should show itself so squeamish in adopting a similar resolution about us. Why should it not, at least, pass a resolution of sympathy for us? Why should it fight shy of us? Last year, it did pass a resolution, but it was only about the interned. Does it not know that they will be automatically released after the cessation of the war? Why did not they feel anything for people like us rotting in the jail for so many years? They had not a tear to shed for us, seated as they are in the spacious, airy and well-appointed pandal of the Indian National Congress—for us who were, in contrast, doomed to spend our lives in a dark dungeon, away from our hearths and homes, and in solitary confinement! While their hearts melted with pity for those interned during the war, why should they ignore other political prisoners, who had suffered for their country more than they, and for a number of years, and whose number was by far greater than that of the interned? For, the very reason that the political prisoners would not be free with the cessation of war, and that the interned would be, the Congress should have exerted more for political prisoners like us than for their brothers, the interned ones. Yes, but the members of the Indian National Congress were sticklers for prestige and tradition and were afraid of the rulers. And there was the rub. To talk about the interned is not so dangerous, but they would not utter a word about us who were revolutionaries. For, that would bring them into ill-odour with the rulers, and injure their prestige with the Europeans. It is the duty of the Congress to be the spokesman of the people and not merely the mouthpiece of a few tall poppies among its members. That when so many newspapers and conferences in the country had demanded the release of revolutionary political prisoners like us, the leaders of the Congress should speak not a word about them does not become an institution or a body that calls itself national. The world expects the Indian National Congress to pass a resolution demanding the release of its own leaders; the world expects that it shall exert pressure for its country and bring about the release of its political prisoners, as similar bodies in Ireland, South Africa and Austria did work for their countrymen. That the Indian National Congress should do nothing of the kind is not creditable to her. We must compel the Congress to be bold and aggressive. If the elder leaders tremble in their shoes at this prospect, let them absent themselves from the Congress at the time she passes a resolution in our favour. Because a few men are cowards, the whole nation should not be allowed to bear the stigma of this guilty silence."

In passing such resolutions, one must be careful on one or two points. Many a newspaper, writing upon us, bear the word 'caution' very well in its mind, so that the government does not know what the paper exactly means by its comments. Sometimes they write so dubiously that it may mean that they are writing in favour of the interned, or those who are deported, or those who are sent across the seas. Seldom do they clearly state that they mean those who are convicted for political or revolutionary crime or the class of political prisoners as a whole. General Botha is now the Prime Minister of South Africa, and Mr. Redmond is a leader of the Constitutional Party in Ireland and a member of Parliament. Yet Botha released those who had rebelled against the Government. And Mr. Redmond brought about the release of members belonging to the opposite party. But the members of the National Congress consider themselves so great that they do not condescend even to utter the names of revolutionaries like us! They are really afraid of committing such a crime. Those who are petitioners on the outskirts of the town seem to think of their self-importance and are afraid of losing their prestige more than the Mayor of the town and its other worthies. In these circumstances, it is necessary to give a precise meaning to the word-political prisoners. It must be made to include those, who are inspired by pure political motives to fight for their country's liberation, whether they are convicts or undertrial prisoners, whether they are interned or deported, or whether they have adopted aggressive tactics for personal or national freedom. Whether the fight is personal or national has to be determined by an intention and not by any other test. No action in itself can be declared to be political. For violent action, if it is purely for personal ends, cannot be regarded as political. And no wise man can sympathies with it. It may be no better than robbery or dacoity on a large scale. Of course, if personal motive is put forward merely to preserve certain political rights, then the action comes under a different category altogether. The bands of thugs may give a fight on a big scale, but that does not make them either patriots or saviours of their country. But a suffragette in England, who goes about administering a whip to the Premier of England, and breaks shop windows, and sets fire to a building, is recognised by that Government as a 'political'. For, the suffragette was a woman fighting for political rights and if she occasionally indulged in whipping and incendiarism there was no motive of personal revenge or profit behind it. She worked for a public cause, though she resorted to violent action. As I have said above, it is the intention and motive that count and there is no moral turpitude attaching the action. And if the intention is proved to be to serve a public cause, then the offender is a political prisoner and must be classed as such.

I have entered into this long digression, that in case a general amnesty is declared—though I have no hope of it, and least hope that the political prisoners will be covered by that amnesty—the decision may not go against us for want of a clear-cut definition of the term 'a political prisoner', and that the Government be compelled to recognise us as political prisoners, and further in case amnesty comes, we should not be excluded from it. I would, therefore, like you to take up the question with writers in newspapers on the strength of my letter, and start agitation in favour of the release of political prisoners, while there is yet time to do so.

I shall now state seriatim what we need to do in the important question now looming large before India.

"As regards sending an open letter to the Government, I have already sent you the details of it by a political prisoner released from this jail. The letter must be endorsed by thousands of signatures. And the agitation for our release must be organised on a definite plan. What the plan is my friend must have already unfolded to you. The open letter must be sent at once; there should be no delay in that matter,

"Meetings should be held all over the country to support the release. They must be held throughout the year, one after another. The wheel must be kept rolling. On the whole, a sustained agitation must be kept up through the Congress, the Conferences, the newspaper press, public petitions and personal representations, through the Imperial Legislative Council and Provincial Legislatures, right up to the British Parliament. The question of political agitators must loom large before the public eye, must be kept in the forefront of all political reform. Carry on the agitation so widely and intensively that it will be impossible to ignore the question any longer. And on every public occasion, you must see to it that my definition of a Political prisoner is thoroughly explained to the audience.

"I must frankly state to you that I have discussed the whole question with you on a higher plane of moral justice than from the viewpoint of immediate gain or success to our cause. I have already stated in my representation to the Government that 'the question of amnesty to all, political prisoners is inevitably bound up with the consideration of progressive, political reforms to be introduced in the government of the country as a whole.' So, amnesty for prisoners is not an immediate question. Though we cannot hope for such instant relief to every political prisoner, the efforts for such release must be started from now onwards for these are bound to exercise a great moral pressure on the public mind and on national conscience. People will remember again the martyrs, the soldiers and the heroes, who fought bravely for the liberation of our country, and the agitation is bound to awaken in their hearts a feeling of deep sympathy for their sufferings to make them realise the sincerity of their motives, and to inspire them to fight continually till victory comes to the cause near their hearts. To remember the services rendered in the past with gratitude is an incentive to new action, and is a means of attracting young recruits to the army that was to keep up the fight to the end.

"In my letter to the Viceroy and Mr. Montague, to which I have already referred in this discussion, I have insisted on the following points: First, if they really intend establishing in India a free and progressive form of government, there is no meaning in keeping us behind the prison bars. Secondly, if free and liberal form of government was to be the crux of the new reforms, much of their importance will be lost upon India, if the political prisoners were not to be granted amnesty simultaneously with them. Already the people have lost their faith in the British Government, and new political reforms will not help to restore that faith. The country may gain by the grant of self-government, but the discontent in every household in India, as the result of thousands of political prisoners rotting in the jails, will not be allayed. How can one expect contentment in a land where brother is separated from brother, where men in thousands who are patriots are yet rotting in jail—in solitary cells, or iron cages—or are wandering as exiles across the seas, and where every family has its son, brother, friend, parent, or lover taken away from it to burn in the Sahara of separation and grief? On the other hand, it has to be borne in mind that mere amnesty to political prisoners, unaccompanied by substantial reforms leading up to self-government, will fail of its good effect on the hearts of the Indian people. I have stated this bare truth in my letter to them, though it may come in the way of my personal freedom. For, how can I be free in a country that enjoys no freedom? How can life be endurable in a land, where every attempt to push the country a step forward may mean an offence, a trial and going back to prison? How is life worth living when a move forward is construed as an insult to the Sultan, and where every step backward is an injury to one's self-respect and conscience? Can one walk safely in a place full of traps and pitfalls? Thus, it was evident that the grant of self-government and amnesty to prisoners must go together to produce the desired effect. They cannot be divorced, one from the other; if one is to succeed, the other must accompany it. I did not, however, fail to stress the fact that my object in forwarding the petition was not to secure my own freedom, but the freedom of all the political prisoners, and if it was granted to them, I shall not be sorry to be detained behind. I pledge my word for it. If they were keeping back my friends for the simple reason that I shall have to be let off along with them, then I shall be happy in their liberation and will not insist on going out with them. I have further told them that if they granted real self-government to India with substantial elected majority in the Central Legislature and with no incubus of the Council of State upon it, and if they further granted full amnesty to Indian political prisoners in the country and outside, in India and in the Andamans, and to exiles in Europe and America, myself and many more like me will accept the new dispensation and, if elected to the Legislature, will exert to make the reforms a success. The Legislature that had all along treated me with scorn and indifference, and that excited an equal contempt in our hearts for it, will, thenceforward, be our scene of action, where we shall be proud to work and co-operate for the fulfillment of our aim. For, I knew that Mr. Montague had insisted in all his communications upon knowing definitely how his proposals would react upon our minds, and if we would accept them. He had hoped that his proposals would bring back the revolutionaries to the path of peaceful progress. In answer to his hope, I have written that none was so foolish as to plunge in fire for the mere fun of it; none would go into the jaws of danger recklessly. Sometimes, and in some cases, it may so happen. But a sincere patriot with love of humanity in his heart will rarely enter on the path of violence, terrorism and bloodshed, or will revel in them, when a door is opened for him to attain the goal by peaceful and constitutional means. When there is no such door open to him in any form or shape, it is idle to talk to him of constitutional action. When such constitutional progress is made possible for him by the opening of such a path by the establishment of free institutions in India on the model of England and America, to talk of revolution and revolutionary activity, as if it were a bed of roses, would be a cruel irony of fate and nothing short of wickedness." This is the gist of the letter I have sent to Mr. Montague.

"You asked me in your last letter what facilities I had won by my promotion to Class 2 in this prison. In the Andamans a prisoner was usually put in Class 2 after a term of five years and in class I after a period of ten years, when ticket was given to him to make an independent home for himself in the colony. Was I free to go out of prison? No. Was I free to do independent literary work? No. Was I free to talk with my brother or stay with him? No. Was I free from the daily routine of hard labour? No. Did they make me a warder; did they stop putting me in the lock up? No. Did they treat me better? No. Did they show me any respect? No. Did they give me freedom to write more than one letter home? No. Did they allow me to receive any parcel from home? No. All these concessions are made at the end of five years, to other prisoners in the jail. But to me, who is running my eighth year in this prison, none of these facilities are granted. What then is the meaning of the phrase that I am now in Class 2, you will ask me? To which my answer would be: I am in Class 2 because I am in Class 2. Nothing more and nothing else. No better and no worse. Do you understand me, my doctor?

"This is all about outward facilities in that prison. And it was endurable so long as my health was all right. But this year it has fallen to my lot to suffer from ill-health. My health is completely shattered. You know that. Usually, I do not write to you about it. But now I feel I must not hide the fact from you. I know that you, my dear, will not easily succumb to fear. You have trained yourself to bear all and suffer all by the study of the Bhagwadgita. My dear Bal, at least one day in a year, used to be to me a day of undiluted joy. That was the day of my writing this letter to you home. And although even today while writing this letter to you, my heart rejoiced in calling to my mind your dear faces and remembering my gratitude to you, I could not enjoy the sweetness and pleasure in the excessive strain it was to my body and brain to write this letter. In March last, I weighed 119 pounds. This year, I weigh only 98 pounds. Dysentery has become more acute, and is sapping my health for want of proper nursing and timely treatment. My body has become a skeleton of my former self. I have borne the burden of prison life for eight long years. I have suffered from hardships too many and too varied to write on. And I have not informed you of them. I now feel I have reached the breaking point. Fears, threats, adverse fortune and abuse, tears and sighs, a vicious and sorrow-laden atmosphere, I am afraid, will snuff out my life's candle. At least, they have altogether stifled me. God has still given me the fortitude to bear up against them all and to keep my soul. He has enabled me to fight with circumstance. But now the human machine has begun to fail, and day by day I feel it breaking down under the heavy blows it is bearing. It is but very recently that the Medical Superintendent has begun to attend to my health; and though I have still to pass through my daily routine of labour, I get better food from the hospital, which is well-boiled rice and milk. My great fear is that this ever-growing weakness will hand me over one day to the care of her elder sister T.B. Only one thing is able to remove this fear, and that is change, rest and different mode of living. Not the kind of change registered in the prison parlance. For, in it change means change for the worse. Change ought to mean removal from this place to a better prison in India, where I can have more of light and more of fresh air and a change of scene. This dull monotony has tired me completely. But do not be unnecessarily alarmed. The environment has become bad enough for me, but it is not disheartening. A prison is a place tenacious of its inmates. It may gnaw the flesh of its victims bit-by-bit, but it does not kill. It makes you suffer, but it does not destroy. It may reduce you and consume you, but it does not burn you into ashes. It preserves you in order to torture you. I have known prisoners in this place who have lived to be eighty years old. And these are not rare instances, by no means. Therefore, I pray that you should not think if I am shattered in health, there is any danger to my life here. Unless something untoward happens, there is nothing in this to make you nervous about me.

"And this about my physical being only. For, though it will be ridiculous on my part to say that I will fight with the flames thrown up by the funeral pile, on which I am tied up; though it would be an idle boast now, still I can say with confidence even today, that my soul has yet force in it to hold together this trembling flesh of a shaken body. It is ready still to face for a long time dire suffering, any trials and tribulations that life may impose upon it. It is determined to resist it with fortitude and patience. My elder brother is better than I, though owing to repeated attacks of hemicrany, his weight has gone down to 106 pounds."

These extracts from the memorandum sent by me to Mr. Montague from this prison in 1918, and quoted in the letter to my brother, show how I was striving all along for the release of the political prisoners, and they also reveal the state of my health and general feelings at the time. My brother made copies of that letter and sent them to all the delegates of that year's session of the Indian National Congress. Extracts from the letter were also published in papers like 'Amrita Bazar Patrika', 'The Bengali' and in other English newspapers in India, as also in the vernacular press and monthly magazines. The state of my poor health roused considerable sympathy, and drew the attention of the people to the political prisoners in the Andamans. My brother carried on ceaseless agitation on the lines I had laid down for him in my annual letter.

And through it public opinion began to assert itself in favour of all the political prisoners in India and outside. If I had joined the strike at the instance of a few of my friends in this jail, I would not have been enabled to do the work I did for my colleagues. I would have been denied permission to address personally to Mr. Montague. But as I could write that letter, and convey its contents to my brother as well, this material helped considerably arm my brother to carry on a campaign in India on behalf of them all, and to show up their misery and suffering in this jail. Some leaders, I learnt later on, wept while reading them. An article in the 'Patrika' headed "Outrageous Treatment of a Political Prisoner", created a sensation. Through the courtesy of a friend I got to read it here.

In the official letter, I could not give any account or our personal grievances connected with the treatment in jail. But this I could embody in my private letter, as also in letters addressed to my friends in India through our usual secret agencies. I drafted a letter and took out many type-written copies of it, and sent them in packets addressed to Pandit Madan Mohan Malaviya, Mrs. Annie Besant and other leaders as also to all the elected members of the Central Legislative Council by every boat. Some reached them and some were lost. One gentleman, Dr. Damodar, returned from the Andamans to India and reported all that he had seen and personally noted down. He had already written anonymously a series of articles on the subject to the 'New India', and to two Indian magazines. Therefore, the authorities in the Andamans were jealously watching his movements. Dr. Damodar was a man of independent views. He was one of our secret organisation to carry news from Port Blair to India. He was one of those who had helped us selflessly for a number of years in the Andamans. Dr. Damodar was one of the untouchables from Madras, fine in features, educated, full of self-respect, bold and independent-minded. When I saw him, I felt how unjust we had been to a class, which could produce such a man. How we had weakened our nation and its power by this curse of untouchability upon a community capable of giving us such men. We had dwarfed them and consequently had dragged ourselves down. If only an opportunity were given to them, they were bound to rise and advance in a manner that would put to shame many of the best products in Hindu Society. This was what I felt sincerely every time I saw and met this stalwart from the depressed classes. He was an independent man and the officers above him were always afraid of him. People complained that he did not salute everyone he met on the way, specially if he happened to be a European. Dr. Damodar returned to India and fell a victim to the Influenza Epidemic of 1918. Now that he is no more I am free to give this open tribute to his memory. He had finished his life's work already. Ours was the loss and his was the glory of it.

A Manuscript Daily in the Prison

The strike in our prison was going on with full vigour. The men on strike were not given their normal ration of prison-food. There were big-bodied persons among them who had found the usual ration insufficient to feed their hunger. And their plight because of the penalty of reduced ration was worse than ever. To make up for this want of food, they feasted on heapfuls of coconut from the prison store-house supplied to them by helpful prisoners, warders, and petty officers on our side. They were given this nourishment in plate-fuls in their own rooms by our help-mates. Every two or three days we got a daily or a weekly newspaper to read in this prison supplied through our usual source. How it came to us is an interesting story. It entered the gate of our prison through a water pipe, or sewn into a prisoner's waist-coat, or hidden beneath the plank or covering of a cart carrying the rubbish in and out of the prison; or it came openly in the pocket of a bold man willing to take the risk. And then, it was conveniently smuggled into our block. We culled important news from the newspaper; we wrote it on a separate sheet of paper; and it became a circulating daily of our prison. Someone from his cell would hand over the sheet to the warder who read it with interest while on his round and in such light as he found on the way. So, we got our daily news of the war even during the days of the strike when a stricter watch was kept on our movements and by British soldiers, for they distrusted black men at the time. These Tommies soon became friends with us and showed great sympathy towards us, and I cannot say that it was not some of them who gave us the news that we were so eager to have from the outside. They were transferred when detected in the act. But others who took their place acted towards us in the same kind manner. "One touch of nature makes the whole world kin." Does it not?

The Postage that I Had to Pay

In this hurry and bustle, sometimes the man who brought us the paper was caught in the act. And his face was pitiable to look at. We mediated for him with the petty officer, the *jamadar* and Mr. Barrie to save him from punishment. Many a time, I must say it to the credit of Mr. Barrie that the prisoner was connived at by him, and let go scot-free. And I must mention the fact also to compliment myself on the art of appeal, which I had learnt so well at the time. And with all this, if a charge was framed and I was punished along with the prisoner, well, I took it as a matter of course. Once for such a sin, I was made to stand one whole week in my room hung up by the chains on my hands. When Mr. Barrie came to my room, he said, full of satire and pointing to my handcuffs, "Oh, what is this new thing?" I replied, "It is the postage I have to pay." He retorted, "Is it not a bit too heavy?" I paid back, "Not in the least, it is so very cheap." "Newspapers have to be paid for inclusive of postage; here I get the newspaper and pay only the postage for it." "Once I pay this postage of a week in handcuffs, and I get for six months after, newspapers to read, free of any charge."

Some Demands Granted, the Strike Ends

The political prisoners, under the weight of handcuffs and shackles, and in solitary confinement for six months on end, discovered that some of them had completely gone down in health. One or two of them showed evident symptoms of T.B. Many a prisoner in the Andamans is found easily to succumb to this fell disease. The able-bodied, muscular, tall class of Sikh peasants and workers had all gone down in health and it was clear from the symptoms that they had developed, that before long, they would be an easy prey to consumption. One or two, in that plight, gave clear indications of insanity. I, therefore, advised the strikers to go back on light work and end the strike. For, that would give them comparative work and change also. After much heated discussion and opposition, they at least came round and ended the strike. Stubborn as most of them were, they at last listened to my advice and resumed their work. Excepting our demand for equal rights with political prisoners in England, the Indian Government agreed to grant us all the demands in the statement submitted by us before going on strike. We secured the right to send long letters home; we secured the right of sweet water for bathing; of soap and oil for the Sikhs; of better food for prisoners; and, last, of light work as our daily routine. We had gained our main object in going on strike which was to draw the attention of the people and leaders in India, in a striking manner to the wretched condition and the hardship of our life in this prison. Although Mr. Barrie was not brought to book for the beating he had given to Bhan Singh, we knew that an enquiry was made into his conduct and he had a very hard time of it to escape from the charge. He was so much pulled up for what he had done, that he had no spirit left in him to play the old game over again. If the Government were to be compelled to hold an open trial and punish, only the Legislature and the press combined could do so. The political prisoners had done all that was in their power to expose him.

The fourth strike in this prison had almost washed out Mr. Barrie. He was disgraced throughout India. The Government had begun to look upon him with suspicion; and the political prisoners, who had won almost all their demands had become unmanageable by him. So, the demigod of Port Blair inspired no fear, but was reduced to be no more than an image of stock or stone. In this plight he was recently found to be ever melancholy. Enough of that authority, of that terror, he wanted to fill up his remaining days and retire in peace. Formerly, he used to accost me thus: "Well, Savarkar, you keep on making the same demands, but your persistence is no better than dashing your head against a stone-wall." And, now, as demand after demand was being conceded to us, I used to say to Mr. Barrie, "Let us see if my persistence ends in breaking my head against the stone-wall, or it leads another to do It. I have not lost, that is what our colleagues say, and the oil-mill at a stand-still is a witness to the fact."

Mukunda

The entire aspect of the war had begun to change by this time. The advance of Germany had come to stand still and her former strength was showing clear signs of decline and breakdown. Correspondingly, our hopes had also sunk low. The bubbling point had already spent itself and coldness had already begun to invade us. Even the late arrivals among us had some blind believers in the slogan: "Tomorrow we clear off, we quit this place." That the rule of Great Britain over India was bound to collapse in a week or two was the faith of them all; in one man alone, I found a singular exception to the general rule. The prisoner was an old Maratha, Mukunda by name. He was a man of firm will and steady nerve. He told them positively that British rule in India was not going to disappear that way. He was a fighter; he was full of daring; he had made three attempts to escape from the Andamans. He had already served his ten years in the prison, and had effected his escape. But he killed the man who was responsible for his first sentence and imprisonment, and was sentenced to transportation for life for the second offence. He again escaped from the prison. He was wandering all alone in a boat for one long month, and was caught just when the boat had touched Madras. Foiled in this way, he had lost all hope of release, and as the other prisoners had been elated with hope, Mukunda was depressed by defeat. Whenever anyone said in his presence that Britain was bound to lose in this war, Mukunda went at him with fury, "I have seen three successive wars, and I have heard fifty times that there was no hope for Britain to win the war. But all that had proved a vain hope; all shame. Britain will never lose. He who says so is a liar." Not that he asserted this out of love for England or Englishmen. He had arranged a plot to avenge himself upon an Englishman He was caught attempting on the life of the Chief Commissioner himself.

A tragedy happened in this prison during the strike, which must find a place in these pages. A Punjabi Brahmin, Ramraksha by name, happened to be involved in a conspiracy to spread sedition in the army and bring about an armed revolution in Siam and Rangoon. The man had travelled far and wide in China and Japan before reaching Rangoon and Siam. He was tried and convicted for the offence and had undergone great hardship in those countries. When he stepped as a prisoner in the jail of the Andamans, he was asked, according to the prison rules, to surrender his sacred thread, which he would not do. Being a widely-travelled man, he was not orthodox in his views. But a Brahmin to be asked to do away with his sacred thread was, in his eyes, a sacrilege; and, on no account, was he going to put up with it. It was to him the symbol of his religion and he was not going to destroy it. He, therefore, straightaway refused to obey that order. It was to be noted here that the officers did not trifle with the sentiment of the Mussulman in this respect, though they did not scruple to trample under foot a similar demand by a Hindu prisoner. They tore off the thread from the body of that Hindu prisoner. To protest against this outrage on his religious sentiment, the Brahmin, at once, went on hunger strike. He said that so long as he had not the sacred thread on his person he would not touch his food. Ramraksha not only said this but affirmed it as a solemn vow. Food and water, he gave them up both in fulfillment of that vow. Without a particle of food or a drop of water he lay in his cell for days together. After a fortnight, they tried to feed him through the nose. A month passed after this. The man began to get emaciated, resolved to die, and never to surrender his will or prove false to his vow. The hardships he had suffered in Siam, and, added to this, a fast unto death in the prison of the Andamans had done him up completely. He developed pain in the chest and the doctor declared that consumption had set in. Everyone begged of him to take food, but he would not yield. He was at the death's door when I wrote to him to give up his fast. It was with great difficulty that I persuaded him to take his meal. But unfortunately, the disease developed fast, and in two months he died of it.

Dharmavir Ramraksha

But the episode did not end there. The matter was taken up to the higher officials, to the Indian press, and before a special Commission appointed to examine into the state of prison administration in India. As a result, a Brahmin was allowed to wear his sacred thread even as a prisoner. But, for this trifle, Dharmavir Ramraksha had to lay down his life! Now prisoners of all sects in Hindu Society, and not Brahmins alone, are permitted to wear the sacred thread as a symbol of their faith.

As the war began to draw to its close, the defeat of Germany became an evident fact. In the early years of the war, the Englishmen here were given to spreading false reports of England's advance against Germany. Now there grew a tendency among the prisoners of this jail to spread fantastic stories of German victories in order to blunt the edge of their own despair. The stories became so extravagant during the concluding period of the war that, after the war, the officers thought it expedient to provide the prisoners with newspapers in order to remove that illusion. For, the newspapers would not publish fantastic reports like the fall of Londan, or the Amir's capture of Lahore. The Superintendent gave me from this time a copy of the weekly edition of the 'London Times', so that I might be enabled to remove their misapprehension as also to read news that would interest me. The defeat of Turkey filled me with joy, though the news was a bitter pill to swallow not only for the Mussulmans but for all other prisoners in this jail. But soon they realised the cause of my satisfaction. I reported about Germany's defeats as faithfully as I had read about them; but they were very angry with the reporter himself, and yet they could not resist the temptation of asking far the news. If I said to them that I was not going to give them any news at all, and they had better not ask for it, because to report something that was not true I considered reprehensible, they used to supplicate me for it. In order to enlighten them on the point, I used to take up the subject of the enemy's defeat for a talk at our weekly meetings. "To hear favourable news only is the part of a fool. A brave and forceful man likes to know first of his reverses, for to meet them fearlessly is his first task. Napoleon Bonaparte had strict orders for his staff never to delay the news that went against him but to report at once, even if it be at the dead of night when he happened to be fast asleep. It was no matter if good news were kept back from him till the following morning. India has not yet gone through the discipline and preparation for the coming in of good news to her. It is her destiny to hear bad news for a good long time to come. But she must be fortified to know the truth, for she has to face it. In good old days, our kings used to reward those who brought them good news with the gift of golden bracelets. And the report of reverses could come to them only from the mouth of the victorious enemy when he entered the palace and mounted on his chest. It does not pay one to be such a coward." I gently rebuked my fellow prisoners in this manner and prepared their minds to hear any news that came to them in natural course. The wise among them became used, in the aftermath of war, to hear and understand everything. They began to realise how the defeat of Turkey was a good dose to our Mussulman friends in this prison, to take off their self-conceit and to change their angle of vision towards India.

Yet, the war was not without its detrimental effect on the health of all prisoners in this jail, including the political prisoners, whom it affected the most. Some suffered from continuous solitary confinement; others from the insanitary conditions and the bad climate of the Andamans, and all from lack of fresh air and wholesome food all along. There were strong, well-built men of rugged constitution among the Panjabi and the Sikh political prisoners, who were the last to come in this jail. But they also suffered from complete collapse of health in the conditions created by war. Within three or four years, the tallest among them were stricken with T.B., and became thin in body; others fell victims to chronic dysentery, and others, again, thought seriously of suicide. Three or four Sikhs died from T.B. before my very eyes. And I was kept for observation in the hospital suspected of the same disease. I was sorely grieved when I saw them dropping off one after another like dry autumnal leaves. I was to go the same way soon—I felt within myself. It was, indeed, a miracle that, when they had dwindled and died within three or four years, I could hold out for these eight or nine years. I will be reborn and come back.

Babu Jotish Chandra

A young man, Jotish Chandra by name, lay in ambush for the arrival of a German submarine to take him off from the hands of the police, who were on his track for revolutionary crime in Bengal. He was a Bengali and a member of the revolutionary organisation in India. The police detected him and in the clash that followed, Jotish Chandra received a bullet wound in the leg. He was, thereafter, caught, tried and sentenced for transportation to the Andamans. One evening during the strike, the warder took the food to him to be served on his plate. The prisoner in the room asked the warder first to remove the chamber pot and clean it. And then he would take the food that the warder had brought for him. I have already told you how the prisoner had to sit for stools in his own room when he was locked inside. The warder asked him to go back into his room and with the help of *jamadars* and other officers managed to put the food inside and left. Mr. Barrie made no inquiries about the incident. Jotish had to sleep the whole night beside the stinking stools and in a small, ill-ventilated and closed room. This was not the first experience of its kind for us, political prisoners, in this jail. But Jotish Babu's patience had reached its breaking point. It was the proverbial last straw for him. He threw away the food and went on hunger strike. Within a few days, he started passing blood in his stools; and he was removed to the hospital. We were all pressing him hard to resume taking food. And I compelled him personally to break the fast. But the chord that was snapped could not be made whole again. The excitement had gone to his head, his brain was affected by it and within a month he became entirely mad. He was then removed to the mental hospital where he lingered for a year. It is said that he had recovered from the malady. But here is what we read what was published after his death. It is from a message that he had sent to his relatives: "Do not think that my soul is fast asleep in heaven. If my love for the country is passionate and sincere, I shall take birth immediately and return to my country to serve her. Be sure of it."

Poor Jotish, they say he was sane at the time of his death. But if he is the real writer of this message, I cannot say of him that he was sane, or that the madness had been but a temporary phase of his life.

Lala Ramcharandas

One more instance of a fine, generous-hearted man, a staunch supporter of Hindu Sangathan, and a Punjabi political prisoner, who was similarly caught in the jaws of death and had suffered in jail from consumption and insanity. This man had developed sleeplessness as the result of shattered nerves, and continuous headache, along with many other political prisoners at that time. I received a note from him in the hospital, in which he had written to me that he was tired of life, that, in the circumstances he had described to me, he had no other alternative than committing suicide. I dissuaded him, for the time being, from that reckless act, by pointing out to him that it was our duty to serve our country by our suffering and we must live for it. My friend was spared to me by this effort, and within two years he recovered his health and began to move about and to do light work.

As if to give us, the political revolutionaries, one more blow during the desperate condition of our life in this period, the superior officers sent me a letter to read, written by Lala Har Dayal. Those who would formerly inflict upon us the punishment of a week's detention in handcuffs for finding even a scrap of paper on our person, gave us matter to read which they felt would be bad news for us. After the great war Lala Har Dayal had written to the daily press that the revolutionaries of India should be let alone and she should co-operate with England and strive to attain swaraj under her aegis, and that he had been convinced that India could attain the goal only by that means. Mr. Barrie called me and my friends and gave me that newspaper cutting to read. And he asked what I thought of it. I said, "I know that Lala Har Dayal is a sincere man, and I believe what he had written is an honest expression of his opinion." I returned to my place in the hospital adding that I would say nothing more on it. In our next meeting, I had taken that letter as a subject for discussion with our political friends. I told my friends the whole story of Har Dayal's life and the many phases through which it had passed. It was the habit of his mind to be depressed for the time being by any adverse situation he had to pass through, and what he said at the time was said by him honestly. And so, he had changed his opinions from time to time. But the reaction had been with him but a temporary phase and had never lasted long. This letter was but another illustration of that passing mood. My friends agreed with me in that conclusion. Some protested that the letter itself was far from genuine, it was a fabricated document put on to us, as a newspaper cutting, just to fathom our minds. I disagreed with them. The analysis in that letter of Turkish ambition and of the attitude of the Amir of Afghanistan, along with the feelings of the Mussulmans towards India and the cause of their opposition to national demand, were absolutely convincing. I had been telling them the same thing all these years. The letter had no effect, beyond this, on anyone of us.

The slogan "Today we leave, tomorrow we are sure to go" had now fallen behind, discredited by facts. The hopes it had roused had been dashed to the ground. If the slogan and the forecast behind it had proved true, everyone would have been reckoned among us as a prophet, like so many other prophets, who go about the world. But the tide had turned and the opportunity was no more. All of them were full of gloom. But there was another straw to catch at. The victory of Great Britain in this war must inevitably lead to general amnesty and pardon from which we cannot be excluded. This now became the talk of the prison, and the mind swayed back like a pendulum from despair to new hope. Just at this time, India was discussing the Andamans and its climate as detrimental to the health of prisoners. What I had written about it in my last letter had contributed largely to raise the controversy in the newspaper world of India. And they wrote about me personally that I should be transferred from this place to some prison in India for reasons of health. Instantly, a rumour found currency in this prison that old political prisoners in the Andamans were soon to be taken back to India. What of me, then? The rumour had it that I was to be sent to Singapore! And a few days after, I found Mr. Wamanrao Joshi and two more with him getting ready to leave for India. They somehow managed to see me in the hospital in order to bid me good-bye. These loyal colleagues, who had fought and suffered with me in a common cause took leave of us, and with a heavy heart, I said farewell to them. They had gone and now I was alone and left behind. For my brother and me, I had never expected any change from one place to another, any turn of fortune in our favour. And, therefore, we had no occasion to be crushed by the despair, which is the reaction of fond hope. We could stand up to anything because we had expected nothing.

The only hope that now remained to many of us in this prison hanged round the slender thread of the celebration of victory. But it proved a dupe like a proverbial mountain in labour. Every prisoner got from it no better solace than the remission of one month's sentence in a year. Some very old and aged prisoners were, of course, let off and the political prisoners were not excluded from the list of those who had got remission of one month's sentence per year.

But for me, what was my good fortune? As in the past, so now onwards! Not a day's reduction in my sentence—no mention of my release or transfer anywhere.

□

6

On Death-Bed

While all these activities were carried on with zest during the later years of the war, I found my health completely shattered, as I wrote in the letter I had sent to my brother; and I was removed to the hospital for rest and treatment. When my fever was ever hundred degrees on my body, and the dysentery had become very acute, the hospital authorities began to attend to me with greater care and undertook regular treatment of my disease. Every prisoner, when taken to the hospital, does get some rest in that place, and, therefore, it was no wonder that I got it because when I went in I was worse in health than any other prisoner. It was in the eighth year of my residence in this jail that they gave me this relief. Otherwise, whenever I was ill before, the only treatment for me was solitary confinement.

Once removed to the hospital, the Superintendent saw to it that I was well-cared for. They changed my food from time to time to find out what suited me best in the present state of my health. This change in prison management, it must be pointed out, was the result of the criticism passed upon it in the Legislature and in the newspaper world of India; and my letters had helped materially in ventilating that grievance. But this reform had come so late that, speaking for myself, the care that the hospital bestowed upon me did not lead to any change for the better in my declining health. My fever did not abate, although they gave me dose after dose of quinine to drive it out of my body. And the quinine brought on dysentery and blood in the stools in a very acute form. I was unable to digest rice and milk which passed out as it had gone in. In the Andamans and especially at Port Blair, T.B., Malaria and dysentery marched on together. They stalked the land and took heavy toll of its inhabitants. I was already in the grip of dysentery and malaria, and six or seven months later, the doctor himself suspected that I had a touch of T.B. In the hospital, there were many patients around me who were stronger and better-built and yet affected by these three maladies. I had passed eight long years of imprisonment and hard labour, and my constitution had completely gone under. It would have been no surprise, if I had suffered from all three of them. Dysentery took off my appetite for food, and I could not digest it. Want of food added to my weakness and shattered my nerves; the fever was continuously on me; only the last enemy was yet to come, though he was very near. In the prison hospital, I had nothing to entertain me except reading. And that was the only solace of my life. But my nervous debility made reading and light conversation a heavy tax on my constitution. The slightest indulgence in these brought on fever which rose to 102 degrees. So, I gave up reading altogether, did not keep any books near me to avoid the temptation, and lay on my cot with eyes shut. Time, already a tedious factor in the jail, became too long and too heavy to bear and I had to spend the tedium to the accompaniment of griping pain in the stomach, and of burning fever on the body. Even then I was doing all those things that I have described in the last chapter.

Sometimes, I thought that, due to my illness in the prison, I had come to regard prison-life as a hell on earth and that to be outside would have been better for me. But how? Do people not suffer from all these maladies outside, and is it wise to lay all the blame for them on the jail? People suffer from dysentery, malaria and consumption even in palaces. Epidemics like bubonic plague and influenza sweep over big cities adorned with theatres, and pleasure-haunts, and blazing with electric light. And groanings and cries of pain are heard in a thousand homes through them. The city of Bombay suffered from such epidemic, and every home in it had four beds of patients stricken with influenza. Why should I then bewail my lot in this prison because I am in its hospital down with malaria and dysentery? Pain and disease are rampant everywhere. There are a thousand villages and a thousand huts of poor families, which, stricken down with similar ailments, do not find any medical aid near at hand to relieve them. You have in this hospital a medical officer, medicine and nursing of which these poor folk have not the slightest notion or expectation. Your lot in this dependent state is much better than theirs though they are free; their lot, in these circumstances, is, any day, harder to bear than yours. So, be patient and put up with it calmly. Do not grumble because you have to pass through it as a prisoner. Do not add to your pain by this idle pining. It is right for you to think that freedom is better than imprisonment, but for other reasons. But now that you are in prison and are ill, you had better not think of it. For, disease and death haunt the prison too often, no doubt, but not that they don't stalk the outside world as well. Life in this prison, intrinsically, is not more 'flat, weary, stale and unprofitable' than the usages of the world outside, for have we not all to pass our days in 'the vast prison that is this world', and is not this prison a part of it?

That is as a part of philosophy. But is the reality so different after all? The struggles for national freedom and the individual struggle for existence are both hard and serious things. Is not life in prison equally hard and serious? It is worth while striving to live up to your noble ideal for which yourself with thousand others like you, and some of them your friends, have had to come in this prison. It is for that, that you had to pass through these trials, practise these austerities, and go through this kind of self-abnegation. And these will shine in the world by their reflected splendour, things great and small, like great and dazzling achievements of other men on the theatre of the world. People read with as much eagerness and interest the accounts of the prisoners transported to Siberia for the political crime of shooting Czar Alexander, as they may gloat over pages of a book describing the life of Czar Nicholas, or of the hypocritical priest, full of romance, mystery, lust and dupery, Rasputin. And they certainly cherish greater sympathy and reverence for the former than they pity or hate the latter. People's eyes are fastened less upon the domes of luxurious palaces than they are rivetted upon the cottages of the exiled and on the jails of people imprisoned for political crime. And even were it not so, we, the worshipers of freedom must count the hour and mark the day in this dark night for the arrival of the dawn for which we had dedicated our all. It is a solemn duty for it is a solemn vow. Then why should I consider this life as meaner and more futile than the life without?

Free life? What is it, and who is free? Is it without the walls where these people toil? Outside these walls are the huge walls of Universe and Nature. Mind alone is free. It is imprisoned only by the skies overhead and by the horizons stretching before its eyes. If you feel pinned down and limited by this prison, ask those who are free, and they will tell you that they are as much pinned down by the giant circumstance. In short, what is here is also without, more or less, but in no way different.

And nothing to entertain here, you think? No, friend, you have plenty of it. Look at this book; within its two pages the ants have built their capital city.

This much about my ailment. What about the tedium? Nothing more and nothing less. We find life in prison dull, monotonous and useless. But what is life in the world intrinsically? You are a prisoner and your jailor and Superintendent are not. But what is the difference between their life and yours? They rise from their bed everyday; they sit in their office and write; they eat and they sleep; again, they wake up, and again they go to bed. How have they made their lives, and what have they made of it? Marriage, children, retirement and pension—that is the sum total of it. Is that life's fulfillment? Do children not enact the same part in their sport? How is this sort of life better than that of the children at play? Can you really say that it is better from your observation and analysis of that life? Your life and theirs run in the same groove and are cast in the same mould, though they are free and you are a prisoner. We grow on our parents' knees; we burn or bury them in due time; then we dangle and rear up our own children; and we go to our graves finally. And what is all this for? Is not the wheel of life a weary round, after all? The great Shankaracharya asked the question, "What next?" And it is a question very pertinent to ask of life in this world as also of my life hereafter. And even to a mighty cataclysm like the great war just ended. France and Germany have indulged in this game many times before the Franks attacked the Gauls, and from that day onwards, how many times, across the ages, have they not played the same role? And victory has made sport of them both, sometimes swinging to one side and sometime swinging to another. France is victorious once; and Germany is victorious next, and France going in sackcloth and ashes before her. Today, the great Napoleon Bonaparte; tomorrow Louis Napoleon III! Today, Austerlitz, tomorrow Sedan! One fine morning Bajirao I, another dark evening Bajirao II! In their uniformity, in their commotion and confusion, whose life was being reared and built up? Why all this ambition, this strife, this rivalry, this struggle for mastery, this lust for power? Whither has it all led? Everywhere the same scene, and the same sequel, and the same end. Futility and weariness are not the signposts of prison alone. These words mark not the sign posts of prison alone. They are writ large on the portals of a palace, on the dome of the Taj, on the summit of a mountain, and on the surface of the sea.

"What then? What is all this for?"—This is writ large on the tablet of eternity. Why then pine, that you are in prison and your life is running to waste? For, what is in prison, that is not also in the world?

Then about the news, about the lust for news. The prisoner is sorry that he gets no news in the prison while the outside world is full of it. That makes life tolerable. But you have to look at it from another point of view. Does any news give you ever entire satisfaction? Say, you know that India is free. But consider well, if it satisfies you. For, your mind will begin to think how long will that freedom last and on what terms. For, India once was free; that freedom brought her glory and greatness; the greatness and glory made her lethargic; and lethargy made her lose freedom. Look at her history and you know the truth of the matter. One generation fights for freedom, another enjoys the fruits of freedom, and the third generation loses it. Suffer, fight, die, enjoy, lose—that cycle sums up the history of every nation, dynasty, community and society. These three or four words contain the story that we call history. Is all news not the quintessence of these basic truths? Do you not think that there is nothing more to hear than this? Why national history? Even the history of the universe is summed up in these five significant words. For, all the ups and downs of this universe end, after all, in deluge. Its origin, its creation was the first news that has now grown so time worn, so stale. The end of the universe that news, broadcast will surely thrill the world of man as nothing else can, any day or at any time. From creation to dissolution the phrase sums up neatly the story of the universe. And you know them both—the beginning and the end. Why then worry that you don't get news here? The philosopher shall find no delight in sports that satisfy the child. All the detailed news must swing like a pendulum between these two extremes—birth and death; creation and dissolution; flux and reflux. And the news are so transitional, transient and passing, that not one of them satisfied any man, and his thirst for it never ends—whether one is in prison or free like the wind to blow where it listeth. The last man's news excites your curiosity in this prison as the last week's news attracts the American. For, in America, every three hours a newspaper comes to birth and the latest news is welcomed as the best. America wants no stale news. The American mind is anxious to know the latest. The Stock Exchange and the Wall Street are the two barometers of the American temper. If tomorrow, we are able to procure news from all sides of the universe, the human mind will be anxious to know what happened on the Planet Mars, as it is eager to know today what happens in the world, of man, or as you are anxious about news from India.

So that, philosophically speaking, your life is not altogether useless or any worse than that of the so-called freeman in this world. Behold that city of ants within the pages of that book. How it bustles with life and activity like the great Pataliputra of ancient history. Look at those eggs, look at their queen, look at their princess, and at their army of ants ready to fight and sting; their standing army, and their divisions and classes, and their division of labour. Look at the film of gnats floating before your eyes in the light of the sky. It is a nation of wanderers like the Jews. They fly together in swarms from region to region and settle nowhere. Do not regard them as insignificant beings. You call yourself a man, but you have no wings to fly. But the gnat, which is one-tenth the size of the sesame, has wings and it flies. How fine the nerves and feelers? How intrinsically small and yet efficient for work? This is God's great miracle, learn it and be wise. This is real diversion to your distracted mind. Great scientists spend a life to understand the infinitely small in the Universe. They study insects and worms, or the animal world, beasts of the earth and the fowls of the air, their life, their ways and habits, and record them. They watch an ant-hill or a beehive for years on end to know and write on the evolution of life. And their life, no one can say, is spent uselessly. If it is not a trifle, why do you look upon your life in this prison as futile or as wasted?

Behold another thing. The cats after midnight mew and cry. They are out caterwauling. A rival comes on the scene, and the love-song changes into a war-song. Terrible is the fight and screaming. So shrill and piercing the sound, that it jars on your nerves. You feel it contemptible, and ridiculous. But if you think of it, what else is our Ramayana? Like these two cats, the two men fight for the possession of a woman. Smitten with love, Ravana kidnaps Sita. In pursuit of love, Rama fights and carries her back. These cats fight with their claws and make terrible noise. Those men fought with their bows and arrows, sword and trident, and sounded their kettle-drums. The passion and the impulse, the instinct and the behaviour, are the same. The cats must have taken this fight between two tom-cats to be as epic as we regard the battle between Rama and Ravana. To talk in the language of evolution this battle of the tom-cats was the origin of the heroic duel between Rama and Ravana. Speaking of evolution, there are two basic facts of life that it enunciates. One is known as the struggle for existence and the other as the preservation of the race. Hunger and sex are its elements. According to this then, the Ramayana or the battle between Rama and Ravana may well be traced in its genesis to the fight of the two cats. And according to another basic fact, the love of Mary for Christ or of Yashoda for Krishna is the evolution of the primitive instinct of the mother-cat for her kitten. Look at the courtyard of the doctor's bungalow, and see there the hen with her brood of chicken. How she plays with them, crows to them and saves them from the swoop of the eagle or the kite. Yashoda trembled and wept not so much when Putana swooped upon Krishna, as this Madame Partelett must have crowed when the kite swooped down upon her little ones. What a wonderful thing is this world! Elders purchase tickets to witness the sports of children and competitions among schools. Here is the gathering of these chickens, jumping, cackling, picking up corn with their little beaks, their dodging one another, their running and their pursuing one another. Is it not as interesting as the school sports and the school competitions? The same feeling throbs in their hearts, the same joy thrills their being that we find in children and school boys playing. The whole life is a symphony of love, and joy, of instinct and appetite. Nothing is mean and nothing is great. The animal is as much human as the human is animal. Only we must look at both with a sympathetic eye and we must live to see it.

After a year in the hospital, I was sent back to chawl number five, and on its third floor. I was kept by myself and all alone, and I whiled away the hours in musings like these. I overcame the weakness of body and mind by these meditations. Sometimes I felt everyday that the body could not hold out any longer because one ailment after another was attacking it. This garment of the flesh seemed to be completely tattered and torn so that the soul could no longer wear it. At another time, I felt a distinct improvement in my health. But how long am I to linger thus? So, a year-and-a half had rolled on. Dysentery, blood in stools, fever and something else followed in succession and I bore it all. So, I resolved to put an end to my life. For, I was in no doubt that this prison and myself were never to part company and so long as this continued my health would never improve. We all struggle for happiness and none could weep for all time and continue suffering to the end of the chapter. I wanted to know how many days I suffered and how many days I was without suffering. So, I made a month's chart and marked on it days when wearing a body was a joy and when it was intense pain. I marked this on the wall, the day of suffering from one ailment or another, and the day free from any ailment. This went on for two months and then I made a reckoning. I found out that of sixty days, fifteen days were relatively better, and the rest were all worse. So, I concluded that things were not after all so I dark, and I must put off the thought of suicide.

But who would, thus, continue to live on the far-off interest of tears? The castles in the air are, after all, shadowy, unsubstantial things. And the mind recoils on reality after building them long enough. So, I was pulled back on 'the earth, earthy' and was kept hanging on the borderland of suicide. In the hospital, my weight had fallen down to 95 pounds, I could take no solid food; I felt distant symptoms of this is. Fever did not abate; and there was none whom I could call mine near me. During the three following months, I became worse, what with the atmosphere of hostility common to all political prisoners around me; what with disrespect and stark despair, with none to talk to me words of kindness and of love, and with no freedom of movement from one place to another. So much so that I knew not when death would pounce upon me and snap the chord of my life. I realised that the time had come when, with all my will to live, I must pass away.

Am I, then, to die in the hospital? This thought began to haunt me all along. I reviewed in my mind the philosophy of the world and its conclusion on the subject. From Buddha's doctrine of Nirvana and nescience to the Yoga doctrine of Knowledge; from the materialism of Science to the Monism of Haeckel and Spencer, and to the evolution theory of 'Substance' propounded by them, I searched them all for light on death and immortality. From the Mimansa doctrine of the Vedanta to Mill's Utilitarianism, I ransacked in my mind their conclusions about religion, and about the triple faith of God, Immortality and Duty. And as the fruit of them all came forth my poem "On my bed facing death". I wrote it while on bed in the hospital, and I had no hope that I should survive to read it.

When I was first arrested, and when in England I had expected the sentence of death, I had composed the two poems titled "My Will", and "First offering". And this I wrote on the threshold of death. In the last I have woven an imaginary conversation between death and myself. All the three poems find a place in the book, "Echo from the Andamans", published subsequently.

First Meeting with My Family

This year, my brother and myself got the permission to see our own people in the Andamans. Others were allowed to meet their own people after five years, and they stayed together with the members of their families for a couple of days, and in some cases, for weeks together. I got the permission at the end of eight years. I could obtain it after much worry and effort and with great difficulty. At last, my younger brother and my wife started from Bombay for Calcutta when they received a wire that the permission was withdrawn. It was a cruel joke, indeed. When one wrote to the Government of Bombay, it directed him to enquire at Port Blair. If the Commissioner of Port Blair was approached on the subject, he referred us to the Government of India. If one wrote to the Government of India, it wrote back to say that the final decision rested with the Government of Bombay. Things went on like this till 1918-19, when, at last, we met each other. I met them in the prison, and in the, presence of the prison-superintendent, and also within the hearing of the Marathi-knowing warder concealed behind, so that they may discover from our conversation if we were hatching up a new plot, conspirators as we were by the nature of our imprisonment. I met them after eight years—my wife, my brother and his wife. I was glad to see him hale and hearty. We talked to each other for an hour and a half full of joy and with the abandonment of a marriage festival. We suppressed for the time being all the dark memories of the past, thoughts of the rueful present, and fears for the unknown future. We dwelt on the immediate before us, and, as if carefree, gave ourselves up to the delight of the moment. But why did not my elder brother's wife come along with them? She had borne the heaviest burden of work in our political activities and in the never failing dangers of those activities. With what superb courage and an amount of patience had she faced them all? She was my childhood's companion, she was a loving mother to me in my adolescence, she was my trusted coworker in all political planning and execution, and for seven long years, I had been pining to see her. Why did she not come? Her eyes had closed on the scene, as I was to learn soon; they had closed after a long vigil with the lighted lamp of her love constantly kept burning. The lamp had flickered, the light had failed, the vigil was over, and she had gone to her maker; hopes deferred had not only made the heart sick but had broken it. Burning in the sacrificial fire of the country's liberation, and of her own separation from one dearest to her heart, she was at last reduced to ashes, and had expired. The wire, that she was permitted to visit her husband in the Andamans, from the kind Government at Delhi, had come a day too late!

The story was told me by my younger brother, and I swallowed it, without a word, like bitter poison. The world is always changing; what is today, tomorrow is not. Those, who are united, are bound to be separated at sometimes, sooner or later. God was kind to keep us together so long, and myself am entering on the decline of life. From the drama of life, one character after another must depart. They are bound to make their exit from the stage of this world. Are they mounting up to appear on the stage of the next world? Who knows? Each one to his faith. My elder brother believes in life after death and in rebirth. According to his faith, the soul of his dear and departed wife was hovering over this family reunion in the prison of the Andamans, and it must have heard us all. A man like me may not have that faith and for me the chapter has ended here. A woman fighting bravely for the freedom of her Motherland, dies on the battlefield and is said to go straight to heaven. What does it mean? It means that she is freed from all cares, all struggles, all pining, that she finds peace. She is extinguished like the flame of fire, disappears, vanishes completely. She goes beyond the pale of sorrow and joy. She attains salvation. On any ground, we ought not to weep for her. The sorrow is our own, for we can see her no more. I consoled myself, thus and dropped the topic. I turned on other subjects of national, religious and domestic importance. I indulged in humour and laughter within the time at our disposal. I do not know whence I gathered so much strength, in my exhausted condition, to say what I said. We three brothers had met together after twelve years! We were standing together on the pier near the boat that was to take me to England. That was in 1906 and we had met now in Port Blair and in prison in the year 1919, and that only for an hour-and- a half!

Permission was given to me to meet my wife alone for half an hour. After the meeting was over, my younger brother and the other members of my family were instantly put on the boat at Port Blair. As if their stay here for a week more to see the Andamans would have been dangerous, and involved some plot to spirit me away from this place by a boat or in an aeroplane! My brother's arrival had made many people anxious to meet him, but no one else was allowed to see him. But my fellow-prisoners saw him in spite of the ban, and did not shrink from presenting him with fruit and flowers.

Well, my people had left. It was like a happy dream in deep sleep on a night when the body is burning with fever; and like waking up from that shortlived experience and relief, to toss restlessly on my bed again. I found myself all alone once more, locked up on the third floor of chawl number five of my prison-house in the Andamans. At this time, I was removed from the hospital and put in this place. It was a solitary place, but I saw from it, the broad ocean and the open sky, and the island of Ras on the bosom of the ocean. I had never before been put in a room so airy and so open to view. And I was permitted, besides, to move freely in the verandas and the square of that circle of chawl. I used to sit and watch the island stretching out in front of me, and I often passed into a reverie. It put a strain on my mind to be lost in thought thus. Sometimes emotions bubbled over and overthrew thought, and I had to surrender myself to them till the storm had passed over me and I was again cooled down. A conflict and anarchy was the result of these surging waves, and then I had to take the helm, ride the storm and let thought resume its seat as before. That my heart should not be so entirely swayed by them, I directed my attention deliberately to the most ordinary things about me like the cows grazing in the compounder's ground like crows picking up and making away with coconut pieces, in concert and phalanx; or like little boats sailing towards the island of Ras. In the prison, the mind becomes so introspective that it is hard for one to push it out and direct it to objects without. We lose the habit of observing the world around us, and contract the vicious habit of brooding, again and again, over the same old thoughts.

Reading was impossible, for the brain was too fagged for it. Serious thinking and concentration on Yogic practices was out of question. While contemplating the sea and watching the rise and fall of the rolling waves, suddenly the mind itself like the waves was lost in the depths of reverie, and a mood of concentration would follow. Sometimes deep silence came over me as I kept on looking at the island of Ras, shining like an emerald in that sea, and adorned by the Church and its spire pointing heavenward. It reminded me of the Father in Heaven, for whose prayer and adoration it was reared on that solitary island. But that deep concentration, that solemn all-embracing silence, and that exhilaration of solitude became too much for my enfeebled body and my shattered nerves. My desolate heart could not bear them. After I had come to myself, my head would begin to ache, I felt their strain upon my brain and my nerves, and I felt weaker than before. Hence, even this exhilaration I could not have. I was reminded in these moments of Lord Buddha. Recovering from the memorable fast, he had fainted, and he had to regain the lost, strength of his body, and his power of concentrated thought and meditation. He had to eat whatever nourished his body like butter sugar candy, rice, milk and sugar boiled together, and whatever he got on the way. What then of a person like me! In the depressed state of mind and body, reading, thinking, concentration, meditation—all were out of court. Serious work was denied to me by my failing health; while the prison-hardships denied to me the calmness of mind as well. Without a friend, without play and without the opportunity of a stroll, the prison had become a nightmare. I could look at the hens of the doctor in the opposite compound. I could watch the birds flying and I could hear the mosquitoes humming. That was my relief; that was my recreation in this prison.

Yes, speaking of birds, I am reminded of bulbuls, the Indian nightingales, in the Andamans. Their melody was a real joy to my heart. They are very beautiful birds indeed. Tiny, well-proportioned, and alert. How playful and how sweet is their music, how quick their movements. Swarms of them hovered over the heaps of coconut fruit and swooped down upon them. They picked and ate the pieces to their fill. They continuously chirped round and about our chawls. The bulbuls entertained me when there was nothing else to entertain. I could even know their language and that of the jay or maina. The ten to fifteen notes of the maina I could clearly follow. So soon as the note fell upon my ears, I at once recognised it. The notes were different for different moods. A simple note, a note of hide and seek, a note of deep yearning, a note of alarm and fear, a note of deep happiness and peace, a note of passionate love, of motherly love and affection, of invitation to the mate, of ultimatums, and last, a note of fierce fight and finale—I had learnt and mastered them all. They were regular like words of human speech. I could not teach them my language but they taught me theirs—prisoners were not allowed to cage a bird as their companion. It was an offence. Or else I could have kept them in my room. I would have taught them songs of patriotism. And then! Why, other prisoners would have directed enquirers to my room as the great Shankaracharya was directed to the house of the learned Mandan Mishra, by pointing it as a house that had in its window a parrot and a maina discussing Vedanta! If a bulbul came in search of my cell, the prisoners would have guided it by saying, "Behold the room, at the bar of which the maina and bulbul sing their songs of patriotism and freedom, and know that it is the cell of the rebel Mandan Mishra Savarkar."

The crows were my familiar friends. A Mussulman prisoner kept a crow secretly with my connivance. But within a few days, I found that it was the food of the Burmese. For, the Burmese and the Mussulmans in that prison, being non-vegetarians, often killed crows to make a meal of them. They cooked his flesh on the fire in the factories and ate it. They sold it to one another at the rate of one anna per roasted piece or four tobacco leaves in exchange for it. The crow was tamed and kept by the Mussulman prisoner with the same end in view. And my suspicion came true when I found him the next day giving it to the Burmese prisoners for making a dish of it!

I was all alone in the prison, confined in a solitary cell, when I came here first. But then I could pass my time in writing poetry. Eight years after, while my fellow prisoners could move freely and be warders on tens of their fellows, I alone was put back to rot in a lonely room, and could not beguile the hours in writing poetry. I had stopped writing it when I found that I had better work to occupy my time here. But now nervous prostration had made it impossible to resume my old pastime. And I had to give it up almost. The three or four thousand lines I had composed, I now found it hard to commit to my memory. How then could I compose any new poems? Even then every week, I recited the old ones and fixed them well in my mind. The whole of my poetry took me one full day and one full night to recite. I used to repeat it line by line and continuously, barring the time for meals. But I realised, as I recited it now from my memory, how much of it I had forgotten during the two years of my continuous illness.

This is the story of my serious illness and the enforced rest that followed it. And yet I had not discontinued activity altogether. All old activities like *Shuddhi*, *Sangathan*, education and political awakening were spreading far and wide and were kept on so spreading by me.

In this lonely chawl and on its third floor, prisoners came to see me and incurred the displeasure of the officers and were put in handcuffs for eight days for breaking the prison regulation. They rendered me all the service they could, with all the difficulties that faced them in it. I cannot close this story without putting on record my gratitude to them in these pages.

The main object of the doctor and the other officers in this prison in bringing me on the third floor of chawl No. 5 was, I must admit, to give me the advantage of fresh sea-breeze and the open prospect in front of it. This change, along with better food and better treatment, that I got during my two years' illness, enabled me to tide over it, and to improve my health after it. Gradually, I began to digest my food, I gained in weight, shook off fever, and got over the signs that had marked me out as a sure victim of tuberculosis. And in the end I rolled up my bed and was confident that I had beaten off death.

My Brother suffers from T.B.

But the bed that I had rolled up I had to spread out once more. And this time it was for my elder brother. His health had been failing for a long time, but it collapsed completely by the time I had recovered my own. And it gives me pain to put down here that he was not looked after so well as I had been till almost the last day of his life in prison. I shall recall the scene: my brother going to the hospital in black coat of coarse blanket and bent down with the disease that had attacked him; with pain in the stomach indicating bad liver and spleen; standing before an insolent Madrasi "the sly-boots" of a doctor; the doctor pretending to examine him and to put him odd questions; and at last dismissing him with the remark that nothing was wrong with him! My brother, taking it as an insult resolved that, even for the life of him, he would never step into the hospital. He was taken back to his room coughing and groaning, clad in the same coarse garment, and was left to be there unattended, unnursed and uncured. The Madrasi was afterwards sternly warned for his rudeness and indifference. Later on, the Superintendent got his sputum examined, and at last, a specialist, who had been sent from India to inspect the hospital and offer his suggestions for improving it, declared that my brother had a patch on his back and was clearly a patient of tuberculosis. Even then, while in prison, he did not get the treatment that he needed for its cure. Sometimes he had such a fit of coughing, that the sound was heard in the two blocks of building near his own. And that obstinate cough would exhaust him completely so that he could hardly breathe, and he felt that it was choking the life out of him. And fever rose everyday from hundred to hundred and two degrees.

And his damaged liver made it impossible for him to walk erect. Add to all this a very bad type of chronic dysentery—and you will be surprised how he could pull on in that prison for the last year and a half of his term of imprisonment.

During that year and a half, about a hundred and fifty political prisoners on life-sentence, and about five hundred of worst convicts like robbers and dacoits—some of whom had not been there even for one year—were released on the occasion of the Victory Celebration of the last war and for amnesty granted in connection with an event to which we shall presently refer. But my brother, who had put ten years of hard labour and declining health in it, and whom bad health and overwork had made prematurely old, got no advantage either of the Victory Celebration or of the amnesty following it. And what was the Government's objection to his release? That he had written a pamphlet of ten pages for which offence he had been sentenced to transportation far life. And the other and the main crime was that he was my brother. So that though he was suffering from tuberculosis, there could be no amnesty for him.

And yet that Karma Yogi, that sufferer, never lost his confidence, never gave way to fear and nervousness, never surrendered his principles, and did not budge an inch when he saw death approaching to claim him as its own.

But this is only about the Andamans. When he was transferred from this jail to a jail in India, he had to undergo hardships still more terrible. Fate had in store for him untold suffering in comparison with what he had got in the Andamans, which was almost nothing. He was reserved by Providence to face them.

□

7

Riots in Punjab and Gujarat (1919-1920)

The war had ended and its reaction on India was just coming to a close, when news came in the Andamans about riots in Punjab and Gujarat. We were taken by surprise to read that news. In the tremendous upheaval of the great war and its repercussion on the world, nothing cataclysmic could happen in India. And now these riots—on a day after the fair, an uprising of sleepers awakened and struggling for commotion, after the tide had turned! Ahmedabad, Viramgaon, and Delhi and towns in the Punjab rioting, for what? Presently were drafted in this prison martial law convicts from Punjab and Gujarat. No Muslim political convicts had yet been reported to the Andamans. But in this batch from Gujarat and Punjab, there were a few Muslim political convicts as well. All of them had sentences passed on them, which ranged from two years' rigorous imprisonment to transportation for life.

In 1911, when I was transported to the Andamans, on board a steamer, in a chalan from India, I had said to the prisoners that a time would come before long when the whole steamer would be full of political prisoners transported from India. They were then mourning that I was transported for life, and the only political convict among them. I then prophesied that India would win her freedom when prisoners with life sentences like me would fill the whole Silver Jail of the Andamans, and that increasing number of prisoners like me was the thermometer of India's rising temper and living conscience. I remembered those words now. For, two steamers had now anchored in the harbour of Port Blair, and they were all political prisoners, who got down from them. The number of political prisoners in the Silver Jail had gone up to two hundred. And most of them were here on ten years' term of imprisonment or on imprisonment for life. And they were all spirited men, not to be cowered down by anything in the world. What a change in the temper of my country during a period of ten years! Prior to that date, if a patriot or political leader were sentenced to a year or a year-and-a-half's rigorous imprisonment, he was reckoned as a martyr by the whole of India. And now men go in prison and suffer ten years' imprisonment in the cause of their country as a matter of course, as if there was nothing unusual in it.

And it has become such a common occurrence now, that nobody even thinks of it. And what of one year's imprisonment? It is taken as if it was as good as free. "Only two years!" has now become an expression to mean nothing.

With all this, freedom has not come nearer. And it will demand tremendous sacrifice on the part of her people and an amount of suffering to accompany it, till India can hope to be free. That is the price of her victory.

Naland Vihar

This was the lesson of my preaching to all prisoners in the Andamans. And that made them stand up against any hardship that fell upon them. The newcomers were all drawn from the villages. They were all uneducated, ignorant people but no whit less patriotic on that account. I began to tell them that now that they were to be in prison for a number of years, it was up to them to add knowledge to their patriotism. Let them enforce their love for their country with rational sentiment behind it. Let them read, let them study, let them grasp and understand, so that patriotism would not be with them a vague sentiment or a mere emotion. The prison was a university for such study. It was our 'Naland Vihar'—a Buddhist temple of study and retirement. Train yourself, discipline yourself and acquire learning. And I and my old colleagues began to instruct them accordingly. We started with alphabets for these newcomers—shopkeepers, farmers, and villagers, all of them. Some of them were Gujaratis, and I procured books for them in Gujarati. Others were Punjabis and I made them read through Gurumukhi. The rest took their lessons in Hindusthani. I mixed with them partly in the morning and partly in the evening, and used my time with them in imparting lessons. Every chawl was humming with life. And all our members applied themselves seriously to that task. Most of them had heard my name and that counted much with them.

One of these newcomers told me, and I had heard it from others also, that when, during the war and in the early part of it, American warships went along the route of the Andamans, the Indians on board raised their hands in salute in front of Port Blair in honour of the political prisoners imprisoned in this jail. When I heard stories like these, I used to recall the words I uttered almost in the second week of my residence here. I had said then, "Do not be depressed by insults and humiliation. A day will dawn when they will raise their hands in salutes to you in this very place." I have already mentioned this in the first part of my narrative. That stimulant, that tonic dose, which I had administered then to my colleagues against their darkest mood of despondency—those words, which had painted the golden morrow on the midnight sky of sorrow—had not proved altogether useless. Some portion of our dear India still remembered us! India had not altogether forgotten us.

After the three 'R's, the new comers were given lessons in history and geography. Every evening after dinner, I talked to them for half an hour on Indian history, on the new reforms, on European history, and on elements of political economy. And I continued the topic with a batch of twenty-five men in turn in our Sunday Meetings. In these days the programme of national education was carried out with special vigour and intensity. Songs from the 'Gadar' were freely sung and all came out in their respective chawls and stood listening to them; prisoners, warders, petty officers, *jamadars* and all.

Well, we went even further. In the shade adjoining the prison factory, they had begun to learn and practise the art of wrestling as a pastime after their day's work. Among the newcomers, there were one or two trained and renowned gymnasts who readily agreed to undertake the task.

During the course of instruction, I had, sometimes, very strange and unwelcome experience. And not unoften, it amused me. Among the Gujarati prisoners, I found that I had to bribe one of them with a little tobacco that he should offer himself to teach Gujarati to a Mussulman fellow-prisoner. There was a Brahmin prisoner from a village in Punjab, who struck me as a double-distilled rascal. He was one of the convicts in the Punjab riots. Well, he not only demanded the usual fee of tobacco to teach a fellow-prisoner, but occasionally claimed as his special charge for doing the work, a portion of the milk that came to me from the hospital as my ration of food everyday. And yet he always shirked the task. When he found me nearby, he did his lessons in a loud voice. Otherwise, he avoided it as much as he could. The Brahmin had passed his fiftieth year but had not overcome his childish pranks. If I failed to give him tobacco, he would straightaway tell me that he had lost the slate and pencil, though I knew but too well that he had concealed them. And when my back was turned upon him, he would sing a skit which ran thus: "The Babuji is duped, duped is the gentleman Babuji." I was amused by it, and if I wanted him to repeat it to me, I had to give him another pinch of tobacco for it. Others threatened to thrash him for this joke at me, and I had to intervene and let him go. I still hum the tune to myself: "Babuji is taken in; the gentleman is taken in."

Several times, I had to run after them with slate, pencil and horn-book to make them learn. Some systematically avoided me as a pest. I remember giving a lesson in Gujarati alphabet to a forty-year-old peasant from that province, Jiva by name, forty times before he could learn it. The rest of them burst with laughter, but the best of it was that Jiva had learnt the lesson. They were so dull, so averse, and so ignorant. But they had, all of them, hearts of gold. Pure, devoted, simple, humble and obedient they were, except in learning, what I wanted them to learn, and what I insisted teaching them. They had wounds from bullet shots, all of them, which now survived as stains or scars. I always used to pass my hand gently on these scars and say with pride, "Behold our soldiers and the medals they wear. They are more precious in my eyes than medals of gold. They are more honestly won than those, and will last forever."

Exit of Mr. Barrie

Where was Mr. Barrie, when all these changes were going on in this prison, in all the bustle of its political prisoners? Where was now the demi-god of Port Blair, who once made the political prisoners look down when he looked up, and look up when he looked down, who roared and fumed every moment of the waking hour, and insulted him every moment of his life? Where was he? Nowhere. He was the jailor; he was in his office, like dead stone, harmful if one dashed his head against it; otherwise immovable and harmless. Ten years of endless wrangling, of strikes of newspaper cries and controversies, his loss of prestige, the grief that it had brought him had tired him out completely. The superior officers had also adopted towards the political prisoners, considering their growing number, their consolidation and their defiant attitude, the policy of let-alonism of tolerating them as an inevitable nuisance. Where we could hardly meet together and talk in a company of four, now we hold open meetings of twenty-five and more, and defy anyone to stop or disperse us. Mr. Barrie saw this, but wanted the petty officers to refrain from any action. "Let them not gather together and hold their meetings under our very nose, and that is enough. Give them light work, do not do anything and let them not do anything that may raise a commotion and a storm. And that will do. Let those devils do what they like. See that you manage them for yourself." That was the tone of his advice to them.

Moreover, ten years of education had made the petty officers, warders and *jamadar*s of our way of thinking. They had ceased carrying tales about us to their superiors. At least, but a few of them did that dirty work now. Hence, Mr. Barrie was ignorant of many things that were happening in the prison. I may give only one instance in point. A Gujarati convict, sentenced for murder in some dispute about agricultural holding, had been in this prison long before my arrival. From the time I came to know him, he had become my confirmed disciple and devout admirer. He had completely absorbed my teaching and had turned a nationalist. In the days of complete strike, he did his work punctually. As a prisoner, he used to pass chits from one political prisoner to another, hidden in the shreds of coconut shell. As a warder, he was put on the work of supervising the gang detailed to take rubbish out of the prison. And he distributed newspapers to different parts of the prison hidden in the baskets for carrying the rubbish. For, that service to us, he went among us by the name of 'the postman'. In the height of his power, Mr. Barrie would not let us have even a scrap of paper or the broken end of a pencil. We then communicated with each other by writing with a pointed piece of brick on our pot of drinking water, and the warder was our carrier of news. He easily passed us one another's pots. Leaves of trees were being systematically thrown on the rubbish and this man signed us to pick them up. And they brought us news scrawled on them by means of thorns, and without exciting the slightest suspicion. The tree is now cut down by order of the authorities. He had, thus, proved our loyal lieutenant and volunteer, helping us in all public activities. In course of time, by sheer honesty and merit, he rose to the position of a *jamadar*. He had learnt his Gujarati alphabet from me and in his turn he at my instance used to lead others to read and write. As a *jamadar*, he had to do it cautiously, for he was liable to be punished for it. That he was a straightforward man and an honest worker was known to all of us. He was without any vice and observed the prison discipline with meticulous care. He was suspect of Mr. Barrie because he was so sympathetic to us, but he rose to be a *jamadar* in spite of that suspicion. That speaks volumes of him.

As men trained by our organisation began to spread all over the Andamans and influenced the working in the prison itself, and, as orders from above had directed that the political convicts were to be kept in peace as much as possible, Mr. Barrie's position in his office was no better than that of an extinct volcano. He had always a long cigar in his mouth which he kept on smoking and puffing all the time that he was in the office. The fire that went up in curls of smoke from his cigar was the only sign of his volcanic temper. All else was as cold as snow. And, in these days, his health also had considerably gone down. He had lumbago of which he was constantly complaining, and he was fed up with it. At last, he had got long leave, for which he had applied, and he was making ready to depart from Port Blair.

He had been at Port Blair for twenty to thirty years and, therefore, packing up his things was a long process. He was now on the eve of retirement, and leave prior to it was already granted to him. It will not be out of place, therefore, to refer here to a past story, when four years ago, he had applied for similar leave to proceed home to Ireland. When he came to India from Ireland, as the report goes, he had come a poor man and was going back to Ireland with a few thousand rupees in his pocket. He then used to say to me, "Mr. Savarkar, I have completed my twenty years of transportation to the Andamans, and am now going back. For, was I not bound up to this place as much as you?" He decided to start, but the very harsh treatment that he had given during that career to the political convicts of that jail, made him afraid of traveling via India. Those were the days, when an official or two like him were despatched to heaven by the political prisoner's knife or bullet, and the news of such happenings in India had reached the ears of Mr. Barrie. One day, discussion arose on this subject in his office between Mr. Barrie and his European friends. They came to the conclusion that it was dangerous for Mr. Barrie to travel via Calcutta, for, in that case, he ran the risk of being done to death by an anarchist in India, who knew the treatment he had meted out to political prisoners in this jail. It was decided, therefore, that he should proceed to Ireland by a different route. This news was conveyed to me by a clerk in his office. I realised the fact that it was a wise decision for him to take at that time. Mr. Barrie was much flattered by the discussion. That evening he came to my room and said, full of self-importance, "Well, Savarkar, I hear that your friends in India are going to throw a bomb at me, as soon as I step on her shores. Is it a fact?" I replied to him in the same ironical tone, "I don't think so. They don't waste their bombs in killing crows and sparrows. I don't think there is such a fool among revolutionaries there who would waste his powder on these poor birds when he can kill a tiger with it." Mr. Barrie's pride melted away like a clod of earth in a pool of water. I do not know what happened to his fear about us. Of course, he knows it all right.

This is all about his last leave. The story of his recent leave stands on a different footing. He was to leave us this time for good. He was so much reduced in health that he was not sure he would live long after reaching his native Ireland. Suffering from the curses of hundreds of political prisoners in that Silver Jail, Mr. Barrie had to be lifted up by two men into the steamer that was to take off from Port Blair. In this dying condition, he reached India. And there, after great physical suffering, he breathed his last. He is remembered because the political prisoners, whom he had persecuted so cruelly, had helped keep his memory alive. And, it will live so long as this book lives, otherwise, it would have soon passed into oblivion. And verily it should have been so. For Mr. Barrie was but a tool in the hands of the Government to inflict horrible cruelty on us. And his role, as the jailor of the Andamans, brought him too much notoriety. In recording all the horrors and kindness, as of an institution, the man, who is unwittingly or wittingly its instrument, must need find mention, and, hence, Mr. Barrie must come in along with the story of our life in the Andamans. Otherwise, in themselves, neither his merits nor his demerits were of a character that would bring him notoriety or fame.

This reference to Mr. Barrie must not end with out an expression of my sincere gratitude to him, his wife and child for the kind words he spoke at times to me and for the deep sympathy his wife and daughter ever felt for me during the ten years of the hard life I had to pass in that prison. If I had met him in different circumstances, perhaps, he would have been one of my sincere admirers. And this thought is enforced in my mind by reading his jottings about me in his own diary.

After Mr. Barrie, Mirza Khan

We have done with Mr. Barrie. Let us now turn to his lieutenant, Mirza Khan. Where the volcano had itself become extinct, what of him who depended for his heat upon the fire in that volcano? The rising strength of the political prisoners, the fact of his isolation, one by one, from his Pathan, Sindhi and Baluchi confreres, and the substitution in their place of men of discipline and order, of gentle and good behaviour, in all the keyposts of the prison and the Andamans, had shorn Mirza Khan of all his former power. His beard inspired no terror in the heart of the prisoners, and, if he was at all to survive as a *jamadar*, he must now earn the goodwill of the very prisoners, whom he had ruthlessly trampled under his foot. His very fanaticism had now become his bugbear. He feared that, as he had so far done by the kafirs, so now they would do unto him. A funny incident will prove to you the truth of what I say. In these days, he had some disease affecting his hand. Whatever he did, the pain would not stop. As Mr. Barrie's whole body had suffered from the atrophy of limbs, so was it with Mirza Khan's hand. The foolish and fanatical Mirza Khan took it into his head that I had done something to it by my miraculous powers. The spectacled Bada Babu of Chawl No. 7 was the cause of it! He had no doubt about it. Mr. Barrie was free from this kind of superstition. But Mirza Khan went about telling that he and his master suffered from the magic I had practised upon them. He, therefore, sent me a message to beg my pardon for all his hundred sins. "Let Savarkar Babu but forgive me, and all will be well with me." That is what he kept on harping. "Do please request him to restore me my hand. Let him do me that kind turn," he repeated to all of them. I tried to convince him that I had nothing whatever to do with his ailment, that I had done no magic, and I did not believe in magic. But he would not listen. And just to please him, I said I would try to cure him. I called him and said, "If you have such faith in my power to cure you, well, then, I say sincerely that I bear no ill-will to you, and may God cure you." In course of time, Mirza Khan got back the strength in his hand he had lost, and he was cured not by me but by the medicine he had used. However, he thought that I had done the trick. Six months after he left the prison with three or four hundred others, who had got their discharge on account of the victory celebrations. But the serpent sneaked out with his fangs taken out. One, who was a terror to Hindu prisoners, had become a lamb before them, before he had left the Silver Jail. All his former allies—the Baluchis, the Sindhis, and the Pathans—had paled into insignificance. Tyranny had been beaten, the tyrants had gone, and the rest of them simply dragged on their existence. The warder, the havaldar, the *jamadar*, the clerk in the office, the doctor, the compounder, in the prison and out in the Andamans—the best part of this phalanx had now been recruited from the Hindus. And they were chosen for their merit, their honesty and straightforwardness, and for their good record as prisoners. The few Pathans that remained, as these new recruits won favour with their officers, said, "It is now Hindu Raj; and what can one say of it!"

Now, it is Hindu Raj

Some old Pathan prisoners used to complain about the new order of things in the following words: "Sahib, today it is Hindu Raj at Port Blair; we are afraid, very much afraid, that the Hindus may trump up some false charge against us!" As if, when these Pathans were in power, they had not trumped up any charges against the Hindu prisoners in order to persecute them! For, these men to fear now a similar treatment from the Hindus was nothing short of a reflection of their own wickedness. The Hindu warders, petty officers and *jamadars* never persecuted their Mussulman fellow-prisoners. On the other hand, it was a rule with us always to support such Mussulmans as were free from bigotry, and behaved with prudence. I used to teach them, and used my influence to promote their interests. I had written petitions in their behalf, I had helped them in their work, and when, later on, I had some power in this pinch beck Raj, I treated them with the utmost fairness and justice. Later on, I will quote their own words about it in its due place.

After the exit of Mr. Barrie, his post was temporarily filled by successive European officers, on permanent or temporary service. Some of them were local men and others were sent from India. One of them began to treat the prisoners as Mr. Barrie had treated them in his early career of high-handedness and utmost rigour. He had, however, lost sight of the ignoble failure of Mr. Barrie's last days. He sent some of the mildest of Gujarati prisoners to work the oil-mill. And another equally shallow-pated officer supported him. The political prisoners had almost sabotaged the oil-mill. The officer sought this opportunity to revive it. However, he did not choose for that purpose the tough and the strong ones among us. He allotted the task to those who were constitutionally weak, and who were of a mild and meek disposition. Who he hoped would not refuse to do it. Most of them were agriculturists, and yet on the very first day, they offered non-violent resistance, for, they had known the past history of the notorious Kolu. Two of them had their rooms in my chawi. And I had directed them how to proceed in the matter. Enraged by this resistance, he outheroded Herod. He roared and fumed like Mr. Barrie and yoked the two in our chawl, whom he regarded as their ring-leaders, to the handle of the mill as if they were bullocks, and asked others to turn it round. As others ran, these two had either to run with them or to be dragged along the ground behind them. One of them preferred the latter course. He lay flat on the ground, and as his hands were tied to the handle, he was pulled along the ground with the body bruised, broken and lacerated. In a moment, the news had reached all the wings of the prison. It was the time of our morning meal, and it was also the hour of our taking counsels together. I sent round word to ascertain if the news that had come to us was a fact. When matters had reached this point, the jailor arrived on the scene. And he saw each one of us standing beside his door, thali in hand, and refusing to take his food till the matter was finally decided. This was the first experience of the new jailor, but he realised at once, with whom he had to deal. First, he denied point-blank that the prisoner was tied to the Kolu. The boldest and the strongest of the Punjabi prisoners, who had taken the lead in the last strike, came forward to contradict the jailor. "Was the Gujarati prisoner lying then?" he asked the jailor. He lifted up the iron plate like a mace and threatened that he would break the head of him, who had lied. Let him beware who dares this outrage against us, he added. The jailor went back without uttering a word. He ordered the release of the prisoners and sent us a message to take our food. He promised that no further trouble would follow. A few days after, the two prisoners were put on picking oakum. And the threatened strike came to an end.

It was during the regime of this jailor, if I remember rightly, that a prisoner was thrashed in spite of the prison regulation that had stopped such beating. The victim was an ordinary prisoner, who heartily took part in all our public activities and always gave all the help he could to political prisoners. I have referred to this young man in my account of the *Shuddhi* movement in an earlier chapter. The officer had always an eye on such persons. The young man was an earnest man and fond of study. He was found reading, taken to the office and was severely rated by our new jailor. In the prison jargon, the epithet that the jailor used was as common as an article in English before a common noun. But eight years had seen a vast change in the mentality of the prisoners. What they would have tolerated before, as a matter of course, they would not put up with now. The jailor abused the prisoner and the prisoner returned the compliment with equal vehemence. The jailor was in a rage, he had the prisoner pinioned by two of his warders and had him beaten with fisticuffs on the chest. Blow after blow was rained upon his mouth and chest. The prisoner's face got swollen and blood came from his mouth. He was then let off. The prisoner was suffering from scrofula, it has to be mentioned here. The jailor was pleased that he had his full vengeance upon the prisoner. Other ordinary prisoners advised the young man to take it all patiently. They said to him, "We are ordinary prisoners. We cannot fight the jailor as political prisoners do. Go quickly to the doctor, tell him that you had a fall and get your wound treated by him. Or else, you will be beaten again. We are such insignificant fellows—a common fry after all." But the young man was no chicken-hearted fellow. He had a black eye and his face was all swollen. He told the doctor that the jailor had beaten him. The doctor, for fear of the jailor, would not entertain the complaint, and the jailor would not allow the prisoner to see the Superintendent. One of us resolved, thereupon, to bring the thing into light. The Chief Commissioner was to visit the prison the same week, and the jailor was in a fright. He begged that the matter should end there. But the young man told the whole incident to the Commissioner without fear or favour. The jailor was sternly rebuked for his conduct, and no more did such a thing happen again during the remainder of my stay in that prison. Eight years back, it was a common thing for the jailor to call upon his myrmidons to teach the prisoner a severe lesson. "Make him straight"—that was the watch word. But the old order had changed. The incident narrated above was the last of its kind under that order. For the rest of the time—a year-and-a half—that I had to pass, nothing of that kind ever happened again. The young man, for all the beating that he had got for it, did not give up his work for us. He had already filled his fourteen years in that prison and had not come out when I left the Silver Jail. What happened to him later, I do not know.

Mr. Diggins

After many transfers and changes, one Mr. Diggins came to be appointed jailor in the Andamans on a permanent basis. He was the brother-in-law of Mr. Barrie and had filled several offices in the Andamans before he was promoted to this post. Even a good man could not continue to be good in the reactionary official atmosphere of the Andamans. It was all the more creditable, for Mr. Diggins to have worked in the several responsible offices he had filled so far, with justice and fair-play. As such, his appointment as jailor was a matter of rejoicing for us all. Mr. Barrie was the best hated man in the prison-world of this place, while his brother-in-law, Mr. Diggins, was all along looked up to with gratitude. He had high regard for Hindu culture. He was an Irishman and a theosophist. I have already quoted a depreciating remark of Mr. Barrie on theosophy in connection with the story of Indu Bhushan, that its reading had a softening effect on a man's brain and ultimately led to insanity. Mr. Diggins was a long and devoted student of theosophical writings and there was no sign in his behaviour of actual or approaching insanity. The Government that had appointed him to several offices in the settlement felt absolutely sure that he had a sound brain. Mr. Diggins was a lover of learning and a man of culture. He was a strict and an honest officer, and while he maintained strict discipline in the prison in his charge, he never allowed himself to forget that the convicts were human beings and were to be ruled for their intellectual and moral well-being, and the jail was a penitentiary and a house of correction, and was not to be used for turning them into beasts of burden and to their utter demoralisation. He worked steadily on that plan, of course, within his limits, and, several times, had to incur the displeasure of his superiors on that account.

The Jail Commission

While the jail administration was passing through this transition, news came to us that the Government of India had appointed a Commission to visit the Andamans and report on the reforms in the colony and the jail of these islands. One of the problems before the Commission was the future of the settlement as a whole. One of the prime causes that had led to the appointment of such a Commission was, no doubt, the agitation we had carried on in the prison and outside during the last eight years to draw the attention of India and the world to the wretched condition of all the prisoners at Port Blair. The officials at Port Blair now busied themselves in preparing evidence that would throw a veil over the past, and show that after all there was nothing very wrong here and things should be allowed to continue as they were. They set up machinery for white-washing and window-dressing the entire administration. And they selected for that purpose renegades and flatterers, from among us to be tutored to appear before the Commission and give the evidence they liked. They took particular care to shut out direct complaints by the prisoners against the officers concerned. On the side of the political prisoners, on the other hand, we had started work that would enable us to put the whole case before the Commission in order that nothing that was needed to bring about a radical change in this institution should escape their attention. We started correspondence and sent messages throughout the settlement that the evidence to be led before the Commission of grievances and demands, that these should be of a straight and uniform character. Each district and part of the settlement was to prepare its own case and represent it to the Commission. But all of them seemed to be very keen that I should lead the deputation on behalf of them all. For they had confidence that I alone could put the whole case before the Commission in written and oral evidence as none of them could do it.

But I had definite information that the Commission was being sent to the Andamans with one object in view. And that was to investigate into and review the cases of its political prisoners and to report on the discharge of as many of them as they thought fit for that mercy by the evidence placed before them. It was obvious, in these circumstances, that if I led the deputation and exposed the administration, the Commission, mainly composed of officials, would be heavily prejudiced against me, and I would lose my chance of freedom from this jail. Should I take that risk or should I not? That was the question before me.

On the other hand, if I failed the political prisoners in their hour of need, I would be rightly charged with ingratitude for the whole-hearted support they had given to me in all the activities that I had started in the prison. They had faced opposition and passed through hardships for my sake during the eight years of my close association with them. Moreover, by my abstention, I would be throwing away the opportunity of a life-time to crown all the activities I had started here with the simple aim of putting an end to the inhuman cruelty practised as a policy by the administrators of this prison. It was not only the question of ten thousand and odd present prisoners in that jail and their just grievances, but of the improvement that would affect all those that might happen to be sent in this place hereafter. Should I fail them now, I would lose all that I had done in the past. For, this enquiry and this Commission were in themselves the fruit of our endeavours, sufferings and resistance in this jail. I knew in my heart that none could render them better service in the present juncture than I do. To back out now was to let them down. I, therefore, decided to lead the deputation whatever be its consequences to me personally.

It was my principle of action in the Andamans to ever observe the golden mean. Whatever good I could do in the Andamans or whatever awakening I might bring about among its people was nothing in comparison with what I could do in India as a free man. On the other hand, in order to win my freedom, I would not stoop low or lend myself to anything mean or treacherous such as would bring disgrace on my country or be a blot on her fair name. Freedom, thus, obtained would have harmed the cause and would have been, as I regarded it, an immoral act.

Barring this, I had determined to miss no opportunity of release, and to pass my days in working for the uplift and consolidation of the prisoners in the midst of whom fate had thrown me, till the time I got the chance I was waiting for. With this aim, I got my work done through those whom the authorities did not regard with suspicion or anger. When I found none, on whom I could cast that responsibility in a particular case or in a particular kind of work, I came forward to shoulder the responsibility without fear or favour. My policy had been not to forego the slightest chance of release; at the same time, that if I was not sure of it, not to take it lying low, and never to be a silent spectator of the ills from which others were suffering, I knew thoroughly well that my freedom was not to come through my good conduct so much as it would come through revolutionary changes in India; and through the pressure of political events on the Government itself. Before that change and pressure in India, even those of our political prisoners, who had turned themselves toadies of Mr. Barrie, rotted in the jail along with us. The authorities regarded them as sensible men precisely because others had dared to condemn their conduct. They treated them better because others would not countenance their tyranny and oppression. And they came to be regarded as gentle because others would not be poltroons. The Government was not so foolish or simple-minded as to set political prisoners free for the mere fact that they were meek and mild men. Obedience would not have won for them what they had achieved by firm resistance. If at all they were freed, it would be no more than an act of policy forced upon them by political circumstances in India, and not as a concession to their good behaviour, or as an indication of their magnanimity. I knew it too well for anyone to take me in. I had realised it from my knowledge of history as also from my experience of prison-life.

According to that policy, I decided to steer the middle course also on this occasion. I agreed to appear as a witness before the Commission, for I knew that no one else could put the case of thousands of prisoners and their sufferings before the Commission as effectively as myself. But, I decided, at the same time, that I would do so only on the invitation of the Commission itself, and, further that I would state before them facts as I knew them. If the Government would not release me because I had told the truth on the invitation of the Commission itself, still regarding me as a dangerous man, I would regard the act as a mere excuse to detain me, in that case, not to be of use to the prisoners was nothing short of failure to do my duty.

At last, when the Commission actually came to go round our prison, it came straight into my room as I had expected. That Commission included Mr. Jackson, who had worked all his life as an Inspector of Prisons in the Presidency of Bombay. The Raja of Pangal was one of its other members. They opened a discussion with me on the settlement in the Andamans, on the administration of the Silver Jail, and on political convicts generally. I had made full preparation for such an enquiry. And I quote here a few specimens of the conversation on the subject between the members of the Commission and me.

I gave them the full story of Bhan Singh's persecution in the jail, which I have already narrated in an early chapter of this work. In that conversation an Indian member of the Commission spoke to me more angrily and insolently than its European members. He put me the following questions:

"How do you know, Mr. Savarkar, that the scars on Bhan Singh's body were the result of the thrashing that he got in this prison?"

I: "Because none could take for granted that they were there without any cause."

On this, another member put in, "Bhan Singh had fallen from the staircase while he was giddy. May the scars not be of the wounds he had received in that fall?" "Were you an eyewitness to his thrashing? Mere hearsay is of no avail." I: "May I ask you, Sir, if you were there when he had a fall? Of course, you were not. And you, in that case, depend upon hearsay report as much as I do. And if that cannot be entertained, this also is out of court. It is more untrustworthy than mine for you were miles away from this place when this incident happened, while I was only divided from him by a partition wall. I heard his cries. I heard the words, 'Beat him, beat him.' I saw the excitement and consternation that followed, and, within five minutes, those who had seen it, brought the report to me."

Member: "Of course, we depend upon what the authorities have reported to us."

I: "And I depend upon what the political prisoners conveyed to me. I do not think that they are less trust worthy than the officers of this prison. The petty officers of this place are themselves very negligent and they are more likely to give garbled news than my friends the political prisoners. The superior officers were not on the spot when the incident happened. Besides, I had personally seen the cut of a cane on the person of Bhan Singh when he was removed to hospital."

Another, who was discussing me aside with a colleague, said, "What will you do if you are set free from this prison?" Before I could answer him, a member interposed ironically, "Of course, he will go on with his old business, that of spreading sedition in the country." I replied, "You seem to be knowing my mind too much. Otherwise, you would not have ventured that remark. Supposing I carry on as before, can you not put me back in the jail again? Will you keep a convict for ever in jail for fear that if he is discharged, he will begin his old game again? It is fair that you release me in pursuance of your own regulations. There has not been a single complaint against me during the last five years. Those, who had tried several times to break away from the prison, have not been kept in the Silver Jail for more than one year. I would abide by every condition you lay down for me even if you make me free in India, instead of transferring me from this prison to any other in India. If you forbid me from entering into politics, I shall do social and literary work in India. I shall try to serve mankind in many other ways. And if I break any condition that you may impose upon me you are free to send me back to this prison on transportation for life. Your law is so comprehensive and your power is so all-embracing."

Member: "Not so, for so long as you evade the law, the law cannot cover you on the charge of breaking it. You may not be caught and preceded against for high treason. But that will not mean that you have not committed it."

I: "But then, you cannot also say positively that I have committed it." So long as you don't catch a thief in the very act, or you have no ground to suspect him of theft, you cannot arrest him for theft. And the same rule applies to a case of treason. I have several times forwarded my opinions to the Governor General in Council. The constitutional reforms will enable me to do some constructive work for the country. And I would try to do my work in a constitutional manner. If the reforms prove fruitful that way, and clear the path to the goal all have in view, a political revolutionary like myself will prefer that path to bloodshed and unnecessary murder. Surely, he is not so tired of his life as to risk it in that way. We followed that dangerous course in utter desperation and not because we were in love with it. And if you don't take me at my word, then I would give you in writing that I will take no part in politics for a stipulated period. Many of my friends will bind themselves down in writing like me. Let us be made free even with that restriction upon us. For, we have much else to do in the service of our country in the field of literature and social reform. Why do you prevent us from doing it? Why do you keep so many useful, honest, brave and self-sacrificing persons behind the prison-bars and its stone walls? You have let off the Irish Sin-feiners ten times. They broke your conditions ten times and yet you have made them free on the same conditions the eleventh time. Why not trust us then at least once? Why not give us a chance?"

In this strain, the conversation went on for one hour and a half. I narrated to them the whole story of my experience in this prison, much of which I have already woven in this narrative.

I also covered the whole ground of Criminal Law and Penology. I traced the whole system of prison administration from the Borstal system in England to the latest experiment in America and on the continent of Europe. We had a long discussion on it. And, last, I embodied the gist of it all in a written petition. With this last direction, the Commission took leave of me.

The Commission had called for similar written statements from three or four of other political prisoners. Petitions were sent to the

Commission from all parts of the settlement through the leaders of the prisoners working in the colony, as was previously arranged by us. These referred to matters special to the districts, they worked in. Two of the statements by political prisoners were very plain-spoken. All of us spoke with one voice and had unanimously made out a case for our release. And we had all demanded a thorough overhauling of the system of prison administration in the islands of the Andamans. A major portion of the political prisoners had represented that the Andamans should no longer be used as a prison settlement. In the newspaper world of India, there was a similar appeal for closing up the settlement. In the 'Bengali' of Calcutta, a series of articles had appeared in support of that policy. For, no one in India knew in detail the exact difference between mending and ending the system as a whole. The prisoners in India were totally ignorant about it. Therefore, the case for ending it was not so well made out in Indian newspapers in that matter of opinion. In my own statement on the subject, I had given all the facts relevant to the point at issue. This difference of viewpoint led, later on, to the sharp opposition by me to the general tendency among the prisoners of the Andamans. I give below an outline of my statement on prison administration as also on the legal and the practical aspect of the whole question:

"The ideal of the administration should be to improve the prisoner, to level him up physically, intellectually and morally, and not merely to punish him as a matter of revenge. The punishment and discipline should be strictly enforced only with an eye to that improvement."

"The punishment should be deterrent and not excessive. It is needed because human nature has not yet completely shed off its cruel and beastly instincts, and only the fear of punishment can make the ordinary class of prisoners abstain from crime. Moral responsibility has no share in it. Therefore, the punishment and discipline should be in strict proportion to the nature of the crime and to the nature and propensities of the prisoner himself. As far as possible, caning and hanging should be the rarest of all punishments, if their total abolition is found to be impossible today. Those convicts alone should be visited by that extreme penalty of the law, who are found to be absolutely irreclaimable. The juvenile criminals should not be classed with ordinary prisoners. Their youth, their impressionable disposition, their repentence, should be taken into particular consideration in the sentence to be passed upon them, and as regards the prisoner, with whom they should be herded.

They are more to be pitied than punished for their offences, and they should be weeded out for a kindlier and more sympathetic treatment. A milder attitude towards them is eminently desirable, while those who appear to be distinctly anti-social may be reserved for stricter discipline and severe punishment. As they improve, the latter may be included in the former class of prisoners, as individual cases, as the former may change places, individually, if they show no sign of improvement whatever.

"The object of hard labour allotted to the prisoner should not be to bring in large profits to the jail he is confined. It should be to improve him that he may return an honest man and a good citizen. He should be made to learn, in addition to doing his allotted labour. In the Andamans, there is no provision for the general education of prisoners in charge. On the other hand, the authorities discourage and try to put down any such private effort. The practice is not only inhuman but devilish. Education in prison should be more compulsory than hard labour. And it should concentrate on the building up of character; it should bring about a change in his mental and moral outlook on life, and in the society in which he lives, moves and has his being.

"Prisoners, up to the age of twenty-two, should not be regarded as hopeless, whatever be the nature of their offence in the eye of the law. The aim of punishment should be to reclaim them as future citizens. All discipline should be directed to that purpose. They should be trained vocationally, so that they might have some useful occupation to fall back upon when they came out in life. By way of recreation, every prison should be provided with amenities like cinema and music, which will make them both human and responsible citizens.

"Of course, the prison ought never to be a place for an easy way of life. The prisoners must feel that they are segregated from the world not for ease, indolence and enjoyment, but for severe self-discipline and for realisation that the kind of life they had led was not desirable or worth while for them to continue further. If they want freedom, they must deserve it; and the sooner they learn the lesson, the better it would be for them in the near or remote future. Prisons are penitentiaries and not places of inquisition and torture.

There are very few races and families, of whom one can say positively that they are a race or a family of hereditary criminals. They should be treated as exceptions. The normal rule should be that the convict is sent to a prison to go back a better man. As heredity and race are not yet final facts like other facts of Science, no penal legislation should be built up on its conclusions as if they were uncontroverted truths."

This is only the barest outline of what I had stated in my petition. And the reader may object to parts of that statement. But I explained the objections fully in my oral evidence. My final conclusion about the Andamans came to this: That today it was not a place of health because of the sea-winds blowing into it. But engineering and sanitation may turn it into a healthy resort before long. If sanitation, drainage, anti-malarial measures succeed in improving it, it may be a colony for settlers who aspire to longevity and sound health. Even as things were today in that settlement, the European settlers are found to thrive there and enjoy perfect health.

Those people, who are proved to be exceptionally cruel in their propensities and who, by their anti-social activities, stand self-condemned as the out-laws of society, should be compelled by law to settle in the Andamans and should be made to develop the settlement, and to help social uplift under strict supervision and discipline rather than be made to rot uselessly in the jail of that place. This will be nationally fruitful, as it will give their lives some social bias, and make their own life happier and better than it could ever be in the prison itself. For, if they are enemies of civilised society, they can, within the area of the settlement, develop a social sentiment and mutual aid under strict regimentation. By well-appointed work, many of their rebellious instincts can be brought under control and directed in fruitful channels of duty and responsibility. They can be, thus, moulded into a social organisation all their own. The most cruel, and selfish convicts are found to turn into men soft as clay under the hard discipline of prison-life today. They have become obedient slaves of the tyrants, who rule them. But it is of no use to them to be broken thus. If, on the other hand, they are put as free men on the settlement, if they are allowed to marry and manage things for themselves, their meekness and obedience will bear good fruit, and they will not be a burden and a drag on society. And their progeny will be immensely better than themselves. The children, under proper training, may become good citizens. To bury so many prisoners in jail for a term of fourteen or more years is to destroy the possibility of marriage and progeny which is a great loss to the country. While if they are made to colonise and develop the settlement on the basis of independent, hard-working and self-supporting families, in a generation or two the nation gains in number and in good citizens. Canada and Australia are living instances of such beneficent policy. They were, to start with, prisoners' settlements. Now they have grown into prosperous, self-contained and civilised dominions. The cruel and domineering temper of men in civilised countries proves useful in the development of back-wood regions peopled by savages. The qualities of head and heart that are a nuisance in older countries are assets in these regions. So that the prisoners can be best utilised for developing a settlement like the Andamans, first, to their personal advantage, and next, as a fine colony of the mother-country. This is the policy that the Government of India should adopt towards the development of the Andamans."

For these reasons, I am not in favour of closing the Andamans as a prison-colony, but I wish the whole nature of it to be changed from harsh and cruel methods of jail life that prevail in it today. The prison-regulations today border on savagery and slavery for the prisoners and entourage despotism and tyranny on the part of the officers in charge. The aim should not be to exact as much work as you can. This ought to change into treatment of each prisoner according to individual merit or demerit. They should be classed together according to their past record of crimes and their present behaviour in the prison. And they should be so governed that by their permanent settlement in the colony they should become good citizens and their progeny a grade higher than they. Thereby, they will be contributing a new chapter to the cultural and social growth of India.

By this reform, the Government will be more than repaid for the crores of rupees it has so far sunk in the Andamans and in maintaining there the Silver Jail. There will be no ground for it to think that by the change they shall be wasting that money. For, the Andamans will rise in importance and the new arrangement will turn it into an asset for the country.

From the day that I stepped on the shores of the Andamans, I had begun to realise that it could be fortified into a great naval base for the defence of India, and, before long, it was to become an area for the location of her naval and air forces. In case an enemy were to attack India from this side with its fleet, warships and aeroplanes, this base will checkmate them first, and constitute its strongest fortification to beat back the attack. (See Part I, Chapter VII).

My memorandum to the Commission consisted of these and similar other proposals. My discussion with them about the Andamans struck them as a new light on the subject. Some of them did not take it seriously, but all of them were deeply impressed by it. When they used to come up to me on the third floor of the chawl, they would laugh and, pointing to the shore, ejaculate, "Behold your naval base and fortification and the warships floating up and down the waves." And I would reply, "You and I may not live to behold them; but our children will very probably witness them."

This discussion between the Commission and myself took place about 1919-1920. I had said then that our children would see the Andamans transformed into a naval base and fortification for the defence of India. In 1926, when I am writing this, I feel I myself shall see it so converted. I read only in November last, in a newspaper in India the following, to confirm my opinion on the subject:

"The Andamans will no longer be used as a settlement for the convicts. The Indian Government has sanctioned an annual grant of rupees four lakh and a half in order to turn it into a self-supporting colony and to use it as a base for naval and air-forces as also for a wireless station."

Suffice it to say here that it will give me great pleasure to see my vision of the Andamans since I stepped on its shores in 1910, and my suggestions all along, to turn it into a reality, as the report from a newspaper, which I have quoted above, goes to show that it will be so. I may, however, remark that in order to make the Andamans a naval and an air base for the future defence of India, it is not necessary to cancel it as a prison settlement, of course, on the lines indicated by me in my written statement and my oral evidence before the Jail Commission. If both the plans were properly correlated and vigorously carried out, they would largely contribute both to the prosperity and military strength of the Andamans. That was the opinion I held in 1919-20, and that is what I hold and maintain even today.

□

8
Amnesty and Political Prisoners

The Jail Commission had left the Andamans. There was, no doubt, in my mind that the members of the Commission were considerably impressed by the statement I had submitted, and the discussion I had with them. And I have reason to believe that they did not suggest my release because, though I had plainly put it to them that if the new reforms proved a success, the revolutionaries would follow the path of peace. I had introduced many ifs and buts to qualify that general proposition, and they were angered by them.

All the same, I had the deep satisfaction of realising that I had done all that I could for the well-being of thousands of my fellow prisoners and the Government had no rational explanation to offer for my detention in that prison.

While the Jail Commission was engaged in its work in this prison and afterwards, a great movement had been started in India for the release of political prisoners in the country and outside. It made the release a great national issue. The 'National Union' of Bombay had submitted to the Government of India a monster petition signed by 70,000 persons, demanding their release. I always insisted on the need of such a petition to bring home to the Government the keenness of public opinion on this vital matter. It is clear to the reader from what I have written about it in the foregoing pages as also from the extracts I have quoted in them from the annual letter I had sent to my brother in India. Our leaders in Bombay and Maharashtra by their strenuous efforts had at last fulfilled that desire. The Government had always maintained that politicals like us had absolutely no following, much less any sympathy from other parties in the country; that the country was indifferent to our fate. They went further and asserted that the mass of people regarded us as wicked and self-centred revolutionaries, no better than other criminals in the country. The representation, made by the 'National Union' on behalf of 70,000 signatories to it, was a conclusive answer to the position the Government had taken. It had a great moral effect in the country, as a vindication of the opinion that the people regarded the revolutionaries as good patriots as those who differed from them in their methods of work, and in their approach to the great national issue. It showed further that the people were full of gratitude to them for their daring and sacrifice in the public cause. The representation was bound to create a great moral force so much needed to persuade the Government to do justice by us. I had said as much to my brother in his visit to me in the Andamans. The. 'National Union' of Bombay had rendered a great service to the country by preparing the petition and taking as many as 70,000 signatures upon it, covering in its activity a wide area from Bombay to a far off village like Bhagur, within the period of a fortnight, an activity in which ladies took such a great part in distributing leaflets and collecting signatures from door-to-door. It may be rightly described as a landmark in the history of political convicts in India. I may be allowed to say here that my younger brother had done a fine piece of work in promoting the agitation, which had fructified in that petition. The petition was also an indication of the great national awakening in the country and the courageous attitude of the people behind it. There was a time in our national movement when the word political prisoners was a terror to the people, and even great national leaders uttered his name without using behind it the appellation due to him as a gentleman, as if he was no better than the most condemned miscreant in society.

The petition had demanded the release of all political convicts including the revolutionaries. And it had made a special mention of me and my brother, precisely because the Government bore a special grudge to us, as deserving such a release. Most of the signatures were taken from people in Maharashtra, as there was very little time for the 'National Union' to approach the people of other provinces. The monster petition submitted by the 'National Union' would surely have grown into a grand remonstrance containing ten times the signatures it bore, if there was time enough to pursue the activity far and wide, throughout the whole country. And yet the petition had on it signatures of representative leaders of all the provinces in India.

What we in the Andamans felt about it is well expressed in my letter to India, written in 1920. I give the following extract from the letter here for the information of my readers.

"Many thanks, I am grateful to all the leaders and patriots and, especially, to the members of the Bombay 'National Union'" for undertaking the task of preparing a petition on behalf of all the political convicts, signed by 75,000 persons and forwarding it to the Parliament. You have achieved the task within such a short time that it deserves all the greater praise for it. It is bound to weigh with the Government, if not directly, at least indirectly. To say the least of it, the petition had raised the moral status of political prisoners all round, as also of the work for which many had fought and failed. I shall now welcome release, if it were to come to me. For, people themselves have expressed their desire to have me back among them. I do not find words adequate enough to express all that I feel about it. The gratitude is overwhelming and the joy inexpressible. They have given me more than I deserve from them. I have no doubt about it."

Within a few days, the Government announced its decision to let off all political prisoners, in accordance with the terms of general amnesty.

The credit of it all goes as much to the petition submitted by the Bombay 'National Union' as it goes deservedly to the work behind it of an all-round agitation and awakening in the country about the political prisoners' condition in the Andamans.

One evening, before the day's work was over, I was standing with other prisoners around me, when one of my Sikh friends came running up to me and said clapping his hands, "Babuji, you are free, orders have come for the release of all the political prisoners in this jail. You are free, Babuji, you are free."

What the word 'freedom' really means and what joy it brings, only the heart of him can tell, who has been sentenced to transportation for life, or who is waiting in his cell to be taken to the gallows.

All the prisoners in our section stood rooted to the spot; the unexpected had happened, and they kept on whispering to one another the word 'deliverance'. But I had heard the word so often, and so many times had it been broken to my heart, that my joy of it could not last long; my heart failed to respond to it. In 1911, on the occasion of the King's' coronation, a prisoner had come up to me all agog with similar news. And prisoners had rolled up their beds and kept themselves ready to depart. Eight or nine years had rolled by since that day, and I was in the same prison now as I was then. So many political prisoners had come and gone during the period!

Therefore, I asked my Sikh friend pointedly, what his source of the news was, whence had it come and how. Had it come by wire or otherwise? Our organisation for getting the news had been so efficient now that whenever the officers received any order or information from India, that order or information was being instantly communicated to us; the copy of the printed order or information would reach our hands at the same time that the original fell into the hands of the officers concerned, crossing all the barriers of the seven seas, watches, walls, locks and bars that would keep it away from us. A copy of the wire had similarly passed into the hands of a warder who had handed it over for me to the Sikh prisoner. As soon as I put him the question, he put the telegram in my hands and smiled. He then asked, "Well, are you now satisfied? Do you or do you not believe me now?" And full of joy and in a victorious mood, he gave me a hearty shake.

I read the wire. The political prisoner was not to be free. I read the sentence to my friend, which ran 'so far as it is compatible with public safety'. The meaning of the qualifying clause was clear as daylight. The amnesty was granted compatible with public safety, from which I was sure that myself and my brother, and other fiery prisoners like us were not to get the benefit of the general pardon. In spite of my doubt about it, lost in joy they would not believe me.

Everyone of them waited, morning and evening, for the order of their delivery from that jail. I told them frequently that many of them were, no doubt, to be set free, and that was, indeed, a matter of sincere rejoicing and personal victory for all of them. But let them not delude themselves that all of them were to go out, for their despair would be sharper and more unbearable. The one thing certain was that we must live, struggle, pine away and die here. The thing that was not so certain was anything else beside it.

And it turned out as I foretold. The amnesty was not only not applied to me, but also to most of those political convicts who came there many years after me.

Some of them are still rotting in different jails in India. Heaven only knows when they shall be free.

Those who were released included by far the largest number of political convicts from Punjab and Gujarat. Most of them were soldiers and had fomented riots in that part of India. They had been in this prison, at the most, for two years-and-a-half. The pure revolutionaries transported for life—political prisoners strictly so called—who got the benefit of general amnesty, all hailed from Bengal and were involved in the Maniktola Bomb Case; and others, who were convicted in the Punjab and the Benares trials for conspiracy and sedition. It was, indeed, a day of universal rejoicing for us all. But in the midst of this rejoicing, I did not fail to point out the fly in the ointment, which was that India was not yet free, that they had fought and suffered for her freedom which was the national goal. And so long as that battle was not won, this rejoicing could not but have its dark shadow of grief, and the rejoicing may be but momentary, to be followed by similar hundred battles, and sufferings and incarcerations. Many still have to die fighting for the cause which my trusted friends and colleagues should never lose sight of.

I also drew their pointed attention to a matter of deep significance locally, and it was that among those released were some fire-eaters, one of whom had resounded the whole chawl with his songs of patriotism called from the revolutionary journal 'Gadar', and made crowds of prisoners hang on his lips while he sang those passionate songs. I may give here just one bit from them to show how fiery they were. Here is the catch: "Open your eyes, O, Indians, the nation is reeling and sinking." I can never forget this refrain; I can hear its sound even today. That such vehement persons should get their pardon was an indication of change in the national temper, and the change in the policy of the Government dictated by that temper. It was not the reward for the good conduct of prisoners in the Andamans. I kept on hammering this fact because, the amnesty would otherwise have been construed as the reward of obedience, and of abstention from any activity in the prison for the unity and uplift of its inmates. And this feeling would have reacted detrimentally on the conduct of the spirited persons among political prisoners as also on that of other nationally-minded prisoners in that jail. That would have bred in them cowardice to make them withdraw from many a useful activity which I had kept going in that jail.

Leaving alone this aspect of the matter, I was very glad that the Bengali friends, who had tome the borne of the revolutionary struggle and suffered terribly for it, shoulder to shoulder with my elder brother, had got their release from this prison as a consequence of the general amnesty proclaimed by the Government. I saw them personally, and felicitated them upon their good fortune. There were among them some who were more intimate with me and who were trusted friends and ardent patriots. They were all transported here for life but had only served four years of their term. The Sikhs, who happened to be released in a batch began singing patriotic songs on their march to the harbour.

On them, the Chief Commissioner had said in his report, so the rumour went then: "These devils were bound to return to the Andamans once again with a life-sentence passed upon them." It was very likely, indeed, for they were proud and rebellious spirits, everyone of them.

All these discharged prisoners had to sign a pledge that they would abstain from politics and revolutionary activity for a certain number of years. And, if again they were tried and found guilty of treason, they would come back to the Andamans to serve the remainder of their life sentence.

Since the receipt of the wire, to which I have already referred to on a previous page, a hot discussion went on among us, whether we should at all sign such a pledge for procuring our release. My advice to my friends was that there was nothing wrong in it, as it referred to a future contingency and was in the best national interest. I quoted to them instances from the life of Shivaji, of his dealing with Jay Singh and Afzulkhan; I told them of Guru Govind and his flight after the incident of Chamkore; nay I drew upon the life of Lord Krishna himself, in order to convince them of the correctness of the step they were taking. The most obstinately proud among them would not be persuaded even by these parallels from the past. Their stubbornness on this subject, after all that they had suffered for the cause, inspired me with great hope for the future of my country. But, at last, I could convince them of my point of view, and they all signed the pledge without demur, and thus, broke open the lock of the jail in the Andamans.

So many followed them out in regular batches. Of them, all the deliverance from jail of Bhai Parmanand made all of us extremely happy. For, though he was only five years in that jail, life there, and the wickedness of the place and its atmosphere, had filled him with such horrid disgust that he could breathe in it with difficulty; and already a month had expired since he had gone on fast unto death. I was all along trying to make him desist from that course and they had begun to feed him through the nose. After things had gone on like this for a few days more, news of general amnesty fell on our ears. I thought that the name of Bhai Parmanand was sure to be included in that pardon. Hope rose high and he resumed taking his food. A few days after the incident, news came of Bhai Parmanand's release. He came to me full of feeling and affection and said, "You should have been the first to be released; how I feel restrained to go out without you." As he said this tears rolled down from his eyes. At last, he bid me adieu left the prison. I returned the compliment with the sincerest good wishes, and took, leave of him with the words, that seeing him leave the place was such a great joy to me that in it was completely drowned the thought that I was to be here after he had gone.

Graduates of Naland Vihar

From the day I saw every possibility for a large number of political convicts to be released under general amnesty from this jail, I carried on among them in every meeting and on every occasion throughout the week till the last batch of prisoners had gone out, a vigorous campaign of education. We discussed the line of work we ought to follow, now that we were being free, for national awakening and in favour of national freedom. When these batches had stepped into the Silver Jail years ago they were only lovers of their country full of the spirit of self-sacrifice. But within five or ten years of their life here, they were completely transformed by self-education and study to such an extent that I may sincerely say of them that they were going out as full-fledged graduates of our "Home University" of "Naland Vihar", as I have preferred to designate our educational centre in this jail. They were no more mere soldiers in our army but they richly deserved to be promoted, some of the best among them, to the rank of captains and generals. For, their patriotism was no longer a passing emotion or mere fervour, but had deepened by self-discipline and study into a steady flame—"the pale flame of strenuous self-possession". Years of hard work and patience had brought them that rich reward, and when I saw the flame burning with its rich glow, I felt an indescribable joy within me for the transformation I had witnessed in them. I felt that through them the fruit of my labour and service will pass on to my country, and my power and my way of thinking will spread throughout the land. That these were sure to be implemented through them made me so cheerful and happy. There were some among them whom I had saved from the brink of suicide. And I was particularly pleased that their lives would now be dedicated to the service and uplift of the nation. The thought that it would be so, made me glad beyond measure, and reconciled me to my present position in this prison.

After all of them had gone out in their respective batches, only thirty political convicts remained behind, of whom myself and my elder brother formed inevitable company. Putting our case aside, as out of question, I did not understand the logic of keeping the rest still in that jail, when those who had been known to be hardened criminals and daredevils, any day worse than they, had been given the advantage of the proclaimed amnesty. This may have happened, I laid the flattering unction to my soul, for want of impartial and close scrutiny of every individual case, as worthy or unworthy of pardon, and because there was no fixed standard by which every prisoner should be weighed in the balance. As a result, some of them, who really deserved release, had been kept behind; and the worthy had to suffer with the unworthy.

Ten years of intensive and widespread agitation had at last helped turn the tide in favour of all political prisoners in the country, but my brother and myself were once more left high and dry to linger on the shore behind. Those who had come with me on transportation for life, those who had been sent here on life sentence some eight years after me, had left the prison after only two years of incarceration. But we two continued to rot here without even a day's pardon in the period of our sentence. Of course, the treatment meted out to both of us was not without its due effect on the mind of the Indian people. The more the Government tried to repress us, the more the people thought of us and remembered us. Questions were put in the Imperial Legislative Council at Delhi why an exception was being made in our individual cases, when almost all of the political convicts had been discharged from prison under the terms of the general amnesty. The newspapers kept up the same cry. The Working Committee of the Indian National Congress passed a resolution "demanding the release of Savarkar brothers and of two others from Punjab, namely Boga and Ratan Choudhari".

But, at last, we also had our chance; Dame Fortune smiled upon us too. We were discharged in the Silver Jail in the Andamans.

But from where and how? When others were taken out of that jail, we were taken out of our respective solitary cells in the chawls, and made to stay in the courtyard of the prison. After some ten to fifteen representations, we were removed near the door of its office. I was given the work to note down the names of the prisoners in the prescribed forms, to take those forms from and to the office, and to stay near the door. I was not allowed to enter it.

Once even that door was shut against me. Not for any fault of my own, sure enough. One of the political prisoners was writing a letter to be sent to India, when he was caught in the act by the warder in charge. The prisoner had written in that letter information for newspapers in India about the condition of prisoners in this jail. The warder and the writer of the letter were duly punished for the offence, but I also suffered along with them. For a few days more, I was forbidden from taking my seat near the office door.

This was ever the hitch in my way. Whenever anything untoward happened in the jail, I was made a scape-goat for all the sins, and had to pay heavily for them.

With all this useless lamentation on wrongs done to me continuing, I was again brought near the office door, and at last, stepped into the office itself. But that again proved to be a step and nothing more.

I had by this time finished ten years of my sentence in this prison. To be more accurate, I had certainly completed my nine years. I then began petitioning to the authorities that, as some of those who had come into the prison along with me, had already been given permission to go out of the prison for a stroll, and one of them was granted leave to stay in the settlement, and as others who had followed me years after, were detailed for different kinds of work outside it, like, for instance, higher work in the factories and the printing press, I should be given the permit to move out and sit all to myself in some place for some part of the day. When hundreds of political convicts on life sentence and ordinary prisoners on two years rigorous imprisonment had been discharged only after two years' hard labour in the jail, a convict like me, who had been there for ten consecutive years, should, at least, not be denied such a ticket. The answer to my petition was a point-blank 'no'; and the ground was that I had not yet completed my ten years!

The regulations, which went against me had always been observed meticulously; while those which went in my favour were far from being so strictly applied. According to the rule, I should have met my kith and kin after five years, but I did not secure the permission to see them till after seven or eight years. And now, as I had technically completed my ten years, the permit I had applied for was being withheld from me!

But was the rule at all observed strictly? By no means. Ten years had passed, the time for granting the ticket was already overdue, and I was lingering in that jail yet!

A Foreman

But now, I came to be appointed a foreman, and I drew for the appointment the handsome salary of rupee one per month! And that was, again, an act of favour. I am sincerely thankful to the individual officer, who did me that kind turn. Never mind, I am a foreman all the same. Some of them spoke to me by way of a jibe, "Many others after you are now occupying higher jobs here; they are 'Babus' and are exercising their authority as such. While your good self! You are only a foreman in an oil depot!"

I used to give them an equally curt answer: "You do not realise the power that I possess. What of the Babu? A prisoner, a Superintendent, a Commissioner—each of them is only a 'man'. While I am a 'foreman', that is the leader of men. The Government has at last seen my worth, and honoured me as I deserved. The honour, which even the Viceroy did not have, they have bestowed upon me. A foreman, the leader of men—what better title should I aspire after?"

As a foreman, I was in charge of the big oil depot of the factory. In the prison world, the office had its singular importance. The oil-depot contained hundreds of casks of coconut oil containing a month's produce of thousands of pounds of oil ready for export abroad. This was the main and a great source of income in the Andamans—its coconut gardens and the oil manufactured out of them. Three big reservoirs were full of oil ground out of the oil-mill in that prison. Big casks were filled with oil on order for export abroad. They went to Calcutta and Rangoon and returned to the treasury an income to be calculated in thousands. The oil depot was the centre of all these transactions from month to month and throughout the year. It was the nerve-centre of the Silver Jail—its thews and sinews. And others were naturally jealous that I was put in charge of the job. So, they began to twit me. Indeed, it was a key—job, an important job and I was dressed in that authority!

What the job meant and what I made of it had better be told in an independent and a new chapter.

□

9

The Spread of Hindi in the Andamans

I had begun my work to obtain for Hindi the status of the national language of India, and to popularise it by every means at my disposal from the year 1906, when I was in England. The members of the Abhinav Bharat in England repeated the pledge every night before they retired for sleep, to 'make India independent, to weld her into one nation, to turn her into a republic, and last and the fourth, to make Hindi the national language of India and Devanagari the script in which it should be written'.

Accordingly, when I found in the Andamans a suitable opportunity for consolidation and propaganda work, I drew up a plan in 1911, in which I gave a prominent place to the spread of Hindi in these islands.

The very idea of making Hindi India's national language seemed so preposterous at that time that the so-called great leaders of India simply pooh-poohed it. The man in the street had no notion about it. Lokamanya Tilak and Mahatma Gandhi openly espoused it only after an agitation in its favour had gathered momentum and weighed behind it. And that was long after 1906. Only the Nagari Pracharini Sabha of Benares and some members of the Arya Samaj were the first agitators in its favour. The first credit of propaganda in favour of Hindi as India's national language, as also of writing patriotically in that language goes to Swami Dayanand Saraswati, the great founder of the Arya Samaj of India.

It was in this stage of the public mind that I undertook in 1911 the task of persuading all the prisoners at Port Blair to study Hindi. I had to begin at the beginning, that is, with a discussion whether Hindi was at all a language after all. To the inhabitants of Maharashtra and of the South of India, the word 'Hindi' itself was a strange word. They would designate Hindi as 'the language of the Mussulmans'. For, in the South, the Mussulmans often used it as a mother-tongue, or, at least, as a language peculiar to their own community. Prisoners, hailing from the North, knew it not only as the common language of the Hindus but had come to realise that eight crore Hindus and Mussulmans together had begun to adopt and use it as their common mother-tongue. Even these, however, used to say that it was not a language fit enough to be the national language of India. Some said it had no grammar, other alleged that it had no literature. It was natural for people from Madras to fight shy of it. But the prisoners from Bengal were as averse from it as those from Madras. For, the Bengalis cherished the ambition of making their own mother-tongue the language of India. In fact, next to Hindi, it is the Bengali language that deserves the honour of becoming the national language of India. In point of number, four crore the inhabitants of India speak in Bengali, and it is as advanced in literature as the Marathi language on our side. But a Bengali gentleman by the name Mitra had given his approval to Hindi as the coming national language—the lingua franca—of India. He had gone the length of conducting a magazine in Hindi in furtherance of that object.

I had met all these objections and to prove to them that it had grammar, literature, richness of vocabulary and style, and all other qualities capable of making it common language of India. And it had behind it the overwhelming strength of numbers, who used it as their language of common speech. I brought for that purpose some classical works in the Hindi language and pointed out, though it was at the time lacking in modern literature, how it was fast making up that deficiency. And, further, that if all of them would put their shoulders to the wheel, in five years' time, we should be able to give that language its proper status in the world of letters. Again, Hindi had always been the 'lingua franca' of India; we had not to create it afresh to enjoy that status. The dervish from Rameshwar, as also the merchant, carried on intercourse with each other at Hardwar in that common language from the days of Prithviraj or even earlier. With these and similar arguments, I, at last, brought them round to the study of the Hindi language. I tackled prisoners in the jail by a similar persuasive method.

The courses of study we followed were as follows: Every prisoner should learn the languages of provinces other than his own. The

Andamans offered a rare opportunity to them for such a study. I used to teach, accordingly, the Bengali prisoners Hindi and Marathi; to prisoners from Maharashtra, I taught Hindi and Bengali; and to the Punjabi I taught Hindi as well as his own Gurumukhi. I carried on this pursuit throughout my stay in this jail. The Gujaratis were the last to come there, but I taught them, all the same, the Hindi alphabet and equipped them, within the brief period at my disposal, to read and write. Others I taught Hindi first and any other language after it. For ten long years, I stuck to that work and my colleagues gave me their fullest co-operation in that self-imposed task.

In a former chapter, I have already informed the reader of the circulating library of Hindi books we had started under our organisation and also of the manner in which books were passed from hand-to-hand for that purpose. Our colleagues were teaching Hindi to some well-meaning Madrasi officers in a secret and silent manner. One doctor taught Hindi to his wife and son, and made them talk to each other in Hindi that it might become the common language of all Indians. He contributed ₹ 5 to 10, from time to time, to our fund for the propagation of that language. I may give here an instance or two of how we collected funds for the purpose, apart from the generous help that some of these officers gave us, a convict by name Divan, sometime an Arya Samajist, had been transported for life to the Andamans. He was a peasant by caste and was convicted in a trial for dacoity. He became my devoted disciple soon after his arrival in the Silver Jail. He did a lot of work for our secret organisation. He had a power of easily influencing the people. Unfortunately, Divan died in the prime of youth, succumbing to the insalubrious climate of these islands as also to the exhausting hard labour in the prison itself. Some friends decided to celebrate the anniversary of his death by a big dinner. I advised them to divert the collection of money for that purpose to the purchase of Hindi books for the use of prisoners. They agreed and the money was spent in the purchase of Hindi primers and other books, which were distributed freely among needy prisoners in the name of the deceased. A man named Bihari was sentenced to death. He made a vow to God to give some money as donation if the sentence was commuted for life imprisonment. By a turn of fortune, he got what he had prayed for, when he asked me how he could donate the money he had vowed for. The dinner was out of question here since I had discountenanced it. I asked him to spend the sum on the purchase of books. But there was a great hurdle here in the way to jump over. Every section claimed the donation to purchase books in his own language. Thus, Urdu and English books claimed it at the time. My championship of Hindi was attributed to my desire to kill the Bengali and the Punjabi languages. I told them that I would not sanction the sum for Urdu or English books and I would not claim it for Marathi either. And nobody would charge me with the motive of killing Marathi. Why do I then ask for the money to purchase Hindi books, when I love Bengali, know Marathi, have learnt Gurumukhi and can teach in all of these? Precisely because what is national must be preferred to what is local and provincial. We must sacrifice our personal bias in the interest of the country as a whole. At last, I persuaded them to use the hundred rupees, which the man with the vow had set apart, towards the purchase of Hindi books. I bought out of the sum the Hindi writings of Al-Udal down to many a book published by the Nagari Pracharini Sabha of Benares. I must say that Al-Udal was my favourite author in Hindi.

I used to impress upon the minds of my Bengali friends, who maintained that Hindi was not a well-developed language or had no literature worth the name, that it was a growing language by bringing to their notice the best works in it as were published by the Gurukul in Punjab and by similar other publishing houses. Sometime they were considerably annoyed by my persistence, and attributed my efforts to a bad motive. But, at last, I won and made the prisoners realise the value of Hindi as the national language of India. Henceforward, the matter was no longer under dispute but had become an accepted proposition. I had to use a different line of argument to convince the Sikhs about it. They did not know that the best writings of Guru Govind were written in pure Hindi, like his drama 'Vichitra Natak' and history named 'Surya Prakash'; they were written in Brija Bhasha—which is the purest Hindi and the language of Tulsidas. I convinced them in this manner that Hindi was the language of their religion, and Gurumukhi was only a script and a dialect. So, they realised the worth of it not only as a national language but as the language of their panth.

About Gurumukhi, I was of the opinion from what I had read on the subject in the prison, that it was not a script invented by Gurus, as tradition maintained, but it was only an older script common in Punjab among merchants and persons of average literacy, as Modi is to Marathi. Historical investigation went to prove that, out of many similar scripts current in Punjab, a Guru chose the older one and stamped it with his own authority as the script to be followed. Hence its nomenclature Gurumukhi. The religious scriptures of the Sikhs, instead of being written in Shastric or Nagari script, were written in the common script known as Gurumukhi for use by common people even as Buddha wrote them in Pali script with the same end in view. This is a subject by itself. I have referred to it here in the context of Hindi alone. This origin of Gurumukhi, I know, has not yet been accepted by accredited scholarship. Whether it is historically correct or otherwise, I must say that the credit of that finding, so far as I know it, is entirely mine. I have, however, discussed the matter so often with Sikh scholars of language and history.

I did not allow anyone of another province to study Marathi in the first instance. My order of study for all the prisoners was first their mother-tongue, next Hindi, and last, the language of any province other than their own. I encouraged all of them to study at least one provincial language other than their own. I could make no provision for teaching the Dravidian languages of Tamil province including Malayali, Andhra, Tamil and Canarese, for I did not know these languages myself and there was none among the prisoners competent enough to teach them, and to collect the necessary literature in them in order that their study could be properly conducted. I was ever conscious of this defect in our common programme of teaching languages, and I have not yet been able to remove it. Otherwise, during the last ten years, I have made the prisoners study all other languages like Marathi, Punjabi and Bengali in addition to the common language Hindi and their respective mother-tongue. Most of them could read important works in the Marathi language. I used to collect information about standard works in Dravidian languages, and, through the Superintendent, was able to get permission to purchase elementary textbooks in that language. I had made a list of them and had provided money for that purpose. But my sudden departure from the Silver Jail put an end to all these projects. Today, I cannot say, what has been the upshot of these plans of mine.

Urdu Given A Setback

The Andamans is a colony of men drawn from different provinces of India; as such its lingua franca is Hindi. The progeny of the prisoners who had settled in that colony, also uses Hindi as its language of common speech. Intermarriages among their families had given Hindi its natural prominence among them. Most of the settlers are Hindus by religion and race. As such the medium of instruction in schools for their children should have been Hindi, as, for all practical purposes, Hindi has been their mother-tongue at home. But from its early years, the Muslims appointed as teachers in these schools hailed, most of them, from Punjab and Delhi and were familiar with Urdu script and language. The result has been that Urdu had become the common medium, of instruction in all the schools of the Andamans. Another source of this tradition was that the writers in the prison office were recruited from Muslim prisoners, and Urdu had become the language of the office records. Those who came out of these schools had all got their education in Urdu, as such, those who learnt Urdu came to be regarded in the Andamans as having the stamp of education upon them. Hindi as a medium of instruction naturally fell into the background and, later OB, came to be altogether ignored. As schools grew in number, Urdu grew in importance along with them. As a matter of fact, there was very little difference between Hindi and Urdu, except for the script. Hindi, written in Persian characters, becomes Urdu. So the point of difference between the two lay in the question of script. Most of the boys and girls learning in these schools being drawn from Hindus and having Hindi as their mother-tongue at home, should have been taught Hindi in the schools through the Devnagari script. That was proper and desirable from the common standpoint of nationality and religion. The schools were built up on the taxes paid by the Hindus; and the wonder of it was that their children were forced to learn Urdu script in schools, which were meant for them, and which were maintained from taxes paid by their parents. Hindu boys and girls educated in such schools did not know the a, b, c of the Hindi alphabet; they could not read Tulsidas' Ramayana or slokas from the Bhagvadgita, while they were familiar with couplets from Persian poets. They knew nothing of Kalidas. Let alone Kalidas, they knew not a line from Surdas or Prema Sagar. The Hindi primer or first book was as strange to them as Latin. The boy, however, read an Urdu newspaper with facility and ease. All his ideas and images were drawn from rivers in Persia and Arabia. He knew more about heroes from those countries. About the Pandavas, or Bharat, or Ramayana, or Bhagwat, he knew practically nothing, for he could not spell a letter out of them. When I went to the Andamans, I saw this state of thing in these islands. If Hindu culture and Hindu tradition were to be saved from extinction in these parts, I felt that the first step to be taken was to make every child learn Hindi script at home, and to talk and read in Hindi alone. I, therefore, thought that an agitation was necessary to bring about this change first in the mind of the Hindu settlers of the place, and then in the schools where their children were being sent for education.

I maintained that the medium of instruction in these schools should be, as a rule, Hindi written in Devnagari script. And for Muslim pupils in such schools Urdu may be accepted for instruction only as special case.

But a change in the schools implied a change, in the first instance, in the mind of the people themselves. For, the Hindu settlers in the Andamans had but little sense of nationality in public life, and their notions of Hindu religion were no better than foolish customs from the past. The survival of Hinduism in them was but rigid adherence to these time worn superstitions. They never realised that Hindi was their national language; much less did they appreciate that it had to be preserved and learnt by them as the language of their sacred books. For, after Sanskrit, these were written for common people in Hindi language. The Devnagari script and the Hindi language were their sacred trust, but they knew nothing about their responsibility in that respect; they were not even remotely conscious of that trust. For two or three generations, Urdu had dominated the place and had monopolised their attention. They had embraced that language with pride, and had lost touch with their real mother-tongue, an attitude suicidal to them as Hindus in race and nationality. I, therefore, sent round men of my way of thinking among these settlers. I made them visit their houses from door to door, that they might be awakened to their own responsibility in this vital task. I began this task with great determination and pursued it with a tenacity of will and action.

How the awakening was brought about by our organisation and through its agencies among the prisoners and the permanent settlers of the place through discussions, through the spread of literature, through the popularisation of national songs, through secret meetings and lectures, has already been narrated to the reader in a former chapter of this work. The main plank in our programme throughout was to spread among the people the knowledge of Hindi language and literature, and to make them love it as their national tongue. Five years of intensive campaign in this direction brought about a tremendous awakening among them. We sent special teachers to several Hindu families to teach boys and girls the Hindi language written in the Nagari script. In 1920, when I was appointed foreman of the oil depot in our prison, I began to come into intimate contact with many merchants in the settlement, who had to come on business in the jail and in connection with the purchase and sale of coconut oil in my charge. Some came only to pay me a visit, others came to deal in oil and coconut cakes. To all of them my constant talk had been, "You are Hindus, Hindi is not only your national language but the language of your religion. You must teach Hindi to your sons and daughters, and that not in Urdu but in Nagari script. You ought to submit a petition to the authorities and assert your right, that it shall be used as a medium of instruction in all the schools of the Andamans." This combined and consolidated action would alone bring about the change. No private and individual effort could cope with such a large problem. All the same, so long as that was not being done, they should not fail to instruct their children at home to read and write Hindi and in Nagari script. That was the least that they owed to their children and to themselves as Hindus. If any one of these visitors seemed agreeable, our volunteers were ready to undertake the task. They would go to his house and begin teaching his children. Of course, they had to do it on the sly, for the prisoners were forbidden from having anything to do with independent settlers, and the latter could not speak openly to the prisoners. It was my constant advice to everyone I met, be he a Munshi, be he a clerk, be he a doctor, if he was a Hindu, I always told him, "Go and learn Hindi." That was my exhortation to them, that the burden of my song.

As the knowledge of Hindi began to spread among these independent Hindu settlers, I distributed freely to boys and girls of their families elementary readers, copies of the Hindi version of Mahabharata, life of Shivaji and other historical personages written in Hindi. I sent Hindi newspapers to them and made them read or hear them, as they were read out to them. Those soldiers and merchants, whom I met in the prison during my last days in jail, I taught them Hindi myself. Thus, the idea that Hindi was their language, both by nationality and religion, took a firm root in the heart of these settlers and a movement began to frame petition to the Government that it should be used as a medium of instruction in all the schools of that settlement.

But so long as the Government records were kept in Urdu, it was but natural that boys should be attracted to the study of Urdu. The next and the most urgent step, therefore, was that Hindi should supersede Urdu in these offices and in their records. I, therefore, directed my energy to that work. As a rule, all proceedings and records were in English in these offices, but the clerks being men from the North of India and most of the prisoners being more familiar with Urdu than with English, statements came to be taken down and recorded in Urdu and the tradition had continued to our day. These records were in bulk made up of documents in connection with prisoners that were sent out in every steamer from India to Port Blair. The Munshi took down their statements in Urdu. Hence, my first move was to ask the authorities that the prisoners should be permitted to submit their statements and other documents in their own native language, and not in Urdu only. Days passed before permission was obtained thus for Marathi and Gurumukhi. The Munshi knew only English and Urdu. And until the Munshi had passed the letter as 'unobjectionable', it would neither enter the prison nor go out of it. After the permission was granted, the prisoner could put the contents in any language he knew. Urdu was the common language of communication in Punjab, Lucknow and parts of Northern India. And I had to persuade those who sent their letters from those places, and those who sent their letters from here to them, to write them invariably in Hindi. My Marathi and Bengali friends also sent and received letters in Hindi. The authorities had, perforce, to appoint Hindi-knowing Munshis to scrutinise their contents before the letters passed in or out of the prison. The older Urdu-knowing officers now began to study Hindi. If no clerk was found to write a letter in Hindi, our volunteers did it for him. Formerly, ninety percent of the letters were in Urdu script. But at the end of our campaign, ninety percent were in other languages, the bulk of them being in Hindi, and only the rest in Urdu script, As the officers with powers to appoint clerks in offices under them became members of Hindu Sangathan, they appointed Hindi-knowing Hindu clerks in these places. It became a rule in the prison thenceforward that a Hindu must write either in Hindi or in his own native tongue. The Mussulman was free to write in Urdu. No compulsion was to be exercised on him to the contrary. But a Hindu could no longer be compelled to send or receive letters in Urdu. When I was admitted to the office, I saw through all the letters coming in and going out, to note how many of the Hindus still persisted in corresponding in Urdu script. And if I found out anyone still doing so,

I lost no time in dissuading him from that habit. In course of time, things had so changed in this prison, that it was full of Hindu Munshis at the top and all correspondence in and out was carried on in Hindi and in Nagari script. Letters addressed to us from outside were also written in Hindi, for we had directed our relatives, abroad to write to us in Hindi. So, correspondence in Hindi and other provincial languages went on multiplying and Urdu began to dwindle proportionately. Consequently, the staff of clerks in the office showed an increasingly larger percentage of Hindus, and the prestige of Urdu began to diminish and it sank in popularity.

Only the political convicts had to write compulsorily in English, as their correspondence was personally gone through by European officers. But as their number increased by hundreds, they were also permitted to write and receive letters in their mother-tongue, for many of them could not speak or write in English. It was after tremendous effort that this concession was made to them, though, to the last, I had to write in English alone.

The same change came over the noting down of names and preparing their list. In fact, all work in the office came to be done in Hindi, miscellaneous official correspondence and every other kind of writing. All this was being done till then in Urdu script. Thus, Hindi and Nagari won the place of honour in the work of this jail and though it did not entirely oust Urdu, it promised to be, before long, its official language.

In the settlement and among free settlers, all invitation cards used to be printed so long in Urdu; then a few ventured to issue them in Hindi, but very many could not read them, for an educated Hindu meant one who knew Urdu. I insisted upon them all the same to go on issuing the invitations in Hindi and, if necessary, in Urdu on the side of the card or letter. If one could not but write in Urdu, I exhorted every Hindu to begin the letter of invitation or the card with the letter "Om" at the top, and end it also with some lines written in Hindi and in Nagari alphabets. I set that new tradition in the writing of invitation cards as the minimum that, as Hindus, they owed to their national language.

It was not a matter for surprise that there was still opposition to the establishment of Hindi as the common language of Hindus in the Andamans. The wonder of it was that the opposition came more from

European than from Mussulman officers of the place. It was partly due to the fact that most of them knew Urdu and were ignorant of Hindi. But the main reason of their opposition lay in the fact that I was the supporter of the campaign in favour of Hindi; and it was on that account that they were suspicious of it. A prisoner once asked for books in Hindi, when one of the officers questioned him why he had changed from Urdu to Hindi, and tried to make him go in for Urdu books as before. And when the movement was started to substitute Hindi for Urdu in the schools, the reporters, the C.I.D. officers and the Mussulman *jamadars* openly informed the higher authorities in the jail that I was at the back of it, and, if it succeeded, I would grow in influence and power throughout the entire settlement.

The agitation, in favour of the Hindi language and the Nagari script, was organised and led by the Arya Samajists, by persons who had sponsored the *Shuddhi* and the Sangathan movements, by civil resisters to jail tyranny, and by those who had striven hard for the education of prisoners. They were all set down in the black list of the officers "as dangerous agitators of a highly suspicious character". This 'unnecessary' suspicion of the Government prevented Hindi from becoming the medium of instruction in the schools of the settlement though the demand for the change had come from the independent settlers of the Andamans. The Hindu boys and girls had yet to learn in the schools in Urdu script, and not in Hindi alone as their mother-tongue, during the time I was in that jail. It was my continuous plea to the inhabitants that they should continue agitating for it, and bring it to the notice of the authorities that their suspicious attitude to Hindi was unjustified, and that at length they would succeed in giving Hindi its proper place in the education of their children, and the Government could no longer withhold their permission to the introduction of Hindi in their schools at least as regards its Hindu pupils.

If I did not succeed in making Hindi indispensable in schools for boys, I did succeed in that respect in schools just started for girls. Even the girls would have been compelled to read and write Urdu script, and Hindi and Nagari would have been given the go-by. But I remonstrated with the parents not to tolerate this sort of tyranny. I put them to shame for acquiescing in such a course. I dissuaded them from sending their daughters as Hindus to learn the Urdu alphabet from a Mohomedan moulvi, and compelled the authorities to introduce Hindi and Nagari script in schools for Hindu girls from their very start.

The political convicts from Punjab, it need not be told, began writing home in Hindi rather than in Urdu or Persian. There were many noted writers and good poets among them who composed fine poems in Urdu. They strongly resented my action. But when I brought home to them as Hindus, how by their prepossession for Urdu, they were letting that foreign script and language thrust out Hindi from its high position as the national language of India, they took a vow that never with their pens would they write anything in Urdu, but devote all their talents towards writing in Hindi alone. I had to teach them such simple words in the beginning as "akasha" (sky) and "vyayama" (exercise). So much was their mind steeped in Urdu, but it must be said to their credit that they gladly went through that toil and began to master classic Hindi. My campaign against Urdu was not dictated by malice or hatred. I myself had learnt Urdu and can still lisp some words in that language and spell its rudiments. I understand Urdu even today when it is read out to me. And I had no objection to its survival as a dialect between Mussulmans and Hindus. I shall cherish it with love as the language of our Muslim fellow countrymen. But that Urdu should be a dominant language of Hindusthan, and that by the patronage and encouragement of the Hindus themselves was more than I could bear. I shall never tolerate Urdu if it tells me to cast off Hindi and to enthrone itself in its place as the national language of India. If it threatens me that way, then I will overthrow it. To that extent alone, I will resist Urdu. I carried on agitation against Urdu in the Andamans because it was imposed upon schools run and maintained by the Hindu community of that place. I insisted that in those schools Hindi and Nagari must have their unchallenged place as medium of instruction. To force Hindu children to learn Urdu was to denationalise them. It was an inroad upon the Hindu culture. As mere language and script everyone was free to learn it. As we learn German, so we may learn Urdu. But as mother-tongue and national language, it had no place in Hindu culture, and could not displace Hindi, which traces its pedigree from Sanskrit and has so many cultural associations with what we love as Hinduism. To let Urdu dominate us in this manner was highly ruinous to us.

I have already written about the stocking and circulation of Hindi books throughout these islands in my chapter on libraries in Part I of this book. I bought for these roving libraries, so to say, choicest books in Hindi on politics, political economy, and the history of our national movement so that those who studied them became really conversant with these important subjects. Most ordinary prisoners passing through this training became, at the end of it, entirely different men. I made them study particularly Satyartha Prakasha of Swami Dayanand Saraswati. Political convicts especially were made to read, re-read, and read it over again. That work of Dayanand, apart from the heat and dust of controversy that occasionally mar it, is a monumental contribution to the proper understanding of our Hindu religion and Hindu culture. It is a bold and courageous vindication of its national importance, and is, in itself, a fine propaganda in its favour. I bestowed scholarships on prisoners and free men for the study of Hindi. I had to hold out this bait to them at the beginning, but soon they became so fond of reading Hindi books that the stock of books fell far short of the demand, and whatever books we had were never found lying idle on their shelves. They were constantly moving from hand to hand and were read over and over again. I had to warn them to use the books carefully and not to lose them in any circumstance. I even preferred the books being tattered and torn by use to their remaining covered with dust on the library shelves.

The Andamans, which knew no other language than Urdu, and where Hindu girls talking to each other spontaneously uttered the word 'shadi' to indicate marriage and knew not its Sanskrit or Hindi equivalent, now saw a transformation that was indeed, a miracle. There every Hindu now began to revere Hindi as his national language or the language of his religion, and the idea seized not only the elders but caught the imagination of boys and girls. And the credit of this transformation goes entirely to the enthusiasm and devotion of my fellow-workers in the prison as well as in the settlement at large.

But the full fruition of that agitation was yet to come. And for it, Hindi and Nagari must spread throughout the education centres of those islands. I made but a beginning. What its sequel has been, we shall see as we go on.

□

10
Miniature Hindu Raj

When I stepped into the Andamans there was in it, in prison and outside, what one may rightly call, Pathan Raj. Dressed in brief authority, the Pathan dominated the scene. It was overthrown, as I have described in this story, by the time that my stay in the prison had come nearly to an end. The Pathan Raj was gone and Hindu Raj had taken its place. If that was no more than a span, this was no better than one and one-fourth that span. The capital of that Raj was the oil depot of the prison and, as I have already mentioned before, I was its foreman and, therefore, the monarch of that Raj. I sat in my capital on a throne which was no other than the chair with a broken arm in front of that depot. Our story has been brought so far, and now we proceed in it.

The oil depot being the main source of income for the Silver Jail, the man in charge of it was a person of great importance. In Mr. Barrie's regime, no other person than a Mussulman or a Pathan was appointed to that office, for the Pathans were the only prisoners who enjoyed his confidence then. This was more so after political convicts had begun to arrive in large number in the Silver Jail. Naturally, the top man selected his own man to manage the whole establishment. As such, everyone connected with the oil depot from top to bottom was a Mussulman, and mostly a Pathan. As the prisoners were to measure out everyday their quota of oil to the foreman and to the officers under him, all of them were a terror to the prisoners put on the Kolu to do their day's work of crushing coconut for oil. The foreman could make the prisoner shake in his shoes by the simple words: "The quantity of oil is not up to your quota." And thc *jamadar*, the petty officer and all under him shuddered along with them. The foreman of the godown had the prescriptive right of beating the prisoners. If Mr. Barrie listened to anyone without a demur, it was to the godown keeper or the foreman of that warehouse of oil. Hence, he was the foremost person to carry tales against the prisoners. The wiliest, the intensely selfish, the most cunning and the most wicked person in the prison was often chosen for the job. During my seven to eight years of prison-life, an array of such men had adorned the seat. Now, in my ninth year, the seat had come to me.

All the Mussulman tindals, petty officers and warders, who had still remained in that jail, were full of fear that I was appointed to that office. The demigod presiding over the oil depot could only be propitiated by offerings in gold and silver. If the prisoners desired not to be ground down in the oil mill of that place, they had perforce to propitiate its deity. Up to this time, the Hindu prisoners in that jail could not escape persecution by him whether they did or did not flatter the deity, for if they refused any offering to him, he was punished for the sin of omission, and if they subscribed to his wishes they came in for harsh treatment because they were kafirs. Now, the position had gone to a Hindu—one who was the most condemned in their eyes for movements like *Shuddhi*, which were gall and wormwood to them. This bespectacled man was now to boss it over them! Why should they not be alarmed and tremble in their shoes? Every single tindal began to approach me from now onwards with bated breath and in whispering humbleness. And these were the persons who had no scruples whatever to thrash the prisoners enslaved to them! Nay, they had vied with each other in punishing and persecuting them. And they now began to say to me on bended knee and with folded hands, "Bada Babu, save us."

Salute; to say Ram Ram is an Offence!

I have deliberately referred to the fact that the Mussulman petty officers and tindals approached me with 'folded hands'. Thereby hangs a tale. When I went to the Andamans, I found the Hindu greeting the Mussulman with a salam, and the Hindus greeted each other in a similar fashion. The Mussulman, however, never hailed the Hindu with 'Ram Ram'. A Maratha warder told me one day that when he had politely said 'Ram Ram' to Mirza Khan, the latter gave him a severe reproof. Said Mirza Khan to the Maratha warder, "Oh, Kafir, do not utter the name of Rama within my hearing. Say always 'salam". There upon I made up my mind never to address a Mussulman with a 'salam' so long as he did not accost me with the name of Rama. If a Mussulman greeted with the name of Rama—and there were many Mussulmans from Maharashtra, who, till then, had no objection to utter that word-I would salute him ten times with the word 'salam'. But such fanatics as would neither hear nor utter that word, and compelled the Hindus to say 'salam' to them, I was determined to resist and I persuaded other Hindu prisoners to do accordingly. Of course, this led to petty quarrels at the start, but many a resolute prisoner on our side invariably returned the Muslim's 'salam' with the Hindu's 'Ram Ram'. The Mussulmans had been, therefore, fully aware, when I became a foreman, what I expected of them, that I was particularly proud of the Hindu way of greeting and of the words used along with that greeting like 'Ram Ram', 'Namaskar', 'Vande Mataram', so on and so forth. The Mussulmans, full of tremor at my appointment as the head of the oil depot, were anxious to conciliate me at any cost. Hence, they approached me with a greeting that was so long an anathema to them. They folded their hands before me and said 'Namaskar' to me. For my part, I had never insisted that they should not salute me with a 'salam'. It was their right to say 'salam' as it was the right of the Hindus to greet them with 'Namaskar' and 'Ram Ram'. If the Mussulmans would utter 'Ram Ram', I would, of course, return the compliment with a 'salam'.

They also tried their usual methods to humour me, in order that no harm should come to them through me. Prisoners, tindals and other persons in the jail were used as agents for that purpose. I wanted to put an end to such dishonest practices once for all. So, I went to the oil factory and called all of them to meet me. In plain words, I addressed them as follows: "Give up the fear that I will give you the slightest trouble because you are Mussulmans. On the other hand, you should not harm, or create trouble for any prisoner because he happens to be a Hindu. I would not accept even a pie from you. Do your work well and as thoroughly as you can. I shall see to it that you are not unnecessarily harassed for it. But if you conspire to give me less work than is your due, because I am a Hindu, or harass, persecute or extort money from Hindu prisoners under you, then beware, I am not the man to put up with such a conduct."

So long as I was on the job, I treated them accordingly. One or two of the hardened ones among them made away with a quantity of oil and had intended to involve me in that affair. But I caught them on the spot and sacked them, and none dared do the same thing again. Thereafter, all of them proved as submissive as lambs. I appointed Hindu warders in place of those I had to dismiss. The Kolu, which had come to be looked upon in the early years of my prison experience as an engine of torture more terrible than the gallows—for if one was to be persuaded to hang himself, the right way to do it was to put him on the Kolu—became under my supervision and control just an ordinary oil mill. I had not put anyone in handcuffs or even give a slap in the face, or offer any tip that it may be turned properly and yield its normal quantity of oil per day. The oil depot was stocked well and the income had not gone down. This was the period when Mr. Diggins—Mr. Barrie's brother-in-law—was the jailor in charge. Under his kind, civil and generous treatment, the normal work of the prison went on without a hitch, and the prisoners had nothing to complain of. Mr. Diggins was a great help to me in doing away with the many horrors of the Kolu in my charge. The Hindu prisoners were particularly grateful to me and words failed them to express what they felt. I was touched by their simple faith and by their devotion to me. What I had done for them? Nothing out of the way. They were drawn to me because I did not treat them badly. That was all. Pleased with that little, they expressed their gratitude to me; and that made me cry, betimes; and tears flowed from my eyes.

We had to drink Water with Nostrils Closed

During the time that I was in charge of the oil depot, the greatest satisfaction that I had was that I could do a good turn to those who in our direst days as prisoners had been so helpful to us. I could also render assistance to the fittest men and families among the free settlers of that island and made gratitude a thing of joy. None of them could be persecuted as in the past. The old and heartless method of sending prisoners to answer the call of nature in a row of eight standing in a queue, who were compelled to come out from the closet at the bidding of the *jamadar* whether they had done the thing and cleared the parts or not, or without water enough to clean them, had become an antiquity. This is only one instance of the many disabilities they had to put up with. From that bestial, savage and inhuman state of things, we had been extricated for good. In those days, if a Mussulman warder saw a Hindu prisoner helping himself to water in the reservoir, he, at once, plunged his feet into it and if the Hindu used the dirty water, he would chaff at him to his heart's content. He went about telling others what a fine thing he had done and often boasted about it. All this had stopped now. The

Mussulmans ceased to be shamelessly insolent and every chawl got its supply of pure water. And that reminds me of an episode in our earlier years in this prison, when water was not brought from a distance for drinking purposes in the prison, and we had to drink it from a closed well. The water was dirty and stinked so horribly that to be able to gulp it down we had often to close the nostrils with our fingers. All this was due to the sheer indifference on the part of Mr. Barrie. But the prisoners dared not complain against him to the Superintendent, for Mr. Barrie was sure to deny it entirely. Once I stored up that water in my tin-pot and concealed the pot beyond discovery. When the Superintendent came, a complaint was lodged that we were made to drink water from a neighbouring well, into which rubbish was being thrown and which had not been cleared for a long time. Mr. Barrie, as usual, denied the fact on oath, and no *jamadar* dared contradict him, and speak the truth in our favour. All of us were, thus, put in a false position with the Superintendent when I took out the pot from a corner of the room. Of course, the water in it stinked horribly. The Superintendent censured Mr. Barrie in our presence and rated him severely in his own office. That kind of stagnant water was never given to us for drinking after that episode. The prisoners, who had to pass their lives in such horrid conditions, found them remarkably altered during the regime of Mr. Diggins, one indication of which was that there was not a single case of even attempted suicide in the prison after it, while not a month or two had passed without a case of suicide during the administration of Mr. Barrie both in prison and in the settlement outside. The change was the result of our persistent agitation for reform during the ten years that I was in that jail.

The officers of the settlement had realised by then that they must change their outlook on prison administration and that it would not do to carry on along the old lines. Another reason was that from the beginning of the great war of 1914, prisoners were looking forward to general amnesty and hope made them desist from putting an end to their own lives by suicide. The fall in the number of suicides was one of the items in my evidence before the jail Commission and I drew the attention of its members to it giving reasons for the change.

Kolu was A School for Scavengers

My office as the foreman of the oil depot was, of course, of great use to me in furthering the movements of *Shuddhi*, Sangathan and education started for an all-round improvement in the Andamans. I may give a few instances in point. A Hindu scavenger, who had been converted to Islam, had been taken back into Hinduism, according to our *Shuddhi* movement. He had grown his tuft of hair, and, therefore, the Mussulmans would not let him dine with them. The Hindus would not sit for dinner in the same line with him because he was a scavenger, and an untouchable. One day, I sent for him on business in the oil depot. I had called him after his day's work was over. I made him bathe and wash his body clean with soap. I gave him fresh and clean garments to wear and I made him sit down for food beside me. The example set by me and by other friends in the prison emboldened the untouchable to sit down for food in a line with other Hindus and they gradually ceased objecting to his presence. He was, thus, saved from compulsory reconversion to Islam. The untouchable recited everyday the bhajans of Tulsidas. In days past, even high caste Hindus applied for scavenger's work to save themselves from the exhausting labour of turning the oil mill. And the Burmese outdid them all in such a demand. Hence, the Kolu was nicknamed as the school for scavengers, and the whole prison recognised it by that name. And now that the Kolu had ceased to be a terror, these very people would not let the poor untouchable sit beside them!

The News of Lokamanya Tilak's Death

Just at this time, news reached the Andamans that Lokamanya Tilak had breathed his last. The news came to us at night as floating rumour, and the following morning, it was definitely confirmed. My heart was deeply afflicted by the news and my soul found no peace. How were we to express the great grief that we felt? It was decided at eight o'clock in the morning that throughout the Andamans, they should observe complete fast for the day, and they should hold condolence meetings in groups on the day following. I communicated the decision to my colleagues and workers. They passed it on all over the island and in the prison through our usual channels. The news and the resolution flashed like the wireless throughout the Andamans. At the dinner time, it was found that everyone of them had refused to take food, from the inmates of the Silver Jail to inhabitants on the far-off island of Ras. The officers could not make out what it was. But none would enlighten them on it. For, to say that they fasted as a mark of mourning was to talk politics; and the prisoner in the Andamans has no politics as the cow has no soul. The prisoner has no politics, that is, he has no national feeling. If he were to talk and act politics of absolute loyalty to the Government, he was allowed to do so; nay, he was often compelled to indulge in such politics. In the days of war, he was asked to contribute his mite to swell the war-chest of his rulers, and to prevent that treasure of gold from going bankrupt. And after the war and in celebration of peace, the officers had compelled the prisoners to observe half-an-hour's complete silence in the prison. But they had no right whatever to express their mourning openly for the death of Lokamanya Tilak. If they were to declare that they had gone on fast for the day to express their grief, it would be construed as treason and may lead to trial, and punishment for the offence.

The prisoners were, therefore, enjoined to maintain silence on that point. But the officers learnt, during the course of that day, the reason for this observance. That the whole prison world of the Andamans should, within two hours of the news, go on absolute fast in honour of Lokmanya Tilak, filled the officers with surprise and anger. That it was a surprise was, no doubt, a fact. No prisoner in the Andamans knew even the name of Mr. Tilak nine years ago. Not one in a thousand on hard labour could have been found then to go on a complete fast on a day of national mourning. In the same Andamans, the lapse of nine years had made such a difference. It had brought a tremendous political awakening and unity among the prisoners and free men throughout the settlement. So that, within two hours, the news could be carried all over the place and thousands of prisoners could observe a fast regarding the day as a day of national mourning.

The same was the case with our meetings. Some of the prominent prisoners among us used to hold meetings in the settlement outside to create an awakening and to educate people in politics by lectures and discussions. Of course, to do so was to run a great risk and we had to proceed cautiously. For, prisoners were forbidden to go from one district to another. In these meetings, about **a** hundred prisoners used to come together, and they came from all parts of the settlement. This was possible because the officers and the prisoners were in alliance with us. But, at times, the plan would fail and the whole batch exposed itself to be caught. And that was the occasion when the leaders were put on their severest trial. A stampede followed, and then rallying the men back was a matter of great tact and prudent management. I may quote one episode by way of illustration. There was one district in the Andamans known as Pinnsbeg. We decided to hold a meeting in that district. Prisoners came there from distant localities on one excuse or another. And we had to watch and ward at strategic points so that the meeting should pass off safely and without detection by the authorities. While the meeting was getting into full swing, one of the men on the watch discovered a police officer, known to all, approaching the place. And the result was a rout. Everyone tried to hide himself and escape from the place as he could. The speakers, the listeners, and the national fervour—all vanished in a moment. Some hid themselves behind tall grass, others behind boulders of stone, some jumped across the fences and went into their respective chawls from their rear. Most of them had made their escape. Only two of them were caught while jumping across. The officer was our friend. He had come there because the higher authorities, informed of our projected meeting by interested persons, had sent him. Otherwise, of himself he would never have turned his steps in that direction or been found in its near vicinity. Those who happened to be caught by him belonged to the same district. He only rebuked them, and as it was a Sunday when prisoners could meet freely, he let them go with a warning. He did not ask them for other names and reported to the headquarters that there was nothing like a meeting in the place, where he was sent to look into the matter. But the episode did not end there. One Maratha prisoner, who had attended the meeting and who was one of our leading men, was degraded from his job as a writer and put on hard labour by way of punishment. Within two weeks, we were able to restore him to his old job through the influence we had with the authorities.

Inter-caste Dinners and Dassera and Divali in the Andamans

As in India, so in the Andamans, the Hindus celebrate Dassera, Divali and Holi with great eclat. There are three Hindu temples in that place well-known to all. One belongs to the Hindus, another to the Sikhs, and the third to the Arya Samajists. All prisoners have a holiday on these three days in the year. And they are allowed to move as free men from morn till eve in its thoroughfares. The prisoners in the Silver Jail had the holidays but were not allowed so far to leave the prison. I used these holidays and the fairs connected with them for purposes of our propaganda among the people. Those outside used these occasions for organising lectures and conversations on subjects of national importance. In the temples, the priest and the Puranik were often persuaded to help us in the task. We arranged inter-caste dinners in connection with these celebrations. And the dinners always began with a national prayer. The prisoners were induced to arrange discourses on the Bhagvad Gita and to recite Bhajans composed by the Arya Samaj. Hundreds of illiterate and ignorant Hindu prisoners imbibed on these sacred days the spirit of nationality and came to know something of national politics. Seeds were sown on the occasion and curiosity was roused among them, which did not all go in vain. I am tempted here to mention some names. They were those who had come first in the Silver Jail, and after serving their term had gone out as writers or factory inspectors in the colony where they carried on our mission with sincerity and zeal. I owe a tribute to them for the excellent public work they had done. But I must refrain from naming them, at least, for the time being, and as regards the first edition of this book, in their own interest. I may, however, state that some were educated men and political convicts from Dharwar, Akola and Bihar. Others came from the class of thieves and dacoits and were ignorant at the start. These latter were, indeed, criminals with dangerous propensities. But through our propaganda and education, they had been completely transformed and their souls were free from the taint of their former sins. It gave me great joy to notice this change in them, and, further, to record here, that they exposed themselves many times to trial and punishment while arranging and holding meetings and doing the constructive work that we had chalked out for them. As agitators, some of them had undergone a summary trial in this prison and sentences from six months to a year were passed on them, and they had to serve this sentence of hard labour in the prison itself, for which they were withdrawn from their appointed work in the settlement. But they bore it all, and their conduct in the prison since their transformation into public workers was honest and beyond all praise.

How bold and enterprising they were will be clear to the reader from the following story. I have already narrated how risky it was to exchange even a word with a man known as a political convict. Some of the ordinary prisoners had to lose their jobs for such misdemeanour. Others were removed from their writing work and were put to work on the oil-mill. Yet, when a large number of ex-soldiers had begun to come here as political convicts, these enterprising men entertained them with fruit on their way from the steamer to the jail, eluding all the police precaution against such course. And they did the same kind turn to political convicts on their release and on their way back to the steamer. They carried to them eatables from people in the Andamans, they brought them new clothes to put on, and they helped them with little money to be of use on the way. And all this they did in a secret, silent manner. For, if the matter was known to the authorities, they were sure to be punished severely for the offence, and they were sure to be completely ruined. And all this good work they continued doing by subscribing for it from their own slender purses.

The first Primary School in the Jail

I decided to utilise my comparative freedom and power as foreman of the oil depot, towards the systematic spread of education among the prisoners. I had always striven for it against tremendous odds as the prisoners had but known too well before. And when I wanted to launch upon a new endeavour, they openly came out to support me. I discussed the project with them and decided to start a school in the prison itself for the instruction of its juvenile offenders. I appointed an educated political convict as a teacher above them. I knew from my knowledge of prison administration in other countries of the world, that, under proper training, the juvenile class of criminals turned out into good citizens. The teacher carried out his task with great efficiency. He was not content to teach them merely the three Rs, but instructed them, according to the programme, drawn by us, in subjects, which made them sound in their morals and well-grounded in all that concerned national education. A sloka from the Gita, some important extracts inculcating sound principles of religion, drawn from our religious books, political news these were the daily items of education in the classroom. They were to read and write in Hindi and in Nagari script. They were made to repeat and recite some of the national songs, which I had specially written in Hindi for the use of free people in the Andamans. They were also taught many other national songs in Hindi that had a vogue in these islands.

After the establishment of this primary school for juveniles, I arranged for a similar school in the depot itself for the instruction of other class of prisoners. What I had done so far only secretly I now began to do openly for them. I had some 150 prisoners detailed for work on the coconuts directly under my supervision. I gave them two hours' leave during the day for attendance in the school. There they learnt in small batches and by turns. On Sundays, according to the new order of things, all of them could freely come together and attend the school at the same time. Hence, our Sunday classes became a regular and accepted feature of prison organisation. We had no fear now, and we had not to be on the run. Did this free atmosphere make the prisoners insolent and disobedient? Did they neglect their regular work or do less of it? Did it interfere with or spoil the discipline of the place? By no means. What, before, had to be enforced on them as compulsion, they now performed as a part of their duty. If one in ten among them showed the slightest tendency for breach of discipline or an inclination to come to blows, others would check them instantly saying, "O you fool, how dare you behave thus under the mild regime of Mr. Diggins and the kind treatment of Babuji—meaning myself. Have you so soon forgotten Mr. Barrie and how he treated us?" And everything began to run normally again.

We celebrate the birth-anniversary of Guru Govind

Whatever public work I could do under the new prison regulations, I did openly. For the rest we did it in our own secret way as before. For instance, we decided this year to celebrate in prison the birthday of Guru Govind Singh. I intended that the anniversary celebration should be on a grand scale so that the Hindus and the Sikhs might come closer to one another and the bond of unity among them might be strengthened, by the understanding and appreciation by them both of their common culture. The day fell on Sunday, and the prisoners in each wing of the jail could assemble together for the celebration. But as the prisoners in one wing could not go to prisoners in another wing, every school had to arrange for the celebration at different hour. All of them were, however, equally eager to hear my speech on Guru Govind. So, I found occasion to visit two or three chawls by turns and delivered in each place a lecture on the great Guru of the Sikhs. In these anniversary celebrations of different chawls of the same prison, the Sikhs and the Hindus participated as brothers. They sang bhajans together, they heard lectures on the life of the Guru together; they listened to various anecdotes from his life together; and they pleaded for solidarity among them with unanimity and fervour. On that day, I had in the depot puja and prasad. This prasad known as 'Kada Prasad' was distributed among all the prisoners of the place without distinction of caste and creed. According to the common practice on Sundays, the prisoners had to go back to their respective cells and be locked in it at a particular hour. That day, I managed that they may be sent to their room, but the door be kept open. And when all the higher officers had left the place, I assembled them in the open courtyard and addressed the meeting. Prisoners from different chawls had come out to hear me, and petty officers and others, who had now been converts to our views, watched all about to warn us in time against the surprise visit of any higher officer of that place. A hundred of them had spread themselves out to keep guard. Others were at the meeting. We sang national songs on the occasion and then they heard my speech with rapt attention. The thing to note is this: We celebrated the birthday of Guru Govind in a place, where a few years before it was an offence for one prisoner to meet and talk to another. To swear by India as mother land was, of course, then out of question. And it has also to be admitted that not one in a hundred could have understood us then, if we were to speak to them of one country, one nation and one mother-tongue.

To encourage the prisoners in the training and development of their mind I would always put such of them on easier work in the prison as showed themselves apt pupils and as would regularly attend our meetings. When we started the classes, the pupils were given slates, pencils and readers from the funds at our disposal. But when an educated man and a lover of learning like Mr. Diggins became the head of the institution, I approached him with a petition that the Government should provide slates and books for our pupils.

At last, after considerable correspondence and repeated petitions, the Government issued orders and they got slates and books at Government expense. I drew the attention of the officer to the zest, with which the prisoners were using books and slates supplied to them. I also obtained permission for other prisoners to obtain books from the political prisoners' library. I then suggested that the Government should purchase books and stock them in the prisoners' library. The task of making a list of such books being entrusted to me, I chose as many books of national views as I could, and included in the list a large number of Hindi books. Some of them were marked as undesirable, when the list was finally approved by the authorities. Such books I included for purchase in our own collection. Thus, I kept on working for national ends either by the help of the Government or through our secret organisation till the end of my period in the Andamans. I included in the library, a large collection of books in Tamil, Andhra, Malayalam and Canarese languages, as I regarded them as essentially of Hindu stock, and as helpful to the promotion of national solidarity and national sentiment among the people.

Eighty Percent Literacy among the Prisoners

An officer of the prison once asked me what was the fruit of it all. And in order to ascertain results, I went into prison statistics, counting the total number of prisoners, and the percentage among them of those who knew reading and writing, and those again who had learnt it after they had been admitted into this jail. I knew from this investigation that eighty percent of them were literates, while out of these ninety percent had learnt to read and write only after they had entered this prison. I conveyed the information to the officer in question, who, in order to test it, paid a surprise visit to our chawls one Sunday morning. And what did he witness? When he went over the chawls room by room, he saw the prisoners absorbed in reading books on various subjects or in singing national songs. Ten years ago, he had seen prisoners in the same place on a Sunday playing at dice, gambling or quarrelling with one another or whiling away their leisure in similar degrading pastime. He was an officer, who had spent years in that jail and he was simply surprised to notice the change between the past and the present.

An Education enough for a Voter

I have only mentioned the percentage of average literacy in the prison, but considering the method of education, we had followed and the subjects included in our scheme, I can say that as he was taught everything about his country and of current politics, he was so widely-read and well-informed that he was capable of understanding how to exercise his right as a voter. Of such, there were at least forty percent, in our prison. In any European country, a voter does not generally know more than this. Our prisoners had been rendered fit by our training to be included in any electorate for a Legislative Council, or to cast his vote correctly in the election of any village panchayat.

With My Elder Brother in the Moonlight

My post as a foreman had enabled me to enjoy personal freedom, at least to some extent. I could come out of my room not only in the morning, but long before day-break. It was then that I stood out in the open with the flood of moonlight all around me. After nearly ten years of buried life, what an exhilaration of spirit it brought me. Though I enjoyed the night immensely, it was not without its shadow upon my soul; for, was it not, after all, moonlight behind the prison-bars as good as the moonlight in a burial ground or at a burning ghat?

A few days after, I had for my companion under such moonlight my elder brother. I could sit with him, thus, for hours under the moon, but only to talk over the sufferings he had to pass through and weep for these sufferings. For his constitution had been thoroughly undermined, he was coughing all the while and T.B. had already come near him. For an hour, when the fit came, he had absolutely no respite. I see him before me even now, seated on a tattered ratten chair with his long coat of coarse blanket on him, a tall, thin, worn-out man, a true patriot and devoted worker, a prisoner piteous to look at, yet himself unbent under the blows that had fallen on him.

Enjoying the moonlight, and this limited freedom in jail, I had determined not to pine for what was not, and to go on persistently with my self-imposed task. As I was living my life thus, one morning my elder brother hurriedly came up to me and put a cutting from a newspaper on my table. I had to read it unnoticed by anyone else. I read it and found in it the news that the Government had resolved to close the Andamans as a colony for prisoners, that no fresh prisoners were to be sent in its Silver Jail, and the old ones were to be transferred to prisons in India in case they would not agree to stay in the Andamans on some specific conditions.

Andamans Closed as Prison Colony

The news, of course, gratified me for it was the ful-filment of the work we had started and carried on for the last ten years. I had stated before the Jail Commission all the grievances of the prisoners at Port Blair; and the manner in which I had championed their cause before the Commission, I had no doubt, it had cost me my freedom from this jail, and was the main reason of my exclusion from the general amnesty that was proclaimed subsequently. Therefore, I had the self-satisfaction that, though I had not won my freedom, I had done all I could in the best interests of all other prisoners in that jail, and was instrumental, at least partially, in the success that had come to them.

Hundreds of prisoners in the jail showered their gratitude upon me. All of them knew one thing very well, and it was that during ten years of my association with them, I had carried on incessant agitation in the Silver Jail and outside for giving them an organised existence. I had carried on agitation in the press, through petitions, through civil resistance, through questions asked in the Imperial Legislature at Delhi, through protests, correspondence and personal letters, to draw the pointed attention of India and its Central Government to their condition in the Andamans. And it was my persistence at it that had made the matter a live issue before the Jail Commission. To those who would felicitate me, I said, "At last, the Andamans as a prison colony is no more, the Silver Jail is dismantled. This change is not the result of any single-handed endeavour. It is the reward of ten years of continuous and all-sided agitation, to the success of which all of you, and especially the political convicts, have made a tremendous contribution by your trials and tribulations throughout this period. And if it has succeeded even partially, the credit is yours." I told them so and offered my sincerest felicitations to them in return.

I added how fine it would have been for Mr. Barrie to be alive that day. Mr. Barrie used to taunt me that all my efforts were to go for nought and add that I was dashing my head against a stonewall, that was not the wall that would break, but that my head would break. I could have told him that day as follows: "Mr. Barrie, my head had received many bruises by my dashing it continuously against your prison walls. No doubt about it. But behold! The wall of your prison has now been cracked and will soon crumble down. And I am here alive with all the bruises I have received in the fight."

I spent the whole night in thinking over the news, and made up my mind as to where I would oppose the Government in that move, and where I would support it heartily from the standpoint of India's interest in that affair. I, at once, realised that the stand I was going to take would cost me at the start in popularity with my own people. But I must be prepared for this opposition, if I was to serve them well. Had I not passed through a similar experience of adverse criticism when I first launched the *Shuddhi* movement in the Andamans?

I was in favour of Prison-Colony

I was, from the start, against breaking up the prison-colony in the

Andamans. What I had insisted upon breaking was the administration of it by harsh, hard-hearted, reactionary, and unsympathetic prison regulations, so harmful to the prisoners coming under its jurisdiction. The colony and the settlement should have been continued on the lines of Canada and Australia, where England had sent its prisoners who made those colonies into thriving dominions. The worst felons were deported from England to Canada. And the fierce qualities of the criminals sent to Canada proved useful in conquering that land for cultivation and development from the aborigines of that country and the wild animals that had infested it. These fierce qualities, tamed by proper discipline and control, have many times helped the convict settlers to turn the land by proper cultivation into a dominion smiling with plenty and power peace and progress. The colonial policy ought to aim at making the prisoners useful and honest citizens and not to kill their spirit or destroy their usefulness. The policy should not be that of revenge but improvement all round. In Canada, partly in America, and to a larger extent in Africa, the convicts sent from England were kept free, though under severe discipline, and their enterprise and daring were utilised to good purpose. They colonised and brought under cultivation the wild and barren places of those continents. The human material that was running to waste in the old country grew in these new countries to hundred times its strength, and the growing population had turned these dominions into independent nations. England's man power and its power as an empire grew with their growth and expansion. I felt from the point of view of India as a nation that the Andamans, instead of being abandoned, should be developed through its prisoners along similar lines.

It was not the policy of our agitation to denude and destroy the Andamans. It was, we felt, to lose all the labour and money that had been spent on that soil for so many years in the past. It should be developed along national lines. For, prisoners, deported to the Andamans on a long or a life-sentence, were bound to rot for fourteen years in the jails of India. Life would be a misery for them in these new conditions as bad as that in the Andamans, if not worse than that. And society would get no benefit whatever of the better part of their criminal propensities like courage, enterprise, daring and recklessness of life. From the national point of view, the very qualities that stink in our nostrils as criminal, furnish rich manure for the soil where the prisoners are transplanted as free men; or are like explosives which, if wisely handled, become powerful weapons of defence. And the greatest harm of it all was that the seed falling on rocky soil was run to waste, while cast on fertile soil might multiply a hundredfold. The nation loses immensely from the disuse of this potentiality for man-power when a prisoner is condemned to rot in the jail, whereas as a free man in a new settlement, he could marry, prosper and multiply to the immense advantage of the country he hails from.

Crime is hereditary only in a limited sense

In my opinion, heredity and crime were not so inviolably bound up as scientists had tried to make it. If there was any truth in this proposition, it was nothing better than half-truth. Not every criminal or sinner transmitted his sin and crime to his children as heredity would seek to prove. A man or woman became a criminal not as the result of heredity alone. That may be attributed to many other causes. Education, circumstances, associations, and several other causes act upon a person to turn him into a criminal and develop or kill the instinct of crime he might inherit from his parents. If virtue and vice were invariably to pass from father to son, there would never have been a son like Sambhaji to a king like Shivaji, or the political convicts deported to Canada would never have been able to give us a nation like Canada as from generation to generation. As a poet does not necessarily beget a poet, so a criminal father does not necessarily give birth to a criminal son.

Prisoners on Life-Sentence should be allowed to Marry

Therefore, to put a ban upon prisoners transported for life against marriage was virtually to punish the nation. It is not only to punish them individually but to penalise the country, for it is a distinct setback to the growth of her population. Instead of this policy of cruelty and castration, it would be wise to continue the settlement as a free colony of prisoners who, under strict discipline, may be allowed to make a home in it, marry and multiply, and turn the settlement into a thriving and prosperous concern. From generations born of them, men who grow up in social virtues should be made entirely free so that the settlement and the country, to which it belongs, may both reap the rich benefits flowing from such a policy.

My work of awakening in the Andamans had been all along guided by this far-sighted aim. To improve the life of the convicts, to make their children good and capable citizens by education and association, must be the policy of the Government, charged with the administration of the Andamans. The regulations ought to be so framed as would contribute to this self-sufficient development. This was the purpose of my mission in the Silver Jail, my self-imposed task during the ten years I had been there. And I had definitely formulated it in my oral evidence, as also in my written statement, before the Jail Commission. And I had strongly emphasised the need for action accordingly.

But the Government Resolution on the subject had altogether brushed aside the constructive part of my evidence and statement, though it had fully accepted the damaging criticism I had made upon the existing method and scope of administering the Andamans. As such, it had proposed the closing down of the colony for prisoners from India and Burma. It had proposed to transfer the prisoners in the Andamans to the respective jails in India. This was a way of doing things, which was no remedy at all for the existing evil, and did not provide in any way for future good of the colony, as well as for the good of the present prisoners in it. I had, therefore, decided to open a campaign against it in the Andamans and in India.

Unfortunately, this time it was clear to me that those who were against me formerly would be out to support me while those who had all along gone with me would be against me. For, the British officers, who had settled in the Andamans thought like me that the colony should not be broken up; at least, they felt that thousands of prisoners who had settled there should not be dislodged from that place. The reason might be different with them. The British officers, from the overseers right up to the Chief Commissioner, did not want to lose their jobs, did not desire to be unsettled in life; they felt that their removal from the Andamans meant that they could no longer rule as they had ruled in the Andamans with unquestioned authority over thousands of prisoners, and, perhaps, would have to be content with positions much inferior to those that they held in these islands. Hence, these high officials were trying to bring pressure upon the authorities in India, with the consent of the prisoners concerned, not to put that resolution into effect. I also began working in my own way that the present prison settlers in the Andamans should not be sent out of the colony into India. In the same cause, yet for different reasons, myself and the officers went on well together.

But this strange ailiance created suspicion in the minds of those prisoners who had so long worked hand in glove with me. It must be admitted that our agitation and activities against the Government had created in them a frame of mind that regarded everything coming from the official side with great suspicion and as having some sinister motive behind it. It is ever true of ignorant persons that such a prejudice in them makes them incapable of judging an action as good or bad on its own merits. They hesitate to accept even a good thing from those against whom they are prejudiced, and they ever suspect something sinister behind it. Common people take their politics as a young and untried wrestler faces a practised man in it. The latter holds forth his hand and the novice would not catch it, ever suspecting some dodge behind the preferred hand. He knows not how to meet a move with a counter-move to checkmate it. The ordinary man in politics and similar affairs misses much and perhaps loses a great deal by such over-suspicion. And exactly similar was the attitude of many prisoners in the Andamans towards me because they felt that I was siding this time with the officers instead of opposing them. The more the local officers persuaded them to stay on in the Andamans, the more eager they became to leave that place. They felt that their interests lay in abandoning the place because the officers, who often deceived them, now importunated them to stick to it. And when I joined my voice to theirs adding, that going back to India was not desirable, that staying there was more advantageous to them because of the new concessions. They were surprised and puzzled in mind, and went the length of suspecting me as they had so long suspected the officers. And in this way, those, who were my staunch friends and devoted disciples till then, prepared themselves to lead an open opposition to my advice and action on this particular question, albeit they did it most reluctantly.

Those who strive for the good of the people are ever ready to sacrifice for it their property and even their life; but they dare not sacrifice popularity for it; they often shrink from such a sacrifice, as I have found from many instances in my own experience of public life. Not to forego popularity at any cost has been the grave of many a good cause in this world. Knowing as I did this side of public life but too well, I have striven to the best of my power, never to succumb to this temptation, and have sacrificed popularity as I have sacrificed myself whenever I found it necessary to do so. I know that it has caused me a severe wrench of the heart. But I have borne the agony of it for the sake of what I was convinced to be my duty. As to that, there was no doubt in my mind.

The prisoners sent to me, under one pretext or another, their respective leaders, one after another, to know my real mind on the subject. To one and all of them, I gave the same advice.

I said to them, "Most of the prisoners in the settlement are drawn from the lowest and the most poverty-stricken strata of society. If they were taken back to India and were but set free at once, without being made to rot in the jails of India, how will they be the better for such freedom? That they shall not be so set free was a certainty, for they were bound to serve out their fourteen years' term of imprisonment in India, if not in the Andamans. The breaking up of the colony in the Andamans by no means implied such a pardon for them. Granted that they were free they will inevitably go back to poverty, which will hold them in its grip. If they happened to have a small piece of land, they will find that their kith and kin had already swallowed it. Homeless they will either fight for them in the law courts, or, worse than that, quarrel with them and beat them. And if they did not do so, they shall have to beg for their subsistence and, at last, lapse into a career of crime. This state of things was good neither for them, nor for their country.

"On the other hand, to settle in the Andamans, and to make the fullest use of the new opportunity opened out to them to own and cultivate the land and to earn an independent living, was to bring into existence a prosperous colony, which would be both an individual and a national gain. The greatest drawback in the past life of the Andamans had been the dearth of females, and, therefore, little or no scope, whatever, for marriage and home life. But if in years to come—say in five years—the officers permit and encourage prisoners to marry and make a home for themselves, then the difficulty on that score was bound to disappear. Many of them would, in that case, bring their families from India or marry women of the Andamans. So long the prisoners were forbidden from having any contact with free men and their families in these islands. But that ban would not be there under the new order of things. Would it not be better, in these circumstances, to stay here and improve their social and economic position than to go back either to rot in the jail, or to carry on litigation for a small piece of land and, thus, quarrel with their kith and kin? Here was free land open for their occupation. They had better settle on it, cultivate it, reap a new harvest from it, live and be happy. The so-called free men here were the progeny of prisoners, who had come to the Andamans a generation back. They were their blood and bone. To establish marriage alliance with them would be addition to that progeny. To live here in contentment was better than anything they were going to do in India. It would be hard for them to win any status there to settle, to marry, to make a home for themselves, have children in the family, and make a little money on their own. Why! In India their caste would shun them as pariahs. Those who had returned from Fiji to India in similar circumstances preferred to go back, for in India conditions were hard for them to endure. They were labourers, while the prisoners will go back branded as convicts or ex-convicts. Was it not better, therefore, for them to obtain their freedom after ten years in the Andamans, which in former days came to them after twenty years of penal servitude? Was it not better to use that freedom to improve their lot by settling here, for which they would get a ticket on mere application? Now the ticket was being given only after three years of imprisonment in the jail here. Turn farmers, cultivate the soil, be independent, earn your living and be happy. Take it that you have come to this foreign country to make your fortune.

"You will, thus, not only serve yourselves, avoiding all the hardships of imprisonment, but you will also be helping to add to India, if you make full use of your opportunities and work as an organised unit, a colony as prosperous and enlightened, in the course of a few generations, as Canada or Cape Colony. That will mean Greater India, not unlike Greater Britain, though an a smaller scale. For, your stay in the Andamans ultimately means to keep the flag of India flying on these shores. It will be the expansion of India from the cultural and religious point of view.

"Look at Nicobar. It originally was an offshoot of India. Now it belongs to the Burmese and the Malayans because the Hindus refused to settle and colonise it. It is lost for good to Hindu culture. And the same thing will happen in the Andamans as soon as the Hindu prisoners are removed from it, and their settlement here is broken up for good. The Burmese, and the Malayans are sure to put themselves in possession of it. And the three generations of Hindus, which had sown the seed and spilt their blood in its development, will disappear in no time. It will be lost to their children and the toil and sweat of their ancestors shall have been in vain. Lost to Hinduism and Hindu culture by such expropriation, the Andamans may remain a possession of India, yet its soul will belong to the Chinese, the Malayans and other races of Mongolian stock and culture.

"You already know the political importance of the Andamans to India. These islands are to be the fortification line of India in the future, a base for her navy and air-force to guard her from foreign invasion. If the Hindu prisoners remain in occupation of these islands, their children will be Hindus by blood and social heritage and it will be theirs, as coming generations, to guard this island fortress of India."

Stay here even if you are free

That is the glorious future that awaits you all. Today, you are fallen, outcast and condemned but this heritage is a golden opportunity that you should not let go. Hence, the few among you, who aspire in India to attain a higher status, must stay here in order to lead and guide you, and make you raise these islands to the status of a great colony and attach it to mother India. This is a service they owe to their motherland, for which they must make this sacrifice. This is a task that is indeed the fulfilment of a life time. Every land demands leaders who would stick to the Spot and carry on propaganda, and who would work to realise the ideal. They spend themselves for the cause that it may fructify. Why can you not be the conquerers of Andamans for India in a similar manner?

I talked to them repeatedly in the same strain. I used almost the same words and language over and over again till all my former co-workers and colleagues came over to my side as the result of these private talks. They, at last, realised that to be sent back to India did not mean freedom for them. It was to be taken to prisons where they would be under stricter confinement. Some of them caught from me the fervent spirit of nationalism and the sense of duty that went with it.

Yet in order that the Government be compelled to give as many concessions as possible to them. I made all of them to say to it that they would stay in the Andamans only under certain conditions or else they should be sent back straight to India. I wanted them to take up that position in their own interest. The authorities allowed us to hold meetings to express our opinion on the subject. Taking advantage of this facility, I began to speak at these meetings to the fullest extent on Sangathan and general politics of the country.

If going to India means no freedom, we prefer to stay here

In order to set an example to the rest, I sent a petition to the Government of India: "If I was not to be set free on my stepping into India, I preferred to be kept back in the Andamans to serve my whole term of imprisonment. Only as I had finished ten years in the jail, for the rest of my time, I should be allowed to settle in the Andamans as a free person with my family, or alone on a ticket granted for that purpose."

In former years, I had submitted representations for the transfer of prisoners from the Andamans to India. I had done so, as the reader will notice from what I have written about them in the pages of this book, on grounds of health and other facilities they would get in India. But today the whole aspect had changed in the Andamans and hundreds of prisoners stood to gain from residence in these islands. And their colonial development and expansion was sure to benefit India as a whole politically and nationally. I, therefore, had made up my mind to pass my days in the Andamans to help that process of expansion and development. My example inspired others to stay there along with me.

My strenuous efforts to stabilise the Andamans as a prison colony filled the free inhabitants of the place with gratitude for me. These were only a handful, who owned lands and plantations. They were farmers and their living depended on the existence of prisoners in that colony. If all the prisoners were turned out from these islands, they would suffer most. They began to submit petitions to Government on the lands they cultivated and on the rights of ownership about them. They complained about the taxes levied on them and the irregularities about them. They protested against arbitrary eviction from these lands, and they tried to organise a regular campaign in support of their grievances. The prisoners often used to say and suggest as if they would be none the better for freedom in the Andamans. In order to bring home to them the advantage of such freedom, the Government was bound to treat those, who were already living as free inhabitants in these islands, with consideration, adopt a well-thought-out policy of action towards them. But in order that they may be enabled to take full advantage of the policy, continuous agitation was indispensable. Their leaders used to see me often and I used to see the representations they submitted and even improve them.

The repercussion of jejune Indian politics on the Andamans

The main topic of politics that year was the Khilafat and the Non-Cooperation movements in India. In our discussions of that topic, I condemned them outright. I said, "The death of Lokmanya Tilak in India gave a fillip to these movements. It is a belief current among us that when a great man dies, nature herself is unable to bear the shock and she erupts in hurricanes and typhoons, in pestilence and epidemics full of evil portent to the world. The exit from the Indian world of a powerful personality like Lokmanya Tilak ushered in the mad intoxication of Khilafat agitation conspiring with the cult of the Charka as a way to Swaraj in one year. It is to be won by the perverse doctrine of non-violence and truth. The Non-Cooperation Movement for Swaraj based on these twin principles was a movement without power and was bound to destroy the power of the country. It is an illusion, a hallucination, not unlike the hurricane that sweeps over a land only to destroy it. It is a disease of insanity, an epidemic and megalomania."

I was the first to protest against the Khilafat movement in India. I denounced it as dangerous to the nation. I did not style it 'Khilafat' but 'afat'—a menace to the country. Every house in the Andamans knew it as 'afat' or a calamity. And that definition of non-violence, which was no definition but its perversion! And what shall we say of truth but that it was downright falsehood, a cant, a sham and a bunkum! I discussed the movement and its everyday incidents and exposed its hollowness before hundreds of my listeners in spite of their strong prejudice in its favour and, therefore, of their bitter opposition to me. I calmly bore it all, and gradually convinced them of its useless hair-splitting and its unreality and hollowness all round. It was bound to do more harm than good to the country and could never bring in Swaraj in one year as it was pledged to do. That I was speaking to them the barest truth was brought home to me by many an incident that followed. I may mention here only one of these.

Two vevolutionaries and political convicts, whose names I may not mention, had just been sent to the Andamans. They had warrants issued against them as involved in the riots in Punjab, but they had gone underground and the police had no clue about them. For six months, they moved freely in the country carrying on their usual work, but no trace was found about them. And like Babu Guru Datta Singh they could have gone on for years defying the C.I.D. to catch them. But they went and saw Gandhiji, the leader of the Non-Cooperation Movement, and as ill luck would have it, narrated to him the story of their life. The great leader was in rage and denounced them. He said, "It is sheer cowardice to be in hiding and to evade warrants against them. Go instantly and deliver yourselves in the hands of the Magistrate. I cannot countenance such untruthful conduct." They asked him plainly if that action was not cooperation with the Government. They said to him, "We are making the law inoperative, we are practicing civil disobedience in the right way. As we are carrying on our work, you cannot say of us that we are in hiding and elude the law out of fear. To act as you would have us act is to help the Government and help the law to have its own course." Before they had finished the argument, Gandhiji reprimanded, "That will not do, I order you to appear before the Magistrate and surrender yourselves. Do it instantly." Poor men! They returned to the North at their own expense and appeared before the Delhi Magistrate. After arrest and trial, they now find themselves on life-sentence in the Andaman jail.

And now they censured Gandhiji and had repented for their ever having committed the blunder of seeing him. I plainly told them that he alone was not to blame in that affair. Those who had the weakness to obey him implicitly were as much to blame and deserved as much censure as he. Why did they listen to him; why did they not exercise their reason, and think, and act for themselves?

I add only two sentences to this disquisition without referring in detail to other incidents and episodes to give the reader a picture of my notions at that time and of my line of work then. Summing up the discussion, I said, "We revolutionaries ought always to remember one thing and guide ourselves by one principle that politics worth the name is neither cooperation nor non-cooperation. It is responsive cooperation, and morally it can be no other. If we win a step by cooperation, then let us cooperate with the opposition. If we feel certain that cooperation is useless, then let us resort to non-cooperation. At one point of time, non-cooperation has to be non-violent. At another time, it cannot help being violent. And even violence or resort to terrorism ought to be only a temporary measure. Non-cooperation cannot be a principle, it is only a remedy for the time being. Co-operation with all and in the best interests of all is a positive doctrine. And when it works for all and promotes the good of all, and is acted upon, according to time and circumstance, it is rightly described as responsive cooperation."

I had pointed out even then to my fellow-prisoners how far this chameleon would go; what would be the extent of its jump. I had warned them how the alliance of non-cooperation with the Khilafat agitation was bound to end in disaster, that it was sure to raise in the country a wave of fanaticism and plunge the whole movement into conflagration, with its consequences to the country too terrible to imagine. I continued impressing the fact upon my colleagues and fellow prisoners, as long as I was in the Andamans.

□

11

I Meet My Family Again

Last days in the Andamans

Just about this time, my younger brother paid me a visit in the Andamans. There was no hope then of my release from that place. My elder brother had continued to be failing in health. And, therefore, the first thought that struck us when we three met together was that perhaps that was the last meeting together of us three. For, the next time that such a permission would be granted to us would be only after the lapse of one year. And one year was such an interminable period for a person like my elder brother who had found himself so thinned in body and so gone down in health that it was hard to imagine he would last long. Everyday was such a difficult day for that emaciated body to pull on with. As such, I told my younger brother the bitterest truth in plain words. I said, "Bal, truth is always harsh but I am sure you are not so weak-minded and cowardly as not to face it with fortitude. I see, therefore, no reason to conceal it from you. On the other hand, the sorrow that comes with perceptible and slow steps is easier to bear than any calamity that comes down upon us with a sudden blow. Be prepared to hear the worst of us any day in the future. I don't think we can pull on for a long time now. Do not forget, however, that even the unexpected sometimes happens. Who knows we may survive from this. But the chances are very remote for that. Take it that this is our last meeting together on this side of the world!" Every word that I uttered went like a burning brand to my heart. The face of Bal, my younger brother had completely darkened and his countenance fell. But he realised that words were like heartbeats, and harsh though they were, they were but echoes of truth. I had uttered them as the voice of my conscience, and he heard them intently.

As I had by now completed my period of ten years in that prison, I had petitioned to the Government to grant me the ticket I was entitled to. The reply that I got was that I had been granted the ticket, but in the prison itself. To have a ticket itself meant freedom to live outside the prison, and to make a home and live in it by earning one's independent livelihood. Others had got such tickets on the expiry of three years in the Silver Jail. I got it at the end of ten years. But a ticket to live in the prison itself was indeed a travesty of terms. That really meant that I was to pass all my days in the prison itself, not in the free life of the Andamans, without a home of my own, and yet it was a ticket that they had given me! That was bitter irony indeed. That was lacerating a bruised heart. I was to be made an exception to all the rules operating in these islands; I was to get no benefit of any word or plea I had advanced to improve the lot of the prisoners in that jail.

Cornered thus on all sides, life for me and for other political prisoners in that jail would sometimes become a burden too hard to bear. In order to save them and myself from suicide, we had hatched up a secret plot among the most trusted and confidential friends of our group. We had included in that dark conspiracy some of the ordinary prisoners as well. Whenever we found that there was no hope whatsoever for this, that, or the other of the political convicts in that jail, when the last thread of hope had perished, then these convicts together were to...

So a day passed, a long, lingering day! The bell tolled announcing the coming of evening. A day of pining had gone by! Relief, rest, sleep, forgetfulness, and the approach of release nearer by a day. But release meant death as well. A day that passed was one day less from the sentence, sure enough. But it was one day less also from the lease of life. That also kept on haunting the mind.

One of such days the hour was evening; the bell had rung; and I had made ready to return to my cell. I locked the oil depot and had handed over the keys to the *jamadar*. Though on ticket, every evening I had to return to my solitary confinement in the appointed room. I gave the keys and was winding my way to the room for the night. A warder came up to me and slipped a chit into my palms. He smiled full of joy and hinted that it was good news. And he went away. I opened the note and I read that an order had come from the Indian Government in the head office of the Commissioner that day that Savarkar brothers were to be sent back to India. The Government of Bombay had asked for their recall!

Such news had been brought to me several times before, and had ended there. And I had remained in the prison all the while. Hence, I had never put any faith in these reports. My friends knew it and, therefore, had added that they had seen the order with their own eyes, and there was no humbug about it.

The news may be true, for aught I thought to the contrary. For, where prisoners had got their tickets after three years, I had got it after ten, and my ticket brought me no freedom, but permit to rot in the jail for all time to come. I realised that this farce could not continue for long and the shamelessness must end. There were only two alternatives to this dirty conduct—either I must be free in the Andamans, or, as the report went, must be sent back to India. The authorities would prefer any day to take me back to India and put me in jail there. They would not have me on them as a free man in the Andamans. What I did not get for the asking, I was to get now from them without asking for it. For, this concession would enable them to detain me in the prison in India after ten years in the Andamans. And that, in the name of mercy again, as an act of kindness towards me! For, my transportation to India would be hailed by all, who did not know the other side of the matter. They would regard it as an act of grace.

These were my night-thoughts on that date. Next morning, the jailor sent for me in the office and ordered me to pack up my things. I then felt sure that this was a prelude to my departure for India.

The Andamans were all agog with the happy news, for they knew not that my send-off from here was to be my imprisonment in India. The people welcomed the news as an order of release and freedom. Wish was father to the thought and they protested, "Babuji, none is going to put you back in the jail again. So soon as you step in India, you are free. That is a certainty." Taking the wish for the deed, they showered on me messages of congratulations from all sides.

But the more I thought of it, the more indifferent I grew to that news. In the Andamans, I had the consolation of staying together with my brother. In India, we were sure to be separated and housed in different jails. I had made intimate friends in the Andamans during the last ten years. I had already secured the ticket, and the chance was that, before long, I could live here as a free man in a home and a family of my own. In India, I would again be confined to prison and as a solitary man. I would lose my friends, the ties would be sundered. And I felt the same wrench of separation that I had felt when I took leave of my friends in India and was transported to the Andamans.

I felt as miserable and unhappy as I was ten years ago when I left India. And now that I was leaving the Andamans, I felt that I was being sent back on transportation for life once again.

I packed up my books. I gave many of them to the prison library. I distributed others among prisoners and friends. On the last day, there was a crowd of men to pay me their last visit. They kept on coming to me from morning till evening. Every moment I feared that the officers might misunderstand the crowd and might arrest anyone of them again. But all went off smoothly and the officers paid no attention to the crowd. Everyone was free that day to go out and come in as he liked. The prisoners ceased to be afraid of the officers, and the officers in their turn did not over-do their part as custodians of the place. In spite of my repeated protests and when many of them could not personally meet me, they brought to the prison gate gifts of all kinds—fruits, flowers, sweetmeats, soda water bottles, tins of biscuits, there were in any number, heaps of them. And who were they that showered these presents upon me? Free men in the Andamans as well as prisoners. What was their worth? Most of them earned no more than ten rupees a month. But what loyalty and what devotion there were in the act! Unsought and unrestricted they came with their gift of a plantain, a watermelon, and a flower to deposit it near the prison gate. I went in the afternoon to the door, and I distributed them all among those whom I found near the gate. I only kept such of them as none would take back from me. I administered the pledge of service to a few of my choice friends who lingered behind. The pledge of our association contained the following words:

"One God, one country, one goal"
"One caste, one life, one language."
We stand by these.

I gave this mantra to him and explained to him its deeper significance. For the fulfilment of this hope, for the attainment of this goal, every Hindu, who is one with the ideal, must be ready, if an occasion arises, even to sacrifice his life fighting for it. I told him in detail what and how to do it. Before every Hindu individually and collectively can summon up strength for this supreme sacrifice and even during the process of it, he must carry out in the present circumstances certain tasks in the

Andamans and I told him in detail the tasks devolving on all of them severally in that connection.

Just then a warder came to inform me that the Sahib was coming, as also the party of policemen that was to fetch me away from that jail.

I got up, and I had the unalloyed gratification that on the last day of my life here I could convey to the men to whom I had just spoken the vow that I had taken when I was but eleven years old. I had buried my hope alive in that prison for ten years and on the day that its door was to open to let me out, my last act on the last day and at the last moment was no other than the message I gave to the prisoner in that jail. I had to step into this prison because I had given that mantra to young India, and now that I was leaving it after ten years, God had spared me to leave the same message behind to inspire young men in the Andamans.

"One God, one country, one hope,

"One caste, one life, one language."

These words were on my lips all along

My brother and myself were made to stand before the prison gate. The jailor handed us over to the police party in order to take us on the steamer bound for India. The kind jailor asked them not to put fetters on us. We were marched along and, at last, the iron door of that horrible prison opened its jaws to let us out into the spacious atmosphere of the world outside.

It had opened in 1909 and closed after swallowing up my elder brother. In 1911, the same horrible jaw opened out again and shut so soon as it had gulped me down. We had no hope then that we could come out of it alive. The iron portal that had shut upon us in 1911, turned on its hinges with a grating sound in 1921, the jaw opened and we came out of it.

The iron theshold of that iron gate, as we crossed it, made us aware that we were leaving the Andamans alive. I said to my brother, "This little threshold is a borderland between life and death. From death we are crossing into life only by stepping athwart the threshold. Yes we have crossed it and stepped into the land of the living. And now? We do not mind very much. Let the future take care of itself."

A garland of white champaka flowers.

The outside of the prison was strictly guarded against the crowd that had gathered to give me a send-off. A large number of people had come there only to have a sight of me. The prisoners scattered over the settlement were scrupulously kept at their work that day. And yet many had come under some excuse or another and lay in hiding to have a look at me. We had walked only a few steps on our way to Port Blair and under an escort when a Maratha prisoner by name Kushaba, who had been raised to the position of a *jamadar* and who was shortly to receive his ticket of freedom, suddenly rushed forward and defying the escort that guarded us put a garland of Champaka flowers round my neck on behalf of all the prisoners present. While the police party was about to raise a cry, he had already left after cheering my name and prostrating himself at my feet. He was liable to lose his job and be punished for such a sacrilege. But he seemed not to mind it.

I still visualise the scene. The Maratha prisoner intent on garlanding me, and the baffled police officers straining to pull me off and handcuff me. The police officer was a symbol of twenty years' effort on the part of the authorities to blot me out from the memory of the people, to prevent one and all of them from having any photograph or book in their houses, or any relic to remind them of me and my work. All these years, they had branded these actions as punishable offences. And now the police officer taking me to the steamer was making his last effort to prevent the prisoners from honouring me. On the other hand, the garland of Champaka flowers and the *jamadar*, who gave it to me, were a token of the love and veneration in which thousands of my fellow-countrymen still continued to hold me. My life and life work had all along been the battleground between these two contending forces and of their action and reaction. And the manifestation in my life constituted so many symbolic expressions of the whole story. That was how I felt about the scene before me, and I expressed it in so many words to my brother beside me.

More precious than a jewel necklace

This garland of flowers was an invaluable recognition of our efforts during the last ten years for uplift of the Andamans. We felt our efforts rewarded by this token of love and reverence. It was dearer to us than any necklace of jewels. As he garlanded me, the crowd expressed its joy by clapping. These plaudits betokened loving gratitude that went home to my heart. It was a conclusive answer to the efforts of the authorities to inspire fear and disaffection about me among the settlers in the Andamans.

I found sometimes to talk confidentially to my friends and chief co-workers before being taken up into the steamer. Through them I gave my parting advice to the dwellers in the Andamans. I told them, "Stay in the Andamans, cultivate the soil, inter-marry, multiply, and add to the growth and expansion of the Hindu culture in those islands." I also chalked out for them the work they were to do. As I climbed the ascent ten years ago from Port Blair to the Silver Jail, I had never imagined that time would come when I was to descend from that place and go back to India. But now I had climbed down and was stepping into the steamer that was to take me back to India.

As the thoughts were passing in my mind, the steamer 'Maharaja' had arrived. She was bound for Calcutta. We went up and I felt a strange sensation coming over me. I was to lose the little freedom I was beginning to enjoy in the Silver Jail, and, when in India, I may be put under severe custody as if I was to run my whole sentence once again beginning from it first day. As I stepped into the steamer, I was taken to the cage for prisoners on the ground floor. It was in the same cage that I was locked on my first voyage to the Andamans. A shiver passed over my entire body as I remembered it. And my elder brother was to be with me now, a thin, emaciated scare-crow of a man hiccoughing without rest or relief. We were both put in together.

Put in the cage of maniacs

The cage we were locked up in was packed full of lunatics. The insane in the Andamans were all being despatched to India by the same steamer. And in their company, we were bound for voyage to India and in the same cage with them! The lunatics were pouring forth foul abuses on one another and were crying aloud in turns. Some were holding their throats in the grip of their hands as if to throttle themselves. The man put in charge of these madmen was one of themselves, who had recovered from that ailment. He used to hammer them all one by one. There was not even moving space for us two in this medley. And my brother was burning with fever and so emaciated in body, and he was herded among this pack.

What the madmen saw and spoke they believed for the time being as gospel truth. Some imagined that the mice were running all over their body and mounting up their chests. Some believed that all the people around were shouting out abuse towards them, and they would wake up at night, sit on the neighbour's chest, each one of them, and were about to belabour them with fisticuffs. Others were rolling pell-mell in their own vomits and urine. And we planted ourselves in their midst!

Who are mad, whom can you call mad?

For a moment, I could not help asking myself the question: Who is really mad and who is not? How do we know that what our senses apprehend is really the truth? Perhaps, what the senses of these madmen perceive may be the reality! On the side of the sane as on the side of the insane, the senses alone constitute the witness. And someone's sense alone is to determine that the other sense reports correctly. If the senses of us all were like the senses of these lunatics, we should have felt like them the mice running over our bodies. Why then should we take it that we are right? Perhaps, they may be right and we, seated in the midst of their vomiting and discharges, are deluded that we are in that foul and dirty place! For aught we know, we are mad and they are in their senses!

These musings gave me a shock. In the whirring noise of the rolling steamer, in those offals around me, in the obscene chatter of the lunatics thereby, and in the fetid and oppressive atmosphere of the place, I felt my life choking within me. I had often the fear and the feeling that this philosophic reverie may be the first intimation of lunacy creeping over my being and under it things visible may be rapidly melting away into illusion.

I felt the weakness of my shattered nerves at the time, as I had never felt them during the ten years of my life in prison. The weak nerves were due to that life, no doubt, but I felt it overwhelmingly in the steamer and at that moment as I had never experienced them before.

I appealed and protested to the officers on board the steamer to remove us from that place. There was a part of the steamer occupied by other Indian passengers bound for India, and they also interceded on our behalf. Their efforts and chiefly the persuasion of one, who shall remain unnamed, secured for both of us seats in the other half of the compartment, and somewhat detached from the space allotted to the lunatics.

But there was no breeze on that side. There were other prisoners carried by the same steamer to India and among them were some consumptive, dacoits and robbers. These convicts were accommodated on the deck so that they might get fresh air to breathe. My brother, who was more sick than anyone of them, had to rot in the cage on the lower deck—the cellar of the ship as it were—and in the cage I have already described. He was consumptive, his body was burning with fever, and I suffered from hard breathing due to chronic bronchitis, and we two were placed in that stuffy atmosphere.

Again, I appealed for fresh air; again I wrote to them that we needed very badly some fresh air to breathe in.

From the following day, a sort of ventilator was improvised to let down fresh air from the deck above two times during the day. A heavy gunny bag was suspended from the top downwards open at both ends, from which air passed downwards from the deck above. Later on, we were taken on the deck, under guard, for half-an-hour everyday to sit there and inhale fresh air.

The passengers on the deck and officers, at times, came in the cellar below to have a talk with us on the sly. The Indians among them were full of sympathy for us, even some Europeans treated us with respect. One educated Anglo-Indian gave me a living proof of it by presenting me a copy of my favourite book, "Thomas A Kempis' 'Imitation of Christ' ", which he asked me to cherish as a keep sake from him. They sent us by private arrangement good food to eat. I sent back out of it soda-water bottles, ice, and sweetmeat as not wanted by me. Some of them would force us to accept gifts in money, which we thankfully refused. I told them, that we were sure to be back in prison in India where we had no use for money. I distributed the sweetmeat among our fellow-passenger—the lunatics on board.

At night, my brother would narrate to me the story of his prison life. I left India for England in 1906. And from that date till fourteen years after, we were not in one room for a single day or night, so that we could talk together and exchange our thoughts. He told me how the movement of Abhinav Bharat had spread in the country after I had left for England, the names of members enrolled in it; how he happened to be arrested; how he was persecuted by the police to force from him the information necessary to round up all of them; how he breathed not a word about them and their whereabouts; how, at last, he had fainted under the torture, so on and so forth. They tried to get out from him information about conspiracies in Maharashtra and Bengal, but they failed. I heard that thrilling narrative with rapt attention.

While on that steamer, I constantly remembered the friends I had left behind in the Andamans! And the thought brought home to me the void in my life that their separation had made. I often had the yearning that I should go back to the Andamans and meet them! Oh, for the touch of a vanished hand!

On the fifth day, as I was seated on the deck for half-an-hour's daily draught of fresh air, I saw a fortified wall right in front of me. A fellow-passenger told me that we were almost in India and the fortified wall was its boundary. I startled. The fortress of India. The embankment, sighting for which I had kept my body and soul together during all the hard years I had passed in the Andamans, was right in front of me and I was soon to be landed on it! This was Mother India, whom I was seeing again with my eyes. Her holy feet I was touching with my head. In this very life, I was seeing and touching them. I turned round to my brother and ejaculated, "Dear brother, behold our dear Bharat once again! Behold her feet washed by the blue waters of the sea around."

We both got up from our seats full of adoration and worship. We folded our hands with reverence and devotion. We felt a thrill passing through us, and we uttered the following prayer:

"Victory to the Goddess of Freedom."

"Vande Mataram!"

□

12
Lock-up at the Alipore Jail

As we alighted from the steamer and touched the port at Calcutta, we were put in the lock-up at the Alipore Jail. The fear that I had felt on leaving the Andamans in the morning had but proved too true. My brother and I were put in different cells. Wearing our prison garments and holding our bedding under the armpit and our pots and pans in one hand, we were both marching together like thieves directed by our escort of sepoys, when my elder brother was directed along a side passage by the sepoy in charge, and I was taken in different direction by another. Then I felt that I and my brother were parted for good one from the other.

I heard him coughing hard, as he was being moved away from me, and for a good long time after. Wearing his long coat of coarse wool and carrying his bed under the pain. "Whatever will happen to him? Who will care for him?"—that was what kept me thinking. When he turned into the side passage, I felt that he had not merely left me, but that he was taking the road to death while leaving me back on the road of life, and that I was having the last sight of him.

I cast my glance to have the last look of him, and walked silently on, though, within me, I was crying for the loss. I was taken to a lonely room in the prison's wing, which was entirely vacated for me, and I was locked up therein. How sad and woebegone I felt then!

Along with the sepoys appointed to keep guard over me, there used to come a warder, who was convicted for fourteen years' transportation for life, but was promoted to the place of the warder after serving only three years of that sentence and had, thus, become relatively a free man. How I envied him for that freedom! I had served my term of nearly twelve years and all while in solitary confinement, and had not been free from restrictions of prison life yet. Nor was I relieved of hardships bound up with that life. On the other hand, they threatened to be all the more oppressive now. I was standing near the door holding its bars. The evening was passing into darkness and night. A sepoy was speaking something in an undertone. I gathered from one remark in that talk a partial proof of the foolishness that had run rampant in the politics of the day. Expressing his own notion of political agitation in Calcutta and other part of the country, he had remarked, "We are going to have Swaraj in two months. For, a powerful Yogi of the name of Gandhi has begun his fight with the Government. The British are helpless against him. For, a bullet shot does not hurt him. If put in prison, he knows how to come out of it. Such superhuman powers he possesses. He vanishes from his cell and is seen standing beyond the outer wall. Such is the magic he wields. This has happened several times. Mahatma Gandhi had gone into prison several times, and, time-after-time, after short sentences, he had been let off." This fact had reflected itself in the mind of this man and in the minds of several persons like him in this queer fashion. I said to the sepoy smilingly, "What you say is correct. For when the Mahatma is seen standing outside the prison wall and near its gate, it is precisely the time when he is released after running his sentence. He thinks of coming out and showing himself on the day when the Government lets him out of the prison."

A young Chinaman was later put in a cell near my own on the charge of selling cocaine. He danced, sang and frolicked for he imagined that within two days, he was to be free. I had not the good fortune like him of cherishing that hope.

Does a shot wound you?

The Chinaman knew the name of Sun-Yat-Sen. As I talked to him, I knew that he was not unfamiliar with my name. He could not believe his eyes when I told him that I was that Savarkar he had heard of. How could a big man be contained in the ordinary cell of a prison! His idea of a big man was that he must be a man of abnormal size. Ordinary people have always similar notion of greatness and when they see that the great man before them does not come up to their notion of him, they are often shocked and disillusioned. So, the Chinaman put me the question, "Does a gunshot pierce your body?" I answered, "No doubt, it will." And a deep disappointment was visible on his face.

Another sepoy asked me, "How many days and nights were you

swimming in the sea?" Of course, he meant at Marseilles. I answered, "What of days and nights? I swam, only for ten minutes before I reached the shore across." This reply gave a rude shock to his admiration for me, and to the miraculous powers he attributed to me. If I had bragged and lied to him, he would not have received any shock, but the barest truth that I told him seemed to put him out. My habit of reporting correctly what happened at Marseilles had lost me many friendships in life and their reverence for me.

Within a week, I was despatched from Calcutta elsewhere. I did not know to what prison I was being taken. In the train, I had the same experience that I had on my way from the Silver Jail to Port Blair. People used to put in my compartment fruit and newspapers from station to station and quietly went away. Sometime, they would gather in large crowds to have a look at me. From the scenes I witnessed as I passed through, I could not help thinking that the news of my departure from Calcutta must have been communicated abroad by wire. As our train reached Nagpur and beyond, I saw newspapers with big headlines announcing my release from the Andamans and expressing their joy for the event. I also saw leaders and articles written upon it. A person sitting on a bench behind me in the same compartment had held a newspaper open and was reading it. He held it deliberately in a manner that I may also be able to see it. The writing was in Marathi and the Anglo-Indian officer in charge could not make any head or tail of the writing. The impression I gathered from what I read in the newspaper was that the report indicated that I would be released within a week. But I knew how the matter stood at the time. The gentleman in question was travelling by the same compartment out of deep sympathy for me, and helped me the best he could, without being noticed by the officer-in-charge. He read the news items aloud that I could follow him.

The Anglo-Indian officers in charge gave me no trouble on the way and, at last, I reached Bombay. Our train reached Nasik at night, as I learnt from the words 'Nasik', 'Nasik' falling upon my ears. The shutters of my compartment had already been let down and I was seated in the centre between officers on either side. In the next compartment some passengers from Nasik got in. Twelve years had passed since. I had left Nasik and now I was passing it in a train! A new generation had grown up during the interval, and who was there that could know and recognise me after such a long interval? And yet the word 'Nasik' itself raised such a flood, tide of thoughts in my mind. So many send-offs and entertainments on that very station; journeys to college and back, and packets of fried grains mixed together; watermelons, faces of friends lit up with joy, friends who had come on the station to see me off to England, and their tears of leave-taking; their cries of "Victory to the Goddess of Freedom"; and now their transformation into prisoners in fetters; and some of them sent to the gallows—these pictures passed rapidly before my mind not unlike the moving pictures of today in a cinematograph.

In Bombay, I was put straightaway on a steamer. At the end of the voyage, I was again locked up in jail at about ten o'clock at night.

The Jail at Ratnagiri

I can no more describe in detail and one after another my experiences in the jail at Ratnagiri. Circumstances prevent me from doing it. The main reason for my reticence is that they are very recent matters and concern a jail in our own province. I shall finish the whole by stating what I have to say about the matter in the briefest outline.

The first two or three weeks in the jail at Ratnagiri passed away very badly for me. In the Andamans during my last days I was given well-cooked food and milk along with it, which had helped improve considerably my digestion and my general constitution. I was just looking up and had recovered from serious illness. When sent to Ratnagiri jail, milk was denied to me, even in the small quantity that was allowed to me in the Andamans. And I had to fall back once again upon the usual ration of prison life, which was hard and ill-baked bread. This bad food had brought on continual illness to me for two years in the Andamans, and I was almost dying. The most experienced doctors had, therefore, prescribed for me milk and well-cooked food, as I have already told my reader in a previous chapter. But now my representation proved of no avail.

To add to my misery, I was kept here all alone, segregated from other prisoners and locked up in the solitary cell assigned to me. All the concessions granted to me after twelve years of imprisonment at Port Blair were now withdrawn. They had given me in the Silver Jail at the end of that period full clothing, freedom from hard labour, mere writing work to do, paper and pencil to write with, and liberty to mix with others. Here I was made to wear the prison uniform, which was given to me on the first day of my sentence, I had on my chest the iron plate marking the year of the completion of my sentence—1960—and I was put in solitary confinement. This change from the Andamans to Ratnagiri was so unbearable to me, I felt that I was made to start running my sentence from its very first day.

Again, I could get no news here of my elder brother. I thought that he must have been passing through the same ordeal as I. My condition here made me remember my friends in the Andamans with greater poignancy. The work given to me was that of cotton spinning. Not being habituated to it, I could not finish it in time. I was not allowed to read and I found time dull and heavy.

The last impulse of suicide

You may wonder, O Reader, but every moment in this prison was an agony of mind. For twelve long years—nay, since the time I went to England—life had been for me a series of unexpected, unendurable mishaps and dangers, a continuous torture to my body and soul, with the result that my mind had been stretched on a rack all the time, and my nerves were completely shattered. And this new and additional strain on them was like the proverbial straw. I feared that it would end in utter collapse. One day, I felt so dejected that my second thoughts could not come to my rescue. How long should I bear such life? What was the use of such a life? It was no use rotting thus now. Suddenly, in this mood of mind, I got up. High up in that cell was a barred window as in the jail of the Andamans. I thought out in my mind how to reach my hand to that window and how to put an end to my life by hanging myself by a rope to its bars. The thread of my life was to be snapped by straining it from the bars of the window above my head. The cord tied to the one was to break the thread tied to the other. My mind was overcast with complete darkness. And every moment that passed deepened the gloom and added to the darkness.

I am writing these pages in imprisonment at Ratnagiri. Only within call from that place is the jail where I experienced the most tragic moment of my life, very similar to one or two experiences during my fourteen years' stay in the Andamans. This was the last and the darkest of these moments.

But it was the day when this last fit came upon me. And I had to wait for the night to act accordingly. And during the interval, I gradually recovered the usual balance of my mind. I argued with myself as follows, "In the Andamans, from Indu Bhushan to Professor Parmanand, you had dissuaded several of the Bengali, the Punjab and the Sikh political convicts, who had suffered as many agonies as you do now, from committing suicide. For the same reason, you must desist today from putting an end to your own life. According to your own precept, you must exact cent percent compensation for such an act. You must, at least, kill one enemy of the country as an exchange for parting with your own life. But is it possible now for you to act up to that precept?"

The night came and I spent the whole of it in reviewing my whole life and its outcome. I was completely absorbed in that task. I scanned minutely with as much detachment and concentration of mind as was possible for me, the steps I had taken one-by-one towards reaching the supreme ideal of my life, and other minor goals subservient to it, and dictated by particular circumstances through, which I had to pass. I definitely visualised my duty in relation to them, and I outlined the course I was to follow in the light of that duty.

I must bear it all

Therefore, I decided to suffer all, to endure all as a supreme national duty in the situation of the moment. I was also to continue doing what little I could, while bearing all that I could not possibly avoid. What cannot be cured must be endured.

That was my final resolve. From the following day, I took up the thread of the poem that I had begun in similar conditions of loneliness years ago, and I planned the writing of the story of my life from the day of my arrest in England down to my removal to Ratnagiri. I brought together all its threads in my mind and working out its outline in my mind, I divided it into parts and chapters and headings and committed the facts, recalling them, one by one, to memory, as if I was immediately putting them down on paper. I repeated the process page by page, concentrating my mind fully on the events as I recalled them. I, then, recorded them, with a piece of pointed brick, on the walls and stones of my prison house using all my leisure from my usual work for that purpose, and according to the opportunity I got for executing the task. These jottings of the principal topics in my story occupied me for successive months, and I accomplished the work full of zest and earnestness.

This work is the outcome of that task

Those writings on the wall and those jottings from memory have given birth to these printed pages. During the three months I was busy with the task, a great change came about in my circumstances. I got better food to eat. The Calcutta weekly, 'The Capital', had written an article connecting my name with the German plot of the submarine Emden. My brother having threatened the paper with prosecution, it apologised and withdrew its statement. This affair had lasted for a few days since my arrival at Ratnagiri, and I also received parcels sent to me by members of my family.

The trouble of the Khilafat

Some convicts from Sindh and other parts of the country, involved in the Non-Cooperation Movement and the Khilafat agitation, both Hindus and Mussulmans, came to the Ratnagiri jail soon after my arrival there. Their notions of the Khilafat movement, of Hindu-Muslim unity and of politics in general struck me as vitiated and eccentric. And I had to carry on endless discussion with them on these topics and vigorously attack their misconceptions. A few days after, I arranged in that jail for talks and for weekly lectures and meetings on the line I had followed in the Andamans. We had been together at Ratnagiri for a year and a half. When I happened to meet them for the first time, I happened to hear one of them shouting: that "The Mussulmans had not done the atrocities in Malabar that were being fathered upon them." Another friend echoed loudly: "It did not matter in the least if they had done them; whatever had happened should be treated as dead past; Hindus may convert themselves to Islam; what mattered most was Swaraj and it must be won." There was no end to the perversion of the definitions of truth and non-violence among them. I may narrate here an episode of a political convict in this prison as a specimen of the mentality of almost all the non-cooperating and the Khilafatist patriots I came across in this jail during that time.

The confusion of Gandhism

We used the devices that we had employed in the Andamans to get news in the jail at Ratnagiri. We could, thus, procure scraps or newspaper from outside, carried to us through dustbins or by prisoners sent on work outside the prison. My friends among the non-cooperators often used to read these scraps as I read them also. Twice or thrice some of them were found reading them while moving about in the open courtyard. One of us warned them against this practice, as we were forbidden to read newspapers in prison, and if noticed by officers, our secret would be out, and all means of getting them would be instantly stopped. To this a non-cooperator replied, "Do you mean to say that I should read this in secret? I am a non-cooperator. Whatever is done secretly is against the doctrine of truth and I will not do it." We did not argue the matter with him. We only stopped giving him any scrap of paper to read. He was in rage with us. And he told us that they were to report the matter the next day to the officer, telling him that they were smuggling newspapers in the jail in the same manner that some prisoners were smuggling tobacco. To hide a fact was sin, which no non-cooperator, as a follower of truth, would commit.

We told him that he knew when he was reading those scraps that he got them from a secret source. Why did he read them then if he felt that it went against his conception of truth? Why did he not say he should have nothing to do with such a course? And was it not a betrayal of confidence on his part to tell the officer the name of the prisoner who had rendered that service to him? If this were truth, then Narendra Goswami must be worshipped by him as a sincere non-cooperator.

No doubt, the man was taken aback by this counterargument. He did not act as he had threatened. But he kept on maintaining that getting news in a secret manner was a sin, that founders of secret societies like Mazzini were all sinners. He asserted that whatever a non-cooperator did, he did openly, and there was no secrecy or one word behind his single action. He went about spinning long yarns on the subject.

One day, in order to make a fun of him, we adopted a plan just when we were dining together. The gentleman in question always managed to eat a 'chapati' by flattering the cook in charge, while all of us were being served at dinner with rice. On the day in question, while the gentleman was eating his 'chapati' as usual, one of us raised an alarm that the Superintendent was coming. The man instantly concealed the 'chapati' under a dinner plate near him and began quietly eating his rice. There was a roar of laughter raised around him, and all began cross-questioning him. "O, fellow, is it not a sin to conceal the 'chapati' as you have done it? Is it following truth, according to your article of the creed, to eat the 'chapati' stealthily?" Another answered on his behalf, of course, ironically, "A non-cooperator lover of truth, does not regard it as a violation to eat a small 'chapati' even stealthily, to feed his stomach. For, that is an act of necessity, while your getting news surreptitiously and reading it is violation of truth as harmful to the national cause." Surely, it is no cowardice to eat forbidden food in order to live; that is not a lie or an evil act. To lie for the sake of a nation is, surely enough, an unpardonable sin, and an act of down right cowardice.

I would not have referred to the story if it were an isolated and exceptional incident. But I found this attitude but too common among the non-cooperators and Khilafatists I met in this jail. Hence, I found it worthwhile to mention it in this narrative.

That they may take in correctly the situation in Malabar, I spoke to them in several lectures on that momentous topic, dealing at large with the whole history of the question. Our friends in that prison were dead against my *Sangathan* movement. I convinced them of their inconsistent attitude in the light of the unity they were working after. For, the larger unity was impossible so long as we were weak and divided among ourselves as Hindus. As to discussion on politics, there was no end to it here.

The *Shuddhi* Movement at Ratnagiri

Before long I discovered in the jail at Ratnagiri that the Pathan and the Muslim convicts sent there from Bombay were practising the same methods of converting the Hindu juvenile offenders to Islam that were current in the Andamans. The officers of the prison had no inkling about the matter. As I knew their ways and means of doing this business, I at once forestalled it. I started the *Shuddhi* movement to reclaim such converts for Hinduism. Two old prisoners from U.P. and some juveniles I reconverted into Hindus. I gave all the monetary help they needed. In course of time, a high dispute arose over the matter. The controversy was carried up to the Superintendent of the jail. There were at the time too many Muslim prisoners in the jail including Pathans and Sindhis. They made things hot for the Maratha warders and their superior officers. I had to join battle with them. Some of them were my immediate neighbours in that jail and they threatened to give me a sound thrashing. I give here one instance in point to show how they harassed me.

Some of them started proclaiming "baang" at dawn just to annoy their Hindu brethren. All of them were worse characters and notorious thieves and robbers, and they never did their *namaz* and never uttered the name of Allah. Yet they shouted out early in the morning inviting Muslims for prayer and disturbed the sleep of the rest of us. It became a great nuisance and when the Superintendent remonstrated with them they pleaded that it was a matter of religion and he dare not object to it. The superior officers could do nothing to stop them. Then I tried my own remedy against the nuisance. I took in hand two of the worst Hindu convicts, the ringleaders of dacoits and thieves in that jail. One of them had passed his whole life there. Four or five times he had been heavily sentenced on charges of theft and had, at last, come to regard this prison as his home. He had lost his one tooth and was advanced in age. I tutored him to utter the name of Ram with a loud voice so soon as the Muslims began to cry "baang". He sang couplets from Tulsidas and in uttering Ramanama, raised his voice louder than the Muslims. The warders would rebuke him sternly when I would intervene and say, "Why should you object to his prayer? Either stop all of them or let everyone be free to pray as he likes." If a Mussulman prisoner was found doing his *namaz* at night, the Hindu followed suit with his bhajan. The Mussulmans were full of fury but they were helpless to prevent us. As they disturbed the sleep of the Hindus, the Hindus paid them back in their own coin. So the whole dispute ended by itself. One nuisance cancelled the other. What punishment could not stop, counter-*goondas*im had silenced. I silenced a Khilafatist editor-prisoner by a similar counter-move. He used to touch water for the Hindus on the plea that Muslims were as much human beings as they, I entirely agreed with him on the point and I called upon an untouchable and scavenger to dip his pot and take water from a vessel of water for the Muslims. And the Khilafatist, who was preaching broad humanitarian principle, at once went at the untouchable and would not touch the water as being unholy for the *namaz*. When I had exposed them two or three times, they quietly took their water from a Hindu water-carrier and stopped touching the water reserved for the Hindus.

Riot in the Ratnagiri Jail

During this period, a great quarrel arose between the insolent Pathans and the cunning Sindhi Mussulmans on the one side, and the

Jail Superintendent on the other. The point in dispute was about the strict enforcement of prison discipline. And the matter came to such a pass that these *goondas* decided to break into a riot to checkmate the Superintendent. In the riot they had conspired to beat all the Hindu prisoners in the jail, including the sepoys, the warders and the political convicts like us, who were leaders of *Sangathan* in that jail. One day after our usual meal was over, the Mussulmans suddenly kicked up a row and began attacking the Hindus. Having already warned the Hindus beforehand against this onslaught, they were ready to meet it though it had come on sudden. Some Hindu warders got a beating to the point of bleeding, but the Mussulman *goondas* did not go unscathed. They also got their share of sound hammering. They began to leave out and to flourish their sticks and fisticuffs, and in order to attack us sought to force their way inside the chawls. I stood ready near my room to meet them and all along incited the Hindus prisoners to take the offensive against them. In the meanwhile, somebody sounded the alarm bell. A regular fight ensured between the two sides along with the usual cries to accompany it. The Superintendent came on the same followed by a posse of soldiers. He threatened to give order for shooting. The Mussulman *goondas* were in a fright. They were all rounded up. Most of them had received sound thrashing from the Hindus and were bathed in blood. Prosecutions were launched, trials followed, and the rioters were duly punished. The Hindu warders, who had saved their fellow-prisoners and themselves from the attack and had fought on the side of law and order, received due meed of praise.

This incident and its sequel made those who were considering me an outcast because I was the leader of the *Shuddhi* movement, converted to that movement. And soon we succeeded in converting a Mussulman to Hindu faith. Of course, for this sacrilege, the Mussulmans dragged me into a suit. After the usual argument and counter-argument, the court decided against forcible conversions on either side. Thus ended the Mussulman's game of converting Hindu lads to their faith. I was always on my guard against those who had designed against my life. The prisoners who had before this worked for the Khilafat movement as its partisans and had subscribed freely to its funds, now became champions of the *Shuddhi* and the *Sangathan* movements. Their eyes were opened to the truth of the matter by what they had witnessed with their own eyes in this prison. And as they began at last to examine everything through the insight given to them by the *Sangathan* movement, their politics changed from non-cooperation into responsive co-operation. Out of this jail and free, they became in their respective provinces staunch supporters of Hindu *Sangathan*.

As in the Andamans so at Ratnagiri, I went on with my work of instruction for the ordinary prisoners in that jail. Some of these I taught myself. I gave from my own purse prizes and scholarships to encourage them to read good books. The prison library had no books worth the name. I petitioned to the Bombay Government for the sanction of books and at length succeeded in getting from them a grant of five hundred rupees for the purchase of books for the library. I made a list of books, and I sent the list through the Superintendent for approval by the educational department of the Government. And after the list was approved of by that body, the books were at once purchased and kept in the library. The prisoners developed so great fondness for reading them that during the course of a year and a half the Superintendent had to make a special mention of it in his report as the main cause of the remarkable decline in that jail of the propensity of the prisoners to quarrel, fight and come to blows.

A public holiday for the Muslims on the day of Eid was marked in the jail by the permission to them for general prayer. The prayer was led on such an occasion by a moulvi from outside. The Christian prisoners had a similar privilege on their great holidays. Only the Hindus were without this right. The political convicts, therefore, petitioned to the authorities that the Hindu prisoners be granted a similar concession to celebrate their public holidays. The Government granted the permission asked for, and we decided to celebrate the Gokulashtami day as a great Hindu holiday. We fixed upon holding a *kirtan* that day, and the Government did not object to it. They gave us things to eat suitable to the fast that we observed and the kirtan was done in the jail as a public function.

The practice overthrown

As has been already pointed in another place, the manner of sending prisoners to answer the call of nature in prison-administration was extremely barbarous and highly objectionable. There was no partition and no door to the latrines arranged in a line, and the prisoners were made to sit down rubbing shoulders with one another. There was no roof overhead either in the rains or in the hot seasons. No water was allowed to be taken into the latrine. All were to get up after the function and to go to a water-tap at a distance to wash and clean their parts. The political prisoners agitated for reform in these matters with the result that this hideousness and dirt disappeared for good and the prisoners began to lead a clean and disciplined life. There was improvement in food and the general mode of living, and order was strictly maintained, as laid down by the prison regulations.

One more thing was being carried out in the jail at Ratnagiri. It had remained unfinished in the Andamans. When I knew that I could no longer do any national work I had resolved, as the reader may remember, to finish a poem and had begun composing it in my own mind. But as other work grew upon my hands, this project lay in abeyance. At Ratnagiri, I resumed the task and completed the poems I had proposed to write. I gathered together the smaller poems previously composed by me. I wrote longer poems and gave a complete notion of what I meant by 'Hinduism'. Some of the writings I had already despatched home from the Andamans. My brother brought out from these writings complete editions of three poems which were.

Kamala, Saptarshi and Gomantak

These three poems were published anonymously. The fourth was a miscellany of my minor poems, which had also gone to the press but it contained so many misprints as I was not on the spot to see it through, and I stopped its publication altogether. The miscellany was entitled 'Virahoswasa', the sighs of separation. I had to withdraw the complete edition of that book from the market. 'Kamala', 'Saptarshi' and 'Mahasagara' were portions of the epic I had contemplated to write. These survive as independent poems themselves, but the main tree, of which they were to be branches, is not yet even in the process of creation. It has been so with me—work that is undertaken under duress is often part finished and part destroyed.

After the completion of these poems, I wrote my work on Hinduism in English, which my friend Mr. Kelkar of Nagpur was kind enough to publish.

In the early days of my stay in the Ratnagiri jail, I was not given a single book to read. After a time, I got the works of Ramdas to read—of these 'Dasabodha', and miscellaneous poems that I had already perused in my younger days. But as my edition of Ramdas contained only these, I read them over and over again in the jail. Later on, they gave me other books and also writing material so that I could do both reading and writing to my satisfaction. I read many great books from beginning to end during this period, like the life of Prithviraj, Puranas, like 'Bhavishya Purana', and Vedic India by Das.

One day, I casually enquired after the health of my elder brother when I learnt that his condition was serious. My brother, after being separated from me at Calcutta, was put in the jail at Bijapur. My younger brother had gone to see him, when he was told that he could enter the prison and see his elder brother only if he would change his Khadi garments.

My brother, of course, refused to accept the condition as highly insulting to himself. He carried the matter up to the Governor and got it cancelled. My elder brother suffered terribly in the jail at Bijapur. He was confined in a dark, damp and deserted room all by himself. I heard, later on, that a political convict had been seized with madness in that very jail. The room had a very bad reaction on my brother's mind and he was removed thence to Ahmedabad. Here he suffered less from solitariness, but he received no treatment and nursing for his growing disease. And, at last, his hardy constitution and his equally strong patience broke down under its terrible inroads. He was then removed from the jail to the prison hospital. We got information about it through the daring of a political convict in that prison. So, my younger brother visited the place and found my brother almost on his death-bed. But his fortitude was remarkable. Nothing could shake it.

When I learnt the news, I felt definitely that my elder brother was passing away without being helped, that he was slipping from our hands. Well, all of us were sojourners here and all had to leave the place sometime. Life was no better than a halt in a caravansari for a day or two. But my brother was dying inch by inch, having suffered and toiled and wasted himself for others, and there was none beside him at the last hour to put an affectionate dropful of water in his mouth. It was the jail that had admitted him, and it was the jail that was swallowing him up.

Alas! I thought, it was the enemy that, at long last, had done him to death! He did not kill him with one stroke, but by a process of slow torture. These had finished him. I could not contain myself. I could hardly breathe, so overwhelming was the feeling of it all.

At that bitter moment, as was the habit with me, I sat up and composed myself. I maintained a quiet frame of mind, and recollected myself. And then I put to myself the question, "Where was the use of all this fretting and storm? My brother dies of hardships imposed upon him by our enemies. He is a victim to the enemies of our country! What help was there now but lamentation over individual loss? Can I avenge myself for it? Nothing but wailing and enquiry!"

I had made up my mind as soon as I was free to avenge myself on those who had victimised my brother, and then I would celebrate his death anniversary. That would be an example to others to do likewise. I felt calm in my mind after I had taken this solemn vow. The perturbation was gone and I was my former self again.

But Baba was released

A few days after this incident, news came that my brother had been let off from the prison. I was full of joy at the news. He got his discharge but had to be brought home in a senseless condition. But that was of no account. I thought the Government had, at last, saved the expenses over his funeral, by setting him free. And the members shall have at least the consolation of paying for it when he dies in the midst of them. Because that was also a matter of doubt. Hence, his release was better than his death in that jail, anyway. It was not release only. It was a rebirth for him from death-in-life in the prison. By the grace of God and as good fortune for the county that lover of his country began gradually to improve in health, and a wave of joy passed over the whole country.

That very year, I believe—though I do not remember correctly at the moment—the Congress session at Coconada adopted a resolution demanding my release. The resolution was moved from the chair and was passed **nem con.** It was a moral gain for all the efforts of my younger brother and for similar agitation of patriots in full sympathy with all the political convicts in the country. I was transferred from the Andamans to Ratnagiri in 1921 and in 1923, I was removed from that place to the Yeravada Jail. That is at least my impression. I cannot be too sure about the dates. I had no opportunity and no time to check the dates. I must say about the whole narrative that there may be discrepancies, here and there about the dates, though in general they may be pretty accurate.

Meeting with friends from the Andamans

This was my second visit to Yeravada Jail. First, I was put there in 1910 and for the second time now in 1923. In those days, the prison was full of convicts, sentenced in the Mulshi Satyagraha case. They came and they went, all of them political prisoners. Some were punished with whipping. Those who had remained behind used to tell me of their severe ordeal in the Yeravada Jail. There were in it prisoners hailing from Sindh and Dharwar who had taken part in the Non-Cooperation and the Khilafat movements. Hindus and Muslims, political convicts, they were all of them. The most wonderful fact of them all was that I met there my friends from the Andamans, whom the Government of India had ordered back to India. Sikhs of the Lahore case and several others on transportation for life to the Andamans I met in the prison. I was strictly forbidden from intercourse with any of them, though I managed secretly to see them, and it gave me as much joy as I would have felt to meet the members of my own family and my near relatives. With tearful eyes, we greeted one another. In the Andamans, we had suffered together. Anyone of us could have won freedom in a day by the betrayal of our friends by giving away the secrets of our society, or by putting the noose round the neck of fellow convicts. But God had saved us from such evil temptation. We revolutionaries had stood our ground bearing tortures as painful as a row of elephants pricked in the head by the good of their rider. They stand rooted to the spot under its severest blows, so we stood up firm and unshaken, to all the mental and physical pain inflicted upon us. We could not take a step forward. We would not go a step backward, so we stood obstinately where we were planted. No doubt, we were cornered and at bay. And all around us were hurled "slings and arrows" of misfortune. The newcomers—the non-cooperators and the Khilafatists—looked down upon these seasoned soldiers, these fighters and revolutionaries, as sinners, because they were members of secret societies, and conspirators. The non-cooperators and the Khilafatists had not seen even two years of prison-life. They were raw, vainglorious men, and they bragged of their suffering before those who had passed through ten years or more of transportation for life in the Silver Jail of the Andamans—the brave Sikhs who had never winced under the severest hardships! They vaunted of their worthless 'Satyagraha' and of their short imprisonment for it before these revolutionaries and presumed to despise them!

I speak from the top of trees

I began here to criticise severely all these followers of Gandhi that their eyes might see clearly. I put collyrium in their eyes. They hated the name of Hindu *Sangathan* as detrimental to the nation. I denounced fiercely these honest but perverse notions. I would go up a tree, others would gather in the courtyard opposite, and political prisoner would keep a watch occupying strategic positions around them. Thus we carried on discussion on politics from day to day. I was then transferred to the courtyard itself, when every alternate day regular meetings were held and discussions carried on to disillusion these novices of their strange notions on politics. I followed the same method here I had adopted in the Andamans, holding meetings, giving lectures and arranging discussions. Gradually, all of them joined in them. Winning Swaraj by Charaka, supporting the Khilafat movement as the duty of the Hindus, and ridiculous definition of non-violence, I exploded them all by invincible logic and by an appeal to history. And these honest young patriots were at last won over to our side from their jejune politics, and from their inexperience and ignorance of the world around them. I made them follow the line of politics and political action that we had laid down for our national soldiers in the Andamans. And these non-cooperators now began to adore the very Sikhs and other revolutionaries they had despised before. They confessed that theirs was the real courage and self-sacrifice in the cause of the nation.

These newcomers and patriots had false notions instilled in their minds about Hindu Sangathan, and they had opposed them in all sincerity and zeal. I argued with them, informed them, talked to them, I explained to them the principles behind our agitation until, at last, they had become the staunch supporters of our work.

Major Murray

My removal to Yeravada synchronised with the appointment of Major Murray as an Inspector of the jail at Yeravada. He was Superintendent of the Silver Jail when I was in the Andamans. And he rose from that position to be the Inspector General of Prisons in Punjab. And now he had come to Yeravada. I cannot say if he had been appointed to the place deliberately while I was there, or it was a mere coincidence. It was a thick rumour that he had been sent there as he knew me well, and all about me in the past, and that he was to report to the Government his opinion about my release or non-release. Whatever it may be, all political convicts in Yeravada jail welcomed his appointment. For, Major Murray had good insight into human nature and was of free and open disposition. It was during his time as Superintendent in the Andamans that political convicts had gone on strike several times and as such he had fully gauged their strength and temper as a class. He had always acceded to our just demands and had never wielded his authority or enforced discipline to the breaking point. He knew when to yield and never let matters to be carried to extremes. As that was his policy in the Andamans, it rejoiced us to see him rule over Yeravada.

Chief of the Quinine Depot

As soon as he took office, he removed me from my cell and appointed me as a chief in charge of the quinine factory in that jail. He gave me permission to teach boys and other workers in that factory. I began to arrange and add to the library at Yeravada as I had done at Ratnagiri. I removed the worm-eaten books from the boxes, which were in the library at Yeravada and replaced them by new ones. I made a complete list of books I needed and got permission of the Government to purchase them for the library. Thus, I had arranged to stock in the Yeravada library the choicest books in Marathi and Hindi languages. I do not know if the books I had ordered had actually come in that library, for I did not stay at Yeravada long after my proposal.

Shuddhi at Yeravada

Along with other activities in that jail, I also started the *Shuddhi* movement there. I would only mention one instance as a specimen of that work. One of the officers here hailed from Madras and dressed himself in tip-top European style. He was a Christian and was proud of his changed religion. He was the doctor of our prison. We had long discussions on the subject and, at last, he was inclined to be reconverted to Hinduism. But he was a married man and had Christian wife. While young the gentleman had dined once or twice with a Christian and so Hindu Brahmins had ex-communicated him. All these facts he had revealed to me frankly in the process of our conversations and discussions with the result that he had decided to become a Hindu. But what was to be done after his conversion about a wife to set up a home for him? His Christian wife had almost deserted him. He went straight with a note from me to my younger brother in Bombay. And the Hindu Missionary

Society arranged for his reconversion. In Bombay he happened to know a nurse who was a Christian like himself. She agreed to be a Hindu along with him. She was an unmarried women, so both agreed to be united in wedlock, the woman in need of a husband and the man in need of a wife. So, their *Shuddhi* and marriage took place in Bombay on the same day under the auspices of the Hindu Missionary Society. The doctor returned to Yeravada with his new wife dressed as a Hindu. With his religion he had left behind his European dress. Instead of a hat he had put on a turban and dhoti and had displaced the trousers. Verily he looked like a Poona Brahmin, when he appeared at Yeravada with his new dress. His doorstep was adorned with 'rangoli'. And the portraits of Ram and Krishna hung on his walls. The vermilion paste marked the forehead of the wife while the 'tilaka' shone on the brow of the husband.

The doctor put me the following question, "Mr. Savarkar, would you mind telling me what more I need to be distinguished as a Hindu?"

"Nothing more," I answered with a smile, "well, you may finish it with a 'puja' of Satyanarayana."

And he performed the puja. All the clerks, the peons and the villagers in Yeravada received invitations for the 'puja" and the 'prasad', and as I had already prepared their minds for it, they had all gone to his house for the occasion. The doctor, who was for twenty-five years out of the fold of Hinduism, now really felt that he was admitted back into it. And he wrote letters to that effect to his own people in Madras. I used to be informed many years after this incident that the man and his wife had made a happy home for themselves as converted Hindus.

Major Murray, our former Superintendent in the Andamans and now an Inspector in the Yeravada jail, often used to ask me what I was going to do in life after I had become a free man. I gave him always a set answer, and that was that it depended always on the circumstances I happened to be discharged in and which alone could shape my future course. The question and the answer never ended there but were invariably followed by a prolonged discussion about the future. And then I would conclude the whole argument with the proposition that if I were released unconditionally I would take my full part in the politics of the country. "What kind of politics?"—that was the question which inevitably followed. I had, then, to say that it also depended on circumstances of the hour. If the reforms were to bear good fruit and naturally lead to the further enlargement of powers granted to the people, I would be for responsive cooperation and work out my goal through the path of peace and constructive constitutional work. If a ban were put on me not to participate in politics for a few years, I would spend the years in other fields of work open to me. I told Major Murray that it was my duty as a follower of responsive cooperation to accept such conditions as would enable me to do better and larger work for my country than I was able to do during the years of imprisonment. I would be free thus to serve my mother country, and I would regurd it as a social duty.

This was not a new phase with me. I used to talk to the officers in the Andamans, when they discussed the matter with me in the same vein. But nothing, so far, had come out of these talks. And I naturally concluded that this discussion would follow the way of all previous conversations on the subject. I had entertained no hopes from the discussion. Of course, human being that I was, I had been exerting my utmost to get free. On the other hand, not banking upon fond hope, I went on with my day-to-day public work in the prison with such patience as I had at my command.

A meeting with Sir George Lloyd

One day when I was in the prison hospital for the treatment of acute pain in the stomach and indisposition, a trusted officer sent me word that Sir George Lloyd, the Governor of Bombay, was coming to see me along with two or three big officials during the course of that week.

The reader remembers the visit of the Home Member of the Government of India, Sir Reginald Craddock and the talk he had with me in the prison of the Andamans. But this had not solved the question of my freedom from that jail. I took it for granted that this visit would not help me in any way in that business. I put before the Governor of Bombay, in my meeting with him at Yeravada, pactically the same view that I had expressed several times before it and to several officers who had interviewed me on the subject of my release. All of them seemed to be dissatisfied with the conditions I had offered to accept. But the Governor, after he had heard me, expressed general satisfaction at what I had told him. Then we discussed together current politics. In that I expressed the same views that I had put down in writing, and had told orally several times and to several persons. I concerned in the following words, "I was compelled to be a revolutionary and a conspirator when I had discovered that there was no peaceful or constitutional method open to me to attain the goal I had in view. But if the present reforms prove to be useful for the furtherance of our hopes in a peaceful way, we shall very willingly turn to constitutional method and pursue gladly the constructive work on the principle of responsive cooperation. Revolutionaries as we were described to be, our policy was as much of responsive co-operation as that of those who swore by other methods. We will utilise to the full the present reforms in pursuance of that principle and with a similar object in view. National good was our sole objective and if peaceful means served that end, we had no reason to cling to our old ways."

But was this convincing enough for the Government concerned? Will it believe in our bona fides? What then were we to do in the matter?

Still, for a stipulated period, I agreed to take no part in politics, that is, in active, day-to-day politics. In prison, I could not, of course, do any Politics at all. But when outside I could do other kind of work, educational, religious and literary and serve my country in diverse fields. Generals, as prisoners of war, cannot conduct the war and come on the battlefield. They are let off on parole after signing the pledge like Lord Krishna, who agreed that he would not wield any arm during the continuance of the war. And it is considered no humiliation on their part to do so, and they consider it their duty to do so, in order that, later on, their services might be available to their nation by way of leading and guidance in other work.

Taking this view of the whole matter, I had advised political convicts in the Andamans to sign a similar pledge to avail themselves of the general amnesty, which had accompanied the new reforms. And hundreds of them had won their liberty by signing the pledge.

Hence, there was no objection for me to sign a pledge of enforced abstinence from current politics. A similar pledge could not obtain freedom for me in the past as they made too much of my past history and of my association in that past with active revolutionary movement in the country. And they had insisted that I should render a full account of them to the authorities. But I told the Governor of Bombay not to rake up the dead past, not to ask me any question about it. Let the dead past bury its dead, and the hatchet be buried along with it. Let him and let me talk of the future. The past had been filed and recorded once for all on either side. Let us think of the future. The Governor did not close the discussion after this categorical statement by me. He kept the topic of release open. He assured me finally that he would do his very best for my liberty on the condition of abstinence from active politics during a stipulated period of time and on condition that some years of my liberty shall be spent like a man on parole within a prescribed area. He added that he would place the whole matter before the coming Governor, Sir Leslie Wilson. With this definite promise to me, Sir George Lloyd bid me good-bye and left the prison along with the other officials who had accompanied him. He had treated me very cordially and had appreciative words for me during the course of the interview. I must say here that Major Murray had strongly supported the case for my release.

A lecture series on our Martyrs

Many days had passed since this interview, and I began to think that this was to be another tilting at the wind like similar and many experiences of the past, lost and vanishing into thin air.

I did not fail, however, to carry on my usual round of self-imposed tasks in this prison. I pursued them with a determined will. I have already narrated on an earlier page how the latest arrivals in this prison—the batch of non-cooperators and Khilafatists—were absolutely ignorant of the history of the revolutionary movements in the country and of the political upheaval following these movements. There were among the newcomers some sincere patriots fired by the desire to serve the country. I started a lecture series on the history of these movements, so that they might learn and profit by the knowledge. I gathered together all of them and expounded to them the meaning and implications of that term political unity, and also elaborated on the consolidation of free India. I gave them full scope for carrying on a debate on these momentous questions. Both Hindus and Mohomedans attended the lecture and took part in the discussion. Among the Muslim prisoners, there were some who happened to be distinguished leaders of the country. And Mahatma Gandhi himself was there beyond the adjoining wall. And consequently, prisoners over here, who often went and saw him, often conveyed to me his opinions on the subject. I never minced matters in attacking his gospel and method of non-cooperation as also in exposing the inside of the Khilafat movement if was mixed up with.

A lecture on Madanlal Dingra

The last of the lectures in that series fell on the last day of my stay at Yeravada. And the subject I chose for it was the life of Madanlal

Dingra. I had already spoken to them of other martyrs to our cause, of those of the Abhinav Bharat Mandal who had either died or had been sent to the gallows. The newcomers had began to appreciate the work of these dead heroes and to feel reverence for them. It was growing day to day till it had reached its height. Some fifty of them had come together in my room and on the verandah to hear me speak to them in that secret meeting. Men were posted at all points to be on the lookout for a possible visit by the officers of the jail. My remarks on the thrilling episodes in the life of Dingra made the political patriots, who heard me, feel the same thrill passing over their frames.

Just as I was in the heart of my subject, one of our men came to us and warned that the gate was being opened and someone was coming. The gathering instantly dispersed and each went his way as if nothing had happened. They had just reached their respective quarters when a sargent seemed to call me. He took me to the head office of the prison, a discussion began between me and the Superintendent about my release. I told him that I was fed up with such endless talk, and that he should inform me if there was any specific order about it, for it was all that really mattered. He said that he had received an order, in which were included all the conditions that I had accepted for my release from jail.

I retorted that I had mentioned the conditions all these years and I could not understand why the Government should make such a mountain out of them.

The Draft Statement

In a moment the Superintendent took out a sheet of paper and wrote on it the conditions of acceptance I had been proposing all these years, and along with it he handed over to me a written statement that he had received from the Government. I read them both. Referring to my letter in the "Echo of the Andamans", written in 1920 (See pages 88 and 89 of that book), I told him that I was willing to make a statement on that line, and that the statement from the Government had to be modified accordingly. I was told by the Superintendent to draft such a statement. He warned me not to introduce any radical changes in it, but just a few as would make the course smooth for my release. He expressed a wish that on no account should I let this rare opportunity slip from my hands.

I drew up my statement. I had added some sentences to clarify the original statement. The Superintendent, having found it too lengthy, abbreviated it. The words that I had introduced in my statement and the meaning thereof I have given in the book "Echo from the Andamans" at pages 88 to 93. The Superintendent assured me that they would be interpreted exactly in the sense I had used them. So, I agreed to the omission of a few sentences I had inserted in my statement. The statement was despatched to the proper authorities and I returned to my room in that prison.

Now the complexion of events seemed to have changed and I could almost say that before long I was going to be free. My friends in the prison and all others were beside themselves with joy. But I often reminded myself and them of the word 'almost', that I was almost sure that I would be free, and none should entirely depend upon it. In my life, I had been so many times disappointed so many times had hopes proved dupes!

□

13

The Last Night of My Sentence

5th January, 1924 was the last night of my imprisonment, of the sentence of transportation for life passed upon me. But I write it so definitely now. I could not say, so on the night that I was in the Yeravada jail. If the night was going to be the last night in that jail and if I had known it to be so, if it was to be the very last in the period of sentence passed upon me by the court, how I would have drawn a pleasant picture of the night that was to follow! At the same hour tomorrow, I would be stretching myself on a bed in a room with window all open to the light of the moon without, and without any warder patrolling along the corridor to disturb my sleep. And if that was not going to be my last night, well then, may it not be so, for some night was sure to be my last night in the prison, the night that will take me away from this world for good.

It was terribly cold that night. Though it was the month of January, we had a sharp shower of rain and we had no sufficient and warm clothing, no blankets to protect ourselves against that cold. Two coarse blankets were not enough to ward off the cold. And the clothing was altogether scanty and the shower of rain had added to the cold weather. Sprays of water began to pour in through the windows of my room, and sleep, in that condition, was impossible. Whatever clothes I had were wet all through. I put myself in a far-off corner of my room, folding up my body and wrapping the half-wet garments as close to it as I could. I kept on napping and dozing in that night till daybreak.

I had passed so many nights in prison in that condition, having my sleep as I coiled myself up in the corner of my cell. I remember this night vividly as it proved to be my last night in prison.

With the morning began my usual routine. I was giving some ten political prisoners an account of Dhingra's life, which I had to leave unfinished. For, on that day, I found no time to arrange for a full meeting and to lecture before it.

Just then, I received a call from the Superintendent to meet him in the office. At the same time, a trusted man sent me a message that I was free.

The political convicts, who had stayed with me, worked with me, and suffered with me, in whose company I had passed so many years of my hard life in the Andamans, were full of joy at the news. Their eyes shone full of tears. But I trembled that I was leaving them behind in that prison. They heartily congratulated me. The Sikhs among them, some of whom were sixty years old, said, "Babuji, come closer to us, do not forget us." And they locked me up in their embrace full of affection and reverence. They added, "You have been on transportation for life long before us. You had passed seven or eight years in the Andamans when we came there. Why then should you be sorry that you go out, while we remain behind! Is it not right that you should precede us? If you are free, we are as good as free. In fact, your freedom will pave the way for us. At least, it will pave the road to freedom for our motherland."

I answered, "It all depends upon the strength that God will give me to complete the task. But, my brothers, you will surely bear me out when I say that—ground down under the sufferings as I was during the fourteen long years that I spent in the Andamans and even to the last day here, I have not flinched or retracted from what I was preaching all my life. I have given you the stories of all our martyrs and I have advised all along to hold firm by our creed of armed resistance if circumstances were to force it upon us" I have kept the flag flying. When I heard the sentence passed upon me fourteen years ago, the words dancing upon my lips were the same that are dancing upon them today. I uttered them then, I have uttered them during my long stay in prison, and they come forth from my mouth today, to be carved on your heart and mind, and to ring in your ears for good. Let us say all of us, "Glory to the Goddess of Freedom; Victory to our Mother." We greeted one another with these words; we hailed our mother and then I parted from them.

As soon as I stepped into the office, the Superintendent read out to me the order of my release. It was that for five years after my release, I was to take no part in politics and stay at Ratnagiri as a prisoner on parole. These two conditions were fundamental and there was no question of my dotting the i's and crossing the t's of these conditions. I was ordered to remove at once from Yeravada and proceed to Ratnagiri. The prisoner's garments were taken off and my own dress was given back to me to wear instead. This was the final order to obey as a prisoner.

I was stripped of my own clothing when I was sent to the jail at Dongri in 1910. I was given them back to wear again on 6th May, 1924.

I felt a feeling of vacancy coming on me and also a sense of relief accompanying it. It was a mood of melancholy dashed with joy. The Superintendent heartily congratulated me on the event. And he frankly warned me to take care in the future. It was Major Murray who did it. His parting words to me, "Take care of the future" summed up the secret of melancholy.

All the inmates of the prison, my fellow-countrymen, prisoners and officers, the youngest as well as the oldest formed a circle round me. They said with one voice, "Savarkar you have been in exile from your country like Rama who went to the forest for fourteen years abandoning his beloved Ayodhya. You have passed through similar trials, sorrows and bereavements. Hail to you, Savarkar, may God bless you. The whole country rejoices today and its joy knows no bounds."

I could not contain myself for the kind words spoken by them and for the affectionate heart they betokened. And I replied, "There is one great omission in this comparison. Rama went into exile, but Rama finished Ravana and won the battle. I have gone into exile and suffered, but Ravana is still alive. I shall feel myself free only when that is accomplished. With God's grace, even that task will accomplish itself like many other minor things I have put my hand to. Some day, some time, that also will happen and you must realise the difference, and it must give you acute pain."

My relative had come to fetch me away. The prison gate was opened and I came out. What varied means I had used to secure my release! And how I felt then that I was escaping, not through the open gate, but through its keyhole.

At last, I was a free man. I looked about me and said to myself I had scored over my life-sentence of fifty years. But who dares say that I may not be sent back to serve it to the full? It was not yet time, I thought, to bid final goodbye to this prison. I must not forget it yet. Was I not free at Marseilles? Had I not made my escape? This may be but the repetition of that experience, for India's battle for freedom has yet to be won, and the struggle must go on.

Indulging in such kind of talk with my friends, and smiling at the same time, I entered the car and it moved on its wheels. It brought me into the land of the living and had left behind my sentence to perish. The boundary line was crossed and I was both alive and free.

The greetings I received from the whole country, as I came back alive to them, made me for a time oblivious of myself. On the very first day of my freedom, I was floating, as it were, in the upper air of my country. When it hailed me as a hero and patted me on the back, all the wounds inflicted on me during my fourteen years of prison life seemed to heal. And the only thing that remained with me were these reminiscences.

Therefore, as I had invoked the Goddess with the words "That another image", in order to fortify myself against the intending shadow of death-sentence and to be prepared to swallow the cup of poison, it was holding out to my lips. I now recall the same Goddess to my mind with deep gratitude for my survival and bowing my head take final leave of her. I pray that the heavenly Goddess may go back, for the time being to her abode.

□

14
Dear Reader

The story is told. The curtain is rung down on it. Two life-sentences have been run. And I have brought together my recollections of them within the cover of this book. They are narrated in brief outline to you; they are put together within the narrowest compass.

When I came into this world, God sent me in it on a sort of life-sentence. It was the span of life allotted to me by Time to stay in this "prison-house of life." This story is but a chapter of that book of life—a longer story not yet ended. As I completed this chapter as a dedication to my great worship of the ideal, so the book of life may end as a dedication to it without break or faltering.

Yes, I am free. The iron fetters on my feet are broken. But the chain of longing that binds my heart still remains. I have come out of the stone-walls that had buried me. But my soul is still imprisoned, for my vision is not yet reached. The horizon that limits it is not yet crossed. It engirdles my soul and stifles it.

Dear Reader, surely you must have been wearied to hear my story, and put out by the endless repetitions it contains. But I am as much tired in writing as you may begin reading it, this weary tale of my life. It has been a long and weary way for me also. How I have suffered and how much fatigue of the mind I have passed through in putting it on paper! But I shall be more than paid for it, if you feel the same disgust for it that I have felt. For, you can finish reading it in a day, while I had to live it for fourteen long years of transportation. And if the story is so tiresome, unendurable and disgusting to you, how much must be the living of it to me! Every moment of those fourteen years in that jail has been an agony of the soul and the body to me, and to my fellow convicts in that jail. It was not only fatiguing, unbearable and futile to us all, it was equally or more excruciating as well to them and to me. And it is only that you may know it, and feel the fatigue, the disgust and the pain of it, as we have felt it, that I have chosen to write it for you. I hope you will have through it some idea of what we have passed through; what we have endured.

Dear Reader, I lay down my pen and take leave of you. My broken pen I cannot put aside, however, without telling you never to forget those who stuck to their task, disheartening and trying though it was; who embraced it to the last; who were nearly burnt up in that fiery ordeal; and who came out of it because nothing could burn them up completely in it, Lest you forget! Dear Reader, I say it to you as my last word, do not forget them. For, sooner or later, the memory of them will serve you and be your salvation; nothing else will avail!

□□□